THE THREE MUSKETEERS

ALEXANDRE DUMAS

THE THREE MUSKETEERS

TRANSLATED, ANNOTATED AND INTRODUCED

BY

Will Hobson

VINTAGE BOOKS

LONDON

Published by Vintage 2013

2 4 6 8 10 9 7 5 3 1

Translation, introduction and notes
copyright © Will Hobson 2013

First published in Great Britain by Vintage in 2013

Vintage
Random House, 20 Vauxhall Bridge Road,
London SW1V 2SA

www.vintage-classics.info

Addresses for companies within The Random House Group Limited can be found at:
www.randomhouse.co.uk/offices.htm

The Random House Group Limited Reg. No. 954009

A CIP catalogue record for this book
is available from the British Library

ISBN 9780099583158

The Random House Group Limited supports the Forest Stewardship
Council® (FSC®), the leading international forest-certification organisation.
Our books carrying the FSC label are printed on FSC®-certified paper.
FSC is the only forest-certification scheme supported by the leading environmental
organisations, including Greenpeace. Our paper procurement policy can be found
at www.randomhouse.co.uk/environment

Typeset in Fournier MT by Palimpsest Book Production Limited,
Falkirk, Stirlingshire
Printed and bound in Germany
by GGP Media GmbH, Pößneck

CONTENTS

THE THREE MUSKETEERS

INTRODUCTION

AN IMMEDIATE, AND COLOSSAL, SUCCESS, *The Three Musketeers* was serialised in the Parisian newspaper *Le Siècle* from March to July 1844 (and promptly followed in August of the same year, in a rival publication, by *The Count of Monte Cristo*). Its sequel, *Twenty Years After*, came out the following year, and the third, and longest, of the d'Artagnan romances, *The Viscount of Bragelonne* (a novel Robert Louis Stevenson loved so much, he read it six times) two years later – not to mention, in the same period, seven plays and fifteen other novels. No wonder Dumas, who had always worked on several things at once but, even by his standards, was now in a golden period, was called the 'inextinguishable volcano' by a contemporary critic. Already renowned, he became wildly famous, earned – and gleefully spent – huge sums of money, had countless affairs, travelled, built a theatre and a mansion, the Château de Monte Cristo, which he was forced by bankruptcy to sell six years later – and never stopped writing. The incredible momentum of *The Three Musketeers* – its repeated cry of *En avant!*, 'Forward!' – is therefore no coincidence. One of the reasons *The Three Musketeers* is so memorable, in fact, is the degree to which it bears the stamp of Dumas's personality. Its relish for life, humour, warmth, flaws, comic bravado, and overriding sense of being undaunted, no matter what storm clouds are brewing, are all distinctly autobiographical.

Alexandre Dumas *père* (1802–1870) was born at Villers-Cotterêts, fifty miles north-east of Paris. His mother, Marie-Louise Labouret, was a local innkeeper's daughter. His father, General Thomas-Alexandre Dumas, was the son of a white, dissolute French aristocrat, Marquis Alexandre-Antoine Davy de la

Pailleterie, and a black slave, Marie Cessette Dumas, born in what is now Haiti.

When Dumas was three and a half, his father died of cancer, an event stirringly described in his memoirs. He had been sent with his two sisters to a neighbour's house on the day of the General's death. At midnight, there was a loud knock on the door. He got out of bed, convinced it was his father coming to say goodbye. The next morning, when he was told his father had died at midnight – or rather, 'that God had taken him back' – he went home, took one of his father's pistols and set off upstairs. When his distraught mother found him on the landing, she asked him what he was doing:

'I am going to heaven!'
'And what are you going to do in heaven, my poor child?'
'I am going to kill God who has killed Papa.'

It is a quintessential Dumas story, winning both for its exaggeration and for the kernel of truth it contains, for in a sense he repeated that scene for the rest of his life – left alone with his mother, whom he idealised, trying to emulate his father, whom he idolised, and permanently going into battle. The Goncourt brothers spoke for their contemporaries when they called him, 'An enormous, overflowing ego, but sparkling with wit and agreeably wrapped up in childish vanity'. Essential qualities for a storyteller, but even Alexandre Dumas *fils*, who did not find it easy being his son, is affectionate when he says, 'My father is a great big child whom I had when I was a boy. [He] was the kind of man who would get up on the back of his own carriage and ride through the fashionable streets of Paris so people would exclaim: "Oh, look, Alexandre Dumas has his own Negro!"'

Fathers are obviously a central theme of *The Three Musketeers*, but *The Black Count* (Harvill Secker, 2012), Tom Reiss's biography of Dumas's actual father, is still electrifying. Thomas-Alexandre had a dizzying rise – joining the army just before the French

Revolution as a private under his mother's name (some scholars have suggested Dumas is in fact not a family name but a slave designation: *du mas* [property] 'of the farm'), he had become General-in-Chief of the French Army of the Alps within seven years. And then an equally dizzying fall – a committed Republican, he quarrelled with Napoleon over the latter's imperial ambitions; sent back to France, he was shipwrecked in Naples and imprisoned for almost two years; returning partly paralysed and deaf in one ear, he was unable to draw a pension and died leaving his wife and three children penniless.

In its derring-do, therefore, *The Three Musketeers* seems to be a homage to Thomas-Alexandre Dumas at the height of his powers, and Porthos Dumas's way of keeping him alive. The bluff soldier dreaming of home comforts, the giant of a man under whose cloak d'Artagnan gets lost like a little boy, the only musketeer to find love and financial security, Porthos was Dumas's favourite character. When the newspaper courier came to pick up one of the last instalments of the trilogy, so the story goes, he emerged from his office in tears, saying, 'I have had to kill Porthos.'

But, of course, *The Three Musketeers* is a myriad other things, not least a supreme piece of storytelling. Besides his gifts for plotting, dialogue, and humour, Dumas's genius as a storyteller lay in his ability to make his autobiographical preoccupations universal. For the first time, a mass audience existed – literacy increased exponentially in the nineteenth century – and technological innovations, notably cheaper paper and the introduction of inked roller press, meant that the first modern newspapers such as *Le Siècle*, funded solely by advertisements, could achieve mass circulation. Dumas knew not only how to entertain with his tales of romance and adventure, but also how to appeal directly to the imaginations of his huge audience then, and ever since; to conjure up the spirit of youth, the challenge of setting out into the world, the need for friendship and loyalty, the openhearted embrace of life, the quest for self-respect.

There's no need, therefore, to know about Dumas's life to respond to his novels. Once hooked, however, his autobiography is a huge pleasure. It is endlessly fascinating to read how, like d'Artagnan, he set off to Paris aged twenty-one with two louis d'or and a letter of introduction in his pocket, there 'to throw himself into literature as his father had thrown himself upon the enemy'; how he was as generous as Athos, as fond of ostentation as Porthos, as quick to respond to a slur, whether racial or literary, as any musketeer. His response to one bigot, for instance, has become famous. 'My father was a mulatto, my grandfather was a Negro, and my great-grandfather a monkey. You see, Sir, my family starts where yours ends.' As Mike Phillips has written, 'Dumas was what he was in a completely unselfconscious way. He emerged new and innovative into a society just recovering from the slaughters of previous decades. Innocent of almost everything but ready for everything, he pushed himself to the top, which is where he wanted to be, and in that sense his life is the most ambitious and interesting of his melodramas.'

Two questions arise: All this talk about men is all very well, but what about women: the damsels in distress; Aramis's dismal nonsense about women being the cause of all evil; Milady, the utterly evil villainess – how is that OK? And how on earth did he publish, for instance, 43,000 pages between 1843 and 1846? Was he a conman?

I don't think that, in a minor sense, Dumas would have tried to defend himself against either of these charges. As I've said, he idealised his mother, whom he brought to Paris as soon as he could – he was supporting her, Laure Labay, Alexandre's mother, Alexandre and himself at the age of twenty-two. He could never form lasting relationships, always falling thunderously in and out of love. But he wasn't proud of it – witness his castigation of d'Artagnan's behaviour. And, in a larger sense, he might appeal to more unfashionable concepts, such as innocence, or that the musketeers' code applies to everyone, not just men; or indeed, he

might plead his childlike egotism and vanity. Milady, after all, is
so central that she is almost the book's anti-heroine, or rather,
another part of her creator. She comes from nowhere, like
d'Artagnan, and fights her way to the top. She is the one imprisoned, like Dumas's father and the Count of Monte Cristo; she is
the one who has to tell a story to survive. But, in any case, Dumas
would have left it up to the reader to judge. As a female admirer
of his plays at the time wrote, 'The great talent of Dumas is to
move souls; one does not worry about the means; one cries and is
happy.' If he didn't move a reader, then obviously he wouldn't
expect to be read.

Similarly, he was quite open about using collaborators, notably
Auguste Maquet, whose arrival in his life triggered his golden
period. And on occasion he definitely signed his names to things
he hadn't written. A book of his was once criticised in his presence, for instance. 'That sounds a very poor novel,' he interjected.
'Who's it by?' When told it was by him, he said, 'Ah. In that case
I shall have to have few words with Maquet.' So, as Stevenson
said, he was 'alas, of doubtful honesty'. Or, to put it in a more
contemporary way, a Pop artist *avant la lettre*, who knew the
signature was all. But when it came to all the countless books
he did write, and for which we have the manuscripts in his
writing, he would have simply explained his method. As the great
Dumas scholar Claude Schopp has written, 'It has been suggested
that Dumas did not have an inventive but a combinative imagination; most of the subjects he developed often came from others
who had nothing more to sell than a primordial idea. Dumas
executed the work, repaired the plan and then his hand took off
on the paper.' Maquet, 'a theatrical jobber with good historical
knowledge', had more to offer. He worked up drafts on Dumas's
instructions, wrote scenes, did research. But then Dumas completely
rewrote them, or rather used them as a starting point for something
completely different. Charles Samaran's annotated edition of *Les
Trois Mousquetaires* published in the Classiques Garnier (Paris,
1956), of which this is a translation, includes passages of Maquet's

draft in an appendix. Maquet's first steps are not unrecognisable from the finished article, but they are totally dead. Dumas is obviously the author of the finished book, and when he and Maquet finally fell out, it was over royalties rather than anything else.

With his historical novels, Dumas sometimes came up with the story first. 'I try to make it romantic, moving, dramatic, and when scope has been found for the emotions and the imagination, I search through the annals of the past to find a frame in which to set it.' But in the case of *The Three Musketeers*, as he says in the preface, the idea came from *The Memoirs of M. d'Artagnan* (1700) by Courtilz de Sandras (1644–1712), which he chanced upon in Marseilles's library. A racy and apocryphal reworking of the more mundane life of Charles de Batz-Castelmore (c.1615–1673), who was a d'Artagnan on his mother's side, Courtilz describes his hero losing his letter of introduction in a quarrel on the way to Paris, meeting Athos, Porthos and Aramis in Monsieur de Tréville's antechamber, falling foul of a ruthless Englishwoman called 'Milédi', travelling to England, and eventually becoming a musketeer. Taking this as his starting point, Dumas read other memoirs, in which he found episodes such as those of the diamond tags and the branding, set Maquet to work, and then, as was his way, told the story he wanted to tell.

Having decided to focus on the siege of La Rochelle in 1627–1628, he gleefully bends chronology to his ends – the historical d'Artagnan was ten in 1625, for instance. Grains of truth sprout in prodigious fashion – Richelieu's memoirs, for instance, suggest Buckingham's feelings for Anne of Austria played a part in his support for La Rochelle; Dumas seizes on this to sweep aside all military and political considerations and make him a man acting solely for love. Partisanship abounds: Richelieu, most obviously, is done a disservice as part of the book's general anti-clericalism, but Buckingham would also be unrecognisable to a seventeenth-century English reader; detested for his military incompetence, his assassination by John Felton was popularly acclaimed.

In a word, Dumas lets nothing get in the way of a good story, and spotting his historical inaccuracies, like his continuity errors, is one of the pleasures of reading him. If he had been a different writer, there would, of course, be no Athos, Porthos and Aramis. They are mentioned briefly in Courtilz, and their historical names are known – Athos was Armand de Sillègue d'Athos d'Autevielle, Porthos Isaac de Portau, and Aramis Henri d'Aramitz – but Dumas would have had nothing to go on if he had confined himself to historical fact.

His style is similarly beholden to no one. As Robert Louis Stevenson says about *The Viscount of Bragelonne*, 'Good souls, I suppose, must sometimes read it in the blackguard travesty of a translation. But there is no style so untranslatable; light as a whipped trifle, strong as silk; wordy like a village tale; pat like a general's despatch; with every fault, yet never tedious; with no merit, yet inimitably right.' It should be read in French, therefore. But, failing that, William Barrow, *The Three Musketeers*'s first translator in 1846, rose to the occasion, and Richard Pevear, its most recent and best in 2006, soared.

Pevear, of course, is renowned for his and Larissa Volokhonsky's translations of Russian writers such as Tolstoy, so I turned eventually to his version with trepidation. It is, unsurprisingly, immaculate, resolving all the textual questions and triumphantly bringing the English text up to date. Apart from anything else, it reverses a bowdlerising tendency on the part of its Victorian translators to cast a veil over the musketeers' amorous exploits. In this, and every other respect, it is wonderful. But, such is the nature of translation, the number of minute literary judgements it involves (I have translated the text's stream of oaths and irreverent expostulations rather than leave them in French, for instance), I was not left feeling I had nothing to offer. The reader, of course, will be the judge of whether I was correct to do so.

Translating Dumas is partly a question of getting out of the way. His language, while occasionally purple (especially when indulging in the pathetic fallacy – 'It was a dark and stormy night'!), is plain and direct. His dialogue is sparkling, all parry and riposte. His way with action is unparalleled. But unsurprisingly, given the speed at which he wrote (no time to put in accents, or, indeed, any form of punctuation), his exposition sometimes suffers from the faults of which Stevenson speaks – pile ups, relative clauses stretching into the far distance, and so on. He was notably blithe about these. When one of his secretaries, for instance, drew his attention to a sentence in which the syntax was so muddled it was impossible to tell what he meant, he joked, '*Il n'y a que des tirets qui puissent nous tirer de là,*' which, without the pun, could be translated as, 'Dashes are our only hope here.'

Taking this as my cue, therefore, I have inserted dashes, actual and metaphorical, where they have seemed appropriate. In terms of diction, I have tried to steer a course between excessive fruitiness and dusty bookishness. Immediacy rather than notional period colour; pace rather than clunkiness. Anything that failed to capture the book as it reads in French – namely, as a supremely compelling and entertaining piece of storytelling for all ages – I avoided.

As I say, I look up to Pevear, not only for his translation but also his notes. David Coward's wonderful annotated edition (Oxford University Press, 1991) has been invaluable. His introduction, like those of Anthony Burgess, Allan Massie, George Macdonald Fraser and Keith Wren, has been revelatory. This translation would also have been impossible, and without any merit, without Dominique Buchan, Frances Macmillan, Lorna Russell, Laura Hassan, Charlotte Marsden, Catherine Tice, Rachel Pole, Giles O'Bryen, Emma Kay, Derek Linzey, Roland Chambers, Annie Pesskin, Doug Lavin, Lusiné Kerobyan and Anthony Hobson. I am very grateful to them all.

Will Hobson, 2013

THE THREE MUSKETEERS

PREFACE

In which it is established that, despite their names ending in -os, and -is, the heroes of the story we shall have the honour of telling our readers are not remotely mythical.

A YEAR OR SO AGO, while I was researching my history of Louis XIV[1] in the Bibliothèque Royale, I chanced upon the *Memoirs of M d'Artagnan*, which was printed — like the great majority of works from that period, when authors were keen to tell the truth without having to take a turn of any duration in the Bastille — in Amsterdam, by Pierre Rouge. The title caught my fancy; I took the memoirs home, with the librarian's permission of course, and devoured them.

My purpose here is not to analyse this curious work; I will simply refer those readers of mine who appreciate picturesque evocations of the time to its pages. There they will find portraits drawn by a masterly hand, and, although the sketches are mostly rendered on barrack doors and tavern walls, they will nonetheless recognise the likenesses of Louis XIII, Anne of Austria, Richelieu, Mazarin and most of the courtiers of the age, all as true to life as their equivalents in Monsieur Anquetil's history[2].

But, as we know, what strikes the poet's capricious mind is not always what makes an impression on the general reader. Now, whilst admiring, as others no doubt will also admire, the details we have mentioned, the thing that preoccupied us most is something to which certainly no one before us had paid the least attention.

D'Artagnan relates that, on his first visit to Monsieur de Tréville, the captain of the king's musketeers, he met three young men in his antechamber who were serving in the illustrious corps, into which he was requesting the honour of being admitted, and who were called Athos, Porthos and Aramis.

We confess we were struck by these three strange names, and it immediately occurred to us that they were pseudonyms employed by d'Artagnan to disguise genuine, possibly illustrious alternatives – unless, that is, the bearers of these assumed names hadn't themselves chosen them on the day when, out of caprice, dissatisfaction or lack of fortune, they had donned the simple tabard of a musketeer.

From that moment on we did not rest until we had found in other works of the period some trace of these extraordinary names, which had roused our curiosity to such a pitch.

The catalogue of books we read to achieve this goal would in itself fill an entire instalment[3], which might be highly educational but certainly not highly entertaining for our readers. We will, therefore, simply inform them that, just as we were about to abandon our researches, discouraged by endless unrewarding enquiry, we finally found, guided by the advice of our illustrious and erudite friend Paulin Paris, a manuscript folio numbered 4772 or 4773 – we don't remember this detail very clearly – entitled:

Memoirs of the Count de La Fère, concerning some of the events that transpired in France towards the end of the reign of King Louis XIII and the start of the reign of King Louis XIV.

One may imagine our jubilation when, leafing through this manuscript, our last hope, we found on the twentieth page the name Athos, on the twenty-seventh the name Porthos, and on the thirty-first the name Aramis.

The discovery of a completely unknown manuscript, in an age when historical science has progressed to such a high level, seemed well-nigh miraculous to us. We therefore hastened to request permission to have it printed, with the aim of presenting ourselves one day at the Académie des Inscriptions et Belles Lettres with other men's baggage, in the unlikely event of us not having succeeded in entering the Académie Française[4] with our own. This permission, we are duty bound to say, was graciously granted;

which fact we here put on record to publicly refute those malicious persons who claim that we are living under a government that is less than entirely sympathetic to men of letters.

Now, it is the first part of this precious manuscript we are offering today to our readers; we have reinstated the title that suits it and if, as we have no doubt, this first part meets with the success it deserves, we undertake to publish the second forthwith[5].

In the meantime, as a godfather is a second father, we ask our readers to hold us, rather than the Count de La Fère, responsible for their pleasure or tedium.

This being granted, let us proceed to our story.

I

THE THREE GIFTS OF MONSIEUR D'ARTAGNAN PÈRE

O N THE FIRST MONDAY in the month of April 1625, the little
market town of Meung[1], birthplace of the author of *The
Romance of the Rose*, appeared to be in the throes of as full-blown
a revolution as if the Huguenots had come to make it a second La
Rochelle. Several townsmen, seeing women running off in the
direction of the High Street and hearing children wailing on doorsteps, hurriedly strapped on their breastplates and, stiffening their
somewhat uncertain resolve with a musket or a halberd, made for
the Honest Miller inn[2], in front of which swarmed a dense, noisy,
intensely curious throng that was growing larger by the minute.

Alarms were frequent in those times, and few days passed
without one or other town recording an event of this sort in its
archives. There were the nobles, who were warring among themselves; there was the king, who was making war on the cardinal;
there were the Spanish, who were making war on the king[3]. And
then, besides these veiled or public, clandestine or overt wars, there
were also the robbers, the beggars, the Huguenots, the wolves and
the lackeys, who made war on everybody. The townspeople always
armed themselves against the robbers, the wolves and the lackeys;
more often than not against the nobles and the Huguenots; occasionally against the king; but never against the cardinal and the
Spanish. This settled way of doing things meant, therefore, that
when the townspeople heard a commotion on the aforesaid first
Monday in April 1625 and saw neither the yellow and red flag[4] nor
the Duke de Richelieu's livery, they rushed to the Honest Miller.

When they got there, the cause of the uproar was plain for all
to see and identify.

A young man . . . Let's sketch his likeness with a quick stroke
of the pen. Imagine Don Quixote at eighteen, Don Quixote not

in body armour, without coat of mail, without cuisses, Don Quixote in a woollen doublet that had once been blue but was now an indefinable shade of wine dregs and azure. He had a long, tanned face, high cheekbones – a sign of astuteness – bulging jaw muscles – a sure-fire way to recognise a Gascon, even when there's no beret in evidence, and our young man was wearing a beret adorned with a feather of some sort – alert, intelligent eyes, and a finely chiselled, if hooked, nose. Too tall for an adolescent, too short for a grown man, an unseasoned observer might have taken him for a farmer's son on a journey if it weren't for the long sword hanging from a leather baldric that banged against its owner's calves when he walked, and against his mount's shaggy coat when he rode.

For our young man had a mount – he had such a remarkable mount, in fact, that it did not go unremarked. It was a little Béarnais nag, about thirteen years old, with a yellow coat, no hair on its tail, no lack of sores on its legs, and the ability, despite walking with its head below its knees, which made the use of the martingale pointless, to plod along for its regulation eight leagues a day. Unfortunately this steed's qualities were so well concealed under its strange coat and bizarre gait that, in an age when everyone was an expert on horses, the appearance of the aforementioned little nag in Meung, into which it had ridden a quarter of an hour earlier by the Beaugency gate, caused a sensation that reflected equally badly on its rider.

This sensation had been all the more mortifying for young d'Artagnan (as this Rocinante's[5] Don Quixote was called) because he was under no illusions as to how ridiculous such a mount made him look, however good a horseman he might be. Consequently he had accepted it as a present from the elder Monsieur d'Artagnan with a heavy sigh. He was not blind to the fact that such an animal was worth at least twenty livres, but it was equally true that the speech accompanying its presentation had been beyond price.

'My son,' the Gascon gentleman had said in that thick Béarnais twang[6] Henri IV had never managed to shake off, 'this horse was born in your father's household getting on for thirteen years ago, and it has remained here ever since – this alone should give you grounds to love it. Never sell it, let it die peacefully and honourably of old age, and if you take it on a campaign, nurse it as you would an old servant. At court,' the elder Monsieur d'Artagnan continued, 'if, that is, you have the honour to go – an honour to which, incidentally, your ancient lineage entitles you – uphold with dignity your noble name, which has been borne by your ancestors with dignity for over five hundred years. For your sake and for that of your kind – by your kind, I mean your relations and your friends – don't stand for anything from anyone except the cardinal and the king. You have to understand that it is by his courage – by his courage alone – that a gentleman makes his way today. A man who trembles for a second may let slip the prize that at that very second fortune is holding out to him. You are young and you should be brave for two reasons: first, because you are Gascon, and second, because you are my son. Never be afraid of opportunities, always be on the lookout for adventures. I have taught you to handle a sword, you have legs of iron and a fist of steel, so fight at every turn – and be all the more ready to fight because duels are forbidden and hence require double the courage. All I have to give you, my son, is fifteen écus, my horse and the advice you've just heard. Your mother will add the recipe of a certain balm she got from a Bohemian woman, which has a wondrous healing effect on any wound that has not reached the heart. Make the most of everything, and live happily and to an old age. I have only one thing to add, to offer you an example – not mine, because for my part I have never appeared at court, and only served in the wars of religion[7] as a volunteer. No, I mean Monsieur de Tréville's, who was my neighbour once, and who had the honour when he was a little child of playing with our king, Louis XIII, may God preserve him! Sometimes their games degenerated into scraps and the king didn't always prove to be the strongest. The blows he received gave him a good deal of esteem and affection for Monsieur de Tréville. Later, on his first trip to Paris, Monsieur de Tréville fought five duels; from the death of the late king until the young heir's coming of age, setting aside wars and sieges, he fought a further seven, and from that majority until today, perhaps a hundred more!

'And so, despite all the edicts, ordinances and decrees, here he is, captain of the musketeers – that is, commander of a legion of Caesars which the king sets great store by and the cardinal stands in dread of, although he is a gentleman who, as everyone knows, stands in dread of very little. Furthermore, Monsieur de Tréville makes ten thousand écus a year, so he is a very great lord. He started out like you; go and see him with this letter, and model yourself on him so that you may attain all that he has accomplished.'

With this, Monsieur d'Artagnan père girded his own sword round his son's waist, tenderly kissed him on both cheeks and gave him his blessing.

Leaving his father's room, the young man found his mother waiting for him with the famous recipe, which, thanks to the advice we have just reported, was sure to enjoy regular use. The farewells in this instance were longer and more tender than they had been in the previous one, not because Monsieur d'Artagnan did not love his son, who was his only child, but because Monsieur d'Artagnan was a man and he would have considered it unworthy for a man to give in to his feelings, whereas Madame d'Artagnan was a woman and, what's more, a mother.

She wept abundantly and, we say this in praise of the younger Monsieur d'Artagnan, however hard he tried to be staunch, as befitted a future musketeer, nature won out and he shed copious tears, half of which he managed with a great effort to hide.

The young man set out that same day, equipped with his father's three gifts, which, as we have said, consisted of fifteen écus, the horse and the letter for Monsieur de Tréville. The advice, understandably enough, was included by way of a supplement.

With such a vade-mecum, d'Artagnan was, mentally as well as physically, the very double of Cervantes' hero to whom we compared him so felicitously when our historian's duty impelled us to sketch his likeness. Don Quixote took the windmills for giants and the sheep for armies; d'Artagnan, for his part, took every smile for an insult and every look for a provocation. He thus had his fist clenched the whole way from Tarbes to Meung and clapped his hand to his sword on average ten times a day, and yet this fist of his didn't land on any jaw, nor did this sword ever leave its scabbard. This wasn't because the sight of the unfortunate yellow pony didn't engender plenty of smiles on passers-by's faces, but rather that, since a sword of respectable size clanked above this mount and an eye glinted with ferocity rather than pride above this sword, the passers-by repressed their mirth – or, if their mirth got the better of their prudence, they at least tried to laugh out of only one side of their mouths, like classical masks. And so d'Artagnan proceeded majestically on his way, his finer feelings intact, until the unfortunate town of Meung[8].

But there, as he was dismounting at the gate of the Honest Miller without anyone, innkeeper, waiter or stable boy, coming to hold his stirrup at the mounting-block, d'Artagnan spotted a gentleman at an open window on the ground floor – a haughty-looking, fine figure of a man, with a somewhat dour expression, who was conversing with two individuals who appeared to be hanging deferentially on his every word. D'Artagnan naturally assumed, as was his habit, that he was the subject of their conversation, and listened in. This time he was only partly mistaken; they weren't talking about him, but they were talking about his horse. The gentleman appeared to be enumerating all its qualities for his listeners' benefit and since, as I've said, his audience was inordinately deferential, they were constantly roaring with laughter. Now, as the intimation of a smile was enough to rouse the young man's ire, it is easy to understand the effect such rollicking hilarity had on him.

Before anything, though, d'Artagnan wanted to examine the features of the impertinent fellow who was ridiculing him. He trained his proud gaze on the stranger and saw a man aged between forty and forty-five with black, piercing eyes, a pale complexion, a strongly pronounced nose, and an impeccably trimmed, black moustache. He was dressed in violet breeches and a violet doublet with tags of similarly coloured lace, which was plain apart from the usual slashes for the shirt. Although new, the breeches and doublet looked rumpled, like travelling clothes that had been kept folded away in a portmanteau for a long time. D'Artagnan took in all these details with the alacrity of the most meticulous observer, no doubt also instinctively sensing that this stranger would have a great effect on the course his life was to take.

Now, since d'Artagnan trained his gaze on the gentleman in the violet doublet just as the object of his scrutiny was propounding one of his most erudite and profound theories about the Béarnais nag, the two men listening burst out laughing, and, contrary to his usual practice, the gentleman himself allowed a bleak smile to visibly hover, if one may use that expression, over his face. This time it was conclusive: d'Artagnan had genuinely been insulted. Convinced of this, he therefore pulled his beret down over his eyes and, attempting to copy some of the courtly airs he had seen displayed by noblemen on their travels in Gascony, stepped forward with one hand on his sword-hilt and the other on his hip. Unfortunately the further he went, the more his anger blinded him, so that instead of the dignified, lordly speech he had prepared to issue his challenge, at the moment of truth all he found on the tip of his tongue was a crude personal remark which he accompanied with a furious gesture.

'Hey, sir!' he cried. 'You sir, skulking there behind that shutter . . . yes, you! Tell me a jot of what's making you laugh and we can all laugh together.'

The gentleman slowly raised his eyes from mount to rider, as if he needed some time to take in the fact that such a strange rebuke was being addressed to him, and then, when there was no longer any room for doubt, his brow furrowed slightly, and after a rather long pause, with an indescribable note of irony and insolence in his voice, he replied to d'Artagnan, 'I am not speaking to you, sir.'

'I am, though!' the young man cried out, exasperated by this mixture of insolence and good manners, of etiquette and contempt. 'I am speaking to you.'

The stranger looked at him for another moment with his faint smile and then, stepping away from the window, sauntered out of the tavern to station himself in front of the horse, a few paces away from d'Artagnan. His serene air and mocking expression had provoked even greater hilarity among his companions who remained by the window.

D'Artagnan, seeing him come out, drew his sword a foot from its scabbard.

'This horse unquestionably is, or has been in its youth, a buttercup,' said the stranger, continuing his disquisitions which he addressed to his listeners at the window, apparently oblivious to the mounting exasperation of d'Artagnan, even though he was drawing himself up to his full height between the man and his audience. 'It's a very common shade in botany, but, as yet, very rarely found in horses.'

'A man laughs at a horse who wouldn't dare laugh at its master!' Tréville's emulator cried furiously.

'I don't laugh much, sir,' replied the stranger, 'as you can see yourself from the cast of my features. But I am keen nevertheless to retain the privilege of laughing when it pleases me.'

'And I,' cried d'Artagnan, 'I do not want people laughing when it displeases me!'

'Indeed, sir?' said the stranger, calmer than ever. 'Well, that's perfectly reasonable.' And with that, he turned on his heel and made to go back into the inn by the main entrance, under which d'Artagnan had noticed on his arrival a saddled horse.

But d'Artagnan wasn't the type to let a man who had had the impudence to laugh at him just saunter away. He drew his sword fully from its scabbard and set off after him, crying, 'Turn, turn, won't you, Mr Snide, unless you wish me to strike you in the back.'

'Strike me!' said the other, swivelling on his heels and looking at the young man with equal parts surprise and contempt. 'Come now, what nonsense, dear boy, you're mad!' Then, in a low voice, as if he were talking to himself, he went on, 'It's tiresome – what a find for His Majesty in his quest for stout fellows to recruit into his musketeers.'

He had barely finished when d'Artagnan aimed such a furious thrust at him that, if he hadn't smartly jumped back, in all probability he would have made his last crack. The stranger saw then that matters had gone beyond a joke, and, drawing his sword, he saluted his adversary and gravely put himself on guard. But as he did so his two listeners, with the innkeeper in tow, fell on d'Artagnan and began belabouring him with sticks, shovels and tongs. Theirs was such a rapid and comprehensive diversionary attack that while d'Artagnan turned to face the hail of blows, his adversary sheathed his sword with the same crisp snap and reverted from would-be participant in the fight to spectator, a role he performed with his habitual impassivity, although not without muttering, 'A plague on these Gascons! Put him back on his orange horse and let him be on his way.'

'Not before I've killed you, you coward!' cried d'Artagnan, bearing up as best he could and not yielding an inch to his three enemies who were pounding him with blows.

'More Gascon bluster,' muttered the gentleman. 'On my honour, these Gascons are incorrigible! Well, on with the dance then, since he has his heart set on it. He'll say he's had enough when he gets tired.'

But the stranger didn't know what manner of pig-headed individual he was dealing with yet; d'Artagnan wasn't a man to seek quarter in any circumstances. So the fight went on for a few more seconds until finally, exhausted, d'Artagnan lost his grip on his sword which was broken in two by the blow of a stick. Another blow almost simultaneously split open his forehead and laid him out on the ground, barely conscious and covered in blood.

It was at this point that the townspeople came flocking from all sides on to the scene. Fearing a scandal, the landlord carried the wounded man with the help of his stable boys into the kitchen where he was given some rudimentary attention.

As for the gentleman, he resumed his place at the window and stared out with a certain impatience at the great throng, which seemed by its continued presence to annoy him keenly.

'Well, how is that mad dog?' he said, turning when he heard the door open and addressing the innkeeper who had come to inquire after his health.

'Your Excellency is safe and sound?' inquired the landlord.

'Yes, perfectly safe and sound, my dear innkeeper, that's why I'm asking for news of our young man.'

'He's better,' said the landlord. 'He has fainted dead away.'

'Really?' said the gentleman.

'But before he did, he summoned up all his strength to challenge and defy you in one and the same breath.'

'My God, this strapping lad is the devil himself,' cried the stranger.

'Oh no, Your Excellency, the devil he is not,' replied the landlord with a grimace of contempt. 'We searched him when he was out cold and all he has is a shirt in his bundle and twelve écus[9] in his purse. Not that that prevented him saying as he was going under that if such a thing had happened in Paris, you would have repented of it immediately, whereas here you'll only repent of it at your leisure.'

'Then he must be some prince of the blood in disguise,' the stranger said coldly.

'I thought I should inform you of this, sir,' said the landlord, 'so you could be on your guard.'

'He didn't mention any names in his rant?'

'He did. He slapped his pocket and said, "We'll see what Monsieur de Tréville thinks of this insult to his protégé."'

'Monsieur de Tréville?' said the stranger, pricking up his ears. 'He slapped his pocket and uttered Monsieur de Tréville's name? Look here, my dear innkeeper, while this young man of yours was dead to the world, I'm sure you didn't omit to have a look in that pocket as well. What did it contain?'

'A letter addressed to Monsieur de Tréville, captain of the musketeers.'

'Indeed.'

'It is as I have the honour to tell you, Excellency.'

The landlord, who wasn't endowed with great perspicacity, didn't notice the expression his words had produced on the stranger's face. The man moved away from the windowsill, which he had been leaning on with his elbow, and furrowed his brow like a worried man.

'Confound it,' he muttered, 'could Tréville have sent this Gascon after me? He's very young! Still, a sword thrust is a sword thrust, however old the person who deals it, and one's always less wary of a child. Sometimes a flimsy obstacle is enough to thwart a great plan.'

The stranger fell to thinking for a few minutes.

'Come now, innkeeper,' he said, 'can't you get rid of this maniac for me? In all conscience, I can't kill him, and yet,' he added with a coldly menacing expression, 'yet he bothers me. Where is he?'

'In my wife's room having his wounds dressed, on the first floor.'

'His clothes and bundle are with him? He hasn't taken off his doublet?'

'No, all that's downstairs in the kitchen. But since he bothers you, this young lunatic . . .'

'Most certainly. He's caused a scandal in your hostelry that no decent person could tolerate. Go up to your room, make out my bill and tell my valet.'

'What, monsieur is leaving us already?'

'You know that perfectly well since I've given you orders to have my horse saddled. Haven't they been obeyed?'

'They have, and as Your Excellency perhaps saw, his horse is under the main gate, accoutred and ready for the road.'

'All right. Do as I've told you then.'

Oh my word, the landlord thought, could he be afraid of this little lad? But an imperious glance from the stranger stopped him in his tracks. He bowed humbly and left the room.

'Milady[10] mustn't be seen by that joker,' continued the stranger.

'It can't be long before she gets here; she's already late in fact . . .
I should mount up and go to meet her, that would be best . . . If
only I could find out the contents of this letter to Tréville . . .'

Still muttering to himself, the stranger headed towards the
kitchen.

The innkeeper, meanwhile, who was certain it was the young
lad's presence that was driving the stranger from his establishment,
had gone up to his wife's room and discovered that d'Artagnan
had finally come round. Impressing upon him that there was every
chance the police would give him a beating for picking a quarrel
with a lord – because, in the innkeeper's opinion, the stranger
couldn't be anything but a lord – he convinced him, despite his
weakened state, that he should get up and be on his way.
D'Artagnan, therefore, half-stunned, without his doublet, his head
swathed in bandages, got up and, with the innkeeper shoving him
in the back, started down the stairs. But, when he got to the kitchen,
the first thing he saw was his antagonist who was quietly conversing
at the step of a heavy carriage drawn by two big Norman horses.

The person he was talking to, whose head was framed by the
door, was a woman of around twenty or twenty-two. We have
already said how quickly and appraisingly d'Artagnan took in the
whole cast of a person's features, and so he saw at a glance that
the woman was young and beautiful. Her beauty struck him all
the more forcibly because it was entirely alien to the southern parts
of the country he had lived in until then. The woman was pale
and blonde, with long curly hair that fell on her shoulders, large,
languorous blue eyes, rosy lips and hands like alabaster. She was
talking very animatedly to the stranger.

'So, His Eminence bids me . . .' she was saying.

'To return immediately to England and inform him directly if
the duke" should leave London.'

'And my other instructions?' asked the beautiful traveller.

'They are in this box which you are not to open until you've
crossed the Channel.'

'Very well. What about you, what will you do?'

'I'm going back to Paris.'

'Without chastising that insolent little boy?' asked the woman.

The stranger was going to reply but, as he was opening his mouth, d'Artagnan, who had heard everything, rushed out to the doorway.

'That insolent little boy is the one who will mete out chastisement,' he cried, 'and I hope this time the man he has to chastise won't escape him as he did before.'

'Won't escape him?' the stranger repeated, frowning.

'No, I assume you wouldn't dare run away in front of a lady.'

'Think,' cried Milady, seeing the gentleman clapping his hand to his sword, 'even a slight delay could ruin everything.'

'You're right,' cried the gentleman. 'You go off your way and I'll go mine.'

With a nod of farewell to the woman, he leapt on to his horse while the coachman vigorously whipped his team. And then the two interlocutors set off at a gallop, each departing in opposite directions down the street.

'Ho there, your bill!' yelled the landlord, whose affection for the traveller was turning into deep contempt at the sight of him receding into the distance without having settled up.

'Pay, you good-for-nothing,' the traveller, without slackening his pace, yelled at his valet, who threw two or three silver coins at the innkeeper's feet, and then started off at a gallop after his master.

'Oh, you coward! You villain! You impostor!' cried d'Artagnan, taking off in turn after the valet.

But the wounded man was still too weak to take such a buffeting. He had barely gone ten paces before his ears were buzzing, he felt dizzy, a cloud of blood passed before his eyes, and he fell off his horse in the middle of the street, still shouting, 'Coward! Coward! Coward!'

'Such a coward, I agree,' murmured the landlord, going up to d'Artagnan, and attempting by this piece of flattery, like the heron and the snail[12] in the fable, to patch things up with the poor lad.

'Yes, an unqualified coward,' murmured d'Artagnan. 'Ah, but she, an unqualified beauty.'

'She who?' asked the innkeeper.

'Milady,' stammered d'Artagnan.

And then he passed out a second time.

It's much of a muchness, reflected the innkeeper. Two of them have packed their bags, but this one remains and I should be able to hang on to him for at least a few days. So that still leaves me eleven écus to the good.

Eleven écus, as we know, was the exact amount left in d'Artagnan's purse.

The innkeeper had reckoned on a convalescence of eleven days at an écu a day; he hadn't, however, reckoned on his traveller. The next day d'Artagnan got up at five in the morning, made his own way down to the kitchen and asked for a list of ingredients, which, apart from those that have not been vouchsafed to posterity, included some wine, some oil and some rosemary. Then, his mother's recipe in hand, he prepared a balm with which he anointed his numerous wounds, and, refusing the assistance of a doctor, changed the compresses himself. Thanks, no doubt, to the efficacy of the Bohemian balm, and possibly also to the lack of any intervention from a medical practitioner, d'Artagnan was back on his feet that evening and virtually cured the followed day.

But when he came to pay for the rosemary, oil and wine, which were the only extra expenses he had incurred (he had observed a starvation diet, whereas his yellow horse, according to the innkeeper at least, had eaten three times more than one would reasonably expect for an animal its size), all that d'Artagnan found in his pocket was his little worn velvet purse and the eleven écus it contained. As for the letter addressed to Monsieur de Tréville, that had disappeared.

The young man started by looking for this letter very patiently, turning out his pockets and fobs twenty times, repeatedly searching through his bundle, opening and shutting his purse, but when he was convinced it was gone for good, he flew into a third fit of rage which almost earned him a fresh dose of the spiced wine and oil. When they saw this young renegade getting into a lather and threatening to smash everything in the establishment if his letter wasn't found, the landlord reached for a pike, his wife for a broom handle and his waiters for the sticks that had served them the day before yesterday.

'My letter of introduction!' cried d'Artagnan. 'My letter of introduction, God's blood, or I'll skewer you all like ortolans[13]!'

Unfortunately a circumstance militated against the young man carrying out his threat; namely that, as we've said, his sword had been snapped in two in the first set-to, a detail that had entirely slipped his mind. So when d'Artagnan came to draw in earnest, he found himself armed simply and solely with a sword-stump eight or so inches long, which had been carefully replaced in its scabbard by the innkeeper. As for the rest of the blade, the chef had deftly made off with it to use as a larding pin.

This reversal probably wouldn't have stopped our impetuous young man, however, if the innkeeper hadn't considered his guest's request perfectly reasonable.

'Now you say it,' he said, lowering his pike, 'where is this letter?'

'Yes, where is it?' cried d'Artagnan. 'First, I'll have you know, this letter is for Monsieur de Tréville and it must be found; otherwise, if you don't find it, he will have it found.'

This threat thoroughly intimidated the innkeeper. After the king and the cardinal, Monsieur de Tréville was the man whose name was probably most often on the soldiers', and even the townspeople's, lips. Father Joseph[14] was another candidate for that title, certainly, but his name was only ever spoken in a whisper, such was the terror inspired by the Grey Eminence, as the cardinal's familiar was called.

So, throwing down his pike and telling his wife to do the same with her broom handle and his servants with their sticks, the innkeeper led by example and starting looking for the lost letter himself.

'Did it contain anything valuable?' he asked after a bout of fruitless rummaging.

'Beggar's blood, I should think so!' cried the Gascon, who was counting on the letter to help him make his way at court. 'It contained my whole fortune.'

'Savings bonds?' asked the innkeeper anxiously.

'Bonds on His Majesty's private treasury,' replied d'Artagnan who, hoping as he did that this letter of introduction would be his entry into the king's service, thought he could hazard this slightly rash response without actually telling a lie.

'Confound it!' said the landlord, in complete despair.

'Never mind though,' continued d'Artagnan with his native aplomb, 'never mind, the money was nothing; the letter was everything. I would sooner have lost a thousand pistoles than lose it.'

He might just as well have said twenty thousand but a certain youthful reticence restrained him.

A ray of light suddenly struck the innkeeper's mind as he was cursing his failure to find anything.

'This letter isn't lost at all!' he cried.

'Ah!' said d'Artagnan.

'No, it's been taken from you.'

'Taken? By whom?'

'By the gentleman from yesterday. He went down to the kitchen where your doublet was. He was alone there. I'll lay odds he stole it.'

'Do you think so?' d'Artagnan replied noncommittally, since he knew better than anyone the letter's purely personal significance, and didn't see how it could tempt the covetous. The fact was, none of the servants or travellers there stood to gain anything from possessing that piece of paper.

'So you're saying,' d'Artagnan went on, 'you suspect that impertinent gentleman?'

'I tell you I'm certain of it,' said the innkeeper. 'When I told him Your Lordship was Monsieur de Tréville's protégé, and that you even had a letter for this illustrious gentleman, he seemed very troubled, asked me where this letter was, and immediately went down to the kitchen where he knew your doublet had been left.'

'Then he's my thief,' replied d'Artagnan. 'I shall complain to Monsieur de Tréville, and Monsieur de Tréville shall complain to the king.' Saying this, he majestically drew two écus from his pocket and gave them to the innkeeper, who accompanied him, hat in hand, to the gate. He remounted his yellow horse which conveyed him without further incident to Paris's Porte Saint-Antoine, where it was sold by its owner for three écus, an excellent price, considering that d'Artagnan had exhausted the animal on the last stage of his journey. The horse dealer to whom d'Artagnan gave up the horse for the aforesaid nine livres left the young man in no doubt that he was only paying this exorbitant sum because of the originality of its colour.

D'Artagnan thus entered Paris on foot, carrying his little bundle under his arm, and he kept walking until he found a room to rent that suited his slender means. This room was a sort of garret in Rue des Fossoyeurs[15], near the Luxembourg.

As soon as he had paid the key money, d'Artagnan took possession of his lodgings and spent the rest of the daylight hours sewing on to his doublet and stockings a set of lace trimmings that his mother had unpicked from one of the elder Monsieur d'Artagnan's all-but-new doublets, and given to him in secret. He then went to the Quai de La Ferraille[16] to have his sword fitted with a new blade, and afterwards returned to the Louvre to inquire of the first musketeer he met the whereabouts of Monsieur de Tréville's residence. This proved to be on Rue du Vieux-Colombier[17], that's to say in the vicinity of the room that d'Artagnan had rented, a circumstance that seemed to him to bode well for the success of his journey.

After which, satisfied with the way he had conducted himself at Meung, free of remorse for the past, confident in the present, and full of hope for the future, he went to bed and slept the sleep of the just.

This sleep, still every inch a country fellow's, saw him through to nine o'clock the next morning, at which hour he rose to make his way to the residence of the celebrated Monsieur de Tréville, in his father's estimation the third most eminent personage in the kingdom.

II

MONSIEUR DE TRÉVILLE'S ANTECHAMBER

MONSIEUR DE TROISVILLES, as his family was still called in Gascony, or Monsieur de Tréville, as he had ended up choosing to call himself in Paris, genuinely had started out like d'Artagnan, that's to say without two pennies to rub together, but with that store of audacity, wit and good judgement that means that the poorest Gascon squireling often receives more in his expectations than the richest gentleman from Périgord or Berry does in reality. His insolent bravery and if anything still more insolent good fortune at a time when blows rained down like hail had seen him rise to the top of that slippery ladder known as the favour of the court, and he had scaled it four rungs at a time.

He was counted a friend by the king, who, as is well known, revered the memory of his father Henri IV. Monsieur de Tréville's father had served the latter so faithfully in his wars against the League[1] that, lacking ready cash – something the Béarnais was short of all his life, constantly paying his debts with the only thing he never needed to borrow, namely wit – lacking ready cash, as we were saying, the king had granted him, after the surrender of Paris, the right to take as his coat of arms[2] a lion passant or on a field gules, with the motto *Fidelis et fortis*. This was a great boon for his honour, but only a middling one for his wellbeing. Consequently, when the great Henri's illustrious companion died, all he left his son were his sword and his motto. Thanks to this twofold legacy and the spotless name that went with it, Monsieur de Tréville was admitted into the young prince's household, where he served him so well with his sword and was so faithful to his motto that Louis XIII, one of the finest swordsmen of the realm, was in the habit of saying that, if a friend of his had contracted to fight a duel and was looking for a second, his advice would be to choose him first and Tréville next, or perhaps even the other way round.

Louis XIII thus felt genuine affection for Tréville: affection of a regal, egotistical kind, it is true, but no less affection for all that. People went to great lengths in those ill-starred times to surround themselves with men of Tréville's stamp. Many gentlemen could take as their motto the epithet 'strong', which formed the second part of his device, but few could claim the epithet 'faithful', which formed the first. Tréville was one of them: his was one of those rare natures, as obedient and intelligent as a mastiff, possessed of blind courage, a quick eye and a ready hand, and it seemed as if he had been given the gift of sight solely to see if the king was displeased with someone, and that of strength solely to strike the offending party, a Besme, a Maurevers, a Poltrot de Méré or a Vitry[3]. In short, all Tréville needed in time was an opportunity, but he watched for it and promised himself he would grab it by its three hairs if it ever came within reach. And so Louis XIII made Tréville captain of his musketeers[4], which in their devotion, or rather their fanaticism, were Louis XIII's equivalent of Henri III's regulars or Louis XI's Scots Guard[5].

The cardinal, for his part, did not lag behind the king in this respect. When he saw the formidable elite with which Louis XIII was surrounding himself, this second, or rather this first, king of France wanted a guard of his own. Thus he had his musketeers, as Louis XIII had his, and the two rival potentates could be seen scouting all the provinces of France, and even all the foreign states, picking out renowned swordsmen to enter their service. Over their evening game of chess, Richelieu and Louis XIII would frequently debate their servants' merits. Each boasted of the demeanour and courage of his men, and while railing in public against duels and brawls, in private they urged them to fight, and felt genuine sorrow and unbridled joy at their respective defeats and victories. Or so at least we are told by the memoirs of a man who participated in a number of these defeats and a great deal of these victories.

Tréville knew how to play on his master's weakness, a skill that earned him the long and constant favour of a king who has not left a reputation for being very faithful to his friendships. He paraded his musketeers in front of Cardinal Armand du Plessis with a mocking air that made His Eminence's grey moustache bristle with rage. Tréville unerringly understood the nature of war in those times when, if you weren't living at your enemy's, you were living at your countrymen's expense, and his soldiers formed a legion of lawless devils, who ran riot except when he called them to order.

Slovenly, drunken, scarred, the king's musketeers, or rather Monsieur de Tréville's, ranged through the taverns, the public walks and the gaming houses, yelling and twirling their moustaches, rattling their swords, gleefully barging into the cardinal's guards whenever they encountered them, then drawing their swords in the middle of the street with a thousand quips, sometimes to be killed, but certain in that case to be mourned and avenged, and often to kill, in which case they were certain not to rot in prison, since Monsieur de Tréville was there to claim them. And so Monsieur de Tréville was praised in every register, hymned in every key, by these men who adored him and who, thoroughgoing scoundrels though they were, trembled before him like schoolboys in the presence of their master, obeying his least word, and ready to go to their deaths to clear themselves of his least reproach.

Monsieur de Tréville had used this powerful lever primarily for the benefit of the king and the king's friends, and only second-arily for himself and his friends. Besides, in none of the memoirs of a time that has left so many memoirs, does one find this worthy gentleman accused, even by his enemies – and he had as many of those among men of letters as he did among men at arms – nowhere, as we were saying, does one find this worthy gentleman accused of profiting personally from his fanatical adherents' support. Despite a rare gift for intrigue, which made him a match for the finest intriguers, he had remained an honest man. Furthermore, despite the swingeing swordplay that gives a soldier his stiff-hipped gait, and the endless, gruelling drills, he had become one of the most feted socialites, one of the most discriminating ladies' men, and one of the most honeyed and most delicate word-spinners of his age. People spoke of Tréville's conquests as they'd spoken twenty years earlier of Bassompierre's, and that is saying a great deal. Thus the captain of the musketeers was admired, feared and loved, which constitutes the apogee of human fortunes.

Whereas Louis XIV absorbed the light of all the lesser stars of his court into his vast effulgence, his father, a sun *pluribus impar*[6], transmitted his personal splendour to each of his favourites, his individual merit to each of his courtiers. Apart from the levees of the king and the cardinal, Paris at the time numbered over two hundred smaller, relatively select levees. And of these two hundred smaller levees, Tréville's was one of the best attended.

From six o'clock in the morning in summer, and from eight o'clock in winter, the courtyard of his mansion on Rue du Vieux-Colombier resembled an army camp. Fifty to sixty musketeers, who seemed to take it in turns to maintain an imposing throng, paraded about constantly, armed as if for war and ready for every eventuality. Up and down the stairs – one of those great flights of steps that soar over an expanse our civilisation would consider fit for a whole house – flowed the petitioners from Paris, bent on securing some favour or other, the gentlemen from the provinces, with their eager hopes of enlistment, and the valets decked out in every colour, bearing their masters' messages for Monsieur de Tréville. In the antechamber, on long circular benches, reclined the elect, that is, those who had been summoned for an interview. A buzz of voices lasted there from morning till night, while Monsieur de Tréville, in his office adjoining the antechamber, received visits, heard complaints, gave orders and, like the king from his balcony at the Louvre, only had to go to his window to review his men and their arms.

The day d'Artagnan presented himself, the crowd was daunting, especially to a country lad just up from his province – although it is true that, in this case, the country lad was a Gascon, and, in those times particularly, d'Artagnan's countrymen had a reputation for not being easily intimidated. But still, once one had gone through the massive door, studded with long square-headed nails, one found oneself in the midst of a mass of swordsmen milling around in the courtyard, hailing, quarrelling and playing games with one another. To clear a path through that eddying tide, one would have had to be an officer, a great lord or a pretty woman.

It was in the thick of this press and confusion that our young man made his way, his heart racing, tucking his long rapier down by his thin legs and holding one hand to the brim of his felt hat with the half-smile of the embarrassed provincial who wants to cut a good figure. Every time he passed a gang, he breathed more freely, but he sensed them turning round to look at him, and, for the first time in his life, d'Artagnan, who until then had entertained a fairly high opinion of himself, felt ridiculous.

When he reached the stairs, it was even worse. The bottom steps were occupied by four musketeers who were amusing themselves with the following exercise, while ten or twelve of their comrades waited on the landing until it was their turn to take part in the game.

The player on the upper step, drawn sword in hand, had to prevent, or at least try to prevent, the three others from ascending, while they went at him with a will, swords flying.

At first d'Artagnan took their weapons for fencing foils and assumed they were buttoned, but he soon realised from various nicks that in fact every blade was flawlessly whetted and sharpened. Whenever someone took a hit, not only the spectators but the protagonists themselves found it uproariously funny.

The fellow occupying the upper step at that moment was wonderfully adept at keeping his adversaries at arm's length. A circle formed around them. The rules were that every time someone was hit, he would leave the game and surrender his turn on

Monsieur de Tréville's waiting list to the scorer. Within five
minutes, the defender of the step had nicked three of his attackers,
one on the wrist, another on the chin, and another on the ear,
without getting a scratch in return – a display of skill which,
according to the conventions, meant he jumped three places in the
queue.

However blasé he aspired to be, rather than actually was, our
young traveller was astonished by this pastime. He had seen a fair
few preludes to duels in his province, which after all is a land where
feelings are inordinately quick to run high, and yet the bravado
of these four players seemed more fearless than anything he
had heard of, even in Gascony. He thought he had been transported
to that famous land of giants where Gulliver was to go later and be
so terrified[7]. And yet that wasn't the end of it. The landing and
the antechamber were still to come.

On the landing, the fighting was forgotten; instead they told
stories of women, and in the antechamber, stories of court. On
the landing, d'Artagnan blushed, and in the antechamber, he shuddered. His vivid, roving imagination, which in Gascony had made
him the scourge of young chambermaids, and sometimes even of
their young mistresses, had never dreamt, even in its moments of
wildest delirium, of half of these amorous marvels or a quarter
of these feats of seduction, embellished with the most celebrated
names and the least cryptic descriptions. But if his love of virtue
was shocked on the landing, his respect for the cardinal was scan-
dalised in the antechamber. There, to his complete astonishment,
d'Artagnan heard openly criticised not only the politics that made
all Europe tremble, but also the cardinal's private life, which so
many eminent, powerful lords had been punished for trying to
delve into. This great man, whom the elder Monsieur d'Artagnan
held in such reverence, was the laughing stock of Monsieur de
Tréville's musketeers. They mocked his bandy legs and round
shoulders, sang halleluiahs about Madame d'Aiguillon, his mistress,
and Madame de Combalet, his niece[8], and plotted forays against
the cardinal-duke's pages and guards, all things which struck

d'Artagnan as monstrous impossibilities. But when the king's name cropped up unexpectedly in the middle of all these cardinal-like gibes, a sort of gag muffled the mocking mouths for a minute. Everyone looked hesitantly around and seemed to fear the indiscretion of Monsieur de Tréville's office wall. But in no time an allusion would bring the conversation back to His Eminence, and then the sallies would start up with a vengeance and every possible light would be shone on his deeds.

These people are going to be thrown in the Bastille and strung up by the neck, every one of them, thought d'Artagnan, terrified, and I am too – of course I am, I've listened to them now and heard what they're saying, so I'll be accused of being their accomplice. My father gave me such strict instructions to respect the cardinal. What would he say if he knew I was in the company of such heathens?

Consequently, as you will have guessed without my needing to spell it out, d'Artagnan did not dare join in the conversation. He simply watched and listened, eagerly straining all his five senses so as not to miss a thing, and despite his faith in his father's advice, found himself prompted by his tastes and inclined by his instincts to praise rather than blame the extraordinary behaviour he was witnessing.

As he was a complete stranger to Monsieur de Tréville's throng of courtiers, however, and this was the first time anyone had seen him in the place, someone came to inquire what he wanted. D'Artagnan very humbly gave his name, relying on the title of fellow countryman, and asked the valet, who had come to put this question, to solicit a moment's audience of Monsieur de Tréville on his behalf. In a patronising voice, the valet said he would pass on the request at an appropriate juncture.

Somewhat recovered from his initial surprise, d'Artagnan then had an opportunity to study a little the outfits and faces in the room.

In the middle of the most animated group was a tall musketeer, with a haughty face and an outlandish get-up that made him the centre of attention. He was not wearing a musketeer's tabard at the time – an item of uniform, incidentally, which was not absolutely obligatory in that age of lesser freedom but greater independence – but a sky-blue jerkin, ever so slightly faded and worn, and over this jacket, a magnificent gold-embroidered baldric that glittered like a fish's scales dripping with water in the noonday sun. A long crimson velvet cloak was draped gracefully over his shoulders, framing the front of the splendid baldric from which hung a gigantic rapier.

This musketeer, who had come off guard that minute, was complaining of a cold and coughing pointedly from time and time. Hence the decision to wear the cloak, he told all and sundry, and as he talked at the top of his voice and disdainfully curled up the ends of his moustache, everyone enthusiastically admired the embroidered baldric, d'Artagnan most of all.

'What would you have me do?' the musketeer was saying. 'Fashion has come to this. It's foolishness, I know, but it's the fashion. Besides, one has to spend one's inheritance on something.'

'Ah, Porthos!' cried out one of the onlookers. 'Don't try to make us believe it was fatherly generosity that added this baldric to your wardrobe. Surely it was the veiled lady I met you with the other Sunday near the Porte Saint-Honoré who gave it to you.'

'No, on my honour, and as I am a gentleman, I bought it myself, with my own money,' replied the man who had just been called Porthos.

'Yes indeed, just as I bought this purse with what my mistress put in the old one,' said another musketeer.

'No, it's true,' said Porthos, 'and the proof is I paid twelve pistoles.'

The general admiration increased, although some doubt seemed to persist.

'Isn't that so, Aramis?' said Porthos, turning to another musketeer.

This musketeer formed a perfect contrast to the individual who, in putting the question, had called him Aramis. He was a young man of barely twenty-two or twenty-three, with an artless, cherubic face – almost cloyingly so – black, gentle eyes, and rosy cheeks as downy as an autumn peach. His thin moustache traced a perfectly straight line along his upper lip; his hands seemed to be afraid to fall below the vertical lest their veins swelled, and from time to time he pinched the tip of his ears to make sure they remained a tender, transparent pink. He spoke sparingly and slowly, bowed a great deal, and laughed noiselessly, showing his teeth, which were handsome and apparently, like the rest of his person, the object of lavish care. He responded with an affirmative nod of the head to his friend's question.

This affirmation seemed to have resolved all doubt about the baldric. It continued to be admired, but no one talked about it any more, and by one of those sudden changes of thought, the conversation abruptly turned to another subject.

'What do you think of the story of Chalais's equerry?' asked another musketeer, throwing the question out to the assembled company rather than addressing anyone in particular.

'What story is this?' asked Porthos condescendingly.

'He says he found Rochefort, the Cardinal's hound, in Brussels, disguised as a Capuchin friar, and that, thanks to this disguise, that cursed Rochefort had played Monsieur de Laigues like the fool he is.'

'A cap-and-bells fool,' said Porthos. 'Do we know this for a fact though?'

'I have it from Aramis,' replied the musketeer.

'Really?'

'You know all about this, Porthos,' said Aramis. 'I told you the story yesterday, I made a point of it. So let's talk about something else.'

'Your opinion is that we should talk about something else?' retorted Porthos. 'Let's talk about something else! By God, you wrap things up quickly! What, the cardinal gives orders for a gentleman to be spied on, has his correspondence stolen by a traitor, a felon, a gallows-bird, and then, with the help of this spy and by means of this correspondence, manages to have Chalais beheaded on the ridiculous grounds that he wanted to kill the king and marry the queen to the king's brother! No one had an inkling of this riddle. You told it to us yesterday, to the stupefaction of all, and today, while we're still reeling from the news, you come out and say, "Let's talk about something else!"'

'Very well, let's not talk about something else then, if you'd rather not,' Aramis said patiently.

'That Rochefort,' cried Porthos, 'if I was poor Chalais's equerry, would pass a nasty moment or two in my company.'

'And you would pass an awkward quarter of an hour in the Red Duke's,' said Aramis.

'Ah, "the Red Duke"! Bravo, bravo,' replied Porthos, clapping his hands and nodding approvingly. 'The "Red Duke" is charming. I will circulate the witticism, my dear fellow, don't you worry. Oh Aramis, what a wit! It's such a pity you couldn't pursue your vocation, my dear fellow. What a delightful priest you would have made.'

'Oh, it's only a temporary delay,' replied Aramis. 'I will be one, one day. You know I have kept up my theology studies, Porthos.'

'He'll be as good as his word,' said Porthos. 'Sooner or later, it will happen.'

'Sooner,' said Aramis.

'He is only waiting for one thing to convince him,' said a musketeer, 'then he'll dust down the cassock that's hanging up behind his uniform.'

'And what is that?' asked another.

'He is waiting for the queen to provide the crown of France with an heir[9].'

'Let's have no joking on that subject, gentlemen,' said Porthos. 'God be thanked, the queen is still of an age to do so.'

'They say the Duke of Buckingham is in France . . .' said Aramis, with a sardonic laugh that made his ostensibly innocuous remark sound more than a little scandalous.

'Aramis, my friend, you've blundered this time,' interrupted Porthos. 'Your obsession with wit always makes you go too far. If Monsieur de Tréville heard you, you'd be in trouble for that remark.'

'Don't lecture me, Porthos!' cried Aramis, a flash of something like lightning passing through his mild eyes.

'My dear fellow, be a musketeer or a priest! Be one or the other, but not one and the other,' replied Porthos. 'Wait, Athos said it again the other day: you have a foot in every camp. Ah, let's not lose our tempers, please, that won't serve any purpose, you know what we agreed, Athos, you, and I. You go to Madame d'Aiguillon's and you pay her court; then you go to Madame de Bois-Tracy's[10], Madame de Chevreuse's cousin, and word has it that you stand very high in that lady's good graces too. Oh, my God, don't confess your good fortunes! No one's asking you to reveal your secrets, everyone knows your discretion. But since you are capable of this virtue, hang it, then apply it to Her Majesty. Anyone can treat the king and the cardinal in any way they please, but the queen is sacred, and if one is going to talk about her, then let it be in good part.'

'I tell you, Porthos, you are as vain as Narcissus,' replied Aramis. 'You know I hate moralising, except when it comes from Athos. Besides, my dear fellow, you have far too magnificent a baldric for morals to be your strong point. I will be a priest if it suits me. In the meantime, I am a musketeer. And as such, I say what I please, and, at this moment, it pleases me to say that I am out of patience with you.'

'Aramis!'

'Porthos!'

'Ho there, gentlemen, gentlemen,' exclaimed the people around them.

'Monsieur de Tréville awaits Monsieur d'Artagnan,' interrupted the valet, opening the office door.

At this announcement, during which the door remained open, a hush fell on the room, and, in complete silence, the young Gascon walked part of the length of the antechamber and went in to the captain of the musketeers' office, heartily congratulating himself on having escaped by the skin of his teeth the conclusion of that strange quarrel.

III

THE AUDIENCE

D ESPITE BEING IN A FOUL MOOD at that particular moment, Monsieur de Tréville still politely greeted the young man, who bowed to the ground, and smilingly accepted his compliments, the Béarnais accent of which reminded him of both his youth and his birthplace, twin memories that will bring a smile to a man's face whatever his age. But then, he almost immediately went over to the antechamber and, holding up his hand to d'Artagnan, as if asking his permission to finish some outstanding business before starting on his, he called out three times, increasingly loudly, his voice covering all the tones between imperative and exasperated, 'Athos! Porthos! Aramis!'

The two musketeers, whose acquaintance we have already made and who answered to the last two of those three names, immediately left the groups they were part of and made their way to the office, the door of which closed behind them as soon as they had stepped over the threshold. Although not entirely unruffled, their free and easy manner, dignified and submissive in equal measure, filled d'Artagnan with admiration. They reminded him of demigods and their leader of an Olympian Jupiter, armed with his panoply of thunderbolts.

When the two musketeers had gone in, when the door had closed behind them, when the buzzing murmur of the antechamber had started up again, no doubt afforded fresh fuel by the summons just made, and when, finally, Monsieur de Tréville had paced up and down his office three or four times, silent and frowning, passing each time in front of Porthos and Aramis, who stood ramrod straight and silent as if on parade, he suddenly stopped so that he was staring them in the face, scanned them from head to foot with an irritated look, and cried, 'Do you know what the king said to me, as recently as yesterday evening? Do you know, gentlemen?'

'No,' replied the two musketeers after a moment's silence. 'No, sir, we do not know.'

'But I hope you will do us the honour of telling us,' added Aramis, in his politest tone and with a most gracious bow.

'He told me that from now on he was going to recruit his musketeers from the cardinal's guards!'

'From the cardinal's guards? And why is that?' Porthos demanded warmly.

'Because he could see his cooking wine needed bucking up with a decent vintage.'

The two musketeers blushed to the roots of their hair. D'Artagnan felt completely lost and wished himself a hundred feet under ground.

'Yes, yes,' Monsieur de Tréville continued, increasingly incensed, 'and His Majesty was right, because, on my honour, it's true the musketeers cut a sorry figure at court. Yesterday, at his game of chess with the king, the cardinal told me with an air of commiseration, which displeased me profoundly, that the previous day those cursed musketeers, those devils incarnate – he gave the words an ironic stress, which displeased me even more – those swaggerers, he added, looking at me with his tiger-cat expression, had been found carousing in the early hours in a tavern on Rue Férou[1], and a watch patrol of his guardsmen – I thought he was going to laugh in my face – were forced to arrest them for disturbing the peace. Confound it, you must know something about this business. Musketeers being arrested! You were there, sirs, don't deny it, you were recognised and the cardinal mentioned you by name. Ah, this is all down to me. Yes, yes, it's all my doing, since I'm the one who chooses my men. Look here, you, Aramis, why the devil did you ask me for a tabard when a cassock would have suited you better? And you, Porthos, come now, do you own such a beautiful gold baldric just so you can hang a straw sword off it? And Athos? I don't see Athos. Where is he?'

'Sir,' Aramis replied sadly, 'he is ill, seriously ill.'

'Ill, seriously ill, you say? With what?'

'They're afraid it might be the smallpox,' answered Porthos, eager to add his bit to the conversation, 'which would be unfortunate, since it would certainly do his looks no favours.'

'Smallpox! Here's another tall tale you have for me, Porthos. Sick with the smallpox at his age? No, for pity's sake. But wounded, I daresay, dying, that may be . . . Ah, if I'd known . . . God's blood, musketeers, gentlemen, I won't have you frequenting scurrilous places like this, picking quarrels in the street and indulging in swordplay at the crossroads. And, above all, I won't have you making yourselves the laughing stock of the cardinal's guards, who are worthy, peaceable, clever fellows, who never put themselves in a position to be arrested, and, in any case, would never let themselves be arrested even if they did. I'm sure of it. They would rather die where they stand than yield an inch. Bolting, cutting and running, taking to their heels in headlong flight – that's what the king's musketeers do!'

Porthos and Aramis shook with rage. They would gladly have strangled Monsieur de Tréville if they hadn't sensed deep down that it was his great love for them that was making him talk to them like that. They drummed their feet on the carpet, bit their lips hard enough to draw blood, and gripped their sword hilts with all their might. The throng outside, as we've said, had heard Athos, Porthos and Aramis being summoned, and had surmised from Monsieur de Tréville's tone that he was in a towering rage. Ten curious heads pressed to the curtain hanging over his office door were paling with fury, as their ears glued to the tapestry caught every syllable of what was being said and their mouths relayed the captain's every insulting word to the antechamber's assembled company. Within an instant the entire building, from the door of the office to the door on to the street, was in uproar.

'So, the king's musketeers allow themselves to be arrested by the cardinal's guards,' continued Monsieur de Tréville, no less furious than his men, but speaking in a staccato, plunging his words one by one, as it were, like so many dagger thrusts into his listeners' breasts. 'Ah, six of His Eminence's guards arrest six of His Majesty's guards! By heaven, I've made my decision: I shall go to the Louvre this instant, I shall hand in my resignation as captain of the king's musketeers and request a lieutenancy in the cardinal's guards, and if he refuses me, by heaven, I shall turn priest!'

At these words, the murmurs outside erupted; oaths and curses were all that could be heard on every side. The cries of 'By heaven', 'God's blood' and 'Death to all the devils in hell' crossed in mid-air. D'Artagnan looked for a tapestry to hide behind and felt an overwhelming desire to crawl under the desk.

'Well, captain,' Porthos said, beside himself, 'it's true we were six against six, but they caught us off guard, and before we had time to draw our swords, two of our men had already fallen dead, and Athos, who was gravely wounded, wasn't much better off. You know Athos: well, captain, twice he tried to get up from his knees and twice he fell back down. But we didn't surrender for a moment – they were dragging us off by force when we managed to get away. As for Athos, we thought he was dead, and we left him in peace on the field of battle, not thinking it worth the effort to carry him away. And that's the whole story! Hang it, captain, you can't win every battle. The great Pompey lost Pharsalus, and King François I, although, from what I hear, he was a match for any man, still lost the battle at Pavia.'

'And I have the honour to assure you that I killed one of them with his own sword,' said Aramis, 'since mine had broken on the first parry. Killed or stabbed, sir, as you wish.'

'I didn't know that,' replied Monsieur de Tréville in a milder tone. 'The cardinal exaggerated, I see.'

'For pity's sake though, sir,' continued Aramis, who, seeing his captain somewhat appeased, ventured to make a request, 'don't say Athos was wounded. He would be in despair if it reached the king's ears and, as it is very serious, since the sword-point went down through his shoulder into his chest, it is to be feared . . .'

At that moment, the door curtain lifted and a noble, handsome, shockingly pale face appeared under its fringe.

'Athos!' cried the two musketeers.

'Athos!' repeated Monsieur de Tréville.

'You sent for me, sir,' Athos said to Monsieur de Tréville in a weakened but perfectly composed voice. 'You requested my presence, my comrades tell me, and I hasten to obey your orders. Here I am, sir, what do you wish of me?'

With these words, the musketeer, impeccably dressed and as buttoned up tight in his uniform as ever, stepped firmly into the office. Profoundly moved by this show of courage, Monsieur de Tréville rushed towards him.

'I was saying to these gentlemen,' he said, 'that I forbid my musketeers to expose their lives needlessly because brave men are very dear to the king, and the king knows that his musketeers are the bravest on earth. Your hand, Athos.'

And without waiting for the new arrival to respond to this display of affection, Monsieur de Tréville seized his right hand and shook it with all his might without noticing that Athos, for all his powers of self-control, couldn't help wincing with pain and growing even paler, something one might have thought impossible.

The door had been left ajar, such was the sensation produced by the arrival of Athos whose wound, despite being kept a secret, was known to all. A brouhaha of satisfaction greeted the captain's last words and two or three faces, carried away by their enthusiasm, appeared through the openings in the tapestry. Monsieur de Tréville was undoubtedly about to sharply correct this breach of etiquette when he suddenly felt Athos's hand clench in his own, and, looking round, saw he was about to faint. At the same moment Athos, who had summoned up all his strength to fight the pain, was finally undone and fell to the floor as though dead.

'A surgeon!' cried Monsieur de Tréville. 'Mine, the king's, the best! A surgeon, or, God's blood, my brave Athos will die!'

At Monsieur de Tréville's shouts, everyone rushed into his office before it occurred to him to shut the door on any of them and crowded round the wounded man. But all this zeal would have been futile if the requested doctor hadn't already been in the building. He elbowed his way through the crowd, went up to the still-unconscious figure of Athos and, as it was too hard for him to work in that noise and crush, asked first, and most urgently, that the musketeer be moved to a neighbouring room. Monsieur de Tréville immediately opened a door and pointed the way to Porthos and Aramis, who carried off their comrade in their arms. Behind this group walked the surgeon, and behind the surgeon the door closed.

Then Monsieur de Tréville's office, ordinarily such a revered sanctum, became a temporary extension of the antechamber. Everyone speechified and spouted their opinions and talked at the tops of their voices, cursing and blinding and wishing the cardinal and his guards in hell.

Moments later, Porthos and Aramis reappeared; the surgeon and Monsieur de Tréville had stayed on their own with the wounded man.

Eventually Monsieur de Tréville also reappeared. The invalid had regained consciousness. The surgeon declared that there was nothing in his condition for his friends to be alarmed about; he had merely fainted from loss of blood.

At a wave of Monsieur de Tréville's hand, everyone then withdrew, except d'Artagnan, who had not forgotten he had an audience and, with his characteristic Gascon tenacity, had not stirred an inch.

When everyone had left and the door had been closed again, Monsieur de Tréville turned and found himself alone with the young man. Recent events had made him lose the thread of his thoughts a little. He inquired what the stubborn petitioner wanted. D'Artagnan gave his name and Monsieur de Tréville, recalling in an instant all his memories of the present and of the past, understood the situation.

'Forgive me,' he said, smiling, 'forgive me, my dear country-man, but I had completely forgotten you. What would you have me do? A captain is merely a father of a family with greater responsibilities than an ordinary paterfamilias. Soldiers are over-grown children, you know. But since I insist that the king's and, above all, the cardinal's orders are carried out . . .'

D'Artagnan couldn't repress a smile. Seeing it, Monsieur de Tréville realised he wasn't dealing with an idiot, and, changing the subject, came straight to the point. 'I loved your father very much,' he said. 'What can I do for his son? Be quick, my time isn't mine.'

'Sir,' said d'Artagnan, 'when I left Tarbes to come here, I intended, in remembrance of that friendship which lives on in your memory, to ask you for a musketeer's tabard. But after everything I've seen in the last two hours, I realise that that would be an enormous favour and am very much afraid I would not merit it.'

'It is a favour, certainly, young man,' replied Monsieur de Tréville, 'but it may not be so very far out of your reach as you think, or at least appear to. A ruling by His Majesty, however, has anticipated this situation, and I regret to tell you that no one can be admitted into the musketeers before passing a preliminary test, either by fighting several campaigns, performing certain feats of arms, or serving for two years in another less favoured regiment.'

D'Artagnan bowed without replying. The difficulties to be surmounted in acquiring the musketeer's uniform only made him all the keener to wear it.

'However,' continued Tréville, fixing his fellow countryman with such a piercing gaze it was as if he wanted to read to the depths of his heart, 'in consideration of your father, my old companion, I want, as I said, to do something for you, young man. Our cadets from Béarn tend not to be rich, and I doubt things have changed drastically since I left the province. You cannot therefore have too much of the money you brought with you left to live on.'

D'Artagnan drew himself up with a proud air signifying that he would never ask for alms from anyone.

'All right, young man, all right,' continued Tréville, 'I know that look. I came to Paris with four écus in my pocket, and I'd have fought any man who implied I couldn't buy the Louvre.'

D'Artagnan drew himself up still further. Thanks to the sale of his horse, he was embarking on his career with four écus more than Monsieur de Tréville had had in his pockets when he'd started his.

'So I'm sure, as I was saying, you need to nurse the funds you already have, however healthy they may be. But I'm equally sure you need to refine your mastery of the accomplishments that become a gentleman. I will write a letter to the director of the Académie Royale² today and tomorrow he will take you on without a fee. Don't refuse this small consideration. Gentlemen from the noblest, wealthiest families have been to known to solicit it in vain. You will learn horsemanship, fencing and dancing; you will form desirable acquaintances, and from time to time you will come back to see me and tell me how you are progressing, and whether there is anything I can do for you.'

Unversed as he was in the ways of the court, d'Artagnan still thought he noticed a certain coolness about this reception.

'Alas, sir,' he said, 'I see how grievously I miss my father's letter of introduction to you.'

'I am surprised, it's true,' remarked Monsieur de Tréville, 'that you embarked on such a long journey without this essential viaticum, the only capital we Béarnais have.'

'I had it, sir, and everything was in order, thank God,' exclaimed d'Artagnan. 'But I was treacherously robbed of it.'

Then he recounted the events at Meung, describing the unknown gentleman in minute detail, and did so with a warmth and a sincerity that delighted Monsieur de Tréville.

'That's strange,' said the latter thoughtfully. 'So you spoke about me openly?'

'Yes, sir, doubtless I was that reckless. But how could I be otherwise? A name as illustrious as yours was to be my shield on my travels. You may imagine how often I sheltered behind it.'

Flattery was extremely common in those days, and Monsieur de Tréville loved fulsome praise as much as a king or a cardinal. He couldn't, therefore, help smiling with visible satisfaction, but his smile soon faded and, returning of his own accord to the incident at Meung, he asked, 'Tell me, this gentleman didn't have a slight scar on his temple, did he?'

'Yes, the sort of mark that could have been made by a bullet grazing it.'

'Was he a good-looking man?'

'Yes.'

'Tall?'

'Yes.'

'Pale complexion, brown hair?'

'Yes, yes, that's the one. How is it, sir, that you know this man? Ah, if ever I find him, and I will find him, I swear, even if it's in hell . . .'

'He was waiting for a woman?' continued Tréville.

'At least he left after conversing for a moment with the woman he was waiting for.'

'You don't know what they were talking about?'

'He gave her a box, said it contained her instructions, and told her not to open it until she was in London.'

'This woman was English?'

'He called her "Milady".'

'It's he!' muttered Tréville. 'It's he. I thought he was still in Brussels!'

'Oh sir, if you know this man,' cried d'Artagnan, 'tell me who he is and where he's from, and I will acquit you of any responsibility you might have to me, even of your promise to have me enrolled in the musketeers, because I must be avenged, that's all that matters to me.'

'Don't even think of it, young man!' cried Tréville. 'If you see him coming on one side of the street, cross to the other. Don't dash yourself on a rock like that, he will shatter you like glass.'

'Nevertheless,' said d'Artagnan, 'if I ever find him . . .'

'But don't go looking for him in the meantime,' said Tréville, 'if I have one piece of advice to give you . . .'

Tréville suddenly paused, struck by a sudden suspicion. This loathing the young traveller was giving vent to in such emphatic terms for a man who supposedly, but hardly very plausibly, had robbed him of his father's letter – couldn't this be a cover for some deviousness? Couldn't His Eminence have sent this young man? Couldn't he have come to lay a trap? Couldn't the cardinal be trying to introduce an agent, this so-called d'Artagnan, into his household, his intimate circle, with a view to ferreting out his secrets and then turning them against him, as had been attempted so many times before? Tréville studied d'Artagnan again, more intently this time than the first. He was only moderately reassured by his expression, sparkling with shrewd wit and affected humility.

I know he's a Gascon, he thought, but he could just as easily be the cardinal's Gascon as mine. Well, let's put him to the test.

'My friend,' he said slowly, 'I want, as you are the son of my old friend, since I believe this story of the lost letter to be true, I want, as I say, as recompense for the coolness you noticed at first in your reception, to let you into the secret of politics here. The king and the cardinal are the best of friends; their apparent differences are merely distractions to deceive fools. I do not intend for a fellow countryman, a dashing young spark, a brave lad with all the prerequisites to rise high, to be taken in by all these feints and walk dumbly into the trap, following in the footsteps of so many others who have gone that way to their ruin. Always bear in mind that I am devoted to these two all-powerful masters, and no serious undertaking of mine could ever have any other aim than to serve the king and the cardinal, who is one of the most illustrious geniuses France has ever produced. So now, young man, be guided by this, and if, either from family, or relations, or even instinct, you have conceived one of those enmities for the cardinal that we see flare up among the nobility, then bid me farewell and let us part. I will

help you in a thousand circumstances, but without attaching you
to my person. At all events, I trust that my frankness will make
you my friend, for you are the only young man I have ever spoken
to this way.'

If the cardinal did send me this young fox, Tréville thought to
himself, he is bound, knowing how I execrate him, to have told his
spy that the best way to court me is to enumerate his worst failings.
So, despite my protestations, his cunning accomplice is now going
to tell me he abominates the Eminence.

In fact, turning Tréville's expectations on their head,
d'Artagnan replied with the utmost simplicity, 'Sir, I have come
to Paris with exactly the same intentions. My father told me not
to stand for anything from anyone except the king, the cardinal
and you, whom he considers the three pre-eminent men of
France.'

It will be noticed that d'Artagnan included Monsieur de
Tréville in his list with the other two, but he didn't think the addition could do any harm.

'Therefore I hold the cardinal in highest veneration,' he
continued, 'and I have the most profound respect for his actions.
It is all the better for me, sir, if, as you say, you speak frankly to
me; you will then be doing me the honour of respecting this affinity
of taste between us. But if you entertain any misgivings with
regards to me, as would be all too natural, I sense telling the truth
will be my undoing. But there it is: you will esteem me all the
same, and I value that more above all else.'

Monsieur de Tréville was taken completely by surprise. Such
acumen, such candour, indeed, commanded his admiration, without
entirely allaying his doubts: the greater this young man's merits
compared to others his age, the more of a threat he posed if he
misjudged him. Nevertheless he shook d'Artagnan's hand and said
to him, 'You are an honest fellow, but at present I can only do
what I offered just now. My door will always be open to you. In
time, with leave to ask for me at any hour and so avail yourself
of every opportunity, I am certain you will attain what you desire.'

'In other words, sir,' said d'Artagnan, 'you are waiting for me to prove myself worthy. Well, don't worry,' he added with Gascon familiarity, 'you won't have to wait long.'

And then, with a bow, he made to leave, as if it was all up to him from now on.

'Wait,' Monsieur de Tréville said, stopping him, 'I promised you a letter for the director of the Academy. Are you too proud to accept it, my young gentleman?'

'No, sir,' said d'Artagnan. 'And I promise you it won't meet the same fate as the previous one. I shall take such good care of it that nothing, I swear, will prevent it reaching its destination, and heaven help the person who tries to take it from me!'

Monsieur de Tréville smiled at this fanfaronade, and, leaving his young companion in the embrasure of the window where they had been talking, he went to sit at his desk and started to write the promised testimonial. D'Artagnan, meanwhile, having nothing better to do, began rapping out a march on the window-panes and looking at the occasional musketeer who left the building, watching them until they disappeared around the corner of the street.

When he had written the letter, Monsieur de Tréville sealed it, got to his feet and went over to the young man to give it to him. But just as d'Artagnan was holding out his hand to take it, Monsieur de Tréville was amazed to see his would-be protégé start, flush with rage, and then storm out of the office, yelling, 'Ah, God's blood, he won't escape me this time!'

'Who?' asked Monsieur de Tréville.

'He, my thief,' replied d'Artagnan. 'Ah, you snake!'

Then he disappeared.

'Mad devil,' muttered Monsieur de Tréville. 'Unless that was a ruse to get away when he saw his plan hadn't worked.'

IV

ATHOS'S SHOULDER, PORTHOS'S BALDRIC AND ARAMIS'S HANDKERCHIEF

D'ARTAGNAN HAD CROSSED THE ANTECHAMBER in three furious bounds and was rushing towards the stairs, intending to take them four at a time, when, caught up in the heat of chase, he crashed into a musketeer who was coming out of Monsieur de Tréville's office by a side door, and, colliding headfirst with the man's shoulder, caused him to let out a cry, or rather, a howl.

'Excuse me,' said d'Artagnan, trying to race off, 'excuse me, but I'm in a hurry.'

He had barely gone down the first step before an iron fist seized him by his sash and stopped him in his tracks.

'You're in a hurry,' cried the musketeer, white as a sheet. 'On that pretext, you bang into me, and say, "Excuse me," and you think that's enough? Not quite, young man. Do you think, because you heard Monsieur de Tréville speak somewhat cavalierly to us today, that anyone can treat us in that fashion? Wake up, friend, you are not Monsieur de Tréville.'

'My faith,' replied d'Artagnan, recognising Athos who was returning to his lodgings after being bandaged up by the doctor, 'I didn't do it on purpose, and, not having done so, I said, "Excuse me". So, yes, that does seem enough to me. But I'll say again – and perhaps this is more than enough – on my word of honour, I am in a hurry, a great hurry. So let me go, please, and allow me to go about my business.'

'Sir,' said Athos, letting him go, 'you are not polite. One can see you come from far away.'

D'Artagnan had already leapt down three or four steps but Athos's remark brought him up short.

'Good grief, sir!' he said. 'However far away I've come from, it won't be you who gives me a lesson in manners, I'll have you know.'

'Perhaps,' said Athos.

'Ah, if I weren't in such a hurry,' cried d'Artagnan, 'if I weren't running after someone . . .'

'Mr I'm-in-a-hurry, you won't need to run to find me, do you understand?'

'And where, if you please, will I do that?'

'Near the Carmes-Déschaux[1].'

'When?'

'Around midday.'

'Around midday, very well. I'll be there.'

'Try not to keep me waiting because at a quarter past, I warn you, I'll be the one running after you and I'll cut off your ears at full tilt.'

'Good!' d'Artagnan called to him. 'I'll be there at ten to.'

And then he broke into a run as if the devil were at his back, still hoping to find his stranger, whose leisurely pace couldn't have taken him very far.

At the street door, however, Porthos was talking with one of the guards. There was a space between the two talkers more or less the width of a man. Thinking this should give him ample room, d'Artagnan picked up speed to fly like an arrow between the two of them. But he hadn't allowed for the wind. As he was about to charge through the gap, a gust caught Porthos's long cloak and d'Artagnan sailed straight into it. Porthos must have had his reasons not to be parted from this essential piece of his attire because, rather than let go of the side he was holding, he yanked it towards him so stubbornly that d'Artagnan was spun round and rolled up in the velvet.

Hearing the musketeer cursing, d'Artagnan struggled to free himself, blindly seeking a way through the billowing cloak. More than anything, he was afraid he had marred the pristine, dazzling baldric with which we are familiar, but when he timidly opened his eyes, he found himself with his nose jammed between Porthos's shoulder blades, that is, directly against this item.

Alas, like most of the things of this world that are merely outward show, the baldric was gold in front and plain buff-leather behind. Confirmed peacock that he was, if he couldn't have a complete gold baldric, Porthos was going to at least have half one, which explained the strategic importance of his cold and the indispensable nature of his cloak.

'God's teeth!' cried Porthos, making strenuous efforts to disentangle himself from d'Artagnan who was squirming around behind his back, 'You must be mad, throwing yourself on people like this.'

'Excuse me,' said d'Artagnan, reappearing under the giant's shoulder, 'but I am in a great hurry, I am running after someone and . . .'

'Do you forget your eyes when you're running, by any chance?'

'Not at all,' d'Artagnan replied, taking offence. 'They even show me things other people don't see.'

Whether Porthos understood this or not, he still lost his temper, declaring, 'You will earn yourself a trouncing, sir, I tell you, if you provoke musketeers in this fashion.'

'Trouncing, sir,' said d'Artagnan. 'That's a strong word.'

'It is the right word for a man who is accustomed to looking his enemies in the face.'

'Ah, by God, I know you won't turn your back on yours!'

And then, delighted with his waggishness, the young man set off, laughing uproariously.

Foaming with rage, Porthos made as if to hurl himself at d'Artagnan.

'Later, later,' d'Artagnan cried, 'when you've got rid of your cloak.'

'At one o'clock then, behind the Luxembourg.'

'Very good, at one o'clock,' replied d'Artagnan, turning the corner.

But he didn't see a soul, either in the street he had run down, or in the one he now took in at a glance. However slowly the stranger had been walking, he had still gone a fair way, or perhaps he had ducked into one of the houses. D'Artagnan inquired after

him of everyone he met, went down to the ferry[2], came back up
Rue de Seine and Rue la Croix-Rouge, but nothing, not a sniff.
All this running, however, was helpful to him because, even as his
forehead became bathed in sweat, so his ardour cooled.

Then he began to reflect on the recent sequence of events: a
great deal had happened, all of it inauspicious. It was barely eleven
o'clock in the morning, and already the day had brought his fall
from favour with Monsieur de Tréville, who was bound to have
thought his exit a little off-hand.

Furthermore, he had acquired two prime duels with two men,
each of whom was capable of killing three d'Artagnans. To cap
it all, they were two musketeers, that is, two of those beings he
held in such high esteem that, in his heart and mind, he placed
them above all other mortals.

It was a sorry state of affairs. Certain he'd be killed by Athos,
the young man, understandably enough, didn't trouble himself
greatly about Porthos. However, as hope is the last thing to be
extinguished in a man's heart, hope began to stir in his that he
might have a chance of surviving, with terrible wounds, of course,
these two duels, and, if so, he took himself to task as to his future
conduct in the following terms: 'What a featherbrain I was, and
what a clumsy lout I am! That brave, unfortunate Athos was
wounded in the very shoulder I had to butt into like a ram. The
only surprise is that he didn't kill me there and then; he had every
right to, and he must be in agony. As for Porthos . . . Ah, as for
Porthos, gracious me . . .'

And in spite of himself the young man started laughing, while
looking round to check that this solitary and, to an onlooker,
apparently groundless laughter wasn't going to offend any
passers-by.

'As for Porthos, that's a funnier business, but I am no less of
a hair-brained wretch. Does one throw oneself on people like this
without warning them? No! Does one look under their cloak to
see what's missing? He would have certainly forgiven me . . . He
would have forgiven me if I hadn't mentioned that cursed baldric.

I only alluded to it, it's true . . . yes, that was beautifully done! Ah, cursed Gascon that I am, I would make witticisms as I leapt from the frying pan into the fire. Come on now, d'Artagnan my friend,' he continued, addressing himself with all the amiability he felt was his due, 'If you get through this, which is not likely, the thing to do in future is be impeccably polite. From now on you must be admired, you must be held up as a model. There's nothing cowardly about being considerate and courteous. Look at Aramis: Aramis is gentleness itself, grace personified. Well then, has anyone ever taken it into his head to say Aramis is a coward? No, certainly not. So, from now on that's whom I shall model myself on in every respect. Ah, speaking of which, here he is.'

Striding along, talking to himself as he went, d'Artagnan had come to within a few paces of the d'Aiguillon mansion³ and had caught sight of Aramis in front of this building, merrily chatting with three gentlemen of the king's guards. Aramis had caught sight of d'Artagnan too, but since he hadn't forgotten it was in this young man's presence that Monsieur de Tréville had flown into such a rage that morning, and since a witness to the musketeers' upbraiding did not appeal to him in the slightest, he pretended not to see him. D'Artagnan could not have felt more differently. Full of his newfound resolve to radiate goodwill and courtesy, he approached the four young men with a low bow and his most winning smile. Aramis inclined his head slightly, but did not return the smile, and, at the same moment, all four men broke off their conversation.

D'Artagnan was not so obtuse as to fail to see that he was intruding, but nor was he sufficiently experienced in the ways of fashionable society to be able to extract himself elegantly from the sort of awkward situation that tends to arise when a man goes up to people he barely knows and joins in a conversation that doesn't concern him. He was thinking how to effect as poised a retreat as possible when he noticed that Aramis had dropped his handkerchief and, no doubt inadvertently, had stepped on it. This seemed to be his opportunity to make amends for his gracelessness. He bent

down and, with all the civility he could muster, pulled the handkerchief out from under the musketeer's foot, despite encountering
some resistance, and said, as he handed it back to him, 'I believe,
sir, this is a handkerchief you would be sorry to lose.'

The handkerchief was indeed richly embroidered and had a
coronet and arms in one corner. Aramis blushed violently and
snatched rather than took it from the Gascon's hands.

'Aha!' cried one of the guardsmen. 'Aramis, you discreet soul,
are you still going to insist you are on bad terms with Madame de
Bois-Tracy when this gracious lady is so kind as to lend you her
handkerchiefs?'

Aramis shot d'Artagnan one of those looks which tell a man he
has acquired a mortal enemy, and then, reverting to his soft-spoken
self, smoothly replied, 'You are labouring under a misapprehension,
gentlemen. The handkerchief doesn't belong to me, and I don't
know why the fancy took monsieur to give it to me rather than to
one of you – and here, as proof of this, is mine in my pocket.'

Saying which, he produced his own handkerchief, which was
equally elegant and of fine cambric, an expensive material at the
time, but lacking embroidery or arms, and, for decoration, having
merely its owner's monogram.

D'Artagnan didn't utter a word this time, realising his blunder,
but Aramis's friends weren't satisfied with his denials, and one of
them, addressing the young musketeer with feigned solemnity,
declared, 'If what you claim is true, then I should be compelled,
my dear Aramis, to request you return the handkerchief because,
as you know, Bois-Tracy is one of my intimates and I will not
have people sporting his wife's personal effects as trophies.'

'You phrase your request poorly,' replied Aramis, 'so, while I
might acknowledge its essential soundness, I should be obliged to
refuse it on a point of form.'

'The fact is,' d'Artagnan ventured timidly, 'that I didn't see
the handkerchief come out of Monsieur Aramis's pocket. He had
his foot on it, that's all, and I thought that, since he had his foot
on it, the handkerchief was his.'

'And you were mistaken, my dear sir,' Aramis replied coldly, impervious to his attempt to make amends. Then, turning to the guardsman who had declared he was a friend of Bois-Tracy, he said, 'Besides, my dear intimate of Bois-Tracy, I think that my friendship with him cannot be any the less tender than yours, which means, strictly speaking, that this handkerchief could just as easily have come out of your pocket as out of mine.'

'No, on my honour!' cried His Majesty's guardsman.

'You will swear on your honour and I on my word, and evidently one of the two of us will be lying. Wait, there's a better way. Monteran, let's each take half.'

'Of the handkerchief?'

'Yes.'

'Perfect!' cried the two other guardsmen. 'The Judgement of Solomon. Aramis, you are wise beyond your years.'

The young people burst out laughing and, as might be imagined, that was an end to the matter. After a moment, the conversation drew to a close and, with a cordial handshake, the three guards and the musketeer parted, the guards going their way and Aramis going his.

Now's the time to make my peace with this gentleman, d'Artagnan thought to himself, having hung back a little during the last part of the conversation. And, with these good intentions, he went up to Aramis, who was walking off without paying him any more attention, and said, 'Sir, you will forgive me, I trust . . .'

'Ah, sir,' Aramis cut in, 'allow me to observe that you did not conduct yourself as a man of honour in this affair.'

'What, sir!' cried d'Artagnan. 'You suppose . . .'

'I suppose, sir, that you are not an idiot, and that you are well aware, even though you've only just arrived from Gascony, that one does not tread on pocket handkerchiefs without a reason. Hang it, Paris is not paved with cambric!'

'It is wrong of you to seek to humiliate me, sir,' said d'Artagnan, his quarrelsome nature getting the better of his pacifist intentions. 'I am from Gascony, it's true, and since you know as much, I hardly need tell you that Gascons are not very long-suffering, so that when they have apologised once, even if it is for a stupid blunder, they are convinced they have not only done what they ought, but half as much again.'

'My remarks, sir, are not intended to pick a quarrel,' replied Aramis. 'I am no brawler, thank God, and as I am merely a provisional musketeer, I only fight when I am compelled to, and always with the utmost repugnance. But this is a serious business, since a lady has here been compromised by you.'

'By us, you mean,' cried d'Artagnan.

'Why were you so indiscreet as to give me the handkerchief?'

'Why were you to drop it?'

'I have said, and I will say again, sir, that this handkerchief did not come out of my pocket.'

'Well then, you have lied twice, sir, because I saw it come out of there with my own eyes!'

'Ah, so this is the tone you take with me, is it, Monsieur le Gascon? Well then, I will give you a lesson in manners.'

'And I will send you back to your mass, Monsieur l'abbé! Draw, if you please, this instant.'

'No indeed, if you please, my fair friend . . . Not here, at least. Can't you see we are outside the d'Aiguillon place, which is teeming with the cardinal's creatures? In point of fact, who's to say His Eminence didn't order you to bring him my head? Now, I am ridiculously attached to it, my head that is, since it seems to go pretty well with my shoulders. So I am looking forward to killing you, don't worry on that score, but I wish to do so in peace and quiet, in a closed and covered place, where you won't be able to brag about your demise to any onlookers.'

'As you wish, but I wouldn't be too confident of the outcome. And bring that handkerchief with you, whether it's yours or not: you may have a chance to use it.'

'Monsieur wouldn't be a Gascon, would he?' asked Aramis.

'He would. Monsieur wouldn't be putting off a meeting out of prudence, would he?'

'Prudence, sir, is a fairly superfluous virtue for a musketeer, I know, but it is indispensable for the clergy, and as I am only a musketeer temporarily, I am keen to remain prudent. I will have the honour, therefore, of expecting you at Monsieur de Tréville's at two o'clock. I will direct you to suitable places from there.'

The two young men bowed to each other, then Aramis went away up the street leading to the Luxembourg, while d'Artagnan, seeing time was getting on, set off for Carmes-Déschaux, saying to himself, There's no escaping now, but at least if I'm killed, I'll be killed by a musketeer.

V

THE KING'S MUSKETEERS AND THE CARDINAL'S GUARDS

D'ARTAGNAN DIDN'T KNOW A SOUL in Paris. So he went to meet Athos without taking a second, ready to make do with those his adversary had chosen. In any case, he had made up his mind to offer the brave musketeer all the appropriate apologies, with all due staunchness, because he was afraid their duel would have the unfortunate outcome that always attends affairs of this sort, when a young, vigorous man takes on a wounded, weakened adversary: if he is defeated, his opponent's triumph is all the greater, while if he is victorious, he is accused of a breach of honour and posturing.

Now, unless we have failed to convey the character of our adventure seeker, our reader will already have gathered that d'Artagnan wasn't an ordinary man. Hence, while he kept telling himself his death was inevitable, he wasn't in the least resigned to going meekly to his grave, as another less courageous, more moderate person would have been in his place. Instead he turned over his adversaries' respective characters in his mind and began to see his situation more clearly. Through the sincere apologies he

intended to offer Athos, he hoped to make a friend of this
gentleman, whose aristocratic air and austere manner pleased him
greatly. He flattered himself that he had put the wind up Porthos
with the baldric episode, on which he could, if he wasn't killed on
the spot, dine out. Judiciously heightened for effect, the story
should cover Porthos with ridicule. And finally, as for Aramis the
fox, he wasn't that scared of him and, assuming he made it that
far, he undertook to dispatch him fair and square, or, at the very
least, strike him in the face, as Caesar had told his men to do to
Pompey's soldiers[1], and so rob him forever of those good looks
on which he prided himself so much.

D'Artagnan could draw on that unwavering store of resolve
which his father's advice had fixed in his heart, advice which, in
essence, declared: 'Don't stand for anything from anyone except
the king, the cardinal and Monsieur de Tréville.' So he flew more
than walked towards the Convent of the Carmes Déchaussés, or
rather Déschaux as it was known then, a windowless building that
was a chapel of ease for the Pré-aux-Clercs[2], which was surrounded
by barren fields that served as a duelling ground for people in a
hurry.

When d'Artagnan caught sight of the stretch of waste ground
at the foot of the convent, Athos had only been waiting for five
minutes and it was striking midday. He was thus as punctual as
the Samaritaine clock[3], and the most demanding expert in duelling
protocol could not have faulted him.

Athos, who was still suffering acutely from his wound, despite
its dressing having been changed by Monsieur de Tréville's
surgeon, had sat down on a boundary-stone to await his adversary
with his perennial calm expression and dignified air. Seeing
d'Artagnan, he stood up and politely took several steps to meet
him. D'Artagnan approached his adversary with his hat in his hand
and its plume trailing on the ground.

'Sir,' said Athos, 'I have sent word to two of my friends who
will act as my seconds, but they haven't arrived yet. I'm surprised
they're late; it's not like them.'

'I haven't any seconds myself, sir,' said d'Artagnan. 'Having only arrived in Paris yesterday, I haven't made the acquaintance of anyone except Monsieur de Tréville, to whom I was referred by my father who, in some small measure, has the honour of being one of his friends.'

Athos reflected for a moment.

'Monsieur de Tréville is the only person you know?' he asked.

'Yes, sir, I know no one else.'

'Ah, but then . . .' continued Athos, half to himself and half to d'Artagnan, 'if I kill you, people will think I am a monster who preys on children.'

'Not entirely, sir,' d'Artagnan replied with a bow which was not devoid of dignity, 'since you do me the honour of crossing swords while afflicted by a wound that must put you to great inconvenience.'

'My word, to extreme inconvenience. I am in infernal pain thanks to you, I have to say. But I will use my left hand, as I usually do in such circumstances, so you mustn't think I'm doing you a favour: I can draw equally well with both hands. It may even put you at a disadvantage. A left-handed opponent is extremely awkward, especially if one isn't prepared. In fact, I regret not informing you of this sooner.'

'You are a model of courtesy, sir,' said d'Artagnan, bowing again, 'I am most grateful to you.'

'This is too much,' demurred Athos with his gentlemanly air. 'Please, let us turn to another subject, as long as that is not disagreeable to you. Ah, God's blood, you hurt me! My shoulder is on fire.'

'Would you allow me . . .' d'Artagnan inquired timidly.

'What, sir?'

'I have a balm that has a marvellous effect on wounds, a balm I was given by my mother and have tried out on myself.'

'And?'

'And I am sure that this balm will have cured you in less than

three days, and, in three days, when you are well, sir, it will be
just as great an honour to be your man.'

D'Artagnan said these words with a simplicity that did honour
to his courtliness without in any way compromising his courage.

'By God, sir,' said Athos, 'there's a proposal I like . . . Not
that I accept it, but you can tell its author is a gentleman a mile
away. This was how those valiant knights spoke and acted in the
time of Charlemagne, those exemplars on whom every gentleman
should seek to model himself. Unfortunately we no longer live in
the time of the great emperor. This is the time of the cardinal,
and in three days everyone would know, however closely the secret
might be guarded – everyone, I tell you, would know we were
contracted to fight, and they would prevent us . . . Heavens above,
are those saunterers coming or not?'

'If you are in a hurry, sir,' d'Artagnan said to Athos with the
same simplicity with which a moment earlier he had suggested
they postpone their duel for three days, 'and would like to dispatch
me without further ado, don't stand on ceremony, I beg you.'

'There's another remark to my liking,' said Athos, graciously
nodding to d'Artagnan. 'A man who says such a thing cannot fail
to have a head on his shoulders, and he clearly has a noble heart
in his breast. Sir, I love gentlemen of your ilk, and I can see that
if we do not kill one another, I will in future take great pleasure
in your conversation. But please, let us wait for these gentlemen;
I have plenty of time and it would be better form. Ah, here's one
of them, I think.'

And, sure enough, the gigantic figure of Porthos hove into
view at that moment on Rue de Vaugirard.

'What!' cried d'Artagnan. 'Your first witness is Monsieur
Porthos?'

'Yes. Does that displease you?'

'No, not at all.'

'And here's the second.'

D'Artagnan turned in the direction Athos was pointing and
saw Aramis.

'What!' he cried, even more surprised than before. 'Your second witness is Monsieur Aramis?'

'Certainly. Don't you know that one of us is never seen without the others, and that we're known in the musketeers and the guards, at court and in town, as Athos, Porthos and Aramis, or the Three Inseparables? Still, as you have only just come up from Dax or Pau . . .'

'Tarbes,' said d'Artagnan.

'. . . you may be forgiven for not knowing this minor detail,' said Athos.

'My faith, the name is apt, gentlemen,' said d'Artagnan, 'and if word gets out about my adventures, it will at least go to prove that your alliance is not founded on contraries.'

Porthos had joined them in the meantime, waved to Athos in greeting, and then, turning to d'Artagnan, had stopped short, astonished.

We should add in passing that he had changed out of his baldric and dispensed with his cloak.

'Ah!' he exclaimed. 'What's this?'

'This is the gentleman I am going to fight,' said Athos, indicating d'Artagnan with his hand and saluting him as he did so.

'This is whom I am fighting too,' said Porthos.

'But not till one o'clock,' said d'Artagnan.

'And I am fighting him as well,' said Aramis, arriving in his turn on the scene.

'But not till two o'clock,' d'Artagnan said, equally calmly.

'Why are you fighting, Athos?' asked Aramis.

'My faith, I'm not too sure; he hurt my shoulder. What about you, Porthos?'

'My faith, I am fighting because I am fighting,' Porthos replied, blushing.

Athos, who saw everything, noticed a faint smile on the Gascon's lips.

'We had a disagreement about dress,' said the young man.

'And you, Aramis?' asked Athos.

'I am fighting over a matter of theology,' replied Aramis, signalling to d'Artagnan that he wanted him to keep the cause of their duel secret. Athos saw a second smile hover over d'Artagnan's lips.

'Indeed,' said Athos.

'Yes, a point of St Augustine on which we do not see eye to eye,' said the Gascon.

'He has a nice wit, clearly,' murmured Athos.

'Now you are gathered here, gentlemen,' said d'Artagnan, 'allow me to offer you my apologies.'

At the word 'apologies', a shadow passed over Athos's brow, a haughty smile curled Porthos's lip and Aramis waved his hand by way of response.

'You misunderstand me, gentlemen,' said d'Artagnan, holding up his head on which a ray of sunshine played at that moment, gilding his fine, bold features. 'I ask you to accept my apologies in case I cannot discharge my debt to all three of you, since Monsieur Athos has the right to kill me first, which significantly devalues your claim, Monsieur Porthos, and renders yours virtually worthless, Monsieur Aramis. So now, gentlemen, I say again, my apologies, but only in this respect . . . And, on guard!'

At these words, with the most cavalier gesture imaginable, d'Artagnan drew his sword.

D'Artagnan's blood was up, and at that moment he would have drawn his sword against all the musketeers of the realm, let alone Athos, Porthos and Aramis.

It was a quarter past midday. The sun was at its zenith and the place chosen as the scene of the duel was exposed to its full ardour.

'It is very hot,' said Athos, drawing his sword in turn, 'and yet I cannot take off my doublet because I felt my wound bleeding again just now, and I would be afraid to put monsieur out by showing him any blood he hadn't drawn himself.'

'It is true, sir,' said d'Artagnan. 'Whether drawn by another or by myself, I assure you that it will always be with considerable regret that I see the blood of so brave a gentleman. I shall fight in my doublet, then, like you.'

'Come now,' said Porthos. 'Enough of these compliments. Remember we're waiting our turn . . .'

'Speak for yourself, Porthos, if you must be so crass,' interrupted Aramis. 'For my part, I find these gentlemen's remarks very elegant and entirely worthy of two men of honour.'

'Whenever you wish, sir,' said Athos, putting himself on guard.

'I was awaiting your orders,' said d'Artagnan, crossing swords.

But the two rapiers had barely rung out and returned to the horizontal when a troop of His Eminence's guards under the command of Monsieur de Jussac appeared at the corner of the convent.

'The cardinal's guards!' Porthos and Aramis cried simultaneously. 'Sheathe your swords, gentlemen! Sheathe swords!'

But it was too late. The two combatants had already been seen in a pose that left no doubt as to their intentions.

'Ho there!' cried Jussac, marching towards them and signalling to his men to do likewise. 'Ho there, musketeers, duelling here, are we? What of the edicts – are we paying those no mind?'

'You are very generous, guardsmen, sirs,' Athos said bitterly, since Jussac had been one of the assailants from the day before yesterday. 'If we saw you fighting, I promise you we would do our utmost not to interfere. Let us get on, therefore, and you will have a modicum of pleasure without going to any pains.'

'Gentlemen,' said Jussac, 'I very much regret to inform you that what you ask is impossible. Duty always comes first. Sheathe your swords, therefore, if you please, and follow us.'

'Sir,' Aramis said, parodying Jussac. 'We would very much like to accept your gracious invitation, if the decision were ours to make, but unfortunately we must inform you that what you ask is impossible: Monsieur de Tréville has forbidden it. So go about your business, sir, that's your best plan.'

This mockery infuriated Jussac.

'We will charge you, then,' he said, 'if you disobey.'

'There are five of them,' Athos said in a low voice, 'and only three of us. They will beat us again and we will have to die here because, on my word, I shall never again appear in the captain's presence a defeated man.'

Athos, Porthos and Aramis went into a huddle together for a moment, while Jussac lined up his men.

That brief moment was enough for d'Artagnan to make up his mind. It was one of those junctures that decide a man's life: a choice had to be made between the king and the cardinal, and, once made, it had to be seen through. Fighting meant disobeying the law, risking his life, and, in one fell swoop, making an enemy of a minister more powerful than the king himself. The young man saw all this and, to his credit, didn't hesitate for a second. Turning towards Athos and his friends, he said, 'Gentlemen, I will take you up on something you said, if I may. You declared there were only three of you, whereas I think there are four.'

'But you're not one of us,' said Porthos.

'It's true I lack the uniform,' replied d'Artagnan, 'but I have the soul. My heart is a musketeer's. I feel it, sir, and it urges me on.'

'Get out of here, young man,' shouted Jussac, no doubt guessing d'Artagnan's intentions from his gestures and the expression on his face. 'You may retire from the field, you have our permission. Off you go, quick, save your skin.'

D'Artagnan didn't move a muscle.

'Good lad,' said Athos, shaking the young man's hand.

'Come on, come on, let's have a decision!' Jussac said.

'Right,' Porthos and Aramis said, 'we must do something.'

'Monsieur is full of generosity,' Athos complimented d'Artagnan, but, like the other two musketeers, he was thinking about his youth and worrying about his inexperience. 'We would only be three, one wounded, and a boy,' he continued. 'And yet it will be said we were four men.'

'Yes, but yield . . .' said Porthos.

'Not easy,' said Athos.

D'Artagnan understood their indecision.

'At least try me, gentlemen,' he said, 'and I swear on my honour that I shall not leave this place if we are defeated.'

'What is your name, my fine fellow?' said Athos.

'D'Artagnan, sir.'

'Well then, Athos, Porthos, Aramis and d'Artagnan, forward!' cried Athos.

'Come now, gentlemen, are you minded to make up your mind?' Jussac cried again.

'It is settled, gentlemen,' said Athos.

'And what is your decision?' demanded Jussac.

'We shall have the honour of charging you,' replied Aramis, doffing his hat with one hand and drawing his sword with the other.

'Ah, you're resisting!' cried Jussac.

'God's blood, does that surprise you?'

Then the nine combatants rushed at one another with a fury that was not entirely without method.

Athos took Cahusac, the cardinal's favourite, Porthos singled out Biscarat[4], and Aramis faced off against two adversaries. As for d'Artagnan, he found himself charging straight at Jussac himself.

The young Gascon's heart beat hard enough to break his rib cage, not from fear though – thank God, he didn't have a flicker of that – but from ambition. He fought like an enraged tiger, circling ten times round his adversary, changing twenty times his guard and his ground. Jussac had an appetite for the blade, as they used to say in those days, and a wealth of experience, but he still had the utmost difficulty defending himself against an agile, quick-footed adversary who constantly departed from received practice, attacking on all sides at once and parrying like a man who has the greatest respect for his skin.

Eventually the struggle exhausted Jussac's patience. Furious at being held at bay by someone he had thought of as a child, the blood went to his head and he started to make mistakes. D'Artagnan, compensating in theory for what he lacked in practice, responded with ever greater feats of agility. Wanting to be done with it, Jussac lunged full length to deliver his adversary a terrible blow, but d'Artagnan parried in prime and, as Jussac was straightening up, slipped like a snake under his blade and ran his sword through his body. Jussac fell in a heap upon the ground.

D'Artagnan glanced quickly and anxiously round the battlefield.

Aramis had already killed one of his opponents; the other was pressing him hard, but he was still in a good position and could defend himself. Biscarat and Porthos had wounded one another moments before, Porthos taking a sword thrust in the arm, and Biscarat one in the thigh. But, as neither of the wounds was serious, they were only fighting all the more fiercely. Athos, wounded afresh by Cahusac, was paling visibly but not giving an inch; he had simply swapped sword-arms and was fighting left-handed.

According to the duelling laws of the time, d'Artagnan was allowed to go to someone's assistance. As he was looking to see which of his companions needed him to rally round, he caught a glance from Athos. It was sublimely eloquent. Athos would have died rather than call for help, but he could look, and with a look ask for support. D'Artagnan guessed as much, sprang forward with a terrible leap and fell on Cahusac's flank, crying, 'To me, guardsman sir, I will kill you!'

Cahusac turned round, not a moment too soon. Athos, who was only standing through sheer courage, slumped on to one knee.

'God's blood!' he cried to d'Artagnan, 'don't kill him, young man, I beg you. I have outstanding business to settle with him when I am mended and well. Just disarm him, bind your blade round his sword . . . that's right . . . good . . . excellent!'

This exclamation was torn from Athos by the sight of Cahusac's sword flying twenty paces off to one side. D'Artagnan and Cahusac took to their heels, one to recover the sword, the other to make it his own, but d'Artagnan was nimbler and, getting there first, put his foot on it.

Cahusac ran to the guardsman Aramis had killed, took his rapier, and headed back to d'Artagnan, but, on the way, he was confronted by Athos who, during the moment's respite d'Artagnan had earned him, had caught his breath and, fearing that d'Artagnan would kill his enemy, wanted to resume the fight.

D'Artagnan realised it would be discourteous not to let Athos have his way. And sure enough, a few seconds later, Cahusac fell with a sword thrust to the throat.

At the same moment, Aramis pressed his sword-point into the chest of his fallen opponent and compelled him to ask for quarter.

That only left Porthos and Biscarat. Porthos was making a thousand boasts, asking Biscarat what o'clock it could possibly be and complimenting him on his brother's new command in the Navarre regiment. But, for all his mockery, he was getting nowhere. Biscarat was one of those men of iron who only yield when they fall down dead.

But they had to wrap it up. The watch could arrive at any moment and arrest all the combatants, wounded or not, royalist or cardinalist. Athos, Aramis and d'Artagnan surrounded Biscarat and called on him to surrender. Biscarat was determined to hold out, despite being alone against them all and with a sword thrust through his thigh, but Jussac, who had raised himself up on an elbow, called to him to yield. Biscarat was a Gascon like d'Artagnan – turning a deaf ear, he simply laughed and, in between parries, found time to point to a spot on the ground with his sword-tip, and, parodying a verse in the Bible, say, 'Here shall die Biscarat, alone of all who are with him.'

'But there are four of them against the one of you,' shouted Jussac. 'End it, I order you.'

'Ah, if it's an order, then that's different,' said Biscarat. 'Since you are my commander, I must obey.'

And jumping backwards, he broke his sword over his knee so as not to surrender it, threw the pieces over the convent wall, crossed his arms and whistled a cardinalist air.

Bravery is always respected, even in an enemy. The musketeers saluted Biscarat with their swords, then sheathed them. D'Artagnan did likewise and then with the help of Biscarat, the only one of their adversaries still standing, carried Jussac, Cahusac and the guardsman Aramis had wounded under the porch of the convent. The fourth guardsman, as we've said, was dead. Then they rang the bell, and, carrying off four out of the five swords, headed back to Monsieur de Tréville's, mad with joy. They swaggered along arm in arm, taking up the whole street, greeting every musketeer they met, and, by the end, their progress had become a triumphal procession. His heart reeling with happiness, d'Artagnan walked between Athos and Porthos, embracing them tenderly.

'I may not be a musketeer yet,' he said to his new friends as they entered the courtyard of Monsieur de Tréville's residence, 'but at least this means I've begun my apprenticeship, doesn't it?'

VI

HIS MAJESTY KING LOUIS XIII[1]

THE AFFAIR CAUSED A GREAT STIR. Monsieur de Tréville publicly took his musketeers to task in the strongest terms, while congratulating them in private, but then, as the king had to be informed immediately, wasted no time before hurrying off to the Louvre. It was already too late: the king was closeted with the cardinal, and Monsieur de Tréville was told he was working and couldn't see anyone at present. That evening, Monsieur de Tréville attended the king's gaming table[2]. The king was winning and, since His Majesty was a terrible miser, he was in an excellent mood. Catching sight of Monsieur de Tréville across the room, he called out, 'Come here, captain, come here so I can reprimand you. Are you aware His Eminence has been to see me to complain about your musketeers, and that he did so with such feeling that he is too ill to come this evening? Heavens above, those musketeers of yours are lawless devils, utter gallows-birds.'

'No, Sire,' replied Tréville, who saw at a glance where the

matter was heading. 'Quite the contrary, they are good creatures, as meek as lambs, and they would like nothing better than never to have to draw their swords except on His Majesty's service. But what would you have them do? The cardinal's guards are constantly trying to pick quarrels with them and so, for the honour of their corps, the poor young men are forced to defend themselves.'

'Listen to Monsieur de Tréville,' said the king. 'You would think he was talking about a religious community. Truly, my dear captain, I have a mind to relieve you of your command and give it to Mademoiselle de Chémerault, to whom I've promised an abbey. But don't think I'm just going to take your word for it. They call me Louis the Just, Monsieur de Tréville, so we shall see in a moment, in just a matter of moments.'

'Ah, Sire, it's because I have faith in this unswerving justice that I shall patiently and calmly await Your Majesty's convenience.'

'Wait then, sir, wait,' said the king. 'I shall not keep you waiting long.'

And indeed, his luck turned, and as the king started to lose what he had won, he was not sorry to have an excuse – if we may be allowed to use a gambling expression, the origins of which, we confess, we do not know – to make Charlemagne[3]. The king got up after a minute and, pocketing the money in front of him, the majority of which was his winnings, said, 'La Vieuville, take my place, I have to speak to Monsieur de Tréville on a matter of importance. Ah, I had eighty louis d'or in my pile[4]. Put in the same sum, so that those who have lost won't have anything to complain about. Justice before all things.'

Then, turning back to Monsieur de Tréville and walking with him to the embrasure of a window, he continued, 'Now then, sir, you say it was the most eminent cardinal's guards who picked a quarrel with your musketeers?'

'Yes, Sire, as usual.'

'And how did it come about? As you know, my dear captain, a judge must hear both sides.'

'Good Lord, in the simplest and most natural of ways. Three

of my best soldiers, whom Your Majesty knows by name and whose
loyalty he has commended on more than one occasion – and who
serve him, I can assure His Majesty, with all their hearts – three
of my best soldiers, as I was saying, Messrs Athos, Porthos and
Aramis, had arranged a jaunt with a young cadet from Gascony
whom I'd introduced them to that morning. Their destination was
Saint-Germain, I believe, and they had agreed to meet at the
Carmes-Déschaux when they were interrupted by Monsieur de
Jussac, Messrs Cahusac and Biscarat and two other guards, who
cannot have gone there in such numbers without some suspect
designs on the edicts.'

'Ah, you've set me thinking,' said the king. 'No doubt they
were coming to fight themselves.'

'I am not accusing them, Sire, but I shall let Your Majesty be
the judge of what five armed men might be going to do in a place
as deserted as the Convent des Carmes.'

'Yes, you're right, Tréville, you're right.'

'So, when they saw my musketeers, they changed their minds
and replaced their individual hatreds with hatred for our corps,
since Your Majesty cannot be blind to the fact that the musketeers,
who are the king's men, and his alone, are natural enemies of the
guards, who are the cardinal's.'

'Yes, Tréville, yes,' said the king melancholically, 'and it is very
sad, believe me, to see two factions in France like this, two heads
vying for the royal crown. But this will change, Tréville, this will
all change. So, you say the guards provoked a quarrel with the
musketeers?'

'I say it is likely that is what happened, but I do not swear to
it, Sire. You know how difficult it is to get to the truth unless one
is endowed with that admirable instinct which has earned Louis
XIII his title "the Just" . . .'

'Quite right, Tréville. But they weren't alone, your musketeers,
there was a boy with them?'

'Yes, Sire, and one of them was wounded, so that three of the
king's musketeers, one a wounded man, and a boy, not only held

their own against five of the cardinal's most formidable guards, but laid four of them low.'

'Why, that's a victory!' cried the king, absolutely radiant. 'An outright victory!'

'Yes, Sire, as outright as that of the Pont de Cé⁵.'

'Four men, one of them wounded, and a boy, you say?'

'A young man, but only just. He conducted himself so impeccably in this affair that I shall take the liberty of commending him to Your Majesty.'

'What is his name?'

'D'Artagnan, Sire. He is the son of one of my oldest friends; the son of a man who fought with your father the king, of glorious memory, in the partisan war.'

'And you say he conducted himself well, this young man?' asked King Louis XIII, proudly twirling his moustache and striking an attitude. 'Tell me, Tréville – you know how I love tales of war and arms.'

'Well, Sire,' replied Tréville, 'as I said, Monsieur d'Artagnan is little more than a boy and, since he does not have the honour of being a musketeer, he was in plain clothes. The cardinal's guards, seeing not only his tender years but also that he didn't belong to the corps, invited him to retire from the field before they attacked.'

'So you see, Tréville,' interrupted the king, 'it was they who attacked.'

'Very true, Sire; that confirms it. Well, they called on him to withdraw, but he replied that he was a musketeer at heart and devoted to His Majesty so he was going to remain at the musketeers' side.'

'Brave young fellow,' murmured the king.

'And, true to his word, he stayed with them, and Your Majesty has there such a stout champion that it was he who gave Jussac the terrible sword thrust that has driven the cardinal into a towering rage.'

'He wounded Jussac?' cried the king. 'Him, a boy? That can't be, Tréville!'

'It is as I have the honour of telling Your Majesty.'

'Jussac, one of the finest blades of the realm!'

'He has met his master now, Sire.'

'I wish to see this young man, Tréville. I wish to see him, and if we can do anything, well, we will attend to it.'

'When will Your Majesty deign to receive him?'

'Tomorrow at midday, Tréville.'

'Shall I bring him on his own?'

'No, bring all four of them together. I want to thank them all at the same time. Loyal men are rare, Tréville, and loyalty must be rewarded.'

'We will be at the Louvre at midday.'

'Ah, but come by the back stairs, Tréville, the back stairs. There's no need for the cardinal to know . . .'

'Yes, Sire.'

'You understand, Tréville, an edict is still an edict. When all's said and done, duelling is prohibited.'

'But this encounter, Sire, bears no resemblance to an ordinary duel. It was a brawl, and the proof is that there were five of the cardinal's guards against my three musketeers and Monsieur d'Artagnan.'

'That's true,' said the king. 'No matter, Tréville, come by the back stairs all the same.'

Tréville smiled. But, as it was a considerable coup to have persuaded this child to rebel against his master at all, he respectfully saluted the king and with his permission took his leave.

The three musketeers were informed that evening of the honour they had been granted. As they had known the king for a long time, they took the news in their stride, but d'Artagnan, with his Gascon imagination, saw it as the key to his fortunes and spent the night dreaming of gold. By eight o'clock the following morning, he was at Athos's door.

D'Artagnan found the musketeer dressed and ready to go out. As their audience with the king wasn't until midday, he had arranged with Porthos and Aramis to have a game of tennis[6] on a court just by the Luxembourg's stables. Athos invited d'Artagnan to come too and, despite his ignorance of the game, which he'd never played, he accepted, not knowing what to do with his time from nine o'clock in the morning – or not even – until midday.

The two musketeers had already got there and were knocking up. Athos, who excelled at all athletic pursuits, went to the other side of the net with d'Artagnan and challenged them to a game. But the first time he went for a shot, although he was playing left-handed, he realised his wound was still too recent to allow for such exertions. D'Artagnan was left on his own, therefore, and, as he said he was too ham-fisted to play a proper game, they simply played rallies without keeping score. But one ball, propelled by Porthos's Herculean wrist, passed so close to d'Artagnan's face that he saw his chances of an audience going up in smoke; if the ball had hit him rather than skim inches past, he would never have been able to appear before the king. And since his whole future, in his Gascon imagination, depended on this audience, he bowed politely to Porthos and Aramis, announced that he would only continue when he could hold his own with them, and went to sit down in the gallery by the net.

Unfortunately for d'Artagnan, among the spectators was one of His Eminence's guards who, still smarting from his comrades' defeat the previous day, had sworn to seize the first opportunity to avenge it. Thinking his moment had now come, he turned to his neighbour and said, 'Hardly surprising this young man is scared of a ball; he looks like an apprentice musketeer.'

D'Artagnan swung round as if he had been bitten by a snake and glared at the guardsman who had just made this impertinent crack.

'By God,' the fellow continued, insolently twirling his moustache, 'look at me as much you want, little man, I said what I said.'

'And since you expressed yourself too clearly for your words to need any clarification,' replied d'Artagnan in a low voice, 'I will thank you to follow me.'

'And when might that be?' asked the guard with the same mocking air.

'At once, if you please.'

'You know who I am, I daresay?'

'I haven't the faintest idea; I am not too concerned either.'

'Well, that's a mistake, since if you knew my name, you might be in less of a hurry.'

'What is it?'

'Bernajoux, at your service.'

'Well then, Monsieur Bernajoux,' d'Artagnan said calmly, 'I'll wait for you at the door.'

'Go ahead, sir, I'll follow you.'

'Don't be in too much of a rush, sir, we don't want people to see us leave together. For our purposes, you understand, too much of a crowd would be awkward.'

'Very well,' replied the guard, surprised his name hadn't had more of an effect on the young man.

In fact, d'Artagnan may have been the only person not to know the name of Bernajoux since he was one of the most frequent participants in the daily brawls that all the edicts of the king and the cardinal were powerless to stop.

Porthos and Aramis were so involved in their game and Athos was watching them so attentively that they didn't even see their young companion leave. As he had told His Eminence's guardsman, he waited at the door, and after a moment, the latter left his seat too. D'Artagnan had no time to waste since the audience with the king was set for midday, so he glanced round and, seeing the street deserted, said to his opponent, 'My faith, you may be called Bernajoux, but you're still very fortunate only to be dealing with an apprentice musketeer. Don't worry though, I will give it my best. On guard!'

'I hardly think this a very good choice of place,' said the man d'Artagnan was taunting. 'We'd be better off behind the Abbey of Saint-Germain or in the Pré-aux-Clercs.'

'There is a lot of sense to that,' replied d'Artagnan.

'Unfortunately I am short of time, since I have an engagement at midday precisely. So, on guard, sir, on guard.'

Bernajoux was not a man to require such a compliment to be repeated. In an instant his sword glittered in his hand and, hoping to intimidate such a stripling, he was upon his adversary.

But d'Artagnan had served his apprenticeship the previous day, and fresh from his victory, exhilarated by his prospects of royal favour, he was determined not to yield an inch. The two swords engaged up to their hilts, but as d'Artagnan held firm, it was his opponent who took a step back. As Bernajoux did so, his sword deviated from the vertical and, seizing his moment, d'Artagnan disengaged, lunged, and wounded his adversary in the shoulder. He immediately took a step back in turn and raised his sword, but Bernajoux cried that it was nothing and, lunging blindly at him, caused himself to be impaled on d'Artagnan's sword. He didn't fall to the ground, however, or concede defeat, but just ran towards the residence of Monsieur de La Trémouille, in whose service he had a relative, so d'Artagnan, not knowing the severity of the last wound his adversary had received, pressed him hotly. He was doubtless going to finish him off with a third thrust when the noise they were making reached the tennis court and two of the guards-man's friends, who had seen him leave after an exchange of words with d'Artagnan, rushed out, swords in hand, and fell on the victor. But Athos, Porthos and Aramis immediately appeared as well and, just as the two guards were attacking their young comrade, they forced them to turn. At that moment, Bernajoux collapsed and, as the guards were only two against four, they cried out, 'To us, de La Trémouille!' At their cries, everyone in the building poured out and threw themselves on the four companions, who, for their part, started shouting, 'To us, musketeers!'

This cry did not go unheeded as a rule, since the musketeers were known to be enemies of His Eminence and loved for the hatred they bore him, so guardsmen from companies which did not owe allegiance to the Red Duke, as Aramis had called him, generally took the king's musketeers' part in such quarrels. In this case, three guards from Monsieur des Essarts's company happened to be passing just then. Two came to the assistance of the four companions while the other ran to Monsieur de Tréville's, crying, 'To us, musketeers, to us!' As ever, Monsieur de Tréville's residence was full of soldiers of that branch and they ran to help their comrades. A battle royal ensued, but the musketeers had the upper hand. The cardinal's guards and Monsieur de La Trémouille's men retreated, shutting the gates of his residence in time to stop their enemies bursting in. As for the wounded man, he had been carried inside first and, as we have said, he was in a very bad way.

In a fever of agitation, the musketeers and their allies were already deliberating whether to set fire to Monsieur de La Trémouille's mansion as punishment for the insolence his retainers had shown in attacking the king's musketeers. This proposal had been aired and enthusiastically received when fortunately it struck eleven o'clock. D'Artagnan and his companions remembered their audience and, as they would have been sorry not to take part in such a tour de force, they managed to calm tempers. The men then made do with throwing a few paving stones at the gates, but the gates held and they grew tired after a while. In any case, those who were entitled to be considered the leaders of the enterprise had left the group moments earlier and were making their way to the residence of Monsieur de Tréville who was waiting for them, already apprised of their escapade.

'Quick, to the Louvre,' he said, 'to the Louvre without losing an instant, and let's try to see the king before the cardinal prejudices him against us. We will describe this affair as a consequence of yesterday's and the two will be excused together.'

Accompanied by the four young men, Monsieur de Tréville made his way to the Louvre, but, to the captain of the musketeers' astonishment, on their arrival he was told that the king had gone stag hunting in Saint-Germain Forest. Monsieur de Tréville required this piece of information to be repeated twice, and each time his companions saw his face darken with anger.

'Did His Majesty plan to go on this hunt yesterday?' he inquired.

'No, Your Excellency,' replied the valet. 'The Master of the Royal Hunt came this morning to report they had tracked a stag to its lair for him last night. At first he said he wouldn't go, but then he wasn't able to resist the pleasure this hunt promised and set out after dinner.'

'And has the king seen the cardinal?' asked Monsieur de Tréville.

'Very probably,' replied the valet, 'because I saw His Eminence's horses harnessed to his carriage this morning, and when I asked where it was going, I was told to Saint-Germain.'

'We have been forestalled,' said Monsieur de Tréville. 'Gentlemen, I will see the king this evening but, in your case, I would advise you not to risk it.'

This counsel was too reasonable and, above all, came from a man who knew the king too well for the four young men to think to oppose it. So Monsieur de Tréville asked them to go to their respective homes and wait to hear from him.

When he reached his residence, Monsieur de Tréville thought it would be wise to steal a march by lodging a complaint first. He therefore sent one of his servants with a letter for Monsieur de La Trémouille requesting he turn the cardinal's guardsman out of his house and reprimand his men for their temerity in assaulting his musketeers. But Monsieur de La Trémouille, having been given a version of events by his equerry who, as we know, was a relative of Bernajoux, sent a letter by reply saying neither Monsieur de Tréville nor his musketeers were in any position to complain – far from it, the right was his, since the musketeers had set on his men and threatened to burn down his residence. As this dispute between the two noblemen could have dragged on a long time, each naturally being obliged to stubbornly maintain his opinion, Monsieur de Tréville thought one way to resolve the matter would be to go and see Monsieur de La Trémouille himself.

So he went to his residence immediately and had himself announced.

The two noblemen greeted each other politely, for, while they may not have felt friendship, they at least felt esteem for one another. Both were men of courage and honour, and since Monsieur de La Trémouille, who was Protestant and rarely saw the king, did not ally himself with any party, his social dealings were free from prejudice. But, although polite, his welcome this time was colder than usual.

'Sir,' said Monsieur de Tréville, 'we each think we have cause for complaint against the other, and so I have come in person in order that, between us, we may elicit the truth of this matter.'

'I will be glad to,' replied Monsieur de La Trémouille. 'But I must warn you that I am in possession of the facts and the fault is entirely your musketeers.'

'You are too just and reasonable a man, sir,' said Monsieur de Tréville, 'not to accept the proposal I wish to put to you.'

'Go ahead, sir, I am listening.'

'How is Monsieur Bernajoux, your equerry's relative?'

'Why, in a very poor way, sir. Besides the sword thrust he received in his arm, which was not very dangerous, he received another that punctured his lung, and the doctor is not optimistic about his prospects.'

'But the wounded man's still conscious?'

'He is indeed.'

'He can talk?'

'With difficulty, but yes, he can.'

'Well then, sir, let us go to him and entreat him, in the name of the God into whose presence he may be about to be summoned, to tell the truth. I acknowledge him as judge in his own cause, sir, and I shall believe whatever he says.'

Monsieur de La Trémouille thought for a minute, and then, as it would have been difficult to counter with anything more reasonable, he agreed.

Both went down to the wounded man's room. Seeing these two noble lords come to pay him a visit, Bernajoux tried to sit up in bed, but he was too weak and, exhausted by the effort, fell back almost unconscious.

Monsieur de La Trémouille went over to him and gave him some smelling salts, which brought him round. Then Monsieur de Tréville, keen to avoid accusations of influencing the sick man, invited Monsieur de La Trémouille to question him himself.

The result was just as Monsieur de Tréville had predicted. Suspended between life and death as he was, it didn't occur to Bernajoux for a moment to conceal the truth and he gave the two noblemen a faithful account of events.

It was everything Monsieur de Tréville could have hoped for. He wished Bernajoux a speedy recovery, took his leave of Monsieur de La Trémouille, returned to his residence, and immediately sent word to the four friends that he expected them for dinner.

Monsieur de Tréville kept excellent company, and all anti-cardinalist to boot. Understandably enough, therefore, the conversation throughout dinner turned on the two reversals His Eminence's guards had just suffered. As d'Artagnan had been the hero of these two battles, it was upon him that all the congratulations fell, and Athos, Porthos and Aramis surrendered them to him not only as good comrades, but also as men who had had enough of their share of acclaim to be able to allow him his.

Around six o'clock, Monsieur de Tréville announced that he had to go to the Louvre. But as the time of the audience originally granted by His Majesty had passed, rather than crave admittance by the back stairs, he and the four young men took their place in the antechamber. The king hadn't returned from the hunt. Our youngsters had barely waited half an hour among the crowd of courtiers, however, before all the doors were flung open and His Majesty was announced.

At these words, d'Artagnan felt himself tremble in every limb. The next few moments would very likely determine the entire course of his life. In a fever of anxiety, he fixed his eyes on the door through which the king was to enter.

Louis XIII swept in first, ahead of his retinue, dressed in hunting clothes still covered in dust and tall boots and with a riding crop in his hand. D'Artagnan saw at a glance that the king was in a stormy mood.

Although His Majesty's humour was written across his face, the courtiers still lined up as he passed: in royal antechambers, it is better to be seen by an irritated eye than not be seen at all. Without a moment's hesitation, the three musketeers took a step forward – while d'Artagnan did the opposite, and hid behind them – but although the king knew Athos, Porthos and Aramis personally, he strode past them without a word or glance in their direction, as if he had never seen them in his life. When his eyes rested on Monsieur de Tréville for a moment, however, the latter held his gaze so firmly that it was the king who looked away and then, muttering to himself, disappeared into his apartments.

'Things have taken a turn for the worse,' Athos said with a smile. 'We're not going to be knighted this time.'

'Wait here for ten minutes,' said Monsieur de Tréville, 'and if I haven't come out by then, go back to Rue du Vieux-Colombier, since there'll be no point waiting for me any longer.'

The four young men waited ten minutes, a quarter of an hour, twenty minutes, until finally, when there was still no sight of Monsieur de Tréville, they left, very worried about how it would all turn out.

Monsieur de Tréville had marched firmly into the king's study and found His Majesty in a filthy temper, sitting in an armchair and rapping his boots with the handle of his whip, a sight that had not prevented him from calmly inquiring after the king's health.

'Poor, sir, poor,' replied His Majesty. 'I am bored.'

This was Louis XIII's worst affliction, in fact. He often singled out one of his courtiers, drew him to a window and said, 'Come, sir, let us be bored together.'

'What, Your Majesty is bored?' said Monsieur de Tréville. 'Didn't he indulge in the pleasure of the chase today?'

'A fine pleasure, sir. On my soul, everything's going from bad to worse, and I don't know if it's the game that has no scent these days or the dogs that have no sense of smell. We started a ten-branched stag, ran it for six hours and then, when it was there for the taking, just as Saint-Simon was bringing the horn to his lips to blow the mort, *pffft*, the whole pack picks up the wrong scent and takes off after a brocket! Soon, you'll see, I'll have to give up hunting just as I have hawking. Ah, I am a very unfortunate king, Monsieur de Tréville. I only had one gerfalcon left, and it died the day before yesterday.'

'I understand your despair, Sire; that is indeed a grievous blow. I believe you still have a good number of falcons, sparrowhawks and tiercels, though.'

'And no one to train them. The falconers are dying out; I'm the only one left who knows the true art of hunting. When I'm gone, it will all be over; people will hunt with traps, snares and pitfalls. If only I still had time to train apprentices! But of course there he is, the cardinal, not giving me a minute's peace, talking to me about Spain, talking to me about Austria, talking to me about England! Ah, speaking of the cardinal, I am vexed with you, Monsieur de Tréville . . .'

Monsieur de Tréville had been expecting this remark. Having known the king for a long time, he had realised that all his complaints were merely a preface, a sort of stimulus to urge him on, and that he had now come to the point he had been driving at all along.

'How have I been so unfortunate as to incur Your Majesty's displeasure?' asked Monsieur de Tréville, feigning the utmost surprise.

'Is this how you discharge your duties, sir?' continued the king without directly answering Monsieur de Tréville's question. 'Is this why I made you captain of my musketeers, so that they could murder a man, convulse a whole neighbourhood and threaten to burn down Paris without you saying a word? However, no doubt I am too quick to accuse you, no doubt the rioters are in prison and you have come to inform me that justice has been done.'

'On the contrary, Sire,' Monsieur de Tréville replied calmly, 'I have come to seek justice.'

'From whom?' cried the king.

'The slanderers,' said Monsieur de Tréville.

'Ah, this is new,' said the king. 'You're not going to tell me your three confounded musketeers Athos, Porthos and Aramis and your youngster from Béarn didn't throw themselves like maniacs on poor Bernajoux and cut him up so badly he is probably departing this life as we speak? You're not going to tell me they didn't then lay siege to the Duke de La Trémouille's residence and try to burn it down? Which may not have been so very unfortunate in wartime, since it's a nest of Huguenots, but which sets a terrible precedent in peacetime. Tell me, you're not going to deny all that?'

'And who told you this fine story, Sire?' Monsieur de Tréville asked calmly.

'Who told me this fine story, sir? Who could it be other than he who watches while I sleep, who toils while I play, who administers everything within the kingdom and without, in France and in Spain?'

'His Majesty is referring to God, no doubt,' said Monsieur de Tréville, 'because apart from God, I know of no other being who could so far outshine His Majesty.'

'No, sir, I am referring to the State's prop and stay, to my only servant, my only friend, the cardinal.'

'His Eminence is not His Holiness, Sire.'

'What do you mean by that, sir?'

'That only the Pope is infallible[7], and that this infallibility does not extend to his cardinals.'

'You mean he is deceiving me, you mean he is betraying me. You are accusing him then. Come on, say it. Openly admit that you are accusing him.'

'No, Sire, but I do say he is deceiving himself, I do say he has been misinformed, I do say he has been overhasty to accuse Your Majesty's musketeers, whom he wrongs, and that he does not have his information on good authority.'

'The accusation comes from Monsieur de La Trémouille, from the duke himself. What do you say to that?'

'I could say, Sire, that he is too interested in the matter to be a wholly impartial witness, but that would be very far from the truth. I know the duke to be a loyal gentleman, Sire, and I will take his word for it, but on one condition, Sire.'

'Namely?'

'That Your Majesty will send for him and question him personally, in private, without witnesses, and then see me immediately after he has seen the duke.'

'Excellent, yes,' said the king. 'And you will take Monsieur de La Trémouille's word for it?'

'Yes, Sire.'

'You will accept his judgement?'

'Without question.'

'And you will submit to any reparations he asks for?'

'I will indeed.'

'La Chesnaye!' called the king. 'La Chesnaye!'

Louis XIII's most trusted valet, who as usual was posted outside the door, came in.

'La Chesnaye,' said the King, 'send someone to fetch Monsieur de La Trémouille immediately. I wish to speak with him this evening.'

'Your Majesty gives me his word that he won't see anyone between Monsieur de La Trémouille and me?'

'No one, as I am a gentleman.'

'Goodbye till tomorrow then, Sire.'

'Goodbye, sir.'

'At what time will it please Your Majesty?'

'At whatever time you wish.'

'But I'm afraid, if I come too early, I may wake Your Majesty.'

'Wake me? Do I sleep? I don't sleep any more, sir. Sometimes I dream, but that's all. So come as early as you please, at seven o'clock if you wish. Look out if your musketeers are guilty, though.'

'If my musketeers are guilty, Sire, the culprits will be handed over to Your Majesty to dispose of at his pleasure. Does Your Majesty require anything further? Let him speak, I shall obey.'

'No, sir, no. It is not without reason that I am called Louis the Just. Goodbye until tomorrow then, sir, goodbye.'

'God keep Your Majesty until then.'

However poorly the king may have slept, Monsieur de Tréville slept even worse. He had sent word that evening to the three musketeers and their companion to be at his residence at half-past six the following morning. They set off immediately. He made no definite pronouncements about their situation, didn't promise them anything, nor did he gloss over the fact that their favour, and perhaps even his own, rested on the throw of a dice.

When they got to the foot of the king's private staircase, he told them to wait. If the king was still irritated with them, they could leave without being seen, and if he consented to receive them, they could simply be sent for.

Monsieur de Tréville went up to the king's private antechamber and saw La Chesnaye, who told him the Duke de La Trémouille hadn't been found at home the previous evening. Having returned too late to appear at the Louvre, he had only just arrived and was with the king at present.

This turn of events pleased Monsieur de Tréville greatly, since it meant he could be sure a third party wouldn't have the chance to make insinuations between Monsieur de La Trémouille's testimony and his audience.

In fact, it was barely ten minutes before the door of the king's office opened, Monsieur de La Trémouille emerged, came up to Monsieur de Tréville and said, 'Monsieur de Tréville, His Majesty has summoned me to find out what happened yesterday morning at my residence. I told him the truth, that my men were at fault, and that I was ready to offer you my apologies. As we have now met, please accept them, and always consider me one of your friends.'

'Your Grace,' said Monsieur de Tréville, 'I had such confidence in your loyalty that I hadn't wanted any other counsel for the defence before His Majesty than yourself. I see I was not mistaken, and I thank you that there is still a man in France of whom one can safely say what I have said of you.'

'That's good, very good!' said the king, who had listened to this exchange of compliments. 'But tell him, Tréville, since he claims to be one of your friends, that I would like to be one of his too if it weren't for the fact that he neglects me. It is nearly three years since I saw him and I only ever do so when I send for him. Tell him all this for me, since these are things a king cannot say himself.'

'Thank you, Sire, thank you,' said the duke. 'But Your Majesty may be assured that it is not those – I am not referring to Monsieur de Tréville here in the least – it is not those he sees at every hour of the day who are the most devoted to him.'

'Ah, you've heard what I said. I am very glad, Your Grace, very glad,' said the king, walking to the door. 'Ah, it's you, Tréville! Where are your musketeers? I told you the day before yesterday to bring them to me. Why haven't you done so?'

'They are downstairs, Sire, and with your permission La Chesnaye will have them come up.'

'Yes, yes, fetch them immediately; it will soon be eight and I'm expecting a visitor at nine. Go, Your Grace, but, more importantly, come back. Come in, Tréville.'

The duke bowed and went out. As he was opening the door, the three musketeers and d'Artagnan, led by La Chesnaye, appeared at the top of the stairs.

'Come here, my brave fellows,' said the king, 'I need to give you a talking to.'

The musketeers approached, bowing, d'Artagnan following close behind.

'Confound it,' the king went on, 'seven of His Eminence's guards laid low in two days by you four! It's too much, gentlemen, too much. At this rate, His Eminence would be compelled to replace his company every three weeks, and I to see the edicts were enforced in their full rigour. If it was only one, an accident, I wouldn't mention it, but seven in two days, I say it again, it's too much, far too much.'

'Which is why, Sire, Your Majesty sees that they have come, full of contrition and repentance, to offer him their apologies.'

'Full of contrition and repentance! Hmm . . .' said the king. 'I don't trust their hypocritical faces, particularly not that Gascon countenance over there. Come here, sir.'

Understanding this compliment was addressed to him, d'Artagnan stepped forward and assumed his most desperately apologetic air.

'What, didn't you tell me he was a young man? He's a child, Monsieur de Tréville, a veritable child! And he's the one who caught Jussac that swingeing blow?'

'And gave Bernajoux those two fine sword thrusts.'

'Indeed.'

'Not counting the fact,' said Athos, 'that if he hadn't rescued me from Biscarat's clutches, I would certainly not have the honour now of bowing most humbly to Your Majesty.'

'By the holy grey belly[8], as my father the king would have said, he's an absolute demon, this Béarnais, Monsieur de Tréville. With that sort of skill, a man will shred a fair few doublets and break a fair few swords in his lifetime. The Gascons are still poor, though, aren't they?'

'Well, Sire, I have to admit no goldmines have been discovered in their mountains as yet, although the Lord certainly owes them such a miracle as reward for the support they gave your father the king's cause.'

'Which means it's the Gascons who made me king too, doesn't it, Tréville, since I'm my father's son? Well, that's fine; I've nothing against it. La Chesnaye, go and have a rummage through my pockets and see if you cannot find forty pistoles. If you do, bring them to me. And now, come on young man, hand on heart, how did it transpire?'

D'Artagnan related the previous day's adventures in their every detail: how, unable to sleep for excitement at the prospect of seeing His Majesty, he had arrived at his friend's lodgings three hours before their audience; how they had both gone to the tennis court,

and how, when he was afraid of a ball hitting him in the face, he
was mocked by Bernajoux, who had almost paid for this mockery
with the loss of his life and Monsieur de La Trémouille, who had
nothing to do with it, with the loss of his residence.

'That's right,' murmured the king. 'Yes, that's just what the
duke told me. Poor cardinal! Seven men in two days, some favourites of his among them. But that's enough of all this, gentlemen,
do you hear, it's enough. You have more than taken your revenge
for Rue Férou; you should be satisfied.'

'If Your Majesty is,' said Tréville, 'then we are.'

'I am,' replied the king, taking a fistful of gold from La
Chesnaye's hand and putting it in d'Artagnan's. 'Here, a token of
my satisfaction.'

Contemporary notions of self-respect weren't the fashion in
those days. A gentleman could be handed money by the king
without feeling in the least humiliated. So d'Artagnan put the forty
pistoles in his pocket without any further ado – quite the opposite,
in fact – and effusively thanked His Majesty.

'There,' said the king looking at his clock. 'There we are. And
now it is half-past eight and time for you to be on your way, because,
as I told you, I am expecting someone at nine. Thank you for your
loyalty, gentlemen. I can count on it, can't I?'

'Oh, Sire,' the four companions cried together, 'we would
gladly be cut to pieces for Your Majesty.'

'Good, good. Stay in one piece though. It is better as a rule,
and you will be of more use to me that way . . . . Tréville,' added
the king in a low voice as the others went out, 'as you have no
room in the musketeers, and, besides, we've decided on an apprenticeship before anyone can enter your corps, put this young man in
your brother-in-law Monsieur des Essarts's company of the guards.
Ah, by God, Tréville, I cannot wait to see the look on the cardinal's
face. He will be furious, but I don't care. I am within my rights.'

And then, with a wave of his hand, the king saluted Tréville,
who went out and rejoined the musketeers, whom he found sharing
out the forty pistoles with d'Artagnan.

The cardinal was indeed furious, as His Majesty had predicted, so furious that for eight days he stayed away from the king's gaming table, which did not prevent the king from observing him with the most charming expression in the world whenever they met, and inquiring in his most caressing voice, 'Tell me, cardinal, how are poor Bernajoux and poor Jussac, those men of yours?'

VII

THE MUSKETEERS AT HOME

WHEN D'ARTAGNAN HAD EMERGED from the Louvre and asked his friends what he should do with his share of the forty pistoles, Athos advised him to order a first-rate meal at the Pine Cone[1], Porthos to hire a valet, and Aramis to acquire a suitable mistress.

The meal was served that day, and the valet waited at table. Athos had chosen the menu and Porthos had provided the manservant, a Picard whom the vainglorious musketeer had engaged for the occasion that morning when he came across him spitting over the edge of the Pont de La Tournelle[2], making rings in the water.

Porthos had claimed this pursuit was the sign of a thoughtful, serious-minded nature and took him on without further testimonials. The magnificent appearance of the gentleman he assumed was to be his master had enchanted the Picard, whose name was Planchet. It was a mild disappointment, therefore, when he found out the position was already occupied by a colleague named Mousqueton – Porthos duly informing him that although his domestic arrangements were lavish, they did not run to two servants, and that in fact he was to enter a certain d'Artagnan's service. But when he attended the dinner thrown by his new master, and saw him take a handful of gold from his pocket to pay the bill, he thought his fortunes were made, and thanked heaven for having found his way into the employ of such a Croesus. He maintained this opinion until the feast had ended and he had remedied some long spells of abstinence with its leftovers. But when he was turning down his master's bed that evening, Planchet's illusions crumbled. The bed was the only one of its kind in the lodgings, which comprised an antechamber and a bedroom. He was to sleep in the antechamber on a blanket taken from his master's bed, and d'Artagnan would make do with fewer covers.

Athos, for his part, had a valet called Grimaud whom he had trained to serve him in a highly idiosyncratic manner. He was extremely reserved, this worthy nobleman – we're talking about Athos, of course. In the five or six years in which he had lived on terms of the greatest intimacy with his friends Porthos and Aramis, they could call to mind numerous occasions on which they had seen him smile, but none on which they had heard him laugh. His utterances were brief and expressive, always saying what he meant to say and nothing more: no embellishments, no embroideries, no arabesques. As practised by him, conversation was factual rather than discursive.

Although Athos was barely thirty years old and extremely prepossessing, both in looks and turn of mind, no one had ever known him to have a mistress. He never talked about women. He didn't actively object to their being discussed in his presence, but it was plain that this sort of conversation, to which his sole contribution was bitter remarks and misanthropic observations, was thoroughly disagreeable to him. With his guarded, unsociable, taciturn manner, he was almost like an old man and so, to avoid changing his ways even slightly, he had trained Grimaud to obey simple gestures or lip movements. He only talked to him in exceptional circumstances.

Occasionally Grimaud, who felt great affection for his master and revered his intellect, while at the same time living in mortal dread of him, would think he had understood perfectly what he wanted, rush off to carry out his orders, and do the exact opposite. Then Athos would shrug his shoulders and, without losing his temper, beat Grimaud. He did say a few words on those occasions.

Porthos's character, as will have been apparent, was the polar opposite of Athos's: he not only talked a great deal, but also in a booming voice. To give him his due, he didn't actually care whether anyone listened to him or not; he talked solely for the pleasure of talking and for the pleasure of hearing himself do so, and would speak on every subject except the sciences, pleading in this regard an inveterate hatred for savants, which he claimed to have harboured since childhood. He had a less imposing presence than Athos, an evident inferiority that, when they first got to know one another, often made him unjust towards this gentleman, whom he would try to outdo with the splendour of his attire. But in his simple musketeer's tabard, Athos only had to throw back his head or put out a foot to assume his rightful place and overshadow Porthos and his showy ways. Porthos consoled himself by making Monsieur de Tréville's antechamber and the Louvre's guardroom ring with tales of his conquests, a subject Athos never discussed. The latest news was that, having graduated from the professions to the nobility, from lawyer's wife to baroness, his affections were now trained on nothing less than a foreign princess, who was extravagantly fond of him.

'Like master, like man,' as an old proverb has it. So let us pass from Athos's valet to Porthos's valet, from Grimaud to Mousqueton.

Mousqueton was a Norman whose master had changed his name from the peaceable Boniface to its present, infinitely more sonorous and bellicose incarnation – Mousqueton being a type of musket with a shortened barrel. When he took him on, Porthos had only offered to house and clothe him, but in magnificent style, and, in return, Mousqueton's one request had been to have two hours a day to devote to activities that would provide for his other needs. Porthos had accepted his terms; the arrangement suited him perfectly. He had doublets made for Mousqueton from his cast-offs and spare cloaks, and thanks to a very clever tailor who made his worn clothes look new again by turning them inside out – and whose wife was suspected of wanting Porthos to lower his aristocratic sights – Mousqueton cut an extremely fine figure in his master's train.

As for Aramis, whose character we think we have sufficiently
described – a character that, in any case, like those of his companions, we will be able to follow as it develops – his valet was called
Bazin. Thanks to his master's hopes of taking orders one day, he
was always dressed in black, as befitted a servant of a man of the
Church. He was between thirty-five and forty years old and from
Berry, a mild, quiet, plump individual who spent his every spare
moment reading pious works and would, if strictly necessary,
prepare dinner for the two of them, drawing on a small but excellent
culinary repertoire. He was also unswervingly loyal, and corres-
pondingly deaf, dumb and blind.

Now we that we are acquainted, at least superficially, with the
masters and their valets, let us turn to their places of residence.

Athos lived on Rue Férou, a stone's throw from the
Luxembourg. His quarters consisted of two nicely appointed,
spick-and-span little rooms in a furnished house, the landlady of
which, a genuine beauty still in the prime of her youth, frequently
gave him meaningful looks, but to no avail. A few fragments of
bygone splendour glittered here and there on the walls of his
modest lodgings. There was a richly damascened sword in the
style of François I's reign, for example, with a jewel-encrusted
handle that alone must have been worth at least two hundred
pistoles, which, even when he was in the direst financial straits,
Athos had never been persuaded to pawn or sell. It had long been
coveted by Porthos, and he would have given six years of his life
to get his hands on this heirloom. One day, when he had an
assignation with a duchess, he had even gone so far as to ask
Athos if he could borrow it. Without a word, Athos had emptied
his pockets, gathered up all his jewels, purses, tagged lace and
gold chains, and offered them all to Porthos, but as for the sword,
he said, it was nailed in its place and could only leave it when its
owner left his lodgings.

Besides the sword, there was a portrait of a nobleman from
the time of Henri III, dressed with the greatest of elegance and
wearing the Order of the Holy Spirit[3]. The cast of his features,

and a general family resemblance, suggested this great lord, a knight of the royal order, was an ancestor of Athos.

Finally, a magnificent gold-worked chest bearing the same arms as the sword and the portrait dominated the mantelpiece, clashing terribly with the rest of the furnishings. Athos always carried the key to it on him. But he had opened it one day in Porthos's presence, and Porthos had been able to see for himself that it only contained letters and papers – love letters and family papers, no doubt.

Porthos lived in a very vast, very sumptuous-looking set of rooms on Rue du Vieux-Colombier. Every time he and a friend passed its windows, at which Mousqueton would invariably be standing in full livery, Porthos would raise his head and hand, and declare, 'My abode!' But he was never to be found at home, nor did he ever invite anyone to come up, so no one had been able to gain any sense of how much genuine wealth lay behind this opulent façade.

Aramis, meanwhile, lived in a little ground-floor lodgings consisting of a drawing room, a dining room and a bedroom, which gave on to a small garden, a cool, green, shaded sanctuary hidden from the neighbours' eyes.

As for d'Artagnan, we are familiar with his accommodation and we have already made the acquaintance of his valet, Master Planchet.

An intensely curious soul, as, incidentally, people with a gift for intrigue always are, d'Artagnan tried his utmost to find out Athos's, Porthos's and Aramis's real identities, since under these assumed names each of the young men surely hid a noble lineage – Athos's aristocratic blood, in particular, stood out a mile. He therefore pressed Porthos for information about Athos and Aramis, and Aramis for details about Porthos.

Unfortunately, Porthos only knew the vague reports about his silent companion's life that were in general circulation. It was said that Athos had suffered terrible misfortunes in love, and that a horrific betrayal had poisoned the life of this honourable man forever. But what this betrayal was, no one knew.

As for Porthos, apart from his real name, which, like those of his two comrades, had only been vouchsafed to Monsieur de Tréville, he was an easy man to get to know. Vain and indiscreet, he was as transparent as glass. A tendency to believe all the good things he said about himself was the only thing that might have led the investigator astray.

Aramis, meanwhile, despite his ingenuous air, was steeped in mystery, restricting himself to laconic answers when asked about the others, and evading the question when asked about himself. One day, after quizzing him at length about Porthos and learning of the rumour of the musketeer's success with a princess, d'Artagnan wanted to know what to make of his interlocutor's romantic exploits, and so asked, 'What about you, my dear friend, who talk about other men's baronesses, countesses and princesses, what . . .'

'Excuse me,' interrupted Aramis. 'I spoke out because Porthos makes a point of doing so himself, regaling me with these fine tales. Believe me, my dear Monsieur d'Artagnan, if I had heard it from someone else, or if he had told it to me in confidence, he could not have had a more discreet confessor.'

'I don't doubt it,' d'Artagnan replied. 'But still, I think you cannot be unfamiliar with coats of arms yourself, as a certain embroidered handkerchief, to which I owe the honour of your acquaintance, bears witness.'

Aramis wasn't put out at all this time. Instead, assuming his most modest air, he replied affectionately, 'My dear friend, don't forget that my heart is set on going into the Church and that I shun worldly pleasures. The handkerchief you saw was forgotten in my lodgings by one of my friends. I was obliged to pick it up so as not to compromise him or the lady he loves. For my part, I do not have, nor do I want to have, a mistress, and in this I follow the very judicious example of Athos who doesn't have one any more than I do.'

'Confound it, you're not a priest though, you're a musketeer!'

'Acting musketeer, as the cardinal says; a musketeer under

sufferance, but believe me, at heart a man of the Church. Athos
and Porthos got me mixed up in all this to keep me occupied. When
I was being ordained, I had a little difficulty with . . . But that's
hardly going to interest you, and I'm wasting your valuable time.'

'Not at all, it interests me very much,' cried d'Artagnan, 'and
for the moment I have absolutely nothing to do.'

'Ah yes, but I have my breviary to recite,' replied Aramis, 'and
then some verses to compose that Madame d'Aiguillon has
requested, and after that I have to go to Rue Saint-Honoré to buy
some rouge for Madame de Chevreuse. So you see, my dear friend,
while you may have no pressing business, I have nothing but.'

And with that, Aramis affectionately held out his hand to his
young companion and took his leave.

Despite his best efforts, this was all d'Artagnan could find out
about his three new friends. So he resolved for the present to
believe everything they said about their pasts, while hoping for
more reliable and extensive revelations in the future. In the meantime, he thought of Athos as another Achilles, Porthos as another
Ajax and Aramis as another Joseph[4].

Life in general was a joyous affair for the four young men.
Athos gambled, always unluckily, but never borrowed a sou from
his friends, although his purse was constantly at their disposal, and
when he gambled on his word, always woke his creditor at six in
the morning to pay the previous day's debt.

Porthos was prone to fits of passion: if he won on those days,
he was to be seen all over town, an insolent, dazzling figure, whereas
if he lost, he would vanish off the face of the earth for several
days and then reappear, ashen and long-faced, but with money in
his pockets.

As for Aramis, he never gambled. He was easily the worst
musketeer and sorriest table-companion imaginable. He had a
perpetual need to work. Sometimes in the middle of a dinner when
the others, inflamed by the headiness of the wine and the ardour
of the conversation, thought they would be at table for another
two or three hours, Aramis would look at his watch, get up with

a graceful smile and take his leave of the company, in order, so he said, to consult a theologian with whom he had an appointment. Or else he would return to his lodgings to write a thesis and would ask his friends not to disturb him. Then Athos would smile the charming, melancholic smile that suited his noble face so well, and Porthos would drink and swear that Aramis would never amount to anything more than a village priest.

Planchet, d'Artagnan's valet, bore good fortune manfully. He was paid thirty sous a day and, for a month, he was the soul of affability to his master, coming back to their lodgings as blithe as a lark. But when the winds of adversity began to blow on the Rue des Fossoyeurs household – when, that is, King Louis XIII's forty pistoles were used up, or as good as – he began making complaints which Athos found nauseating, Porthos indecent and Aramis ridiculous. Athos advised d'Artagnan to sack the strange bird, Porthos thought he should be given a thrashing first, and Aramis claimed that servants shouldn't address a word to their masters unless it was to pay them a compliment.

'That's very easy for all you to say,' said d'Artagnan, 'Athos, when you live in complete silence with Grimaud and forbid him to speak, so you never have words with him. And you, Porthos, who live in magnificent style and are a god to your valet Mousqueton. And finally you, Aramis, always absorbed in your theological studies, who inspire a profound respect in your servant Bazin, a gentle, religious man. But I, who lack both standing and resources, who am neither a musketeer nor even a guard, how am I to inspire either affection, terror or respect in Planchet?'

'They're a serious business, these domestic matters,' the three friends opined, adding that valets were like wives and that you had to start them off on the right footing. 'You should give it some thought,' they advised.

D'Artagnan duly thought it over and decided to beat Planchet provisionally, a task he performed with the conscientiousness he applied to everything, and then, having given him a good going over, he forbade him to leave his service without his permission.

'Because,' he added, 'the future cannot fail me; I inevitably expect better times. So your fortune is made if you stay at my side, and I am too good a master to make you forfeit your prosperity by allowing you to give notice.'

This approach filled the musketeers with respect for d'Artagnan's policies; Planchet was equally admiring and made no further mention of leaving his employ.

In time, the four young men came to do everything together, and d'Artagnan, having no settled habits of his own, since he had just arrived from the country and found himself in an entirely new world, promptly adopted those of his friends.

They rose at around eight o'clock in winter, and six in summer, and went straight to Monsieur de Tréville's to get the day's password and see how things stood. D'Artagnan, although not a musketeer, performed the duties of one with touching punctuality. He was always on guard because he was always keeping one of his three friends who was on duty company. All the musketeers knew him and thought him a good comrade. Monsieur de Tréville, who had recognised his merit on sight and bore him real affection, constantly commended him to the king.

For their part, the three musketeers genuinely loved their young comrade. The bonds of friendship between these four men and their need to see each other three or four times a day, whether for a duel or for business or for pleasure, meant they chased after one another constantly like shadows, and the inseparables were always to be found looking for one another between the Luxembourg and Place Saint-Sulpice, or Rue du Vieux-Colombier and the Luxembourg.

Meanwhile Monsieur de Tréville's promises were coming good. One fine day, the king commanded the Chevalier des Essarts to take on d'Artagnan as a cadet in his company of guards. With a sigh, d'Artagnan donned the uniform that he would have given ten years of his life to trade for a musketeer's tabard. But Monsieur de Tréville promised to grant him this favour after he had served a two-year apprenticeship – an apprenticeship, furthermore, that could be curtailed if he had the opportunity to render a service to the king or perform some brilliant feat of arms. D'Artagnan left with this promise ringing in his ears, and the following day began his service.

Henceforth it was Athos's, Porthos's and Aramis's turn to mount guard with d'Artagnan when he was on duty. And so the Chevalier des Essarts's company acquired four new recruits rather than simply one, the day it took on d'Artagnan.

VIII

A COURT INTRIGUE

THE FORTY PISTOLES FROM KING LOUIS XIII, however, like all the things of this world, having had a beginning, had subsequently also had an end, and since that end our four companions had fallen on difficult times. First Athos had supported the fellowship for a while with his own money. Then Porthos had stepped in and, by means of one of those vanishing acts they had become accustomed to, provided for the others for almost a fortnight. Finally Aramis's turn had come round, and he had acquitted himself with good grace, managing, so he said, to secure a few pistoles by selling some works of theology.

Their next port of call, as ever, was Monsieur de Tréville, who advanced them some money against their wages, but the sums could not tide over for very long three musketeers who already had a mass of accounts in arrears and a guardsman who was yet to acquire any.

Finally, when they saw they were going to run out of funds completely, eight or ten pistoles were scraped together with one last effort and given to Porthos to wager. Unfortunately he was on a bad run; he lost them all, as well as twenty-five pistoles on credit.

Difficult times then became dire straits. Famished, they and their valets were to be seen roaming the embankments and guard-rooms, calling in all the dinners they could from their circle of friends. Their watchword, following Aramis's advice, was that you should sow meals left, right and centre in days of prosperity so that you could reap a few in days of trouble.

Athos was invited out four times and took his friends and their valets with him on each occasion. Porthos received six invitations, and similarly shared his good fortune with his comrades. And Aramis struck lucky no less than eight times: he was a man who, as will already have been apparent, was almost no talk and almost all action.

As for d'Artagnan, who didn't know anyone in the capital yet, all he could drum up was the offer of a cup of hot chocolate for breakfast from a fellow Gascon, a priest, and an invitation to dinner from a cornet of the guards. He took his army to the priest's, where they devoured two months' worth of provisions, and to the cornet's, who worked wonders, but, as Planchet said, no matter how high you heap your plate, you only ever eat one meal at a time.

D'Artagnan found it pretty humiliating not being able to offer his friends more than a meal and a half – breakfast with the priest could only be counted as half – in return for all the feasts they had provided. He felt a burden on them all, forgetting in his youthful selflessness that he had fed everyone for a month, and his troubled mind busily set to work. It seemed to him that a coalition like theirs of four brave, enterprising, dynamic young men needed more of a purpose than just swaggering about town, taking fencing lessons and indulging in more or less humorous banter.

Clearly, four men such as they, who were ready to sacrifice everything, from their purses to their lives, for the common good; four comrades, who would support one another at every turn and never yield as they executed, either singly or in concert, their joint resolutions; four sword-arms that could threaten the four cardinal points or be trained in a single direction – whether openly or covertly, by mine or trench, through stratagem or force, clearly it was inevitable the four of them would cut a way through to any goal they set themselves, no matter how well defended or distant it might be. The only thing that surprised d'Artagnan was that his companions had never thought of this before.

He was giving it some serious thought, racking his brains to find an application for this unique fourfold force with which he was sure, like Archimedes's lever[1], one could move the whole world, when there was a quiet knock at his front door. D'Artagnan woke up Planchet and told him to let the visitor in.

D'Artagnan woke up Planchet: these words shouldn't lead the reader to suppose it was night-time or the early hours of the morning. Far from it – it had only just struck four in the afternoon. Two hours earlier, Planchet had come to ask his master if there was any food and had been answered with the proverb 'Who sleeps, dines.' He had, therefore, taken a nap for his dinner.

He showed in a fairly plainly dressed individual with the air of a townsman. By way of dessert, he was very keen to hear the subsequent conversation, but the townsman informed d'Artagnan that he had an important and confidential matter to discuss, and so wished to have a private interview.

D'Artagnan therefore dismissed Planchet and showed his visitor to a chair.

There was a moment's silence during which the two men looked at one another as if becoming preliminarily acquainted, and then d'Artagnan bowed to indicate he was listening.

'I have heard reports describing Monsieur d'Artagnan as an extremely brave young man,' said the townsman, 'and prompted, therefore, by his thoroughly deserved reputation, I have come to confide a secret in him.'

'Unburden yourself, sir,' said d'Artagnan, instinctively sensing something to his advantage.

The townsman paused again, before continuing, 'I have a wife who is a seamstress to the queen, sir, and lacks neither virtue nor beauty. I was induced to marry her almost three years ago to the day, despite her modest dowry, because Monsieur de La Porte[2], the queen's cloak-bearer, is her godfather and patron . . .'

'Well, sir?' prompted d'Artagnan.

'Well,' replied the townsman. 'Well, sir, my wife was abducted yesterday morning as she was leaving her workroom.'

'And by whom was your wife abducted?'

'I don't know for certain, sir, but there's someone I suspect.'

'And who is this person whom you suspect?'

'A man who has been pursuing her for a long time.'

'Confound him!'

'If I may say, sir,' continued the townsman, 'I think politics plays more of a part in all this than love.'

'Politics plays more of a part in all this than love . . .' d'Artagnan repeated with a ruminative air. 'And whom do you suspect?'

'I don't know if I should tell you . . .'

'Let me remind you, sir, that I am not asking you for anything. It is you who have come to my door, you who have told me you have a secret to confide in me. Do as you please, therefore. There's still time for you to draw back.'

'No, no, sir. You strike me as a young man of honour, and I shall trust you. So, what I believe is that my wife has not been seized on account of any liaison she has embarked on, but on account of one of a lady of nobler blood.'

'Aha, would this be a liaison of Madame de Bois-Tracy?' asked d'Artagnan, who wanted the townsman to think he was conversant with court affairs.

'Higher, sir, higher.'

'Of Madame d'Aiguillon?'

'Higher still.'

'Of Madame de Chevreuse?'

'Higher, much higher!'

'Of the . . .' d'Artagnan paused.

'Yes, sir,' replied the scared townsman, almost inaudibly.

'And with whom?'

'Who could it be other than the Duke of . . .'

'The Duke of . . .'

'Yes, sir,' replied the townsman in an even more muffled voice.

'But how do you know all this?'

'Ah . . . How do I know it?'

'Yes, who told you? No half-measures or . . . you understand.'

'My wife told me, sir, my wife in person.'

'And who told her?'

'Monsieur de La Porte. Didn't I tell you she was the goddaughter of Monsieur de La Porte, the queen's confidential agent? Well, Monsieur de La Porte gave her a position at Her Majesty's side so that there would at least be someone our poor queen could trust, abandoned as she is by the king, spied on as she is by the cardinal, betrayed as she is at every turn.'

'Aha, it's taking shape,' said d'Artagnan.

'So, my wife came to visit me four days ago, sir. One of the terms of her employment was that she could see me twice a week, because, I am honoured to say, my wife loves me a great deal. So she came and confided in me that the queen is very afraid at present.'

'Indeed?'

'Yes, apparently the cardinal is hounding and persecuting her more than ever. He cannot forgive her the saraband incident[3]. You know about the saraband incident?'

'I should think so, by God,' replied d'Artagnan, who knew nothing about it whatsoever but wanted to appear well informed.

'So now it's not just hatred, it's revenge.'

'Indeed?'

'And the queen believes . . .'

'Well, what does the queen believe?'

'She believes a letter has been written to the Duke of Buckingham in her name.'

'In the queen's name?'

'Yes, to bring him to Paris and then lure him into a trap.'

'Hang it! But, my dear sir, what does your wife have to do with all this?'

'They know how devoted she is to the queen, so either they want to part her from her mistress, or intimidate her into revealing Her Majesty's secrets, or seduce her to use her as a spy.'

'That could well be,' said d'Artagnan. 'But do you know the man who abducted her?'

'As I said, I think so.'

'What is his name?'

'I don't know. All I know is he's a creature of the cardinal, his hound.'

'You've seen him though?'

'Yes, my wife pointed him out to me one day.'

'Would he be easy to recognise?'

'Oh, certainly, he's a nobleman with a haughty air, black hair, a swarthy complexion, piercing eyes, white teeth, and a scar on his temple.'

'A scar on his temple!' cried d'Artagnan. 'Along with white teeth, piercing eyes, swarthy complexion, black hair, and a haughty air – why, that's my man from Meung!'

'He's your man, you say?'

'Yes, yes, but that has nothing to with this . . . Wait, no, it makes it all much simpler. If your man is mine, I will simply avenge two wrongs at a stroke, that's all. Where is this man to be found though?'

'I have no idea.'

'You have no knowledge as to where he lives?'

'None. One day, when I was escorting my wife back to the Louvre, he came out as she was about to go in, and she pointed him out to me.'

'Confound it, this is all very vague,' muttered d'Artagnan. 'Who told you about your wife's abduction?'

'Monsieur de La Porte.'

'Did he give any details?'

'He didn't know any.'

'And you haven't learnt anything from any other source?'

'Yes, I have. I received . . .'

'What?'

'Perhaps I am being very rash though . . .'

'That line again. I should point out that it is a bit late to turn back this time, though.'

'God's teeth, then there'll be no turning back!' cried the townsman, swearing to give himself courage. 'Besides, on the honour of the Bonacieux . . .⁴'

'You're called Bonacieux?' interrupted d'Artagnan.

'Yes, that's my name.'

'You were saying, "On the honour of the Bonacieux". . . Forgive me for interrupting, but I've a feeling I've heard that name before.'

'That may be, sir. I am your landlord.'

'Aha!' exclaimed d'Artagnan, half rising to his feet and bowing, 'You're my landlord?'

'Yes, sir, I am. And seeing as you've been in my house for three months and, no doubt distracted by important matters, you have forgotten to pay my rent; seeing, as I say, that I have not pestered you once, I thought you would take my tact into consideration.'

'Why of course, my dear Bonacieux,' cried d'Artagnan, 'I am very grateful for such treatment, believe me, and, as I say, if I can be of any use to you . . .'

'I believe you, sir, I do, and as I was going to say, on the honour of the Bonacieux, I trust you too.'

'Then finish what you've started to tell me.'

The townsman produced a piece of paper from his pocket and gave it to d'Artagnan.

'A letter!' said the young man.

'Which I received this morning.'

D'Artagnan opened it and, as the light was going, went to the window. The townsman followed.

'"Don't go looking for your wife,"' d'Artagnan read out. '"She will be restored to you when she is no longer needed. If you make any attempt to find her, you are lost." That's plain enough,' d'Artagnan went on. 'Still, it's just a threat.'

'But it terrifies me, sir. I'm not a swordsman in any shape or form, and I'm scared of the Bastille.'

'Hmm . . . I don't care for the Bastille any more than you do,' said d'Artagnan. 'A sword thrust is another matter; I wouldn't have any objection to that.'

'But, sir, I had been really counting on your support in this affair.'

'You had?'

'Seeing you always in the company of the haughtiest of musketeers, who I recognised as Monsieur de Tréville's men, and so enemies of the cardinal, I thought, while doing our poor queen justice, you and your friends would be delighted to cause His Eminence some mischief.'

'I daresay.'

'I also thought that, since you owe me three months' rent that I've never mentioned . . .'

'Yes, yes, you've already given me that reason and I find it very compelling.'

'And intending, as long as you do me the honour of staying with me, never to mention your rent in the future . . .'

'Very good.'

'Intending also to give you fifty pistoles on the off-chance, far-fetched as it may seem, that you found yourself in difficulties at present.'

'Wonderful. So you're a rich man, my dear Monsieur Bonacieux?'

'I am comfortable, sir, that's the word for it. I have accumulated something like two or three thousand écus a year in small wares, in particular from an investment in the last voyage of the celebrated navigator, Jean Mocquet[5], so, you understand, sir . . . Hey!' cried the townsman.

'What?' asked d'Artagnan.

'What's that I see there?'

'Where?'

'In the street, directly opposite, in that doorway: a man wrapped in a cloak.'

'It's he!' d'Artagnan and the townsman cried out in unison, each recognising his man at the same moment.

'Ah, he won't escape me this time,' cried d'Artagnan, flying for his sword, and then, drawing it, he rushed out of the room.

On the stairs, he met Athos and Porthos who were coming to see him. They stepped aside and d'Artagnan shot between them like a bullet.

'Heavens, where are you running off to like this?' the two musketeers shouted as one.

'The man from Meung!' d'Artagnan replied, and then disappeared.

D'Artagnan had told his friends on more than one occasion about his run-in with the stranger and the arrival of the beautiful traveller, to whom the man had been able to entrust a vital communication.

Athos was of the opinion that d'Artagnan had lost his letter of introduction in the free-for-all. According to him, a gentleman – and from d'Artagnan's description of the stranger, he couldn't be anything but a gentleman – could never stoop so low as to steal a letter.

Porthos had seen the affair as nothing more than a tryst that had been granted by a lady to her beau, or vice versa, and then interrupted by d'Artagnan and his yellow horse.

Aramis, finally, had declared that those sorts of things were always mysterious, so it was better not to go into them too deeply.

They therefore gathered what was afoot from d'Artagnan's terse exclamation, and reasoning that he would come back home at some point, regardless of whether he caught up with his man or lost him from sight, they continued on their way.

When they entered d'Artagnan's room, they found it empty. Fearing the consequences of the encounter that was doubtless about to take place between the young man and the stranger, the landlord had shown the character traits he had alluded to himself and judged it prudent to clear off at the double.

IX

D'ARTAGNAN SHOWS HIMSELF

As Athos and Porthos had anticipated, d'Artagnan came back after half an hour. Disappearing as if by magic, his man had again given him the slip. He had run round all the neighbouring streets, sword in hand, without finding anyone remotely resembling his quarry. Finally he had gone back to do what he perhaps should have done first, namely knock on the door the stranger had been leaning against, but he had given the knocker ten or twelve firm raps to no avail. No one had answered, and some neighbours attracted by the noise, who had come out on to their doorsteps or poked their noses out of their windows, had assured him that the house, which was shuttered and boarded up tight, had stood empty for six months.

While d'Artagnan was scouring the streets and knocking on doors, Aramis had joined his two friends so that, when he got home, d'Artagnan found the whole band in attendance.

'Well?' the three musketeers inquired in unison as they saw d'Artagnan come in, his forehead dripping with sweat, a distracted, furious look on his face.

'Well,' he cried, throwing his sword on the bed, 'he must be the devil himself, that fellow. He vanished like a phantom, a shadow, a spectre.'

'Do you believe in ghosts?' Athos asked Porthos.

'I only believe what I've seen with my two eyes, and as I've never seen a ghost, I don't believe in them.'

'But the Bible tells us to,' said Aramis. 'Samuel's spirit appeared to Saul', and I would be sorry for this article of faith to be called into question, Porthos.'

'In any case,' said d'Artagnan, 'mortal or devil, flesh or spirit, illusion or reality, that man has been put on this earth to torment me. His escape has cost us a superb piece of business, gentlemen, an affair that could have earned us a hundred pistoles, perhaps more.'

'How so?' Porthos and Aramis asked with one voice, while Athos, true to his policy of silence, merely looked inquiringly at d'Artagnan.

'Planchet,' d'Artagnan called to his servant, who had just squeezed his head round the door in an attempt to catch some snippets of their conversation. 'Go down to my landlord, Monsieur Bonacieux, and tell him to send us up half a dozen bottles of the Beaugency — that's my favourite.'

'Goodness, you've got a line of credit with your landlord now, have you?' asked Porthos.

'Yes, from today,' replied d'Artagnan, 'and don't worry, if his wine is no good, we'll have him fetch up another one.'

'One must use, not abuse,' Aramis remarked sententiously.

'I've always said, of us four, d'Artagnan is the one with a good head on his shoulders,' declared Athos, and then, having expressed himself of this opinion, which d'Artagnan responded to with a bow, he immediately lapsed back into his customary silence.

'Enough beating about the bush — what is this business?' asked Porthos.

'Yes,' said Aramis, 'confide in us, my dear friend, unless the confidence concerns a lady's honour, in which case you'd best keep it to yourself.'

'I assure you,' said d'Artagnan. 'no one's honour will be compromised by what I am going to tell you.'

Then he relayed word for word the conversation he had just had with his landlord, and concluded with the fact that the man who had abducted the worthy mercer's wife was the individual he had quarrelled with at the Honest Miller inn.

'Not too shabby, this business of yours,' said Athos, after taking an appraising sip of the wine and indicating his approval with a nod of the head, 'and we'll be able to get fifty or sixty pistoles from this good fellow. The question is whether it's worth risking four lives for fifty or sixty pistoles.'

'Aren't you paying attention?' cried d'Artagnan. 'A woman is involved – a woman who has been abducted, and is undoubtedly being threatened, perhaps even tortured, as we speak, simply because she is loyal to her mistress!'

'Careful now, d'Artagnan,' said Aramis. 'You seem to be getting a little too worked up over the fate of Madame Bonacieux in my opinion. Womankind was put on earth to be our downfall. They are the source of all our troubles.'

Athos frowned and bit his lip at this sententious remark of Aramis's.

'It's not Madame Bonacieux I'm worried about!' cried d'Artagnan. 'It's the queen, who is abandoned by the king and persecuted by the cardinal, and watches on as, one by one, her friends' heads roll.'

'Why does she love what we most detest, the Spanish and the English?'

'Spain is her native country,' replied d'Artagnan, 'so there is no mystery to her love of the Spanish, who are children of the same land as her. As for your second reproach, I have heard it said it is not the English, but an Englishman that she loves.'

'And, my faith, you have to admit this Englishman is worthy of it,' said Athos, 'I have never seen a nobler air.'

'Not to mention that he dresses better than any man alive,' said Porthos. 'I was at the Louvre once, when he scattered his pearls[2], and by God, I sold the two I picked up for ten pistoles a piece. What about you, Aramis, do you know him?'

'As well as you, gentlemen, since I was one of the men who arrested him in the garden at Amiens[3], after the queen's equerry, Monsieur Putange, let me pass. I was in the seminary at the time, and I thought the adventure was hard on the king.'

'Nevertheless,' said d'Artagnan, 'if I knew where the Duke of Buckingham was, I would still take him by the hand and conduct him to the queen, even if simply to enrage the cardinal – for our real, our only, our eternal enemy, gentlemen, is the cardinal, and if we could find a way of causing him some mischief, I confess, I would be only too happy to risk my life in it.'

'And the mercer also told you, did he, d'Artagnan,' asked Athos, 'that the queen thought Buckingham had been brought over under false pretences?'

'She fears so.'

'Wait, wait . . .' said Aramis.

'What?' asked Porthos.

'No, go on. I'm just trying to remember some details.'

'Now I'm convinced,' said d'Artagnan, 'this abduction of a woman from the queen's retinue is connected to the events we are talking about, and perhaps also to the Duke of Buckingham being in Paris.'

'The Gascon is so imaginative,' Porthos said admiringly.

'I like hearing him talk,' said Athos. 'His twang amuses me.'

'Gentlemen,' Aramis resumed. 'Listen to this . . .'

'Aramis has the floor!' exclaimed the three friends.

'Yesterday I was at the house of a learned doctor of theology whom I sometimes consult for my studies . . .'

Athos smiled.

'He lives in a deserted part of town,' Aramis went on. 'His tastes, his calling require it. Now, just as I was coming out of his house . . .'

Aramis paused.

'Well?' asked his listeners. 'Just as you were coming out of his house?'

Aramis seemed to be exercising all his powers of self-control like a man who, midway through a lie, finds himself confounded by an unforeseen obstacle. But the eyes of his three companions were fixed upon him, their ears pricked up. There was no turning back.

'This doctor has a niece . . .' Aramis resumed.

'Ah, he has a niece!' interrupted Porthos.

'An eminently respectable lady,' said Aramis.

The three friends started laughing.

'Oh, if you're going to laugh or be sceptical,' said Aramis, 'you won't learn anything.'

'We are as full of belief as the Mahometan and as silent as the tomb,' said Athos.

'I'll go on then,' said Aramis. 'This niece sometimes pays her uncle a visit. Well, she and I happened to coincide yesterday, and I was obliged to offer to show her to her carriage.'

'Ah, she has a carriage, the doctor's niece?' interrupted Porthos, one of whose failings was an inability to hold his tongue. 'That's a good acquaintance to have, my friend.'

'Porthos,' said Aramis, 'I've already pointed out to you several times that you are extremely indiscreet, a quality that does not endear you to women.'

'Gentlemen, gentlemen,' cried d'Artagnan, who sensed what lay behind the story. 'This is serious, let's try not to joke if possible. Go on, Aramis, go on.'

'Suddenly, a tall, dark-haired man with a gentleman's manners . . . why, rather like your fellow, d'Artagnan.'

'The same one, perhaps,' the latter said.

'That may be,' replied Aramis. 'At any rate, this gentleman approached me, with five or six characters ten paces behind him, and very politely said, "Your Grace, and you, madam," addressing the lady I had on my arm . . .'

'The doctor's niece?'

'Peace there, Porthos!' said Athos. 'You are infuriating.'

'Would you be so good as to get into this carriage, without putting up any resistance or making a sound?'

'He took you for Buckingham!' cried d'Artagnan.

'I believe so,' replied Aramis.

'And the lady?' asked Porthos.

'He took her for the queen!' said d'Artagnan.

'Precisely,' said Aramis.

'He's a devil, this Gascon,' cried Athos. 'Nothing gets past him.'

'It's true,' said Porthos, 'Aramis is the same height as the handsome duke and has something of his figure, but still, I would have thought a musketeer's uniform . . .'

'I had on a huge cloak,' said Aramis.

'In July?' said Porthos. 'Heavens, was the doctor afraid you'd be recognised?'

'I can understand the spy being misled by your figure,' said Athos, 'but your face . . .'

'I had on a big hat,' said Aramis.

'Oh, my God,' cried Porthos, 'such precautions for a theology lesson!'

'Gentlemen, gentlemen,' said d'Artagnan, 'let's not waste our time bantering. Let's spread out and search for the mercer's wife, she's the key to the intrigue.'

'A woman of such lowly station? Do you think so, d'Artagnan?' said Porthos, pursing his lips disdainfully.

'She's the goddaughter of La Porte, the queen's confidential valet. Haven't I said that already, gentlemen? Besides, perhaps it was intentional on Her Majesty's behalf to have sought support so low this time. The high and mighty can be seen a long way off, and the cardinal has good eyesight.'

'Well, agree a price with the mercer first then,' said Porthos, 'a good one.'

'No need,' said d'Artagnan. 'If he doesn't pay us, I am certain we will be handsomely remunerated from another quarter.'

At that moment, a noise of hurrying feet echoed in the stairwell, the door opened with a crash, and the unfortunate mercer rushed into the room where the council was in progress.

'Ah, gentlemen, save me, in heaven's name, save me!' he cried. 'Four men are coming to arrest me. Save me!'

Porthos and Aramis leapt to their feet.

'One moment,' cried d'Artagnan, motioning them to sheathe

their half-drawn swords, 'what's needed here is caution rather than courage.'

'But,' cried Porthos, 'we're not going to let . . .'

'You're going to let d'Artagnan carry on,' Athos interrupted. 'Of all of us, I repeat, he is the one with the head on his shoulders, and, for my part, I declare I shall obey him. Act as you see fit, d'Artagnan.'

At that moment, four guards appeared at the door of the ante-chamber, but, seeing four musketeers standing there with swords at their sides, they hesitated to go any further.

'Come in, gentlemen, come in,' cried d'Artagnan. 'This is my home and we are all loyal servants of the king and the cardinal here.'

'So you won't try to stop us carrying out our orders, gentlemen?' asked the man who appeared to be the leader of the party.

'On the contrary, gentlemen. We will lend a hand if need be.'

'What's he saying?' muttered Porthos.

'You're a fool,' said Athos. 'Keep quiet.'

'But you promised . . .' whispered the poor mercer.

'We can only help you if we're free,' d'Artagnan replied quickly in a low voice, 'and if we seem to be defending you, they'll arrest us too.'

'I think though . . .'

'Carry on, gentlemen,' said d'Artagnan loudly. 'I have no reason to defend this man. Today is the first time I've clapped eyes on him, and he can tell you what business he came on – to ask me for my rent! Isn't that true, Monsieur Bonacieux? Answer!'

'It is the plain truth,' exclaimed the mercer, 'but this gentleman is not saying . . .'

'Not a word about me,' d'Artagnan whispered, 'not a word about my friends, and, above all, not a word about the queen, otherwise you will ruin us all without saving yourself. Go on, gentlemen,' he added at the top of his voice, 'remove this man!'

And then he pushed the stunned mercer into the arms of the guards, saying, 'You are a rascal, my dear sir. You come and ask me for money – *me*, a musketeer! Off to jail with him, gentlemen, I repeat – take the fellow off to jail and keep him under lock and key as long as you can – that will allow me to pay my rent.'

Thanking him effusively, the officers of the law made off with their prey.

As they were going down the stairs, d'Artagnan slapped their leader on the shoulder and, filling two glasses with the Beaugency he owed to Monsieur Bonacieux's generosity, asked, 'Why don't we toast one another's health?'

'It would be a great honour,' said the constable. 'I gratefully accept.'

'So, your health, sir . . . What is your name?'

'Boisrenard.'

'Monsieur Boisrenard!'

'To you, sir! Now, in return, what is your name, if you please?'

'D'Artagnan.'

'Your health, Monsieur d'Artagnan!'

'And above all,' cried d'Artagnan, as if carried away by enthusiasm, 'the king's and the cardinal's health!'

The constable might have doubted d'Artagnan's sincerity if the wine had been bad, but it was excellent and he was convinced.

'What fiendish act of villainy have you committed here?' protested Porthos, when the chief officer had rejoined his companions and the four friends were alone again. 'Aaargh, four musketeers allow a wretch begging for help to be arrested in their midst! A gentleman takes a drink with a bailiff's man!'

'Porthos,' said Aramis, 'Athos has already told you you're a fool, and I am of the same opinion. D'Artagnan, you are a great man, and when you succeed Monsieur de Tréville, I shall ask for your support when I apply to an abbey.'

'Wait, goodness, now I'm completely lost!' said Porthos. 'You approve of what d'Artagnan just did?'

'By heaven, I should think so,' said Athos. 'And not only do I approve, I heartily congratulate him on it.'

'And now, gentlemen,' said d'Artagnan, without troubling to explain himself to Porthos, '"All for one, one for all!" – that is our motto, is it not?'

'But . . .' said Porthos.

'Put out your hand and swear!' Athos and Aramis exclaimed as one.

Succumbing to his peers, Porthos put out his hand, grumbling softly, and the four friends repeated with one voice the creed dictated by d'Artagnan: 'All for one, one for all!'

'Good, now let's all go home,' said d'Artagnan, as if he had done nothing but command his entire life, 'and be on our guard, because from now on we are at war with the cardinal.'

X

A SEVENTEENTH-CENTURY MOUSETRAP

THE MOUSETRAP IS NOT a modern invention. As soon as human societies came up with some form of police force in the course of their evolution, the police in turn came up with the mousetrap.

But as our readers may not yet be familiar with Rue de Jérusalem[1] slang, and since it is the first time in the fifteen years we have been writing that we have used the word in this context, let us explain to them what a mousetrap is.

When an individual suspected of a crime is arrested in a dwelling of any sort, the arrest may be kept secret, and four or five men posted in ambush in the front room; when visitors knock, they are let in, the door is closed behind them, and they are arrested; and, by these means, within two or three days more or less everyone who regularly frequents the place will be detained.

That is a mousetrap.

And that is what became of Monsieur Bonacieux's lodgings. Anyone who put in an appearance there was seized and questioned by the cardinal's men. Naturally, since a separate alley led to d'Artagnan's rooms on the first floor, his visitors were spared their attentions.

In any case, he had no visitors apart from the three musketeers. They had all started searching, each pursuing their own course, but hadn't come up with anything or made any discoveries. Athos had gone so far as to question Monsieur de Tréville, which, considering the worthy musketeer's habitual silence, had astonished his captain. But Monsieur de Tréville didn't know anything, apart from the fact that the last time he had seen the cardinal, the king and the queen, the cardinal had worn a worried look, the king was uneasy and the queen's red eyes indicated that she had either not been sleeping or that she had been crying. But the latter circumstance hadn't struck him particularly because, since her marriage, the queen often lay awake and cried a great deal[2].

At all events, Monsieur de Tréville charged Athos to serve the king and, above all, the queen, and begged him to instruct his comrades to do likewise.

D'Artagnan, meanwhile, didn't stir from his lodgings. He had converted his room into an observation post. From its windows he could see when a new arrival was about to be caught in the trap, and, having removed some floor tiles and taken up the parquet so that only a simple ceiling separated him from the room below in which the questioning took place, he could then hear everything that passed between the inquisitors and the accused.

The person arrested would first be searched meticulously and then asked, almost word for word, the following questions:

'Did Madame Bonacieux give you anything for her husband or for some other person?'

'Did Monsieur Bonacieux give you anything for his wife or for some other person?'

'Did either of them confide anything to you by word of mouth?'

They wouldn't be questioning them like this if they knew anything, d'Artagnan thought to himself. So, what are they trying to find out? Whether the Duke of Buckingham is in Paris, and whether he has either had or is due to have some interview with the queen?

D'Artagnan fastened on this idea, which, from all he had heard, did not seem implausible.

Meanwhile the mousetrap worked away day and night, and d'Artagnan's vigilance likewise.

The evening after poor Bonacieux's arrest, Athos had just left d'Artagnan to go to Monsieur de Tréville's; it had just struck nine, and Planchet, who had not made up his master's bed, was setting to work, when knocking was heard on the front door. It was immediately opened and then closed again; another person had been caught in the mousetrap.

D'Artagnan rushed to the spot where he had taken up the tiles, lay face-down on the floor and listened.

Cries soon rang out, followed by groans, which the police attempted to stifle. There was no indication of their questioning anyone.

Confound it, that sounds like a woman, d'Artagnan said to himself. They're searching her, she's resisting, they're forcing her – the blackguards!

Despite his innate prudence, it took all d'Artagnan's self-control to stop himself intervening in the scene unfolding below.

'But I tell you that I am the mistress of this house, gentlemen, I am Madame Bonacieux, I am part of the queen's retinue,' cried the unfortunate woman.

'Madame Bonacieux!' murmured d'Artagnan. 'Could I be lucky enough to have found the prize everyone is searching for?'

'We've been waiting for you,' declared the interrogators.

The voice became more and more stifled; there was a sound of struggling, crashes against the panelling. The victim was resisting as much as a woman can resist against four men.

'Excuse me, gentlemen, excu—' murmured the voice, after which it only produced inarticulate sounds.

'They're gagging her, they're going to take her away,' cried d'Artagnan, bounding to his feet like a spring. 'My sword . . . Good, it is at my side. Planchet!'

'Sir?'

'Run and find Athos, Porthos and Aramis. One of them is bound to be at home, perhaps all three will be by now. Tell them to arm themselves and come here at the double, ah, I remember, Athos is at Monsieur de Tréville's . . .'

'Where are you going, sir?'

'I am taking the window,' cried d'Artagnan. 'It will be quicker. Put the tiles back, sweep the floor, leave by the door and hare off to where I've told you.'

'Oh master, you'll kill yourself,' cried Planchet.

'Tush, you fool,' said d'Artagnan, and hanging by a hand from the windowsill, he dropped from the first floor, which fortunately was not high, without getting a scratch.

Then he went immediately to knock on the door, muttering, 'Now it's my turn to get caught in the mousetrap. Woe betide any cats who provoke this mouse.'

The knocker had barely rung out at the young man's touch before the uproar ceased, steps approached, the door opened, and d'Artagnan, blade drawn, dashed into Monsieur Bonacieux's lodgings. No doubt moved by a spring, the door closed of its own accord behind him.

Then the remaining residents of the unfortunate Bonacieux house and their immediate neighbours heard a tremendous shouting, stamping of feet, clashing of swords and smashing of furniture. Moments later, those who had been startled by the noise and come to their windows to learn the cause were greeted by the sight of the door opening and four men dressed in black flying rather than emerging from it like frightened crows, leaving feathers from their wings – or rather, strips of their uniforms and pieces of their cloaks – strewn on the ground and caught on the corners of tables.

D'Artagnan had not had too much trouble winning the day, it has to be said, because only one of the constables was armed and he defended himself purely for form's sake. The other three had tried to knock the living daylights out of the young man with chairs, stools and crockery, it is true, but two or three scratches from the Gascon's blade had terrified them. Ten minutes had been enough to vanquish them and leave d'Artagnan master of the field.

The neighbours, who had opened their windows with the coolness peculiar to Paris's inhabitants in those times of constant rioting and brawling, closed them as soon as they saw the four men in black run away. Their instincts told them the show was over for the moment.

In any case, it was getting late and then, as now, people living near the Luxembourg went to bed early.

Left alone with Madame Bonacieux, d'Artagnan turned towards her: the poor woman was slumped in a chair, half-unconscious. D'Artagnan looked her over with a quick glance.

She was a charming woman of between twenty-five or twenty-six with brown hair and blue eyes, a slightly upturned nose, pearlescent teeth and a complexion of marbled rose and opal. These were the only features, however, that might have led one to mistake her for a noblewoman. Although white, her hands lacked finesse, nor did her feet indicate a woman of quality. Fortunately d'Artagnan hadn't got round to caring about such details yet.

As he was looking at Madame Bonacieux – an inspection that, as we've said, had reached her feet – he saw a handsome cambric handkerchief on the floor. He picked it up, as he had a habit of doing, and recognised in one corner the same mark he had seen on the handkerchief which had almost got him his throat cut by Aramis.

D'Artagnan had been wary of handkerchiefs with heraldic bearings ever since, so he put the one he'd picked up back in Madame Bonacieux's pocket without saying anything.

As he did so, Madame Bonacieux came to. She opened her eyes, looked round, terrified, and saw the room was empty and that she was alone with her deliverer. She immediately smiled and held out her hands. Madame Bonacieux had the sweetest smile in the world.

'Ah, sir,' she said, 'you have saved me; allow me to thank you.'

'Madam,' said d'Artagnan, 'I only did what any gentleman would have done in my place. You owe me no thanks.'

'I do, sir, I do, and I hope to prove to you that you have not rendered an ingrate a service. What did those men want from me though? I thought they were thieves at first. And why isn't Monsieur Bonacieux here?'

'Madam, those men were agents of the cardinal, so far more dangerous than thieves could ever be. As for your husband, Monsieur Bonacieux, he is not here because yesterday they came and took him off to the Bastille.'

'My husband in the Bastille!' cried Madame Bonacieux, 'Oh, my God, what has he done? That poor, dear man . . . innocence itself!'

The hint of a smile appeared on the young woman's still terrified face.

'What has he done, madam?' said d'Artagnan. 'I believe his only crime is to have both the good and the ill fortune of being your husband.'

'So, sir, you know . . .'

'I know you were abducted, madam.'

'And by whom? Do you know that? Oh, if you do, tell me.'

'By a man between forty and forty-five years old, with black hair, a dark complexion, and a scar on his left temple.'

'That's right, that's right. What is his name though?'

'Ah, his name – I haven't found that out.'

'Did my husband know I had been abducted?'

'He was told in a letter from the kidnapper himself.'

'And does he suspect why it might have happened?' asked Madame Bonacieux with some embarrassment.

'He attributed it, I believe, to a political matter.'

'I wasn't sure at first, but now I think the same. So, dear Monsieur Bonacieux did not suspect me for a moment . . . ?'

'Ah, far from it, madam, he prided himself on your good sense and above all on your love.'

A second, almost invisible smile played on the beautiful young woman's rosy lips.

'But how did you come to escape?' d'Artagnan went on.

'I was left alone for a moment, and as I knew from this morning what to make of my abduction, I used my sheets to climb out of a window. I thought my husband would be at home, so I ran all the way here.'

'To put yourself under his protection?'

'Oh no, the poor dear man, I knew he couldn't protect me, but since he could be of service in another matter, I wanted to tell him.'

'About what?'

'Oh, that is not my secret to tell.'

'I apologise, madam, if my guardsman's nature prompts me to remind you of the need for caution,' said d'Artagnan, 'but I don't think this is a suitable place to exchange confidences anyway. The men I drove off will return with reinforcements, and if they find us here we are lost. I sent word to three of my friends, but who knows if they were at home.'

'Yes, yes, you are right,' Madame Bonacieux cried, frightened, 'let's go, we must fly from here.'

Saying this, she put her arm under d'Artagnan's and pulled him away.

'But where shall we go?' said d'Artagnan. 'Where shall we fly to?'

'Let's get away from this house first, then we'll see.'

Then the young man and the young woman left the house without even troubling to shut the door, quickly went down Rue des Fossoyeurs, turned into Rue des Fosses Monsieur-le-Prince and stopped at Place Saint-Sulpice.

'What shall we do now?' asked d'Artagnan. 'Where do you want me to take you?'

'I am very embarrassed to tell it, I admit,' said Madame Bonacieux, 'but my plan was to get word to Monsieur de La Porte through my husband, so that Monsieur de La Porte could tell us exactly what has been happening in the Louvre for the last three days, and whether it would be dangerous for me to go there.'

'I can do that,' said d'Artagnan. 'I can get word to Monsieur de La Porte.'

'I dare say. There is only one difficulty: Monsieur Bonacieux is known at the Louvre and would be let in, whereas you are not, and they would close the door on you.'

'Bah,' said d'Artagnan, 'you must have a concierge at one of the Louvre's gates who is devoted to you and who, with a password . . .'

Madame Bonacieux looked intently at the young man.

'And if I gave you the password,' she said, 'would you forget it as soon as you had used it?'

'On my word of honour, and as I am a gentleman!' d'Artagnan declared with unmistakable sincerity.

'Why, I believe you. You seem a fine young man, and besides, your devotion may be the cause of your fortune.'

'I don't need any promises – I shall do as a matter of conscience all I can to serve the king and be agreeable to the queen,' said d'Artagnan. 'I am at your service as a friend.'

'But what about me? Where will you keep me in the meantime?'

'Isn't there a house you can go to and wait for Monsieur de La Porte?'

'No, I don't want to have to rely on anyone.'

'Wait,' said d'Artagnan, 'we are nearly at Athos's door. Yes, this is the way.'

'Who is Athos?'

'One of my friends.'

'But what if he is at home and sees me?'

'He isn't, and I'll take the key after I have let you into his rooms.'

'But what if he comes back?'

'He won't. Besides, he would find out that I had brought a woman, and that she is in his rooms.'

'But that will be very compromising for me, you know.'

'Why does that matter? No one knows you. Besides, our position requires us to overlook niceties.'

'Let's go to your friend's then. Where does he live?'

'Rue Férou, two minutes from here.'

'On, on!'

They both set off again. As d'Artagnan had predicted, Athos was not at home. He took the key, which the concierge was in the habit of giving him as a friend of the family, climbed the stairs and showed Madame Bonacieux into the small set of rooms we have already described.

'You can feel at home here,' he said. 'Wait, lock the door from the inside and don't open it to anyone, unless you hear three knocks like this.' He knocked three times, twice quite loud, in quick succession, and then once more softly after a gap.

'Fine,' said Madame Bonacieux. 'Now it's my turn to give instructions.'

'I'm listening.'

'Go to the Louvre's gate on the Rue de l'Échelle and ask for Germain.'

'Very well. And then?'

'He will ask you what you want and you will answer with two words: "Tours" and "Brussels". He will immediately await your orders.'

'Which will be?'

'To find Monsieur de La Porte, the queen's valet.'

'And when he has done that and Monsieur de La Porte has appeared?'

'Send him to me.'

'Very well. But where and how am I going to see you again?'

'Do you want to do so very much?'

'Of course!'

'Well then, rely on me to arrange it, don't worry.'

'I am counting on you.'

'Count away.'

D'Artagnan bowed to Madame Bonacieux, giving her the most

loving look he could possibly concentrate on her charming little being, and took his leave. As he went down the stairs, he heard the door being double-locked behind him. In two bounds he was at the Louvre. He entered the Rue de l'Échelle gate as it was striking ten o'clock. All the events we have just related had succeeded one another in half an hour.

Everything went off just as Madame Bonacieux had said it would. Hearing the agreed password, Germain bowed; ten minutes later, La Porte was in the porter's lodge; in a few words, d'Artagnan brought him up to date and told him where Madame Bonacieux was. La Porte confirmed the address twice and then ran off. He had barely gone ten paces, however, before he came back.

'Young man,' he said to d'Artagnan, 'a word of advice.'

'What?'

'You could have the police on your track for this.'

'Do you think so?'

'Yes. Do you have a friend with a clock that runs slow?'

'Why?'

'Go and see him so he can testify you were with him at nine-thirty. That's what the law calls an alibi.'

D'Artagnan thought it sensible advice. Taking to his heels, he ran to Monsieur de Tréville's but there, instead of going into the drawing room with all the others, he asked to be shown into his office. As d'Artagnan was a regular visitor, no objections were raised, and someone went to inform Monsieur de Tréville that his young compatriot had something important to tell him and was requesting a private audience. Five minutes later, Monsieur de Tréville was inquiring how he could be of service to d'Artagnan and what had earned him a visit at such a late hour.

'Forgive me, sir,' said d'Artagnan, who had used the moment he had been left alone to put the clock back three quarters of an hour, 'I thought that because it was only twenty-five past nine, it wouldn't be too late to pay you a visit.'

'Twenty-five past nine,' cried Monsieur de Tréville looking at his clock. 'That can't be.'

'But you see, sir,' said d'Artagnan. 'There's the evidence.'

'That's right. I would have thought it was later,' said Monsieur de Tréville. 'Anyway, come now, what do you want from me?'

Then d'Artagnan told Monsieur de Tréville a long story about the queen. He described his fears on Her Majesty's behalf, and told him what he had heard about the cardinal's designs concerning Buckingham, all with a calmness and aplomb that Monsieur de Tréville was all the more taken in by, given that he, as we have said, had himself noticed something new between the cardinal, king and queen.

On the stroke of ten, d'Artagnan took his leave of Monsieur de Tréville, who thanked him for the information, charged him to serve the king and the queen with all his heart, and returned to his drawing room. But at the foot of the stairs, d'Artagnan remembered he had forgotten his walking stick. He hurriedly retraced his steps, went back into the office and, with a flick of his finger, set the clock back to the correct time, so that the following day there would be no sign that it had been tampered with. And then, satisfied that he now had a witness who could confirm his alibi, he went back downstairs and soon found himself out on the street.

XI

THE INTRIGUE GROWS TANGLED

H IS VISIT TO MONSIEUR DE TRÉVILLE over, d'Artagnan took the longest way home, deep in thought.

What was d'Artagnan thinking about to make him stray from his usual route like this and stare up at the stars in the sky, sighing one moment and smiling the next?

He was thinking about Madame Bonacieux. For an apprentice musketeer, the young woman was close to love's dream. Pretty, mysterious and privy to almost all the secrets of the court, which lent her graceful features such a charming air of gravity, he sensed she wasn't entirely indifferent to him, which is an irresistible attraction for novices in love. Moreover, he had delivered her from the clutches of those demons who were bent on searching and manhandling her, and this notable service had established between them one of those feelings of gratitude that can so easily assume a more tender nature.

D'Artagnan already saw himself, so fast do dreams travel on the wings of imagination, being accosted by a messenger from the young woman, bringing a note arranging a meeting, perhaps, or a gold chain, or a diamond. We have already said that young gentlemen felt no shame at taking money from the king; let us now add that, in this time of loose morals, they felt no more compunction with regard to their mistresses, who almost always gave them valuable and durable mementos, as if trying to overcome the fragility of their feelings with the solidity of their gifts.

Men unblushingly made their way by means of women in those days. Those who were simply beautiful gave their beauty, which is no doubt the origin of the proverb that the most beautiful girl in the world can only give what she has. And those who were rich added a share of their money, and one could list a good number of the heroes of that gallant age who would not have won their spurs first, or their battles afterwards, if it weren't for the more or less well-lined purses their mistresses had tied to the pommels of their saddles.

D'Artagnan hadn't a sou to his name, and his provincial reticence, like a thin varnish, an ephemeral bloom or the down of a peach, had long since been scattered by the winds of the unorthodox advice the three musketeers had given him as his friends. In keeping with the strange customs of the time, therefore, he thought of himself as if he were on campaign in Paris, no more nor less than if he had been in Flanders: there the Spanish, here women. Everywhere there was an enemy to fight and contributions to be imposed.

But may we also say that d'Artagnan was motivated at present by more noble and disinterested sentiments. The mercer had told him he was rich, and the young man had been able to guess that, with a fool like Monsieur Bonacieux, the wife would be the one holding the purse strings. But this hadn't influenced his feelings when he saw Madame Bonacieux in the slightest, and self-interest had played almost no part in the stirrings of love that had ensued. We say almost, because the idea of a young woman who is not only beautiful, graceful and witty, but also rich does not diminish love's first stirrings – quite the contrary, it strengthens them.

Affluence, after all, affords a wealth of aristocratic attentions and caprices that suit beauty. A sheer white stocking, a silk dress, a lace chemisette, a pretty slipper on the foot, a gauzy ribbon in the hair – such articles cannot make an ugly woman pretty, but they can make a pretty woman beautiful. Not to mention the hands that benefit from all this: the hands that, in women particularly, need to remain idle to be beautiful.

Moreover d'Artagnan, as the reader well knows, since we haven't concealed the state of his fortunes for him – d'Artagnan was not a millionaire. He had every hope of becoming one some day, but the date he set for this happy development lay in the fairly distant future. In the meantime, what agony to see the woman one loves desiring those thousand trifles of which a woman's happiness is composed but not be able to provide them! At least when the woman is rich and the lover isn't, she can give herself what he cannot, and although ordinarily it is her husband's money that enables her to do so, her husband is rarely the one who gets the gratitude.

Primed as he was to be the most tender of lovers, d'Artagnan remained in the meantime a most devoted friend. In the midst of his amorous plans concerning the mercer's wife, he did not forget his comrades. The pretty Madame Bonacieux was just the woman, he thought, to take on an outing to the Saint-Denis plain or the Saint-Germain fair with Athos, Porthos and Aramis, and he would be proud to show off such a conquest to them. And then, after one has been walking for a long time, hunger sets in – d'Artagnan had noticed that for a while now. They could have one of those charming little dinners when, on one side, one touches a friend's hand, and, on the other, the mistress's foot. And finally, in tight corners or drastic need, d'Artagnan would come to his friends' rescue.

But what of Monsieur Bonacieux, whom d'Artagnan had openly repudiated as he thrust him into the officers' clutches, while promising in a whisper to save him? We must confess to our readers that d'Artagnan didn't think about him at all – or rather, if he did think about him, it was to tell himself that he was better off where he was, wherever that might be. Love is the most selfish of all the passions.

Our readers need not worry, however. D'Artagnan may have forgotten his landlord, or have pretended to on the grounds that he did not know where he had been taken, but we haven't forgotten him, and we know his whereabouts. For the moment, though, let us imitate our lovestruck Gascon – we will come back to the worthy mercer later.

Thinking about the love that lay in store, talking to the night, smiling at the stars, d'Artagnan headed up Rue du Cherche-Midi[1], or Chasse-Midi as it was called at the time. Finding himself in Aramis's neighbourhood, he decided to pay his friend a visit to explain why he had sent Planchet with the invitation to hurry to the mousetrap. If Planchet had found him at home, Aramis would undoubtedly have run to Rue des Fossoyeurs to find nobody but his two other friends, and neither he nor they would have known what to make of it. This imposition deserved some explanation, d'Artagnan reasoned.

But he also felt it would be a chance to talk about the pretty little Madame Bonacieux, of whom his mind, if not his heart, was already overflowing. You cannot ask for discretion when it comes to a first love. First love is always attended by such overwhelming feelings of joy that they have to spill over, otherwise they would suffocate you.

Paris had been dark for two hours and was starting to empty. All the clocks in the Faubourg Saint-Germain were striking eleven, and it was a mild and balmy night. D'Artagnan was walking along a lane on the site of what is today the Rue d'Assas, inhaling the fragrant air coming from Rue de La Vaugirard, where the gardens breathed out their scents, refreshed by the evening dew and the night breeze. The sound of drinkers singing in taverns lost on the plain, muffled as it was by stout shutters, could be heard in the distance. When he reached the end of the lane, d'Artagnan turned left. The house Aramis lived in lay between Rue Cassette and Rue Servandoni[2].

D'Artagnan had just passed Rue Cassette and had already spotted the door of his friend's house, which was buried under a swelling mass of sycamores and clematis, when he saw something like a shadow coming out of Rue Servandoni. This something was swathed in a cloak, and at first d'Artagnan took it for a man, but he soon realised, from its diminutive stature, uncertain gait and hesitant step, that it was a woman. He also noticed that she didn't seem entirely certain which house she was looking for; she kept looking up as if to get her bearings, stopping, turning back and then going on. D'Artagnan was intrigued.

What if I went to offer her my services? he wondered. By her bearing, she is clearly young; perhaps she is pretty too. Oh, yes. But a woman roaming the streets at this hour is almost bound to be going to see her lover. Lord, interrupting trysts is no sort of door through which to enter into relations with someone!

The young woman continued down the street, counting the houses and windows as she went. This wasn't, incidentally, a difficult or lengthy undertaking. There were only three buildings to be seen, and, of those, only two had windows facing on to the street – the house parallel to Aramis's, and Aramis's itself.

By God, thought d'Artagnan, remembering the theologian's niece. It would be funny if this dove running late was looking for the home of our friend. On my soul though, it looks very much as if she is! Ah, my dear Aramis, I will get to the bottom of it all this time.

And, making himself as slight as possible, d'Artagnan hid on the darker side of the street, near a stone bench at the back of a niche.

He could tell the young woman was still walking because, apart from the unmistakable light step, she had just given a little cough that suggested she had a very pure voice. D'Artagnan thought this cough must be a signal.

Suddenly, however, whether because an answering signal had resolved the nocturnal searcher's doubts, or whether because she had recognised her journey's end without another's help, the woman strode resolutely up to Aramis's shutter and tapped on it three times at equal intervals with her bent finger.

'That's Aramis's house,' murmured d'Artagnan. 'Ah, Mr Hypocrite, I've caught you studying your theology!'

She had scarcely knocked before the inner casement opened and a light appeared through the slats of shutter.

'Aha!' said the eavesdropper to himself. 'The visit was expected. Come on, now the shutter's going to be opened and the lady will climb in. Very good.'

But, to d'Artagnan's astonishment, the shutter remained closed. What's more, the light that had flared up for a minute disappeared and everything returned to darkness.

D'Artagnan thought that couldn't be the end of it, and continued watching and listening, straining his eyes and ears.

He was right. After a few seconds, two sharp knocks rang out from inside.

The young woman in the street knocked once in response, and the shutter opened a crack.

The reader will judge how avidly d'Artagnan watched and listened.

Unfortunately the light had been moved to another room. But the young man's eyes had grown accustomed to the night. In any case, it is a property of Gascons' eyes, so we're told, that they can see in the dark, like cats.

D'Artagnan then saw the young woman take something white from her pocket, which she quickly unfolded, whereupon it assumed the form of a handkerchief. She then drew her interlocutor's attention to one of its corners.

D'Artagnan was reminded of the handkerchief he had found at Madame Bonacieux's feet, which had in turn reminded him of the one he had found at Aramis's feet.

What the devil could these handkerchiefs mean?

From his vantage point, d'Artagnan couldn't see Aramis's face – we say Aramis, because the young man was in no doubt his friend was inside talking to the woman outside – and his curiosity soon got the better of his prudence. Taking advantage of the absorption into which the two figures we have staged were apparently plunged by the sight of the handkerchief, he left his hiding place, and, quick as lightning, but still muffling his steps, he went and flattened himself against a corner of the wall, from where he could see into Aramis's rooms.

Once in place, d'Artagnan almost let out a cry of surprise. It wasn't Aramis who was talking to the nocturnal visitor, it was a woman. But d'Artagnan could only see enough to recognise the shape of her clothes, and not her features.

At the same moment, the woman in the apartment drew a second handkerchief from her pocket and swapped it for the one she had just been shown. Then a few words were exchanged by the two women. Finally the shutter closed again. The woman who found herself outside the window turned and passed within four steps of d'Artagnan, pulling down the hood of her cloak as she did so. But this precaution was too late; d'Artagnan had already recognised Madame Bonacieux.

Madame Bonacieux! A suspicion it might be her had already crossed his mind when she produced the handkerchief from her pocket. But how likely was it that, after sending for Monsieur de La Porte to escort her back to the Louvre, Madame Bonacieux would be roaming the streets of Paris at half-past eleven at night, at the risk of being abducted a second time?

That meant it had to be a matter of great importance. And what is of most importance to a woman of twenty-five? Love.

On whose behalf was she running such risks – her own or someone else's? That was the question the young man asked

himself, as the demons of jealousy gnawed at his heart just as
fiercely as if he were a recognised lover.

There was a very simple way to be sure of where Madame
Bonacieux was going, though, and that was to follow her. It was
so simple that d'Artagnan adopted it entirely naturally and
instinctively.

But at the sight of the young man emerging from the wall like
a statue from a niche, and at the sound of the footsteps echoing
behind her, Madame Bonacieux gave a little scream and fled.

D'Artagnan ran after her. It wasn't difficult for him to catch
up with a woman entangled in her cloak, and he did so a third of
the way down the street she had taken. The poor thing was
exhausted from terror rather than tiredness, and when d'Artagnan
put his hand on her shoulder, she fell on one knee, crying out in
a choked voice, 'Kill me if you wish, you won't learn a thing!'

Putting his arm round her waist, d'Artagnan lifted her to her
feet, and then, feeling from her dead weight that she was about to
pass out, hastened to reassure her with protestations of his devotion. These meant nothing to Madame Bonacieux in themselves –
such protestations can be made with the worst intentions in the
world – but the voice changed everything. The young woman
thought she recognised it. She opened her eyes again, glanced at
the man who had filled her with such terror and, recognising
d'Artagnan, let out a cry of joy. 'Oh, it's you, it's you! My God,
thank you!'

'Yes, it's me,' said d'Artagnan, 'whom God has sent to watch
over you.'

'Is that why you followed me?' the young woman asked with
a coquettish smile, her mildly sarcastic nature reasserting itself.
All her fear had vanished the moment she recognised as a friend
he whom she had taken for an enemy.

'No,' said d'Artagnan, 'I confess it was chance that set me
on your path. I saw a woman knocking on one of my friends'
windows . . .'

'One of your friends?' interrupted Madame Bonacieux.

'Certainly. Aramis is one of my best friends.'

'Aramis! Who is that?'

'Come now, are you going to tell me you don't know Aramis?'

'This is the first time I've heard that name.'

'So this is also the first time you've come to this house?'

'Certainly.'

'And you didn't know a young man lives here?'

'No.'

'A musketeer?'

'Not for a moment.'

'So it wasn't him you were looking for?'

'Not at all. Besides, you saw for yourself, the person I was talking to was a woman.'

'That is true, but surely she is a friend of Aramis?'

'I wouldn't know.'

'Seeing as she lodges with him.'

'That is not my concern.'

'But who is she?'

'Oh, that is not my secret.'

'Dear Madame Bonacieux, you are charming, but you are also the most mysterious woman . . .'

'Does that count against me?'

'Far from it, you are entrancing.'

'Well then, give me your arm.'

'Gladly. And now?'

'Now, lead on.'

'Where to?'

'To where I'm going.'

'But where are you going?'

'You'll see, since you're going to drop me at the door.'

'Should I wait for you?'

'There will be no need.'

'You will come back on your own, then?'

'Perhaps I will, perhaps I won't.'

'But who will accompany you, then – a man or a woman?'

'I don't know yet.'

'Well, I'll find out then.'

'How?'

'I'll wait until you come out.'

'In that case, goodbye!'

'Why?'

'I don't need you.'

'But you asked . . .'

'To be helped by a gentleman, not watched by a spy.'

'That's putting it a little harshly!'

'What do you call someone who follows a person against their will?'

'Indiscreet.'

'That is putting it a little mildly.'

'Ah, madam, I see your wishes must be obeyed.'

'Why did you deprive yourself of the merit of doing so straightaway?'

'Is there nothing to be gained from repenting, then?'

'Do you sincerely repent?'

'I don't know. But what I do know is that I promise you I'll do anything you want if you let me accompany you to where you are going.'

'And you'll leave me afterwards?'

'Yes.'

'Without spying on me when I come out?'

'Yes.'

'On your word of honour?'

'As I am a gentleman!'

'Then take my arm and let's go.'

D'Artagnan offered his arm to Madame Bonacieux, who clung to it, half laughing, half trembling, and they both headed up Rue de La Harpe. When they got to the top of the street, the young woman seemed to hesitate, as she had done before in Rue de Vaugirard. But then, from certain signs, she appeared to recognise a door, and approaching it, she said, 'And now, sir, this is where

I am expected. A thousand thanks for your honourable company, which has saved me from all the dangers I would have been exposed to had I been alone. But now the moment has come for you to keep your word, I have reached my destination.'

'You won't have anything to fear on your way back?'

'Only thieves.'

'Aren't they anything?'

'What could they take? I don't have a sou on me.'

'You're forgetting that beautiful handkerchief embroidered with a coat of arms.'

'Which one?'

'The one I found at your feet and put back in your pocket.'

'Be quiet, be quiet, you wretch!' cried the young woman. 'Do you want to ruin me?'

'Clearly you're still in danger if a word can make you tremble, and you confess that if anyone heard it you would be ruined. Ah, stay, madam,' d'Artagnan cried out, seizing her hand and looking at her ardently. 'Hold! Be more generous, confide in me. Haven't you read in my eyes that there's only devotion and sympathy in my heart?'

'I have,' replied Madame Bonacieux. 'Ask me my secrets then, and I will share them with you. But other people's are another matter.'

'Very well, then I shall discover them myself,' said d'Artagnan. 'Since they can affect your life, I have to make them mine.'

'Don't even think of it!' cried the young woman with a seriousness that made d'Artagnan shiver in spite of himself. 'Oh, don't meddle in anything that concerns me! Don't try to help me in what I'm doing, I ask you this in the name of the interest I inspire in you, in the name of the service you have rendered me, which I will never forget all my life. You must believe what I am telling you. Don't concern yourself about me any more; I no longer exist for you; let it be as if you'd never seen me.'

'Must Aramis do the same, madam?' asked d'Artagnan, stung.

'That's the second or third time you have mentioned that name, sir, and yet I have told you that I don't know it.'

'You don't know the man whose shutter you knocked on? Come, madam, you think me very credulous!'

'Admit that you're inventing this story and creating this character to make me talk.'

'I'm inventing nothing, madam, creating nothing. This is the plain truth.'

'And you say that one of your friends lives in that house?'

'I do, and I shall say it for a third time: that house is inhabited by a friend of mine, and that friend is Aramis.'

'All this will become clear later,' murmured the young woman, 'but for now, sir, keep quiet.'

'If my heart was laid bare for you to see,' said d'Artagnan, 'you'd read so much curiosity in it that you'd have pity on me, and so much love, that you would instantly satisfy my curiosity. You have nothing to fear from those who love you.'

'You are very quick to talk of love, sir!' said the young woman with a shake of her head.

'That is because love has come to me quickly and for the first time, and I'm not yet twenty.'

The young woman looked at him furtively.

'Listen, I'm already on the trail,' said d'Artagnan. 'Three months ago, I nearly fought a duel with Aramis over a handkerchief like the one you showed to the woman who was in his house, a handkerchief with the same markings, I am sure.'

'Sir,' said the young woman, 'I swear you are wearing me to the bone with these questions.'

'But you who are so prudent, madam, think, if you were arrested with that handkerchief, and if it were seized, wouldn't you be compromised?'

'Why, aren't the initials mine – CB, Constance Bonacieux[3]?'

'Or Camille de Bois-Tracy.'

'Silence, sir, again silence! Ah, since the risks I am running cannot stop you, think of those you run yourself.'

'I?'

'Yes, you. You risk prison, you risk death knowing me.'

'Then I'll never leave your side.'

'Sir,' said the young woman, clasping her hands and imploring him, 'sir, in the name of heaven, in the name of a soldier's honour, in the name of a gentleman's courtesy, go away . . . Wait, it's striking midnight; that is the hour I am expected.'

'Madam,' said the young man, bowing, 'I cannot refuse anyone who makes such a request of me. You can be content, I am going on my way.'

'You won't follow me, you won't spy on me?'

'I'm going home this minute.'

'Ah, I knew you were a fine young man,' cried Madame Bonacieux, holding out one hand to him and placing the other on the latch of a little door that was almost invisible in the wall.

D'Artagnan seized the hand held out to him and kissed it passionately.

'Oh, I wish I'd never seen you!' cried d'Artagnan, with that naive brutality women often prefer to the affectations of politeness, because it reveals a person's truest thoughts and proves that feelings have prevailed over reason.

'Well,' said Madame Bonacieux in an almost caressing voice, squeezing d'Artagnan's hand, which had not let go of hers, 'well, I won't go that far. What is lost today is not lost for the future. Who knows, if one day I'm free, whether I won't gratify your curiosity?'

'Do you promise as much for my love?' cried d'Artagnan, overjoyed.

'Oh, I can't commit myself to that. That will depend on the feelings you are able to stir in me.'

'So, today, madam . . .'

'Today, sir, my heart is simply full of gratitude.'

'Oh, you're too charming,' said d'Artagnan sadly, 'and you take advantage of my love.'

'No, I benefit from your generosity, that's all. But believe me, with some people everything comes good.'

'Oh, you make me the happiest of men. Do not forget this evening, do not forget this promise.'

'Don't worry, when the time and place are right, I will remember everything. But now go, in heaven's name, go! I was expected at midnight exactly and I'm late.'

'Five minutes.'

'Yes, but in some circumstances five minutes are five centuries.'

'When you're in love.'

'And who told you I'm not going to see a lover?'

'So it's a man expecting you?' cried d'Artagnan. 'A man!'

'Oh no, now the discussions are going to start again,' said Madame Bonacieux with a half-smile which was not without a hint of impatience.

'No, I'm leaving, I'm going, I believe in you, I wish to earn all the merit of my devotion, even if it is folly. Goodbye, madam, goodbye!'

And as if he felt he would only be strong enough to free himself from the hand he was holding by jerking away, he ran off while Madame Bonacieux knocked three times, slowly and evenly, on the door, as she had done on the shutter. When he got to the corner of the street, he turned. The door had opened and closed, and the pretty mercer's wife had disappeared.

D'Artagnan carried on his way. He had given his word not to spy on Madame Bonacieux, and even if his life had depended on the place she was going to, or the person who would accompany her, d'Artagnan would still have gone home because he had said he would. Five minutes later he was in Rue des Fossoyeurs.

'Poor Athos,' he said. 'He won't know what all this means. He will either have fallen asleep waiting for me or gone back home, and then found out a woman had been there. A woman in Athos's house! . . . Still,' d'Artagnan went on, 'there was one in Aramis's house. All this is very strange, and I'll be very curious to know how it will turn out.'

'Badly, sir, badly,' responded a voice the young man recognised as Planchet's, for while he was talking to himself out loud, as very preoccupied people have a habit of doing, he had turned into the alley at the end of which were the stairs leading to his lodgings.

'Badly, how? What do you mean, imbecile?' asked d'Artagnan. 'What has happened?'

'All manner of misfortunes.'

'What?'

'First, Monsieur Athos has been arrested.'

'Arrested? Athos arrested? Why?'

'They found him in your rooms, and thought he was you.'

'Who did?'

'The guards the men in black went to find when you sent them packing.'

'Why didn't he tell them his name? Why didn't he say he had nothing to do with the affair?'

'He went out of his way not to, sir. Instead he came over to me and said, "Your master's the one who needs his freedom now, not me, because he knows everything and I know nothing. They'll think he's been arrested and that will give him time. In three days I will say who I am and they'll have to let me go."'

'Bravo, Athos! Noble heart,' murmured d'Artagnan. 'It's just like him. What did the officers do?'

'Four of them took him off somewhere, the Bastille or For-l'Évêque[4], two stayed with the men in black, who searched everywhere and took all the papers, and the last two stood guard at the door throughout the expedition. When it was over, they went off, leaving the house empty and open to the four winds.'

'What about Porthos and Aramis?'

'I haven't found them, they didn't come.'

'But they still may at any moment, because you left word that I was expecting them?'

'Yes, sir.'

'Well then, don't move from here. If they come, tell them what's happened to me and that they should wait for me at the Pine Cone. Here's too dangerous, the house may be watched. I'll run to Monsieur de Tréville and tell him everything, then I'll meet them there.'

'Right, sir,' said Planchet.

'You're going to stay here though, aren't you? You're not going to be afraid?' said d'Artagnan, coming back to exhort his valet to be brave.

'Don't worry, sir,' said Planchet. 'You don't know me yet, I am courageous when I set my mind to it. Setting my mind to it is all it is. Besides, I'm a Picard.'

'It's settled, then,' said d'Artagnan. 'You'll lay down your life sooner than abandon your post.'

'Yes, sir, and there's nothing I wouldn't do to prove to monsieur how attached I am to him.'

Good, d'Artagnan thought to himself. I certainly seem to have used the right approach with this lad. I'll use it again when the opportunity presents itself.

And then, as fast as his legs, which were already a little tired from the day's exertions, could carry him, d'Artagnan headed for Rue du Vieux-Colombier.

Monsieur de Tréville wasn't at home. His company was on guard duty at the Louvre and he was there with them.

He had to see Monsieur de Tréville; it was vital he was told what was happening. D'Artagnan decided to try to gain entry to the Louvre; his uniform as a guard in Monsieur des Essarts's company would serve as passport.

He went down Rue des Petits-Augustins and back up the embankment to cross the Pont-Neuf. He thought of taking the ferry for a moment, but when he got to the water's edge, he mechanically put his hand in his pocket and realised he didn't have any money to pay the ferryman with.

As he came level with Rue Guénégaud he saw a couple of people whose appearance caught his attention.

The two people were a man and a woman.

The woman had the figure of Madame Bonacieux and the man was the very image of Aramis.

There was another thing: the woman was wearing the black mantle that d'Artagnan could still see in his mind's eye outlined against the shutter in Rue de Vaugirard and the door in Rue de La Harpe.

And another thing: the man was wearing a musketeer's uniform.

The woman's hood was pulled down, and the man held his handkerchief to his face: two sets of precautions that indicated they were both anxious not to be recognised.

They took the bridge – that was the way d'Artagnan was going, because he was bound for the Louvre. D'Artagnan followed them.

D'Artagnan had not gone twenty paces before he was convinced that the woman was Madame Bonacieux and the man was Aramis.

In an instant his jealous heart was seething with suspicion.

He was doubly betrayed: by his friend and by the woman he already loved as a mistress. Madame Bonacieux had sworn to him by the great gods that she didn't know Aramis, and yet here she was, a quarter of an hour after she had sworn him this oath, on Aramis's arm.

It didn't even occur to d'Artagnan that he had only known the pretty mercer's wife for three hours, that she owed him nothing other than a minor debt of gratitude for freeing her from the men in black who'd been trying to abduct her, and that she hadn't promised him anything. As far as he was concerned, he was an offended, betrayed, ridiculed lover. The blood and rage rose to his face, and he resolved to make everything clear.

Noticing they were being followed, the young woman and the young man had started walking faster. D'Artagnan broke into a run, overtook them, then swung round when they were in front of the Samaritaine clock, caught in the light of a street lamp, which illuminated that whole part of the bridge.

D'Artagnan stopped, facing them, and they stopped, facing him.

'What do you want, sir?' the musketeer asked, taking a step

back and speaking in a foreign accent which proved to d'Artagnan that he had been mistaken in part of his conjectures.

'It's not Aramis!' he cried.

'No, sir, it is not Aramis, and by your exclamation I perceive that you have taken me for someone else, and I excuse you.'

'You excuse me?' cried d'Artagnan.

'Yes,' replied the stranger. 'So now let me pass, since your business is not with me.'

'You're right, sir,' said d'Artagnan. 'My business is not with you, it is with madame.'

'Madame? You don't know her,' said the stranger.

'You're mistaken, sir, I do.'

'Oh!' Madame Bonacieux said reproachfully. 'Oh sir! You gave me your word as a soldier and your honour as a gentleman; I was hoping I could count on them.'

'And I, madam,' said d'Artagnan, embarrassed, 'you had promised me . . .'

'Take my arm, madam,' said the stranger, 'and let us carry on our way.'

But d'Artagnan, stunned, appalled, shattered by everything that was happening to him, remained where he was, his arms crossed, blocking the musketeer and Madame Bonacieux's path.

The musketeer took two steps forward and moved d'Artagnan aside with his hand.

D'Artagnan jumped back and drew his sword.

At the same moment, with lightning speed, the stranger drew his.

'In heaven's name, my lord,' cried Madame Bonacieux, throwing herself between the combatants and grabbing their swords with her hands.

'My lord!' cried d'Artagnan, in a sudden flash of enlightenment. 'My lord, forgive me, sir, but would you be . . .'

'My Lord Duke of Buckingham,' said Madame Bonacieux in a low voice. 'Now you can ruin us all.'

'My lord, madam, a thousand pardons, but I loved her, my

lord, and I was jealous. You know what it's like to love someone, my lord. Forgive me, and tell me how I may lay down my life for your lordship.'

'You are a fine young man,' said Buckingham, holding out his hand to d'Artagnan, who shook it respectfully. 'You offer me your services, and I accept them. Let us go on twenty paces, then follow us to the Louvre, and if anyone spies on us, kill them.'

D'Artagnan tucked his bare sword under his arm, allowed Madame Bonacieux and the duke a head start of twenty paces and then followed them, ready to carry out to the letter the instructions of Charles I's noble and elegant minister.

Fortunately, however, the young acolyte didn't have a chance to give the duke this proof of his loyalty, and the young woman and the handsome musketeer entered the Louvre by the gate on the Rue de l'Échelle without being bothered.

As for d'Artagnan, he went straight to the Pine Cone, where he found Porthos and Aramis waiting for him.

But, rather than enlightening them any further as to why he'd put them to trouble, he simply said he hadn't needed their help, as he had thought he would for a moment, and had resolved his business on his own.

And so now, caught up as we are in our tale, let us leave our three friends to return to their respective homes and follow the Duke of Buckingham and his guide through the mazy intricacies of the Louvre.

XII

GEORGE VILLIERS, THE DUKE OF BUCKINGHAM

MADAME BONACIEUX AND THE DUKE had no trouble entering the Louvre, since Madame Bonacieux was known to be part of the queen's retinue, and the duke was wearing the uniform of Monsieur de Tréville's musketeers, who, as we have said, were on guard duty that evening. In any case, Germain was devoted to the queen, and if anything happened, Madame Bonacieux would simply be accused of having smuggled her lover into the Louvre. She would take all the responsibility for the crime on herself. Her reputation would be ruined, it was true, but, after all, what value did the reputation of a little mercer's wife have in the world?

Once they were in the courtyard, the duke and the young woman followed the base of the wall for roughly twenty-five paces. Having covered this distance, Madame Bonacieux pushed a little service door, which was open in the day but ordinarily shut at night. The door yielded, and they both went in and found themselves in darkness, but Madame Bonacieux knew all the twists and turns of this part of the Louvre, which was reserved for attendants. She closed the door behind her, took the duke by the hand, groped her way forward for a few paces, grasped a banister, felt for a step with her foot and then began to climb a staircase; the duke counted two floors. Then she turned to the right, followed a long corridor, went back down a floor, took another few steps, inserted a key in a lock, opened a door, and pushed the duke into a room lit only by a nightlight, saying, 'Stay here, my lord, someone will come.' Then she went out by the same door and she locked it so that the duke found himself literally a prisoner.

Isolated though he was, it has to be said that the Duke of Buckingham didn't feel a flicker of fear; one of the salient features of his character was his perpetual quest for adventure and love of romance. Courageous, bold, enterprising, this was not the first time he had risked his life in such endeavours. He had found out that the alleged message from Anne of Austria, which had brought him to Paris, was a trap, but instead of returning to England, he had made the most of the position he had been put in and told the queen he wouldn't leave without seeing her. The queen had categorically refused at first, but then she grew afraid the duke would commit some act of folly in his exasperation. She had already made up her mind to see him and beg him to leave immediately, when, on the evening of her decision, Madame Bonacieux, who had been entrusted with the task of fetching the duke and guiding him to the Louvre, was abducted. For two days no one knew what had happened to her, and everything was left hanging in the air. But once she was free and back in contact with La Porte, things had resumed their course, and she had just carried out the perilous enterprise, which she would have carried out three days earlier if she had not been abducted.

Left alone, Buckingham went over to a mirror. The musketeer's uniform suited him to perfection.

Aged thirty-five, as he then was, he was rightly considered the most handsome gentleman and the most elegant cavalier in all France and England.

The favourite of two kings, worth millions, all-powerful in a kingdom that he threw into uproar at his fancy and calmed at his whim, George Villiers, Duke of Buckingham, had embarked on one of those fabulous existences[1] that resonate down the centuries to astonish posterity.

Utterly sure of himself, convinced of his power, certain that the laws that govern other men couldn't touch him, he made straight for any goal he set himself, however rarefied and dazzling, even if it were folly for anyone else even to consider it. Thus he had managed to approach the beautiful, proud Anne of Austria on several occasions and dazzle her into loving him.

So George Villiers stood in front of a mirror, as we have said, restored the waves to his beautiful blond hair that his hat had flattened, twisted up his moustache, and, his heart swelling with joy, happy and proud to have arrived at the moment he had so long desired, smiled proudly and hopefully at his reflection.

At that moment, a door hidden in the tapestry opened and a woman appeared. Buckingham saw this apparition in the mirror, and uttered a cry: it was the queen!

Anne of Austria was then twenty-six or twenty-seven years old; that is, in the full bloom of her beauty.

She carried herself like a queen or a goddess, and her eyes, which glinted emerald in the light, were immaculately beautiful, full of both sweetness and majesty.

Her mouth was small and rosy, and although her lower lip, like those of the princes of the house of Austria, stuck out slightly, she was both eminently gracious in her smile, and profoundly disdainful in her contempt.

Her skin was a byword for its velvet softness, her hands and arms were startlingly beautiful, hymned by all the poets of the age as without compare.

Lastly her hair, which had been blonde when she was younger and was now chestnut, and which she wore curled and floating, with plenty of powder, admirably framed her face – a countenance in which the most rigid censor might only have perhaps wished for a little less rouge, and the most demanding sculptor for a little more finesse to the nose.

Buckingham remained dazzled for a moment. Never had Anne of Austria looked as beautiful at the finest balls, feasts and carousels as she did to him at that moment, dressed in a simple white satin dress and accompanied by Doña Estefania, the only one of her Spanish women who had not been driven away by the king's jealousy and Richelieu's persecutions.

Anne of Austria took two steps forward, Buckingham fell to his knees and, before the queen could stop him, kissed the hem of her dress.

'Duke, you already know it wasn't I who wrote to you.'

'Oh yes, madam, yes, Your Majesty,' cried the duke. 'I know I was a fool, a madman, to believe that snow could quicken, marble grow warm. But how could I help myself? When one loves, one is quick to believe in love. Besides, the journey has not been hopeless since I am seeing you.'

'Yes,' Anne replied. 'But you know why and how I am seeing you, my lord. I am seeing you out of pity; I am seeing you because, insensible to all my sufferings, you have insisted on remaining in a city where, by staying, you risk your life and cause me to risk my honour; I am seeing you to tell you that everything separates us, the depths of the sea, the enmity of kingdoms, the sanctity of oaths. It is sacrilege to fight against so much, my lord. I am seeing you, finally, to tell you that we must no longer see each other.'

'Speak, madam, speak, queen,' said Buckingham. 'The sweetness of your voice veils the harshness of your words. You speak of sacrilege. True sacrilege is when hearts that God has made for one another are parted.'

'My lord,' the queen cried out, 'you forget I have never told you I loved you.'

'But you have not told me you did not love me either. And truly saying such words to me would be too great an act of ingratitude on Your Majesty's behalf. Because, tell me, where can you find a love like mine, a love that neither time, nor absence, nor despair can extinguish; a love which contents itself with a mislaid ribbon, a stray look, an inadvertent word? It was three years ago, madam, that I saw you for the first time, and for three years I have loved you like this. Do you want me to tell you how you were dressed the first time I saw you? Do you want me to list the ornaments of your attire? Wait, I can still see you. You were sitting on cushions, in the Spanish style; you wore a green satin dress with gold and silver embroideries and hanging sleeves tied back over your beautiful arms, these exquisite arms, with large diamonds; you had a fastened ruff, and on your head a little hat, the colour of your dress, and on this hat you wore a heron feather. Oh, wait, wait, I close my eyes and I see you as you were then . . . Then I open them and I see you as you are now, that is, a hundred times more beautiful!'

'What madness,' murmured Anne of Austria, who couldn't find it in her to begrudge the duke for storing up her portrait so faithfully in his heart. 'What madness to nourish a useless passion with such memories!'

'What would you have me live on? All I have are memories. They are my happiness, my treasure, my hopes. Each time I see you it is one more diamond that I store in the casket of my heart. This is the fourth you have dropped and I have picked up; for in three years, madam, I have only seen you four times. The first, which I have just mentioned, the second at Madame de Chevreuse, the third in the gardens at Amiens.'

'Duke,' said the queen, blushing, 'do not speak of that evening.'

'Oh, on the contrary, let us speak of it, madam, let us, please. It was the happiest, most radiant evening of my life. Do you remember what a beautiful night it was? How soft and fragrant the air, how blue and all enamelled with stars the sky? Ah, madam, then I was able to be alone with you for a moment; then you were ready to tell me everything, the loneliness of your life, the sorrows of your heart. You leant on my arm, look, on this arm. I felt, as I bent my head towards you, your beautiful hair brush my face, and every time I felt it, I shivered from head to foot. Oh, queen, queen! Oh, you don't know all the felicities of heaven, the joys of paradise contained in such a moment! I would give all my possessions, my fortune, my glory, all the days I have left for a moment and a night like that! For that night, madam, that night you loved me, I swear.'

'My lord, it is possible, yes, that the influence of the place, the charm of that beautiful evening, the fascination of your gaze, in a word, that all those thousand circumstances that sometimes combine to ruin a woman gathered themselves around me on that fatal evening, but you saw, my lord, how the queen came to the rescue of the woman who was weakening. At the first word you dared utter, the first boldness I had to answer, I called out.'

'Oh, yes, yes, that is true. And any other love than mine would have failed that test, but my love, the love I feel in my heart, emerged from it more ardent and more eternal. You thought you could escape me by returning to Paris, you thought I wouldn't dare leave the treasure my master has charged me to watch over. Ah, what do all the treasures in the world and all the kings on earth matter to me? Eight days later I returned, madam. This time you had nothing to say to me. I had risked my favour, my life, to see you for a second. I didn't even touch your hand, and you pardoned me seeing me so submissive and repentant.'

'Yes, but calumny seized on all these follies in which, as you well know, my lord, I played no part. Goaded by the cardinal, the king made a terrible scandal: Madame de Vernet was driven away, Putange exiled, Madame de Chevreuse fell into disfavour, and when you tried to return to France as ambassador, the king himself, you remember, my lord, the king himself opposed it.'

'Yes, and France will pay for her king's refusal with war. I cannot see you any more, madam. Well then, I will have you hear about me every day. What do you think has been the purpose of this expedition against the Île de Ré and of this league with the Protestants of La Rochelle I am planning? The pleasure of seeing you! I have no hope of entering Paris by force of arms, I know that, but this war may bring a peace, this peace will require a negotiator, and this negotiator will be me. They will not dare refuse me then, and I will return to Paris, and I will see you again, and I will be happy for a moment. Thousands of men, it is true, will have paid for my happiness with their lives, but what will that matter to me, as long as I can see you again? This may all be very foolish, very mad, but tell me, what woman has a more loving lover? What queen has ever had a more ardent servant?'

'My lord, my lord, you invoke things in your defence that condemn you still further. My lord, all these proofs of love you wish to give me are as good as crimes.'

'Because you don't love me, madam. If you loved me, you would see all this differently . . . if you loved me. Oh, if you loved me. That would have been too much happiness and I would have gone mad. Ah, Madame de Chevreuse whom you mentioned just now, Madame de Chevreuse was less cruel than you. Holland[2] loved her, and she returned his love.'

'Madame de Chevreuse was not a queen,' murmured Anne of Austria, overcome in spite of herself by the profession of so deep a love.

'You would love me then if you weren't one yourself, madam? Tell me, would you love me then? Can I believe that it is solely the dignity of your rank that makes you cruel to me? Can I believe that if you had been Madame de Chevreuse, poor Buckingham could

have hoped? Thank you for these sweet words, oh my beautiful
Majesty, thank you a thousand times.'

'Ah, Your Grace, you have misunderstood, you have misinter-
preted me. I didn't mean . . .'

'Shh, shh,' said the duke. 'If I am happy through a mistake,
don't be so cruel as to disillusion me. You said it yourself, I have
been lured into a trap and perhaps it will cost me my life, since,
it's strange, you know, for some time I have been having presentiments that I am going to die.' And the duke smiled a smile that
was at once sad and charming.

'Oh, my God!' cried Anne of Austria, with a note of terror
which proved how much more of an interest she took in the duke
than she wished to admit.

'I do not say that to scare you, madam, no. It's ridiculous I
say it at all, in fact, and believe me I don't concern myself about
such dreams in the least. But those words you have just said, that
hope you have almost given me would have paid for everything,
even my life.'

'Well,' said Anne of Austria, 'I too have presentiments, duke,
I too have dreams. I thought I saw you lying bleeding and
wounded . . .'

'In the left side, wasn't it, with a knife?' Buckingham
interrupted.

'Yes, that's right, my lord, that's right, in the left side with a
knife. Who could have told you I had that dream? I confided it to
God alone, in my prayers.'

'I want nothing more. You love me, madam, all is well.'

'I love you?'

'Yes, you do. Would God send you the same dreams as me if
you did not love me? Would we have the same presentiments if
our lives were not joined at the heart? You love me, O queen, and
you will weep for me?'

'Oh, my God! My God!' cried Anne of Austria, 'this is more
than I can bear. Here, duke, for heaven's sake, go, leave, I do not
know if I love you or if I do not love you, but what I do know

is that I will not break my marriage vows. So take pity on me, and go. Oh, if you were struck down in France, if you died in France, if I thought your love for me was the cause of your death, I would never forgive myself, I would go mad. So go, go, I beg you.'

'Oh how beautiful you are like this! Oh, how I love you!' said Buckingham.

'Go! Go! I beg you, and return later; return as an ambassador, return as a minister, return surrounded by guards who will defend you, servants who will watch over you, and then I will no longer fear for your days, and I will be glad to see you again.'

'Oh, is it true what you say?'

'Yes . . .'

'Well then, give me a pledge of your indulgence, an object that comes from you and that reminds me that I have not been dreaming, something you've worn and that I can wear in my turn, a ring, a necklace, a chain.'

'Then you will go – you will go, if I give you what you ask?'

'Yes.'

'This instant?'

'Yes.'

'You will leave France, you will return to England?'

'Yes, I swear!'

'Wait, then, wait.'

Anne of Austria went back into her apartment and came back out almost immediately, holding in her hand a small rosewood box bearing her monogram, all inlaid with gold.

'Here, my lord, here,' she said, 'keep this in memory of me.'

Buckingham took the box and fell to his knees a second time.

'You promised to leave,' said the queen.

'And I shall keep my word. Your hand, your hand, madam, then I will leave.'

Anne of Austria held out a hand, closing her eyes and leaning on Estefania with her other hand because she felt her strength was about to give out.

Buckingham pressed his lips passionately to that beautiful hand, then, getting to his feet, he said, 'Within six months, if I am not dead, I will see you again, madam, even if I have to turn the world on its head to do so.'

And then, true to his promise, he rushed out of the room.

In the corridor he found Madame Bonacieux, who was waiting for him, and who, with the same precautions and the same good fortune, escorted him out of the Louvre.

XIII

MONSIEUR BONACIEUX

THERE HAS BEEN ONE CHARACTER in all this, the reader may have noticed, in whom, despite his precarious situation, we seem to have shown a very sketchy interest. That is Monsieur Bonacieux, respectable martyr of the political and amorous intrigues that became so easily entangled in that age which was at once so chivalrous and so gallant.

Fortunately, as the reader may or may not recall, we promised not to lose sight of him.

The attendants who had arrested him took him straight to the Bastille where he was led, trembling from head to foot, past a platoon of soldiers who were loading their muskets.

From there, hustled into a passage that was partly underground, he was subjected to the grossest insults and most brutal man-handling by his escort. The officers saw they were not dealing with a gentleman and treated him as the lowliest nonentity.

After half an hour or so, a clerk of the court came to put an end to his tortures, but not to his anxieties, by giving orders that Monsieur Bonacieux should be taken to the interrogation room. Ordinarily prisoners were questioned in their cell, but such niceties were not observed with Monsieur Bonacieux.

Two guards laid hold of the mercer, led him across a courtyard, steered him into a corridor where three sentries stood guard, opened a door and pushed him into a low room, in which the only furnishings were a table, a chair and a commissary. The commissary was sitting on the chair and was busy writing on the table.

The two guards marched the prisoner up to the table and then, at a signal from the commissary, retreated out of earshot.

The commissary, who had kept his head bowed over his papers until then, raised it to see who he was dealing with. He was a forbidding-looking individual, this commissary, with a pointed nose, yellow, jutting cheekbones, eyes that were small but lively and searching, and a general air somewhere between that of a weasel and a fox. His head, supported on a long, mobile neck, emerged from his full, black robe with a swaying movement not unlike that of a tortoise poking its head out of its shell.

He began by asking Monsieur Bonacieux his family name and first names, his age, his profession and his place of residence.

The accused replied that his name was Jacques-Michel Bonacieux, he was fifty-one, a retired mercer, and lived at 11, Rue des Fossoyeurs.

Instead of continuing to question him, the commissary then delivered a long speech on how dangerous it was for an obscure townsman to involve himself in public affairs.

Treating this merely as an introduction, he further elaborated his theme with an exposition of the power and deeds of the cardinal, that incomparable minister, that vanquisher of ministers past, that example for ministers to come – deeds and power that no one could flout with impunity.

After this second part of his speech, fixing his hawk-like gaze on poor Bonacieux, he invited him to reflect on the gravity of his situation.

The mercer's reflections needed no prompting. He cursed the moment Monsieur de La Porte had had the notion of marrying him to his goddaughter, and, above all, the moment when this goddaughter had been taken into the queen's household as a seamstress.

The essence of Monsieur Bonacieux's character was profound

egotism and sordid greed, with a seasoning of extreme cowardice. The love his young wife had inspired, being an entirely secondary feeling, could not therefore contend with the primary sentiments we have just enumerated.

Bonacieux reflected in earnest on what he had just been told.

'But, Mr Commissary,' he said timidly, 'believe me, I know and I value more than anyone the merit of the incomparable Eminence by which we have the honour of being governed.'

'Indeed?' the commissary asked doubtfully. 'But if that were really so, why would you be in the Bastille?'

'How I come to be here, or rather why I come to be here,' Monsieur Bonacieux replied, 'is something I am completely incapable of telling you, since I do not know myself. But certainly it is not for having offended the cardinal, at least not knowingly.'

'But you must have committed a crime though, since you have been accused of high treason.'

'Of high treason!' cried Bonacieux, terrified. 'High treason! And how do you think a poor mercer who detests the Huguenots and who abhors the Spanish can be accused of high treason? Consider, sir, the thing is physically impossible.'

'Monsieur Bonacieux,' said the commissary looking at the accused as if his little eyes could read the profoundest depths of the human heart. 'You have a wife?'

'Yes, sir,' replied the mercer, trembling and feeling that this was where matters were going to become complicated. 'That is to say, I had one.'

'What? You had one! What did you do with her, if you don't have her any more?'

'She was abducted from me, sir.'

'She was abducted from you?' repeated the commissary. 'Ah!'

At this 'Ah!' Bonacieux felt matters becoming increasingly complicated.

'She was abducted from you!' said the commissary. 'And do you know who is the man who carried out this abduction?'

'I think so.'

'Who is it?'

'Remember that I am not asserting anything, Mr Commissary, I only suspect.'

'Whom do you suspect? Come on, answer frankly.'

Monsieur Bonacieux was in the greatest perplexity. Should he deny everything or tell all? By denying everything, it might seem he knew too much to admit; by telling all, he would give proof of goodwill. So he decided to tell all.

'I suspect,' he said, 'a tall, dark-haired man with a haughty expression, who looks every bit a great nobleman. I thought he followed us several times, when I was waiting for my wife at the gate of the Louvre to escort her home.'

The commissary appeared uneasy.

'And his name?' he said.

'Oh, I have no idea what his name is, but if I ever meet him, I will recognise him at once, I promise you, even in a crowd of a thousand.'

The commissary's forehead darkened.

'You would recognise him out of a thousand, you say?' he continued.

'That is,' replied Bonacieux, who saw he was on the wrong track, 'that is . . .'

'You said you would recognise him,' said the commissary. 'Fine, that's enough for today. Before we continue, I must pass on the information that you know your wife's abductor.'

'But I didn't tell you I knew him!' cried Bonacieux, in despair. 'Far from it, I told you that . . .'

'Take the prisoner away,' the commissary said to two guards.

'Where should we take him?' asked the clerk.

'A cell.'

'Which one?'

'Oh God, the first one you come to, as long as it's got a good lock,' replied the commissary with an indifference that filled poor Bonacieux with horror.

'Alas! alas!' he said to himself. 'Misfortunes are gathering over my head! My wife must have committed some terrible crime. They think I'm her accomplice and I will be punished with her. She must have talked, she must have said she told me everything, women are so weak. A cell, the first one they come to . . . This is it, a night passes so fast, and then tomorrow, the wheel, the gallows! Oh, my God, my God, have mercy on me!'

Without paying any mind to Monsieur Bonacieux's lamentations, lamentations which in any case they must have been used to, the two guards took the prisoner by the arms and led him away, while the commissary dashed off a letter as his clerk waited.

Bonacieux didn't close his eyes, not because his cell was so unpleasant but because his anxieties were too great. He sat on his stool all night, shuddering at the slightest noise; and when the first rays of sunshine slipped into his cell, dawn seemed to him to have taken on funereal shades.

Suddenly he heard the bolts being drawn back and started terribly. He thought they were coming to take him to the scaffold, so when he saw, rather than the executioner he was expecting, just the commissary and his clerk from the previous day, he was within a whisker of throwing his arms round their necks.

'Your case has become very complicated since yesterday evening, my good man,' said the commissary, 'and I advise you to tell the whole truth, for only your repentance can avert the cardinal's anger.'

'But I am ready to tell all,' cried Bonacieux, 'at least all that I know. Question me, please.'

'Firstly, where is your wife?'

'But I've told you she was abducted.'

'Yes, but since five o'clock yesterday afternoon, thanks to you, she has escaped.'

'My wife has escaped!' cried Bonacieux. 'Oh, the wretch! Sir, it is not my fault if she has escaped, I swear.'

'Then why did you visit the lodgings of Monsieur d'Artagnan, that neighbour of yours with whom you had a long conference during the day?'

'Ah, yes, Mr Commissary, yes, that is true, and I admit that I was wrong. I did go to Monsieur d'Artagnan's.'

'What was the purpose of this visit?'

'To ask him to help me find my wife. I thought I was entitled to demand her return. I was wrong, it seems, and I heartily beg your pardon for this.'

'And what answer did Monsieur d'Artagnan give you?'

'Monsieur d'Artagnan promised me his help, but I soon realised he was betraying me.'

'You are attempting to deceive the law! Monsieur d'Artagnan made a pact with you, and, in accordance with that pact, drove off the policemen who had arrested your wife and conveyed her beyond the reach of justice.'

'Monsieur d'Artagnan abducted my wife! Ah, what is this you are telling me?'

'Fortunately Monsieur d'Artagnan is in our hands, and you are going to confront him.'

'Ah, my faith, I'd like nothing better,' cried Bonacieux. 'I shan't be sorry to see a familiar face.'

'Bring in Monsieur d'Artagnan,' said the commissary to the two guards.

The two guards brought in Athos.

'Monsieur d'Artagnan,' said the commissary, addressing Athos, 'state what happened between you and this gentleman.'

'But this man you've got here is not Monsieur d'Artagnan!' cried Bonacieux.

'What, this is not Monsieur d'Artagnan?' cried the commissary.

'Certainly not,' replied Bonacieux.

'What is the gentleman's name?' asked the commissary.

'I cannot tell you. I do not know him.'

'What, you don't know him?'

'No.'

'You've never seen him before?'

'I have, but I do not know what he is called.'

'Your name?' asked the commissary.

'Athos,' replied the musketeer.

'But that's not a man's name, that's the name of a mountain!' cried the poor investigator, feeling as if he was going out of his mind.

'It is my name,' said Athos, calmly.

'But you said your name was d'Artagnan.'

'I?'

'Yes, you.'

'Well, in fact, someone said to me, "You are Monsieur d'Artagnan?" I replied, "You think so?" My guards shouted they were sure of it and I did not want to upset them. But I could have been mistaken.'

'Sir, you insult the majesty of the law.'

'Not at all,' said Athos calmly.

'You are Monsieur d'Artagnan.'

'You see, you're telling me so again.'

'But I tell you, Mr Commissary,' Monsieur Bonacieux cried in turn, 'there isn't a shadow of a doubt. Monsieur d'Artagnan is my tenant and so, although he doesn't pay me the rent, or rather for that very reason, I ought to know him. Monsieur d'Artagnan is a young man of barely nineteen or twenty and this gentleman is thirty at least. Monsieur d'Artagnan is in Monsieur des Essarts's guards, and this gentleman is in Monsieur de Tréville's company of musketeers. Look at the uniform, Mr Commissary, the uniform.'

'It's true,' murmured the commissary, 'by God, it's true.'

At that moment the door opened quickly, and a messenger, introduced by one of the Bastille's turnkeys, gave the commissary a letter.

'Oh, the wretch!' cried the commissary.

'What? What are you saying? Who are you talking about? It is not my wife, I hope!'

'It most certainly is. You're in up to your neck, you know.'

'Ah,' cried the mercer in exasperation, 'be so kind as to tell me, sir, how my case can get worse because of something my wife has done while I'm in jail!'

'Because what she is doing is the result of a plan agreed between you, an infernal plan!'

'I swear, Mr Commissary, that you are profoundly mistaken, that I have no idea what my wife is meant to be doing, that I have nothing to do with her actions, and that, if she has done anything foolish, I renounce her, I disown her, I curse her!'

'I was thinking,' Athos said to the commissary, 'if you don't need me any more, perhaps you could send me somewhere? He is very dull, your Monsieur Bonacieux.'

'Take the prisoners back to their cells,' the commissary said, including Athos and Bonacieux in the same gesture, 'and see they are guarded more strictly than ever.'

'But,' Athos said with his habitual calm, 'if your business is with Monsieur d'Artagnan, I don't quite see how I can replace him.'

'Do as I say,' cried the commissary. 'And I want it to remain completely secret. Understood?'

Athos followed his guards, shrugging his shoulders, as Monsieur Bonacieux poured forth lamentations that would have broken a tiger's heart.

The mercer was taken back to the cell in which he had spent the previous night, and left there all day. All day Bonacieux wept like a true mercer, not being a swordsman in any shape or form, as he has told us himself.

In the evening, around nine o'clock, when he was about to decide to go to bed, he heard steps in the corridor. The steps drew near to his cell, his door opened, guards appeared.

'Follow me,' said an army officer who came in after the guards.

'Follow you!' cried Bonacieux. 'Follow you at this hour! My God, where to?'

'Where we have been ordered to take you.'

'But that's not an answer.'

'It is the only one we can give you.'

'Ah, my God, my God,' murmured the poor mercer, 'now I'm done for!'

And mechanically and without resisting he followed the guards who had come to fetch him.

He took the same corridor he had already taken, went through a first courtyard, then a second part of the building, and finally, at the gate of the front courtyard, found a carriage flanked by four mounted guards. They made him get into the carriage, the officer sat next to him, the door was locked, and they found themselves in a moving prison.

The carriage set off, slow as a hearse. Through the locked grill, the prisoner could only see the houses and pavement. But, true Parisian that he was, Bonacieux recognised each street by its corner posts, signs and street lamps. When they got to Saint-Paul, where the Bastille's condemned were executed, he almost fainted and crossed himself twice. He thought the carriage was going to stop there, but it drove past.

Further on, he was seized by a still greater terror when they drove alongside Saint-Jean cemetery where state criminals were buried. One thing reassured him a little: the fact that before burying them they generally cut their heads off, and his head was still on his shoulders. But when he saw that the carriage was heading to Place de La Grève, when he saw the Hôtel de Ville's pointed roofs, when the carriage turned into an arcade, he thought it was all over for him and tried to make his confession to the officer, and, when he was refused, began screaming so pitifully that the officer declared that if he carried on deafening him like this, he would gag him.

This threat reassured Bonacieux somewhat. If he was to be executed on the Grève, it wasn't worth gagging him since they had almost reached the place of execution. And indeed the carriage crossed the fatal square without stopping. Now all that was left to fear was La Croix-du-Trahoir. The carriage took that very road.

This time there could be no more doubt. La Croix-du-Trahoir was where they executed the lowborn. Bonacieux had flattered himself by believing he was worthy of Saint-Paul or Place de La Grève – it was at La Croix-du-Trahoir that his journey and his destiny were to end! He couldn't see the unfortunate cross yet, but he could somehow feel it coming to meet him. When it was no more than twenty paces away, he heard a commotion and the carriage stopped. Crushed by the successive waves of emotion[1] he had already experienced, it was more than poor Bonacieux could stand: he uttered a feeble groan, like the last sigh of a dying man, and passed out.

XIV

THE MAN FROM MEUNG

RATHER THAN WAITING FOR A MAN to be hanged, the gathering in question was contemplating one who already hung from the gibbet.

Having been held up for a moment, therefore, the coach set off again, passed through the crowd, continued on its way, went down Rue Saint-Honoré, turned into Rue des Bons-Enfants and stopped in front of a low door.

The carriage door opened and two guards caught Bonacieux, who was supported by the officer. He was pushed into an alley, made to climb a flight of stairs, and deposited in an antechamber.

His body performed all these movements as if he were a automaton.

He had walked as you walk in a dream, glimpsing objects through a fog, his ears perceiving sounds without understanding them. They could have executed him at that moment and he wouldn't have made a move to try to defend himself or uttered a cry to beg for mercy.

So he stayed exactly where the guards had deposited him on a bench, his back pressed against the wall, his arms dangling at his sides.

However, as he looked around him and saw no menacing objects, as nothing suggested he was in any real danger, as the bench was pleasingly upholstered, as the wall was covered with beautiful Cordovan leather, as huge red damask curtains hung at the window, held back by gold loops, he gradually realised that his terror was exaggerated, and began to move his head from left to right and up and down.

With this movement, which no one tried to stop, he gained a little courage and ventured to flex one leg, then the other. Finally, with the help of both his hands, he pushed himself off the bench and found himself on his feet.

At that moment, a kindly-looking officer lifted a door curtain, still talking to someone in the next room, and then, turning towards the prisoner, said, 'Are you the fellow called Bonacieux?'

'Yes, officer, sir,' stammered the mercer, more dead than alive. 'At your service.'

'Come in,' said the officer.

And he stepped back to let the mercer pass. The latter obeyed in silence and entered a room where he seemed to be expected.

It was a large study, with walls lined with offensive and defensive weapons and a blazing fire, even though it was only September, which made it close and stuffy. A square table covered with books and papers, on which a huge map of the city of La Rochelle was unrolled, occupied the centre of the room.

Standing in front of the fireplace was a man of medium height[1] with a haughty, proud bearing, piercing eyes, a broad forehead, and a long, thin face that was lengthened still further by an imperial[2] topped with a pair of moustaches. Although he was barely thirty-six or thirty-seven, his hair, moustaches and imperial were already greying. Even without the sword, he looked every inch a soldier and the light covering of dust on his buff-leather boots indicated he had been riding that day.

This was Armand-Jean du Plessis, Cardinal Richelieu[3], not as he is usually represented to us, as a shattered old man, suffering like a martyr, his body broken, his voice extinct, buried in a great armchair as if in an imminent grave, clinging to life merely by the strength of his genius and only sustaining the fight against Europe by the eternal application of his mind. No, this is what he was really like at the time, that is, a skilful, gallant cavalier, already weak of body but sustained by that moral power that made him one of the most extraordinary men that have ever existed. Having supported the Duke de Nevers[4] in his duchy at Mantua, having taken Nîmes, Castres and Uzès, now he was finally preparing to drive the English out of the Île de Ré and lay siege to La Rochelle.

At first sight, then, nothing marked him out as cardinal, and it was impossible for those who did not know to guess in whose presence they found themselves.

The poor mercer remained standing by the door, while the eyes of the person we have just described were fixed on him and seemed to want to penetrate into the depths of the past.

'This is that Bonacieux?' he asked after a moment's silence.

'Yes, my lord,' replied the officer.

'Fine. Give me those papers and leave us.'

The officer fetched the papers in question from the table, gave them to his master, bowed to the ground, and left.

Bonacieux recognised the papers from his interrogation in the Bastille. From time to time, the man by the fireplace raised his eyes from the documents, and plunged them like daggers deep into the poor mercer's heart.

After ten minutes' reading and ten seconds' examination, the cardinal had made up his mind.

'That is the face of a man who has never plotted in his life,' he murmured, 'but no matter, let's see anyway.'

'You are accused of high treason,' the cardinal said slowly.

'This is what I've been told, my lord,' cried Bonacieux, addressing his interrogator by the title he had heard the officer use, 'but I swear I was in the dark about it.'

The cardinal repressed a smile.

'You conspired with your wife, with Madame de Chevreuse, and with His Grace the Duke of Buckingham.'

'Actually, my lord,' replied the mercer, 'I have heard her mention those names.'

'On what occasion?'

'She said that Cardinal Richelieu had lured the Duke of Buckingham to Paris to ruin him and the queen with him.'

'She said that?' cried the cardinal vehemently.

'Yes, my lord, but I told her she was wrong to make such remarks, and that His Eminence was incapable . . .'

'Hold your tongue, you imbecile,' said the cardinal.

'That is exactly what my wife said, my lord.'

'Do you know who abducted your wife?'

'No, my lord.'

'But you have your suspicions?'

'Yes, my lord, but these suspicions appeared to upset the commissary, so I don't have them any more.'

'Your wife has escaped, did you know that?'

'No, my lord, I have only heard of it since I have been in prison through the good offices of the commissary . . . a most amiable gentleman!'

The cardinal repressed a second smile.

'Then you do not know what has happened to your wife since her escape?'

'Not a thing, my lord, but she is bound to have gone back to the Louvre.'

'She hadn't returned at one o'clock in the morning.'

'Ah, my God! What has become of her then?'

'We will find out, do not worry. No one hides anything from the cardinal; the cardinal knows everything.'

'In that case, my lord, do you think the cardinal will consent to tell me what has become of my wife?'

'Perhaps, but you must first confess everything you know about your wife's relations with Madame de Chevreuse.'

'But, my lord, I don't know anything about them; I've never seen her.'

'When you went to fetch your wife from the Louvre, would she go straight home?'

'Very rarely: she had business with linen-drapers, and I would take her to their establishments.'

'And how many linen-drapers were there?'

'Two, my lord.'

'Where do they reside?'

'One in Rue de Vaugirard, the other in Rue de La Harpe.'

'Would you go into their shops with her?'

'Never, my lord. I waited for her at the door.'

'And what excuse did she give you for going in alone like that?'

'She didn't. She told me to wait, and I waited.'

'You are an obliging husband, my dear Monsieur Bonacieux,' said the cardinal.

He calls me his dear sir, the mercer said to himself. My word, things are going well!

'Would you recognise their doors?'

'Yes.'

'Do you know the numbers?'

'Yes.'

'What are they?'

'25 in Rue de Vaugirard, and 75 in Rue de La Harpe.'

'Good,' said the cardinal.

At these words, he picked up a little silver bell, and rang. The officer came back in.

'Go and find Rochefort for me,' he said in a low voice. 'Have him come at once if he's back.'

'The count is here,' the officer said. 'He urgently requires to speak to Your Eminence.'

'To Your Eminence!' murmured Bonacieux, who knew this was the cardinal's usual title, '. . . to Your Eminence!'

'Let him come in, then, let him come in,' Richelieu said sharply.

The officer rushed out of the room with the haste the cardinal's servants generally employed in obeying him.

'To Your Eminence!' murmured Bonacieux, wildly rolling his eyes.

Five seconds had scarcely elapsed since the officer's disappearance before the door opened and a new character came in.

'It is he,' cried Bonacieux.

'Who?' asked the cardinal.

'The man who abducted my wife.'

The cardinal rang a second time. The officer reappeared.

'Return this man to the care of his two guards, and have him wait until I send for him.'

'No, my lord! No, it's not he!' cried Bonacieux. 'No, I was wrong: it was someone else who doesn't resemble him in the slightest! This gentleman is an honest man.'

'Take this imbecile away,' said the cardinal.

The officer took Bonacieux by the arm, and led him back into the antechamber, where he found his two guards.

The new character who had just been shown in watched Bonacieux impatiently until he left. As soon as the door had closed behind him, he stepped smartly up to the cardinal and declared, 'They've seen each other.'

'Who?' asked His Eminence.

'She and he.'

'The queen and the duke?' cried Richelieu.

'Yes.'

'And where was that?'

'At the Louvre.'

'Are you sure?'

'Absolutely sure.'

'Who told you?'

'Madame de Lannoy, who is Your Eminence's loyal servant, as you know.'

'Why didn't she say this sooner?'

'By chance or mistrust, the queen had Madame de Fargis sleep in her room with her, and kept her with her all day.'

'All right, we are beaten. Let us try to take our revenge.'

'I will help you with all my soul, my lord, rest assured of that.'

'What happened?'

'At half-past twelve the queen was with her women . . .'

'Where?'

'In her bedroom . . .'

'Right.'

'When someone came to give her a handkerchief on the part of her seamstress . . .'

'And then?'

'The queen was immediately overcome with emotion and, even under her rouge, grew pale.'

'And then? And then?'

'Nevertheless she stood up and said in a faltering voice, "Ladies, wait for me, I shall be back in ten minutes." Then she opened the door to her alcove and went out.'

'Why didn't Madame de Lannoy come and tell you then?'

'Nothing was definite at that point, and, besides, the queen had said, "Ladies, wait for me," and she did not dare disobey.'

'And how long was the queen out of the room?'

'Three quarters of an hour.'

'None of her ladies-in-waiting accompanied her?'

'Only Doña Estefania.'

'And then she came back?'

'Yes, but only to get a little rosewood box bearing her monogram, and then leave immediately.'

'And when she came back later, did she bring back the box?'

'No.'

'Did Madame de Lannoy know what was in the box?'

'Yes. The diamond tags His Majesty gave the queen⁵.'

'And she came back without this box?'

'Yes.'

'Madame de Lannoy is of the opinion that she gave them then to Buckingham?'

'She is sure of it.'

'How?'

'During the day, in her capacity as lady-in-waiting to the queen, Madame de Lannoy looked for the box, feigned anxiousness when she couldn't find it, and finally inquired after it of the queen.'

'And then the queen . . . ?'

'The queen went very red and said that she had broken one of her tags the day before and so had sent it to her jeweller to be mended.'

'Someone should see him to find out if that's true or not.'

'I already have.'

'Well, the jeweller?'

'The jeweller knows nothing about it.'

'Good, good! Rochefort, all is not lost, and perhaps . . . perhaps all is for the best.'

'I do not doubt that Your Eminence's genius . . .'

'Will make up for his agent's incompetence, is that it?'

'That is exactly what I was going to say if Your Eminence had let me complete my sentence.'

'Now, do you know where the Duchess de Chevreuse and the Duke of Buckingham were hiding?'

'No, my lord, my men could not give me any definite information as to that.'

'I know.'

'You, my lord?'

'Yes, or at least I suspect it. One was staying at 25, Rue de Vaugirard, and the other at 75, Rue de La Harpe.'

'Does Your Eminence want me to have them both arrested?'

'It will be too late, they will be gone.'

'No matter, we can make sure.'

'Take ten of my guards, and search the two houses.'

'I'm on my way, my lord.'

Then Rochefort rushed out of the room.

Left on his own, the cardinal reflected for a moment, then rang a third time.

The same officer appeared.

'Bring in the prisoner,' said the cardinal.

Monsieur Bonacieux was shown in again, and, at a sign from the cardinal, the officer withdrew.

'You have deceived me,' the cardinal said sternly.

'I?' cried Bonacieux. 'I deceive Your Eminence?'

'When she went to Rue de Vaugirard and Rue de La Harpe, your wife was not going to see linen-drapers.'

'Then, God of Justice, whom was she going to see?'

'She was going to see the Duchess de Chevreuse and the Duke of Buckingham.'

'Ah yes!' said Bonacieux, his memories coming back to him. 'That's it, Your Eminence is right. I said several times to my wife that it was surprising drapers lived in such houses, in houses with no signs, and each time my wife started laughing. Ah, monsieur,' cried Bonacieux throwing himself at His Eminence's feet, 'you are indeed the cardinal, the great cardinal, the man of genius everyone reveres.'

Paltry though his triumph was over such a vulgar creature as Bonacieux, the cardinal nevertheless relished it for a moment. But then almost instantly, as if a new thought had presented itself to his mind, a smile creased his lips, and holding out his hand to the mercer, he said to him, 'Get up, my friend. You are a fine fellow.'

'The cardinal touched my hand! I've touched the great man's hand!' cried Bonacieux. 'The great man has called me "my friend".'

'Yes, my friend, yes,' said the cardinal, in that paternal tone he could adopt on occasion, which only deceived those who didn't know him. 'And since you have been unjustly suspected, well, you need to be compensated. Here, take this bag of a hundred pistoles, and forgive me.'

'I forgive you, Your Eminence?' said Bonacieux, hesitating to take the bag, doubtless fearing the alleged gift was a joke. 'But you were quite within your rights to have me arrested. You would be quite within your rights to have me tortured, you would be quite within your rights to have me hanged: you are the master, and I wouldn't have had a word to say against it. Forgive you, Your Eminence? Come now, such a thing can't have crossed your mind!'

'Ah, my dear Monsieur Bonacieux, you are being generous, I see, and I thank you for it. So, will you take this bag and leave not too discontented?'

'I shall leave enchanted, Your Eminence.'

'Farewell then, or rather goodbye until the next time, because I hope we will see each other again.'

'As often as Your Eminence shall wish, and I am entirely at His Eminence's disposal!'

'It will be often, rest assured, because I found your conversation to have great charm.'

'Oh, Your Eminence!'

'Goodbye, Monsieur Bonacieux, until the next time.'

And the cardinal gestured with his hand, to which Bonacieux responded by bowing down to the ground, then backed his way out and, when he was in the antechamber, the cardinal heard him yelling in his enthusiasm, 'Long live my lord! Long live His Eminence! Long live the great cardinal!' The cardinal listened with a smile to this noisy demonstration of Monsieur Bonacieux's feelings of enthusiasm, then when Bonacieux's cries were lost in the distance, he said, 'Good, there's a man who will die for me from now on.'

And then the cardinal started examining with intense attention the map of La Rochelle, which, as we have said, was spread out on his desk. He marked with a pencil the course of the famous dyke that, eighteen months later, would seal off the port of the besieged city.

When he was deep in his strategic meditations, the door opened again, and Rochefort came back in.

'Well?' snapped the cardinal, straightening up with an alacrity that proved the degree of importance he attached to the mission he had entrusted to the count.

'Well, a young woman between twenty-six and twenty-eight, and a man between thirty-five and forty did indeed reside in the houses indicated by Your Eminence, one for four days and the other for five, but the woman left last night and the man this morning.'

'It was them!' cried the cardinal, looking at the clock. 'And now,' he went on, 'it's too late to send anyone after them; the duchess is in Tours and the duke in Boulogne[6]. We will have to catch up with them in London.'

'What are Your Eminence's orders?'

'Not a word to anyone of what has happened; the queen must feel completely secure, oblivious to the fact that we know her secret, and thinking that we are on the trail of some conspiracy. Send me Séguier, the keeper of seals.'

'And what has Your Eminence done with that fellow?'

'Which one?' asked the cardinal.

'That Bonacieux.'

'I've done everything that could be done with him. I've made him spy on his wife.'

Count de Rochefort bowed like a man acknowledging the effortless superiority of his master, and withdrew.

Left alone, the cardinal sat back down, wrote a letter, sealed it with his private seal, and then rang. The officer entered for the fourth time.

'Send Vitray to me,' he said, 'and tell him to get ready for a trip.'

A moment later, the man he had summoned was standing before him, all booted and spurred.

'Vitray,' he said. 'You are to leave at the double for London. You will not stop for a moment on the way. You will give this letter to Milady. Here's a bond for two hundred pistoles. Go to my paymaster and have him pay you. The same amount will be waiting if you're back here in six days and have done a good job carrying out my commission.'

Without saying a word in response, the messenger bowed, took the letter and the bond for two hundred pistoles and went out.

The letter read as follows:

Milady,
    'Be at the first ball the Duke of Buckingham attends. He will have twelve diamond tags on his doublet. Get close to

him and cut off two. As soon as these tags are in your possession, send word.

XV

MEN OF THE LAW AND MEN OF THE SWORD

THE DAY AFTER THESE EVENTS, as there was still no sign of Athos, d'Artagnan and Porthos informed Monsieur de Tréville of his disappearance. Aramis, meanwhile, had requested five days' leave and was said to have gone to Rouen on a family matter.

Monsieur de Tréville was like a father to his soldiers. No matter how lowly or obscure, the minute one of his men donned the musketeers' uniform, he was as sure of his help and support as Tréville's own brother would have been.

The captain of the musketeers therefore went immediately to the criminal lieutenant[1]. The officer in charge of La Croix-Rouge post was summoned and successive inquiries revealed that Athos was temporarily housed in For-l'Évêque.

Athos had undergone all the trials to which we have seen Bonacieux be subjected.

We have witnessed what happened when the two prisoners were brought face to face. Athos, who had remained silent until then so that d'Artagnan, who had troubles of his own, could have enough time to do what he needed to, declared that henceforth he should be called by his real name rather than by that of d'Artagnan.

He added that he didn't know Monsieur or Madame Bonacieux, that he had never spoken to either of them, and that, while it was true he had paid a visit to his friend Monsieur d'Artagnan around ten o'clock at night, before then he had been at Monsieur de Tréville's, where he had dined. Twenty witnesses could attest to it, he declared, and he named a number of distinguished gentlemen, including the Duke de La Trémouille.

The second commissary was as stunned as the first by the musketeer's clear, firm statement. He had been itching to give him the comeuppance men of the law so love inflicting on men of the sword, but the names of Monsieur de Tréville and the Duke de La Trémouille gave him pause for thought.

So Athos was sent to the cardinal, but unfortunately the cardinal was at the Louvre with the king.

Meanwhile Monsieur de Tréville had gone from the criminal lieutenant to the governor of For-l'Évêque, but he had had no luck finding Athos. Deciding therefore to speak to His Majesty, he was entering the Louvre at that precise moment.

As captain of the musketeers, Monsieur de Tréville could see the king at any hour.

We are familiar with the king's animus against the queen, an animus skilfully nurtured by the cardinal who, where intrigues were concerned, mistrusted women infinitely more than men. One of the main reasons for this animus was Anne of Austria's friendship with Madame de Chevreuse. Those two women worried the cardinal more than the wars with Spain, the quarrels with England and the disarray of the State's finances combined. He was convinced Madame de Chevreuse not only assisted the queen in her political intrigues, but also, and far more troublingly for him, in her intrigues of the heart.

The moment the cardinal had revealed that Madame de Chevreuse, who had been exiled to Tours and so was naturally thought to be in that city, had come to Paris and, outwitting the police, had stayed in the capital for five days, the king had flown into a furious rage. Capricious with others and unfaithful to his wife, the king nevertheless wanted to be known as *Louis the Just* and *Louis the Chaste*. His is not an easy character for posterity to understand, given that history only records his actions, rather than his reasoning.

The cardinal went on to say that not only had Madame de

Chevreuse been in Paris, but that she had also been in contact with the queen by means of one of those mysterious correspondences known in those days as a cabal. He claimed to have been on the verge of unravelling the most arcane threads of this intrigue. In particular, he said, his men had been poised to catch red-handed, with all possible proofs, the queen's emissary in the act of communicating with the exiled woman, when a musketeer had had the temerity to brutally obstruct the course of justice by falling, sword in hand, on honest officers of the law – officers who had been detailed to examine the whole affair impartially so they could bring it to the king's notice. When he heard this, Louis XIII couldn't contain himself any longer. He took a step toward the queen's rooms, consumed by that pale and mute indignation which, when it erupted, drove that prince to acts of the coldest cruelty.

And yet, in all these revelations, the cardinal still hadn't breathed a word about the Duke of Buckingham.

It was then that the impeccably turned-out figure of Monsieur de Tréville strode into the room and bowed with icy politeness.

Apprised of the situation by the cardinal's presence and the change in the king's expression, Monsieur de Tréville felt as strong as Samson[2] joining battle with the Philistines.

Louis XIII was at the door, his hand upon the handle, when he heard Monsieur de Tréville enter and swung round.

'This is timely, sir!' said the king, who was unable to dissemble when his passions had reached a certain pitch. 'I'm learning some fine things about your musketeers.'

'And I,' Monsieur de Tréville replied coldly, 'have some fine things to tell Your Majesty about his officers of the law.'

'Yes?' the king inquired haughtily.

'I have the honour to inform Your Majesty,' Monsieur de Tréville continued in the same tone, 'that a troop of lawyers, commissaries and police – highly estimable people, no doubt, but also, it seems, rabid enemies of the army – made so bold as to arrest in a private residence, march down the middle of the street, and throw into For-l'Évêque – all on orders which they have refused to show me – one of my musketeers, or rather one of yours, Sire, a gentleman of irreproachable conduct and nigh on illustrious reputation, whom Your Majesty knows and favours, Monsieur Athos.'

'Athos,' the king repeated mechanically. 'Yes, in fact, that name is familiar to me.'

'If Your Majesty will recall,' said Monsieur de Tréville, 'Monsieur Athos is the musketeer who had the misfortune to inflict a severe wound on Monsieur Cahusac in the regrettable duel with which you are familiar. Incidentally, my lord,' continued Tréville, addressing the cardinal, 'Monsieur de Cahusac has made a complete recovery, has he not?'

'Thank you, yes,' said the cardinal, angrily pursing his lips.

'So, Monsieur Athos had gone to visit one of his friends and found him not at home,' said Monsieur de Tréville, 'a young Béarnais cadet in His Majesty's guards, in des Essarts's company. But he had hardly made himself comfortable in his friend's rooms and picked up a book to read while he waited when a chaotic swarm of soldiers and minions of the law laid siege to the house, broke down its doors . . .'

The cardinal signalled to the king that this was the business he had just told him about.

'We know all this,' replied the king. 'It was done on our service.'

'Then,' said Tréville, 'it was also on Your Majesty's service that an innocent musketeer of mine was seized, flanked by guards like a common criminal, and frogmarched through an insolent crowd – a man of honour who has ten times shed blood on Your Majesty's service and stands ready to spill more.'

'No!' exclaimed the king, shocked. 'Is that what happened?'

'Monsieur de Tréville does not say,' the cardinal replied with perfect self-possession, 'that this innocent musketeer, this man of honour, had an hour earlier belaboured with his sword four examining commissaries whom I had appointed to investigate a matter of the utmost importance.'

'I defy Your Eminence to prove it,' cried Monsieur de Tréville with his Gascon frankness and soldierly bluntness, 'for an hour earlier Monsieur Athos – a man, I should tell Your Majesty in confidence, of most noble family – had done me the honour of dining with me, then repairing to my reception room with my other guests, the Duke de La Trémouille and the Count de Châlus.'

The king looked at the cardinal.

'A statement is always conclusive,' said the cardinal in reply to His Majesty's tacit question. 'The victims made this report, which I have the honour to transmit to Your Majesty.'

'Is a lawman's report worth a swordsman's word of honour?' Tréville demanded proudly.

'Come, come, Tréville, hush now,' said the king.

'If His Eminence were to suspect one of my musketeers in any way,' said Tréville, 'the cardinal's justice is sufficiently renowned that I should call for an inquiry myself.'

'The house where the raid took place,' the cardinal continued impassively, 'is the lodgings of a Béarnais, I think, a friend of the musketeer.'

'Your Eminence means Monsieur d'Artagnan?'

'I mean a young man who enjoys your patronage, Monsieur de Tréville.'

'Yes, Your Eminence, they are one and the same.'

'Don't you suspect this young man of giving bad advice . . .'

'To Monsieur Athos, a man twice his age?' interrupted Monsieur de Tréville. 'No, I don't, Your Eminence. Besides, Monsieur d'Artagnan spent the evening with me.'

'My, my,' said the cardinal. 'Did everyone enjoy your hospitality that evening?'

'Does His Eminence doubt my word?' said Tréville, flushing with anger.

'No, God forbid,' said the cardinal. 'But could you tell me what time he was with you?'

'Oh, I know that for a fact, Your Eminence, since I noticed when he came in that it was half-past nine by the clock, although I had thought it later.'

'And at what time did he leave your residence?'

'At half-past ten, an hour after the incident.'

'Nevertheless,' said the cardinal, who did not doubt Tréville's sincerity for a moment and felt victory slipping away, 'Athos was arrested in this house on Rue des Fossoyeurs, was he not?'

'Is it forbidden for friends to visit one another? For a musketeer of my company to fraternise with a guard of Monsieur des Essarts's company?'

'It is when the house in which these friends fraternise is under suspicion.'

'Those premises are under suspicion, Tréville,' said the king. 'Perhaps you didn't know that?'

'Indeed I did not, Sire. In any case, the house as a whole may be suspect, but I refuse to accept this suspicion extends to Monsieur d'Artagnan's lodgings, for I assure you, Sire, that, if I am to take him at his word, there is no more loyal servant of His Majesty or more profound admirer of the cardinal than he.'

'Isn't this the d'Artagnan who wounded Jussac in that unfortunate encounter by the Convent of the Carmes-Déschaux?' asked the king, looking at the cardinal, who flushed angrily.

'And Bernajoux the next day. Yes, Sire, it is indeed. Your Majesty has a good memory.'

'Come now, what shall we decide?' said the king.

'That is more a matter for Your Majesty than me,' said the cardinal. 'I assert his guilt.'

'And I deny it,' said Tréville. 'But His Majesty has judges, and his judges will decide.'

'That's right,' said the king, 'let us refer the matter to the judges. It is their business to judge and they shall do so.'

'Things have come to a pretty pass,' said Tréville, 'in these ill-starred times in which we find ourselves, if the most unblemished life, the most indisputable virtue cannot spare a man infamy and persecution! Mark my words, the army will not be very pleased to be treated so harshly in what is a police matter.'

It was a reckless remark, but Monsieur de Tréville had thrown it out deliberately. He wanted an explosion: a blast sets everything on fire, and fires shed light.

'A police matter!' cried the king, repeating Monsieur de Tréville's words. 'A police matter – and what do you know of that, sir? Concern yourself with your musketeers and stop driving me to distraction. Listening to you, one would think that if by some ill fortune a musketeer is arrested, all of France is in peril. What a fuss over one musketeer! God's teeth, I'll have ten arrested, a hundred even, the whole company, why not – and I won't hear a word of complaint!'

'The moment Your Majesty suspects them,' said Tréville, 'my musketeers are guilty. But look, Sire, you see me ready to surrender my sword into your keeping, for after accusing my soldiers, I have no doubt the cardinal will end up accusing me too. So it is better I give myself up to justice like Monsieur Athos, who has already been arrested, and Monsieur d'Artagnan, who no doubt will be any moment.'

'Will you stop this, you Gascon hothead?' said the king.

'Sire,' replied Tréville, without lowering his voice, 'give the order that my musketeer be returned to me or else put on trial.'

'He is to be tried,' said the cardinal.

'Well, so much the better, for then I will ask His Majesty's permission to plead his cause.'

The king feared a scandal.

'If His Eminence,' he said, 'has no reason personally . . .'

The cardinal saw what the king was driving at and met him head on.

'Forgive me,' he said, 'but if for a moment Your Majesty suspects any bias in my judgement, then I must withdraw.'

'Come,' said the king, turning to Treville, 'do you swear by my father that Monsieur Athos was with you during the incident and had no part in it?'

'By your glorious father, and by you yourself, whom I love and revere most in the world, I swear it!'

'Consider, Sire, I beg you,' said the cardinal. 'If we release the prisoner like this, we will no longer be able to find out the truth.'

'Monsieur Athos will always be at hand,' said Monsieur de Tréville, 'and ready to answer the officers of the law whenever they choose to question him. He will not abscond, cardinal, you may rest assured, I will personally guarantee it.'

'Quite right, he will not abscond,' said the king, 'we will always be able to find him, as Monsieur de Tréville says. Besides,' he added, lowering his voice and looking beseechingly at His Eminence, 'let us set their minds at rest: it's politic.'

Richelieu smiled at Louis XIII's notion of what was politic.

'Give the order, Sire,' he said; 'you have the right of pardon.'

'The right of pardon applies only to the guilty,' said Tréville, determined to have the last word, 'and my musketeer is innocent. So it is not a pardon you will be granting, Sire, it is justice.'

'And he is in For-l'Évêque?' said the king.

'Yes, Sire, and in solitary confinement, like the lowest criminal.'

'Confound it, confound it!' murmured the king. 'What is to be done?'

'Sign the order of his release, and that will be an end to it,' said the cardinal. 'Like Your Majesty, I believe Monsieur de Tréville's guarantee will more than suffice.'

Tréville bowed respectfully, with a joy that was not unmixed with fear. He would have preferred obstinate resistance from the cardinal to this sudden compliance.

The king signed the order for release, which Tréville carried off without delay.

Just as he was leaving, the cardinal gave him a friendly smile, and said to the king, 'A fine spirit of harmony reigns between the officers and men in your musketeers, Sire. It is of great benefit to the service and does honour to all concerned.'

He will do me some mischief soon, Tréville thought to himself. You never have the last word with a man like that. But let's hurry, the king can change his mind at any time, and, when all is said and done, it is harder to put a man back in the Bastille or For-l'Évêque once he has been released than it is to keep someone in there who is already held prisoner.

Monsieur de Tréville made a triumphant entrance into For-l'Évêque and released the musketeer, who was as peaceful and indifferent as ever.

The next time Tréville saw d'Artagnan, he said, 'You got away with it by the skin of your teeth. There's your recompense for the sword thrust you gave Jussac. That still leaves the one you gave Bernajoux, but I wouldn't rely on it if I were you.'

Moreover, Monsieur de Tréville was right to mistrust the cardinal and to think that wasn't an end to it, for the captain of the musketeers had scarcely closed the door behind him before His Eminence said to the king, 'Now that it is just the two of us, I think we should have a serious talk, if it please Your Majesty. Sire, the Duke of Buckingham has been in Paris for five days and has only just left this morning.'

XVI

IN WHICH SÉGUIER, THE KEEPER OF THE SEALS, SEARCHES MORE THAN ONCE FOR THE BELL IN ORDER TO RING IT AS HE USED TO

T HOSE FEW WORDS had a prodigious effect on Louis XIII. He flushed and paled by turns, and the cardinal instantly saw he had won back at a single stroke all the ground he had lost.

'The Duke of Buckingham in Paris!' the king cried. 'And why did he come here?'

'No doubt to conspire with our enemies the Huguenots and the Spanish.'

'No, by God! To conspire against my honour with Madame de Chevreuse, Madame de Longueville and the Condés.'

'Oh, Sire, what a notion! The queen is too good and, above all, loves Your Majesty too much.'

'Women are weak, cardinal,' said the king. 'And as for loving me so much, I have my own opinion about those sentiments.'

'I nonetheless maintain,' said the cardinal, 'that the Duke of Buckingham came to Paris for purely political reasons.'

'And I am sure he came for something else, cardinal. But if the queen is guilty, let her tremble!'

'As a matter of fact,' said the cardinal, 'repugnant though it is for me to dwell on such an act of betrayal, Your Majesty has reminded me of something: Madame de Lannoy, whom I have questioned several times at Your Majesty's behest, told me this morning that Her Majesty stayed up very late the night before last, cried a great deal the following morning, and spent the whole day writing.'

'There you are!' said the king. 'To him, no doubt. Cardinal, I must have the queen's papers.'

'But how to get them, Sire? I do not think either I or Your Majesty can undertake such a task.'

'How was it managed with the Maréchale d'Ancre¹?' cried the king in a pitch of fury. 'They searched her wardrobes, then they searched the woman herself.'

'But the Maréchale d'Ancre's wife was just the Maréchale d'Ancre's wife, a Florentine adventuress, Sire, nothing more. Whereas Your Majesty's august consort is Anne of Austria, queen of France – that is, one of the greatest princesses in the world.'

'And so all the more guilty, Your Grace! The more she has forgotten the high position in which she has been placed, the further she has fallen. In any case, I made up my mind a long time ago to put an end to all these petty political and romantic intrigues. She is always in the company of a certain La Porte, for instance . . .'

'Whom I believe to be the linchpin in all this, I confess,' said the cardinal.

'So you think as I do that she is deceiving me?' said the king.

'I believe, and I repeat to Your Majesty, that the queen is conspiring against the power of her king, but I have never said against his honour.'

'And I tell you she is conspiring against both. I tell you the queen does not love me, I tell you she loves another man, I tell you she loves that infamous Duke of Buckingham! Why didn't you have him arrested while he was in Paris?'

'Arrest the duke? Arrest King Charles I's prime minister? What are you thinking, Sire? What a scandal! And then, if there were any substance to Your Majesty's suspicions, which I continue to doubt, what a terrible scandal! What a desperate scandal!'

'But since he showed himself to be a vagabond and a bandit, he ought to . . .'

Louis XIII stopped himself, afraid of what he was going to say, while Richelieu craned his neck and waited in vain for the words that did not cross the king's lips.

'He ought to . . . ?'

'Nothing,' said the king, 'nothing. Now, you didn't lose sight of him while he was in Paris, did you?'

'No, Sire.'

'Where was he staying?'

'At No. 75, Rue de La Harpe.'

'Where is that?'

'Near the Luxembourg.'

'And you're sure he and the queen have not seen each other?'

'I believe the queen takes her duties too much to heart, Sire.'

'But they have corresponded. It was to him the queen spent the whole day writing. Your Grace, I must have those letters!'

'But, Sire . . .'

'Duke, I will have them, no matter what the cost.'

'I would point out to Your Majesty . . .'

'Do you betray me too, cardinal, always opposing my wishes like this? Are you also in league with the Spanish and the English, with Madame de Chevreuse and the queen?'

'Sire,' replied the cardinal, sighing, 'I thought I was immune from such suspicions.'

'You heard me, Your Eminence, I want those letters.'

'There is only one way.'

'Which?'

'To entrust the task to Monsieur Séguier, the keeper of the seals. It falls squarely within the duties of his office.'

'Have him sent for immediately.'

'He should be at my residence, Sire. I asked him to pass by, and when I came to the Louvre, I left instructions to have him wait if he presented himself.'

'Then send someone to fetch him at once.'

'Your Majesty's orders will be carried out. But . . .'

'But what?'

'But the queen may refuse to obey.'

'My orders?'

'Yes, if she is unaware they are the king's.'

'Well then, lest she be in any doubt, I will go and inform her myself.'

'I trust Your Majesty will not forget that I have done everything in my power to prevent a rift.'

'Yes, duke, I know you are very indulgent towards the queen – perhaps too indulgent. I warn you, we will have to talk about that presently.'

'Whenever it pleases Your Majesty, but I will always be happy and proud, Sire, to sacrifice myself to the spirit of complete harmony that I desire to see reign between you and the queen of France.'

'Very well, cardinal, very well. But in the meantime send for the keeper of the seals. I am going to the queen.'

And then Louis XIII opened the communicating door and set off down the passage that led to Anne of Austria's suite of rooms.

The queen was surrounded by her ladies-in-waiting: Madame de Guitaut, Madame de Sablé, Madame de Montbazon and Madame de Guéménée. In a corner was the Spanish maid of honour, Doña Estefania, who had followed her from Madrid. Madame de Guéménée was reading aloud and everyone was listening attentively, apart from the queen. She had organised this entertainment so that, while pretending to listen, she could follow the thread of her thoughts.

Gilded though these thoughts were by a last glow of love, they were no less sad for all that. Deprived of her husband's trust, persecuted by the hatred of the cardinal, who could not forgive her for rejecting his tender feelings, and faced with the example of the queen mother, who had been plagued by this hatred all her life (although Marie de' Medici², if the memoirs of the time are to be believed, had initially reciprocated the feelings that Anne of Austria, when it came to her turn, denied the cardinal), Anne of Austria had seen her most devoted servants, her most intimate confidants and her most beloved favourites struck down on all sides. Like those unfortunate souls endowed with a malign gift, she brought misfortune on everything she touched; her friendship was a deadly mark that called down persecution in its train. Madame de Chevreuse and Madame de Vernet were in exile, and now La Porte admitted to his mistress that he expected to be arrested at any moment.

It was when she was immersed in the deepest and darkest of these thoughts that the door of her chamber opened and the king entered.

The reader broke off immediately, all the ladies-in-waiting stood up, and a profound silence descended on the room.

The king made no show of courtesy, but simply halted in front of the queen and said in a strained voice, 'Madam, you are about to receive a visit from the chancellor, who will inform you of certain matters which I have entrusted to his care.'

The unfortunate queen, who was constantly threatened with divorce, exile and even court proceedings, paled under her rouge and could not help asking, 'But why this visit, Sire? What will the chancellor tell me that Your Majesty cannot tell me himself?'

The king turned on his heel without replying, and at almost exactly the same moment the captain of the guards, Monsieur de Guitaut, announced the chancellor's visit.

When the chancellor appeared, the king had already left by another door.

Séguier entered, half-smiling, half-blushing. As we will probably encounter him again in the course of this story, there is no harm in our readers making his acquaintance now.

This chancellor was a pleasant man. Des Roches le Masle, a canon of Notre Dame and former valet to the cardinal, had recommended him to His Eminence as a man of unimpeachable loyalty. Putting his trust in him, the cardinal found himself well rewarded.

Various stories were told about him, including the following:

After a stormy youth, he had retired to a monastery to atone, at least temporarily, for the follies of his adolescence.

But on entering this holy place, the poor penitent had been unable to slam the door behind him fast enough to keep the passions he was fleeing from entering with him. They plagued him relentlessly, and the head of the monastery – to whom he had confided his disgrace, and who wished to protect him from it as best he could – suggested that, to cast out the tempter, he should run to the bell rope and pull it with all his might. At the telltale ring, the monks would know a brother was beset by temptation and the whole community would fall to prayer.

This seemed good advice to the future chancellor. He warded off the evil one with a barrage of prayers offered up by the monks, but the devil does not readily surrender a fortress he has garrisoned. The more they redoubled their exorcisms, the more he redoubled his temptations, and, the next thing anyone knew, the bell was pealing day and night, broadcasting the penitent's extreme desire for mortification.

The monks no longer had a moment's respite. By day they did nothing but traipse up and down the chapel stairs, and by night, besides compline and matins, they had to leap out of bed twenty times and prostrate themselves on the floor of their cells.

It is not known whether the devil eventually let go or the monks collapsed from exhaustion, but after three months the penitent reappeared in the world with a reputation as the most demonically possessed individual that had ever walked this earth.

When he left the monastery he entered the magistracy and took his uncle's place as a presiding judge. He threw in his lot with the cardinal, which showed no lack of acumen on his part, and, on being appointed chancellor, zealously supported His Eminence in his hatred of the queen mother and vengefulness towards Anne of Austria. He spurred on the judges in the Chalais Affair, encouraged the efforts of Monsieur de Laffemas, Richelieu's chief gamekeeper in France[3], and finally, invested with the cardinal's complete confidence, a confidence he had so richly earned, he was entrusted with the singular mission, the execution of which now brought him to the queen's chamber.

The queen was still standing when he entered, but, almost the moment she caught sight of him, she sat back down in her chair and, motioning her ladies-in-waiting to their cushions and stools, asked in a tone of supreme hauteur, 'What do you want, sir? Why is it that you come here?'

'To conduct in the king's name, ma'am, and with all the respect I am honoured to owe Your Majesty, a thorough examination of your papers.'

'What, sir? An examination of my papers? *Mine?* This is an outrage!'

'Please forgive me, madam, but I am merely the instrument employed by the king in this matter. Did His Majesty not just leave here, and did he not ask you himself to prepare for this visit?'

'Search then, sir. I am a criminal, it seems. Estefania, hand over the keys to my tables and my writing desk.'

For form's sake the chancellor examined these items of furniture, but he knew the queen wouldn't have consigned to their keeping an important letter, which she had spent the day writing.

When he had opened and shut the drawers of the writing desk twenty times, there was nothing for it, however reluctant he felt – there was nothing for it, as I say, but to bring the matter to a close: that is, to search the queen herself. The chancellor walked towards Anne of Austria and, in a very perplexed tone of voice and with a very embarrassed air, announced, 'And now it still remains for me to perform the principal search.'

'Which is?' asked the queen, not understanding, or rather not wanting to understand.

'His Majesty is certain a letter was written by you during the day. He knows it hasn't yet been sent to its recipient. This letter is to be found neither in your table nor in your desk, and yet this letter is somewhere.'

'Would you dare lay a hand on your queen?' said Anne of Austria, drawing herself up to her full height and staring at the chancellor with a look almost of menace in her eyes.

'I am a loyal subject of the king, ma'am, and I shall carry out any order His Majesty sees fit to give.'

'Well, it is true,' said Anne of Austria. 'The cardinal has been well served by his spies. I did write a letter today, and this letter has not been dispatched . . . It is here,' the queen added, bringing her beautiful hand to her bosom.

'Then give me this letter, ma'am,' said the chancellor.

'I will only give it to the king, sir,' said Anne.

'If the king wished this letter to be handed to him, ma'am, he would have asked you for it himself. But, I repeat, he has charged me to ask you for it, and if you do not surrender it . . .'

'Well?'

'He has also charged me to take it from you.'

'What – what do you mean?'

'That my orders are far-reaching, madam, and that I am author-ised to go so far as to search Your Majesty's person for the suspect communication.'

'This is horrific!' cried the queen.

'Please be so kind then, ma'am, as to be more accommodating.'

'This conduct is monstrously violent, are you aware of that, sir?'

'The king has ordered it, ma'am. Forgive me.'

'I will not allow it. No, no, I'd rather die!' cried the queen, the imperious Spanish and Austrian blood in her veins rebelling.

The chancellor made a low bow and then, clearly intent on seeing his mission through to the bitter end, stepped forward like an assistant executioner in a torture chamber as tears of rage could be seen welling up in Anne of Austria's eyes.

The queen was extremely beautiful, as we have said.

The mission could thus be deemed a delicate one, but so virulent was the king's jealousy of Buckingham, it no longer occurred to him to be jealous of anyone else.

No doubt Chancellor Séguier looked around for the rope of the famous bell at that moment, but, unable to find it, he resigned himself to the inevitable and stretched his hand out towards the place where the queen had confessed the letter to be.

Deathly pale, Anne of Austria took a step back, and, leaning her left hand on a table behind her so as not to fall, drew a sheet of paper from her bosom with her right hand and handed it to the keeper of the seals.

'Here, sir, here is the letter,' exclaimed the queen, her voice hoarse and quavering. 'Take it and rid me of your odious presence.'

The chancellor, who for his part was trembling with an emotion that is easy to imagine, took the letter, bowed to the ground and withdrew.

The door had scarcely closed behind him before the queen collapsed, half-unconscious, into the arms of her ladies-in-waiting.

The chancellor delivered the letter to the king[4] without reading a word of it. The king took it, his hand trembling, and looked for the address, which had not been filled in. He grew very pale, opened the letter slowly, and then, seeing from its first words that it was addressed to the King of Spain[5], read it very quickly.

It was an entire plan of attack against the cardinal. The queen urged her brother and the emperor of Austria, galled as they were by Richelieu's politics, by his eternal preoccupation with humbling the House of Austria, to pretend to declare war on France and impose the cardinal's dismissal as a condition of peace. But of love, the letter contained not a single word.

Overjoyed, the king asked if the cardinal was still in the Louvre. He was told His Eminence was awaiting His Majesty's orders in his study.

The king went straight to him.

'So, duke,' he said, 'you were right and it was I who was wrong. The intrigue is entirely political and there was no mention of love in that letter, which I have here. There is, however, considerable mention of you.'

The cardinal took the letter and read it with the greatest attention, and, on reaching the end, read it a second time.

'Well, Your Majesty,' he said, 'you see how far my enemies go – you are threatened with two wars if you do not dismiss me. In truth, Sire, in your place I would yield to such powerful entreaties, and for my part it would be with genuine delight that I should retire from public affairs.'

'What are you saying, duke?'

'I am saying, Sire, that my health is being ruined by these excessive struggles and eternal labours. I am saying that in all probability I won't be able to endure the fatigues of the siege of La Rochelle, and that it would be better if you appointed for it either Monsieur de Condé or Monsieur de Bassompierre or, in short, any valiant man whose profession it is to wage war, and not me, who am a man of the Church and am constantly being distracted from my vocation to apply myself to things for which I have no aptitude. You will be happier at home, Sire, and I've no doubt you will be all the more victorious abroad.'

'Duke,' said the king, 'I understand; you need not worry. All those who are named in this letter will receive the punishment they deserve, including the queen herself.'

'What are you saying, Sire? God forbid that the queen should suffer the least vexation on my account! She has always believed me her enemy, Sire, although Your Majesty can attest that I have always warmly taken her part, even against you. Oh, if she betrayed Your Majesty with regard to his honour, that would be a different matter, and I would be the first to say, "No mercy, Sire, no mercy for the guilty one." Fortunately it isn't so, and Your Majesty has just acquired fresh proof of this.'

'That is true, cardinal,' said the king, 'and you were right, as ever, but the queen nonetheless deserves my full anger.'

'It is you, Sire, who have incurred hers. And, in truth, if she were to refuse to speak to Your Majesty, I would understand it. Your Majesty has treated her with a severity . . .'

'That is how I will always treat my enemies and yours, duke, however prominent they may be and whatever risk I may run in dealing severely with them.'

'The queen is my enemy, but not yours, Sire. On the contrary, she is a devoted, compliant, irreproachable spouse. Allow me, Sire, to intercede on her behalf with Your Majesty.'

'Let her humble herself then, and let her make peace with me first!'

'On the contrary, Sire, set the example. You were in the wrong first, since it was you who suspected the queen.'

'I be the first to make peace?' said the king. 'Never!'

'Sire, I beg you.'

'Besides, how could I make peace first?'

'By doing something you know would give her pleasure.'

'Such as?'

'Throw a ball. You know how much the queen loves dancing. I assure you her sense of grievance will not be able to resist such a show of consideration.'

'Your Eminence, you know I do not love worldly pleasures indiscriminately.'

'The queen will only be the more grateful, since she knows your aversion to this one. Besides, it will be a chance for her to wear those beautiful diamond tags you gave her the other day for her birthday, with which she has not yet had time to adorn herself.'

'We shall see, cardinal, we shall see,' said the king, who, in his joy at finding the queen guilty of a crime he cared little about and innocent of a transgression he feared terribly, was quite ready to make up with her. 'We shall see. But, on my honour, you are too lenient.'

'Sire,' said the cardinal, 'leave severity to your ministers.

Leniency is the royal virtue. Dispense it and you will be rewarded, you will see.'

Upon which the cardinal, hearing the clock strike eleven, bowed low, and, begging the king to make up with the queen, asked his leave to retire.

Anne of Austria, who was expecting to be taken to task after the seizure of her letter, was highly astonished the next day to see the king attempting to be reconciled with her. Her first impulse was to repel his efforts. Her woman's pride and her queen's dignity had both been so grievously wounded that she couldn't make up just like that at the first time of asking. But eventually, swayed by the advice of her ladies-in-waiting, she seemed to be starting to forget. The king seized on this intimation of a change of heart to tell her he was planning to give a fête soon.

A fête was such a rarity for poor Anne of Austria that, at this announcement, as the cardinal had thought, the last trace of resentment disappeared, if not from her heart, then at least from her face. She asked what day the fête would take place, but the king replied that he and the cardinal had yet to agree on that point.

Indeed, every day from then on the king asked the cardinal when the fête would take place, and every day the cardinal, on some pretext or other, put off setting a date.

Ten days passed in this fashion.

On the eighth day after the scene we have described, the cardinal received a letter with a London stamp, which only contained these few lines:

I have them, but I cannot leave London for lack of money. Send me five hundred pistoles, and four or five days after I receive them, I will be in Paris.

The day the cardinal received this letter, the king asked him his customary question.

Richelieu counted on his fingers and said to himself in a low voice, 'She will be here, she says, four or five days after she gets the money. It will take four or five days for the money to arrive, and four or five days for her to return, so that makes ten days. So, let's allow for adverse winds, bad luck and women's fallibility, and round it up to twelve days.'

'Well, duke,' said the king, 'have you done your calculations?'

'Yes, Sire. Today is the twentieth of September. The city aldermen are giving a fête on the third of October. That will be ideal, because it won't look as if you're making overtures to the queen.'

'By the way, Sire,' the cardinal added, 'do not forget to tell Her Majesty on the eve of the ball that you wish to see how her diamond tags suit her.'

XVII
THE BONACIEUX HOUSEHOLD

THIS WAS THE SECOND TIME the cardinal had brought up the matter of the diamond tags with the king. Struck by his insistence, Louis XIII thought this prompting must conceal some mystery.

The king had been humiliated more than once by the cardinal knowing more about what was going on in his own household than he did – the cardinal's police, whilst not having attained the perfection of their modern equivalent, were excellent – and so he decided to talk to Anne of Austria. He hoped to be able to glean enough information from their conversation to go back to His Eminence in possession of a secret, which, regardless of whether the cardinal knew it or not, would raise him immeasurably in his minister's eyes.

So he went to find the queen, and, as was his habit, accosted her with further threats against her entourage. Anne of Austria bowed her head and let the torrent wash over her without responding, hoping it would eventually come to a halt. But that wasn't what Louis XIII wanted. Louis XIII wanted an exchange that would shed some sort of light, convinced as he was that the cardinal had an ulterior motive and was devising one of those terrible surprises for which His Eminence had such a flair. He persisted with his accusations until he achieved his aim.

'But, Sire,' Anne of Austria cried eventually, weary of these vague attacks. 'You are not telling me everything that is in your heart. What have I done? Come, what crime have I committed? Your Majesty surely can't be making all this to-do over a letter written to my brother.'

The king, finding himself in turn under such direct attack, didn't know how to reply. He thought now would be a good moment to deliver the instructions that he was supposed to give only on the eve of the fête.

'Madam,' he declared majestically, 'a ball is shortly to be held at the Hôtel de Ville. To honour our worthy aldermen, I wish you to appear in ceremonial dress, and above all adorned in those diamond tags I gave you for your birthday. There, that is my reply.'

It was a terrible one. Anne of Austria thought that Louis XIII knew everything and that the cardinal had persuaded him to dissemble for seven or eight days, which would in any case have been characteristic of him. She turned inordinately pale, steadied herself on a wall-bracket with her admirably beautiful, waxen hand, and, without uttering a syllable in response, gazed at the king with terrified eyes.

'Do you hear, madam,' said the king, enjoying her confusion to the full, although without suspecting its cause, 'do you hear?'

'Yes, Sire, I hear,' stammered the queen.

'You will appear at the ball?'

'Yes.'

'With your tags?'

'Yes.'

The queen's pallor increased still further, if that were possible. The king noticed this, and savoured it with the cold cruelty that was one of the ugly sides of his character.

'Then it is settled,' said the king. 'And that is all I had to say to you.'

'But what day will the ball take place?' inquired Anne of Austria.

Louis XIII instinctively sensed he oughtn't to answer this question, which the queen had asked in an almost inaudible whisper.

'Why, very shortly, madam,' he said, 'but I have forgotten the exact date. I will ask the cardinal.'

'So it was the cardinal who told you of the ball?' cried the queen.

'Yes, madam,' the king replied, astonished. 'Why?'

'It was he who told you to request that I appear wearing those tags?'

'That is to say, madam . . .'

'It was he, Sire, it was he!'

'Well, what does it matter which of us it was? Is there any crime in this request?'

'No, Sire.'

'Then you will appear?'

'Yes, Sire.'

'Very good,' said the king, making for the door. 'Very good, I shall count on it.'

The queen curtsied, less out of a concern for etiquette than because her knees were giving way beneath her.

The king left the room, delighted.

'I'm done for,' murmured the queen, 'done for, because the cardinal knows everything and he is urging on the king, who hasn't found out yet, but soon will know everything. I'm done for! My God! My God! My God!'

She knelt on a cushion and prayed, her head buried in her quivering arms.

Her situation was indeed terrible. Buckingham had returned to London. Madame de Chevreuse was in Tours. More closely watched than ever, the queen had a nagging sense one of her ladies-in-waiting was betraying her but couldn't say which one.

La Porte couldn't leave the Louvre. There wasn't a soul in the world she could trust.

Faced with imminent ruin, abandoned at every turn, she burst into sobs.

'Can't I be of any service to Your Majesty?' a voice full of gentleness and pity suddenly asked.

The queen swung round, for there was no mistaking that tone: only a friend could speak like that.

And there, in one of the doors that gave on to the queen's apartments, stood the pretty Madame Bonacieux. She had been busy sorting dresses and linen in a closet when the king had made his entrance, and, unable to leave, had heard everything.

The queen let out a piercing shriek at finding herself overheard. In her agitation she did not recognise the young woman who had been given her by La Porte.

'Oh, do not be afraid, ma'am,' said the young woman, clasping her hands, tears welling at the queen's anguish. 'I am Your Majesty's servant, body and soul, and far as I am below her, lowly as my station may be, I believe I have found a way of extricating Your Majesty from her difficulty.'

'You? Oh heaven! You?' exclaimed the queen. 'But come, look me in the eye. I am betrayed on all sides: can I trust you?'

'Oh, ma'am!' cried the young woman, falling to her knees. 'On my soul, I would die for Your Majesty!'

That cry came from the very bottom of her heart, and, as with her first exclamation, its sincerity was unmistakable.

'It's true,' Madame Bonacieux went on, 'it's true there are traitors here, but by the holy name of the Virgin, I swear to you that no one is more devoted to Your Majesty than I. You gave the tags the king is asking for to the Duke of Buckingham, didn't you? Those tags were in a little rosewood box he was holding under his arm? Am I mistaken? Isn't that so?'

'Oh, my God! My God!' murmured the queen, her teeth chattering with terror.

'Well, those tags must be recovered,' continued Madame Bonacieux.

'Yes, without a doubt, they must,' cried the queen, 'but what is to be done? How is it to be managed?'

'Someone must be sent to the duke.'

'But who? Who? Whom can I trust?'

'Trust me, ma'am. Do me this honour, my queen, and I will find the messenger myself.'

'But I'll have to put something in writing.'

'Oh yes! That is vital. A few words in Your Majesty's hand and your personal seal.'

'But those few words will damn me – divorce, exile!'

'Yes, if they fall into malicious hands. But I guarantee those few words will be delivered to their address.'

'Oh, my God, must I then put my life, my honour and my reputation in your hands?'

'Yes, yes, ma'am, you must, and I will preserve them all!'

'But how? At least tell me that.'

'My husband was released two or three days ago; I haven't had time to see him yet. He is a worthy, honest man who is incapable of either hatred or love for anyone. He will do what I want. He will set out on my orders, not knowing what he is carrying, and he will deliver Your Majesty's letter, not even knowing it is Your Majesty's, to the address she indicates.'

Impulsively, the queen grasped both the young woman's hands, gazed at her as if wanting to read to the depths of her heart, and, seeing nothing but sincerity in her beautiful eyes, kissed her tenderly.

'Do that,' she cried, 'and you will have saved my life, you will have saved my honour!'

'Oh, do not exaggerate the service I have the good fortune to render you. I could never save anything of Your Majesty's, who is merely the victim of treacherous plots.'

'That is true, that is true, my child,' said the queen, 'you are right.'

'Give me the letter then, ma'am. Time presses.'

The queen ran to a little table on which there were ink, paper and pens. She wrote a few lines, sealed the letter with her own seal and handed it to Madame Bonacieux.

'And now,' said the queen, 'we are forgetting something essential.'

'Which is?'

'Money.'

Madame Bonacieux blushed.

'Yes, that's true,' she said, 'and I must confess to Your Majesty that my husband . . .'

'Your husband has none, you mean.'

'No, he does, but he is very miserly, it is his failing. But Your Majesty mustn't worry, we will find a way . . .'

'Because I do not have any either,' said the queen (an answer that will come as no surprise to anyone who has read Madame de Motteville's memoirs), 'but wait . . .'

Anne of Austria ran to her jewel case.

'Look,' she said, 'here is a ring I am assured is very valuable. It is from my brother, the King of Spain; it is mine and I can do with it as I wish. Take the ring, convert it into money, and let your husband be on his way.'

'You will be obeyed within the hour.'

'You see the address,' said the queen, speaking so low it was barely possible to hear what she was saying. 'To My Lord the Duke of Buckingham, London.'

'The letter will be given to him in person.'

'Generous child!' cried Anne of Austria.

Madame Bonacieux kissed the queen's hands, hid the paper in her bodice and disappeared, as light as a bird.

Ten minutes later she was at home. As she had told the queen, she had not seen her husband since his release and so was unaware of the change that had come over him regarding the cardinal, a change brought about by His Eminence's flattery and money, and confirmed by two or three subsequent visits from the Count de

Rochefort. The count had become Bonacieux's best friend and had convinced him without great difficulty that there were no reprehensible motives to his wife's abduction, and that it was merely a political precaution.

She found Monsieur Bonacieux alone. The poor man was struggling to get the house back into shape, having found the furniture more or less smashed to pieces and the wardrobes more or less stripped bare, justice not being one of the three things King Solomon spoke of as leaving no trace of their passage[1]. As for the maid, she had fled when her master was arrested. The poor girl had been so terrified that she had walked without stopping from Paris to Burgundy, the province of her birth.

As soon as he had got home, the worthy mercer had sent word of his safe return to his wife, and his wife had replied, congratulating him and telling him that the moment her duties allowed her any time to herself, she would devote it entirely to visiting him.

That moment took five days to arrive, which, in any other circumstances, would have struck Monsieur Bonacieux as rather too long, but his visit to the cardinal and Rochefort's subsequent visits to him had provided him with ample food for thought, and, as we know, nothing makes the time pass like thinking.

Especially because Bonacieux's thoughts were uniformly rose-tinted. Rochefort called him his friend, his dear Bonacieux, and did not tire of reporting that the cardinal set the greatest store by him. The mercer already saw himself on the high road to honour and fortune.

Madame Bonacieux, for her part, had also been thinking, but not, it has to be said, about ambition. Despite herself, her thoughts kept turning to the handsome young man who was so brave and appeared so loving. Married at eighteen to Monsieur Bonacieux, and having spent all her time in the company of her husband's friends, who were unlikely to stir any feelings in a young woman whose heart was more elevated than her position, Madame

Bonacieux had remained indifferent to vulgar seductions. But, in those days especially, the title of gentleman had a great hold over the bourgeoisie, and d'Artagnan was a gentleman. Moreover, he wore the uniform of the guards, which, after the uniform of the musketeers, was the object of women's greatest admiration. He was, we repeat, handsome, young and adventurous, and he spoke of love as a man who loves and yearns to be loved in return. All of which was more than enough to turn a twenty-three-year-old's head, and Madame Bonacieux had just reached that happy time of life.

Although the spouses had not seen each other for over eight days, and during that week significant events had occurred for both of them, their greetings were somewhat preoccupied. Nonetheless, Monsieur Bonacieux appeared genuinely delighted and went up to his wife with open arms.

Madame Bonacieux proffered her brow, and said, 'Let's talk a little.'

'What?' Bonacieux said, surprised.

'Why yes, I have something of the highest importance to tell you.'

'Well, as a matter of fact, I too have some rather serious questions to put to you. Give me some explanation of your abduction, please.'

'That's neither here nor there for the moment,' replied Madame Bonacieux.

'And what is, then? My imprisonment?'

'I heard about it the day it happened, but as you weren't guilty of any crime, as you weren't guilty of any intrigue, and as, finally, you knew nothing that could compromise you or anyone else, I only gave it the importance it deserved.'

'It's very easy for you to talk, madam!' replied Bonacieux, offended by his wife's lack of interest. 'Do you know I was buried away for a day and a night in a cell of the Bastille?'

'A day and a night soon pass. So let's leave your imprisonment to one side and come back to why I am here.'

'What? Why you're here? Isn't it because you want to see the husband you have been parted from for eight days?' demanded the mercer, stung to the quick.

'That first, and then something else.'

'Speak!'

'Something of the greatest consequence on which our future fortunes may depend.'

'Our fortunes have assumed a very different complexion since I last saw you, Madame Bonacieux, and I shouldn't be surprised if in a few months they weren't the envy of many people.'

'Indeed, especially if you follow the instructions I am about to give you.'

'Give me?'

'Yes, give you. There is a good and holy action to be performed, sir, and a great deal of money to be made at the same time.'

Madame Bonacieux knew that, in bringing up money, she was playing on her husband's weakness.

But no one, not even a mercer, is the man he used to be after ten minutes of conversation with Cardinal Richelieu.

'A great deal of money to be made?' Bonacieux pursed his lips.

'Yes, a great deal.'

'How much, roughly?'

'Perhaps a thousand pistoles.'

'So what you are going to ask of me is very serious?'

'Yes.'

'What do I have to do?'

'You'll leave straightaway, I'll give you a letter which you will not let out of your possession on any pretext, and you will give it to the proper person.'

'And where am I to leave for?'

'For London.'

'I go to London? Come now, you're joking, I have no business in London.'

'But others need you to go there.'

'Who are these others? I warn you, I am not doing anything

blindly any more. I want to know not only what I am exposing myself to, but also whom I am exposing myself for.'

'An illustrious person is sending you, an illustrious person is expecting you: the reward will exceed your desires. That's all I can promise you.'

'More intrigues! Always intrigues! Thank you, but I am wary of them now; the cardinal has enlightened me in that regard.'

'The cardinal!' cried Madame Bonacieux. 'You've seen the cardinal?'

'He sent for me,' the mercer replied proudly.

'And you were imprudent enough to go along when he invited you?'

'Strictly speaking, I didn't have a choice whether I went or not because I was marched there between two guards. It is also true that as I wasn't acquainted with His Eminence at that point, I would have been extremely delighted if I could have forgone that visit.'

'So he mistreated you? He threatened you?'

'He gave me his hand and called me his friend – his friend! Do you hear, madam? I am a friend of the great cardinal!'

'Of the great cardinal?'

'Would you dispute his right to that title by any chance, madam?'

'I'm not disputing his right to anything, but I'm telling you that a minister's favour is fleeting, and that one has to be mad to attach oneself to a minister. There are powers higher than his that do not depend on the whim of a man or the outcome of an event. Those are the powers to which one must rally.'

'I am sorry, madam, but I know of no other power than that of the great man whom I have the honour to serve.'

'You serve the cardinal?'

'Yes, madam, and as his servant I will not permit you to engage in plots against the security of the State, or to further the intrigues of a woman who is not French and has a Spanish heart. Fortunately, the great cardinal is there: his vigilant gaze keeps watch and penetrates to the depths of every heart.'

Bonacieux was repeating word for word something he had heard the Count de Rochefort say. But the poor woman, who had counted on her husband and, in that hope, had vouched for him to the queen, shuddered nonetheless, both at the danger into which she had almost blundered and at the helplessness of her predicament. However, knowing the weakness and, above all, the greed of her husband, she did not despair of bringing him round to her ends.

'Ah, you are a cardinalist, sir!' she cried. 'Ah, you serve the party of those who ill-treat your wife and insult your queen!'

'Private interests are nothing compared to the interests of all. I am for whoever protects the State,' Bonacieux ringingly declared.

This was another of the Count de Rochefort's phrases he had remembered and found an opportunity to work into the conversation.

'And do you have any idea what this State is you're talking about?' said Madame Bonacieux, shrugging her shoulders. 'You just go on being a townsman without any discrimination, rallying to whichever side offers you the most benefits.'

'Hey, hey,' said Bonacieux, slapping a bag with a rounded belly that gave off a silvery sound, 'what do you say to this, madam preacher?'

'Where does that money come from?'

'Can't you guess?'

'The cardinal?'

'From him and from my friend, the Count de Rochefort.'

'The Count de Rochefort? But he was the one who abducted me!'

'That may be, madam.'

'And you accept money from that man?'

'Didn't you tell me your abduction was purely political?'

'Yes, but the point of it was to make me betray my mistress, to extract information from me by torture that might compromise the honour, and perhaps even the life of my august mistress.'

'Madam,' said Bonacieux, 'your august mistress is a perfidious Spaniard, and the cardinal is doing the right thing.'

'Sir,' said the young woman, 'I knew you were cowardly, miserly and stupid, but I didn't know you were base!'

'Madam,' said Bonacieux, who had never seen his wife angry and recoiled before such conjugal wrath, 'madam, what are you saying?'

'I'm saying you are a scoundrel!' continued Madame Bonacieux, seeing she was regaining some influence over her husband. 'Ah, you are playing at politics now, are you? Cardinalist politics, to boot? You're selling yourself body and soul to the devil for money!'

'No, to the cardinal.'

'It's the same thing!' cried the young woman. 'Richelieu is another name for Satan.'

'Be quiet, madam, be quiet, someone might hear you!'

'Yes, you're right, and I'd be ashamed for your sake because of your cowardice.'

'But look, what are you asking of me?'

'I've told you: that you set out this very instant, sir; that you loyally carry out the commission I am deigning to entrust to you, and, on condition you do so, I will forget everything, I will forgive you, and, what's more,' she held out her hand, 'I will count you a friend again.'

Bonacieux was a poltroon and a miser, but he loved his wife, and he was moved. A man of fifty does not bear a grudge against a woman of twenty-three for long. Madame Bonacieux saw he was hesitating.

'Well, have you decided?' she said.

'But, my dear friend, think for a moment what you are asking of me. London is a long way from Paris, a very long way, and the commission you are entrusting to me may not be without its dangers.'

'What difference does that make if you evade them?'

'Stop, Madame Bonacieux,' said the mercer. 'Stop, I've decided, I refuse to do it. Intrigues scare me. I have seen the Bastille with

my own eyes. Brrrr, it's frightful, the Bastille! Just thinking about
it makes my flesh creep. They threatened to torture me. Do you
know what torture is? Wooden wedges driven between your legs
until your bones splinter! No, I've made up my mind, I won't
go . . . Good grief, why don't you go yourself? Because, to tell
you the truth, I think I've been mistaken about you until now: I
think you're a man, and one of the maddest there is, at that!'

'And you are a woman, a miserable, stupid, besotted woman.
So, you're scared, are you? Well then, if you don't set out this
very instant, I'll have you arrested on the queen's orders and I'll
have you put in that Bastille you're so afraid of.'

Bonacieux fell into deep thought. He meticulously weighed
the two angers in his brain, the cardinal's and the queen's: the
cardinal's came out overwhelmingly heavier.

'Have me arrested on the queen's behalf,' he said, 'and I will
appeal to His Eminence.'

Madame Bonacieux suddenly saw she had overstepped the mark
and was terrified at having gone so far. She gazed with dread for
a moment at the stupid figure standing there with that unshakeable
resolve that always comes over fools when they are afraid.

'Well then, so be it!' she said. 'Perhaps you are right after all.
A man knows more about politics than women – especially you,
Monsieur Bonacieux, since you talked with the cardinal. And yet
it is very hard,' she added, 'that my husband, that a man on whose
affection I thought I could count, treats me so disgracefully and
won't satisfy a whim of mine.'

'That's because your whims can go too far,' Bonacieux retorted
triumphantly, 'and I don't trust them.'

'I'll give it up then,' said the young woman with a sigh. 'Very
well, let's say no more about it.'

'You could at least tell me what I was going to do in London,'
Bonacieux demurred, remembering a little late that Rochefort had
instructed him to try to learn his wife's secrets.

'There's no point you knowing that,' said the young woman,
drawing back out of an instinctive mistrust. 'It concerned one of

those trifles women are fond of, a purchase in which there was much to gain.'

But the cagier the young woman became, the more importance the secret she was withholding from him assumed in Bonacieux's mind. He decided to run off to the Count de Rochefort's that instant and tell him the queen was looking for a messenger to send to London.

'Excuse me if I leave you, my dear Madame Bonacieux,' he said, 'but not knowing you were coming to see me, I had arranged to meet one of my friends. I'll be back in no time, and if you wouldn't mind waiting for just a second, as soon as I'm done with my friend, I'll come and pick you up, and as it's getting late, I'll escort you back to the Louvre.'

'Thank you, sir,' replied Madame Bonacieux. 'You are not brave enough to be of any use to me, and I will be quite happy making my own way back to the Louvre.'

'As you please, Madame Bonacieux,' replied the former mercer. 'Will I see you again soon?'

'No doubt. Next week I hope my work will allow me some spare time and I will use it to come and put our affairs in order. They must be in some disarray.'

'Very well, I'll expect you. You're not angry with me?'

'I? Not in the slightest.'

'We shall see each other soon, then?'

'We shall.'

Bonacieux kissed his wife's hand and quickly walked away.

'No,' said Madame Bonacieux, when her husband had closed the front door and she was alone, 'that's the final straw, that imbecile is a cardinalist! And I, who'd given my word to the queen, and I, who'd promised my poor mistress . . . Ah, my God, my God! She'll take me for one of those wretches the palace is crawling with, whom they put near her to spy on her. Ah, Monsieur Bonacieux! I've never loved you very much, but now it's far worse: I hate you! And, on my word, you'll pay for it!'

Just as she was saying these words, a knock on the ceiling

made her look up, and a voice called down to her through the floorboards, 'Dear Madame Bonacieux, open the little door to the alley and I will come and join you.'

XVIII
THE LOVER AND THE HUSBAND

'AH, MADAM,' SAID D'ARTAGNAN as he came through the door the young woman held open for him, 'if I may say, you have a sorry excuse for a husband there.'

'You heard our conversation, then?' demanded Madame Bonacieux, looking anxiously at d'Artagnan.

'Every word.'

'My God, how?'

'By a method I know that also allowed me to hear the livelier exchange you had with the cardinal's minions.'

'And what did you gather from what we said?'

'A thousand things: first, that your husband is a simpleton and a fool, thank goodness; then that you were in a quandary, which I was very pleased to hear about because it gives me the chance to put myself at your service, and God knows I would put my hand in the fire for you; lastly that the queen needs a brave, intelligent, loyal man to travel to London. I have at least two of the three qualities you need, and so here I am.'

Madame Bonacieux didn't reply, but joy made her heart race and her eyes shone with a secret hope.

'And what guarantee will you give me,' she asked, 'if I agree to entrust you with this mission?'

'My love for you. So, speak, give your orders: what has to be done?'

'My God! My God!' murmured the young woman. 'Ought I to entrust such a secret to you, sir? You are practically a child!'

'Come, I see you need someone to vouch for me.'

'I admit that would be very reassuring.'

'Do you know Athos?'

'No.'

'Porthos?'

'No.'

'Aramis?'

'No. Who are these gentlemen?'

'King's musketeers. Do you know Monsieur de Tréville, their captain?'

'Oh yes, him I do know – not personally, but I've heard him recommended more than once to the queen as a brave and loyal gentleman.'

'You're not afraid he would betray you to the cardinal, are you?'

'Oh no, certainly not.'

'Well then, reveal your secret to him, and, as important, as precious, as terrible as it may be, ask him whether you may not entrust it to me.'

'But the secret isn't mine and I can't reveal it in such a manner.'

'But you were going to entrust it to Monsieur Bonacieux,' d'Artagnan said resentfully.

'As you'd entrust a letter to the hollow of a tree, or the wing of a pigeon, or the collar of a dog.'

'But you can see I love you!'

'So you say.'

'I am a man of honour.'

'I believe it.'

'I am brave.'

'Oh, that I'm sure of.'

'Try me, then.'

Madame Bonacieux looked at the young man, still wavering slightly. But there was such ardour in his eyes, such persuasiveness in his voice, that she felt impelled to trust him. Besides, she was in one of those situations where you have to risk all to gain all. The queen would be damned by excessive caution just as much as she would be by excessive confidence. And, let's admit it, the involuntary feelings she entertained for her young protector also prompted her to speak out.

'Listen,' she said, 'I bow to your protestations and yield to your assurances. But I swear to you before God who hears us that if you betray me and I am pardoned by my enemies, I will kill myself and accuse you of my murder.'

'And I swear to you before God, madam,' said d'Artagnan, 'that if I am caught carrying out your orders, I will die before doing or saying anything that will compromise anyone.'

Then the young woman confided in him the terrible secret that chance had already partly revealed to him in front of the Samaritaine clock. This was their mutual declaration of love.

D'Artagnan was radiant with joy and pride. Sharing that secret, loving that woman – such trust and love made a giant of him.

'I'll go,' he said. 'I'll go at once.'

'What? You'll just go?' cried Madame Bonacieux. 'What about your regiment, your captain?'

'On my soul, you'd made me forget all that, dear Constance! Yes, you're right, I need a leave of absence.'

'Another obstacle,' Madame Bonacieux murmured sadly.

'Oh, don't worry,' cried d'Artagnan after a moment's thought, 'I'll overcome this one.'

'How?'

'I'll go and find Monsieur de Tréville this evening and charge him on my behalf to ask this favour of his brother-in-law, Monsieur des Essarts.'

'Now, another thing . . .'

'What?' asked d'Artagnan, seeing Madame Bonacieux hesitate.

'Perhaps you have no money?'

'Forget the "perhaps",' d'Artagnan said with a smile.

'Then,' said Madame Bonacieux, opening a wardrobe and taking from it the bag that her husband had been caressing so lovingly half an hour earlier, 'take this bag.'

'The cardinal's?' cried d'Artagnan, bursting into laughter – by removing his floor tiles, we will recall, he hadn't missed a syllable of the mercer's conversation with his wife.

'The cardinal's,' replied Madame Bonacieux. 'It looks quite respectable, as you see.'

'By God,' cried d'Artagnan, 'that will be twice as entertaining, saving the queen with His Eminence's money!'

'You are a kind and charming young man,' said Madame Bonacieux. 'Believe me, Her Majesty will not be ungrateful.'

'Oh, I am already lavishly rewarded!' cried d'Artagnan. 'I love you and you have let me tell you so: that alone is more happiness than I ever dared hope for!'

'Shh!' said Madame Bonacieux, starting.

'What?'

'Someone's talking in the street.'

'That's the voice . . .'

'Of my husband. Yes, I recognised it.'

D'Artagnan ran to the door and shot the bolt.

'He won't come in before I've gone,' he said. 'And once I've gone, you can open up for him.'

'But I ought to be gone too. How will I justify the money's disappearance if I'm here?'

'You're right, you have to leave.'

'Leave how? They'll see us if we go out by the door.'

'Then we'll have to go up to my rooms.'

'Ah,' exclaimed Madame Bonacieux. 'That frightens me, the way you say that!'

There were tears in Madame Bonacieux's eyes as she uttered these words. D'Artagnan saw them and, troubled and moved, fell to his knees.

'You will be as safe in my home,' he said, 'as if you were in a temple. I give you my word as a gentleman.'

'Let's go,' she said. 'I trust you, my friend.'

D'Artagnan carefully drew back the bolt and, light as shadows, the two of them slipped through the inner door into the alley, silently climbed the stairs, and entered d'Artagnan's lodgings.

Once inside, for added security, the young man barricaded the door. Then they both went over to the window, and, through a slat in the shutter, saw Monsieur Bonacieux talking with a man in a cloak.

At the sight of the man in the cloak, d'Artagnan started back and, half-drawing his sword, rushed for the door.

It was the man from Meung.

'What are you going to do?' cried Madame Bonacieux. 'You'll ruin us.'

'But I've sworn to kill that man!' said d'Artagnan.

'Your life is pledged to another now and no longer belongs to you. In the queen's name, I forbid you to expose yourself to any dangers other than those you will meet on your journey.'

'Have you no orders in your name?'

'In my name,' Madame Bonacieux burst out. 'In my name, I beg you not to. But let's listen to what they're saying. I think they're talking about me.'

D'Artagnan went back to the window and cocked an ear.

Monsieur Bonacieux had opened his front door and, seeing no one was at home, had rejoined the man in the cloak whom he had left on his own for a moment.

'She's gone,' he said. 'She'll have returned to the Louvre.'

'You're sure she didn't suspect why you left?' replied the stranger.

'No,' Bonacieux said smugly. 'She's a very superficial woman.'

'Is the cadet of the guards at home?'

'I don't think so. As you see, his shutters are closed, and there's no light coming through the slats.'

'Even so, we have to make sure.'

'How?'

'By knocking on his door.'

'I'll ask his valet.'

'Go on.'

Bonacieux went back inside, passed through the door that had given passage to the two fugitives, went up to d'Artagnan's landing, and knocked.

Nobody answered. To cut a grander figure, Porthos had borrowed Planchet for the evening. As for d'Artagnan, he took care not to give any sign of life.

When Bonacieux's knuckle rang out on the door, the two young people felt their hearts miss a beat.

'There's no one home,' said Bonacieux.

'No matter, let's still go inside: it will be more private than in a doorway.'

'Oh, my God,' murmured Madame Bonacieux, 'we won't hear anything now!'

'On the contrary,' said d'Artagnan, 'we'll hear all the better.'

Taking up the three or four tiles that made his room into another Ear of Dionysius¹, d'Artagnan spread a carpet on the floor, knelt down, and beckoned to Madame Bonacieux to bend down to the opening as he was doing.

'You're sure there's no one here?' asked the stranger.

'I guarantee it,' said Bonacieux.

'And you think your wife . . . ?'

'Has returned to the Louvre.'

'Without speaking to anyone except you?'

'I'm sure of it.'

'It's an important point, you understand?'

'So, the news I brought you is of some value?'

'Very great value, my dear Bonacieux, I will be perfectly frank with you.'

'So the cardinal will be pleased with me?'

'I have no doubt about that.'

'The great cardinal!'

'You are sure that, in her conversation with you, your wife didn't mention any proper names?'

'I don't believe so.'

'She didn't name Madame de Chevreuse or the Duke of Buckingham or Madame de Vernet?'

'No, she just told me she wanted to send me to London to serve the interests of an illustrious person.'

'The traitor!' murmured Madame Bonacieux.

'Shh,' said d'Artagnan, taking her hand, which she unthinkingly surrendered to him.

'All the same,' continued the man in the cloak, 'you're a fool not to have pretended to accept the mission. You'd have the letter now; the State, which is under threat, would be saved, and you . . .'

'And I?'

'Ah, you! The cardinal would have given you letters patent of nobility . . .'

'He told you that?'

'Yes, I know he was planning to surprise you with it.'

'Well, set your mind at rest!' declared Bonacieux. 'My wife adores me, and there is still time.'

'The fool,' murmured Madame Bonacieux.

'Shh,' said d'Artagnan, squeezing her hand more tightly.

'How is there still time?' demanded the man in the cloak.

'I'll go back to the Louvre, ask for Madame Bonacieux, and say I've been thinking, then I'll pick up where we left off, get the letter and then run to the cardinal's.'

'Off you go then, quick. I'll come back soon to find out what comes of your plan.'

The stranger went out.

'The villain!' said Madame Bonacieux, again aiming this epithet at her husband.

'Shh!' d'Artagnan repeated, squeezing her hand still tighter.

A terrible howling interrupted d'Artagnan and Madame Bonacieux's thoughts. It was her husband, who had noticed his bag had gone and was shouting, 'Stop, thief!'

'Oh, my God!' cried Madame Bonacieux. 'He'll bring out the whole neighbourhood.'

Bonacieux shouted for a long time, but as yelling of that sort was such a frequent occurrence that it never attracted anyone's attention

on Rue des Fossoyeurs – and, besides, the mercer's house had been
under something of a cloud for quite a while – he eventually realised
no one was going to come and left the house, still shouting. His voice
could be heard receding in the direction of Rue du Bac.

'And now he is gone, it's your turn to be off,' said Madame
Bonacieux. 'Be brave, but, above all, be careful. Remember that
you serve the queen.'

'Her and you!' cried d'Artagnan. 'Don't worry, beautiful
Constance, I will return worthy of her gratitude, but will I also
return worthy of your love?'

The young woman's only reply was a blush that turned her
cheeks bright red. A few moments later, d'Artagnan left in his
turn, similarly swathed in a great cloak, which was debonairly
hitched up at the back by the scabbard of a long sword.

Madame Bonacieux's eyes followed him with that long, loving
look a woman sends after the man she feels she loves, but when
he had disappeared around the corner of the street, she fell to her
knees, clasped her hands and cried, 'Oh, my God, protect the
queen, protect me!'

XIX

THE PLAN OF CAMPAIGN

D'ARTAGNAN WENT STRAIGHT to Monsieur de Tréville's. He
had assumed the cardinal would be informed in a matter of
minutes by that cursed stranger, who appeared to be his agent, and
rightly thought there wasn't a moment to lose.

The young man's heart was brimming over with joy. An opportunity had presented itself to him in which there was both glory
to be won and money to be gained, and, as a first incentive, had
just brought him together with a woman he adored. Chance
had thus, almost at first blush, done more for him than he would
ever have dared ask of Providence.

Monsieur de Tréville was in his reception room with his usual court of gentlemen. D'Artagnan, who was known as an intimate of the house, went straight to his office and sent word that he was waiting for him on a matter of importance.

D'Artagnan had scarcely been there five minutes before Monsieur de Tréville entered. At a glance, seeing the joy written all over his face, the worthy captain realised something new was clearly afoot.

On his way there, d'Artagnan had debated whether to confide in Monsieur de Tréville or simply ask him to give him a free hand in a secret affair. But Monsieur de Tréville had always been such a pillar of strength in their dealings, he was so unfailingly devoted to the king and queen, and he loathed the cardinal so cordially that the young man resolved to tell him everything.

'You asked for me, my young friend?' said Monsieur de Tréville.

'Yes, sir,' said d'Artagnan, 'and I hope you will forgive the interruption when you hear the important matter it is concerning.'

'Tell me, then, I am listening.'

'At stake,' said d'Artagnan, lowering his voice, 'is nothing less than the queen's honour and perhaps her life.'

'What are you saying?' asked Monsieur de Tréville, looking around to check they were alone and then turning his questioning gaze back to d'Artagnan.

'I am saying, sir, that chance has made me privy to a secret . . .'

'Which you will guard with your life, I trust, young man.'

'But I must confide it to you, sir, because you are the only person who can help in the mission I have just been given by Her Majesty.'

'Is this secret yours?'

'No, sir, it is the queen's.'

'Do you have Her Majesty's permission to tell it to me?'

'No, sir, on the contrary, I have been sworn to the strictest secrecy.'

'And so why were you going to betray it to me?'

'Because, as I say, I can't do anything without you, and I'm afraid you will refuse me the favour I have come to solicit from you if you don't know my reason for doing so.'

'Keep your secret, young man, and tell me what you want.'

'I wish you to obtain a fortnight's leave for me from Monsieur des Essarts.'

'Starting when?'

'Tonight.'

'You are leaving Paris?'

'I am going on a mission.'

'Can you tell me where?'

'To London.'

'Is it in anyone's interest for you not to reach your destination?'

'I believe the cardinal would give anything in the world to prevent me succeeding.'

'And you're going on your own?'

'I am going on my own.'

'In that case, you will not get past Bondy¹, I assure you, on the honour of the Trévilles.'

'Why?'

'You will be assassinated.'

'I will have died doing my duty.'

'But your mission won't have been carried out.'

'That's true,' said d'Artagnan.

'Believe me,' continued Tréville, 'in undertakings of this sort, four men are needed for one to succeed.'

'Ah, you're right, sir,' said d'Artagnan. 'But you know Athos, Porthos and Aramis, and you know I can call on them.'

'Without telling them the secret I have not inquired after?'

'We have sworn blind faith and unfailing devotion to one another. Besides, you can tell them that you have complete confidence in me, and they will be no more incredulous than you.'

'I can simply send each of them a fortnight's leave, so that

Athos, who is still suffering from his wound, can take the waters at Forges², and Porthos and Aramis can accompany their friend, whom they won't want to abandon when he is suffering so painfully. The dispatch of their leaves will be proof that I sanction their journey.'

'Thank you, sir, you are infinitely kind.'

'Go and find them this instant, then, and let everything be done tonight. Ah, but first write the request you want me to put to Monsieur des Essarts. You may have had a spy at your heels, and your visit, which in that case is already known to the cardinal, will be legitimised that way.'

D'Artagnan wrote out his application, and Monsieur de Tréville, taking it from him, assured him that the four leaves would be in the travellers' respective homes by two o'clock in the morning.

'Be so kind as to send mine to Athos's,' said d'Artagnan. 'I'd be afraid of trouble if I went home again.'

'Don't worry. Goodbye, and a good journey to you!' said Monsieur de Tréville, before calling him back. 'By the way . . .'

D'Artagnan retraced his steps.

'Do you have money?'

D'Artagnan jingled the bag he had in his pocket.

'Enough?' asked Monsieur de Tréville.

'Three hundred pistoles.'

'Very good. You can go to the end of the world with that. Away you go, then.'

D'Artagnan bowed to Monsieur de Tréville, who held out his hand to him. D'Artagnan shook it with a mixture of respect and gratitude. Since his arrival in Paris, he had had nothing but praise for this excellent man, whom he had always found to be worthy, loyal and noble.

His first visit was to Aramis. He had not been back to his friend's lodgings since that famous evening when he had followed Madame Bonacieux. Moreover, he had hardly seen the young musketeer since, and each time he had, he had thought he noticed the impress of a profound sadness on his face.

That evening too, Aramis sat up, lost in a sombre reverie. D'Artagnan questioned him a little about this deep melancholy. Aramis apologised, claiming to be very preoccupied by a commentary he had to write in Latin on the eighteenth chapter of St Augustine by the following week.

After the two friends had been talking for a few moments, one of Monsieur de Tréville's servants entered carrying a sealed packet.

'What is this?' asked Aramis.

'The leave of absence monsieur requested,' replied the servant.

'I haven't requested any leave.'

'Be quiet and take it,' said d'Artagnan. 'And you, my friend, here's a half-pistole for your trouble. Tell Monsieur de Tréville that Monsieur Aramis is sincerely grateful to him. Off you go.'

The valet bowed to the ground and left.

'What does this mean?' asked Aramis.

'Take what you'll need for a fortnight's journey and follow me.'

'But I can't leave Paris at present without knowing . . .'

Aramis paused.

'What's become of her, you mean?' continued d'Artagnan.

'Who?' replied Aramis.

'The lady who was here, the lady with the embroidered handkerchief.'

'Who told you there was a lady here?' Aramis retorted, turning deathly pale.

'I saw her.'

'And you know who she is?'

'I think I can guess, at least.'

'Listen,' said Aramis, 'since you know so much, do you know what's become of that lady?'

'I presume she's gone back to Tours.'

'To Tours? Yes, that's right, you do know her. But why did she go back to Tours without saying anything to me?'

'Because she was afraid of being arrested.'

'Why didn't she write to me?'

'Because she was afraid of compromising you.'

'D'Artagnan, you've brought me back to life!' cried Aramis. 'I thought I was scorned, betrayed. I was so happy to see her again! I couldn't believe she'd risked her freedom for me, and yet what other cause could have led her to return to Paris?'

'The same cause that sends us to England today.'

'And what cause is that?' asked Aramis.

'You'll find out one day, Aramis, but for the moment I'll imitate the discretion of the doctor's niece.'

Aramis smiled, remembering the story he had told his friends one evening.

'Well then, since she has left Paris and you are sure of it, d'Artagnan, there's nothing stopping me any more and I am ready to follow you. You say we're going . . .'

'To Athos's for the moment, and if you wish to come, perhaps I could ask you to make haste, because we've already lost a lot of time. Tell Bazin, by the way.'

'Is Bazin coming with us?' asked Aramis.

'Perhaps. In any case, it is well if he comes with us to Athos's for now.'

Aramis called Bazin and, after ordering him to meet them at Athos's, said, 'Let's go then.' He grabbed his cloak, his sword and three pistols, and vainly opened three or four drawers to see if he mightn't find a stray pistole. Then, once he was convinced of the futility of his search, he followed d'Artagnan, wondering how it was that the young cadet of the guards knew as well as he did who the lady to whom he had given hospitality was, and knew better than he did what had become of her.

As they were leaving, Aramis put his hand on d'Artagnan's arm, and, looking intently at him, said, 'You haven't mentioned this lady to anyone?'

'No one in the world.'

'Not even Athos and Porthos?'

'I haven't breathed a single word to them.'

'Well done!'

And then, reassured on this important point, Aramis carried on his way with d'Artagnan, and the two of them were soon at Athos's door.

They found him holding his leave of absence in one hand and Monsieur de Tréville's letter in the other.

'Can you explain to me the meaning of this leave and this letter I've just received?' asked the surprised Athos.

My dear Athos,
    I would like you to take the fortnight's rest your health urgently requires. Go and take the waters at Forges, or anywhere else that suits you, and get well quickly.
        Your affectionate,
        Tréville

'Well, this leave and this letter mean that you have to come with me, Athos.'

'To the waters at Forges?'

'There or somewhere else.'

'On the king's service?'

'The king's or the queen's. Are we not Their Majesties' servants?'

At that moment, Porthos entered.

'By God,' he said, 'here's a strange thing. Since when are musketeers granted leaves of absence they haven't requested?'

'Since they've had friends who request them on their behalf,' said d'Artagnan.

'Aha!' said Porthos. 'It seems there's something new here?'

'Yes, we're leaving,' said Aramis.

'For what country?' asked Porthos.

'My faith, I've no idea,' said Athos. 'Ask d'Artagnan.'

'For London,' said d'Artagnan.

'For London?' cried Porthos. 'And what are we going to do in London?'

'That's what I can't tell you, gentlemen; you'll have to trust me.'

'But you need money to go to London,' added Porthos, 'and I don't have any.'

'Nor do I,' said Aramis.

'Nor do I,' said Athos.

'I do,' replied d'Artagnan, taking his treasure from his pocket and putting it on the table. 'There's three hundred pistoles in that bag. Let's each take seventy-five: that is all you need to go to London and back. Besides, rest assured, not all of us will get to London.'

'And why's that?'

'Because in all probability some of us will be left by the wayside.'

'What, are we going on a campaign?'

'And a most dangerous one, I warn you.'

'Now then, since we're risking our lives,' said Porthos, 'I'd like to at least know why.'

'A lot of good that will do you!' said Athos.

'Nevertheless,' said Aramis, 'I am of Porthos's way of thinking.'

'Is the king in the habit of giving you explanations? No, he just tells you, "Gentlemen, there's fighting in Gascony or in Flanders; go and fight," and you go. Why? You don't even concern yourselves about that.'

'D'Artagnan is right,' Athos said. 'Here are our three leaves from Monsieur de Tréville and here are three hundred pistoles from I don't know where. Let's go and get ourselves killed where we are told to go. Is life worth the trouble of asking so many questions? D'Artagnan, I'm ready to follow you.'

'And I am too,' said Porthos.

'And I am too,' said Aramis. 'In any case, I'm not sorry to leave Paris; I need distractions.'

'Well, you'll have those, gentlemen, don't worry about that,' said d'Artagnan.

'And now, when are we leaving?' said Athos.

'Straightaway,' answered d'Artagnan. 'There isn't a moment to lose.'

'Ho there, Grimaud, Planchet, Mousqueton, Bazin!' the four young men cried, summoning their valets. 'Polish our boots and bring the horses from the stables.'

Indeed, each musketeer left his and his valet's horse at the general stables as if at a barracks.

Planchet, Grimaud, Mousqueton and Bazin set off post-haste.

'Now, let's draw up a plan of campaign,' said Porthos. 'Where are we going first?'

'To Calais,' said d'Artagnan. 'That's the most direct route to London.'

'Well then, here's my opinion,' said Porthos.

'Speak.'

'Four men travelling together would arouse suspicion. So, d'Artagnan will give each of us his instructions: I'll go ahead on the Boulogne road to clear the way; Athos will leave two hours later by the Amiens road; then Aramis will follow us by the Noyon road. As for d'Artagnan, he can take whichever road he pleases, in Planchet's clothes, while Planchet will follow us dressed as d'Artagnan in guard's uniform.'

'Gentlemen,' said Athos, 'in my opinion, it's inadvisable to involve valets at all in an affair of this sort. A secret may accidentally be betrayed by a gentleman, but it will almost always be sold by a valet.'

'Porthos's plan also seems unworkable to me,' said d'Artagnan, 'in that I don't myself know what instructions I can give you. I am the bearer of a letter, that's all. I don't have and I can't make three copies of this letter, since it is sealed, so, in my opinion, that means we have to travel together. The letter is here,' he said, pointing to one of his pockets which contained the letter. 'If I'm killed, one of you will take it and you will carry on your way. If he is killed, it will be someone else's turn, and so on. As long as one of us gets there, that's all that's needed.'

'Bravo, d'Artagnan! We are of the same opinion,' said Athos.

'Besides, we have to be consistent. I'm going to take the waters and you're going to keep me company, but instead of the waters at Forges, I'm going to take the waters at the sea – I'm free to choose. If they try to arrest us, I show Monsieur de Tréville's letter and you show your leaves of absence. If they attack us, we defend ourselves. If we are tried, we stoutly maintain that our only intention was to soak in the sea a certain number of times. They would make short shrift of four men travelling on their own, but four travelling together form a troop. We will arm our four valets with pistols and carbines. If they send an army against us, we will give battle, and whoever survives, as d'Artagnan said, will take the letter.'

'Well said!' cried Aramis. 'You don't speak often, Athos, but when you do, it's like St John Golden Mouth[3]. I adopt Athos's plan. What about you, Porthos?'

'I do too, if it suits d'Artagnan,' said Porthos. 'As bearer of the letter, d'Artagnan is naturally the leader of this enterprise. Let him make the decision and we will carry it out.'

'Well, then,' said d'Artagnan. 'My decision is to adopt Athos's plan and leave in half an hour.'

'Adopted!' the three musketeers chorused.

And then each of them reached a hand out to the bag, took seventy-five pistoles, and set about preparing to leave at the appointed time.

XX

THE JOURNEY

At two o'clock in the morning, our four adventurers left Paris by the Porte Saint-Denis. While the night lasted, they remained silent; despite themselves, they fell under the influence of the darkness and saw ambushes on all sides.

But at the first rays of dawn, their tongues loosened, and with

the sun, their high spirits returned. It was like the eve of a battle:
their hearts beat faster, their eyes laughed, and they felt that this
life they might be about to depart was, all in all, a good thing.

Their caravan, moreover, presented a most formidable aspect:
the black horses of the musketeers, their martial bearing, that
squadron's habit which makes these soldier's noble companions
walk in step – all of this would have betrayed the strictest
incognito.

And behind them rode the valets, armed to the teeth.

All went well until Chantilly, which they reached at about
eight o'clock in the morning. It was breakfast time. They
dismounted outside an inn recommended by a sign showing St
Martin giving half his cloak to a poor man. The valets were
instructed not to unsaddle the horses and to be ready to start again
immediately.

They went into the public room and sat down at the table.

A gentleman who had just arrived by the Dammartin road was
already sitting there having breakfast. He struck up conversation
about this and that; the travellers replied. He drank their health;
the travellers returned the courtesy.

But when Mousqueton came in to announce the horses were
ready and they got up from the table, the stranger proposed to
Porthos that they drink the cardinal's health. Porthos replied that
he would like nothing better provided the stranger drank the king's
health in return. The stranger cried that he knew of no king other
than His Eminence. Porthos called him a drunkard; the stranger
drew his sword.

'That was foolish of you,' said Athos. 'No matter, there's no
turning back now. Kill the man and catch us up as fast as you can.'

And then all three mounted their horses again and sped off,
leaving Porthos promising his adversary he was going to perforate
him with every hit known to fencing.

'One down!' said Athos after they had gone five hundred paces.

'But why did the man attack Porthos in particular?' asked
Aramis.

'Porthos talks louder than the rest of us, so he took him for the leader,' said d'Artagnan.

'I've always said this young Gascon was a fount of wisdom,' murmured Athos.

And then the travellers carried on their way.

At Beauvais they stopped for two hours, as much to let the horses get their breath back as to wait for Porthos. After two hours, when neither Porthos nor any word of him had arrived, they set off again.

A league from Beauvais, in a place where the highway narrowed between two banks, they came upon eight or ten men who, taking advantage of the fact the road was unpaved there, were engaged in some sort of work, digging holes and gouging out muddy ruts.

Aramis, who was afraid of getting his boots dirty in the man-made quagmire, upbraided them sharply. Athos tried to restrain him, but it was too late. The workers began to jeer at the travellers and, with their insolence, managed to make even the imperturbable Athos lose his head and drive his horse at one of them.

At this, each of the men fell back to the ditch and produced a hidden musket, whereupon our seven travellers found themselves literally facing a firing squad. Aramis was hit by a bullet that went through his shoulder and Mousqueton by another that lodged in the fleshy parts beneath the lower back. Only Mousqueton, however, fell off his horse, which indicated not that he was seriously wounded but that, as he couldn't see his wound, he doubtless thought it was more dangerous than was in fact the case.

'It's an ambush,' said d'Artagnan, 'don't return fire, keep going!'

Aramis, severely wounded as he was, clung to the mane of his horse, which carried him off with the others. Catching them up, Mousqueton's mount galloped along riderless in its previous place.

'We'll have a spare horse now,' said Athos.

'I'd rather a spare hat,' said d'Artagnan, 'mine was blown off by a bullet. My faith, it's lucky the letter I'm carrying wasn't inside it.'

'Ah, but they'll kill poor Porthos when he comes along!' said Aramis.

'If Porthos could stand upright, he would have caught us up by now,' said Athos. 'I have a feeling that drunkard will have sobered up once the duel started.'

And then they galloped on for another two hours, although their horses were so tired it was to be feared they might soon withhold their labours.

The travellers cut across country, hoping thereby to run into less trouble that way, but at Crèvecœur, Aramis declared he couldn't go any further. As it was, it had required all the courage he concealed under his natural elegance and polished manners for him to get that far. He was growing paler by the instant and had to be held steady in the saddle. They set him down at the door of a tavern, left Bazin with him, who was, in any case, more of a hindrance than a help in a skirmish, and then set off again, hoping to spend the night in Amiens.

'Good grief!' said Athos, when they were on their way again, their number now reduced to two masters and Grimaud and Planchet. 'Good grief, I won't be their dupe again. Mark my words, they won't make me open my mouth or draw my sword from here to Calais. I swear . . .'

'Instead of swearing,' said d'Artagnan, 'let's gallop – if our horses will consent, that is.'

And then the travellers clapped their spurs into their horses' ribs, which, thus vigorously stimulated, had a second wind. They reached Amiens at midnight and alighted at the Golden Lily.

The innkeeper, who greeted the travellers with his candlestick in one hand and his cotton nightcap in the other, looked like the most honest man on God's earth. He wanted to put each of the travellers in a charming room, the only drawback being that these rooms were at either ends of the inn. D'Artagnan and Athos refused. The host replied that he had no other rooms worthy of Their Excellencies, but the travellers declared they would sleep in the public room, each on a mattress thrown on the floor. The host insisted, the travellers held their ground, and in the end he had to do as they wished.

They had just made up their beds and barricaded their door from inside when someone knocked on the courtyard shutter. On asking who was there, they recognised their valets' voices and opened the window.

It was indeed Planchet and Grimaud.

'Grimaud will be able to guard the horses on his own,' said Planchet. 'If the gentlemen like, I can sleep across their door. That way, they can be sure no one will be able to get to them.'

'And what will you sleep on?' said d'Artagnan.

'Here's my bed,' replied Planchet, pointing to a bundle of straw.

'Come on, then,' said d'Artagnan. 'I agree with you. I don't care for that innkeeper's face, it's too friendly.'

'I don't either,' said Athos.

Planchet climbed through the window and settled down across the door, while Grimaud went to lock himself in the stables, promising that he and the four horses would be ready at five o'clock in the morning.

The night was quiet enough. Someone tried to open the door at two o'clock, but when Planchet awoke with a start and cried, 'Who goes there?' the intruder replied he was mistaken and went away.

At four o'clock in the morning, a great noise was heard coming from the stables. Grimaud had wanted to wake up the stable boys and, for his pains, had received a terrible beating. When they opened the window they saw the poor lad lying unconscious, his head split open by a blow from a pitchfork handle.

Planchet went down into the yard to saddle the horses but found them broken down with exhaustion. The only one that might have carried on was Mousqueton's mount, which had been riderless for five or six hours the previous day, but, by some inconceivable mix-up, the veterinary surgeon, who apparently had been brought to bleed the landlord's horse, had bled Mousqueton's instead.

This was starting to be unnerving: all these accidents coming one after the other might be a coincidence, but they could just as well be the outcome of a plot. Athos and d'Artagnan took a turn in the courtyard, while Planchet went to inquire whether there were three horses for sale locally. At the gate stood two saddled, fresh, vigorous horses. They would be perfect. He asked where their masters were, and was told they had spent the night at the inn and were at that moment settling up with the innkeeper.

Athos went down to pay their bill, while d'Artagnan and Planchet waited at the street door. The innkeeper was in a low, back room, which Athos was sent through to.

Athos entered unsuspectingly and took out two pistoles to pay. The innkeeper was alone and sitting at his desk, one of the drawers of which was half open. He took the money Athos gave him, turned it this way and that in his hands, and then suddenly cried out that the coins were fake and that he was going to have him and his companion arrested as counterfeiters.

'Rascal!' said Athos, marching over to him. 'I'll cut your ears off!'

At the same moment, four men armed to the teeth burst in by side doors and threw themselves on Athos.

'They've got me!' Athos shouted with all the breath in his lungs. 'Get away, d'Artagnan! Go, go!' And he let off two pistol shots.

D'Artagnan and Planchet did not need to be told twice. They untethered the two horses waiting by the gate, sprang into the saddles, dug their spurs into their flanks and rode off at full gallop.

'Do you know what's become of Athos?' d'Artagnan asked Planchet as they raced along.

'Ah, sir,' said Planchet, 'I saw two of them fall at his two shots, and it looked, through the glass door, as if he was clashing swords with the others.'

'Brave Athos,' murmured d'Artagnan. 'And to think we have to abandon him! What's more, the same may be awaiting us a few paces from here. Forward, Planchet, forward! You are a brave man.'

'I told you, sir,' replied Planchet, 'you get to know a Picard over time. Besides, I'm in my own country here, and that puts me on my mettle.'

And then the two of them, spurring on the horses harder than ever, rode to Saint-Omer without stopping. At Saint-Omer, they let the horses rest, the bridles looped over their arms in case of an accident, ate a quick bite standing in the street, and then set off again.

A hundred paces from the gates of Calais, d'Artagnan's horse collapsed beneath him and couldn't be got to its feet. Blood was streaming from its nose and eyes. That left Planchet's horse, but it had halted and nothing could make it budge.

Fortunately, as we have said, they were only a hundred paces from the town, so they left their two mounts on the highway and ran to the port. Planchet pointed out to his master a gentleman who had just arrived with his valet and was only fifty paces or so in front of them.

They walked briskly up to the gentleman, who appeared to be in a tremendous hurry. His boots were covered with dust, and he was inquiring whether he mightn't cross to England immediately.

'Nothing would be easier,' replied the skipper of a vessel ready to sail, 'but an order arrived this morning not to let anyone leave without the express permission of the cardinal.'

'I have that permission,' said the gentleman, taking a paper from his pocket. 'Here it is.'

'Have it countersigned by the governor of the port,' said the skipper, 'then give me your preference.'

'Where shall I find the governor?'

'At his country house.'

'And this country house is situated . . . ?'

'A quarter of a league from town. Look, you can see it from here, at the foot of the little hill – that slate roof.'

'Very good!' said the gentleman.

And then, followed by his valet, he took the road leading to the governor's country house.

D'Artagnan and Planchet followed them at a distance of five hundred paces.

Once they were out of the town, d'Artagnan quickened his pace and caught up with the gentleman as he entered a small wood.

'Sir,' said d'Artagnan, 'you seem in a great hurry?'

'One couldn't be in more of one, sir.'

'I'm very sorry for that,' said d'Artagnan, 'since, as I'm in a great hurry too, I wanted to ask you to do me a service.'

'What?'

'Let me go first.'

'Impossible,' said the gentleman, 'I have travelled sixty leagues in forty-four hours, and I have to be in London by noon tomorrow.'

'I have covered the same distance in forty hours, and I have to be in London by ten o'clock tomorrow morning.'

'Very sorry, sir, but I arrived first and I will not go second.'

'Very sorry, sir, but I arrived second and I will go first.'

'On the king's service!' said the gentleman.

'On my own service!' d'Artagnan.

'This is an ugly quarrel you're trying to pick with me, it seems.'

'By heaven, what would you rather it be?'

'What do you want?'

'Would you like to know?'

'Certainly.'

'Well then, I want the order you're carrying, seeing as I don't have one myself and I have need of it.'

'You're joking, I presume.'

'I never joke.'

'Let me pass!'

'You shall not pass.'

'My brave young man, I'm going to blow your brains out. Ho there, Lubin! My pistols.'

'Planchet,' said d'Artagnan, 'see to the valet, I'll see to the master.'

Planchet, emboldened by his first exploit, leapt on Lubin, and, being a strong, vigorous fellow, he knocked him flat on his back and planted his knee on his chest.

'Attend to your business, sir,' said Planchet. 'I've attended to mine.'

Seeing this, the gentleman drew his sword and fell on d'Artagnan, but he was dealing with a tough customer.

In three seconds d'Artagnan had dealt him three sword thrusts, declaring at each lunge:

'One for Athos, one for Porthos, one for Aramis.'

At the third thrust, the gentleman crumpled in a heap.

D'Artagnan thought he was dead, or at least unconscious, and went over to take the order. But when he reached out a hand to search him, the wounded man, who hadn't let go of his sword, stabbed him in the chest, saying, 'One for you.'

'Yes, one for me!' d'Artagnan cried furiously, pinning him to the ground with a fourth thrust to the stomach. 'Last come, best served!'

This time the gentleman closed his eyes and lost consciousness.

D'Artagnan searched through the pocket where he had seen him put the order of passage and relieved him of the document. It was made out in the name of Count de Wardes[1].

Then, with a last glance at the handsome young man – he could hardly have been twenty-five years old – whom he was leaving sprawled on the ground, unconscious, perhaps dead, he heaved a sigh over the strange fate that leads men to destroy one another in the interests of people who are strangers to them and often have no idea they even exist.

But he was soon distracted from these thoughts by Lubin, who was howling and shouting for help with all his might.

Planchet grabbed his throat and squeezed as hard as he could.

'Sir,' he said, 'as long as I hold him like this, he won't cry out, I'm sure of that. But the minute I let him go, he'll start again. He's a Norman, I can tell, and Normans are a stubborn lot.'

And indeed, despite having the life squeezed out of him, Lubin was still trying to emit a steady noise.

'Wait!' said d'Artagnan.

And taking his handkerchief, he gagged him.

'Now,' said Planchet, 'let's tie him to a tree.'

They made a conscientious job of this, then dragged the Count de Wardes close to his servant. As night was falling and the bound man and wounded man were both a few paces inside the wood, it was clear they would be staying there until the following morning.

'And now,' said d'Artagnan, 'to the governor's!'

'But I think you're wounded, aren't you?' said Planchet.

'It's nothing. Let's deal with what's most pressing first and then we'll come back to my wound, which doesn't, in any case, appear too serious.'

And then they both strode off towards the worthy functionary's country retreat.

The Count de Wardes was announced, and d'Artagnan was shown in.

'You have an order signed by the cardinal?' asked the governor.

'Yes, sir,' answered d'Artagnan. 'Here it is.'

'Ah . . . It is all correct and duly endorsed,' said the governor.

'Naturally,' said d'Artagnan. 'I am one of his most loyal servants.'

'It appears His Eminence wishes to prevent someone reaching England.'

'Yes, a certain d'Artagnan, a gentleman from Béarn who has left Paris with three of his friends, intending to go to London.'

'Do you know him personally?' asked the governor.

'Whom?'

'This d'Artagnan.'

'Extremely well.'

'Give me his description, then.'

'Nothing could be easier.'

Whereupon d'Artagnan gave an exact description of the Count de Wardes.

'Is there anyone with him?' asked the governor.

'Yes, a valet named Lubin.'

'We will keep watch for them, and if we lay hands on them, His Eminence may rest assured that they will be sent back to Paris under tight guard.'

'If you do so, sir,' said d'Artagnan, 'the cardinal will be in your debt.'

'You will see him on your return, my lord?'

'Certainly.'

'Tell him, pray, that I am his humble servant.'

'I shall do so without fail.'

Delighted by this assurance, the governor then countersigned the pass and returned it to d'Artagnan.

Wasting no time on superfluous compliments, d'Artagnan bowed, thanked the governor, and left.

Once outside, he and Planchet hurried off and, making a long detour, they avoided the wood and came back into the town by another gate.

The vessel was still ready to sail and the skipper was waiting on the dock.

'Well?' he said when he saw d'Artagnan.

'Here is my pass countersigned,' said the latter.

'And that other gentleman?'

'He won't be leaving today,' said d'Artagnan. 'But don't worry, I'll pay for both our passages.'

'In that case, let's be off,' said the skipper.

'Let's be off!' repeated d'Artagnan.

And then he leapt into the skiff with Planchet, and five minutes later they were on board.

Not a moment too soon: when they were half a league out to sea, d'Artagnan saw a flash of light and heard a detonation. It was a cannon shot announcing the closure of the port.

The time had come to tend to his wound. Luckily, as d'Artagnan had thought, it wasn't very serious. The sword-point had hit a rib and slid along the bone. Moreover, his shirt had stuck to the wound immediately, so he'd only shed a few drops of blood.

D'Artagnan was worn out. A mattress was laid out for him on deck. He threw himself down on it and fell asleep.

The next day, at daybreak, he found himself still three or four leagues off the English coast. The wind had been weak all night, and they had made little progress.

At ten o'clock the vessel dropped anchor in the port of Dover.

At half-past ten d'Artagnan set foot on English soil, exclaiming, 'Here I am at last!'

But that wasn't an end to it: he still had to get to London. The post roads were relatively well served in England so d'Artagnan and Planchet each took a nag and a postilion galloped ahead of them. Within four hours they were at the gates of the capital.

D'Artagnan didn't know London, nor did he know a word of English, but when he wrote the name Buckingham on a piece of paper, everyone pointed him in the direction of the duke's townhouse.

The duke was hunting at Windsor with the king.

D'Artagnan asked for the duke's confidential valet, who, having accompanied him on all his travels, spoke perfect French. He told him he had come from Paris on a matter of life and death and that he must see his master that instant.

The self-assurance with which d'Artagnan spoke convinced Patrick, as this minister's minister was called. He had two horses saddled and took it upon himself to show the young guard the way. As for Planchet, he had to be helped off his horse as stiff as a board; the poor lad was shattered. D'Artagnan, for his part, seemed made of iron.

They reached the castle, where they learnt the king and Buckingham were hawking in marshes some two or three leagues away.

In twenty minutes they were at the place. Patrick soon heard the voice of his master, who was calling his falcon.

'Whom should I announce to my lord duke?' Patrick asked.

'The young man who sought a quarrel with him one evening on the Pont-Neuf, opposite the Samaritaine clock.'

'A singular introduction!'

'You'll see it's as good as any other.'

Patrick put his horse into a gallop, found the duke, and informed him in the terms we've relayed that a messenger was waiting for him.

Buckingham recognised the name d'Artagnan instantly, and suspecting he was being sent word of events in France, stopped only to ask the whereabouts of the person bringing it. Recognising the guards uniform from a distance, he urged on his horse and galloped straight to d'Artagnan, while Patrick discreetly kept his distance.

'No misfortune has befallen the queen, has it?' cried Buckingham, pouring all his care and all his love into the question.

'I don't believe so. But I believe she is in great danger, from which Your Grace alone can save her.'

'I?' cried Buckingham. 'What is it? I would be happy indeed if I could be of some use to her! Speak! Speak!'

'Take this letter,' said d'Artagnan.

'This letter? Who is this letter from?'

'From Her Majesty, I think.'

'From Her Majesty,' said Buckingham, turning so pale d'Artagnan thought he was about to faint.

And then he broke the seal.

'What's this tear?' he said, showing d'Artagnan where the paper had been run through.

'Aha!' said d'Artagnan, 'I hadn't seen that. Count de Wardes's sword must have left that trophy when it pierced my chest.'

'Are you hurt?' asked Buckingham.

'Oh, it's nothing,' said d'Artagnan, 'a scratch.'

'God's heavens, what's this I am reading?' cried the duke. 'Patrick, stay here – no, go and find the king, wherever he may be, and tell His Majesty that I humbly beg him to excuse me, but

I am called back to London on a matter of the utmost importance. Come, sir, come.'

And then the two of them set off at a gallop on the road to the capital.

XXI
THE COUNTESS DE WINTER

THE DUKE SPENT THE JOURNEY being brought up to date by d'Artagnan about recent events, or rather as much as d'Artagnan knew of them. By comparing what he heard from the young man's lips with his memories, he could form a passably accurate idea of the situation, the gravity of which he had already been able to gauge from the queen's letter, brief and inexplicit though it was. But what most astonished him was that, given the cardinal's interest in the young man not setting foot in England, he hadn't managed to stop him on his way. When he gave voice to this astonishment, d'Artagnan told him the precautions he had taken, and how, thanks to the devotion of his three friends, whom he had left bleeding along the roadside, he had come through unscathed apart from the sword thrust that had pierced the queen's letter, for which he had repaid the Count de Wardes in such terrible coin. As he listened to this account, which was delivered with the utmost simplicity, the duke looked from time to time with astonishment at the young man, as if he could not understand how so much prudence, courage and devotion could be allied to a face that had not yet been marked by the passage of so much as twenty years.

The horses went like the wind, and within minutes they were at the gates of London. D'Artagnan had thought the duke would slow his pace when they reached town, but that wasn't the case. He tore along at break-neck speed, caring little about whether he knocked down anyone in his path. Indeed, as they crossed the city, two or three accidents of this kind occurred, but Buckingham didn't so much as turn his head to see what had become of those he had sent flying. D'Artagnan followed amid shouts that sounded strikingly like curses.

On entering the courtyard of his townhouse¹, Buckingham sprang from his horse and, unconcerned about what would become of the creature, threw the bridle over its neck and rushed towards the steps. D'Artagnan followed suit, although rather more concerned for the wellbeing of those noble animals whose worth he had come to appreciate. He was reassured to see three or four servants had already come running from the kitchens and stables, and were without delay taking charge of the horses.

The duke walked so fast that d'Artagnan had trouble keeping up. He passed through several reception rooms of an elegance that the greatest lords of France couldn't even conceive of, and came finally to a bedroom that was at once a miracle of taste and sumptuousness. In the alcove of this chamber was a door set into the tapestry. The duke opened it with a little gold key that he kept round his neck on a chain of the same metal. D'Artagnan discreetly hung back, but as Buckingham stepped over the threshold, he turned and, seeing the young man's hesitation, said, 'Come, and if you are fortunate enough to be admitted into Her Majesty's presence, tell her what you've seen.'

Encouraged by this invitation, d'Artagnan followed the duke, who closed the door behind them.

The two of them then found themselves in a small chapel all hung with Persian silk and gold brocade, and dazzlingly lit with a multitude of candles. Above a kind of altar, and beneath a blue velvet canopy topped with white and red plumes, hung a life-size portrait of Anne of Austria that was so exact a likeness that d'Artagnan cried out in surprise: the queen looked for all the world as if she were about to speak.

On the altar, and beneath the portrait, was the box containing the diamond tags.

The duke went up to the altar, knelt as a priest might have before Christ, and then opened the box.

'Here,' he said, taking from the box a large blue ribbon bow all sparkling with diamonds, 'these are the precious tags which I had sworn to be buried with. The queen gave them to me, now the queen takes them back from me: her will, like God's, be done in all things.'

Then he began kissing, one by one, the tags from which he was fated to be parted. Suddenly he uttered a terrible cry.

'What is it?' asked d'Artagnan anxiously. 'What has happened to you, my lord?'

'All is lost,' cried Buckingham, turning as pale as a corpse. 'Two of the tags are missing. There are only ten left.'

'Has my lord lost them, or does he think they've been stolen?'

'They've been stolen,' said the duke, 'and it is the cardinal's handiwork. Here, look, the ribbons holding them have been cut with scissors.'

'If my lord had any suspicions as to who committed the theft . . . The person may still have them in his possession.'

'Wait, wait!' cried the duke. 'The only time I wore the tags was at the king's ball eight days ago at Windsor. The Countess de Winter, whom I had fallen out with, came up to me at that ball. Her reconciliation was the revenge of a jealous woman. I haven't seen her since. That woman is an agent of the cardinal.'

'He has them in every corner of the world, then?' cried d'Artagnan.

'Oh, yes, yes,' Buckingham said, grinding his teeth furiously, 'yes, he is a terrible adversary. At all events, when is this ball due to take place?'

'Next Monday.'

'Next Monday! Five days, that's more than enough time for us. Patrick!' cried the duke, opening the door of the chapel. 'Patrick!'

His confidential valet appeared.

'My jeweller and my secretary!'

The valet went out with an alacrity and silence that testified to a habit of blind, wordless obedience.

The jeweller had been sent for first, but it was the secretary – naturally enough, since he lived in the townhouse – who was the first to appear. He found Buckingham sitting at a table in his bedroom, writing orders in his own hand.

'Mr Jackson,' he said, 'you will go at once to the Lord Chancellor's and inform him I am charging him with executing these orders. I wish them to be promulgated immediately.'

'But, my lord, if the Lord Chancellor questions me about Your Grace's motives for so extraordinary a measure, what shall I reply?'

'That such is my good pleasure, and that I have no need to account to anyone for my wishes.'

'Should I also transmit that reply to His Majesty,' the secretary asked with a smile, 'if by chance His Majesty is curious to know why no vessel may leave Great Britain's ports?'

'You're right, sir,' said Buckingham. 'In that case you would tell the king that I have decided on war, and that this measure is my first act of hostility against France.'

The secretary bowed and left.

'There, we can rest easy on that score,' said Buckingham, turning towards d'Artagnan. 'If the tags haven't already left for France, they won't arrive before you now.'

'Why is that?'

'I have just placed an embargo on every ship presently in His Majesty's ports and, without special permission, not one of them will dare weigh anchor.'

D'Artagnan looked with stupefaction at this man, who would place the unlimited power vested in him by a king's confidence at the service of his love. Buckingham saw what the young man was thinking from the expression on his face and smiled.

'Yes,' he said, 'yes, Anne of Austria is my true queen. At a word from her, I would betray my country, I would betray my king, I would betray my God. She asked me not to send the Protestants of La Rochelle the aid I had promised them and I complied. I broke my word, but what does that matter – I obeyed her wish. Tell me, wasn't I richly rewarded for my obedience, since it is to that obedience that I owe her portrait?'

D'Artagnan marvelled at the fragile and unknown threads by which the destinies of nations and the lives of men sometimes hang.

He was lost in thought when the goldsmith entered. An Irishman, one of the most skilled practitioners of his art, he was the first to admit that he earned a hundred thousand livres a year from the Duke of Buckingham.

'Mr O'Reilly,' said the duke, leading him into the chapel, 'take a look at these diamond tags, and tell me what they are worth apiece.'

The jeweller cast a brief glance at the elegant mountings, calculated the average value of the diamonds, and replied without hesitation, 'Fifteen hundred pistoles, my lord.'

'How many days would it take to make two tags like these? You see two are missing.'

'A week, my lord.'

'I'll pay three thousand pistoles apiece for them, but I need them the day after tomorrow.'

'My lord will have them.'

'You are an invaluable man, Mr O'Reilly. But that's not all: these tags cannot be entrusted to anyone, they have to be made here in the palace.'

'Impossible, my lord, I am the only person who can do the work so you won't see the difference between the old and the new tags.'

'In that case, my dear Mr O'Reilly, you are my prisoner and if you wished to leave my palace now, you would be unable to do so. So, make the best of it. Give me the names of the assistants you will need and tell me which tools they are to bring.'

The goldsmith was acquainted with the duke and knew that it would be useless to pass any comment, so he duly made the best of it.

'Will I be permitted to tell my wife?' he asked.

'Oh, you will even be permitted to see her, my dear Mr O'Reilly. Your captivity will be benign, don't worry, and as every inconvenience deserves compensation, here is a bond for a thousand pistoles, in addition to the price of the two tags, to help you forget the trouble I am causing you.'

D'Artagnan could not get over his surprise at this minister, who constantly shuffled men and millions in gold.

As for the goldsmith, he wrote to his wife, enclosing the bond for a thousand pistoles, with instructions to send him in exchange his most skilled apprentice, an assortment of diamonds, of which he specified the weight and the grade, and a list of the tools he needed.

Buckingham showed the goldsmith to the room allocated to him, which was transformed into a workshop in half an hour. Then he posted a sentry at each door, with orders not to let anyone in apart from his valet Patrick. It goes without saying that O'Reilly, the goldsmith, and his assistant were strictly forbidden to leave the room on any pretext whatsoever. Once this was settled, the duke returned to d'Artagnan.

'Now, my young friend,' he said. 'England is ours. What are your wishes, what do you desire?'

'A bed,' replied d'Artagnan. 'I confess that, at the moment, that's what I need most.'

Buckingham gave d'Artagnan a room adjoining his own. He wanted to keep the young man near at hand, not out of any mistrust, but so that he could have someone to talk to constantly about the queen.

An hour later, the order was promulgated in London that no vessel laden for France could leave port, not even the mail ship. Everyone took this as a declaration of war between the two kingdoms.

Two days later, at eleven o'clock, the two diamond tags were finished. They were copied so exactly, and so perfectly identical, that Buckingham could not tell the new tags from the old, and the greatest experts in the field would have been equally deceived.

He immediately sent for d'Artagnan.

'So,' he said, 'here are the diamond tags you came for. Be my witness that I have done everything humanly possible.'

'Rest assured, my lord; I will say what I have seen. But is Your Grace giving me the tags without the box?'

'The box would get in your way. Besides, the box is all the more precious to me now that it is all I have left. You will say that I am keeping it.'

'I shall deliver your message word for word, my lord.'

'And now,' Buckingham said, looking earnestly at the young man, 'how can I ever repay you?'

D'Artagnan blushed to the roots of his hair. He realised the duke was looking for a way to give him a present, and the idea that his and his companions' blood should be paid for in English gold was strangely repugnant to him.

'Let us understand one another, my lord,' replied d'Artagnan, 'and let us carefully weigh the facts in advance so that there is no mistake. I serve the king and queen of France and belong to the guards company of Monsieur des Essarts, who, like his brother-in-law Monsieur de Tréville, is particularly attached to Their Majesties. I have therefore done everything for the queen, and nothing for Your Grace. What's more, I might not have done any of it if I had not wanted to please someone who is my lady, as the queen is yours.'

'Yes,' said the duke, smiling, 'and I even think I know this other person. It is . . .'

'My lord, I have not named her,' the young man interrupted hotly.

'Quite so,' said the duke. 'Then it is to this person that I must be grateful for your devotion.'

'It is, my lord, for, especially now there's talk of war, I must confess that I see in Your Grace only an Englishman and hence an enemy whom I would be even more delighted to encounter on the battlefield than in the park at Windsor or the corridors of the Louvre – not that that will prevent my carrying out my mission in every particular and laying down my life, if need be, to accomplish it. But, I repeat to Your Grace, he personally owes me no more thanks for what I'm doing for myself in this second interview than for what I've already done for him in the first.'

'"Proud as a Scot", we say,' murmured Buckingham.

'And we say "Proud as a Gascon",' replied d'Artagnan. 'The Gascons are the Scots of France.'

And then d'Artagnan bowed to the duke and made as if to leave.

'What, you're going away just like that, are you? Where? And how, exactly?'

'True.'

'Damn me, the French are sure of themselves!'

'I had forgotten that England is an island and that you are its king.'

'Go to the port, ask for the brig *The Sund* and give this letter to the captain. He will take you to a small harbour where you will certainly not be expected, as ordinarily only fishing boats put in there.'

'This port is called . . . ?'

'Saint-Valery . . . But wait: when you get there, you will go into a squalid little inn with no name or sign, a real sailors' pothouse – you can't mistake it, there's only one in the place.'

'And then?'

'You will ask for the landlord, and you will say "Forward" to him.'

'Which means?'

'*En avant* – it's the password. He will give you a saddled horse and show you the road you are to take. You will find four other relays like it along the way. If you wish to leave your address in Paris at each, the four horses will be sent on. You are already familiar with two of them, which I had the impression you appreciated as a keen horseman. Those were the two we rode and, I guarantee, the others won't be in any way inferior. These four horses are equipped for battle. Proud as you may be, you cannot refuse to accept one and have your three companions accept the others. Besides, you can use them to wage war on us. The end justifies the means, as you French say, do you not?'

'Yes, my lord, I accept,' said d'Artagnan, 'and, if it please God, we will make good use of your presents.'

'Now, your hand, young man. We may soon meet on the battlefield, but in the meantime I hope we shall part good friends.'

'Yes, my lord, but in the hope of soon becoming enemies.'

'Don't worry, I can promise you that.'

'I count on your word, my lord.'

D'Artagnan bowed to the duke and hurried off to the port.

Opposite the Tower of London, he found the ship he'd been told about and gave his letter to the captain, who had it countersigned by the governor of the port and then weighed anchor immediately.

Fifty ships were waiting to sail.

As they passed alongside one of them, d'Artagnan thought he recognised the lady from Meung, whom the stranger had called 'Milady' and whom he had thought so beautiful. But thanks to the river's current and the stiff breeze that was blowing, his ship went so fast that they were out of sight in an instant.

The next day, they landed at Saint-Valery at around nine o'clock in the morning.

D'Artagnan headed at once to the tavern indicated to him, which he recognised by the shouts coming from within. The sailors were heralding war between England and France as imminent and inevitable, and, glad at heart, were carousing with a will.

D'Artagnan pushed his way through the crowd, went up to the landlord and said the word 'forward'. The landlord immediately made a sign for him to follow, went out by a door that gave on to a courtyard, led him to a stable where a saddled horse stood waiting for him, and inquired if there was anything else he needed.

'I need to know which road I am to take,' said d'Artagnan.

'Go from here to Blangy, and then from Blangy to Neufchâtel. At Neufchâtel, go into the Golden Harrow inn, give the landlord the password and you'll find a saddled horse like you did here.'

'Do I owe you anything?' asked d'Artagnan.

'Everything is paid for,' said the landlord. 'Handsomely, too. Go, then, and God be with you!'

'Amen,' said the young man, as he galloped away.

Four hours later, he was in Neufchâtel.

He followed the instructions he had been given to the letter. At Neufchâtel, as at Saint-Valery, he found a saddled horse waiting for him. When he went to transfer the pistols from the old saddle to the new one, he saw its holsters were already equipped with identical pistols.

'Your address in Paris?'

'Hôtel des Gardes, des Essarts's company.'

'Very well,' replied the landlord.

'What road should I take?' d'Artagnan asked in his turn.

'The Rouen one, but you're going to leave the city on your right. You'll stop at the small village of Écouis. There's one inn, the Shield of France. Don't judge it by its looks: there will be a horse in its stables every bit the equal of this one.'

'Same password?'

'Exactly.'

'Goodbye, master.'

'Good journey, sir. Do you need anything?'

D'Artagnan shook his head and rode off hell for leather. At Écouis, the scene repeated itself: he found an equally solicitous landlord, a fresh, rested horse. He left his address as before, and set off with equal speed for Pontoise. At Pontoise he changed mounts for the last time, and at nine o'clock came racing into the courtyard of Monsieur de Tréville's residence.

He had covered almost sixty leagues in twelve hours.

Monsieur de Tréville greeted him as if he had seen him that morning, although his handshake was slightly warmer than usual. He informed him that Monsieur des Essarts's company was on guard at the Louvre, and said he could go and take up his post.

XXII
THE BALLET OF THE MERLAISON

THE NEXT DAY, THE ONLY SUBJECT on anyone's lips in Paris was the ball the city aldermen were throwing for the king and queen, at which Their Majesties were to dance the famous ballet of the Merlaison[1], the king's favourite.

Preparations at the Hôtel de Ville for this august occasion had been under way for a week. The city carpenter had put up stands on which the female guests were to sit; the city chandler had decorated the halls with two hundred white wax torches, an unheard-of luxury in those days; finally, twenty violins had been hired and their fee set at double the usual rate, since, word had it, they were to play all night.

At ten o'clock in the morning the Sieur de La Coste, ensign of the royal guards, followed by two officers and several archers of the corps, came to ask Clément, the city clerk, for the keys to all the doors, rooms and offices of the Hôtel de Ville. The keys were handed over at once; each with a label to identify it, and from that moment on the Sieur de La Coste was in charge of guarding all the doors and the drives.

At eleven o'clock, Duhallier, the captain of the guards, came in his turn, bringing with him fifty archers, who immediately fanned out through the Hôtel de Ville to the doors assigned to them.

At three o'clock two companies of guards arrived, one French, the other Swiss. The company of French guards was made up of half Monsieur Duhallier's men and half Monsieur des Essarts's.

At six o'clock in the evening, the guests began to arrive. They were shown straight into the main hall and directed to their seats on the stands prepared for the occasion.

At nine o'clock, the wife of the first president of the parliament of Paris made her entrance. As she was the most prominent guest at the fête after the queen, the city fathers greeted her, and then showed her to a box facing the one the queen was to occupy.

At ten o'clock, in a small room on the side of the church of Saint-Jean, a light meal of sweetmeats was laid out for the king, facing the city silver sideboard, over which four archers stood guard.

At midnight, great cries and waves of cheering were heard: the king was making his way from the Louvre to the Hôtel de Ville along streets all lit up with coloured lanterns.

The aldermen, dressed in their woollen robes and preceded by six sergeants, each of whom was holding a torch, immediately went to receive the king, whom they met on the steps. The provost of the merchants delivered a speech of welcome, to which His Majesty replied by apologising for his lateness, while laying the blame for it on the cardinal, who had kept him discussing affairs of state until eleven o'clock.

His Majesty, in ceremonial dress, was accompanied by his brother – His Royal Highness Monsieur – the Count de Soissons, the Grand Prior, the Duke de Longueville, the Duke d'Elbeuf, the Count d'Harcourt, the Count de La Roche-Guyon, Monsieur de Liancourt, Monsieur de Baradas, the Count de Cramail and the Chevalier de Souveray.

Everybody remarked on the fact that the king looked sad and preoccupied.

A dressing room had been prepared for the king and another for Monsieur, with masquerade costumes laid out in each. Similar provisions had been made for the queen and Madame la Présidente. The lords and ladies of Their Majesties' suite were to dress two at a time in rooms prepared to that end.

Before he went into his dressing room, the king gave instructions that he wished to be informed as soon as the cardinal appeared.

Half an hour after the king's entrance, there was a fresh outbreak of cheering: heralding the queen's arrival. The aldermen did as before, and, preceded by sergeants, went forward to meet their illustrious guest.

The queen entered the hall. It was remarked that, like the king, she looked sad and, above all, tired.

When she entered, the curtains of a small gallery, which until then had remained drawn, were opened, and the pale face of the cardinal, who was dressed as a Spanish cavalier, appeared. His eyes locked on to the queen's and a smile of terrible joy passed over his lips: the queen was not wearing her diamond tags.

The queen stood for some time receiving the compliments of the city fathers and returning the greetings of the ladies.

Suddenly, the king appeared with the cardinal at one of the doors to the hall. The cardinal was speaking softly to him and the king was very pale.

The king pushed through the crowd and, without a mask, the ribbons of his doublet barely tied, he approached the queen and said to her in a strained voice:

'Madam, why, pray, are you not wearing your diamond tags, when you know it would have given me pleasure to see them?'

The queen looked around her and saw the cardinal behind the king's back, smiling a diabolical smile.

'Sire,' she replied, her voice husky, 'because I was afraid something might happen to them in this great crowd.'

'Well, you were wrong, madam! I gave you this gift so you might adorn yourself with it. I tell you, you were wrong.'

The king's voice shook with anger. Everyone looked on and listened in astonishment, not understanding what was happening at all.

'Sire,' said the queen, 'I can send for them to the Louvre, which is where they are, and thus fulfill Your Majesty's wishes.'

'Do so, madam, do so, and with all possible haste, for the ballet will commence in an hour.'

The queen bowed in token of submission and followed the ladies who were to show her to her dressing room.

The king, for his part, returned to his own.

There was a flurry of unease and confusion in the ballroom.

Something had clearly gone on between the king and the queen, but they had both spoken so quietly – and those around them had stepped back a few paces so respectfully – that no one had heard anything. The violins played with all their might, but no one listened.

The king emerged from his dressing room first. He was wearing the most elegant hunting dress, and Monsieur and the other nobles were similarly attired. This was the costume the king carried off best, and, when thus attired, he truly looked the finest gentleman of his kingdom.

The cardinal approached the king and gave him a box. The king opened it and found two diamond tags.

'What does this mean?' he asked the cardinal.

'Nothing,' the latter replied. 'But if the queen has the tags, which I doubt, count them, Sire, and if you only find ten, ask Her Majesty who can have robbed her of these two.'

The king looked quizzically at the cardinal, but, before he could question him, a cry of admiration burst from every mouth. If the king looked the finest gentleman of his kingdom, the queen was unquestionably the most beautiful woman in France.

Her huntress's outfit became her to perfection, it is true. She was wearing a felt hat with blue feathers, a pearl-grey velvet jacket fastened with diamond clasps, and a skirt of blue satin covered in silver embroidery. On her left shoulder the tags sparkled on a bow the same colour as her feathers and her skirt.

The king trembled with joy and the cardinal with anger, but they were too far from the queen to count the tags. The queen had them, but did she have ten or did she have twelve?

At that moment the violins gave the signal for the ballet to start. The king went up to Madame la Présidente, who was to be his partner, and His Royal Highness Monsieur to the queen. Everyone took their places, and the ballet began.

The king danced opposite the queen, and each time he came near her, he gazed voraciously at the tags, without being able to work out how many of them there were. A cold sweat stood out on the cardinal's brow.

The ballet lasted an hour, and had sixteen figures.

When the ballet ended to applause from the whole hall, each of the men escorted his partner back to her seat. The king, however, took advantage of the privilege afforded him to leave his partner where she was and walked smartly up to the queen.

'I thank you, madam,' he said, 'for the deference you have shown to my wishes, but I believe you are missing two tags and so I am returning them to you.'

Saying which, he handed the queen the two tags that the cardinal had given him.

'What, Sire?' cried the young queen, feigning surprise. 'Are you giving me another two? But that will mean I have fourteen!'

The king duly counted and saw all twelve tags on Her Majesty's shoulder.

The king summoned the cardinal.

'Well, cardinal, what does this signify?' he asked severely.

'It signifies, Sire,' replied the cardinal, 'that I wished Her Majesty to accept these two tags as a gift, and not daring to give them to her myself, I adopted this method.'

'And I am all the more grateful to Your Eminence,' Anne of Austria replied with a smile that proved she wasn't taken in by his ingenious gallantry, 'since I'm sure those two tags alone cost you as much as the other twelve cost His Majesty.'

And then, bowing to the king and the cardinal, the queen went back to the room where she had put on her costume and was now to change.

The attention we have been obliged to devote to the illustrious personages we have introduced at the start of this chapter has briefly diverted us from the individual to whom Anne of Austria owed her unprecedented triumph over the cardinal. Self-conscious, ignored, lost in the crowd at one of the doors, he had watched this scene that was only comprehensible to four people: the king, the queen, His Eminence, and him.

The queen had just returned to her dressing room, and d'Artagnan was preparing to leave, when he felt a gentle tap on his shoulder. He turned and saw a young woman gesturing for him to follow her. The young woman's face was covered by a black velvet mask, but despite this precaution, which in any case was for others rather than for him, he instantly recognised his habitual guide, the lissom and witty Madame Bonacieux.

They had barely seen each other the previous day at the Swiss gatekeeper Germain's lodge, where d'Artagnan had asked for her. The young woman was in such a hurry to give the queen the wonderful news of her messenger's safe return that the two lovers had only exchanged a few words at most. D'Artagnan was thus gripped by two feelings as he followed Madame Bonacieux: love and curiosity. As they went down increasingly deserted corridors, he constantly tried to stop the young woman, to hold her, to gaze at her, even if only for a moment, but, quick as a bird, she repeatedly slipped from his grasp, and when he tried to speak, the finger she brought to her lips in a small, infinitely charming gesture of command reminded him he was under the sway of a power that he had blindly to obey, and that forbade him even the least complaint. Eventually, after a minute or two of twists and turns, Madame Bonacieux opened a door and ushered him into a pitch-dark dressing room. She gestured again for him to be quiet and then, opening a second door concealed behind a tapestry, through the gaps of which a bright light suddenly fell, she disappeared.

D'Artagnan stood motionless for a moment, wondering where he was, but soon a ray of light coming from the other room, the warm, scented air that reached him, the conversation of two or three women in respectful, elegant language, the word 'majesty' repeated several times, made it clear to him he was in a dressing room adjoining the queen's chamber.

The young man kept to the shadows and waited.

The queen appeared cheerful and happy, which seemed greatly to astonish her entourage, who were used, on the contrary, to seeing her almost permanently care-worn. The queen attributed her feelings of joy to the beauty of the fête, the pleasure she had taken in the ballet, and as it is never permissible to contradict a queen, whether she is smiling or crying, they all went to greater lengths to extol the gallantry of the aldermen of the city of Paris.

Although d'Artagnan did not know the queen, he soon distinguished her voice from the other voices, first by a slight foreign accent, and then by the stamp of authority that is naturally imprinted upon a sovereign's every word. He heard her approach and move away from the open door, and two or three times he even saw the shadow of a body block the light.

Finally, a hand and an arm of exquisite shapeliness and whiteness, suddenly reached through the tapestry. D'Artagnan understood this was his reward. He threw himself on his knees, grasped the hand and respectfully pressed his lips to it. Then the hand withdrew, leaving in his hands an object that he recognised as a ring. The door closed again immediately, and d'Artagnan found himself in the most complete darkness.

D'Artagnan put the ring on his finger, and waited once more. Clearly that wasn't all. First came the reward for his loyalty, then the reward for his love. Besides, although the ballet had been danced, the fête had scarcely begun. Supper was to be taken at three, and the Saint-Jean clock had struck a quarter to three not long ago.

Indeed, the sound of voices in the next room gradually grew quieter, then the women could be heard leaving. Next thing, the door of the dressing room in which d'Artagnan was waiting opened, and Madame Bonacieux rushed in.

'You, at last!' cried d'Artagnan.

'Shhh!' said the young woman, putting her hand to the young man's lips. 'Shhh! And go out the way you came.'

'But where and when shall I see you again?' cried d'Artagnan.

'A note you will find when you get home will tell you. Go, go!'

And with these words she opened the door to the corridor and pushed d'Artagnan out of the dressing room.

D'Artagnan obeyed like a child, unresistingly, without objection, which proves that he really was in love.

XXIII

THE RENDEZVOUS

D'ARTAGNAN RAN ALL THE WAY HOME, and although it was after three in the morning and he had to go through Paris's worst neighbourhoods, he met with no trouble. As everyone knows, there is a god that watches over drunkards and lovers.

He found the door to his alley ajar, climbed his stairs and gently knocked according to the code he and his valet had agreed upon. Planchet, whom he had sent back from the Hôtel de Ville two hours earlier and told to wait up for him, came and opened the door.

'Has anyone brought a letter for me?' d'Artagnan burst out.

'No one brought a letter, sir,' replied Planchet. 'But there's one that came by itself.'

'What do you mean, imbecile?'

'I mean that when I got back, even though I had the key to your lodgings in my pocket, and even though that key hadn't gone anywhere, I found a letter on the green tablecloth in your bedroom.'

'And where is this letter?'

'I left it where it was, sir. It's not natural for letters to get into people's homes like that. If the window had still been open, or even half-open, I wouldn't say a word, but no, everything was shut up tight. Be careful, sir, there's definitely some magic behind it.'

While he was saying this, the young man had rushed into his bedroom and opened the letter. It was from Madame Bonacieux and read:

> We have heartfelt thanks to extend and to convey to you. Be at Saint-Cloud this evening at around ten o'clock, opposite the pavilion that stands at the corner of Monsieur d'Estrées's house.
>
> C. B.

Reading this letter, d'Artagnan felt his heart dilate and contract in one of those delectable spasms which torture and caress the hearts of lovers.

It was the first such note he had received, the first rendezvous that had been granted to him. His heart, full to bursting with rapturous joy, felt as if it were about to give out on the threshold of that earthly paradise known as love.

'Well, sir?' said Planchet, who had seen his master blush and pale successively. 'Well, didn't I guess right? Isn't this some evil business?'

'You are mistaken, Planchet,' said d'Artagnan, 'and, to prove it, here is an écu for you to drink my health.'

'I thank monsieur for the écu he has given me, and promise to strictly follow his instructions, but it's still true that letters that get into locked houses like that . . .'

'Fall from heaven, my friend, fall from heaven.'

'Then monsieur is happy?' asked Planchet.

'My dear Planchet, I am the happiest of men!'

'And I may take advantage of monsieur's happiness to go to bed?'

'Yes, go on.'

'May all the blessings of heaven fall on monsieur, but it's still true that this letter . . .'

And then Planchet retired, shaking his head with a doubtful air that d'Artagnan's liberality hadn't been able to erase completely.

When he was left alone, d'Artagnan read and reread his note, then kissed and kissed again, at least twenty times, those lines written by his beautiful mistress's hand. At last, he went to bed, fell asleep, and dreamt golden dreams.

At seven o'clock in the morning, he got up and called Planchet, who, the second time he was summoned, opened the door, his face still not entirely scrubbed clean of the previous day's anxieties.

'Planchet,' said d'Artagnan, 'I may be gone for the whole day, so you're free until seven o'clock this evening. But at seven, be ready with two horses.'

'Here we go,' said Planchet. 'It looks as if we're going to have our hides skewered in a few places again.'

'You will take your carbine and your pistols.'

'Ah, what was I saying?' cried Planchet. 'There, I was sure of it – that cursed letter!'

'Calm down, imbecile, it's just an outing.'

'Oh, like our jaunt the other day when it rained bullets and sprouted steel traps?'

'But if you're afraid, Monsieur Planchet,' said d'Artagnan, 'I'll go without you. I'd rather travel alone than with a companion who quakes in his boots.'

'Monsieur insults me,' said Planchet. 'I thought he'd seen me at work.'

'Yes, but I assumed you'd used up all your courage in one go.'

'When the time comes, monsieur will see I have more. But, I'll beg monsieur not to be too free with it if he wants my reserves to last.'

'Do you think you've got enough to spend some tonight?'

'I hope so.'

'Well then, I'm counting on you.'

'I'll be ready when you said. But I thought monsieur only had one horse in the guards' stables.'

'There may only be one at the moment, but this evening there will be four.'

'Looks like our journey was to stock up on remounts.'

'Exactly,' said d'Artagnan.

And then, with a last gesture of exhortation for Planchet, he went out.

Monsieur Bonacieux was at his door. D'Artagnan intended to pass by without speaking to the worthy mercer, but Bonacieux bowed to him in such a pleasant and benign fashion that his tenant was compelled not only to return his bow but also to strike up conversation with him.

Besides, how can one not condescend a little to a husband whose wife has arranged to meet you that very evening at Saint-Cloud, opposite Monsieur d'Estrées's pavilion? D'Artagnan approached him with the most amiable air he could assume.

The conversation naturally turned to the poor man's incarceration. Monsieur Bonacieux, who was unaware that d'Artagnan had overheard his conversation with the stranger from Meung, described to his young tenant the persecutions he had endured at the hands of that monster Monsieur de Laffemas – 'the cardinal's executioner', as he insisted on calling him throughout his account – and expatiated at length on the Bastille: its bolts, its peepholes, its air-vents, its bars and its instruments of torture.

D'Artagnan listened with exemplary attention before asking, when he had finally finished, 'And what of Madame Bonacieux – do you know who abducted her? For I haven't forgotten that it is to this unfortunate circumstance that I owe the pleasure of your acquaintance.'

'Ah,' replied Monsieur Bonacieux, 'they took every care not to tell me, and my wife for her part has sworn by all that's sacred that she does not know. But what about you?' Monsieur Bonacieux continued with the utmost affability, 'What's become of you in the last few days? I haven't seen you or your friends, and I can't think it was on the cobblestones of Paris that you picked up all that dust Planchet was brushing off your boots yesterday.'

'You're right, my dear Monsieur Bonacieux, my friends and I went on a little journey.'

'Far from here?'

'Oh, my God, no. Only forty leagues. We had to take Monsieur Athos to the waters at Forges, and my friends have stayed on there.'

'But you've come back, have you not?' said Monsieur Bonacieux, assuming his slyest expression. 'A handsome lad like you does not obtain long leaves of absence from his mistress. We were impatiently expected in Paris, were we not?'

'My faith,' laughed the young man, 'I admit it, especially, my dear Monsieur Bonacieux, because one clearly can't hide anything from you. Yes, I was expected – very impatiently too, I can tell you.'

A slight cloud passed over Bonacieux's brow, but so slight that d'Artagnan did not notice it.

'And we're going to be rewarded for our diligence?' continued the mercer, with a slight catch in his voice, a catch that d'Artagnan did not notice any more than he had the fleeting cloud that had darkened the worthy man's face a moment before.

'Ah, no need to act holier-than-thou,' d'Artagnan said, laughing.

'No, I'm only asking,' protested Bonacieux, 'to find out if we will be coming back late.'

'Why this question, my dear landlord?' asked d'Artagnan. 'Are you planning on waiting up for me?'

'No, it's just that since I was arrested and my house was robbed, I'm scared every time I hear a door open, especially at night. Goodness, how could I not be? I am not a swordsman in any shape or form!'

'Well, don't be scared if I come back at one, or two, or three in the morning. And if I don't come back at all, don't be scared about that either.'

This time Bonacieux turned so pale that d'Artagnan couldn't help but notice, and he asked him what was wrong.

'Nothing,' replied Bonacieux, 'nothing. It's only that since my misfortunes, I am prone to sudden weak spells, and I just felt a chill run down my back. But pay it no mind, your only business is to be happy.'

'Then I must be very busy, because that's what I am.'

'Not yet, wait a while – you said this evening.'

'Ah well, this evening will come, thank God! And perhaps you're looking forward to it as impatiently as I am. Perhaps this evening Madame Bonacieux will pay a visit to the conjugal home.'

'Madame Bonacieux is not free this evening,' the husband replied gravely. 'She is detained at the Louvre by her duties.'

'What a shame for you, my dear landlord, what a shame. When I'm happy, I want the whole world to be too. But apparently that's not possible.'

And then the young man went off, laughing heartily at his joke that he thought only he could understand.

'Enjoy yourself,' Bonacieux replied in a sepulchral tone.

But d'Artagnan was already too far away to hear, and if he had, in the frame of mind he was in, he certainly wouldn't have noticed.

He headed for Monsieur de Tréville's – his visit of the previous day, it will be remembered, having been very brief and less than explanatory.

He found Monsieur de Tréville in a state of high good humour. The king and queen had been charming to him at the ball. The cardinal by contrast, it is true, had been extremely sullen. He had retired at one o'clock in the morning on the pretext of being unwell. As for Their Majesties, they hadn't made their way back to the Louvre until six o'clock in the morning.

'Now,' said Monsieur de Tréville, lowering his voice and examining all the corners of his office to check they were alone, 'now, let's talk about you, my young friend, for obviously your safe return has played some part in the king's joy, the queen's triumph and His Eminence's humiliation. You must take care of yourself.'

'What do I have to be fear,' replied d'Artagnan, 'as long as I am fortunate enough to enjoy Their Majesties' favour?'

'Everything, believe me. The cardinal is not a man to forget a trick if he hasn't settled accounts with the trickster, and the trickster in this case very much seems to me to be a certain Gascon of my acquaintance.'

'Do you think the cardinal is as astute as you and knows I was the one who went to London?'

'What the devil, you've been to London? Did you bring that beautiful diamond sparkling on your finger back from London? Take care, my dear d'Artagnan, a gift from an enemy is not a good thing. Isn't there a Latin verse about that . . . ? Wait . . .'

'Yes, I daresay,' said d'Artagnan, who had never been able to cram the most basic Latin into his brain, driving his tutor to despair with his ignorance, 'yes, I daresay, there must be.'

'There certainly is,' said Monsieur de Tréville, who had a nodding acquaintance with literature, 'and Monsieur Benserade¹ quoted it to me the other day . . . Wait . . . Ah, here it is:

'*Timeo Danaos et dona ferentes.*

'Which means "Beware of the enemy who gives you presents."'

'This diamond isn't from an enemy, sir,' replied d'Artagnan, 'it is from the queen.'

'From the queen? Oho!' said Monsieur de Tréville. 'Yes indeed, that is an eminently regal jewel. It must be worth a thousand pistoles if it is worth a sou. Who did the queen choose as an intermediary to give you this gift?'

'She gave it to me herself.'

'Where?'

'In the dressing room adjoining the room where she changed.'

'How?'

'By giving me her hand to kiss.'

'You kissed the queen's hand?' cried Monsieur de Tréville, staring at d'Artagnan.

'Her Majesty did me the honour of granting me that kindness.'

'And in the presence of witnesses? Recklessness – insane recklessness!'

'No, sir, rest assured, nobody saw it,' replied d'Artagnan, and then he told Monsieur de Tréville what had happened.

'Ah, women, women!' cried the old soldier. 'I know their romantic imaginations. They love everything with a dash of mystery.

So you just saw an arm. If you met the queen, you wouldn't recognise her, and if she met you, she wouldn't know who you are.'

'No, but thanks to this diamond . . .' said the young man.

'Listen,' said Monsieur de Tréville, 'do you want me to give you a piece of advice – good advice, the advice of a friend?'

'You will be doing me an honour, sir,' said d'Artagnan.

'Well, go to the first jeweller's you can find and sell him the diamond for whatever he will give you for it. As Jewish as he may be, you'll still get a good eight hundred pistoles. Pistoles have no name, young man, whereas that ring has a terrible one, and it may betray the man who wears it.'

'Sell this ring? A ring that came from my sovereign? Never!' said d'Artagnan.

'Then turn the stone inside, you poor fool, because everyone knows a Gascon cadet doesn't happen upon those sorts of gems in his mother's jewellery box.'

'So you think I've got something to fear?' asked d'Artagnan.

'Put it this way, young man: a gentleman sleeping on a mine with a lighted fuse should feel safe compared to you.'

'Hang it,' said d'Artagnan, increasingly alarmed by the note of certainty in Monsieur de Tréville's voice. 'Hang it, what am I to do?'

'First and foremost, be on your guard at every moment. The cardinal has a tenacious memory and a long arm – believe me, he will play you some trick.'

'What sort?'

'How would I know? Doesn't he have all the wiles of the devil at his disposal? The least that can happen is that you'll be arrested.'

'What! They'd dare arrest a man in His Majesty's service?'

'By God, they didn't have too many scruples with Athos! In any case, young man, believe a man who has been at court for thirty years: don't lull yourself into a false sense of security or you are done for. Quite the contrary, I can tell you, see enemies at every turn. If someone tries to pick a quarrel with you, don't rise to the bait, even if it's a ten-year-old child trying to pick it;

if you are attacked by night or day, retreat without shame; if you cross a bridge, test the planks for fear one should give way as you take a step; if you walk past a house where there's building work going on, look up for fear a stone should fall on your head; if you come home late, have your valet walk behind you, and let your valet be armed – if you're sure of your valet, that is. Distrust everybody, your friend, your brother, your mistress – your mistress most of all.'

D'Artagnan blushed.

'My mistress,' he repeated mechanically. 'Why her more than anyone else?'

'Because the mistress is one of the cardinal's favourite methods – his most expeditious, in fact. A woman will sell you for ten pistoles. Look at Delilah. You know the Scriptures, don't you?'

D'Artagnan thought of the rendezvous Madame Bonacieux had given him that evening, but, to our hero's credit, we have to say that the low opinion Monsieur de Tréville entertained of women in general did not arouse in him the least suspicion of his pretty landlady.

'By the way,' resumed Monsieur de Tréville, 'what has become of your three companions?'

'I was going to ask if you'd had any news of them.'

'None, sir.'

'Well, I left them along my way: Porthos at Chantilly with a duel on his hands, Aramis at Crèvecœur with a bullet in his shoulder, and Athos at Amiens with an accusation of counterfeiting on his head.'

'You see!' said Monsieur de Tréville. 'So how did you escape?'

'By a miracle, sir, I have to say, with a sword-thrust in the chest, and only after I'd pinned the Count de Wardes to the Calais roadside like a butterfly to a tapestry.'

'There, you see again! De Wardes, one of the cardinal's men, a cousin of Rochefort's. Wait, my dear friend, an idea's coming to me.'

'Tell me, sir.'

'In your place, there's one thing I'd do.'

'What?'

'While His Eminence's men were searching for me in Paris, I would take the road to Picardy again without any fuss, and go to get word of my three companions. Hang it, they surely deserve this small mark of attention on your part.'

'That's good advice, sir. I will leave tomorrow.'

'Tomorrow? And why not this evening?'

'This evening, sir, I am detained in Paris by an indispensable matter.'

'Ah, young man! Young man! Some dalliance? Take care. I'll say it again; it is women who have ruined us, each and every one of us, and it is they who will ruin us again, every last one of us. Believe me, leave this evening.'

'Impossible, sir!'

'You've given your word, then?'

'Yes, sir.'

'Well, that's different. But promise me that if you're not killed tonight, you'll leave tomorrow.'

'I promise.'

'Do you need money?'

'I still have fifty pistoles. That's as much as I'll need, I think.'

'What about your companions?'

'I can't imagine they'll have run short. We each left Paris with seventy-five pistoles in our pockets.'

'Will I see you again before you leave?'

'No, I don't think so, sir, unless there's something new.'

'A good journey to you, then!'

'Thank you, sir.'

And then d'Artagnan took his leave of Monsieur de Tréville, more touched than ever by his fatherly solicitude for his musketeers.

He went to Athos's, Porthos's and Aramis's lodgings in turn. None of them had come back. Their valets were nowhere to be seen either, and no news was to be had of either party.

He would have liked to ask their mistresses, but he didn't know Porthos's or Aramis's, and Athos didn't have one.

As he passed the guards' building, he glanced into the stables. Three out of the four horses had already arrived. Stunned by this turn of events, Planchet was currying them, and had already finished two.

'Ah, sir,' said Planchet, catching sight of d'Artagnan, 'how glad I am to see you!'

'And why is that, Planchet?' asked the young man.

'Do you trust Monsieur Bonacieux, our landlord?'

'Me? Not in the least.'

'Ah, you're very right, sir.'

'But what prompts this question?'

'Well, while you were talking to him, I was watching you without listening to what you were saying. Sir, his face changed colour two or three times!'

'Nonsense!'

'Monsieur did not notice it, preoccupied as he was by the letter he had just received. But I, having been put on my guard by the strange way that letter had got into the house – I didn't miss a single shift in his countenance.'

'And you found it . . . ?'

'Treacherous, sir.'

'Indeed!'

'What's more, as soon as monsieur had left him and disappeared round the corner, Monsieur Bonacieux took his hat, locked his door and hared off down the street in the opposite direction.'

'Ah, of course, you're right, Planchet! That all strikes me as highly suspect. But don't worry: we won't pay him a sou's rent until we've had a full explanation.'

'Monsieur is joking, but monsieur will see.'

'How can I help it, Planchet? Our fates are written.'

'So monsieur isn't going to cancel his outing tonight?'

'Quite the contrary, Planchet: the more I dislike Monsieur Bonacieux, the more determined I am to go to the rendezvous granted me by that letter that worries you so much.'

'Then, if monsieur is resolved . . .'

'Unwaveringly, my friend. So, at nine o'clock, be ready here at the guardhouse. I'll come and fetch you.'

Realising there was no more hope of making his master give up his plan, Planchet heaved a deep sigh and set about currying the third horse.

As for d'Artagnan, who at heart was a very prudent lad, rather than go home, he went to dine with the Gascon priest who, when the four friends were in dire financial straits, had given them hot chocolate for breakfast.

XXIV

THE PAVILION

D'ARTAGNAN WAS AT THE GUARDS' STABLES at nine o'clock, where he found Planchet under arms. The fourth horse had also arrived.

Planchet was armed with his carbine and a pistol; in addition to his sword, d'Artagnan had tucked two pistols in his belt.

Then the two of them mounted up and silently set out. It was after dark, and no one saw them leave. Planchet followed in his master's train, riding ten paces behind him.

D'Artagnan crossed the embankments, went out by the Porte de La Conférence, and took the road – far more beautiful then than now – that leads to Saint-Cloud.

While they were in town, Planchet respectfully kept his self-imposed distance. But once the road became darker and more deserted, he quietly inched closer until, by the time they entered the Bois de Boulogne, he naturally enough found himself riding side by side with his master. Indeed, we mustn't conceal the fact that the swaying of the tall trees and the shimmer of moonlight in the dark copses caused him extreme anxiety. D'Artagnan noticed something strange was afoot with his valet.

'Well, Monsieur Planchet,' he asked him, 'what is bothering us?'

'Don't you find, sir, that woods are like churches?'

'Why is that, Planchet?'

'Because you don't dare raise your voice in either of them.'

'Why don't you dare raise your voice, Planchet? Because you're afraid?'

'Afraid of being heard, yes, sir.'

'Afraid of being heard? But our conversation is quite proper, my dear Planchet. No one could take exception to it.'

'Ah, sir,' said Planchet, returning to his main subject, 'that Monsieur Bonacieux has something shifty about his eyebrows and unpleasant about the play of his lips!'

'What the devil makes you think of Bonacieux?'

'Sir, one thinks of what one can, not of what one will.'

'That's because you're a poltroon, Planchet.'

'Sir, let's not confuse prudence with poltroonery. Prudence is a virtue.'

'And you're a virtuous soul, aren't you, Planchet?'

'Sir, isn't that the barrel of a musket gleaming over there? Shouldn't we duck down?'

'Honestly,' d'Artagnan muttered, remembering Monsieur de Tréville's advice, 'honestly, this creature will end up scaring me.'

And then he put his horse into a trot.

Planchet copied his master's movements as if he were his shadow, and found himself trotting alongside him.

'Are we going to ride like this all night, sir?' he asked.

'No, Planchet, because you've arrived.'

'What do you mean I've arrived? What about monsieur?'

'I'm going on a few paces.'

'And monsieur is leaving me alone here?'

'Are you afraid, Planchet?'

'No, but I'll just point out to monsieur that the night will be very cold, that chills bring on rheumatism and that a valet with rheumatism makes a sorry servant, especially for so agile a master as monsieur.'

'Well then, if you're cold, Planchet, you can go into one of those taverns you see over there and wait for me by the door at six o'clock in the morning.'

'Sir, I dutifully ate and drank the écu you gave me this morning, so I haven't a miserable sou left in case I get cold.'

'Here's a half-pistole. Goodbye until tomorrow.'

D'Artagnan got off his horse, threw the bridle over Planchet's arm and strode away, wrapping his cloak around him.

'God, I'm cold!' exclaimed Planchet once his master was out of sight, and, so urgent was his need to get warm, he didn't waste a moment before knocking at the door of a house adorned with all the attributes of a suburban wine shop.

In the meantime, d'Artagnan, who had plunged down a narrow side road, carried on his way until he reached Saint-Cloud. But, instead of following the main street, he went round to the back of the château and, coming to a very secluded sort of lane, soon found himself facing the pavilion that had been indicated to him. It was in a completely deserted spot. A high wall, at the corner of which stood the pavilion, dominated one side of the lane, and a hedge ran along the other, screening from passers-by a small garden with a wretched little hut at its far end.

He had arrived at the meeting place, and, not having been told to announce his presence by a signal of any sort, he settled down to wait.

Not a sound was to be heard; he could have been a hundred leagues from the capital. Glancing behind him, d'Artagnan leant back against the hedge. Beyond the hedge, the garden and the hut, a dark mist enveloped in its folds the vastness where Paris slept, blank and yawning, a vastness in which a few specks of light glittered, funereal stars in that hell.

But to d'Artagnan every sight bore a cheerful aspect, every thought was wreathed in smiles, every shadow was diaphanous. The hour of his rendezvous was about to strike.

And indeed, a few moments later, the belfry of Saint-Cloud slowly let fall ten strokes from its wide, booming mouth.

There was something lugubrious about that bronze voice uttering its lament in the middle of the night.

But each peal that made up the eagerly awaited hour echoed harmoniously in the young man's heart.

His eyes were fixed on the little pavilion at the corner of the wall, every window of which was shuttered apart from one on the second floor.

A gentle light shone through that window, silvering the trembling foliage of two or three linden trees that stood together in a group outside the park. Clearly the pretty Madame Bonacieux was waiting for him on the other side of that little window with its welcoming light.

Lulled by that sweet thought, d'Artagnan, for his part, waited for half an hour without a tremor of impatience, his eyes fixed on that charming little living room. He could see part of its ceiling, the gilded mouldings of which attested to the elegance of the rest of the interior.

Saint-Cloud's belfry tolled half-past ten.

This time, without his knowing why, a shudder ran through d'Artagnan's veins. Perhaps he was feeling the cold too and had mistaken a purely physical sensation for an intuition.

Then it occurred to him that he had misread the note and that the rendezvous wasn't until eleven o'clock.

He went over to the window, placed himself in a ray of light, took the letter out of his pocket and reread it. No, he hadn't been mistaken: the rendezvous was definitely at ten o'clock.

He resumed his post, slightly uneasy now at the silence and the solitude.

It struck eleven.

D'Artagnan began to be genuinely afraid that something had happened to Madame Bonacieux.

He clapped his hands three times, the usual lovers' signal, but no one answered him, not even an echo.

Then he thought with a flash of annoyance that the young woman might have fallen asleep while she was waiting for him.

He went up to the wall and tried to climb it, but it had recently been roughcast, and d'Artagnan broke his fingernails to no avail.

Just then he noticed the trees, their leaves still silvery in the light, and, as one of them overhung the lane, he thought he would be able to see into the pavilion from amidst its branches.

The tree was easy to climb. Besides, d'Artagnan was barely twenty years old and still remembered his schoolboy activities. In an instant he was among its branches, gazing down through the transparent panes into the interior of the pavilion.

It was an uncanny thing – and it sent a shiver from the soles of d'Artagnan's feet to the roots of his hair – how that gentle light, that serene lamp, lit up a scene of appalling confusion. One of the windowpanes was smashed; the door to the room had been beaten in and hung, half-broken, from its hinges; a table that must have been set with an elegant supper lay upturned on the floor; shattered bottles and trampled fruit littered the parquet. Everything in the room bore witness to a violent and desperate struggle. D'Artagnan thought he even saw amid that strange jumble some shreds of clothing and a few spots of blood spattered on the table-cloth and curtains.

His heart pounding terribly, he climbed hurriedly back down to the street to see if he could find any other signs of violence.

The warm little light still shone out into the peaceful night. D'Artagnan hadn't noticed before – it hadn't occurred to him even to look – but now he saw that the ground, trodden flat here, dug up there, bore confused traces of men's feet and horses' hooves. The wheels of a carriage, moreover, which seemed to have come from Paris, had left deep ruts in the soft soil that went no further than the pavilion and then turned back to Paris.

Finally, as he continued his search, d'Artagnan found a torn woman's glove near the wall. Apart from where it touched the muddy ground, it was immaculate. It was one of those perfumed gloves that lovers delight in pulling off a pretty hand.

As d'Artagnan pursued his investigations, an ever more

abundant and icy sweat beaded his brow, his heart was gripped by a terrible anguish, he gasped for breath – and yet, to reassure himself, he kept thinking that perhaps there was no connection between the pavilion and Madame Bonacieux; that the young woman had arranged to meet him in front of it, not inside it; that she might have been detained in Paris by her work, or perhaps her husband's jealousy.

But all these arguments were beaten down, demolished, over-thrown by that feeling of innermost grief that, on certain occasions, takes hold of our whole being and cries out to us, through every faculty we have of hearing, that a terrible misfortune hangs over us.

Then d'Artagnan almost lost his mind. He ran out on to the main street, headed back the way he had come, went as far as the ferry and questioned the ferryman.

Around seven o'clock that evening, the ferryman had conveyed across the river a woman wrapped in a black cloak who had seemed extremely anxious not to be recognised. But, precisely because of the precautions she had taken, he had paid all the greater attention to her and had noticed she was young and pretty.

There were in those days, as there are now, plenty of young, pretty women who were anxious not to be seen when they went to Saint-Cloud, and yet d'Artagnan didn't doubt for an instant that it was Madame Bonacieux whom the ferryman had noticed.

D'Artagnan took advantage of the lamp burning in the ferry-man's hut to reread Madame Bonacieux's note once more and make sure he hadn't been mistaken, that the rendezvous was definitely at Saint-Cloud and not somewhere else, in front of Monsieur d'Estrées's pavilion and not in some other street.

Everything confirmed to d'Artagnan that his presentiments were not misguided and that a terrible misfortune had occurred.

He ran back towards the château, thinking that in his absence something new might have happened at the pavilion, that some information might be waiting for him there.

But the lane was as deserted as before, and the same calm, gentle light still spilled from the window.

D'Artagnan then thought of that mute and blind hovel, which had doubtless seen and perhaps might speak.

The gate of the enclosure was locked, but he jumped over the hedge and, despite the barking of a dog on a chain, went up to the hut.

His knocking at first received no response. A deathly silence reigned in the hut, as in the pavilion. But, as it was his last resource, he persisted.

Soon he thought he heard a faint noise inside – a timid noise that seemed to tremble at the prospect of being heard.

Then d'Artagnan stopped knocking and began pleading in a tone so full of anxiety and assurances, of terror and cajoling, that his voice would have reassured the most timorous soul. Finally an old, worm-eaten shutter was opened, or rather half-opened, and shut again the minute the light of a pitiful lamp burning in a corner had picked out d'Artagnan's baldric, sword-hilt and pistol butts. But, swift though the movement had been, d'Artagnan had still had time to glimpse an old man's face.

'In heaven's name!' he said. 'Listen to me: I have been waiting for someone who hasn't come. I'm dying of anxiety. Has there been any trouble around here? Speak!'

The window slowly opened again, and the same face reappeared, still paler than before.

D'Artagnan artlessly told the whole story, only omitting names. He said he had had a rendezvous with a woman in front of this pavilion, and, when there was no sign of her, he had climbed the linden tree, and, by the light of the lamp, had seen the bedlam in the room.

The old man listened attentively, gesturing in agreement, and, when d'Artagnan had finished, shook his head ominously.

'What do you mean?' cried d'Artagnan. 'In heaven's name! Come, explain yourself.'

'Oh, sir,' said the old man, 'don't ask me anything. If I told you what I saw, it would not turn out well for me, I can assure you.'

'So you did see something? In that case, in heaven's name,'

replied d'Artagnan, tossing him a pistole, 'tell me, tell me what you saw, and I give you my word as a gentleman that I will bury every word you say in my heart.'

The old man read so much candour and grief in d'Artagnan's face that he motioned for him to listen and then said in a whisper, 'It was about nine o'clock: I had heard some noise in the road and wanted to find out what it could be, but as I was going to my gate I realised someone was trying to get in. As I'm poor and have no fear of being robbed, I went to open it and I saw three men a few paces away. In the shadow was a carriage with horses harnessed to it and some saddle horses. The saddle horses clearly belonged to the three men who were dressed as gentlemen.

'"Ah, my good sirs!" I cried. "What do you require of me?"

'"You must have a ladder?" asked the one who seemed to be the leader of the escort.

'"Yes, sir. The one I use to gather my fruit."

'"Give it to us and go back into your house. Here's an écu for the trouble we're putting you to. But remember that if you say a word of what you're going to see and hear – because you'll watch and listen however we threaten you, I'm sure of that – you are lost."

'At those words, he tossed me an écu, which I picked up, and took my ladder.

'After shutting the hedge gate behind them, I pretended to go back into the house, but then went straight out by the back door and, slipping through the shadows, made my way to that clump of elder, from where I could see everything without being seen myself.

'The three men had silently brought up the carriage. They pulled a little man out of it, fat, stumpy, grey-haired, shabbily dressed in dark clothes, who cautiously climbed the ladder, sneaked a glance into the room, stole back down on tiptoe and muttered in a low voice, "It is she!"

'The one who had spoken to me immediately went up to the door of the pavilion, opened it with a key he had on his person, shut the door behind him and disappeared. Meanwhile, the two others climbed the ladder. The little old man remained standing by the carriage door, the coachman held the carriage horses, and a valet the saddle horses.

'Suddenly there were loud shouts in the pavilion; a woman ran to the window and opened it as if to jump out. But as soon as she saw the two men, she reared back; the two men dived into the room after her.

'After that I couldn't see anything, but I heard the sound of breaking furniture. The woman shouted and called for help, but her cries were soon stifled. The three men came back to the window, carrying the woman in their arms. Two of them climbed down the ladder and took her to the carriage, and the little old man got in after her. The one who had stayed in the pavilion closed the window again, came out of the door a moment later and checked the woman was in the carriage. His two companions were already on their horses, waiting for him. He leapt into the saddle in his turn, the valet took his place beside the coachman; the carriage set off at a gallop escorted by the three horsemen, and then it was all over. I haven't heard or seen anything since.'

Crushed by such terrible news, d'Artagnan stood unmoving and speechless while all the demons of rage and jealousy howled in his heart.

'But, my dear gentleman,' said the old man, clearly more affected by this mute despair than he would have been by cries and tears, 'come, don't grieve so. They didn't kill her, that's the main thing.'

'Do you have any idea,' said d'Artagnan, 'who the man in charge of this infernal expedition was?'

'I don't know him.'

'But, when he spoke to you, you got a look at him.'

'Ah, you're asking for his description?'

'Yes.'

'A tall, lean man, dark-skinned, black moustaches, black eyes, with a gentlemanly air.'

'That's it,' cried d'Artagnan. 'Him again! Always him! He's my evil spirit, it seems! And the other one?'

'Which?'

'The little one.'

'Oh, that one's not a nobleman; you can take my word for it. Besides, he wasn't wearing a sword, and the others treated him without any consideration.'

'Some lackey,' murmured d'Artagnan. 'Ah, poor woman! Poor woman! What have they done to her?'

'You promised this would remain a secret,' said the old man.

'And I renew my promise – don't worry, I'm a gentleman. A gentleman only has his word and I have given you mine.'

D'Artagnan took the road back to the ferry, his soul in anguish. One moment he couldn't believe it was Madame Bonacieux and hoped he would find her the following day at the Louvre, the next he feared she was having an intrigue with someone, and had been surprised by a jealous lover and carried off. He wavered, he grieved, he despaired.

'Oh, if only I had my friends here!' he cried. 'At least I'd have some hope of finding her, but who knows what's become of them either!'

It was almost midnight; the question now was how to find Planchet. D'Artagnan looked into every tavern in which he could see a flicker of light, but didn't find Planchet in any of them.

At the sixth he started to think his search was somewhat foolhardy. D'Artagnan hadn't arranged to meet his valet until six o'clock in the morning, so wherever he was, he was entirely within his rights.

Besides, it occurred to the young man that by staying near the scene of events, he might obtain some enlightenment as to this mysterious affair. At the sixth tavern, as we have said, d'Artagnan therefore stopped, called for a bottle of their finest wine, leant on his elbows in the darkest corner and decided to wait there for it to get light. But his hopes were disappointed this time too, and although he listened, all ears, to the oaths, jeers and insults bandied about by the workers, valets and carters who comprised the honourable company of which he formed a part, he heard nothing that could put him on the trail of the poor abducted woman. So, after drinking the whole bottle for want of anything better to do, so as not to arouse suspicion, there was nothing for it but to try to find the most satisfactory position available in his corner and fall asleep as best he could. D'Artagnan was twenty years old, it will be remembered, and at that age sleep has inalienable rights over even the most desperate hearts, which it imperiously claims.

Around six o'clock in the morning, d'Artagnan awoke feeling that discomfort that generally greets daybreak after a bad night. It didn't take him long to spruce up. He patted himself down to check no one had profited from his sleep to rob him, and having found his diamond ring on his finger, his purse in his pocket, and his pistols in his belt, got up, paid for his wine and went to see whether he might not have better luck searching for his valet in the morning than he had had at night. And indeed, the first thing he saw through the damp, greyish fog was honest Planchet who, with the two horses in hand, was waiting for him at the door of a seedy-looking little wine shop, which d'Artagnan had walked past without even suspecting its existence.

XXV
PORTHOS

R ATHER THAN GO STRAIGHT HOME, d'Artagnan dismounted at Monsieur de Tréville's door and quickly climbed the stairs. This time he was resolved to tell him all that had transpired. No doubt he would give him good advice about the whole affair, but, as Monsieur de Tréville saw the queen almost daily, he might also glean some information from Her Majesty about that poor woman who was undoubtedly being made to pay for her devotion to her mistress.

Monsieur de Tréville listened to the young man's account with a gravity that proved he saw something more than a lovers' intrigue in the whole adventure. Then, when d'Artagnan had finished, he said, 'Hmm, you can smell His Eminence a league away in all this.'

'But what am I to do?' said d'Artagnan.

'Nothing, absolutely nothing for the moment, except leave Paris, as I told you, as soon as possible. I will see the queen, I will inform her of the details of this poor woman's disappearance, of which she is doubtless unaware. Those details will guide her for her part, and, when you come back, perhaps I will have some good news for you. Count on me.'

D'Artagnan knew that, despite his Gascon blood, Monsieur de Tréville was not in the habit of making promises, and that when by chance he did promise something, he more than kept his word. So he bowed to him, full of gratitude for the past and for the future, and the worthy captain, who for his part took a keen interest in this young man, who was so brave and so resolute, affectionately shook his hand and wished him a good journey.

Determined to put Monsieur de Tréville's advice into practice immediately, d'Artagnan made for Rue des Fossoyeurs to see to the packing of his bags. Drawing near the house, he saw Monsieur Bonacieux in his morning attire standing on his doorstep. Everything the prudent Planchet had told him the previous day about his land-lord's sinister character now came back to d'Artagnan, and he studied him more carefully than before. And indeed, besides his yellowish, sickly pallor, which indicated an infiltration of bile into the blood and might in any case be purely accidental, d'Artagnan did notice something slyly treacherous about the wrinkles on his face. A rogue does not laugh in the same fashion as an honest man; a hypocrite does not shed the same tears as a man of good faith. All falsehood is a mask, and no matter how well made the mask, it is always possible with a little attention to distinguish it from the face.

It seemed now to d'Artagnan that Monsieur Bonacieux wore a mask – one of the most unpleasant masks imaginable, in fact.

Overcome by repugnance for the man therefore, he was on the point of walking past him without speaking when Monsieur Bonacieux hailed him as he had done the previous day.

'Well, well, young man,' he said, 'apparently we're burning the candle at both ends. My word, seven o'clock in the morning! You seem to be turning established customs on their head and coming home when other folk venture out.'

'A criticism no one could make of you, Monsieur Bonacieux,' replied the young man. 'Yours is the model of an orderly life. It is true, though, that when you have a young and beautiful wife, you don't need to run after happiness – happiness comes looking for you, doesn't it, Monsieur Bonacieux?'

Turning deathly pale, Bonacieux forced a smile.

'Ha, you're a droll fellow,' said Bonacieux. 'But where the devil were you running around all night, my young master? The back roads were in a state, I gather.'

D'Artagnan glanced down at his filthy boots, but as he did so, his gaze fell on the mercer's shoes and stockings. It looked as if they had been trailed through the exact same quagmire; they were coated with spatters of mud just like his own.

Then a thought suddenly crossed d'Artagnan's mind. That fat, stumpy, grey-haired little man, that sort of lackey dressed in dark clothes who had been treated without any consideration by the swordsmen of the escort – that was Bonacieux himself! The husband had presided over his wife's abduction.

D'Artagnan felt a terrible urge to fling himself at the mercer's throat and strangle him. But, as we've said, he was an extremely prudent lad, so he restrained himself. Nevertheless, the change in his expression was so glaring that Bonacieux was terrified and tried to take a step back, but as he was standing right in front of the closed leaf of the door, he was forced to stay where he was.

'Ah, you may be joking, my good man,' said d'Artagnan. 'But really, if my boots need a good sponge, I think your stockings and your shoes could also do with a good brush. Could it be that you have been out on the prowl too, Monsieur Bonacieux? Hang it, there'd be no excuse for that in a man of your age, especially when he has a wife as young and pretty as yours.'

'Oh, my God, no,' said Bonacieux. 'But yesterday I was in

Saint-Mandé making inquiries about a maid whom I simply can't do without, and as the roads were bad, I brought back all this muck. I haven't had time to clean it off.'

Bonacieux's alleged whereabouts were further evidence in support of d'Artagnan's suspicions. Bonacieux had said Saint-Mandé because Saint-Mandé was in exactly the opposite direction to Saint-Cloud.

The likelihood of this was the first source of consolation to d'Artagnan. If Bonacieux knew where his wife was, then, by extreme means if necessary, it might always be possible to force the mercer to unclench his teeth and let out his secret. It was simply a matter of changing that probability into a certainty.

'Excuse me, my dear Monsieur Bonacieux, if I treat you unceremoniously,' said d'Artagnan, 'but nothing leaves one so parched as lack of sleep and I have a raging thirst. Permit me to help myself to a glass of water indoors; you know one can't refuse a neighbour this favour.'

And then, without waiting for permission from his landlord, d'Artagnan strode into the house and cast a quick glance at the bed. It was still made. Bonacieux hadn't slept in it. So he had only come back an hour or two ago. He had accompanied his wife to wherever they had taken her, or at least to the first relay.

'Thank you, Monsieur Bonacieux,' said d'Artagnan, draining his glass, 'that's all I wanted of you. Now I'll go home, have Planchet brush my boots, and, when he's finished, I'll send him to you, if you like, to give your shoes a brush.'

And then he left the mercer utterly dumbfounded by this strange parting, and wondering, for his part, whether he hadn't given himself away.

At the top of the stairs he found Planchet in a state of extreme agitation.

'Ah, sir!' cried Planchet the minute he saw his master. 'Something else has happened – I've been so desperate for you to come home.'

'What's wrong now?' asked d'Artagnan.

'Ah, I'll give you a hundred goes, sir, a thousand goes, and

you still won't guess whose visit I received on your behalf
while you were gone.'

'When was that?'

'Half an hour ago, while you were at Monsieur de Tréville's.'

'So who did come? Go on, speak.'

'Monsieur de Cavois[1].'

'Monsieur de Cavois?'

'In person.'

'The captain of His Eminence's guards?'

'Himself.'

'He came to arrest me?'

'I suspected so, sir, even with his flattering way.'

'You say he had a flattering way?'

'That is, he was pure honey, sir.'

'Really?'

'He said he came on the part of His Eminence, who wishes you
extremely well, to beg you to accompany him to the Palais-Royal[2].'

'And you answered?'

'That the thing was impossible, since you were out of the
house, as he could see.'

'Then what did he say?'

'That you should not fail to pay him a visit during the day.
Then he added in a very low voice, "Tell your master that His
Eminence is entirely well disposed towards him, and that his fortune
may depend upon this interview."'

'Quite a clumsy trap for the cardinal.' The young man smiled.

'That's why I spotted it, the trap, and said you would be in
despair when you got back.

'"Where has he gone?" asked Monsieur de Cavois. To Troyes
in Champagne, I said. "And when did he leave?" Yesterday
evening . . .'

'Planchet, my friend,' d'Artagnan interrupted, 'You are a truly
invaluable man.'

'You understand, sir, I thought that there'd still be time, if you
wanted to see Monsieur Cavois, to contradict me and say you hadn't

left. Then I'd be the one who'd lied, and, as I am not a gentleman, I can always do that.'

'Don't worry, Planchet, your reputation as a truthful fellow is safe: we're leaving in a quarter of an hour.'

'Exactly the advice I was going to give monsieur. And where are we going, if that's not being too inquisitive?'

'By God, in the opposite direction to the one you said I went in. Besides, aren't you as anxious to have news of Grimaud, Bazin and Mousqueton as I am to know what has become of Athos, Porthos, and Aramis?'

'Yes, I am, sir,' said Planchet, 'and I'll leave whenever you say. Country air will do us a lot more good at the moment, I reckon, than the air of Paris. So then . . .'

'So then, pack our things, Planchet, and let's be off. I'll go on ahead with my hands in my pockets so as not to arouse suspicion. Meet me at the guards' stables. By the way, Planchet, I believe you're right about our landlord: he's unquestionably a ghastly scoundrel.'

'Ah, you should believe me in future, sir. I am a physiognomist – yes I am!'

D'Artagnan went down first, as agreed, and then, so as to have nothing with which to reproach himself, paid a final visit to the lodgings of his three friends. There had been no news of them, but a letter, heavily scented and addressed in an elegant, tiny hand, had arrived for Aramis. D'Artagnan took charge of it. Ten minutes later, Planchet met him at the stables. So as not to waste any time, d'Artagnan had already saddled his horse himself.

'Good,' he said to Planchet, when the latter had put his bags with the other equipment. 'Now saddle up the other three and let's be off.'

'Do you think we'll go faster with two horses apiece?' Planchet inquired with his sardonic air.

'No, Mr Hilarious,' replied d'Artagnan. 'But with our four horses we'll be able to bring back our three friends – if we find them alive, that is.'

'Which would be an incredible stroke of luck,' replied Planchet. 'But still, one must not despair of God's mercy.'

'Amen,' said d'Artagnan, mounting his horse.

And then the two of them emerged from the guards' stables and rode off in opposite directions, one to leave Paris by the Porte de La Villette and the other by the Porte de Montmartre, the plan being to meet up past Saint-Denis. Executed equally promptly by both of them, their strategic manoeuvre was crowned with the most favourable results, and D'Artagnan and Planchet rode into Pierrefitte together.

Planchet, it has to be said, was more courageous during the day than at night.

But his natural prudence never deserted him for a moment. He had forgotten none of the incidents of their first journey, and took everyone he met on the road for an enemy. As a result he had his hat constantly in his hand, which earned him severe rebukes from d'Artagnan, who was afraid such excessive politeness might cause him to be taken for a poor man's valet.

Nevertheless, whether because the passers-by were genuinely impressed by Planchet's urbanity, or because there was no one stationed on the young man's route, our two travellers reached Chantilly without mishap and dismounted at the Great Saint-Martin, the inn where they had stopped on their first journey.

Seeing a young man followed by a valet and two saddle horses, the innkeeper respectfully came to his door. Now, as he had already gone eleven leagues, d'Artagnan thought it would be a good idea to stop, regardless of whether Porthos was in the inn or not. Besides, he reflected, it might not be prudent to ask straight out what had become of the musketeer. Without asking for news of any sort therefore, d'Artagnan dismounted, entrusted the horses to his valet, and went into a small room set aside for those who wished to be alone. He called for a bottle of his host's best wine and the finest breakfast he could provide, a request that further confirmed the high opinion the innkeeper had formed of his traveller at first sight.

D'Artagnan was accordingly served with marvellous alacrity.

The regiment of the guards drew its recruits from the finest families in the realm, and d'Artagnan, with a valet and four magnificent horses in tow, could not fail to cause a sensation, no matter the plainness of his uniform. The innkeeper wished to wait on him himself. Seeing this, d'Artagnan had him bring two glasses and struck up the following conversation:

'My faith, my dear innkeeper,' said d'Artagnan, filling both glasses, 'I asked you for your best wine, and if you've cheated me, you'll reap what you've sown, since, as I hate drinking alone, you are going to drink with me. Take this glass, then, and let's drink. Now, what shall we toast so no one's feelings are hurt? Let's drink to the prosperity of your establishment!'

'Your lordship does me honour,' said the innkeeper, 'and I thank him sincerely for his good wishes.'

'Don't be under any illusions,' said d'Artagnan. 'My toast may be more selfish than you think. One is only properly looked after in thriving establishments. In ailing inns, everything sinks into disarray, and the traveller falls victim to the host's troubles. Now, as I travel a great deal, especially on this road, I'd like to see every innkeeper make his fortune.'

'Indeed,' said the landlord, 'I've a feeling this is not the first time I've had the honour of seeing monsieur.'

'Bah, I've passed through Chantilly ten times perhaps, and out of those ten times I have stopped in your establishment at least three or four. Wait, I was here about ten or twelve days ago. I was giving friends – musketeers – a send off, and the upshot was that one of them got into an argument with a stranger, some unknown man who tried to pick who knows what sort of quarrel with him.'

'Ah, yes indeed,' said the landlord. 'I remember him perfectly. Isn't Your Lordship speaking of Monsieur Porthos?'

'That is exactly what my travelling companion is called. My God, my dear landlord, tell me, has any misfortune befallen him?'

'But Your Lordship must have remarked that he couldn't continue his journey.'

'Indeed, he'd promised to catch us up, but we haven't seen him since.'

'He has done us the honour of staying here.'

'What! He's done you the honour of staying here?'

'Yes, sir, in this hotel. We're even quite concerned.'

'About what?'

'About certain expenses he has run up.'

'Why, if he has run up any expenses, he will pay.'

'Ah, sir, you are pouring a veritable balm into my wounds! We have advanced him some very considerable sums, and only this morning the surgeon declared that if Monsieur Porthos did not pay him, he would go after me, since I was the one who sent for him.'

'But is Porthos wounded, then?'

'I couldn't tell you that, sir.'

'What, you couldn't tell me? You should be better informed than anyone.'

'Yes, but in our profession we don't say everything we know, sir, especially when we've been warned our ears will answer for our tongues.'

'Well then, can I see Porthos?'

'Certainly, sir. Take the stairs, go up to the second floor and knock at number one. But let him know it's you.'

'What! Let him know it's me?'

'Yes, otherwise you might suffer some misfortune.'

'And what misfortune do you expect I'll suffer?'

'Monsieur Porthos might take you for one of the household and, in a fit of anger, pass his sword through your body or blow your brains out.'

'Why, what have you done to him?'

'We asked him for money.'

'Hang it, now I understand. That is a request Porthos takes very badly when he is not in funds. But, as far as I know, he ought to be quite comfortable.'

'That's what we thought too, sir. As this is a very orderly establishment and we do our accounts every week, after eight days we presented him with our bill. But it appears we came at a bad moment, because, at the first word we uttered on the matter, he sent us to all the devils in existence. It's true that he had been playing cards the night before.'

'What! He'd been playing cards the night before? And with whom?'

'Oh, my God, who knows? With some nobleman who was passing through to whom he had proposed a game of lansquenet³.'

'That's it, the poor devil must have lost everything.'

'Including his horse, sir, for when the stranger was about to leave, we noticed that his valet was saddling Monsieur Porthos's horse. We drew his attention to this fact, only to be told we were meddling in matters that didn't concern us and that the horse was his. We immediately informed Monsieur Porthos of what was happening, but he told us we were scoundrels to doubt the word of a gentleman, and that since the man had said the horse was his, it must necessarily be so.'

'That's Porthos,' murmured d'Artagnan.

'Then,' continued the innkeeper, 'I sent back an answer saying that, since we seemed destined not to come to an understanding about payment, I hoped he would at least have the kindness to grant the favour of his custom to my colleague, the proprietor of the Golden Eagle. But Monsieur Porthos replied that, as my hotel was the best, he wished to stay here. This reply was too flattering for me to insist he leave. So I simply asked him to give up his room, which is the most beautiful in the hotel, and settle for a pretty little study on the third floor. But to this Monsieur Porthos replied that, as he was expecting the imminent arrival of his mistress, who was one of the finest ladies at court, I had to understand that even the room he did me the honour of occupying in my establishment was hardly fitting for such a person. Nevertheless, while allowing the truth of what he said, I believed it was my duty to insist. Then, without even troubling to enter into a discussion with me, he took his pistol, set it on his bedside table, and declared that, at the first mention anyone made of a move, either within or without the hotel, he would blow out the brains of whomever would be so imprudent as to meddle in what was solely his concern.

And so, since then, sir, no one has been able to enter his room apart from his servant.'

'Mousqueton is here, then?'

'Yes, sir. Five days after his departure, he came back in an extremely ill humour. It appears he had also suffered some inconvenience on his travels. Unfortunately, however, he is the nimbler of the two of them, and consequently turns everything upside down for his master's sake. He is under the impression we might refuse what he asks for, and so takes everything he needs without asking at all.'

'As a matter of fact,' replied d'Artagnan, 'I have always thought Mousqueton showed a very superior loyalty and intelligence.'

'That may be, sir. But if I were exposed to such intelligence and loyalty just four times a year, I would be ruined.'

'No you won't, because Porthos will pay you.'

'Hmm,' said the innkeeper doubtfully.

'He's the favourite of a lady of great quality who will not leave him in difficulties over a pittance of the sort he owes you.'

'If I only dared say what I think about that . . .'

'What you think?'

'I'll go further – what I know.'

'What you know?'

'And even what I'm sure of.'

'Come now, what are you sure of?'

'I'll go so far as to say I know this great lady.'

'You?'

'Yes, me.'

'And how do you know her?'

'Oh, sir, if I thought I could rely on your discretion . . .'

'Speak, and on my word as a gentleman, you will have no cause to regret your confidence.'

'Well, sir, you understand, anxiety makes one do many things.'

'What have you done?'

'Oh, nothing, in any case, that's not within a creditor's rights.'

'Well?'

'Monsieur Porthos gave us a note for this duchess with instructions to put it in the post. His servant hadn't arrived by then, and, as he was unable to leave his room, he was obliged to entrust us with his errands.'

'Well?'

'Instead of putting the letter in the post, which is never very trustworthy, I took advantage of one of my boys going to Paris, and instructed him to deliver it to the duchess in person. That was carrying out the wishes of Monsieur Porthos, who had commended this letter so forcefully into our care, wasn't it?'

'Up to a point.'

'Well, sir, do you know what this great lady is?'

'No. I've heard Porthos speak of her, that's all.'

'Do you know what this alleged duchess is?'

'I repeat, I don't know her.'

'She is the wife of an old prosecutor from the Châtelet, sir, by the name of Madame Coquenard, who is at least fifty and still puts on a show of being jealous. I thought it was very odd, a princess living in Rue aux Ours[4].'

'How do you know all this?'

'Because she flew into a towering rage when she received the letter, saying that Monsieur Porthos was fickle, and that he'd received this sword thrust over a woman.'

'So he received a sword thrust?'

'Ah, my God, what have I said?'

'You said that Porthos had received a sword thrust.'

'Yes, but he strictly forbade me to say so!'

'Why?'

'By heaven sir, because he had boasted he was going to perforate the stranger with whom you'd left him arguing, and then, quite the opposite, it was the stranger who despite all his bluster, left him stretched out on the tiles. Now, as Monsieur Porthos is an extremely vainglorious man, apart from the duchess, whom he thought would be touched by the story of his adventure, he doesn't want to admit to anyone that he has received a sword thrust.'

'So it is a sword thrust that is keeping him in bed?'

'And a masterly one too, I assure you. He must be tough as nails.'

'You were there, then?'

'I had followed them out of curiosity, sir, so I saw the combat without the combatants seeing me.'

'And what happened?'

'Oh, it wasn't a long affair, I can tell you. They put themselves on guard, the stranger feinted and lunged – all so fast that by the time Monsieur Porthos came to parry, he already had three inches of steel in his chest. He fell over backwards. The stranger immediately brought his sword point to his throat, and Monsieur Porthos, seeing himself at the mercy of his adversary, conceded defeat. Whereupon the stranger asked him his name and, on learning that he was called Monsieur Porthos and not Monsieur d'Artagnan, he gave him his arm, brought him back to the inn, mounted his horse and disappeared.'

'So this stranger had designs on Monsieur d'Artagnan?'

'It seems so.'

'And do you know what's become of him?'

'No, I'd never seen him before that moment, and we haven't seen him since.'

'Very well, I know all I wanted to know. Now, you say Porthos's room is on the second floor, number one?'

'Yes, sir, the finest in the inn, a room I could have filled ten times over by now.'

'Bah, calm down,' laughed d'Artagnan. 'Porthos will pay you with Duchess Coquenard's money.'

'Oh, sir, it would be of no concern whether she were a prosecutor's wife or a duchess as long as she loosened the purse strings, but she stated categorically that she was tired of Monsieur Porthos's demands and infidelities, and that she wouldn't send him a sou.'

'And have you passed on this reply to your guest?'

'We've taken every care not to. He would see how we had carried out his errand.'

'So he's still waiting for his money?'

'Oh, my God, yes! He put pen to paper again yesterday but this time it was his servant who put the letter in the post.'

'And you say the prosecutor's wife is old and ugly!'

'Fifty at least, sir, and no looks at all, according to Pathaud.'

'In that case, don't worry; she will relent. Besides, Porthos can't owe you that much.'

'What, not that much? Twenty pistoles or so already, and that's not counting the doctor. Oh, he doesn't stint himself, that's for sure! You can see he's used to the good life.'

'Well, if his mistress abandons him, he'll find he has friends, I assure you. So, my dear innkeeper, don't worry in the slightest, and go on providing him with all the care his condition demands.'

'Monsieur has promised me he won't mention the prosecutor's wife or speak of the wound.'

'It's settled – you have my word.'

'Oh, because he'd kill me, you see!'

'Don't be afraid: he's not such a devil as he seems.'

Saying which, d'Artagnan went upstairs, leaving his host slightly more reassured about two things he seemed greatly attached to: his balance sheet and his life.

At the top of the stairs, the most conspicuous door in the corridor sported a gigantic number 1 drawn in black ink. D'Artagnan knocked, and on being invited to go about his business by a voice inside, went in.

Porthos was in bed, playing a game of lansquenet with Mousqueton to keep his hand in, while a spit groaning with partridges turned in front of the fire, and, at either corner of the great fireplace, two saucepans simmered on two chafing dishes, releasing the mingled aromas of game fricassee and fish stew that delighted the nose. The top of a desk and the marble slab of a chest of drawers, moreover, were covered with empty bottles.

At the sight of his friend, Porthos let out a great cry of joy and Mousqueton, rising respectfully to his feet, gave up his place to him and went to take a look at the two saucepans, of which he seemed to have personal charge.

'Ah, by God, it's you!' Porthos said to d'Artagnan. 'Welcome, and excuse me if I don't get up to meet you. But,' he added, looking at d'Artagnan with some concern, 'do you know what has happened to me?'

'No.'

'The innkeeper hasn't told you anything?'

'I inquired after you and came straight up.'

Porthos seemed to breathe more freely.

'So what has happened to you, my dear Porthos?' d'Artagnan went on.

'What happened to me was that, as I lunged at my adversary, whom I had already dealt three sword thrusts and wanted to finish off with a fourth, my foot slipped on a stone and I sprained my knee.'

'Really?'

'On my honour! And very fortunate the rascal was too, because otherwise, believe you me, I would have left him dead on the spot.'

'And what has become of him?'

'Oh, I've no notion! He'd had enough and left without further ado. But what about you, my dear d'Artagnan, what's happened to you?'

'So,' d'Artagnan went on, 'it's this sprain that's keeping you in bed, my dear Porthos?'

'Ah, my God, yes, simple as that! Anyhow, I'll be on my feet in a few days.'

'Why didn't you have yourself conveyed to Paris then? You must be excruciatingly bored here.'

'I was planning to – but, my dear friend, there's something I have to confess to you.'

'What?'

'Well, feeling excruciatingly bored, as you say, and having the seventy-five pistoles you gave me in my pocket, as a diversion, I invited up a passing gentleman to keep me company and suggested a game of cards. He agreed and, my faith, my seventy-five pistoles passed from my pocket to his, not to mention my horse, which he took into the bargain. But what about you, my dear d'Artagnan?'

'So it goes, my dear Porthos. You cannot be privileged in every domain,' said d'Artagnan. 'You know the proverb, "Unlucky at cards, lucky in love." You are too lucky in love for the cards not to take their revenge. But what do reverses of fortune matter to you? Don't you have, you lucky beggar – don't you have your duchess, who won't fail to come to your assistance?'

'Ah well, you see, my dear d'Artagnan, I'm having an unlucky run,' Porthos replied with the most nonchalant air in the world. 'I wrote asking her to send me some fifty louis that I had vital need of, given the position I was in . . .'

'And?'

'And she must be on her estates, because she hasn't replied.'

'Really?'

'No. So yesterday I sent her a second more urgent epistle than the first. But here you are, my very dear friend, let's talk about you. I confess I had started to feel a certain anxiety on your account.'

'But your host treats you well, it seems, my dear Porthos,' d'Artagnan said, indicating the full saucepans and the empty bottles to the invalid.

'So-so!' replied Porthos. 'Three or four days ago that impertinent fellow brought up his bill and I slung the two of them out, the man and his bill, so I'm here as a kind of victor, a conqueror of sorts. Which is why, as you can see, always afraid of being stormed in my position, I am armed to the teeth.'

'Nevertheless,' laughed d'Artagnan, 'you seem to make the occasional sortie.'

He pointed to the bottles and saucepans.

'I don't, unfortunately!' said Porthos. 'I'm confined to my bed by this wretched sprain, but Mousqueton scours the country-side and brings back food. Mousqueton, my friend,' Porthos continued, 'you see reinforcements have arrived, we'll need extra supplies.'

'Mousqueton,' said d'Artagnan, 'you must do me a service.'

'What's that, sir?'

'Tell Planchet your recipe. I may find myself besieged in my turn, and I wouldn't object to him treating me to the comforts with which you indulge your master.'

'Oh, goodness, sir,' said Mousqueton modestly, 'nothing could be easier. It is a matter of being handy, that's all. I was raised in the country, and my father was something of a poacher when he had a spare moment.'

'What did he do the rest of the time?'

'He practised a trade, sir, that I have always found rather lucky.'

'What was that?'

'As it was the time of the wars between the Catholics and the Huguenots, and as he saw Catholics wiping out Huguenots and Huguenots wiping out Catholics, all in the name of religion, he adopted a mixed creed which allowed him to be Catholic at one moment and Huguenot the next. Now, he was in the habit of walking with his harquebus⁵ on his shoulder behind the hedgerows by the roadside, and when he saw a lone Catholic coming along, the Protestant faith would immediately gain the upper hand in his mind. He would lower his matchlock in the traveller's direction, and then, when he was ten paces away, strike up a conversation, which almost always ended with the traveller giving up his purse to save his life. I hardly need say that when he saw a Huguenot coming, he was overcome by a Catholic zeal so ardent that it was baffling to him how, a quarter of an hour earlier, he could have doubted the superiority of our holy religion. For I, sir, am a Catholic, since my father, staying true to his principles, made my elder brother a Huguenot.'

'And how did this worthy man end up?' asked d'Artagnan.

'Oh, in the most unfortunate fashion, sir. One day he found himself trapped in a sunken lane between a Huguenot and a Catholic with whom he had already had dealings, and they both recognised him. So they teamed up against him and hanged him from a tree. Then they decided to boast of their fine adventure in the tavern of the first village they came to, where my brother and I were drinking.'

'And what did you do?' said d'Artagnan.

'We let them talk,' replied Mousqueton. 'Then, as they set off in opposite directions when they left the tavern, my brother went to lie in ambush on the Catholic's way, and I on the Protestant's. Two hours later it was all over. We had dealt with them both, and were left full of admiration for the foresight of our poor father, who had taken the precaution of raising us in separate religions.'

'Indeed, as you say, Mousqueton, your father seems to have been an extremely intelligent fellow. And you say that in his spare time the worthy man was a poacher?'

'Yes, sir, and he was the one who taught me how to set a snare and lay a baited line. So, when I saw our rascally host was feeding us a load of coarse meat fit for yokels, which wouldn't suit two stomachs as delicate as ours, I took up my old trade again in a small way. As I went for a walk in the Prince de Condé's woods, I set some snares in the paths, and as I lay on the banks of His Highness's ponds, I slipped some lines into the water. So that now, thank God, we've no shortage, as monsieur can see for himself, of partridges and rabbits, carp and eels – all light and wholesome foods, suitable for invalids.'

'But the wine,' said d'Artagnan. 'Who supplies the wine? Is it your innkeeper?'

'Well, yes and no.'

'How do you mean, yes and no?'

'He supplies it, it's true, but he isn't aware he has that honour.'

'Explain yourself, Mousqueton: your conversation is full of instructive details.'

'This is what it is, sir. I happened to meet a Spaniard on my travels who had seen many countries, including the New World.'

'What connection can there be between the New World and the bottles on this desk and that chest of drawers?'

'Patience, sir, everything will have its turn.'

'Fair enough, Mousqueton. I'll trust you. I'm listening.'

'This Spaniard had a valet in his service who had accompanied him on his journey to Mexico. This valet was a compatriot of mine, which meant we were all the quicker to strike up a friendship because our characters were very alike. We both loved hunting above all things, so he told me how, on the plains of the pampas, the natives of the country hunt tigers and bulls with just a simple noose, which they throw round the necks of these terrible animals. At first I refused to believe anyone could become skillful enough to throw the end of a rope at a target twenty or thirty paces away. But when I saw the proof with my own eyes, I was forced to acknowledge the truth of his story. My friend stood a bottle thirty paces away and snared its neck in the noose with every throw. I took it up, and as nature has given me some abilities, today I can throw a lasso as well as any man in the world. So, do you understand now? Our host has a very well stocked cellar with a key that never leaves his sight – but this cellar has a little window. So I throw the lasso through the window, and knowing the best corner as I do now, I draw up wine from there. And that, sir, is how there comes to be a connection between the New World and the bottles on this chest of drawers and that writing desk. Now, will you be so kind as to taste our wine, and without prejudice, tell us what you think of it?'

'Thank you, my friend, thank you. Unfortunately I have just breakfasted.'

'Well then,' said Porthos. 'Set the table, Mousqueton, and while we two breakfast, d'Artagnan will tell us what has befallen him in the ten days since he left us.'

'Gladly,' said d'Artagnan.

While Porthos and Mousqueton breakfasted with the appetites of convalescents and in that spirit of fraternal cordiality that brings men closer in adversity, d'Artagnan recounted how the wounded Aramis had been forced to stop at Crèvecœur, how he had left Athos at Amiens fighting off four men who accused him of being a counterfeiter, and how he, d'Artagnan, had been forced to run Count de Wardes through the belly to get to England.

But there d'Artagnan's confidences ended. He merely said that, on his return from Great Britain, he had brought four magnificent horses, one for himself and one for each of his companions. Then he concluded by informing Porthos that the one intended for him was already tethered in the inn's stables.

At that moment Planchet entered. He reported to his master that the horses had rested enough, and that they could spend the night in Clermont.

As d'Artagnan was pretty much reassured about Porthos's health, and as he longed to have word of his two other friends, he held his hand out to the invalid, and told him he was setting off again to continue searching. Moreover, as he planned on taking the same route back, if Porthos was still at the Great Saint-Martin in seven to eight days, he would pick him up on the way.

Porthos replied that in all probability his sprain would prevent him from leaving before then. Besides, he had to stay in Chantilly to await a reply from his duchess.

D'Artagnan wished him a swift and favourable reply, and after again commending Porthos to Mousqueton's care and settling up for his part with the landlord, he set off again with Planchet, already relieved of one of his saddle horses.

XXVI
ARAMIS'S THESIS

D'ARTAGNAN HADN'T SAID ANYTHING to Porthos about his wound, or about his prosecutor's wife. For one so young, he was a very canny lad, our Béarnais. Instead he had pretended to believe everything the vainglorious musketeer had told him, convinced that there isn't a friendship that can withstand the revelation of a secret, especially when the secret is a matter of pride. Besides one always has a certain moral superiority over those with whose ways one is acquainted. D'Artagnan would be involved in intrigues in the future, and as he was determined to make his three companions the instruments of his fortune, he did not mind gathering up in advance the invisible threads with which he intended to steer them.

Nevertheless, a profound sadness gripped his heart for the length of his journey. He thought of the young and pretty Madame Bonacieux who was to have conferred on him the reward for his devotion. But, may we quickly add, the young man's sadness was less a matter of regret at his lost happiness than of fear lest any misfortune befall this poor woman. He was in no doubt that she was the victim of the cardinal's vengeance and, as was well known, His Eminence's revenge was terrible. How he had found mercy in the minister's eyes was something he couldn't fathom; no doubt that was what Monsieur Cavois would have revealed if the captain of the guards had found him at home.

Nothing passes the time and shortens a journey like a thought which absorbs into itself all the organising faculties of the person thinking it. External reality resembles a sleep of which that thought is the dream. Under its influence, time loses all measure, space all distance. You leave one place and arrive somewhere else, that is all. Of all the ground covered in between, your memory retains nothing except a vague mist blurring a thousand confused images of trees, mountains and landscapes. Letting his horse go at its own pace, d'Artagnan covered the six or eight leagues between Chantilly and Crèvecœur in the grip of his hallucination, and when he reached the village, could not remember anything he had encountered on the way.

Only there did his memory revive. He shook his head, saw the tavern where he had left Aramis, put his horse into a trot and stopped at its door.

This time it was a landlady rather than a landlord who came to greet him. D'Artagnan was a physiognomist. Taking in the fat, delighted countenance of the mistress of the place at a glance, he saw that he needn't hide anything from her, and had nothing to fear from such a good-humoured face.

'My good lady,' he asked, 'could you tell me what has become of one of my friends whom we were forced to leave here twelve days ago or so?'

'A handsome young man of around twenty-three to twenty-four – gentle, amiable, strappingly built?'

'And wounded in the shoulder, to boot.'

'That's right!'

'The very same.'

'Well, sir, he is still here.'

'Ah, by God, my dear lady,' said d'Artagnan, dismounting and throwing his horse's bridle over Planchet's arm, 'you have brought me back to life! Where is he, that dear Aramis, so I can embrace him? I confess, I'm longing to see him again.'

'Excuse me, sir, but I doubt he can receive you at the moment.'

'Why is that? Because he's with a woman?'

'Oh Lord, what are you saying? The poor lad! No, sir, he is not with a woman.'

'And who is he with then?'

'The curate of Montdidier and the superior of the Jesuits of Amiens.'

'My God,' cried d'Artagnan, 'has the poor lad taken a turn for the worse?'

'No, sir, on the contrary. But, as a result of his illness, he has been touched by grace, and he has decided to take holy orders.'

'That's right,' said d'Artagnan, 'I'd forgotten he was only a temporary musketeer.'

'Does monsieur still insist on seeing him?'

'More than ever.'

'Well then, monsieur only has to take the staircase to the right in the courtyard, third floor, number five.'

D'Artagnan sped off in the direction indicated to him, and found one of those external staircases we still find in the courtyards of old inns. But entering the future priest's presence wasn't as simple as that. The approaches to Aramis's room were guarded as vigilantly as the gardens of Armida¹. Bazin was stationed in the corridor, and he barred d'Artagnan's way all the more fearlessly because, after many years of trials, he finally saw himself on the brink of attaining the outcome he had endlessly coveted.

Indeed, it had always been poor Bazin's dream to serve a man of the Church, and he impatiently awaited the moment, constantly glimpsed in the future, when Aramis would finally throw away his tabard and adopt the cassock. The young man's promise, renewed daily, that this moment was imminent was the only thing that had kept him in the service of a musketeer, a service in which, he used to say, he must surely lose his soul.

Bazin was thus in ecstasy. This time there was every chance his master would not go back on his word. The combination of physical and emotional agony had produced the effect he had so long desired. Suffering in both body and soul, Aramis had finally trained his eyes and thoughts on the Church, and he saw as a warning from heaven the twofold accident he had suffered, namely, the sudden disappearance of his mistress and the wound to his shoulder.

Given this frame of mind, it is understandable that nothing could have been more disagreeable to Bazin than d'Artagnan's arrival, which risked plunging his master back into the whirlwind of worldly ideas that had swept him up for so long. He thus resolved to defend the door stoutly, and since, having been betrayed by the mistress of the inn, he could not say that Aramis was out, he tried to prove to the new arrival that it would be the height of indiscretion to disturb his master in the middle of the pious conference he had embarked upon that morning, and which, Bazin added, couldn't finish before evening.

But d'Artagnan took no notice of Master Bazin's eloquent speech, and, as he didn't care to enter into a debate with his friend's valet, he simply pushed him out of the way with one hand and turned the handle of number five's door with the other.

The door opened, and d'Artagnan went into the room.

Dressed in a black overcoat, his head encased in a round, flat sort of headpiece that bore more than a passing resemblance to a skullcap, Aramis was seated at an oblong table covered with scrolls of paper and enormous folios. On his right sat the superior of the Jesuits and on his left the curate of Montdidier. Half-drawn, the curtains only admitted a mysterious light conducive to devout reverie. All the worldly objects that usually catch the eye when one enters a young man's room, especially when that young man is a musketeer, had vanished as if by enchantment. No doubt afraid the sight of them might reawaken thoughts of this world in his master, Bazin had whisked away the sword, the pistols, the plumed hat and any hint of embroidery or lace.

In their place, d'Artagnan thought he could make out in a dark corner a scourge hanging from a nail in the wall.

At the sound of d'Artagnan opening the door, Aramis raised his head and recognised his friend. But, to the young man's great surprise, his appearance did not seem to make much of an impression on the musketeer, such was his detachment from earthly matters.

'Good day, my dear d'Artagnan,' said Aramis. 'I am glad to see you, believe me.'

'It's mutual,' said d'Artagnan, 'although I'm still not entirely sure I'm talking to Aramis.'

'In person, my friend, in person. But what could make you doubt it?'

'I was afraid I had got the wrong room and thought at first I'd entered the chamber of a man of the Church. Then I fell into error again, finding you in the company of these gentlemen, and thought you might be gravely ill.'

The two men in black, who realised what d'Artagnan was driving at, shot him an almost menacing look, but d'Artagnan remained unruffled.

'Perhaps I'm disturbing you, my dear Aramis,' he continued, 'for, from what I see, I'm inclined to believe you are confessing to these gentlemen.'

Aramis blushed imperceptibly.

'You disturb me? Oh, quite the contrary, my dear friend, I swear. And as proof of it, permit me to rejoice at seeing you safe and sound.'

Ah, he's coming round at last, thought d'Artagnan. And a good job too.

'For monsieur, who is my friend, has just escaped terrible danger,' Aramis continued unctuously, indicating d'Artagnan to the two ecclesiastics.

'Praise God, sir,' they replied, bowing in unison.

'I made a point of it, reverend fathers,' replied the young man, returning their bow.

'You've come at an opportune moment, my dear d'Artagnan,' said Aramis, 'and, by taking part in the discussion, you will illuminate it with your learning. The superior of Amiens, the curate of Montdidier and I are arguing about certain theological questions which have long fascinated us. I would be charmed to have your opinion.'

'A swordsman's opinion really carries very little weight,' protested d'Artagnan, who was starting to feel anxious at the turn things were taking, 'and, believe me, you may depend on these gentlemen's knowledge.'

The two men in black bowed in their turn.

'On the contrary,' said Aramis. 'Your opinion will be invaluable. The question is this: the superior thinks my thesis must, above all, be dogmatic and didactic.'

'Your thesis? So you're doing a thesis?'

'Why, certainly,' replied the Jesuit. 'For the ordination exam, a thesis is obligatory.'

'Ordination?' cried d'Artagnan, who was already having difficulty believing what the landlady and Bazin had told him. 'Ordination!' he repeated, staring, stupefied, at the three characters before him.

'Now,' said Aramis, striking a graceful pose in his chair as if he were in a society salon, and complacently examining his hand, as white and plump as a lady's, which he held up so the blood would drain out of it. 'Now, as you have heard, d'Artagnan, the superior would like my thesis to be dogmatic, whereas I myself would prefer it to be idealist. Which is why the superior has proposed the following subject, which has never been tackled, and which, I acknowledge, contains material for some magnificent developments: *Utraque manus in benedicendo clericis inferioribus necessaria est.'*

D'Artagnan, with whose erudition we are familiar, did not bat an eyelid at this quotation, any more than he had at the one Monsieur de Tréville had dealt him concerning the presents he claimed d'Artagnan had received from the Duke of Buckingham.

'Which means,' said Aramis to make things easier for him, '"Both hands are indispensable for priests of the lower orders when giving the blessing."'

'An admirable subject!' cried the Jesuit.

'Admirable and dogmatic!' repeated the curate, who, having roughly the same grasp of Latin as d'Artagnan, studiously observed the Jesuit so he could keep up with him and repeat like an echo everything he said.

As for d'Artagnan, he remained utterly impervious to the enthusiasm of the two men in black.

'Yes, admirable! *Prorsus admirabile!*2' Aramis went on. 'But it demands careful study of the Fathers and the Scriptures. Now, I have confessed to these learned ecclesiastics, and that in all humility, that guard duty and the king's service have made me neglect my studies a little. I should thus be more comfortable, *facilius natans*, with a subject of my choice, which would stand in relation to these taxing theological questions as morals to metaphysics in philosophy.'

D'Artagnan was profoundly bored, as was the curate.

'Look at that for an exordium!' cried the Jesuit.

'*Exordium*,' repeated the curate to say something.

'*Quemadmodum inter cælorum immensitatem.*'

Glancing in d'Artagnan's direction, Aramis saw his friend was yawning hard enough to dislocate his jaw.

'Let's speak French, father,' he said to the Jesuit, 'Monsieur d'Artagnan will derive a keener enjoyment from our conversation.'

'Yes, I'm tired from the journey,' said d'Artagnan, 'and all this Latin is beyond me.'

'Very well,' said the Jesuit, slightly put out, as the overjoyed priest shot d'Artagnan a grateful look. 'Now then, look at what one can gain from this gloss: Moses, the servant of God . . . he is only a servant, you see? . . . Moses blesses with the hands. Both his arms are held aloft while the Hebrews fight their enemies, so he blesses with both hands. Besides, as the Gospel says: *imponite manus*, not *manum*. Lay on the hands, not the hand.'

'Lay on the hands,' repeated the curate, acting it out.

'To St Peter, on the contrary, whose successors the popes are,' continued the Jesuit, '*porrige digitos*. Stretch out the fingers. Do you follow now?'

'Certainly,' Aramis replied with relish, 'but it's a subtle thing.'

'The fingers!' continued the Jesuit. 'St Peter blessed with the fingers. The Pope thus also blesses with the fingers: And with how many fingers does he bless? With three fingers: one for the Father, one for the Son and one for the Holy Ghost.'

They all crossed themselves, including d'Artagnan, who thought he had better follow suit.

'The Pope is the successor of St Peter and represents the three divine powers. The rest, the *ordines inferiores* of the ecclesiastical hierarchy, bless in the name of the holy archangels and angels. The humblest priests, such as our deacons and sextons, bless with sprinklers, which simulate an indefinite number of blessing fingers. And there you have the bare bones of the subject, *argumentum omni denudatum ornamento*[3]. With it,' the Jesuit went on, 'I could fill two volumes the size of this one.'

And in his enthusiasm he thumped the folio of St Chrysostom, which was causing the table to bow under its weight.

D'Artagnan shuddered.

'Certainly,' said Aramis, 'I give full credit to the beauties of this thesis, but, at the same time, I know it would overwhelm me. I had chosen this text – tell me, dear d'Artagnan, if it is not to your taste – *Non inutile est desiderium in oblatione,* or, better still: A little regret is not unbecoming in an offering to the Lord.'

'Stop!' cried the Jesuit. 'This thesis borders on heresy. There is an almost identical proposition in the *Augustinus* of the heresiarch Jansen[4], whose book sooner or later will be burned at the executioner's hands. Beware, my young friend! You are being lured by false doctrines, my young friend! You will lose your way!'

'You will lose your way,' said the priest, shaking his head sorrowfully.

'You are close to foundering on the famous question of free will, that fatal rock. You are neck and neck with the insinuations of the Pelagians and semi-Pelagians[5].'

'But, reverend father . . .' protested Aramis, slightly dazed by the hail of arguments falling on his head.

'How will you prove,' the Jesuit went on, without giving him time to speak, 'that one must regret the world when one offers oneself to God? Listen to this dilemma: God is God, and the world is the devil. To regret the world is to regret the devil. That's my conclusion.'

'And mine too,' said the priest.

'For pity's sake, though . . .' said Aramis.

'*Desideras diabolum*, you wretch!' cried the Jesuit.

'He regrets the devil! Ah, my young friend,' groaned the priest, 'do not regret the devil, I beg you with all my heart.'

D'Artagnan's brain was turning to mush. He felt as if he were in a madhouse and that he was going to go as mad as the people he could see before him. But he couldn't say anything because he couldn't understand the language they were speaking.

'But, if you'd listen to me for a moment,' Aramis said with a politeness through which a hint of impatience was beginning to be apparent, 'I'm not saying I regret it. No, I would never utter that phrase, that would fly in the face of orthodoxy . . .'

The Jesuit raised his arms to heaven, the curate likewise.

'No, but at least agree that it is ungracious only to offer to the Lord that with which one is thoroughly disgusted. Am I right, d'Artagnan?'

'I should think so, by God!' the latter exclaimed.

The curate and the Jesuit started from their seats.

'Here is my starting point – it is a syllogism. The world does not lack attractions; I am leaving the world; therefore I am making a sacrifice. Now the Scriptures categorically say: Make a sacrifice unto the Lord.'

'That is true,' said the antagonists.

'And besides,' continued Aramis, pinching his ear to make it red, while shaking his hands to make them white. 'And besides, I composed a rondeau on the subject which I communicated to Monsieur Voiture[6] last year, and on which that great man has paid me a thousand compliments.'

'A rondeau?' the Jesuit said disdainfully.

'A rondeau!' the curate said automatically.

'Recite it, recite it,' cried d'Artagnan. 'That will make a change.'

'Ah no, it won't, it's religious,' replied Aramis. 'Theology in verse.'

'Oh hell,' said d'Artagnan.

'Here it is,' said Aramis, with a modest little air which was not entirely free of hypocrisy:

My sad friends, who mourn lost, enchanted years,
And drag out lives ill-starred, ill-fated,
All your misfortunes, like storms, will abate,
When to God alone you offer your tears,
My sad friends.

D'Artagnan and the curate appeared delighted. The Jesuit was unswayed.

'Beware of profane taste in the theological style. Indeed, what does St Augustine say? *Severus sit clericorum sermo*[7].'

'Yes, let the sermon be clear!' said the priest.

'Now,' the Jesuit hastily interrupted, seeing his acolyte going astray, 'now, your thesis will please the ladies, but that is all. It will have the success of one of Master Patru's pleadings[8].'

'Please God!' cried Aramis, in transports.

'You see,' cried the Jesuit, 'the world still speaks in you, at the top of its voice, *altissima voce*. You follow the world, my young friend, and I tremble lest grace won't be effective.'

'Don't worry, father, I can answer for myself.'

'Worldly presumption!'

'I know myself, father – my colours are nailed to the mast.'

'Then you are bent on pursuing that thesis?'

'I feel myself called upon to address it and no other. I shall therefore go on with it and tomorrow I hope you will be satisfied with the corrections I will have made based on your advice.'

'Work slowly,' said the priest, 'we are leaving you in an excellent frame of mind.'

'Yes, the ground is all sown,' said the Jesuit, 'and we have no reason to fear lest some of the grain has fallen on stony ground, some along the path, and that the birds of the sky have eaten the rest, *aves cæli comederunt illam*[9].'

'May the plague choke you with your Latin!' said d'Artagnan, who felt at his wits' end.

'Goodbye, my son,' said the priest, 'till tomorrow.'

'Till tomorrow, you young hothead,' said the Jesuit. 'You promise to be one of the leading lights of the Church. Heaven grant that this light does not become a consuming fire!'

D'Artagnan, who had been biting his nails with impatience for an hour, started on the flesh.

The two men in black rose, bowed to Aramis and d'Artagnan and made for the door. Bazin, who had remained standing, listening to the entire controversy with pious jubilation, sprang forward, took the priest's breviary and the Jesuit's missal, and respectfully set off to clear a path for them.

Aramis saw them to the bottom of the stairs and then immediately went back up to d'Artagnan, who was still lost in thought.

Left alone, the two friends at first maintained an embarrassed silence. One of them had to break it, though, and as d'Artagnan appeared determined to leave that honour to his friend, Aramis said, 'You see, I have returned to my fundamental ideas.'

'Yes, you've been touched by efficient grace[10], as the gentleman said just now.'

'Oh, these plans to retire from the world took shape a long time ago, and you've already heard me talk about them, haven't you, my friend?'

'No doubt, but I must confess I thought you were joking.'

'About these sorts of things? Oh, d'Artagnan!'

'Why not? We joke about death!'

'And we're wrong to, d'Artagnan, for death is the door that leads to perdition or salvation.'

'Quite so. But please, let's not theologise, Aramis you must have had enough for today. For my part, I have pretty much forgotten the little Latin I ever knew. Besides, I must admit, I haven't eaten since ten o'clock this morning, and I'm devilishly hungry.'

'We'll dine presently, my dear friend, only you'll remember that today is Friday, and this day I can neither set eyes on nor partake of meat. If you're willing to make shift with my dinner, it consists of boiled tetragon and fruit.'

'By tetragon, you mean . . .?' d'Artagnan inquired anxiously.

'I mean spinach,' replied Aramis. 'But for you I'll add eggs, and that is a grave infraction of the rule, for eggs, since they produce chickens, strictly speaking, are meat.'

'It's not the most succulent feast, but no matter, I'll submit to it to stay with you.'

'I thank you for your sacrifice,' said Aramis, 'and if it does not profit your body, I assure you it will profit your soul.'

'So you're really going into the Church, Aramis. What will our friends say? What will Monsieur de Tréville say? They'll call you a deserter, I warn you.'

'I am not going into the Church, I am going back to it. It was the Church I deserted for the world, for you know I took the musketeer's tabard against my better instincts.'

'I know nothing of the sort.'

'You are unaware of how I left the seminary?'

'Absolutely.'

'Well then, here's my story. Besides, the Scriptures say, "Confess one to another"[11], and I shall confess to you, d'Artagnan.'

'And I absolve you beforehand – you see, I've got a good heart.'

'Don't joke about sacred matters, my friend.'

'Go on, then, I am listening.'

'I had been at the seminary since I was nine, my twentieth birthday was in three days, I was going to be a priest, everything was settled. One evening I had gone, as was my habit, to a house I enjoyed frequenting – what can you expect, you're young, you're weak – when an officer, who used to look jealously on as I read *The Lives of the Saints* to the mistress of the house, came in suddenly and unannounced. As it happened, that evening I had translated an episode from Judith[12], and had just recited my verses to the lady, who was paying me all sorts of compliments, and, her head on my shoulder, was reading them over again with me. Our attitude, which was rather free, I admit, offended the officer. He didn't say anything, but when I left, he came out after me, caught me up and said, "Monsieur l'abbé, do you like canings?"

'"I can't say, sir," I replied, "since no one has ever dared give me one."

'"Well then, listen, Monsieur l'abbé: if you go back to the house where I met you this evening, I will dare to."

'I think I was afraid. I turned very pale, and felt I'd lost the use of my legs. I searched for some response but couldn't find one, so held my tongue.

'The officer was waiting for this response, and seeing it was slow in coming, he burst out laughing, turned his back on me and went into the house again. I returned to the seminary.

'I am a gentleman and have hot blood, as you may have remarked, my dear d'Artagnan. The insult was terrible, and although it remained hidden from the world, I felt it living and moving deep in my heart. I informed my superiors that I did not feel sufficiently prepared to be ordained, and, at my request, the ceremony was postponed for a year.

'I sought out the best fencing master in Paris, contracted with him to take a fencing lesson every day, and every day for a year I took that lesson. Then, on the anniversary of the day on which I'd been insulted, I hung my cassock on a peg, put on the full costume of a cavalier and went to a ball given by a lady who was a friend of mine, where I knew I should find my man. It was in Rue des Francs-Bourgeois, just by La Force[13].

'And there, indeed, was my officer. I went up to him as he was gazing tenderly at a woman and singing a lover's lay, and interrupted him in the middle of the second verse.

'"Sir," I said to him, "do you still object to my returning to a certain house in Rue Payenne, and will you still give me a caning if I take a fancy to disobey you?"

'The officer looked at me in astonishment, then said, "What do you want of me, sir? I don't know you."

'"I am," I said, "the little priest who reads *The Lives of the Saints* and translates Judith into verse."

'"Aha! I remember," jeered the officer. "What do you want of me?"

'"I would like you to find a moment to take a walk with me."

'"Tomorrow morning, if you wish, and I will do so with the greatest pleasure."

'"No, not tomorrow morning, if you please. Right away."

'"If you absolutely insist . . ."

'"Yes I do, I insist."

'"Let's go, then. Ladies," said the officer, "please don't trouble yourselves. Grant me the time to kill monsieur, and then I shall come back and finish the last verse."

'We went out.

'I directed him to Rue Payenne, to the exact spot where a year before, to the very hour, he had paid me the compliment I have related to you. It was a superb moonlit night. We drew our swords and, at the first pass, I killed him outright.'

'Hellfire!' said d'Artagnan.

'Now,' continued Aramis, 'as the ladies did not see their singer come back, and as he was found in Rue Payenne with a great sword thrust through his body, everyone thought it was I who had cut him up in this fashion and the business caused a scandal. So I was forced to renounce the cassock for a while. Athos, with whom I became acquainted at the time, and Porthos, who, in addition to my fencing lessons, had taught me some lively thrusts, persuaded me to solicit a musketeer's tabard. The king loved my father, who was killed at the siege of Arras, and the tabard was granted to me. So you understand that today the moment has come for me to return to the bosom of the Church.'

'And why today rather than yesterday or tomorrow? What has happened to you today to give you such wretched ideas?'

'This wound, my dear d'Artagnan, has been a warning from heaven.'

'This wound? Pah, it's almost healed, and I'm sure that's not what's causing you the most pain today.'

'And what is?' asked Aramis, blushing.

'You have one in your heart, Aramis, rawer and bloodier, a wound inflicted by a woman.'

Aramis's eye flashed involuntarily.

'Ah!' he said, hiding his feelings under a feigned carelessness. 'Don't talk about such things. Really, me thinking about all that? Suffering lover's heartbreak? *Vanitas vanitatum*! Has my head been turned, in your opinion? And by whom? Some seamstress, some chambermaid I've courted in a garrison? For shame!'

'Forgive me, my dear Aramis, but I thought you set your sights higher.'

'Higher? Who am I to have such ambition? A poor, beggarly, obscure musketeer, who hates servitude and finds himself altogether out of place in the world!'

'Aramis, Aramis!' cried d'Artagnan, looking at his friend doubtfully.

'Dust, I return to dust. Life is full of pain and humiliation,' he continued, sinking into gloom. 'All the threads that bind it to happiness snap in a man's hand, one after the other – the golden threads above all. Oh, my dear d'Artagnan,' continued Aramis, a slight tinge of bitterness in his voice, 'believe me, hide your wounds well. Silence is the last refuge of the unfortunate. Beware of alerting anyone to your pain – the curious suck our tears like flies a wounded deer's blood.'

'Alas, my dear Aramis,' d'Artagnan said, heaving a deep sigh in his turn, 'that is my story you're telling.'

'What?'

'Yes, a woman I loved, I adored, has just been carried off by force. I don't know where she is, where they've taken her. She may be a prisoner, she may be dead.'

'But at least you have the consolation of telling yourself she didn't leave you of her own will; that if you haven't any news of her, it is because all communication with you is forbidden, whereas . . .'

'Whereas . . .'

'Nothing,' said Aramis, 'nothing.'

'So you are giving up the world forever? It's your fixed purpose, your set resolve?'

'Forever and a day. You're my friend today; tomorrow you'll be no more than a shade to me, or rather, you won't even exist. As for the world, it is nothing but a grave.'

'Confound it, that's a very sad thing to say to me.'

'What do you expect? My vocation entices me, it carries me off!'

D'Artagnan smiled and said nothing. Aramis went on, 'And yet, while I still care about this earth, I would have liked to talk with you, about yourself, about our friends.'

'And I,' said d'Artagnan, 'I would have liked to talk with you about yourself, but I find you so detached from everything: you despise love, friends are shades, the world is a grave.'

'Alas! You will see so for yourself,' Aramis said with a sigh.

'Let's say no more about it then,' said d'Artagnan, 'and let's burn this letter, which, no doubt, brings word of some new infidelity on the part of your seamstress or your chambermaid.'

'What letter?' Aramis cried eagerly.

'A letter that came to your lodgings when you were away and was entrusted to me on your behalf.'

'But who is this letter from?'

'Oh, some tearful maidservant, some town girl in despair . . . Madame de Chevreuse's chambermaid perhaps, who was forced to return to Tours with her mistress, and to affect an air of elegance, has taken some scented paper and sealed her letter with a duchess's coronet.'

'What are you saying?'

'Wait, I must have lost it!' said the young man slyly, pretending to search. 'Still, luckily the world is a tomb, and men – and consequently women – are but shadows, and love is a sentiment you despise!'

'Ah, d'Artagnan, d'Artagnan!' cried Aramis. 'You're killing me!'

'Finally, here it is,' said d'Artagnan.

And then he drew the letter from his pocket.

Aramis sprang forward, seized the missive and began to read, or rather devour it, with a radiant expression on his face.

'The maid seems to be a beautiful stylist,' the messenger said nonchalantly.

'Thank you, d'Artagnan!' cried Aramis, almost delirious. 'She was forced to return to Tours, she isn't unfaithful, she still loves me! Come here, my friend, come here so I can embrace you. I can't breathe I'm so happy!'

And then the two friends began to dance around the venerable St Chrysostom, merrily trampling the pages of the thesis that had fallen on to the floor.

At that moment, Bazin entered with the spinach and the omelette.

'Get out of here, you wretch!' cried Aramis, throwing his skullcap in his face. 'Go back where you came from and take those horrible vegetables and ghastly side-dishes with you! Ask for a larded hare, a fat capon, a leg of lamb with garlic and four bottles of old Burgundy.'

Without understanding this change in the slightest, Bazin looked at his master and then melancholically tipped the omelette into the spinach and the spinach on to the floor.

'Now's the time to dedicate your existence to the King of Kings,' said d'Artagnan, 'if you want to pay him a courtesy: *Non inutile desiderium in oblatione.*'

'Go to the devil with your Latin! God's teeth, my dear d'Artagnan, let's drink! Let's drink cool draughts, let's drink deep and long, and, while we're at it, why don't you tell me a little of what's been going on out there.'

XXVII
ATHOS'S WIFE

'NOW WE JUST HAVE TO get word of Athos,' d'Artagnan said to the jubilant Aramis, after he had filled him in on what had been happening in the capital since their departure, and after an excellent dinner had made the one forget his thesis and the other his fatigue.

'So you think he may have suffered some misfortune?' asked Aramis. 'Athos is so imperturbable, so brave, and he handles his sword so ably.'

'Yes, of course, and no one is more ready to acknowledge Athos's courage and skill than I, but I prefer the shock of lances on my sword to that of sticks, and I'm afraid Athos may have taken a beating from that rabble of lackeys. Valets are the sort who hit hard and are in no hurry to stop. That's why, I must confess, I'd like to start out as soon as possible.'

'I'll try to come with you,' said Aramis, 'although I scarcely feel in a fit state to mount a horse. Yesterday I used the scourge you see there on the wall and the pain forced me to give up that pious exercise.'

'Quite apart from the fact, my dear friend, that no one's heard of trying to cure a wound from a musket with the lashes of a whip. But you were ill and illness makes one light-headed, so you are excused.'

'And when are you setting off?'

'Tomorrow at daybreak. Rest as well as you can tonight, and tomorrow, if you are strong enough, we'll set out together.'

'Till tomorrow, then,' said Aramis, 'for, although you're made of iron, you must need some rest.'

On entering Aramis's room the next morning, d'Artagnan found him standing by the window.

'What are you looking at?' he asked.

'My faith,' cried Aramis, 'I'm admiring those three magnificent horses the stable boys are holding by the bridle. It must be a princely pleasure to travel on such creatures.'

'Well then, my dear Aramis, you shall treat yourself to that pleasure, for one of those horses is yours.'

'No! Which one?'

'Whichever of the three you'd like, I have no preference.'

'And the rich caparison covering it belongs to me as well?'

'Certainly.'

'You're joking, d'Artagnan.'

'I haven't made a joke since you started speaking French.'

'Those gilded holsters, that velvet horse-cloth, that silver-studded saddle are mine?'

'Yours and yours alone, just as the horse pawing the ground is mine, and the other one caracoling is Athos's.'

'Heavens above, they're three superb animals!'

'I'm glad they're to your taste.'

'So the king gave you this gift, did he?'

'The cardinal certainly didn't. But don't worry where they came from, just reflect on the fact that one of the three belongs to you.'

'I'll take the one the red-haired valet is holding.'

'Splendid!'

'Thank the Lord,' cried Aramis, 'that's healed the last of my

aches and pains! I could ride him with thirty bullets in my body.
Ah, on my soul, what beautiful stirrups! Ho there, Bazin, come
here this instant.'

Bazin appeared, doleful and listless, in the doorway.

'Polish my sword, straighten my hat, brush my coat, and load
my pistols!' said Aramis.

'No need for that last order,' interrupted d'Artagnan. 'There
are loaded pistols in your holsters.'

Bazin sighed.

'Now then, Master Bazin, don't fret,' said d'Artagnan. 'The
kingdom of heaven is open to those from every walk of life.'

'Monsieur was already such a good theologian,' cried Bazin,
almost in tears. 'He would have become a bishop, perhaps even a
cardinal.'

'Ah, my poor Bazin, come now, think it over a little. What use
is it being a man of the Church, I ask you? It doesn't exempt you
from going to war. You know very well the cardinal is about to
fight his first campaign with a pot-helm on his head and a halberd
in his hand. And what have you to say about Monsieur de Nogaret
de La Valette¹? He's a cardinal too. Ask his valet how many times
he has made lint for bandages.'

'Alas,' Bazin sighed, 'I know, sir, everything is topsy-turvy in
the world today.'

While talking thus, the two young men and the poor valet had
gone downstairs.

'Hold my stirrup, Bazin,' said Aramis.

Aramis sprang into the saddle with his usual grace and light-
ness, but after the noble animal had performed a few capering
turns and leaps into the air, its rider was in such agony that he
grew pale and lost his balance. Foreseeing an accident of this sort,
d'Artagnan hadn't taken his eyes off him. He sprang forward,
caught him in his arms and helped him back to his room.

'It's fine, my dear Aramis, you take care of yourself,' he said.
'I'll go and look for Athos on my own.'

'You are a man of bronze,' said Aramis.

'No, I'm lucky, that's all. Now, what are you going to do in the meantime? No more theses, no more glosses on fingers and blessings, eh?'

Aramis smiled.

'I shall compose verses,' he said.

'Ah yes, verses perfumed with the scent of that note from Madame de Chevreuse's servant. Teach Bazin prosody, then: it will console him. As for the horse, ride him a little every day; you'll get used to his manoeuvring that way.'

'Oh, don't worry about that,' said Aramis, 'you'll find me ready to leave with you.'

They said goodbye, and ten minutes later, after commending his friend to the care of Bazin and the landlady, d'Artagnan was trotting in the direction of Amiens.

What state would he find Athos in? Would he even find him at all?

The position he had left him in was critical; he might easily have been worsted. That thought clouded his brow, wrenched sighs from his breast and caused him to mutter oaths of vengeance. Of all his friends, Athos was the eldest and hence, to all appearances, the furthest removed in his tastes and sympathies.

And yet he had a marked preference for this gentleman. Athos's noble and distinguished air, those flashes of greatness that occasionally blazed forth from the obscurity in which he chose to bury himself, that unfailing equanimity which made him the most easygoing companion on earth, that forced, mordant gaiety, that bravery one might have called blind had it not been the result of the rarest self-possession – such a wealth of qualities inspired more than esteem, more than friendship in d'Artagnan, they inspired his admiration.

Indeed, even when weighed against that elegant and noble courtier, Monsieur de Tréville, on his sanguine days Athos could easily withstand such a comparison. He was of medium height, but that height was so admirably fashioned and proportioned that, in more than one of his wrestling bouts with Porthos, he had bested the giant[2] whose physical strength had become a byword among the musketeers. His face, with its piercing eyes, straight nose and chin like Brutus's, had an indescribable quality of grandeur and grace. His hands, which he neglected completely, were the despair of Aramis, who tended his with prodigious quantities of almond paste and scented oil. The timbre of his voice was at once penetrating and melodious. And then, what was truly indefinable about Athos, who always behaved as if he were of low parentage and no consequence, was his acute knowledge of the world and of the ways of the most glittering society, his habits of good breeding that, seemingly unwittingly, were manifest in every least thing he did.

If there were a dinner, Athos would arrange it better than anyone in the world, allocating to every guest the place and rank that either his ancestors had earned for him or he had earned for himself. If expertise in heraldry were called for, Athos knew all the noble families of the realm, their genealogy, their alliances, their arms and the origin of their arms. Etiquette boasted no minutiae with which he was unfamiliar; he was conversant with all the rights of the great landowners, and so thorough was his knowledge of venery and falconry that, one day, when discoursing on this great art, he had astonished King Louis XIII himself, despite his being a past master on the subject.

Like all the great noblemen of the time, he was an impeccable rider and swordsman. His education, furthermore, had been so little neglected, even with regard to scholastic subjects, which was rare for gentlemen of the time, that he used to smile at the scraps of Latin Aramis dispensed and Porthos pretended to understand. On two or three occasions, to the astonishment of his friends, he had even managed, when Aramis made a rudimentary error, to restore a verb to its rightful tense and a noun to its rightful case. Moreover, his integrity was indisputable, in that age when military men were so quick to compromise with their religion and their consciences, lovers with the rigorous delicacy of our day, and the poor with the Lord's seventh commandment[3].

Athos, therefore, was a very extraordinary man.

And yet it was apparent that so distinguished a nature, so handsome a creature, so refined an essence was sinking insensibly into mindlessness, as old men sink into physical and emotional imbecility. In his times of privation – and there were many of those – everything luminous in Athos would be extinguished and his brilliant side would disappear as if into deep night.

Then, with the demigod vanished, barely a man would remain. Hanging his head, his eyes dull, his speech heavy and painstaking, Athos would spend long hours staring either at his bottle and glass or at Grimaud, who, accustomed to obeying him by signs, would read every least wish in his master's blank gaze and gratify it immediately. If the four friends met during one of those episodes, a single word expelled with a violent effort was Athos's sole contribution to the conversation. In exchange, he would drink enough for four men, while giving no outward sign of it other than a more deeply furrowed brow and a more profound sadness.

D'Artagnan, with whose inquiring and acute mind we are acquainted, had so far been unable, despite an intense desire to satisfy his curiosity on the subject, to assign any cause to this melancholy, or to record its onset. Athos never received letters; Athos never took any step that was not known to all his friends.

It couldn't be said that wine brought on this sadness, for, on the contrary, he only drank to combat it, and then, as we've mentioned, this remedy only made it all the darker. His excess of black bile couldn't be attributed to gambling either, for, unlike Porthos, who greeted the vagaries of chance with songs or oaths, Athos remained equally impassive whether he won or lost. Playing cards with the musketeers, he had been known to win three thousand pistoles in one evening, then lose everything, including the gold embroidered belt he wore on gala days, then win it all back, plus another hundred louis, without his beautiful black eyebrows rising or falling a jot, his hands losing their pearly hue, or his conversation, which was pleasant that evening, ever being less than calm and personable.

Nor was it, as with our neighbours the English, an atmospheric influence that darkened his countenance, because his sadness generally grew more intense at the most beautiful time of the year – June and July were the cruel months for Athos.

He wasn't grieving for anything in the present; he shrugged his shoulders when anyone spoke to him of the future; so his secret must lie in the past, as had vaguely been implied to d'Artagnan.

The mysterious tint that overlay his whole person added to the fascination of this man whose eyes and tongue, even when he was completely drunk, never gave anything away, no matter how skilfully he was questioned.

'Well,' mused d'Artagnan, 'poor Athos may be dead at this moment, and it will be my fault, for it was I who got him into this affair. He didn't know what caused it, he won't know how it turned out, and he never had the chance of profiting from it.'

'Not to mention, sir,' replied Planchet, 'that we very likely owe him our lives. You remember him shouting, "Get away, d'Artagnan, They've got me!" And after loosing off his two pistols, the terrible din he made with his sword! It sounded like twenty men, or rather twenty raging devils!'

These words redoubled d'Artagnan's ardour, and he urged on his horse, which, needing no urging, carried its rider along at a gallop.

Around eleven o'clock in the morning, they caught sight of Amiens. At half-past, they were at the gate of the cursed inn.

D'Artagnan had often contemplated exacting one of those trenchant revenges on the perfidious landlord that, even merely in prospect, afford consolation. He therefore strode into the hostelry with his hat pulled down over his eyes, his left hand on the hilt of his sword, and his riding crop snapping in his right hand.

'Do you recognise me?' he said to the innkeeper, who came forward to greet him.

'I haven't that honour, my lord,' the man replied, his eyes dazzled by d'Artagnan's brilliant turnout.

'Ah, so you don't know me!'

'No, my lord.'

'Well, a word or two will restore your memory. What have you done with the gentleman whom you had the audacity a fortnight ago to accuse of passing off counterfeit money?'

The host grew pale, d'Artagnan having assumed a most threatening attitude and Planchet having copied his master.

'Ah, my lord, don't speak to me of him,' cried the landlord in the most lachrymose voice he could muster. 'Ah, Lord, how I've paid for that mistake! Ah, luckless wretch that I am!'

'I'm asking you, what has become of that gentleman?'

'Deign to listen to me, my lord, and be merciful. Come, sit down, for pity's sake!'

Mute with rage and anxiety, d'Artagnan seated himself, as forbidding as a judge, while Planchet leant haughtily against his chair.

'Here is the story, my lord,' the host went on, trembling all over, 'for I recognise you now. You left when I had that unfortunate dispute with the gentleman you speak of.'

'Yes, I did. So you see you cannot expect any mercy if you do not tell the whole truth.'

'Be so kind as to listen to me, then, and you'll know every last detail of it.'

'I'm listening.'

'I had been warned by the authorities that a notorious counterfeiter would be coming to my inn with several of his companions, all disguised in guards' or musketeers' uniforms. Your horses, your valets, your faces, my lord, had all been described to me.'

'And then? And then?' said d'Artagnan, quickly realising the source of such an exact description.

'Following the authorities' orders, who sent me a reinforcement of six men, I took such measures as I believed imperative to secure the persons of the alleged counterfeiters.'

'Go on!' said d'Artagnan, his ears burning terribly at the term 'counterfeiter'.

'Forgive me, my lord, for saying such things, but that's my

excuse. The authorities had scared me, and you know a landlord must remain on good terms with the authorities.'

'But, I ask you again, where is this gentleman? What has become of him? Is he dead or is he alive?'

'Patience, my lord, we're nearly there. You know what happened next, and your hasty departure,' the host added with a sharpness that did not escape d'Artagnan, 'seemed to justify the outcome. The gentleman – your friend – defended himself desperately. His valet, who, by an unforeseen misfortune, had picked a quarrel with the authorities' men, who were disguised as stable boys . . .'

'Ah, you wretch!' cried d'Artagnan. 'You were all in league – I don't know why I don't wipe you all out!'

'Alas, no, my lord, we were not all in league, as you will soon see. Monsieur your friend (forgive me for not calling him by the honourable name he undoubtedly bears, but we do not know it), monsieur your friend, after putting two men out of action with his two pistol shots, defended himself with his sword while he beat a retreat, crippling another of my men and stunning me with a blow from the flat side.'

'You tormenter, are you ever going to finish?' said d'Artagnan. 'Athos, what has become of Athos?'

'While beating a retreat, as I said to your lordship, he found the stairs to the cellar at his back, and as the door was open, he took the key and barricaded himself inside. Since we knew we'd find him there, we left him to it.'

'Ah yes,' said d'Artagnan, 'you weren't bent on killing him outright, you just wanted to imprison him.'

'God of Justice, imprison him, my lord? He imprisoned himself, I swear. And before he did, he had put his back into his work, I can tell you: one man killed on the spot and two others grievously wounded! The dead man and the two wounded were carried off by their comrades and I haven't heard a word about either party since. As for myself, when I came round, I went to the governor, told him all that had happened, and asked him what

I should do with the prisoner. But the governor seemed dumb-founded. He told me he had no idea what I was talking about, that my orders hadn't come from him, and that if I had the misfortune to tell anyone he had anything to do with this brawl, he would have me hanged. Apparently I was mistaken, sir; I'd arrested the wrong man and the one who should have been arrested had got away.'

'But Athos?' cried d'Artagnan, doubly impatient at the news that the authorities had washed their hands of the matter. 'What has become of Athos?'

'As I was in a hurry to redress the wrongs I had done the prisoner,' said the innkeeper, 'I went to the cellar to set him free again. Ah, sir, I didn't find a man there any more, I found a devil! When I offered him his freedom, he replied that it was a trap and that he was going to impose conditions before he came out. I told him very humbly – because I fully appreciated the predicament I had got myself into by laying hands on one of His Majesty's musketeers – I told him I was ready and willing to submit to his conditions.

'"First," he said, "I want my valet returned to me, fully armed."

'We hastened to obey this order, for, you understand, sir, we were disposed to do everything your friend wished. Monsieur Grimaud (he did tell us his name, not that he's not much of a talker himself), Monsieur Grimaud was therefore taken down to the cellar, heavily wounded as he was. Then his master, having taken him in, barricaded the door again and sent us about our business.'

'Come now,' cried d'Artagnan, 'where is he? Where is Athos?'

'In the cellar, sir.'

'What, you wretch, you've kept him in the cellar all this time?'

'Heavens above, no, sir! Us keep him in the cellar? You don't know what he's doing down there! Ah, if you could make him come out, sir, I would be grateful to you for the rest of my life, I would worship you as my patron saint!'

'So, he's there? I'll find him there?'

'You certainly will, sir, he has doggedly stayed put. Every day we pass him bread on a pitchfork through the air-vent, and meat too when he asks for it, but alas, bread and meat are not his main diet. One day I tried to go down with two of my servants, but he flew into a terrible fury. I heard the click of him cocking his pistols and his valet cocking his carbine. When we asked their intentions, the master replied that he and his valet had forty shots between them, and that they would fire every last one of them sooner than allow a single one of us to set foot in the cellar. So then, sir, I went to complain to the governor, who told me that I had only got what I deserved, and that it would teach me to insult honourable noblemen who lodged under my roof.'

'So that, since then . . .' replied d'Artagnan, who couldn't help laughing at the pitiful expression on his host's face.

'So that, since then, sir,' continued the latter, 'we've been leading the most woeful existence imaginable. For you should know, sir, that all our provisions are in the cellar. There's our wine in bottles and our wine in barrels, our beer, oil and spices, bacon and sausages. And as we are forbidden to go down there, we are forced to refuse food and drink to the travellers who visit us, so that our hostelry loses money every day. Another week with your friend in my cellar, and we're ruined.'

'And that would only be fair, you rogue. Wasn't it obvious from our appearance that we were men of quality and not forgers, eh?'

'Yes, sir, yes, you're right,' said the landlord. 'But wait, wait, there he is flying into a rage.'

'Doubtless someone has disturbed him,' said d'Artagnan.

'But we have to disturb him!' cried the innkeeper. 'Two English gentlemen have just arrived.'

'So?'

'So, the English like good wine, as you know, sir, and these two have called for the best. My wife must have requested Monsieur Athos's permission to enter in order to satisfy these gentlemen, and he must have refused as usual. Ah, heavens above, now the racket's louder than ever!'

Indeed, d'Artagnan heard a great noise coming from the

direction of the cellar. He stood up and, preceded by the landlord, who wrung his hands, and followed by Planchet, who held his carbine cocked, he approached the scene.

The two gentlemen were exasperated. They had ridden a great distance and were dying of hunger and thirst.

'But it's pure tyranny,' they cried in very good French, though with a foreign accent, 'that this madman won't allow these good people the use of their wine. We'll break down the door, and if he's too much of a mad dog, well, we'll kill him.'

'Steady, gentlemen!' said d'Artagnan, drawing his pistols from his belt. 'You won't kill anyone, if you please.'

'Excellent,' said the calm voice of Athos behind the door, 'let those child-eaters come in, then we'll see.'

Despite their apparent bravery, the two English gentlemen looked hesitantly at one another. It was as though the cellar contained one of those ravenous ogres, one of those giant heroes of popular legend, whose cave no one can storm with impunity.

There was a moment's silence, but eventually the two Englishmen were too ashamed to retreat, and the more cantankerous of the two went down the five or six steps of the staircase and gave the door a thunderous kick that would have split open a wall.

'Planchet,' said d'Artagnan, cocking his pistols, 'I'll take care of the one at the top, you take care of the one below. Ha, gentlemen, you want a fight, do you? Well then, we'll give you one!'

'Good God,' cried the hollow voice of Athos, 'I think I hear d'Artagnan.'

'Yes indeed,' said d'Artagnan, raising his voice in turn. 'It is I, my friend.'

'Ah, good,' said Athos. 'Then we'll give these door-breakers a beating.'

Having drawn their swords, the gentlemen found themselves caught between two lines of fire. They hesitated for another moment, but, as before, pride carried the day and a second kick cracked the door from top to bottom.

'Stand back, d'Artagnan, stand back,' cried Athos, 'stand back, I'm going to shoot.'

'Gentlemen,' said d'Artagnan, whose reason never deserted him, 'gentlemen, think it over! – Be patient, Athos – You're getting into a bad business, and you'll be riddled with shot. Here are my valet and I, who will fire three rounds at you, and you'll get the same number from the cellar. Then we'll still have our swords, which, I assure you, my friend and I handle tolerably well. Let me settle your affairs and mine. You'll have something to drink presently, I give you my word.'

'If there's anything left,' growled Athos, in a mocking voice.

The innkeeper felt a trickle of cold sweat run down his spine.

'What does he mean, if there's anything left?' he murmured.

'Confound it, of course there will be,' said d'Artagnan. 'Don't worry, they can't have drunk the whole cellar between them. Gentlemen, sheathe your swords.'

'You tuck your pistols back in your belt, then.'

'Gladly.'

D'Artagnan set an example, and then, turning to Planchet, motioned for him to uncock his musket.

Convinced, the British sheathed their swords, grumbling. They were told the story of Athos's imprisonment. And as they were true gentlemen, they laid the blame on the innkeeper.

'Now, gentlemen,' said d'Artagnan, 'go back up to your rooms, and I give you my word, in ten minutes you will be brought everything you could wish.'

The Englishmen bowed and left.

'Now I'm alone, my dear Athos,' d'Artagnan said, 'open the door for me, I beg you.'

'This very instant,' said Athos.

There followed a great noise of clashing logs and groaning beams: these were Athos's counterscarps and bastions, which the besieged man was demolishing himself.

A moment later, the door edged open, and Athos's pale face appeared, as he scanned the surroundings with a quick glance.

D'Artagnan threw his arms around his neck and embraced him tenderly. But when he set about helping him out of his humid abode, he noticed that Athos was staggering.

'Are you wounded?' he said.

'I? Not in the slightest. I'm dead drunk, that's all, and no man ever did a better job of making himself so. Lord above, my host – speaking for myself, I think I must have got through at least a hundred and fifty bottles.'

'Mercy!' cried the innkeeper. 'If the valet drank only half as much as the master, I'm ruined.'

'Grimaud is too reputable a valet to permit himself the same bill of fare as me. He only drank from the barrel. Wait, I think he forgot to put the spigot back in . . . Do you hear? It's leaking.'

D'Artagnan let out a roar of laughter that turned the landlord's shivers into a raging fever.

At the same time, Grimaud appeared in turn behind his master. With the carbine on his shoulder, his head bobbing, he looked like one of the drunken satyrs in Rubens's[4] paintings. His chest and back were drenched in a greasy liquid that the landlord recognised as his best olive oil.

The procession crossed the public room and went to make itself comfortable in the best room of the inn, which d'Artagnan firmly commandeered.

Meanwhile, the landlord and his wife rushed with lamps down to the cellar that had so long been forbidden them, and found a frightful spectacle awaiting them.

Beyond the fortifications Athos had breached to get out – a mass of logs, planks and empty casks stacked according to the rules of strategic art – they saw the remains of the hams dotted here and there, swimming in pools of oil and wine, a heap of broken bottles clogging the whole left-hand corner of the cellar, and a barrel, the tap of which had been left open, spilling the last drops of its blood. The image of death and devastation, as the ancient poet says, reigned there as on a battlefield.

Fifty sausages had been hanging from the rafters, of which scarcely ten remained.

At that the howls of the landlord and landlady pierced the cellar's vault. Even d'Artagnan himself was moved, but Athos did not so much as turn his head.

Grief, however, promptly gave way to rage. The landlord armed himself with a spit and, in his despair, rushed into the room to which the two friends had retired.

'Wine!' called Athos, at the sight of the landlord.

'Wine?' exclaimed the stupefied landlord. 'Wine? But you've drunk over a hundred pistoles' worth at my expense! I'm a ruined man – lost, destroyed!'

'Bah!' said Athos. 'We were thirsty the whole time.'

'If you'd just drunk it, well . . . but you've broken all the bottles.'

'You pushed me on to a stack of them and made it come clattering to the floor. It's your fault.'

'All my oil is gone!'

'Oil is a sovereign balm for wounds, and poor Grimaud had to bandage the ones you gave him.'

'All my sausages have been gnawed past recognition!'

'It's incredible how many rats there are in that cellar.'

'You're going to pay for everything,' cried the exasperated innkeeper.

'You vile rascal!' said Athos, getting to his feet, then immediately fell back down, his strength exhausted. Raising his riding crop, d'Artagnan came to his assistance.

The host shrank back and dissolved into tears.

'That will teach you to show more courtesy to the guests God sends you,' said d'Artagnan.

'God – you mean the devil!'

'My dear friend,' said d'Artagnan, 'if you keep deafening us, all four of us will lock ourselves in your cellar and see if the damage really is as bad as you say.'

'Very well, gentlemen,' said the landlord, 'I'm wrong, I admit it. But there is mercy for every sin. You are noblemen, and I'm a poor innkeeper – you ought to take pity on me.'

'Ah, you'll break my heart if you talk that way,' said Athos, 'and the tears will flow from my eyes like the wine from your casks. We're not such devils as we seem. Now then, come over here and let's talk.'

The landlord took a tentative step towards him.

'Come here, I say, and don't be afraid,' continued Athos. 'When I was about to pay you, I put my purse on the table.'

'Yes, my lord.'

'That purse contained sixty pistoles. Where is it?'

'Deposited with the town clerk, my lord. It was said to be counterfeit money.'

'Well then, get them to give you back my purse and keep the sixty pistoles.'

'But my lord knows very well that the town clerk never lets go of anything once he has got his hands on it. If it was counterfeit money, there'd still be hope, but unfortunately those coins were good.'

'Arrange it with him, my good man, it is not my concern, particularly since I don't have a livre left.'

'Let's see,' said d'Artagnan, 'where is Athos's old horse?'

'In the stables.'

'How much is he worth?'

'Fifty pistoles at most.'

'He's worth eighty. Take him, and we'll say no more about it.'

'What? You're selling my horse?' said Athos. 'You're selling my Bajazet? And what will I ride on campaign – Grimaud?'

'I've brought you another one,' said d'Artagnan.

'Another one?'

'It's magnificent, too!' cried the landlord.

'Well, if there is another younger and more handsome, take the old stager and let's drink!'

'What would you like?' asked the landlord, his serenity entirely restored.

'The vintage at the back, near the laths. There are still

twenty-five bottles of it left, all the others were broken by my fall. Bring up six.'

Why, he's a hogshead, this man! the innkeeper said to himself. If he'd stay just a fortnight, and pay for what he drinks, my business will be back on its feet.

'And don't forget,' d'Artagnan went on, 'to take four bottles of the same up to the two English noblemen.'

'Now,' said Athos, 'while we wait for them to bring us the wine, come, d'Artagnan, tell me what has become of the others.'

D'Artagnan told him how he had found Porthos in bed with a sprain, and Aramis sitting at his table with a theologian either side. As he was finishing, the landlord entered with the bottles he had asked for and a ham, which, fortunately for him, had been stored somewhere other than the cellar.

'Very good,' said Athos, filling his and d'Artagnan's glasses, 'here's to Porthos and Aramis. But what about you, my friend – what's wrong? What's happened to your good self? I fancy you look downcast.'

'Alas!' said d'Artagnan. 'That's because I am the unhappiest of us all!'

'You, unhappy, d'Artagnan?' said Athos. 'Come now, how are you unhappy? Tell me.'

'Later,' said d'Artagnan.

'Later? And why later? Because you think I'm drunk, d'Artagnan? Remember this in future: I am never clearer-headed than when I'm in my cups. Speak, then, I'm all attention.'

D'Artagnan related his adventure with Madame Bonacieux.

Athos listened without batting an eyelid, and, when he'd finished, said, 'Those are all trifles – mere trifles!'

That was Athos's favourite expression.

'You always dismiss things as "trifles", my dear Athos,' said d'Artagnan. 'It doesn't become you, never having been in love yourself.'

Athos's dead eyes flared up suddenly, but only for a moment, before becoming as dull and vague as before.

'That's true,' he said calmly, 'I have never been in love.'

'You see, then, you heart of stone,' said d'Artagnan, 'you're wrong to be hard on those of us with tender hearts.'

'A tender heart is a broken heart,' said Athos.

'What are you saying?'

'I say that love is a lottery in which the prize is death! You're very fortunate to have lost, believe me, my dear d'Artagnan. And if I have any advice to give you, it's always to lose.'

'She seemed to love me so much!'

'She seemed to.'

'Oh, she did love me!'

'You child! There isn't a man who hasn't believed, like you, that his mistress loved him, and there isn't a man who hasn't been deceived by her.'

'Except you, Athos, who's never had a mistress.'

'That's true,' said Athos, after a moment's silence. 'I've never had one of my own. Let's drink!'

'Well then, philosopher that you are,' said d'Artagnan, 'instruct me, support me; I need wisdom and consolation.'

'Consolation for what?'

'For my misfortune.'

'Your misfortune is laughable,' said Athos, shrugging his shoulders. 'I'd be curious to hear what you'd say if I told you a love story.'

'Involving you?'

'Or one of my friends – what difference does it make?'

'Tell me, Athos, tell me.'

'Let's drink, that's a better idea.'

'Drink and tell the story.'

'That can be done, as a matter of fact,' said Athos, emptying and refilling his glass, 'the two complement one another perfectly.'

'I'm listening,' said d'Artagnan.

Athos collected his thoughts, and as he did so, d'Artagnan saw him turn pale. He had reached that stage of drunkenness when an ordinary drinker would slump to the ground and fall asleep. He, however, was dreaming out loud without being asleep. There was something terrifying about this drunken somnambulism.

'You really want to hear?' he asked.

'I beg you,' said d'Artagnan.

'As you wish, then. One of my friends – a friend, you understand, not myself,' said Athos, interrupting himself with a sombre smile, 'one of the counts of my province – that is, of Berry – who was as noble as a Dandolo or a Montmorency[5], fell in love at the age of twenty-five with a young girl of sixteen. She was as beautiful as love itself. An ardent spirit shone through the naivety of her age, the spirit not of woman but of poet. She did not merely please, she intoxicated. She lived in a little market town with her brother who was a curate. They had both recently arrived in that part of the country. No one knew where they came from, but seeing her so beautiful and her brother so pious, no one thought to ask. Besides, they were said to be of good family. My friend, who was the lord there, could have seduced her or taken her by force if he wished. He was the master. Who would have come to the aid of two strangers, two unknowns? Unfortunately, he was an honest man. He married her. The fool, the simpleton, the imbecile!'

'But why, if he loved her?' asked d'Artagnan.

'Just wait,' said Athos. 'He took her to his château and made her the first lady of the province. And, one must do her justice, she occupied her position admirably.'

'Well?' asked d'Artagnan.

'Well, one day when she was out hunting with her husband,' Athos went on, speaking very fast in a low voice, 'she fell off her horse and fainted. The count rushed to her aid and, as she was suffocating in her clothes, he cut them open with his dagger and bared her shoulder. Guess what was on her shoulder, d'Artagnan,' said Athos with a great gust of laughter.

'How could I know?' asked d'Artagnan.

'A fleur-de-lys,' said Athos. 'She was branded[6].'

And then Athos emptied the glass he was holding in his hand in a single draught.

'That's horrible!' cried d'Artagnan. 'What are you telling me?'

'The truth. My dear friend, the angel was a demon. The poor young girl had been a thief.'

'And what did the count do?'

'The count was a great lord; he had the right to administer low and high justice on his lands. He tore off the rest of the countess's clothes, bound her hands behind her back, and hanged her from a tree.'

'Heavens, Athos, a murder!' cried d'Artagnan.

'Yes, a murder, plain and simple,' said Athos, pale as death. 'Why, they're letting me go without wine, it seems.'

And then Athos seized the last bottle by the neck, brought it to his lips and drained it in one, like an ordinary glass.

Then he let his head sink into his hands. D'Artagnan stared at him, horror-struck.

'That has cured me of beautiful, poetic, loving women,' said Athos, straightening up and forgetting to continue his fable of the count. 'May God grant you the same! Let's drink!'

'So she's dead?' stammered d'Artagnan.

'Yes, by God!' said Athos. 'But come on, hold out your glass. Hey there, ham, you rogue!' cried Athos. 'We can't drink!'

'And her brother?' d'Artagnan added timidly.

'Her brother?' said Athos.

'Yes, the priest?'

'Ah, I searched for him to hang him in his turn, but he had got the start of me. He had fled his parish the previous evening.'

'Did anyone at least find out who the wretch was?'

'Doubtless the beauty's first lover and accomplice, a worthy man who had perhaps pretended to be a priest to see his mistress married and provided for. He will have been quartered by now, I trust.'

'Oh, my God! My God!' said d'Artagnan, stunned by this horrible adventure.

'Have some of this ham, d'Artagnan, it's exquisite,' said Athos, cutting a slice and putting it on the young man's plate. 'What a shame there weren't four like it in the cellar. I'd have drunk another fifty bottles!'

D'Artagnan couldn't take any more of this conversation, otherwise he would have gone mad. He let his head sink into his hands and pretended to fall asleep.

'Young people don't know how to drink these days,' said Athos, looking at him pityingly, 'and yet he's one of the best of them! . . .'

XXVIII

RETURN

D'ARTAGNAN WAS LEFT STUNNED by Athos's terrible secret. Many things, however, still struck him as obscure in this partial revelation. Apart from anything else, it had been made by a man who was completely drunk to one who was half so. And yet, despite the blurriness of the brain caused by the fumes of two or three bottles of Burgundy, when d'Artagnan woke up the next morning, he could remember Athos's every word as clearly as if they had stamped themselves on his mind the moment they fell from his lips. His doubts only made him more anxious to reach some certainty, so he went to his friend's room bent on resuming their conversation of the night before. But there he found Athos his usual self again – that is, the subtlest and most impenetrable of men.

Furthermore, after shaking hands with him, the musketeer anticipated his thoughts.

'I was very drunk yesterday, my dear d'Artagnan,' he said. 'I felt it this morning in my tongue, which was still terribly thick, and in my pulse, which was still terribly agitated. I'll wager I held forth on a thousand extravagant matters.'

Saying this, he looked at his friend with an intentness that embarrassed him.

'Not at all,' replied d'Artagnan. 'If I remember rightly, you said nothing out of the ordinary.'

'Ah, you amaze me! I thought I'd told you a most woeful story.'

And then he looked at the young man as if he would read to the very depths of his heart.

'My faith!' said d'Artagnan. 'Apparently I was even drunker than you, because I don't remember a thing.'

Unconvinced by this, Athos continued, 'You must have noticed, my dear friend, that everyone has his own kind of drunkenness – sad or merry. I have the sad kind, and once I'm fuddled, I have a way of coming out with every doleful story my foolish nurse stuffed into my brain. It's my failing – a capital failing, I agree – but, in all other respects, I am a good drinker.'

Athos said this so naturally that d'Artagnan's conviction wavered.

'Oh, yes, that's right,' said the young man, trying to recover his purchase on the truth, 'I remember – it's like remembering a dream, in fact – we talked about hangings.'

'Ah, you see,' said Athos, turning pale and yet trying to laugh, 'I was sure of it: hanged men are my worst nightmare.'

'Yes, yes,' said d'Artagnan, 'now it's coming back to me, yes, it involved . . . wait . . . it involved a woman.'

'See,' replied Athos, virtually sheet-white, 'it's my great story of the woman with the blonde hair. When I tell it, it means I'm dead drunk.'

'Yes, that's right,' said d'Artagnan, 'the story of the tall, beautiful blonde woman, with blue eyes.'

'Yes, and hanged.'

'By her husband, who was a nobleman of your acquaintance,' continued d'Artagnan, staring fixedly at Athos.

'Well now, look how you can compromise a man when you have no idea what you're saying any more,' replied Athos, shrugging his shoulders, as if he were taking pity on himself. 'Honestly, I want to stop getting drunk, d'Artagnan, it's a terrible habit.'

D'Artagnan kept silent.

'By the way,' Athos said, suddenly changing the subject, 'thank you for that horse you brought me.'

'Is he to your liking?' asked d'Artagnan.

'Yes, but he wasn't a working horse.'

'You're mistaken. I rode ten leagues on him in less than an hour and a half, and he looked as if he'd just taken a turn around Place Saint-Sulpice.'

'Ah, you'll make me have regrets.'

'Regrets?'

'Yes, I got rid of him.'

'How is that?'

'Here's what happened: I woke up this morning at six o'clock. You were dead to the world, and I didn't know what to do. I was still in a complete stupor from our debauch last night. I went down to the public room and saw one of our Englishmen haggling over a horse with a dealer, his own having died yesterday of a stroke. I went up to him, and as I saw he was offering a hundred pistoles for a sorrel, I said to him, "By God, my dear sir, I've got a horse for sale too."

'"And a very handsome one too," said he. "I saw him yesterday, your friend's valet was holding him."

'"Do you think he's worth a hundred pistoles?"

'"Yes. And will you let me have him for that price?"

'"No, but I'll play you for him."

'"You'll play me for him?"

'"Yes."

'"At what?"

'"At dice."

'No sooner said than done, and I lost the horse. Ah, I can tell you, though,' continued Athos, 'I won back the saddle!'

D'Artagnan made a disgruntled face.

'Does that irk you?' said Athos.

'Why, yes, I confess it does,' said d'Artagnan. 'The point of that horse was to allow us to be recognised on the battlefield: it was a token, a souvenir. You did wrong, Athos.'

'Come now, my dear friend, put yourself in my place,' retorted the musketeer. 'I was bored to death. Besides, on my word of honour, I don't like English horses. Look, if it's just a matter of being recognised by someone, well, the saddle will do the job – it's very distinctive. As for the horse, we'll find some excuse to justify its disappearance. Hang it, horses are mortal! Let's say mine had the glanders or farcy.'

D'Artagnan's face did not brighten.

'It's vexing,' Athos went on, 'that you seem so attached to these animals, for I haven't finished my story.'

'What else have you done?'

'After losing my horse – nine against ten, that was the throw – I had the idea of staking yours.'

'Yes, but it was just an idea, I hope?'

'No, I acted on it right away.'

'Ah, I don't believe it!' d'Artagnan exclaimed anxiously.

'I staked him and lost.'

'My horse?'

'Your horse, seven against eight. For lack of a point . . . you know the proverb¹.'

'Athos, I swear you've taken leave of your senses!'

'My dear friend, you should have told me that yesterday, when I was regaling you with my ridiculous stories, rather than this morning. So, I lost him with every conceivable bit of tack and equipment.'

'But this is awful!'

'Wait, there's more. I would make an excellent gambler if I didn't get carried away, but I do get carried away, just as when I drink. So I got carried away . . .'

'But what could you wager? There was nothing left.'

'There was, my friend, there was. We still had that diamond flashing there on your finger, which I remarked yesterday.'

'This diamond!' cried d'Artagnan, quickly covering his ring with his hand.

'And as I am a connoisseur, having had some of my own, I had valued it a thousand pistoles.'

'I hope,' d'Artagnan said gravely, half-dead with fright, 'you didn't mention my diamond?'

'On the contrary, my dear friend. You understand, the diamond was now our only resource. With it I could win back our harnesses and our horses, and, what's more, the money we'll need for our travels.'

'Athos, you're giving me the shudders!' cried d'Artagnan.

'So I mentioned your diamond to my partner, who had also remarked it. Confound it, my dear friend, you can't wear a star fallen from heaven on your finger and expect people not to pay attention to it! It's impossible!'

'Get to the point, my dear friend, get to the point!' said d'Artagnan. 'On my honour, your matter-of-factness is killing me.'

'So then we divided the diamond into ten parts of a hundred pistoles each.'

'Ah, this is a joke to test me, is it?' said d'Artagnan, anger seizing him by the hair as Minerva seized Achilles in the *Iliad*[2].

'God's blood, no, I'm not joking! I'd like to have seen you in my shoes! I hadn't set eyes on a human face for a whole fortnight; I'd been in there the whole time, stupefying myself and parlaying with bottles.'

'That's no reason to wager my diamond,' replied d'Artagnan, nervously clenching his fist.

'Listen to how it turned out, then. Ten parts of a hundred pistoles each, in ten throws, with no rematch. In thirteen throws, I lost everything. Thirteen throws! The number thirteen has always been fatal for me. It was on the thirteenth of July that . . .'

'God's wounds!' cried d'Artagnan, getting up from the table, the morning's story making him forget the one of the night before.

'Patience!' said Athos. 'I had a plan. The Englishman was an eccentric. I'd seen him talking to Grimaud that morning, and Grimaud had told me he had offered to take him on. So I stake Grimaud, the silent Grimaud, divided into ten parts.'

'Ah, what a stroke of genius!' said d'Artagnan, bursting out laughing in spite of himself.

'Grimaud himself, you hear! And then, with the ten parts of Grimaud, which aren't worth a ducat in total, I win back the diamond. Now tell me persistence isn't a virtue.'

'My faith, that's hilarious!' cried a relieved d'Artagnan, shaking with laughter.

'You can understand that, as I was feeling lucky, I immediately staked the diamond again.'

'Oh, hang it,' said d'Artagnan, a pall of gloom descending over him again.

'I won back your harness, then your horse, then my harness, then my horse, and then I lost them all again. In short, I ended up recovering your harness, then mine. And that's where we are now. It was a wonderful throw, so I left it at that.'

D'Artagnan exhaled as if the whole tavern had been lifted off his chest.

'So I still have the diamond?' he said timidly.

'In one piece, my dear friend! Along with your Bucephalus's harness and mine.'

'But what shall we do with our harnesses without horses?'

'I have an idea about that.'

'Athos, you're giving me the shudders.'

'Listen, you haven't gambled for a long time, have you, d'Artagnan?'

'And I have no desire to either.'

'Let's not rule anything out. You haven't gambled for a long time, as I say, so you should be in luck.'

'Well, what of it?'

'Well, the Englishman and his companion are still here. I remarked that they felt very aggrieved about the harnesses. You seem to be attached to your horse. In your place, I'd wager your tack against your horse.'

'But he won't want just one harness.'

'Wager both of them, by God! I am not selfish like you.'

'You'd do that?' wavered d'Artagnan, as Athos's confidence stealthily began to win him over.

'Word of honour, on a single throw.'

'But, since we've lost the horses, I was very keen to keep the harnesses.'

'Wager your diamond, then.'

'Oh no, that's completely different. Never, never!'

'Hang it!' said Athos. 'I'd happily propose you wager Planchet, but as that's been done already, the Englishman may not want a repeat.'

'The truth is, my dear Athos,' d'Artagnan said, 'I'd rather not risk anything.'

'Pity,' said Athos coldly, 'the Englishman is rolling in pistoles. Hey, my God, just try one throw – a throw only takes a second!'

'What if I lose?'

'You'll win.'

'But what if I lose?'

'Well, then you'll give up the harnesses.'

'Fine, one throw, then,' said d'Artagnan.

Athos went looking for the Englishman and found him in the stable, where he was examining the harnesses with a covetous eye. The timing was perfect. He set out his conditions: the two harnesses against either a horse or a hundred pistoles, they could choose which. The Englishman made a quick calculation: the two harnesses together were worth three hundred pistoles. He shook on it.

D'Artagnan tremblingly threw the dice and rolled a three. His pallor frightened Athos, who simply said, 'That's a dismal throw, friend. Sir you will have the horses fully saddled and bridled.'

In his triumph, the Englishman didn't even bother to roll the dice. He just threw them on the table without looking, so certain was he of victory. D'Artagnan had turned his back to conceal his ill humour.

'Well, well, well,' said Athos in his calm voice. 'That's an extraordinary throw of the dice; I've only seen it four times in my life. Two aces!'

The Englishman looked and was seized with astonishment. D'Artagnan looked and was seized with delight.

'Yes,' continued Athos, 'only four times: once at Monsieur de Créquy's, another time at home in the countryside, in my château of . . . when I had a chateau; a third time at Monsieur de Tréville's, where he surprised us all; and finally a fourth time in a tavern, where I was on the receiving end and it cost me a hundred louis and a supper.'

'So, monsieur is taking back his horse?' said the Englishman.

'Certainly,' said d'Artagnan.

'Then there's to be no rematch?'

'Our conditions stated no rematch, you remember?'

'That's true. The horse will be handed over to your servant, sir.'

'One moment,' said Athos. 'With your permission, sir, I request to have a word with my friend.'

'Go ahead.'

Athos drew d'Artagnan aside.

'Well,' said d'Artagnan, 'what do you want of me now, tempter? You want me to keep playing, isn't that it?'

'No, I want you to think.'

'About what?'

'You're going to take back the horse, aren't you?'

'Of course.'

'You're wrong. I'd take the hundred pistoles. You know you wagered the harnesses against your choice of the horse or the hundred pistoles.'

'Yes.'

'I'd take the hundred pistoles.'

'Well, I'm taking the horse.'

'And you're wrong, I repeat. What are we going to do with one horse between the two of us? I can't ride behind you: we'd look like two sons of Aymon[3] who'd lost their brothers. And you can't humiliate me by riding next to me astride that magnificent steed. I would take the hundred pistoles without a moment's hesitation; we need money to get back to Paris.'

'I am very attached to that horse, Athos.'

'And you're wrong to be, my friend. A horse shies, a horse stumbles and damages its knees, a horse eats from a rack where a glandered horse has eaten before him – and that's the last you see of your mount, or rather your hundred pistoles. The master has to feed his horse, whereas a hundred pistoles will feed their master.'

'But how will we get back?'

'On our valets' horses, by God! It will be obvious from our faces that we're men of quality.'

'A fine figure we'll cut on our nags, while Aramis and Porthos caracole on their horses!'

'Aramis? Porthos?' cried Athos, and he started laughing.

'What?' asked d'Artagnan, not understanding his friend's hilarity.

'All right, all right, let's go on,' said Athos.

'So, your advice . . . ?'

'Is to take the hundred pistoles, d'Artagnan. With the hundred pistoles we will feast until the end of the month. We have suffered fatigue, you see, and it will be well for us to rest a little.'

'Rest? Ah, no, Athos, the minute I get to Paris, I shall start searching for that poor woman.'

'Well, do you think your horse will be as useful to you for that as some solid gold louis? Take the hundred pistoles, my friend, take the hundred pistoles.'

D'Artagnan only needed a reason to give in. This one struck him as excellent. Besides, he was afraid if he held out any longer, he'd appear selfish in Athos's eyes. So he agreed and chose the hundred pistoles, which the Englishman counted out right away.

Their only thought after that was to be on their way. The peace treaty they had concluded with the landlord cost six pistoles, in addition to Athos's old horse. D'Artagnan and Athos took Planchet and Grimaud's horses, and the two servants set off on foot, carrying the saddles on their heads.

Poorly mounted though the two friends were, they soon drew ahead of their servants and reached Crèvecœur. From a distance they spied Aramis leaning sadly out of his window and, watching the dusty horizon like 'Sister Anne[4]'.

'Hey, hey, Aramis! What the devil are you doing there?' cried the two friends.

'Ah, it's you, d'Artagnan, it's you, Athos,' said the young man. 'I was thinking how shortlived worldly goods are. My English horse, which ran off and has just disappeared in a whirl of dust, struck me as a living image of the fragility of earthly things. Life itself can be summed up in three words: *Erat, est, fuit*[5].'

'Which means?' asked d'Artagnan, who was beginning to suspect the truth.

'Which means I've just made a fool's bargain: sixty louis for a horse which, judging by the way he moves, could do five leagues an hour at a trot.'

D'Artagnan and Athos burst out laughing.

'My dear d'Artagnan,' Aramis said, 'don't hold it against me too much, I beg you. Necessity knows no law. Besides, I am the first to be punished, since that infamous horse dealer robbed me of at least fifty louis. Ah, you're good husbanders, you two! You come on your valets' horses and have your fine chargers led by hand, slowly and in short stages.'

At that moment a wagon, which for several minutes had been coming into view on the Amiens road, stopped, and Planchet and Grimaud could be seen emerging with their saddles on their heads. The wagon was returning empty to Paris, and in exchange for their ride, the two valets had undertaken to keep the driver in refreshments on the way.

'What's this?' said Aramis, seeing what was happening. 'Just the saddles?'

'You understand now?' said Athos.

'My friends, I was the same. An instinct made me keep the tack. Ho there, Bazin! Put my new harness with these gentlemen's.'

'And what have you done with your priests?' asked d'Artagnan.

'My dear friend, I invited them to dinner the next day,' said

Aramis. 'There's some exquisite wine here, by the way. I proceeded to get them as drunk as I could. Then the priest forbade me to give up the tabard and the Jesuit begged me to get him enrolled as a musketeer.'

'Without a thesis!' cried d'Artagnan. 'Without a thesis! I demand the suppression of the thesis!'

'Since then,' continued Aramis, 'I've been living very agreeably. I began a poem in lines of one syllable. It's rather difficult, but merit in all things depends on their difficulty. The theme is amatory. I'll read you the first canto. It is four hundred lines long and takes a minute to recite.'

'My faith, my dear Aramis,' said d'Artagnan, who loathed verse almost as heartily as Latin, 'add the merit of brevity to that of difficulty and your poem will be sure to have at least two merits.'

'Not to mention,' continued Aramis, 'that it's imbued with seemly passions, as you'll see. Ah, my friends, so we're going back to Paris? Bravo, I'm ready. We shall see the good Porthos again, so much the better. What, you don't believe I missed that great ninny? You wouldn't find him selling his horse, not even for a kingdom. I wish I could see him now, on his beast and in his saddle. I am sure he'd look every inch the Great Mogul.'

They stopped for an hour to allow the horses to rest. Aramis settled his account, and put Bazin in the wagon with his comrades, and then they set off to join Porthos.

They found him up and about, with more colour in his cheeks than when d'Artagnan had seen him on his first visit, and presiding over a table, which, despite his being alone, was laid with a dinner for four. The repast consisted of gallantly trussed meats, choice wines and superb fruits.

'Ah, by God!' he said, getting to his feet. 'Perfect timing, gentlemen, I had just started on the soup. You shall dine with me.'

'Oho!' said d'Artagnan, 'Mousqueton can't have lassoed such bottles as these. And here's a larded fricandeau[6], and a fillet of beef . . .'

'I'm building up my strength,' said Porthos, 'I'm building up my strength. Nothing weakens one like these devilish sprains. Have you ever sprained anything, Athos?'

'Never. But I remember that, during our fracas in Rue Férou, I received a sword thrust that, after fifteen or eighteen days, had exactly the same effect.'

'This dinner wasn't just for you though, was it, my dear Porthos?' said Aramis.

'No,' said Porthos, 'I was expecting some local gentlemen who've just sent word to say they aren't coming. You will take their places and I shall lose nothing by the exchange. Ho there, Mousqueton! Chairs! And double the number of bottles!'

Ten minutes elapsed, then Athos asked, 'Do you know what we're eating here?'

'By God,' replied d'Artagnan, 'I'm eating veal larded with cardoons and marrow.'

'And I, fillets of lamb,' said Porthos.

'And I, breast of chicken,' said Aramis.

'You're all mistaken, gentlemen,' Athos replied gravely. 'You're eating horse.'

'Come now!' said d'Artagnan.

'Horse?' cried Aramis with a grimace of disgust.

Porthos alone remained silent.

'Yes, horse. Isn't that right, Porthos, that we're eating horse? Perhaps even with the trappings!'

'No, gentlemen, I kept the harness,' said Porthos.

'My faith, we're all the same,' Aramis said. 'It's as if we'd spread the word.'

'What would you have me do?' said Porthos. 'That horse was putting my visitors to shame – I didn't want to humiliate them!'

'As well as the fact that your duchess is still taking the waters, is that right?' said d'Artagnan.

'She is,' replied Porthos. 'But, my faith, the governor of the province, one of the gentlemen I was expecting to dinner today, seemed to want the animal so much that I gave it to him.'

'Gave?' cried d'Artagnan.

'Oh, my God, yes, gave! That's the word,' said Porthos, 'for he was certainly worth a hundred and fifty louis, and the miser only wanted to pay me eighty.'

'Without the saddle?' said Aramis.

'Yes, without the saddle.'

'You will notice, gentlemen,' said Athos, 'that once again Porthos has struck the best bargain of us all.'

There was a loud shout of laughter, which completely startled poor Porthos. But the cause of this hilarity was soon explained to him, and he joined in heartily, as was his way.

'So we're all in funds?' said d'Artagnan.

'Not for my part,' said Athos. 'I thought Aramis's Spanish wine so good that I had sixty bottles loaded on to the valet's wagon, which has all but cleared me out.'

'And I,' said Aramis, 'as you can imagine, gave all but my last sou to the church of Montdidier and the Jesuits of Amiens. I'd also entered into engagements, which I had to keep: masses ordered for myself and for you, gentlemen, which will be said and I have no doubt will do wonders for us.'

'And do you think,' said Porthos, 'my sprain cost me nothing? Not to mention Mousqueton's wound, for which I was obliged to have the surgeon come in twice a day, and he charged me double for his visits on the grounds that Mousqueton had caught a bullet in a place that is not ordinarily displayed to apothecaries. I have therefore strongly advised him not to get wounded there again.'

'Well, well,' said Athos, exchanging a smile with d'Artagnan and Aramis. 'I see you have behaved nobly towards the poor boy: that is the mark of a good master.'

'In short,' Porthos went on, 'once I've paid my bill, I'll have a good thirty or so écus left.'

'And I'll have a dozen pistoles,' said Aramis.

'Well, well,' said Athos, 'it seems we're the Croesuses of society. How much of your hundred pistoles is left, d'Artagnan?'

'Of my hundred pistoles? First of all, I gave you fifty.'

'You think so?'

'By God!'

'Ah, that's true, I remember.'

'Then I paid the landlord six.'

'What an animal that landlord was! Why did you give him six pistoles?'

'You told me to.'

'I'm too kind, it's true. In a word, the balance?'

'Twenty-five pistoles,' d'Artagnan said.

'And I,' said Athos, taking some small change from his pocket, 'I . . .'

'You – nothing.'

'My faith, or so little it's not worth putting in the pot.'

'Now, let's calculate how much we have in total. Porthos?'

'Thirty écus.'

'Aramis?'

'Ten pistoles.'

'And you, d'Artagnan?'

'Twenty-five.'

'Which makes in total?' said Athos.

'Four hundred and seventy-five livres!' said d'Artagnan, who calculated like Archimedes.

'When we get to Paris, we'll still have a good four hundred,' said Porthos, 'plus the harnesses.'

'But our regimental horses?' said Aramis.

'Well, of the four valets' mounts, we will make two for masters and draw lots for them. We can use the four hundred livres for half a horse for one of the dismounted, and then we can give the scrapings of our pockets to d'Artagnan, who is in luck, and he will go and stake them in the first gambling den we come to. And there it is!'

'Let's dine,' said Porthos. 'It's getting cold.'

The four friends, calmer now about their future, did honour to the repast, and then the leftovers were given to Messrs Mousqueton, Bazin, Planchet and Grimaud.

On reaching Paris, d'Artagnan found a letter from Monsieur de Tréville informing him that, as per his request, the king had just granted him the favour of joining the musketeers[7].

As that was everything d'Artagnan coveted in the world – apart, of course, from wanting to find Madame Bonacieux again – he ran joyfully to his comrades, whom he had just left half an hour before, and found them very sad and very concerned. They were gathered in council at Athos's, which always indicated circumstances of a certain gravity.

Monsieur de Tréville had just sent word that, as it was His Majesty's firm intention to open the campaign on the first of May, they had to prepare their outfits at once.

The four philosophers were gazing at one another, stunned. Monsieur de Tréville did not joke about matters of discipline.

'And how much do you estimate these outfits cost?' said d'Artagnan.

'Ah, there's no getting around it,' replied Aramis. 'We've just made our calculations with a Spartan parsimony, and we'll need fifteen hundred livres each.'

'Four times fifteen is sixty, that makes six thousand livres,' said Athos.

'I think,' said d'Artagnan, 'that with a thousand livres each – true, I'm not speaking as a Spartan, but as a lawyer . . .'

The word 'lawyer' woke Porthos up.

'Wait, I've got an idea,' he said.

'That's a start; I haven't even the ghost of one,' Athos said coldly. 'But as for d'Artagnan, gentlemen, the joy of being one of us now has driven him mad. A thousand livres! I declare I need two thousand for my part alone.'

'Four times two is eight,' Aramis said then, 'so it's eight thousand livres that we need for our outfits. It's true we already have the saddles.'

'Plus,' said Athos, waiting until d'Artagnan, who was going to thank Monsieur de Tréville, had closed the door, 'plus that beautiful diamond flashing on our friend's finger. Confound it,

d'Artagnan is too good a comrade to leave his brothers in a fix
when he's wearing a king's ransom on his middle finger!'

XXIX
THE HUNT FOR OUTFITS

O F THE FOUR FRIENDS, THE most preoccupied was undoubtedly d'Artagnan, despite the fact that, as a guard, it was
far easier for him to fit himself out than it was for the gentlemen
musketeers, who were noblemen. But, as may already have been
remarked, our Gascon cadet was of a careful, if not actually
miserly, disposition, while also being (explain contraries if you
can) almost vainglorious enough to be a match for Porthos. The
preoccupations of his vanity, however, were now joined by a less
selfish anxiety. Such enquiries as he had been able to make about
Madame Bonacieux had not led to any news. Monsieur de Tréville
had spoken of her to the queen, but the queen didn't know where
the mercer's young wife was. She had promised to instigate a
search but this promise was very vague and of but scant reassur-
ance to d'Artagnan.

Athos, meanwhile, did not leave his rooms. He was resolved
not to take a single step to fit himself out.

'We still have a fortnight,' he told his friends. 'Well then, if, at
the end of that fortnight, I have found nothing – or rather, if
nothing has come to find me – as I am too good a Catholic to blow
my brains out with a pistol, I'll pick a good quarrel with four of
His Eminence's guards or eight Englishmen and fight until one of
them kills me, which, at those odds, should be a foregone conclusion. People will say that I died for the king, so I'll have served
him without needing to fit myself out.'

Porthos continued to pace about with his hands behind his
back, nodding his head up and down, and saying, 'I'll pursue my
idea.'

As for Aramis, wracked with anxiety, his curls a mess, he said nothing.

It will be apparent from these disastrous details that desolation reigned in their little community.

The valets, for their part, like the coursers of Hippolytus[1], shared their masters' bitter affliction. Mousqueton laid in a store of crusts; Bazin, who'd always had a penchant for devotion, spent his every waking moment in church; Planchet watched the flies buzzing about; and Grimaud, who could not be induced by the general distress to break the silence his master had imposed, heaved piteous sighs that would have moved stones to tears.

The three friends – for, as we have said, Athos had sworn not to move a muscle to outfit himself – the three friends went out very early every day and came back very late. They wandered through the streets, scrutinising every paving stone to see if a passer-by had dropped a purse. They could almost have been tracking an animal, so watchful were they at every turn. When they met up, their disconsolate looks seemed to say, 'Have you found anything?'

As Porthos had come up with his idea first, however, and then doggedly pursued it, he was the first to take action. He was a man of deeds, that worthy Porthos. D'Artagnan spotted him one day heading towards the church of Saint-Leu[2] and instinctively followed him. After twisting up his moustache and smoothing down his imperial, always the sign of the most lady-killing of intentions on his part, Porthos entered the holy place believing he was unobserved since d'Artagnan, who had come in behind him, had been careful to hide. He went to loll against one side of a pillar, and d'Artagnan, still unnoticed, leant against the other.

As chance would have it, a sermon was in progress at that moment, which meant the church was very crowded. Porthos took the opportunity to survey the women of the congregation. Through the good offices of Mousqueton, his outward appearance was far from announcing his inner distress. His felt hat was certainly somewhat threadbare, his plume somewhat faded, his embroidery somewhat tarnished, and his lace frayed, but in that subdued light all those trifles disappeared, and Porthos was still the handsome Porthos.

In the pew closest to the pillar, against which he and Porthos were leaning, d'Artagnan remarked a sort of mature beauty, slightly yellow, slightly desiccated, but straight-backed and haughty under her black head-dress. Porthos's eyes furtively alighted on this lady, then fluttered off down the nave.

Blushing from time to time, the lady meanwhile cast lightning glances at the fickle Porthos, at which his eyes fluttered away still more furiously. This little game clearly stung the lady in the black head-dress to the quick, for she started biting her lips until they bled, scratching the tip of her nose and fidgeting desperately in her seat.

When he saw this, Porthos curled his moustache once more, smoothed down his imperial for a second time, and then began signalling to a beautiful lady who was near the choir. She was clearly not only a beautiful, but also a great lady, since she had behind her a black boy who had brought the cushion on which she was kneeling, and a maid, who was carrying the emblazoned bag in which she kept her mass-book.

Following Porthos's gaze through all its rovings, the lady in the black head-dress saw it was trained on the lady with the velvet cushion, the black boy and the maid.

In the meantime, Porthos had been playing a cautious game: a matter of winks, of fingers pressed to the lips, of killing little smiles, which really were killing the scorned beauty.

As a mea culpa, therefore, beating her breast, she uttered such a vigorous 'Hm!' that everyone, even the lady with the red cushion, turned in her direction. But Porthos held fast. Despite understanding perfectly, he feigned deafness.

The lady with the red cushion made a deep impression, by virtue of her great beauty, both on the lady in the black head-dress, who saw in her a truly formidable rival; and on Porthos, who thought her prettier than the lady in the black head-dress; and on d'Artagnan, who recognised her as the lady from Meung, Calais and Dover, whom his persecutor, the man with the scar, had addressed by the name of Milady.

Without losing sight of the lady with the red cushion, d'Artagnan continued to observe Porthos's game, which amused him enormously. He ventured to guess that the lady in the black head-dress was the prosecutor's wife from Rue aux Ours, especially because the church of Saint-Leu wasn't very far from that street.

He further divined by inference that Porthos was seeking revenge for his defeat at Chantilly, when the prosecutor's wife had proved so recalcitrant in regard to her purse.

And yet, in the midst of all this, d'Artagnan also remarked that no one in the church was responding to Porthos's attentions. It was all just chimaeras and illusions – but for a real love, a true jealousy, is there any other reality than chimaeras and illusions?

At the conclusion of the sermon, the prosecutor's wife set off towards the stoop, but Porthos got there first and, instead of a finger, plunged his whole hand in the holy water. The prosecutor's wife smiled, thinking Porthos was putting himself out on her behalf. But she was promptly and cruelly undeceived. When she was only three paces from him, he turned away and stared unwaveringly at the lady with the red cushion, who had stood up and was approaching, followed by her black boy and her lady's maid.

When the lady with the red cushion was close to Porthos, he drew his hand from the stoop, all dripping with holy water. The devout beauty touched Porthos's great hand with her slender fingers, smilingly made the sign of the cross and left the church.

This was too much for the prosecutor's wife. She no longer doubted that the lady and Porthos were having a dalliance. If she had been a great lady, she would have fainted, but as she was only a prosecutor's wife, she merely said with concentrated fury to the musketeer, 'What, Monsieur Porthos, are you not going to offer me any holy water?'

Porthos started at the sound of that voice like a man waking up from a hundred-year sleep.

'Ma . . . madam!' he cried. 'Is it really you? How is your husband, that dear Monsieur Coquenard? Is he still as miserly as ever? Where were my eyes that I did not even notice you in the two hours that sermon lasted?'

'I was a few steps away from you, sir,' replied the prosecutor's wife, 'but you didn't notice me because you only had eyes for the fair lady to whom you have just given the holy water.'

Porthos feigned embarrassment.

'Ah,' he said, 'you noticed . . .'

'One would have had to be blind not to.'

'Yes,' Porthos said nonchalantly, 'she's a friend of mine, a duchess, whom I have great difficulty meeting on account of her husband's jealousy, and who had informed me that, purely for the sake of seeing me, she would be visiting this wretched church today, in the depths of this godforsaken neighbourhood.'

'Monsieur Porthos,' said the prosecutor's wife, 'would you kindly offer me your arm for five minutes? I would be very glad to talk with you.'

'By all means, madam!' said Porthos, winking to himself like a gambler laughing at the dupe he's about to make of someone.

At that moment, d'Artagnan passed in pursuit of Milady. Glancing sidelong at Porthos, he saw the triumphant wink.

'Hey, hey!' he thought to himself, reasoning according to the strangely easy morals of that age of gallantry. There's someone who could be going to fit himself out in time.'

Yielding to the pressure of the arm of his prosecutor's wife as a boat yields to the rudder, Porthos arrived at the cloister of Saint-Magloire[3], an ill-frequented passage enclosed by turnstiles at either end. The only people to be seen in it during the day were either beggars eating or children playing.

'Ah, Monsieur Porthos!' cried the prosecutor's wife, after making sure they couldn't be seen or heard by anyone who was a stranger to the usual inhabitants of the place. 'Ah, Monsieur Porthos, you are a great conqueror, it seems!'

'I, madam?' said Porthos with a swagger. 'And why is that?'

'Those signs just now? The holy water? She must be a princess at least, that lady with her black boy and her lady's maid!'

'You're mistaken. My God, no,' replied Porthos, 'she's merely a duchess.'

'And that attendant waiting at the door, and that carriage with a coachman in full livery waiting on its box?'

Porthos had not seen the attendant or the carriage, but, with her jealous woman's gaze, Madame Coquenard had seen all.

Porthos regretted not having made the lady with the red cushion a princess to start off with.

'Ah, you are the pet of all the beautiful women, Monsieur Porthos!' resumed the prosecutor's wife with a sigh.

'Why,' replied Porthos, 'endowed by nature with a physique such as mine, you can understand that I have no shortage of conquests.'

'My God, how quick men are to forget!' cried the prosecutor's wife, raising her eyes to heaven.

'Not as quick as women, I think,' replied Porthos. 'For, after all, madam, I may say that I was your victim, when, wounded, at death's door, I saw myself abandoned by the surgeons. I, the scion of an illustrious family, who had depended on your friendship, I almost died first of my wounds, and then of hunger, in a wretched tavern in Chantilly, while you did not deign to reply to even one of the burning letters I wrote to you.'

'But, Monsieur Porthos . . .' murmured the prosecutor's wife, who sensed that, judged against the conduct of the great ladies of the time, she was in the wrong.

'I, who had sacrificed the Countess de Penaflor for you . . .'

'I know!'

'The Baroness de . . .'

'Monsieur Porthos, don't overwhelm me.'

'The Duchess de . . .'

'Monsieur Porthos, be generous!'

'You are right, madam, and I shall not be exhaustive.'

'But it is my husband who won't hear of lending.'

'Madame Coquenard,' said Porthos, 'remember the first letter you wrote to me, which I treasure, and have kept graven on my memory.'

The prosecutor's wife uttered a groan.

'But it was also that,' she said, 'the sum you were asking to borrow was really a little steep.'

'Madame Coquenard, I gave you my preference. I only had to write to the Duchess de . . . I do not wish to say her name, for I do not know what it is to compromise a woman. But what I do know is that I only had to write to her for her to send me fifteen hundred.'

The prosecutor's wife shed a tear.

'Monsieur Porthos,' she said, 'I swear that you have punished me severely, and that if, in the future, you should find yourself in a similar position, you have only to ask me.'

'For shame, madam,' cried Porthos, as if disgusted, 'let's not speak of money, please. It is humiliating.'

'So you don't love me any more,' the prosecutor's wife said slowly and sadly.

Porthos maintained a majestic silence.

'Is that your answer? Alas, I understand.'

'Think of the offence you have done me, madam. It has lodged itself here,' said Porthos, placing his hand on his heart and pressing hard.

'Come, my dear Porthos, I will make it right!'

'In any case, what was I asking of you?' continued Porthos with a most good-natured shrug. 'After all, I am not an unreasonable man. I know you are not rich, Madame Coquenard, and that your husband is obliged to suck the blood of his wretched litigants to extract a few wretched écus from them. Oh, if you were a countess, marchioness or duchess, that would be different, and you would be beyond forgiveness.'

The prosecutor's wife was stung.

'Let me tell you, Monsieur Porthos,' she said, 'there's every chance that my strongbox – strongbox of a prosecutor's wife though it may be – is better furnished than all your fine, impoverished ladies' coffers.'

'Then you have doubly offended me,' said Porthos, disengaging the arm of the prosecutor's wife from his, 'for if you are rich, Madame Coquenard, then your refusal is inexcusable.'

'When I say rich,' the prosecutor's wife demurred, realising she had let herself be carried away, 'you must not take the word literally. I am not exactly rich: I am comfortable.'

'Look, madam,' said Porthos, 'let's say no more about it, please. You have slighted me. All fellow-feeling between us is destroyed.'

'Ungrateful man!'

'Ah yes, I'd complain if I were you!' said Porthos.

'Go off with your beautiful duchess then! Don't let me keep you.'

'She still has some flesh on her bones, I believe!'

'Look, Monsieur Porthos, I'll ask you once again, and this is the last time: do you still love me?'

'Alas, madam,' said Porthos in the most melancholy tone he could assume, 'when we are about to go on campaign, a campaign in which I have a presentiment I shall be killed . . .'

'Oh, don't say such things,' cried the prosecutor's wife, bursting into sobs.

'Something tells me it will be so,' continued Porthos, sinking further and further into melancholy.

'Tell me you have a new love rather than that!'

'No, I'll be perfectly frank with you: no new object has touched my affections. I even feel here, at the bottom of my heart, something that speaks for you. But, in a fortnight, as you may or may not know, this fatal campaign will begin; I will be terribly taken up with my outfit. Then I'm going to take a trip to my family, in deepest Brittany, to secure the funds necessary for my departure.'

Porthos sensed a final struggle between love and avarice.

'And,' he went on, 'as the duchess, whom you saw in church just now, has her estates near mine, we will make the journey together. Journeys, you know, are always much shorter when one has company.'

'You have no friends in Paris, then, Monsieur Porthos?' said the prosecutor's wife.

'I thought so,' said Porthos, assuming his melancholy air, 'but I've seen I was mistaken.'

'You do, though, Monsieur Porthos, you do!' protested the prosecutor's wife in a passionate outburst that took even her by surprise. 'Come to the house tomorrow. You are my aunt's son, hence my cousin; you come from Noyon, in Picardy; you have several lawsuits in Paris and no lawyer. Can you remember all that?'

'Perfectly, madam.'

'Come at dinnertime.'

'Very well.'

'And hold your own with my husband, who is sly, despite his seventy-six years.'

'Seventy-six years! Man alive, a fine age!' replied Porthos.

'A great age, you mean, Monsieur Porthos. The poor dear man may therefore leave me a widow at any moment,' the prosecutor's wife continued, giving Porthos a meaningful look. 'Fortunately, by our marriage contract, everything goes to the surviving spouse.'

'Everything?' said Porthos.

'Everything.'

'You are a prudent woman, I see, my dear Madame Coquenard,' said Porthos, tenderly clasping the hand of the prosecutor's wife.

'Then we are reconciled, dear Monsieur Porthos?' she simpered.

'For life!' replied Porthos in the same tone.

'Farewell, then, until our next meeting, my perfidious one!'

'Until our next meeting, my forgetful one!'

'Goodbye until tomorrow, my angel!'

'Until tomorrow, light of my life!'

XXX

MILADY

D'ARTAGNAN HAD FOLLOWED MILADY without her noticing. He saw her get into her carriage, and heard her give the order to her coachman to drive to Saint-Germain[1].

There was no point in trying to follow on foot a carriage carried off at a trot by two vigorous horses, so d'Artagnan returned to Rue Férou.

In Rue de Seine, he met Planchet, who had stopped in front of a pastry-cook's shop and appeared to be in ecstasies over a brioche of most appetising proportions.

He ordered him to go and saddle two horses in Monsieur de Tréville's stables, one for each of them, and meet him at Athos's lodgings – Monsieur de Tréville having placed his stables permanently at d'Artagnan's service.

Planchet made his way to Rue du Vieux-Colombier, and d'Artagnan to Rue Férou. Athos was at home, sadly draining one of the bottles of the famous Spanish wine he had brought back from his travels in Picardy. He signalled for Grimaud to bring a glass for d'Artagnan, and Grimaud obeyed in his customary fashion.

D'Artagnan then told Athos everything that had transpired in church between Porthos and the prosecutor's wife, and observed that, at that moment, their comrade was probably well on his way to outfitting himself.

'Ah, well, for my part,' said Athos, by way of response to the whole story, 'I am quite sure it won't be a woman who bears the cost of my harness.'

'And yet, handsome, refined, peerless nobleman that you are, my dear Athos, surely there can't be a princess or a queen who is safe from the darts of your love?'

'Oh, he's so young, this d'Artagnan!' said Athos, shrugging

his shoulders, and then signalled for Grimaud to bring him a second bottle.

Just then, Planchet modestly poked his head through the half-open door, and announced to his master that he had brought the two horses.

'What horses?' asked Athos.

'Two that Monsieur de Tréville has lent me to ride out; I'm going to take a turn to Saint-Germain with them.'

'And what are you going to do at Saint-Germain?' Athos asked again.

D'Artagnan told him about his encounter in the church, and how, once again, he had come upon that woman who, along with the gentleman in the black cloak with the scar on his temple, was his eternal concern.

'In other words, you're in love with her, just as you were with Madame Bonacieux,' said Athos with a disdainful shrug of his shoulders, as if filled with pity for human weakness.

'I? Not at all!' cried d'Artagnan. 'I'm just curious to explain the mystery with which she envelops herself. I don't know why, but I fancy that this woman, unknown though she is to me, and unknown though I am to her, affects my life in some way.'

'You're right, as a matter of fact,' said Athos. 'I don't know of any woman who is worth looking for once she's been lost. Madame Bonacieux is lost, so much the worse for her! Let her find herself!'

'No, Athos, no, you're wrong,' said d'Artagnan. 'I love my poor Constance more than ever, and if I knew where she was, even if it were at the end of the world, I would set out to free her from her enemies' clutches. But I don't know, and all my searching has been fruitless. What would you have me do? One has to distract oneself.'

'Distract yourself with Milady then, my dear d'Artagnan. I approve wholeheartedly, if it will amuse you.'

'Listen, Athos,' said d'Artagnan, 'instead of keeping yourself locked away in here as if you were under arrest, mount up and take a ride with me to Saint-Germain.'

'My dear friend,' replied Athos, 'I ride my horses when I have them, otherwise I walk.'

'Well,' replied d'Artagnan, smiling at Athos's misanthropy, which, coming from anyone else, would certainly have offended him, 'I'm not so proud as you, I ride what I find. Goodbye, then, my dear Athos.'

'Goodbye,' said the musketeer, signalling to Grimaud to uncork the bottle he had just brought in.

D'Artagnan and Planchet vaulted into the saddle and took the road to Saint-Germain.

All the way there, Athos's remarks about Madame Bonacieux kept coming back to the young man's mind. Although d'Artagnan was not very sentimental by nature, the mercer's pretty wife had made a real impression on his heart. As he said, he would go to the end of the world to find her. But the world has many ends, seeing as it's round, so he didn't know which way to turn.

In the meantime, he was going to attempt to find out who this Milady was. Milady had spoken to the man in the black cloak, which meant she knew him. Now, in d'Artagnan's mind, it was the man in the black cloak who had abducted Madame Bonacieux the second time, as he had done the first. D'Artagnan was therefore only half lying, which is not really lying at all, when he said that in setting out in search for Milady, he was also setting out in search of Constance.

Mulling over matters in this fashion, and occasionally touching his spurs to his horse's ribs, d'Artagnan proceeded on his way and reached Saint-Germain. He had just ridden past the pavilion, in which Louis XIV was to be born ten years later, and was crossing a starkly deserted street, looking to right and left to see if he mightn't discover some trace of his beautiful Englishwoman, when he saw a familiar figure on the ground floor of a pretty house, which, as was the fashion then, had no windows on the street. This figure was walking about on some sort of terrace decorated with flowers. Planchet recognised him first.

'Hey, sir,' he said, addressing d'Artagnan, 'doesn't that face catching flies over there ring any bells?'

'No,' said d'Artagnan. 'And yet I'm certain it's not the first time I've seen it.'

'By God, I should think not,' said Planchet. 'That's that poor Lubin, the Count de Wardes's valet, whom you worked over a month ago in Calais, on the road to the governor's country house.'

'Ah yes,' said d'Artagnan, 'now I recognise him! Do you think he will recognise you?'

'My faith, sir, he was so confused I doubt he's got a very clear memory of me.'

'Well then, go and chat to the lad,' said d'Artagnan, 'and find out in the course of your conversation if his master is dead.'

Planchet got off his horse, walked straight up to Lubin, who indeed did not recognise him, and the two valets struck up the most convivial of conversations while d'Artagnan urged the horses into a lane and, circling round a house, came back to attend to their conference from behind a hazel hedge.

After watching for a moment from behind the hedge, he heard the sound of wheels and saw Milady's carriage stop in front of him. There could be no possibility of a mistake. Milady was inside. D'Artagnan lay down on his horse's neck so he could see everything without being seen.

Milady put her charming blonde head out of the door and gave some orders to her maid.

The latter, a pretty, alert, vivacious girl of around twenty to twenty-two, the model of a fine lady's soubrette, jumped down from the steps, which she had been sitting on as was the custom then, and set off for the terrace where d'Artagnan had seen Lubin.

D'Artagnan followed the soubrette with his eyes and saw her heading towards the terrace. But, as chance would have it, Lubin had been called away by an order from inside, leaving Planchet on his own, looking in all directions to see where d'Artagnan had disappeared to.

The lady's maid went up to Planchet, whom she took for Lubin, and handed him a little note.

'For your master,' she said.

'For my master?' replied Planchet, astonished.

'Yes, and it's very urgent. So be quick about taking it.'

With that she rushed off towards the carriage, which had already turned back the way it had come. She leapt on to the steps, and the carriage sped off.

Planchet turned the note over and over, and then, accustomed to unquestioning obedience, jumped down from the terrace, set off along the lane, and, after twenty paces, came upon d'Artagnan, who, having seen everything, was hurrying to meet him.

'For you, sir,' said Planchet, handing the note to the young man.

'For me?' said d'Artagnan. 'Are you quite sure?'

'By God, am I sure! The soubrette said: "For your master." I have no other master than you, so . . . My faith, she's a pretty little slip of a girl, that soubrette!'

D'Artagnan opened the letter and read these words:

A person who is interested in you more than she can express would like to know when you will be in a fit state to take a walk in the forest. Tomorrow, at the inn of the Field of the Cloth of Gold, a valet in black and red will await your reply.

'Oho!' d'Artagnan said to himself. 'That's a little impetuous. It seems that Milady and I are concerned about the health of the same person. Well then, Planchet, how is this good Count de Wardes? He's not dead, then?'

'No, sir, he is as well as a man with four sword wounds in his body can be – because, meaning no reproach, sir, you dealt that good gentleman four of the best – and still very weak, having lost almost all his blood. As I'd said to monsieur, Lubin did not recognise me, and he related our adventure from start to finish.'

'Excellent, Planchet, you are the king of valets. Now mount up again and let's catch up with the carriage.'

This did not take long. After five minutes they caught sight of the carriage stopped by the side of the road. A richly dressed horseman was standing at the door.

The conversation between Milady and the horseman was so animated that d'Artagnan halted on the other side of the carriage without anyone noticing his presence except the pretty soubrette.

The conversation was conducted in English, a language d'Artagnan did not understand, but from her tone the young man guessed the beautiful Englishwoman was extremely angry. She concluded with a gesture that left him in no doubt as to the nature of the conversation, bringing down her fan with such force that the little feminine accessory flew into a thousand pieces.

The horseman burst out laughing, to the evident exasperation of Milady.

D'Artagnan judged it time to intervene. He approached the other door, and, respectfully doffing his hat, said, 'Madam, will you allow me to offer you my services? It seems to me that this horseman has enraged you. Say the word, madam, and I will undertake to punish him for his lack of courtesy.'

At his first words, Milady had turned and looked at the young man with astonishment. When he had finished, she said in very good French, 'Sir, I would gladly put myself under your protection were the person quarrelling with me not my brother.'

'Ah, my apologies, then,' said d'Artagnan. 'You will understand that I was not aware of that, madam.'

'What is this birdbrain sticking his nose into?' exclaimed the horseman whom Milady had designated as her relative, bending down to the door. 'Why doesn't he carry on his way?'

'Birdbrain yourself,' said d'Artagnan, flattening himself in turn on his horse's neck, and replying through the door from his side, 'I do not carry on my way because it pleases me to stop here.'

The horseman addressed a few words in English to his sister.

'I am speaking French to you,' said d'Artagnan. 'Do me the favour therefore, I pray you, of replying in the same language. You are madam's brother, so be it, but thankfully you're not mine.'

It might have been supposed that Milady, with the customary

trepidation of a woman, would intervene at this initial provocation to prevent the quarrel developing, but, on the contrary, she threw herself back in her carriage and shouted coldly at the coachman, 'Off to town!'

The pretty soubrette cast a worried glance at d'Artagnan, whose good looks seemed to have made an impression on her.

The carriage departed and left the two men face to face, no longer with any material obstacle between them.

The horseman made as if to follow the carriage, but d'Artagnan, whose already-boiling anger had been stoked still further by the realisation that this was the Englishman who had won his horse at Amiens and almost won his diamond from Athos, leapt for his bridle and stopped him.

'Hey, sir!' he said. 'You seem to be even more of a birdbrain than me, for I get the impression you've forgotten there's a little quarrel going on between us.'

'Aha!' said the Englishman. 'It's you, my master. So you always have to be playing some game or other?'

'Yes, and that reminds me I have a rematch to take. We will see, my dear sir, if you handle the rapier as skilfully as the dice cup.'

'You can see that I have no sword,' said the Englishman. 'Do you want to play the hero against an unarmed man?'

'I hope you have one at home,' replied d'Artagnan. 'In any event, I have two, and, if you wish, I'll play you for one.'

'No need,' said the Englishman. 'I'm adequately supplied with such implements.'

'Well then, my worthy gentleman,' said d'Artagnan. 'Choose the longest and come and show it to me this evening.'

'Where, if you please?'

'Behind the Luxembourg. It's a charming neighbourhood for outings of the sort I'm proposing.'

'Very well, I'll be there.'

'Your hour?'

'Six o'clock.'

'Speaking of which, you probably also have one or two friends?'

'Why, I have three who will be greatly honoured to play the same game as myself.'

'Three? Wonderful! How well things turn out,' said d'Artagnan. 'I have the same number.'

'Now, who are you?' asked the Englishman.

'I am Monsieur d'Artagnan, a Gascon gentleman, serving in the guards, in Monsieur des Essarts's company. And you?'

'I am Lord de Winter, Baron of Sheffield.'

'Well then, I am your servant, my lord,' said d'Artagnan, 'however difficult your set of names are to remember.'

And then, spurring his horse, he set off at a gallop and took the road back to Paris.

As was his habit on such occasions, d'Artagnan went straight to Athos's lodgings.

He found Athos reclining on a large sofa, waiting, as he'd said he would, for his outfit to come and find him.

D'Artagnan told Athos everything that had happened, only omitting the letter for Count de Wardes.

Athos was delighted when he found out he was going to fight an Englishman. As we have said it was his dream to do so one day.

They immediately sent valets to fetch Porthos and Aramis and told them the situation.

Porthos drew his sword from its scabbard and started lunging at the wall, stepping back occasionally and performing pliés like a dancer. Aramis, who was still working on his poem, shut himself up in Athos's study and asked not to be disturbed until it was time to draw.

Athos signalled for Grimaud to bring him a bottle.

As for d'Artagnan, he worked out a little plan, the execution of which we will see later. It promised him a congenial adventure, as was evident from the smiles that passed over his face from time to time, lighting up his reverie.

XXXI
ENGLISHMEN AND FRENCHMEN

A T THE APPOINTED HOUR, they went with their four valets to a paddock behind the Luxembourg, which was given over to goats. Athos handed a coin to the goatherd to make himself scarce. The valets were put on lookout.

Soon a silent troop drew near to the paddock, entered it and joined the musketeers. And then, as was the custom across the Channel, introductions were made.

The Englishmen were all men of the highest quality. The bizarre names of their adversaries were thus a cause not only of surprise to them, but of actual concern.

'But, for all that,' said Lord de Winter, when the three friends had identified themselves, 'we still don't know who you are, and we will not fight with such names. Why, those are shepherds' names!'

'And so assumed, as you no doubt rightly suppose, my lord,' said Athos.

'Which makes us all the more eager to know your real names,' replied the Englishman.

'You were quite happy to gamble with us without knowing them,' said Athos, 'so much so that you won our two horses off us.'

'That's true, but we were only risking our pistoles then. Now we are risking our blood. A gentleman gambles with anyone, but he only fights with his equals.'

'Fair's fair,' said Athos, and then took the Englishman he was going to fight off to one side and quietly told him his name.

Porthos and Aramis, for their part, did the same.

'Will that suffice?' Athos asked his adversary. 'Do you find me of noble enough blood to do me the grace of crossing swords with me?'

'Yes, sir,' said the Englishman, bowing.

'And now, do you want me to tell you something?' Athos went on coldly.

'What?' asked the Englishman.

'You would have done better not to require me to make myself known.'

'Why?'

'Because I am thought to be dead, and I have reasons for wanting no one to know I'm alive. I shall therefore be obliged to kill you to prevent my secret getting out.'

The Englishman looked at Athos, thinking he was joking, but Athos wasn't joking in the slightest.

'Gentlemen,' he said, addressing both his companions and their adversaries, 'are we ready?'

'Yes,' the Englishmen and Frenchmen answered with one voice.

'On guard, then!' said Athos.

And immediately eight swords glittered in the rays of the setting sun, and battle was joined with a fury that was wholly natural in men who were enemies twice over.

Athos fenced as calmly and methodically as if he were in a fencing school.

Porthos, no doubt cured of his overconfidence by his adventure in Chantilly, played a game full of guile and watchfulness.

Aramis, who had the third canto of his poem to finish, set to like a man in a tremendous hurry.

Athos was the first to kill his opponent. He only struck him once, but as he'd warned him, the blow was fatal, his sword running him through the heart.

Next Porthos laid out his adversary on the grass, piercing his thigh. As the Englishman surrendered his sword without offering any further resistance, Porthos gathered him up in his arms and carried him to his carriage.

Aramis, meanwhile, pressed his man so vigorously that, after retreating fifty or so paces, he ended up taking to his heels and disappeared to jeers from the valets.

As for d'Artagnan, he played a purely defensive game, until, seeing his opponent becoming exhausted, he sent his sword flying with a vigorous bind thrust. Disarmed, the baron retreated two or three steps, but as he did so, his foot slipped, and he fell over backwards.

D'Artagnan was on him in a single bound. Bringing his sword to his throat, he said to the Englishman, 'I could kill you, sir, you are in my hands, but, for love of your sister, I shall grant you your life.'

D'Artagnan was overjoyed. He had just carried out his plan, the devising of which, as we've mentioned, had caused his face to light up in smiles.

The Englishman, delighted to be dealing with so obliging a gentleman, clasped d'Artagnan in his arms and gave the three musketeers a thousand caresses. As Porthos's adversary was already settled in the carriage and Aramis's had taken to his heels, their only thought then was of the dead man.

While Porthos and Aramis undressed him in the hope his wound might not be fatal, a bulging purse fell from his belt. D'Artagnan picked it up and handed it to Lord de Winter.

'And what the devil do you expect me to do with this?' said the Englishman.

'You can give it to his family,' said d'Artagnan.

'His family won't care about such a pittance; they'll be inheriting an income of fifteen thousand louis. Keep the purse for your valets.'

D'Artagnan put the purse in his pocket.

'And now, my young friend, for you will permit me, I hope, to call you that,' said Lord de Winter, 'this evening, if you will, I'll introduce you to my sister, Lady Clarick, for I want her in her turn to admit you into her good graces, and, as she is not ill-favoured at court, a word from her may not be altogether useless to you in the future.'

Flushing with pleasure, d'Artagnan bowed in assent.

Athos had come up to d'Artagnan in the meantime.

'What do you plan to do with that purse?' he whispered softly in his ear.

'Why, I was planning to give it to you, my dear Athos.'

'To me? Why's that?'

'Well, you killed him: these are the spoils.'

'I, the heir of an enemy?' said Athos. 'Whom do you take me for?'

'It's the custom in war,' said d'Artagnan. 'Why shouldn't it be the custom in a duel?'

'Even on the battlefield,' said Athos, 'I've never done such a thing.'

Porthos shrugged his shoulders, and Aramis pursed his lips in agreement with Athos.

'Then,' said d'Artagnan, 'let's give this money to the valets, as Lord de Winter told us to.'

'Yes,' said Athos, 'let's give this purse, not to our valets, but to their English counterparts.'

Athos took the purse and tossed it to the coachman.

'For you and your comrades.'

Such nobility of spirit in an entirely destitute man struck even Porthos, and this French generosity, related by Lord de Winter and his friend, was hailed by all and sundry, except Messrs Grimaud, Mousqueton, Planchet and Bazin.

On leaving d'Artagnan, Lord de Winter gave him his sister's address. She lived at number six, Place Royale[1], the fashionable part of town in those days. Furthermore, he promised to come and fetch him to introduce him. D'Artagnan arranged that they should meet at eight o'clock at Athos's.

This introduction to Milady[2] weighed heavily on our Gascon's mind. He remembered the strange way this woman had been involved in his destiny. He was convinced she was some creature of the cardinal, and yet, with one of those feelings one can't account for, he felt himself irresistibly drawn to her. His only fear was that Milady would recognise him as the man from Meung and Dover. If so, she would know he was friends with Monsieur de

Tréville and consequently belonged body and soul to the king. That would cost him some of his advantage, since, if Milady knew him as he knew her, they would be evenly matched in their game. As for the nascent intrigue between her and Count de Wardes, that barely concerned our presumptuous hero, despite the fact the marquis was young, handsome, rich, and high in the cardinal's favour. It is not for nothing that one is twenty years old, and, above all, a native of Tarbes.

D'Artagnan went home first and dressed in great style. Then he returned to Athos's, and, as was his habit, told him everything. Athos listened to his plans, then shook his head and, with a sort of bitterness, advised him to be prudent.

'What,' he said, 'you've just lost one woman, whom you said was good, charming, perfect, and now you're already running after another?'

D'Artagnan felt the truth of this reproach.

'I loved Madame Bonacieux with my heart, while I love Milady with my head,' he said. 'The introduction to her house is primarily so I can find out what role she plays at court.'

'By God, what role she plays? It is not difficult to guess from what you've told me. She's some emissary of the cardinal's – a woman who will lure you into a trap, where plainly you'll lose your head.'

'Hang it, my dear Athos, it seems to me you have a very black way of seeing things.'

'My dear friend, I mistrust women – what do you expect? I've paid the price – and blonde women above all. Didn't you say Milady was blonde?'

'She has the most beautiful blonde hair you could ever see.'

'Ah, my poor d'Artagnan,' said Athos.

'Listen, I want to find out. Once I know what I want to know, I'll leave.'

'Find out, then,' Athos said phlegmatically.

Lord de Winter arrived at the appointed hour, but Athos, forewarned, had gone into the other room. He therefore found d'Artagnan alone, and as it was almost eight o'clock, he whisked the young man away.

An elegant carriage was waiting below, and as it was drawn by two excellent horses, they were at Place Royale in an instant.

Milady Clarick received d'Artagnan graciously. Her townhouse was remarkably sumptuous; and although most of the English, driven out by the war, had left France, or were on the point of doing so, Milady had just spent money on her house, which proved that the general measure forcing the English to quit the country did not affect her.

'You see here,' said Lord de Winter, introducing d'Artagnan to his sister, 'a young gentleman who held my life in his hands, and yet did not wish to exploit his advantage, even though we were enemies twice over, since I had insulted him and am English. Thank him, then, madam, if you have any affection for me.'

Milady frowned slightly. A scarcely visible cloud passed over her brow, and a smile appeared on her lips that was so peculiar the young man, who had noticed this triple change, almost shuddered.

The brother didn't notice anything. He had turned round to play with Milady's favourite monkey, which had tugged at his doublet.

'You are welcome, sir,' said Milady, in a voice the singular gentleness of which contrasted with the symptoms of ill humour d'Artagnan had just remarked. 'Today you have acquired an eternal entitlement to my gratitude.'

The Englishman turned round again and described the fight in every last detail. Milady listened with the greatest of attention, but it was obvious, despite the effort she made to hide her feelings, that this story wasn't agreeable to her. The blood rose to her face, and her little foot tapped impatiently under her dress.

Lord de Winter didn't spot any of this. When he had finished, he went over to a table on which a bottle of Spanish wine and some glasses had been laid out on a tray. He filled two glasses and, with a gesture, invited d'Artagnan to drink.

D'Artagnan knew it was the height of impoliteness for an

Englishman to decline his toast. So he went over to the table and took the second glass. He had not lost sight of Milady, however, and looking in the mirror, he saw the change in her expression. Now that she thought no one was looking at her, a feeling akin to ferocity animated her countenance. She violently bit her handkerchief.

The pretty little soubrette, whom d'Artagnan had already noticed, then entered. She said a few words in English to Lord de Winter, who immediately asked d'Artagnan's permission to retire, excusing himself on account of the urgency of the matter that called him away, and charging his sister to obtain his pardon.

D'Artagnan shook hands with Lord de Winter and went back to Milady. With surprising mobility, her face had recovered its gracious expression; only a few small red spots on her handkerchief indicated that she had bitten her lips hard enough to draw blood.

Her lips were magnificent, like coral.

The conversation took a playful turn. Milady seemed to have entirely recovered. She said that Lord de Winter was only her brother-in-law, not her brother; she had married a younger son of the family, who had left her a widow with a child[3]. That child was Lord de Winter's sole heir, if Lord de Winter didn't marry. All this revealed to d'Artagnan a veil that hid something, but what lay behind it he could not yet see.

Moreover, after half an hour's conversation, d'Artagnan was convinced Milady was his compatriot; she spoke French with a purity and an elegance that left no doubt in that regard.

D'Artagnan was profuse in his gallantries and protestations of devotion. At every piece of nonsense that came out of our Gascon's mouth, Milady smiled benevolently. The hour came for him to retire. D'Artagnan took his leave of Milady, and emerged from her drawing room the happiest of men.

On the staircase he met the pretty soubrette, who gently brushed against him as they passed, and, blushing to the roots of her hair, begged his pardon for having touched him, in a voice so sweet that the pardon was instantly granted her.

D'Artagnan returned the next day and was even better received than the evening before. Lord de Winter wasn't there, and this time it was Milady who did all the evening's honours. She seemed to take a great interest in him, asking where he was from, who his friends were, and whether he hadn't ever thought of entering the cardinal's service.

D'Artagnan, who, as we know, was exceptionally prudent for a lad of twenty, remembered his suspicions regarding Milady at this point. He delivered a stirring eulogy of His Eminence and told her he would certainly have entered the cardinal's guards rather than the king's if he had known Monsieur Cavois, for instance, rather than Monsieur de Tréville.

Milady unaffectedly changed the subject, and asked d'Artagnan in the most casual way possible whether he had ever been to England.

D'Artagnan replied that he had been sent there by Monsieur de Tréville to negotiate for a remount of horses, and had even brought back four as a sample.

Milady screwed up her lips two or three times during the conversation; clearly she was dealing with a Gascon who played his cards close to his chest.

D'Artagnan left at the same hour as the previous evening. In the corridor he again met the pretty Kitty – that was the soubrette's name. She looked at him with an expression of kindness that, however enigmatic, was impossible to misconstrue. But d'Artagnan was so preoccupied with the mistress that he only noticed what concerned her.

D'Artagnan returned to Milady's the next day and the day after, and each time Milady's welcome was more gracious.

Each time too, either in the antechamber, or the corridor, or on the stairs, he ran into the pretty soubrette.

But, as we've said, d'Artagnan paid no attention to poor Kitty's persistence.

XXXII
A PROSECUTOR'S DINNER

MEANWHILE, THE DUEL IN WHICH PORTHOS had played such a brilliant part had not caused him to forget the dinner the prosecutor's wife had invited him to. The next day, as one o'clock approached, he had Mousqueton give him a last once-over with a brush and then proceeded to Rue aux Ours with the step of a man who is fortunate on two counts.

His heart was beating fast, but not, like d'Artagnan's, with young, impatient love. No, a more material interest sent the blood pulsing through his veins. At long last he was about to step over the mysterious threshold and climb the unknown staircase that, one after another, Monsieur Coquenard's venerable écus had ascended.

He was going to see in reality a particular chest, the image of which he had seen twenty times in his dreams: a long, deep chest, padlocked, bolted and fixed to the floor; a chest of which he had so often heard tell, which the slightly dry, it's true, but not inelegant hands of the prosecutor's wife would now throw open to his admiring gaze.

And then he, the man condemned to wander the face of this earth, the man without fortune, the man without family, the soldier accustomed to inns, wine shops, taverns, posadas, the gourmet more often than not forced to make do with whatever chance mouthful he could scrounge – then he would savour family meals, enjoy a comfortable home, and indulge in those little attentions that the tougher one is, as old soldiers say, the more pleasurable they are.

To come as a cousin and sit at a good table every day, to smooth the old prosecutor's yellow, wrinkled brow, to fleece the young clerks a little by teaching them the finer points of basset, passe-dix[1] and lansquenet, and then win their monthly savings in lieu of a fee for the hour-long lesson he would give them – all of this appealed tremendously to Porthos.

Certainly the musketeer recalled now and then the dismal stories about prosecutors that were current at the time and have survived them – the stinginess, the trimming, the fasting. But since, all things considered, apart from a few fits of economy that Porthos had always found very ill-timed, the prosecutor's wife in his experience had been more generous than not – for a prosecutor's wife, naturally – he hoped to find a household set up on a pleasing scale.

At the door, however, the musketeer had some misgivings. The exterior was not inviting: a dark, stinking alley, a dim staircase with barred windows through which a grey light filtered from a neighbouring courtyard; a low door on the second floor studded with huge nails like the main gate of the Grand Châtelet prison.

Porthos rapped with his knuckle. A tall, pale clerk buried under a forest of untamed hair came to open the door, and bowed like a man forced to respect in another an imposing nature that indicated strength, a military uniform that indicated social rank, and a scarlet face that indicated a habit of good living.

There was another, smaller clerk behind the first; another, taller clerk behind the second, and a twelve-year-old errand boy behind the third.

In all, three and half clerks, which, in those days, indicated a thriving practice.

Although the musketeer wasn't due to arrive until one o'clock, the prosecutor's wife had been on the lookout since noon, and was counting on the heart, and possibly also the stomach, of her ardent admirer to make him come early.

Madame Coquenard thus came to the door of her private apartment almost at the same time as her guest came to the door on the stairs, and the worthy lady's appearance rescued him from a very awkward situation. The clerks were eying him curiously, and, not knowing what to say to this ascending and descending scale, he was tongue-tied.

'It's my cousin!' cried the prosecutor's wife. 'Come in, come in, do, Monsieur Porthos.'

The name Porthos had its effect on the clerks, who started laughing, until he turned and every face resumed its grave expression.

They reached the prosecutor's study after passing through the antechamber where the clerks were, and the office where they should have been: the latter being a sort of gloomy chamber furnished with old papers. Coming out of the study, they passed the kitchen on their right and went into the reception room.

All those rooms giving on to one another did not put Porthos in a good frame of mind. Conversations would travel a long way through all those open doors. And then he had also, in passing, cast a quick, inquisitive glance into the kitchen, and was forced to admit, to the shame of the prosecutor's wife and to his great regret, that he hadn't seen any of the fire, animation, and bustle that ordinarily reign in this sanctuary of gluttony when a good meal is in the offing.

The prosecutor had no doubt been informed of the visit, for he evinced no surprise at the sight of Porthos, who went up to him with a passably jaunty air and bowed politely.

'We are cousins, it seems, Monsieur Porthos?' said the prosecutor, raising himself up in his cane wheelchair with his arms.

The old man, swathed in a large black doublet, in which his slender body drowned, was green and dry. His little grey eyes gleamed like carbuncles, and, along with his grimacing mouth, seemed the only part of his face still to show any sign of life. The legs, unfortunately, had begun to refuse to serve the whole bony mechanism, and in the five or six months since this incapacity had made itself felt, the worthy prosecutor had more or less become his wife's slave.

The cousin was accepted with resignation, nothing more. A sprightly Monsieur Coquenard would have declined any kinship with Monsieur Porthos.

'Yes, sir, we are cousins,' said the unruffled Porthos, who had, in any case, never expected to be received enthusiastically by the husband.

'On the female side, I believe?' the prosecutor said archly.

Porthos was oblivious to this piece of mockery, which he took for an ingenuous remark and laughed at behind his bushy moustache. Madame Coquenard, however, who knew that an ingenuous prosecutor was an extremely rare variety of the species, smiled slightly and blushed furiously.

Since Porthos's arrival, Monsieur Coquenard had kept glancing anxiously at a large cupboard facing his oak desk. Porthos realised that this piece of furniture, although it didn't correspond physically in the least to the one he'd seen in his dreams, had to be the blessed chest, and he congratulated himself on the fact that the reality was six feet taller than the dream.

Monsieur Coquenard didn't pursue his genealogical investigations. Instead, swinging his anxious gaze from the cabinet to Porthos, he simply said, 'Our cousin will surely grace us with his company at dinner on one occasion before he leaves on campaign, will he not, Madame Coquenard?'

This time Porthos took the blow full in the stomach, and felt it. It seemed Madame Coquenard wasn't insensible to it either, since she added, 'My cousin won't come again if he finds we treat him badly. Moreover, he has too little time in Paris, and thus to see us, for us not to request his presence at every moment he has free before his departure.'

'Oh, my legs! My poor legs, where are you?' murmured Coquenard, attempting a smile.

This assistance, coming to Porthos's aid just as his gastronomic hopes were under attack, filled the musketeer with gratitude towards his prosecutor's wife.

Dinner time soon arrived. They went into the dining room, a large dark room opposite the kitchen.

The clerks, who appeared to have smelled unaccustomed aromas in the house, were military in their punctuality, and held their stools in their hands, poised to sit down. Their jaws could be seen working in anticipation with frightening efficiency.

God's virtue! thought Porthos, glancing at the three famished souls, for the errand boy, as might be supposed, was not admitted to the honours of the master's table, God's virtue, if I were my cousin, I wouldn't keep gourmands like that! They look like castaways who haven't eaten for six weeks.

Monsieur Coquenard entered in his wheelchair, pushed by Madame Coquenard, whom Porthos went in turn to help by rolling her husband to the table.

He was barely in the room before his nose and jaws began twitching just like the clerks'.

'Oho,' he said, 'here's an alluring soup!'

'What the devil do they smell that's so extraordinary in this soup?' said Porthos at the sight of a pale broth, abundant but entirely opaque, in which a few crusts floated like the far-flung islands of an archipelago.

Madame Coquenard smiled, and at a sign from her, everyone eagerly sat down.

Monsieur Coquenard was served first, then Porthos. Then Madame Coquenard filled her bowl, before distributing the crusts, minus the soup, to the impatient clerks.

Just then the door of the dining room opened of its own accord with a creak, and, through the gap, Porthos discerned the little clerk, who, unable to take part in the feast, was eating his bread amid the mingled smells of the kitchen and dining room.

After the soup, the maid brought in a boiled chicken, a display of culinary magnificence that caused the guests' eyes to open so wide they looked as if they might pop.

'One can see you love your family, Madame Coquenard,' said the prosecutor with a well-nigh tragic smile. 'This is indeed a mark of attention you've shown your cousin.'

The poor chicken was scrawny and clad in one of those thick, bristly hides that teeth can never pierce, no matter how hard they try. The search party must have been hunting for a long time before they found her on the perch, to which she had crept away to die of old age.

Hang it, thought Porthos, there's a very sorry sight. I respect old age, but I don't really care for it boiled or roasted.

And then he looked round to see if the others shared his opinion. Quite the contrary – all he saw were flaming eyes, devouring in anticipation the sublime chicken that was the object of his contempt.

Madame Coquenard drew the dish towards her, adroitly detached the two great black feet, which she put on her husband's plate, cut off the neck, which she set aside with the head for herself, removed a wing for Porthos, and then gave the animal back to the serving girl who had just brought it. It returned to the kitchen almost intact, disappearing before the musketeer had time to examine the changes disappointment had wrought on the various faces, according to the characters and temperaments of those suffering it.

In place of the chicken, a dish of beans now made its entrance, a huge dish in which a few mutton bones – at first sight, ostensibly accompanied by some meat – gave the impression of lurking.

But the clerks were not fooled by this ruse, and their lugubrious expressions gave way to looks of resignation.

Madame Coquenard served the dish to the young men with the moderation of a model housewife.

Now it was the turn of the wine. From an extremely thin sandstone bottle, Monsieur Coquenard poured a third of a glass for each of the young men, a roughly equal measure for himself, and then the bottle passed at once to Porthos and Madame Coquenard's side of the table.

The young men topped up their third of wine with water, and having drunk half the glass, topped it up again – and kept on doing so until, by the end of the meal, they were downing a drink that had gone from the colour of ruby to that of burnt topaz.

Porthos timidly ate his chicken wing and shivered as he felt the prosecutor's wife's knee coming to find his own under the table. He too drank half a glass of that carefully husbanded wine, which he recognised as that horrible Montreuil vintage, the terror of experienced palates.

Watching him swallow the wine neat, Monsieur Coquenard let out a sigh.

'Would you like some beans, Cousin Porthos?' Madame Coquenard said, in a tone that meant 'Believe me, I wouldn't.'

'Damned if I'll let them pass my lips!' Porthos muttered under his breath, before saying aloud, 'Thank you, cousin, but I'm no longer hungry.'

Silence fell. Porthos didn't know which way to look. The prosecutor repeated several times, 'Ah, Madame Coquenard, my compliments, your dinner was a veritable feast! God, how I've gorged myself!'

Monsieur Coquenard had eaten his soup, the chicken's black feet, and the only mutton bone with a bit of meat on it.

Porthos thought they were making a fool of him, and started to twirl his moustache and furrow his brow, but Madame Coquenard's knee quietly appeared, counselling patience.

The silence and the disappearance of the maid, which were unintelligible to Porthos, had a terrible significance for the clerks. At a look from the prosecutor, and a smile from Madame Coquenard, they slowly rose from the table, folded their napkins still more slowly, then bowed and left.

'Off you go, young men, go and work off your dinner,' the prosecutor said gravely.

Once the clerks had left, Madame Coquenard got up and took down from a dresser a piece of cheese, some quince preserves and a cake she had made herself out of almonds and honey.

Master Coquenard frowned, because he saw too much food; Porthos screwed up his lips because he saw nothing to dine on.

He looked to see if the dish of beans was still there. The dish of beans had disappeared.

'Decidedly, a feast,' cried Monsieur Coquenard, shifting restlessly in his chair. 'A veritable feast, *epulae epularum*[2]! Lucullus dines with Lucullus.'

Porthos looked at the bottle, which was near him, and hoped that he'd be able to make a dinner out of wine, bread and cheese.

But the wine was gone, the bottle was empty. Monsieur and Madame Coquenard gave no indication of having noticed.

Very well, Porthos said to himself, I've been warned.

He ran his tongue over a little spoonful of preserves and embedded his teeth in Madame Coquenard's sticky pastry.

Now, he said to himself, the sacrifice is complete. Ah, if only I had never hoped to look with Madame Coquenard in her husband's cupboard!

After the delights of such a meal, which he called excessive, Monsieur Coquenard felt the need for a nap. Porthos hoped it would take place at the same sitting, and in the same spot, but the cursed prosecutor wouldn't hear a word of it. He had to be taken to his room, and shouted until he was in front of his cupboard and, to be even safer, had put his feet on the edge of it.

The prosecutor's wife took Porthos into an adjoining room where they began laying the foundations for a reconciliation.

'You can come for dinner three times a week,' said Madame Coquenard.

'Thank you,' said Porthos, 'but I don't like to take advantage. Besides, I have to think about my outfit.'

'That's true,' said the prosecutor's wife, groaning. '. . . It's that wretched outfit.'

'Alas, yes,' said Porthos. 'It is.'

'But what does your corps' equipment consist of, Monsieur Porthos?'

'Oh, lots of things,' said Porthos. 'Musketeers, as you know, are elite soldiers, and they need a lot of objects that would be unnecessary for the guards or the Swiss.'

'But still, list them.'

'Why, it can come to as much as . . .' said Porthos, who preferred discussing the general to the particular.

The prosecutor's wife waited, all a-quiver.

'How much?' she said, 'I truly hope it won't exceed . . .'

She paused, the words failing her.

'Oh no,' said Porthos, 'it won't exceed two thousand five

hundred livres. I even think that, if I economise, I could get by with two thousand livres.'

'Good Lord, two thousand livres,' she cried. 'Why, that's a fortune!'

Porthos grimaced in an intensely meaningful way; Madame Coquenard understood.

'I asked for details,' she said, 'because, having many relatives and clients in trade, I was almost sure I could get the things a hundred per cent cheaper than you would yourself.'

'Aha!' said Porthos. 'Is that what you meant?'

'Yes, dear Monsieur Porthos! So, don't you need a horse first?'

'Yes, a horse.'

'Well, I have the perfect one for you.'

'Ah!' said Porthos, beaming. 'So all's well as far as my horse is concerned. Then I need a complete set of tack, which consists of things only a musketeer can purchase, and, besides, won't come to more than three hundred livres.'

'Three hundred livres. Well, let's say three hundred livres then,' said the prosecutor's wife with a sigh.

Porthos smiled. He had the saddle from Buckingham, it will be remembered, so this was three hundred livres he counted on slipping into his pocket.

'Then,' he went on, 'there's my valet's horse and my travelling case. As for weapons, no need for you to concern yourself about those, I have them.'

'A horse for your valet?' the prosecutor's wife said hesitantly. 'That's very grand, my friend.'

'What, madam?' Porthos said proudly. 'Am I a yokel, by any chance?'

'No, I was just saying that a fine mule sometimes looks as good as a horse, and it seems to me that in procuring you a fine mule for Mousqueton . . .'

'A fine mule it is,' said Porthos. 'You're right; I've seen the cream of Spanish noblemen whose entire suite rode mules. But in that case, you understand, Madame Coquenard, a mule with plumes and bells?'

'Don't worry,' said the prosecutor's wife.

'That leaves the travelling case,' Porthos went on.

'Oh you mustn't worry about that,' exclaimed Madame Coquenard. 'My husband has five or six cases; you can choose the best. There is one in particular he preferred for his travels, which is big enough to hold a whole world.'

'Your case is empty then?' Porthos asked artlessly.

'Certainly it's empty,' the prosecutor's wife replied equally artlessly.

'Ah, but the case I need is a well-furnished one, my dear.'

Madame Coquenard sighed some more. Molière had not yet written his play *The Miser*. Madame Coquenard therefore had a head start on Harpagon[3].

The rest of the equipment was successively haggled over in the same fashion, and, at length, the upshot was that the prosecutor's wife would ask her husband for a loan of eight hundred livres in cash, and would provide the horse and the mule that would have the honour of carrying Porthos and Mousqueton to glory.

With these conditions agreed upon, along with the rate of interest and stipulated time of repayment, Porthos took his leave of Madame Coquenard. She tried to keep him from going by making eyes at him, but Porthos claimed the demands of the service, and the prosecutor's wife had to yield to the king.

The musketeer returned home hungry and in a very bad temper.

XXXIII

SOUBRETTE AND MISTRESS

M EANWHILE, AS WE HAVE SAID, despite the pricking of his conscience and Athos's sage advice, d'Artagnan was falling more in love with Milady by the hour. And so every day, without fail, he went to pay court to her, a court to which the venturesome

Gascon was convinced that sooner or later she could not fail to respond.

One evening when he arrived, sniffing the breeze, as spry as a man who expects gold to shower down from the sky, he bumped into the maid in the coach gate. But rather than simply smiling at him in passing, this time the pretty Kitty gently took his hand.

Good, thought d'Artagnan, she has been entrusted with a message for me from her mistress. She will assign me some rendez-vous that it would have been too brazen to grant me face to face.

And then he looked at the beautiful child with the most triumphant air he could assume.

'I would very much like to have a word with you, sir . . .' stammered the maid.

'Speak, my child, speak,' said d'Artagnan. 'I am listening.'

'It's not possible here. I have too much to say and it is too confidential.'

'Well then, what shall we do?'

'If monsieur would like to come with me,' said Kitty timidly.

'Wherever you wish, my pretty child.'

'Come, then.'

And then Kitty, who had not let go of d'Artagnan's hand, led him up a dark, twisting little staircase, and after ushering him up a dozen or so steps, opened a door.

'Come in, sir,' she said. 'We will be alone here and we can talk.'

'And what room is this, then, my pretty child?' asked d'Artagnan.

'It is mine, sir. It communicates with my mistress's bedroom through that door. But don't worry, she won't be able to hear what we say; she never goes to bed until midnight.'

D'Artagnan glanced around him. The little room was a charming study in taste and cleanliness. Despite himself, however, his eyes fixed themselves on the door Kitty had said communicated with Milady's room.

Kitty guessed what was going on in the young man's soul and gave a sigh.

'So you really like my mistress, sir?' she said.

'Oh, more than I can say! I am mad about her!'

Kitty gave a second sigh.

'Alas, sir,' she said, 'that is a great pity!'

'And what the devil do you think is so unfortunate about it?' asked d'Artagnan.

'The fact, sir,' replied Kitty, 'that my mistress doesn't love you in the least.'

'What?' said d'Artagnan. 'Did she instruct you to tell me so?'

'Oh, no, sir, she didn't! But out of the interest I take in you, I resolved to inform you of this fact.'

'Thank you, my good Kitty, but only for the intention – the revelation itself, you'll agree, is not very agreeable.'

'In other words, you don't believe what I've told you, isn't that so?'

'One always finds it hard to believe such things, my pretty child, if only from vanity.'

'So you don't believe me?'

'I confess that until you deign to give me some proof of what you assert . . .'

'What do you say to this?'

And then Kitty took a small note from her bosom.

'For me?' d'Artagnan said, snatching the letter from her.

'No, for another.'

'For another?'

'Yes.'

'His name? His name?' cried d'Artagnan.

'Look at the address.'

'Count de Wardes.'

The memory of the scene in Saint-Germain immediately came to the presumptuous Gascon's mind. With a movement as swift as thought, he tore open the envelope, despite Kitty's cries as she saw what he was going to do, or rather was doing.

'Oh, my God, sir,' she said, 'what are you doing?'

'I? Nothing!' said d'Artagnan, and then read:

You have not replied to my first note. Are you, then, unwell,
or have you rather forgotten the eyes you made at me at
Madame de Guise's ball? This is your chance, count. Do not
let it escape you.

D'Artagnan grew pale. His vanity was wounded, although he
mistook it for his love.

'Poor dear Monsieur d'Artagnan!' said Kitty, in a voice filled
with compassion, clasping the young man's hand again.

'Do you pity me, you kind child?' said d'Artagnan.

'Oh yes, with all my heart! For I know what love is as well!'

'You know what love is?' said d'Artagnan, looking at her for
the first time with a certain attention.

'Alas, yes!'

'Well then, instead of pitying me, you'd do better to help me
take revenge on your mistress.'

'And what sort of vengeance would you take on her?'

'I wish to win her, supplant my rival.'

'I will never help you with that, sir!' burst out Kitty.

'And why not?' asked d'Artagnan.

'For two reasons.'

'Which are?'

'The first is that my mistress will never love you.'

'How would you know?'

'You have offended her heart.'

'I? How can I have offended her – I who, ever since I have
known her, have lived at her feet like a slave? Speak, I beg you.'

'I would only ever confess that to the man . . . who could read
to the bottom of my soul.'

D'Artagnan looked at Kitty for the second time. The young
girl had a freshness and beauty that many duchesses would have
given their coronet to possess.

'Kitty,' he said, 'I'll read to the bottom of your soul whenever you wish. That need be no obstacle, my dear child.'

And he gave her a kiss, which made the poor child go as red as a cherry.

'Oh no,' cried Kitty, 'you don't love me! It's my mistress you love: you told me so just now.'

'And does that prevent you telling me the second reason?'

'The second reason, sir,' said Kitty, emboldened first by the kiss and then by the expression in the young man's eyes, 'is that, in love, it's everyone for himself.'

Only then did d'Artagnan remember Kitty's languishing glances, the meetings in the antechamber, on the stairs, in the corridor, the way she brushed hands whenever they met, her stifled sighs. Absorbed by his desire to please the great lady, he had disdained the soubrette. He who hunts the eagle pays no mind to the sparrow.

But this time our Gascon saw at a glance all the profit to be gained from this love Kitty had just confessed with such naivety or such boldness – the interception of letters addressed to the Count de Wardes, communications with an ally within the fortress, access at any hour to Kitty's room, which was next to her mistress's. As we can see, in his mind the treacherous soul was already sacrificing the poor girl to get Milady, by fair means or foul.

'Well then,' he said to the young girl, 'do you want me, my dear Kitty, to give you a proof of this love you doubt?'

'Of what love?' asked the young girl.

'The one I am ready and willing to feel for you.'

'And what is this proof?'

'Do you want me to spend the time I ordinarily spend with your mistress with you this evening?'

'Oh yes!' said Kitty, clapping her hands. 'Most willingly!'

'Well then, my dear child,' said d'Artagnan, settling into an armchair, 'come here so I can tell you are the prettiest soubrette I have ever seen!'

And he told it to her at such length and so well that the poor child, who wanted nothing better than to believe him, believed him . . . Even so, to d'Artagnan's great astonishment, the pretty Kitty defended herself with a certain resoluteness.

Time passes quickly when it is spent in attack and defence.

It struck midnight, and as it did so, the bell was heard in Milady's room.

'Good God!' cried Kitty. 'There's my mistress calling me! Leave, quickly!'

D'Artagnan stood up, took his hat as if intending to obey, but then, smartly opening the door of a large wardrobe instead of that to the stairs, squeezed in among Milady's robes and dressing gowns.

'Whatever are you doing?' cried Kitty.

D'Artagnan, who had taken the key beforehand, locked himself in the wardrobe without replying.

'Well,' cried Milady in a sour voice, 'are you sleeping too soundly to come when I ring?'

And then d'Artagnan heard the communicating door violently flung open.

'Here I am, Milady, here I am,' cried Kitty, darting forward to meet her mistress.

The two of them returned to the bedroom and, as the communicating door had been left open, d'Artagnan could hear Milady berate her maid for a while longer. But finally she calmed down, and, while Kitty attended to her mistress, the conversation turned to him.

'Well,' said Milady, 'I haven't seen our Gascon this evening.'

'What, madam,' said Kitty, 'he didn't come? Can he be turning fickle before he has been fortunate?'

'Oh no! Monsieur de Tréville or Monsieur des Essarts must have detained him. I know what I'm doing, Kitty; that one is mine.'

'What will madam do with him?'

'What will I do with him? Don't worry, Kitty: there's

something between this man and me of which he is unaware . . . He almost cost me my standing with His Eminence . . . Oh, I'll have my revenge!'

'I thought madam loved him?'

'I, love him? I detest him! A fool, who has Lord de Winter's life in his hands and, by not killing him, deprives me of an income of three hundred thousand livres!'

'That's true,' said Kitty, 'your son is uncle's sole heir, and until he came of age, his fortune would have been at your disposal.'

D'Artagnan shuddered to the marrow of his bones, hearing this sweet creature reproach him in that strident voice which she had so much trouble concealing in conversation, for not having killed a man he had seen her shower with affection.

'And so,' continued Milady, 'I would already have taken my revenge on him if the cardinal, I don't know why, hadn't instructed me to show him consideration.'

'Oh, yes, but madam didn't show that little woman he was in love with any.'

'Oh, the mercer's wife from Rue des Fossoyeurs? Hasn't he already forgotten she existed? A fine vengeance, my faith!'

Cold sweat ran down d'Artagnan's forehead: she was a monster, this woman.

He resumed listening but unfortunately her preparations for bed were complete.

'That's fine,' said Milady, 'go back to your room, and tomorrow try finally to get a reply to that letter I gave you.'

'For Count de Wardes?' said Kitty.

'Of course for Count de Wardes.'

'There's a man,' said Kitty, 'who strikes me as the exact opposite of that wretched Monsieur d'Artagnan.'

'Leave me, young miss,' said Milady, 'I do not like comments.'

D'Artagnan heard the door shutting again, then the sound of two bolts being drawn across as Milady locked herself in. On her side, Kitty turned the key in the lock as softly as she could. Then d'Artagnan pushed open the door of the wardrobe.

'Oh, my God,' Kitty said in a whisper, 'what's wrong? How pale you are!'

'The abominable creature!' murmured d'Artagnan.

'Quiet! Quiet! Go now,' said Kitty. 'There's only a partition between my room and Milady, and everything you say in one room can be heard in the other.'

'Which is exactly why I won't go,' said d'Artagnan.

'What?' said Kitty, blushing.

'Or at least I'll go . . . later.'

And then he drew Kitty to him. There was no way to resist – resistance makes such a noise! So Kitty gave in.

It was a vengeful impulse against Milady. D'Artagnan discovered the truth in the saying that vengeance is the pleasure of the gods. And so, if he'd had a little heart, he would have been satisfied with this new conquest, but d'Artagnan had nothing but ambition and pride.

However, to his credit, it must be said, the first use he made of his influence over Kitty was to try to find out what had become of Madame Bonacieux. But the poor girl swore on the crucifix that she knew nothing about it, since her mistress only ever let her into the half of her secrets. The only thing she could say for certain was that she wasn't dead.

As for the affair that had cost Milady her influence with the cardinal, Kitty was none the wiser. But this time, d'Artagnan was ahead of her. Having seen Milady on a detained ship when he was leaving England, he suspected that in this case it had to do with the diamond tags.

But what was clearest in all this was that Milady's genuine, profound, inveterate hatred for him was caused by the fact that he had not killed her brother-in-law.

D'Artagnan returned to Milady's the following day. She was in a very ill humour, and d'Artagnan suspected it was the lack of a reply from Count de Wardes that was vexing her in this way. Kitty came in, but was greeted very harshly by Milady. A glance in d'Artagnan's direction seemed to say, 'You see what I suffer for your sake?'

Towards the end of the evening, however, the beautiful lioness softened. She listened to d'Artagnan's sweet nothings with a smile, and even gave him her hand to kiss.

D'Artagnan left, not knowing what to think any more. But as he was a lad who wasn't easily flustered, he had, while paying court to Milady, formed a little plan.

He found Kitty at the door, and, as on the previous evening, he went up to her room to get news. Kitty had been severely told off; she had been accused of negligence. Unable to understand Count de Wardes's silence, Milady had ordered Kitty to come to her room at nine o'clock in the morning to pick up a third letter.

D'Artagnan made Kitty promise to bring him that letter the following morning. The poor girl promised her lover everything he wanted. She was mad.

Events followed the same course as the previous evening. D'Artagnan locked himself in the wardrobe; Milady called, got ready for bed, dismissed Kitty and then closed her door again. As before, d'Artagnan did not return to his lodgings until five o'clock in the morning.

At eleven o'clock, he saw Kitty arrive at his door. She had a new note from Milady. This time, the poor child did not even try to put up a fight, but let d'Artagnan do as he pleased. She belonged body and soul to her handsome soldier.

D'Artagnan opened the note and read the following:

This is the third time I am writing to tell you I love you. Be careful I do not write a fourth to tell you I hate you.

If you repent of the fashion in which you have treated me, the young girl who will give you this note will inform you how a man of honour may obtain his pardon.

D'Artagnan blushed and paled several times reading this note.

'Oh, you still love her!' said Kitty, who had not taken her eyes off the young man's face for a moment.

'No, Kitty, you are mistaken. I don't love her any more. But I do want to avenge myself for her contempt.'

'Yes, I am familiar with your vengeance – you have told me about it.'

'What difference does that make, Kitty? You know full well that I only love you.'

'How can one know that?'

'By the way I'll show her my disdain.'

Kitty sighed.

D'Artagnan took a pen and wrote:

Madam, until now I had doubted that your first two letters were truly addressed to me, so unworthy did I believe myself to be of such an honour. Besides, I was in such pain that I would in any case have hesitated to reply.

But today I am obliged to believe in the excess of your kindness, since not only your letter, but also your servant affirm that I have the good fortune to be loved by you.

She does not need to inform me how a man of honour may obtain his pardon. I shall therefore come to beg you for mine this evening at eleven o'clock. To delay a day longer would now, in my eyes, be to cause you further offence.

He who you have rendered the happiest of men.

Count de Wardes.

The note was first of all a forgery, and then an indelicacy. It was even, from the standpoint of our contemporary morals, bordering on scandalous, but people treated one another with less consideration in those days than they do now. Besides, d'Artagnan knew by her own confession that Milady was guilty of treachery in more important matters, and he had only a very paltry regard for her. And yet, despite this scant esteem, he burned with a mad passion for this woman. A passion intoxicated with contempt, but a passion – or thirst, whichever one prefers – nonetheless.

D'Artagnan's plan was very simple. From Kitty's room he

would gain access to her mistress's, then take advantage of the first moment of surprise, shame and terror to win her. He might fail, it was true, but surely something had to be left to chance. In a week the campaign would begin, and he would have to leave. D'Artagnan did not have time to draw out a textbook courtship.

'Here,' said the young man, handing Kitty the sealed note, 'give this letter to Milady. It is Count de Wardes's reply.'

Poor Kitty turned deathly pale, suspecting the contents of the note.

'Listen, my dear child,' d'Artagnan said to her, 'you understand that all this has to end one way or another. Milady may discover that you gave the first note to my valet instead of the count's valet, and that it was I who opened the other notes which should have been opened by Count de Wardes. Then Milady will dismiss you, and you know she's not a woman to let that suffice.'

'Alas!' said Kitty. 'For whose sake have I exposed myself to all of this?'

'For mine, I know that, my beauty,' said the young man, 'and deeply grateful I am too, I swear.'

'Please though, what does your note say?'

'Milady will tell you.'

'Ah, you don't love me!' cried Kitty. 'I'm so unhappy!'

There is a response to this reproach which always misleads women. D'Artagnan's reply left Kitty labouring under the greatest delusion.

Even so, she cried a great deal before resolving to deliver the letter to Milady. But she finally made up her mind, and that was all d'Artagnan wanted.

Besides, he promised her that he would leave her mistress early that evening, and then come up to see her.

This promise succeeded in consoling poor Kitty.

XXXIV

IN WHICH THE SUBJECT OF ARAMIS'S AND PORTHOS'S OUTFITS IS DISCUSSED

SINCE THE FOUR FRIENDS had embarked on the hunt for their outfits, they no longer met up regularly. They dined on their own wherever they happened to be, or rather wherever they could. Military duty, for its part, also took up its share of their precious time, which was slipping away so fast. Nonetheless they had agreed to meet once a week, around one o'clock, at Athos's lodgings, seeing as the latter, true to his oath, refused to set foot outside.

The day Kitty came to find d'Artagnan in his lodgings was the day of their meeting.

Kitty had barely left before d'Artagnan headed towards Rue Férou.

He found Athos and Aramis philosophising. Aramis was toying with the idea of taking up the cassock again, while Athos, as was his habit, was neither dissuading nor encouraging him. Athos believed everyone should exercise their own free will. He never gave advice unless asked, and always had to be asked twice.

'In general,' he used to say, 'people only ask for advice so they don't have to take it. Or, if they do take it, it's only so they'll have someone to blame for giving it to them.'

Porthos arrived moments after d'Artagnan. The four friends were thus all assembled.

Their four faces expressed four different feelings: Porthos's tranquillity, d'Artagnan's hope, Aramis's anxiety, Athos's insouciance.

After a moment's conversation, in which Porthos hinted that a person of high position had deigned to help him out of his difficulty, Mousqueton entered.

He had come to beg Porthos to pass by his lodgings, where, he declared with an extremely piteous air, his presence was urgently required.

'Is it my equipment?' asked Porthos.

'Yes and no,' replied Mousqueton.

'Now then, what does that mean?'

'Come, sir.'

Porthos got up, bowed to his friends and followed Mousqueton. A moment afterwards, Bazin appeared in the doorway.

'What is it you want, my friend?' said Aramis in that mild tone that was noticeable whenever his thoughts led him back to the Church.

'A man is awaiting monsieur at home,' replied Bazin.

'A man? What man?'

'A beggar.'

'Give him alms, Bazin, and tell him to pray for a poor sinner.'

'This beggar is bent on speaking to you, and claims you will be very glad to see him.'

'Didn't he have a message for me?'

'He did. He said, "If Monsieur Aramis is reluctant to come and find me, tell him that I have just come from Tours."'

'From Tours?' cried Aramis. 'Gentlemen, a thousand pardons, but this man is undoubtedly bringing news I have been expecting.'

And then, leaping to his feet, he quickly left.

Athos and d'Artagnan remained behind.

'I've a feeling those fellows have taken care of their business. What do you reckon, d'Artagnan?' said Athos.

'I know Porthos was making good progress,' said d'Artagnan. 'And, as for Aramis, to tell you the truth, I was never seriously worried about him. But what about you, my dear Athos, after you so generously gave away the Englishmen's pistoles which were your legitimate property, what are you going to do?'

'I am very happy to have killed that rogue, my child, seeing as killing an Englishman is giving him his just deserts. But if I had pocketed his pistoles, they would weigh on me like remorse.'

'Come now, my dear Athos! You really have some inconceivable notions.'

'Let's change the subject! Now, what was I hearing from Monsieur de Tréville, who did me the honour of coming to see me yesterday, about you keeping company with those suspect Englishmen whom the cardinal is protecting?'

'Well, its true, I have been paying visits to an Englishwoman, the one whom I mentioned to you.'

'Ah yes, the blonde woman concerning whom I gave you some advice which naturally you made a point of not taking.'

'I have given you my reasons.'

'Yes. You see a possible source for your equipment in that direction, I believe, from what you've told me.'

'Not at all! I am certain now that this woman had something to do with the abduction of Madame Bonacieux.'

'Yes, and I understand. To find one woman, you court another. It's the longest way round, but the most amusing.'

D'Artagnan was on the verge of telling Athos everything, but one detail stopped him. Athos was rigorous on points of honour, and there were, in the little plan our lover had formed concerning Milady, certain things which, he was sure in advance, would not meet with the Puritan's approval. He preferred therefore to keep silent, and so, as Athos was the least curious man on earth, d'Artagnan's confidences stopped there.

And so we shall leave our two friends, who had nothing of great importance to tell each other, to follow Aramis.

At the news that the man who wanted to talk to him had just come from Tours, we saw how quickly the young man set off after Bazin, or rather raced ahead of him. He therefore got from Rue Férou to Rue de Vaugirard in a single bound.

On entering his lodgings, he found a small man whose intelligent eyes contrasted with the rags in which he was dressed.

'Is it you who is asking for me?' said the musketeer.

'To be precise, I am asking for Monsieur Aramis: do you go by that name?'

'In person. Do you have something to give me?'

'Yes, if you show me a certain embroidered handkerchief.'

'Here it is,' said Aramis taking a key from round his neck and opening a little ebony casket inlaid with mother-of-pearl, 'here, look.'

'Very good,' said the beggar. 'Dismiss your valet.'

Indeed, Bazin, curious to know what the beggar wanted with his master, had matched his pace to the latter's and arrived almost at the same time as him. But such swiftness was not of much use to him; at the beggar's request, his master made a sign for him to retire, and he had no alternative but to obey.

When Bazin had left, the beggar quickly glanced around to make sure no one could see or hear him, and then, opening his ragged jacket, which was loosely cinched by a leather belt, he started unpicking the top of his doublet, from which he drew a letter.

Aramis let out a cry of joy at the sight of the seal, kissed the writing and with almost religious devotion, opened the epistle which contained the following:

> My friend, fate wills it that we should be separated a while longer, but the golden days of youth are not irretrievably lost. Do your duty in camp; I will do mine elsewhere. Take what the bearer will give you; go through the campaign as a fine and noble gentleman, and think of me, who tenderly kisses your black eyes.
>
> Farewell – or rather, until our next meeting!

The beggar continued unpicking his doublet. One by one, he took a hundred and fifty Spanish double pistoles from his dirty clothes and lined them up on the table. Then he opened the door, bowed and left before the stunned young man had dared say a word to him.

Aramis then reread the letter and noticed that it had a postscript:

> P.S. You may make the bearer welcome; he is a count and Spanish grandee.

'Golden dreams!' cried Aramis. 'Oh, beautiful life! Yes, we're young! Yes, we'll have more happy days! Oh, to you, my love, my blood, my life! Everything, everything, everything, my beautiful mistress!'

And then he passionately kissed the letter, without even glancing at the gold that glittered on the table.

Bazin scratched at the door. No longer having any reason to keep him at a distance, Aramis gave him permission to enter.

Dumbfounded by the sight of the gold, Bazin forgot he was meant to announce d'Artagnan, who, curious to find out who this beggar was, had come to Aramis's lodgings after leaving Athos's.

Now, as d'Artagnan did not stand on ceremony with Aramis, seeing that Bazin had forgotten to announce him, he announced himself.

'Ah, what the devil, my dear Aramis,' said d'Artagnan, 'if those are the prunes they send us from Tours, give my compliments to the gardener who picked them.'

'You are mistaken, my dear friend,' said Aramis, discreet as ever, 'it's my bookseller, who has just sent me the money for that poem with lines of one syllable which I began on our travels.'

'Ah, really?' said d'Artagnan. 'Well then, your bookseller is a generous man, my dear Aramis, that is all I can say to you.'

'What, sir,' cried Bazin, 'does a poem fetch such a price? That's incredible! Oh, sir, you can do whatever you wish, you can become the equal of Monsieur de Voiture or Monsieur de Benserade. I like it, yes I do. A poet is almost a priest. Ah, Monsieur Aramis, become a poet, I beg you.'

'Bazin, my friend,' said Aramis, 'I believe you are joining in our conversation.'

Realising he was in the wrong, Bazin bowed his head and left.

'Ah!' said d'Artagnan with a smile, 'you sell your productions by their weight in gold. You are very fortunate, my friend. But watch out, you're going to lose that letter which is sticking out of your tabard and is doubtless also from your bookseller.'

Aramis blushed to the roots of his hair, pushed the letter back into his doublet and buttoned it.

'My dear d'Artagnan,' he said, 'if you have no objection, we'll go and find our friends. And as I'm rich, we'll resume our dinners at once, in anticipation of the time when you will all become rich in your turn.'

'My faith!' said d'Artagnan, 'with great pleasure. It's a long time since we've had a proper dinner, and as I, for my part, have a somewhat risky expedition to undertake tonight, I confess I shall not be sorry to make my blood race a little with some bottles of old Burgundy.'

'Old Burgundy it is. I don't detest it either,' said Aramis, whose notions of retiring from the world had been expunged, as if with a wave of the hand, by the sight of the gold.

And having put two or three double pistoles in his pocket to meet the needs of the moment, he locked the rest in the ebony casket inlaid with mother-of-pearl, which already contained the famous handkerchief that had served him as a talisman.

The two friends went to see Athos first, and, ever faithful to the oath he had sworn not to go out, he undertook to have the dinner delivered to his rooms. As he had a marvellous under-standing of the intricacies of gastronomy, d'Artagnan and Aramis had no objection to leaving this important task to him.

They were on their way to Porthos's rooms, when, at the corner of Rue du Bac, they met Mousqueton, who, with a pitiful air, was driving a mule and a horse before him.

D'Artagnan let out a shout of surprise that was not without its share of joy.

'Ah, my yellow horse!' he cried. 'Aramis, look at this steed!'

'Oh, what a frightful work horse!' said Aramis.

'Well, my friend,' said d'Artagnan, 'that's the horse on which I rode into Paris.'

'What, monsieur knows this horse?' said Mousqueton.

'It's an original colour,' said Aramis. 'I've never seen one with a coat like that before.'

'I can well believe it,' said d'Artagnan. 'I sold it for three écus, and that must have been for the coat because the carcass certainly isn't worth eighteen livres. But how has this horse ended up in your hands, Mousqueton?'

'Ah!' said the valet, 'don't speak to me about it, sir. It's a terrible trick our duchess's husband has played on us!'

'What's that, Mousqueton?'

'Yes, we're looked on very favourably by a lady of quality, the Duchess de . . . But forgive me, my master has enjoined me to be discreet. She insisted we accept a little souvenir, a magnificent Spanish jennet and an Andalusian mule, which were a wonder to behold. The husband found out, confiscated the two magnificent beasts as they were being sent to us, and substituted these horrible animals!'

'Which you are taking back to him?' said d'Artagnan.

'Exactly!' replied Mousqueton. 'You understand that we cannot accept such mounts in exchange for the ones we had been promised.'

'No, by God, although I would have liked to have seen Porthos on my Buttercup. It would have given me an idea of what I was like when I arrived in Paris. But don't let us keep you, Mousqueton. Go and carry out your master's commission, go on. Is he at home?'

'Yes, sir,' said Mousqueton. 'But he's in a very surly temper, I can tell you!'

And then he continued on his way towards the Quai des Grands-Augustins, while the two friends went to ring at the unfortunate Porthos's door. The latter had seen them crossing the courtyard, but the last thing he was going to do was open up for them. Their ringing was therefore in vain.

Meanwhile, Mousqueton carried on his way, and, crossing the Pont-Neuf, still driving the two old screws in front of him, turned into Rue aux Ours. Arriving there, following his master's orders, he tethered the horse and mule to the prosecutor's door knocker. Then, without another thought to their fate, he went back to find Porthos and told him his commission had been carried out.

After a while, the two unfortunate beasts, who hadn't eaten since morning, made such a racket lifting the knocker and letting it fall that the prosecutor ordered his errand boy to inquire in the neighbourhood to whom this horse and mule belonged.

Madame Coquenard recognised her gift, and at first couldn't understand its return in the least. But a visit from Porthos soon enlightened her. The wrath that shone in the musketeer's eyes, despite his attempts at restraint, terrified his sensitive mistress. Indeed, Mousqueton hadn't concealed from his master that he had run into d'Artagnan and Aramis, and that d'Artagnan had recognised the yellow horse as the Béarnais nag he had come to Paris on and sold for three écus.

Porthos left after arranging to meet the prosecutor's wife in the cloister of Saint-Magloire. The prosecutor, seeing Porthos was going, invited him to dinner, an invitation the musketeer refused with the most majestic air.

Madame Coquenard set off for the cloister of Saint-Magloire trembling all over, since she guessed the reproaches awaiting her there. But she was captivated by Porthos's grand manner.

All the curses and reproaches a man whose vanity has been wounded can rain down on a woman's head, Porthos then rained down on the prosecutor's wife's bowed head.

'Alas!' she said. 'I did it for the best. One of our clients is a horse-dealer. He owed the office money and was proving to be recalcitrant. I took the mule and the horse as payment for what he owed us. He had promised me two mounts fit for royalty.'

'Well, madam,' said Porthos, 'if he owed you more than five écus, your horse-coper is a thief.'

'There's no law against seeking a bargain, Monsieur Porthos,' the prosecutor's wife said, trying to excuse herself.

'No, madam, but those who seek a bargain must allow others to look for more generous friends.'

And then, turning on his heel, Porthos took a step to leave.

'Monsieur Porthos! Monsieur Porthos!' cried the prosecutor's wife, 'I was wrong, I admit it. I shouldn't have bargained when it was a matter of outfitting a gentleman such as you!'

Without replying, Porthos took a second step to leave.

The prosecutor's wife fancied she saw him on a glittering cloud, surrounded by duchesses and marchionesses, who were throwing bags of gold at his feet.

'Stop in heaven's name, Monsieur Porthos!' she cried. 'Stop and let us talk.'

'Talking with you brings me bad luck,' said Porthos.

'But tell me, what are you asking for?'

'Nothing, because it amounts to the same as asking you for something.'

The prosecutor's wife hung on Porthos's arm, and, in an outburst of grief, cried out, 'Monsieur Porthos, I am ignorant of all these things. Do I know what a horse is? Do I know what a harness is?'

'You should have left it to me, who do know my way in such matters, madam. But you wished to economise and, consequently, lend at interest.'

'It was wrong of me, Monsieur Porthos, and I will put it right, on my word of honour.'

'And how?' demanded the musketeer.

'Listen. This evening Monsieur Coquenard is going to see the Duke de Chaulnes, who has sent for him. The consultation will last two hours at least. Come to the house, we'll be alone and we shall make up our accounts.'

'Capital! That is real talking, my dear!'

'You will forgive me?'

'We shall see,' said Porthos majestically.

And then the two of them parted company, both saying, 'Till this evening.'

'What the devil!' thought Porthos, as he went away. 'It seems as if at long last I might be getting closer to Monsieur Coquenard's cabinet.'

XXXV

AT NIGHT ALL CATS ARE GREY

T HAT EVENING, SO IMPATIENTLY AWAITED by Porthos and d'Artagnan, finally arrived.

D'Artagnan, as usual, called on Milady around nine o'clock. He found her in a charming mood – never had he been received so well. Our Gascon saw at first glance that his note had been delivered and was having its effect.

Kitty came in bringing water-ices. Her mistress gave her a charming look and smiled her most gracious smile, but alas, the poor girl was so sad she didn't even notice Milady's benevolence.

D'Artagnan looked at the two women in turn, and was compelled to admit that nature had made a mistake in fashioning them: to the great lady it had bequeathed a vile and venal soul, to the soubrette the heart of a duchess.

At ten o'clock Milady began to appear restless. D'Artagnan understood what this meant. She looked at the clock, stood up, sat back down and smiled at d'Artagnan with a look that said, 'You are very amiable, no doubt, but you would be charming if you left!'

D'Artagnan stood up and took his hat. Milady gave him her hand to kiss. The young man felt her press his hand and understood she did so from a feeling not of coquetry but of gratitude that he was leaving.

'She loves him to distraction,' he murmured. Then he left.

This time Kitty wasn't waiting for him, either in the antechamber or in the corridor or in the coach gate. D'Artagnan had to make his way to the staircase and her little room on his own.

Kitty was sitting with her head buried in her hands, weeping.

She heard d'Artagnan come in, but didn't raise her head. The young man went to her and took her hands. Then she burst into sobs.

As d'Artagnan had presumed, when Milady had received the letter, in the delirium of her joy, she had told her maid everything. Then, as reward for the way she had carried out her commission this time, she had given her a purse. On returning to her room, Kitty had thrown the purse in a corner, where it lay wide open, spilling three or four gold coins out on to the carpet.

At the sound of d'Artagnan's voice, the poor girl raised her head. Even d'Artagnan was startled at the look of distress on her face. She clasped his hands with a beseeching look, not daring to say a word.

Unresponsive as d'Artagnan's heart was, he felt touched by this mute sorrow, but he was too attached to his plans in general, and to this one in particular, to make any changes to the programme he had decided on in advance. He therefore gave Kitty no hope of swaying him, but merely presented what he was going to do as a simple act of vengeance.

This vengeance, moreover, seemed all the more straightforward because Milady, no doubt to hide her blushes from her lover, had instructed Kitty to put out all the lights in her apartments, and even in Kitty's own room. Count de Wardes was to leave before daybreak, while it was still dark.

After a moment Milady was heard going to her bedroom. D'Artagnan immediately rushed to his wardrobe. He had barely squeezed into it before the bell rang.

Kitty went into her mistress's room, making a point of shutting the door. But the partition wall was so thin, he could hear almost everything the two women said.

Milady seemed drunk with joy. She had Kitty repeat the minutest details of the alleged interview with de Wardes: how he had received her letter, how he had responded, his expressions, whether he seemed truly in love. And poor Kitty, forced to put a good face on it, replied to all these questions in a choked, mournful voice, which her mistress did not even notice, such is the selfishness of those who are happy.

At length, as the hour of her meeting with the count approached,

Milady had all the lights put out and ordered Kitty to go back to her room and show in de Wardes as soon as he arrived.

Kitty did not have long to wait. D'Artagnan had scarcely seen through the keyhole of his wardrobe that the whole apartment was in darkness before he leapt out of his hiding place, just as Kitty was shutting the communicating door.

'What's that noise?' demanded Milady.

'It is I,' said d'Artagnan in a whisper. 'I, Count de Wardes.'

'Oh, my God! My God!' murmured Kitty 'He couldn't even wait for the hour he had set himself!'

'Well then,' Milady said tremulously, 'why doesn't he enter? Count, count,' she added, 'you know I am waiting for you!'

At these summons, d'Artagnan gently pushed Kitty aside and hurried into Milady's bedroom.

If any soul is prey to the torments of rage and grief, then it is that of the lover who, under another's name, receives protestations of love which are addressed to his favoured rival.

D'Artagnan had not anticipated the painful situation he now found himself in. Jealousy gnawed at his heart, and he suffered almost as acutely as poor Kitty, who at that moment was weeping in the next-door room.

'Yes, count,' Milady said in her sweetest voice, tenderly clasping his hand in hers, 'I am happy for the love your glances and your words have expressed to me every time we have met. I love you too. Oh, tomorrow – tomorrow, I want some token from you that proves you are thinking of me. And, as you might forget me, take this.'

And then she slipped a ring from her finger on to d'Artagnan's.

D'Artagnan remembered seeing this ring on Milady's hand: it was a magnificent sapphire surrounded by diamonds.

D'Artagnan's first impulse was to give it back, but Milady added, 'No, no, keep this ring out of love for me. Besides, in accepting it,' she added in a voice touched with emotion, 'you are doing me a service far greater than you could possibly imagine.'

'This woman is full of mysteries,' d'Artagnan murmured to himself.

At that moment he felt ready to reveal all. He opened his mouth to tell Milady who he was, and with what vengeful intent he had come, but she added, 'Poor angel, whom that Gascon monster almost killed!'

That monster was him.

'Oh,' Milady went on, 'are you still in pain from your wounds?'

'Yes, a great deal,' said d'Artagnan, who wasn't sure how to reply.

'Don't worry,' murmured Milady, 'I will avenge you myself, and cruelly too!'

Damn! thought d'Artagnan, the time for confidences hasn't arrived yet.

D'Artagnan needed some time to recover from this little exchange. But all the thoughts of vengeance he had come with had vanished completely. This woman had an incredible hold over him. He both hated and adored her at the same time; he had never thought that two such contradictory feelings could exist in the same heart, and, in combining, produce a strange, almost diabolical love.

But it had just struck one, and they had to part. D'Artagnan, as he was leaving Milady, felt nothing but a keen regret at going, and in the course of their passionate farewells, a new meeting was agreed upon for the following week. Poor Kitty hoped to be able to address a few words to d'Artagnan as he went through her room, but Milady saw him out herself in the darkness and only left him on the stairs.

The next morning, d'Artagnan ran to Athos's. He was embarked on such a singular adventure, he wanted to ask his advice. As he told him everything, Athos furrowed his brows several times.

'Your Milady,' he said to him, 'strikes me as an infamous creature, but you are no less wrong to deceive her. Now, in one way or another, you have a terrible enemy on your hands.'

And as he spoke to him, Athos looked attentively at the sapphire surrounded with diamonds on d'Artagnan's finger which had taken the place of the queen's ring, which had been carefully put away in a jewellery box.

'You're looking at this ring?' said the Gascon, brimming with

THE THREE MUSKETEERS

pride at being able to show off such a lavish present to his friends.

'Yes,' said Athos, 'it reminds me of a family jewel.'

'It's beautiful, isn't it?' said d'Artagnan.

'Magnificent!' replied Athos. 'I didn't think two sapphires existed of so fine a water. Did you barter your diamond for it?'

'No,' said d'Artagnan. 'It's a present from my beautiful Englishwoman, or rather my beautiful Frenchwoman, for, although I haven't asked her, I'm convinced she was born in France.'

'You got this ring from Milady?' cried Athos, strong emotion clearly discernible in his voice.

'In person. She gave it to me last night.'

'Show me it, then,' said Athos.

'Here it is,' replied d'Artagnan, taking the ring off his finger.

Athos examined it, growing very pale. Then he tried it on the ring-finger of his left hand. It fitted as if it had been made for him. A cloud of anger and vengeance passed over the gentleman's ordinarily calm brow.

'It cannot be the same one,' he said. 'How could this ring end up in the hands of Milady Clarick? And yet it is very hard to imagine that two jewels could be so alike.'

'Are you familiar with this ring?' asked d'Artagnan.

'I thought I recognised it,' said Athos, 'but no doubt I was mistaken.'

And then he gave it back to d'Artagnan, although without ceasing to look at it.

'Look,' he said after a moment, 'd'Artagnan, either take that ring off your finger or turn the stone inside. It brings back such cruel memories that I won't have the wits to talk to you. Didn't you come to ask me for advice? Didn't you say you were perplexed as to what to do? But wait . . . give me that sapphire again. The one I was talking about should have a scratch on one side from an accident.'

D'Artagnan took the ring off his finger again and handed it to Athos.

Athos shuddered.

'Here,' he said, 'you see. Isn't that strange?'

And then he showed d'Artagnan the scratch that he had remembered should be there.

'But who gave you this sapphire, Athos?'

'My mother, who had it from her mother. As I told you, it's an old jewel . . . which should never have left the family.'

'And you . . . sold it?' d'Artagnan asked hesitantly.

'No,' Athos replied with a singular smile. 'I gave it away during a night of love, as it was given to you.'

D'Artagnan grew pensive in his turn. He seemed to see dark, mysterious abysses opening up in Milady's soul.

He put the ring in his pocket rather than back on his finger.

'Listen,' Athos said to him, taking his hand, 'you know I love you, d'Artagnan. If I had a son I couldn't love him any more than you. Well then, believe me, renounce this woman. I don't know her, but a sort of intuition tells me she is a lost creature, and that there is something fatal about her.'

'And you're right to think so,' said d'Artagnan. 'I'll break off with her. I confess, that woman scares me.'

'Will you have the courage?' said Athos.

'I will,' replied d'Artagnan. 'This instant, in fact.'

'Well, I tell you, my boy, you're doing the right thing,' said the gentleman, clasping the Gascon's hand with almost paternal affection. 'May God grant that this woman, who has barely entered into your life, leaves no baleful trace on it!'

And then Athos nodded to d'Artagnan in the way of a man who is keen to convey that he will not be sorry to be left alone with his thoughts.

When he got home, d'Artagnan found Kitty waiting for him. A month's fever couldn't have changed the poor girl more than her night of insomnia and grief.

She had been sent by her mistress to the false de Wardes. Her mistress was mad with love, drunk with joy; she wanted to know when the count would grant her a second interview.

And so poor Kitty, pale and trembling, waited for d'Artagnan's reply.

Athos had a great influence over the young man. The counsels of his friend, coupled with the cries of his own heart, had resolved him, now his pride had been saved and his vengeance satisfied, not to see Milady again. By way of reply, he took a pen and wrote the following letter:

> Do not count on me, madam, for the next rendezvous. Since my convalescence, I have so many commitments of this sort that I have had to put them into a certain order. When your turn comes, I shall have the honour to inform you.
> I kiss your hands.
> Count de Wardes

Not a word about the sapphire. Did the Gascon want to keep it as a weapon against Milady? Or, to speak frankly, wasn't he keeping this sapphire as a last resource for his outfit?

It would be wrong, however, to judge the actions of one era from the perspective of another. What would be regarded today as shameful for a man of honour was in those days an entirely simple and natural thing, and the youngest sons of the best families were regularly kept by their mistresses.

D'Artagnan handed the open letter to Kitty, who read it at first without understanding, and then almost went mad with joy when she read it a second time.

Kitty couldn't believe such happiness. D'Artagnan was obliged to repeat aloud the assurances the letter had given her in writing. And no matter the risks, given Milady's irascible character, the poor girl was running in delivering this note to her mistress, she then returned to Place Royale as fast as her legs could carry her.

Even the best woman's heart is pitiless towards a rival's sorrows. Milady opened the letter with as much alacrity as Kitty had brought it. But, at the first word she read, she became livid, then crumpled up the paper and turned with lightning in her eyes to Kitty.

'What is this letter?' she said.

'But it's the reply to madam's,' replied Kitty, trembling all over.

'Impossible!' cried Milady. 'Impossible for a gentleman to have written a lady such a letter!'

Then shuddering suddenly, she said, 'My God! Could he know . . . ?' And she stopped.

Grinding her teeth, her face ashen, she tried to take a step towards the window to get some air but she could only stretch out her arms. Her legs gave way and she collapsed into a chair.

Thinking she was unwell, Kitty rushed forward to undo her bodice. But Milady quickly picked herself up and said, 'What do you want? Why are you laying your hands on me?'

'I thought madam was feeling unwell and I wanted to help her,' replied the waiting-maid, utterly terrified by the awful expression that had appeared on her mistress's face.

'Unwell? I? I? Do you take me for me some silly little woman? When I'm insulted, I don't feel unwell, I take revenge, do you understand?'

And then, with a wave of her hand, she dismissed Kitty.

XXXVI

THE DREAM OF VENGEANCE

THAT EVENING MILADY, AS WAS her habit, gave orders that Monsieur d'Artagnan should be shown in the moment he arrived. But he did not arrive.

The next day Kitty went to see the young man again and told him what had happened the previous day. D'Artagnan smiled; Milady's jealous rage was his revenge.

That evening Milady was even more impatient than the day before. She repeated her orders regarding the Gascon, but, as the previous day, she waited in vain.

The following day Kitty appeared at d'Artagnan's door, no longer joyful and animated as on the two previous days, but desperately sad.

D'Artagnan asked the poor girl what was the matter but her only response was to take a letter out of her pocket and hand it to him.

This letter was in Milady's writing. But this time it was genuinely addressed to d'Artagnan rather than Count de Wardes.

He opened it and read the following:

Dear Monsieur d'Artagnan, it is wrong to neglect your friends in such a fashion, especially when one is about to leave them for so long. My brother-in-law and I expected you in vain yesterday and the day before. Will it be the same this evening?

Your very grateful,

Lady Clarick

'There's no mystery to it,' said d'Artagnan, 'and I was expecting this letter. My credit rises as the Count de Wardes's falls.'

'Are you going to go?' asked Kitty.

'Listen, my dear child,' said the Gascon, who was trying to excuse himself in his own eyes for breaking his promise to Athos, 'you understand that it would be ill-advised not to accept such an explicit invitation. If Milady saw I was staying away, she wouldn't understand why I'd broken off my visits. She might suspect something, and who can say how far the vengeance of such a woman could go?'

'Oh, my God!' said Kitty. 'You know how to put things so you're always right. But you'll go and pay court to her again, and if you should please her this time under your real name and your own face, it will be far worse than before!'

Instinct allowed the poor girl to guess part of what was going to happen.

D'Artagnan reassured her as best he could and promised to remain impervious to Milady's seductions.

He sent word by reply that he couldn't be more grateful for her kindness and would obey her orders. But he didn't dare write to her lest he fail to disguise his writing sufficiently for eyes as trained as Milady's.

At nine o'clock on the dot, d'Artagnan was at Place Royale. It was obvious that the servants who were waiting for him in the antechamber had been primed, for the moment he appeared, before he had even inquired whether Milady was at home, one of them ran off to announce him.

'Show him in,' said Milady, in a curt voice that was so piercing d'Artagnan heard it from the antechamber.

He was ushered in.

'I am not at home to anyone,' said Milady, 'do you hear? Not to anyone.'

The valet went out.

D'Artagnan glanced curiously at Milady. She was pale and her eyes were tired, either from crying or from insomnia. Fewer lights than usual had been lit, intentionally so, and yet still the young woman couldn't hide the traces of the fever that had consumed her for two days.

D'Artagnan went over to her with his customary gallantry. She made a supreme effort to receive him, but never had a more troubled countenance belied a more amiable smile.

To d'Artagnan's questions about her health, she replied, 'Bad, very bad.'

'Why,' said d'Artagnan, 'then I am being indiscreet. You doubtless need rest, and I shall retire.'

'No, no,' said Milady. 'On the contrary, stay, Monsieur d'Artagnan. Your agreeable company will divert me.'

Oho! thought d'Artagnan. She's never been so charming – let's be wary.

Assuming the most affectionate air she could muster, Milady made her conversation as brilliant as possible. As she did so, the fever that had left her for a moment returned, restoring brightness to her eyes, colour to her cheeks, crimson to her lips. D'Artagnan rediscovered the Circe[1] who had previously enveloped him in her enchantments. The love that he had thought dead, but in fact was only drowsing, reawoke in his heart. Milady smiled, and d'Artagnan felt he would incur damnation for that smile.

For a moment he felt something like a stab of remorse for what he had done to her.

Gradually Milady became more communicative. She asked d'Artagnan if he had a mistress.

'Alas!' said d'Artagnan with the most sentimental air he could assume. 'Can you be so cruel as to ask me such a question – I, who, ever since I saw you, have only breathed and sighed through you and for you?'

Milady smiled a strange smile.

'So you love me?' she said.

'Need I tell you so? Haven't you noticed it?'

'Yes, I have. But, you know, the prouder a heart, the harder it is to win.'

'Oh, difficulties don't scare me!' said d'Artagnan. 'Impossibilities are all I fear.'

'Nothing is impossible,' said Milady, 'for true love.'

'Nothing, madam?'

'Nothing,' replied Milady.

Damn, d'Artagnan said to himself, the tune's changed! Can she by any chance be falling in love with me, the capricious soul? Will she be disposed to give me another sapphire for myself like the one she gave me when she thought I was de Wardes?

D'Artagnan quickly moved his chair closer to Milady's.

'Come now,' she said, 'what would you do to prove this love you speak of?'

'Anything that was required of me. Give your orders, I'm ready.'

'For anything?'

'Anything!' cried d'Artagnan, who knew in advance he was not risking much by making such a commitment.

'Well then, let's talk a little,' Milady said in her turn, moving her chair closer to d'Artagnan's.

'I'm listening, madam,' said the latter.

For a moment Milady remained anxious and seemingly undecided, then, appearing to make up her mind, she said, 'I have an enemy.'

'You, madam?' cried d'Artagnan, feigning surprise. 'Is it possible, my God, beautiful and good as you are!'

'A mortal enemy.'

'Really?'

'An enemy who has insulted me so cruelly that it is war to the death between us. Can I count on you as an ally?'

D'Artagnan instantly understood what the vindictive creature was driving at.

'You can, madam,' he said emphatically. 'My arm and my life are yours, like my love.'

'Then,' said Milady, 'since you are as generous as you are in love . . .'

She paused.

'Well?' asked d'Artagnan.

'Well,' resumed Milady after a moment's silence, 'don't speak of impossibilities from now on.'

'Oh, do not overwhelm me with happiness,' cried d'Artagnan, throwing himself on his knees and covering with kisses the hands that were relinquished to him.

'Avenge me on that detestable de Wardes,' Milady muttered through gritted teeth, 'and I'll have no trouble getting rid of you afterwards, you double fool, you living sword-blade!'

Throw yourself into my arms after jeering at me so brazenly, you dangerous, hypocritical woman, thought d'Artagnan for his part, and then I will laugh at you with the man you want to kill by my hand.

D'Artagnan raised his head.

'I am ready,' he said.

'You've understood me then, my dear Monsieur d'Artagnan?' said Milady.

'I could guess from one of your looks.'

'So you will put your arm, which has already acquired such renown, to work for me?'

'This very instant.'

'But,' said Milady, 'how shall I repay such a service? I am familiar with lovers: they are people who never do something for nothing.'

'You know the only response I desire,' said d'Artagnan, 'the only one that would be worthy of you and me!'

And then he drew her gently towards him.

She barely resisted.

'Schemer!' she said, smiling.

'Ah!' cried d'Artagnan, genuinely swept up by the passion this woman had the gift of inflaming in his heart. 'Ah, it's because my happiness seems so unlikely to me, and as I'm always afraid I'll see it fly away like a dream, I can't wait to make it a reality.'

'Well then, make sure you deserve this so-called happiness.'

'I am yours to command,' said d'Artagnan.

'You're absolutely sure?' asked Milady with a lingering doubt.

'Name the villain who could make your beautiful eyes shed tears.'

'Who told you I shed tears?' she said.

'I fancied . . .'

'Women such as I don't shed tears,' said Milady.

'So much the better! Come, tell me what he is called.'

'Remember his name is my whole secret.'

'I still must know it.'

'Yes, you must. See how I trust you!'

'You fill me with joy. What is he called?'

'You know.'

'Really?'

'Yes.'

'It's not one of my friends?' said d'Artagnan, feigning hesitation to convince her of his ignorance.

'If it was one of your friends, would you hesitate?' cried Milady, a flash of menace lighting up her eyes.

'No, not if it were my brother!' cried d'Artagnan, as if carried away by enthusiasm.

Our Gascon was advancing without risk because he knew where he was going.

'I love your devotion,' said Milady.

'Alas, is that all you love about me?' asked d'Artagnan.

'I love you too,' she said, taking his hand.

And the ardent pressure made d'Artagnan shiver, as if, by touching him, the fever burning up Milady had transmitted itself to him.

'You love me, do you?' he cried. 'Oh, if that were true, it would make me take leave of my senses!'

And then he enfolded her in his arms. She did not try to move her lips away from his kiss, but nor did she return it either.

Her lips were cold; d'Artagnan felt as if he had just kissed a statue.

Nonetheless, he was drunk with joy, electrified with love. He almost believed in Milady's tenderness; he almost believed in de Wardes's crime. If de Wardes had been in his grasp at that moment, he would have killed him.

Milady seized the opportunity.

'He is called . . .' she said in her turn.

'De Wardes, I know,' cried d'Artagnan.

'But how?' demanded Milady, seizing both his hands and trying to read in his eyes the depths of his soul.

D'Artagnan felt he had let himself be carried away and had made a mistake.

'Tell me, tell me, come on, tell me!' repeated Milady. 'How do you know?'

'How do I know?' said d'Artagnan.

'Yes.'

'I know because yesterday de Wardes, in a salon where I happened to be, showed off a ring he said you had given him.'

'The scoundrel!' cried Milady.

This epithet, understandably enough, resonated deep in d'Artagnan's heart.

'Well?' she went on.

'Well, I shall avenge you on that scoundrel,' said d'Artagnan, giving himself the airs of Don Japhet of Armenia[2].

'Thank you, my brave friend!' cried Milady. 'And when shall I be avenged?'

'Tomorrow. At once. Whenever you wish.'

Milady was about to cry out, 'At once!', but she reflected that such haste would not be very gracious to d'Artagnan.

Besides, she had a thousand precautions to take, a thousand pieces of advice to give her defender so that he would avoid explaining himself to the count in front of witnesses. All of this, however, was forestalled by a declaration from d'Artagnan.

'Tomorrow,' he said, 'either you shall be avenged or I shall be dead.'

'No,' she said, 'you will avenge me, and you will not die! He's a coward.'

'With women, perhaps, but not with men. I have first-hand knowledge.'

'But I think that, in your fight with him, you had no cause to complain of your fortune.'

'Fortune is a courtesan. Favourable yesterday, she may betray me tomorrow.'

'Which means you're hesitating.'

'No, I'm not hesitating, God forbid! But would it be fair to let me go to a possible death without giving me at least a little more than just hope?'

Milady replied with a glance that meant, 'Is that all? Well then, speak.'

Then, accompanying the glance with plainer words, she said tenderly, 'You're quite right.'

'Oh, you're an angel!' said the young man.

'So it's all settled?' she said.

'Apart from what I ask of you, my dear soul!'

'Even when I tell you that you can trust my affections?'

'I have no tomorrow to spend waiting.'

'Quiet! I hear my brother. There's no need for him to find you here.'

She rang and Kitty appeared.

'Leave by this door,' she said, pushing open a small jib-door, 'and come back at eleven o'clock. We will finish this conversation then. Kitty will show you into my room.'

The poor child thought she would fall to the floor when she heard these words.

'Well, what are you doing, miss, standing there like a statue? Come, show this gentleman out. And this evening, at eleven o'clock, you heard me!'

Eleven o'clock is apparently her hour for rendezvous, thought d'Artagnan. It's a fixed habit.

Milady held out a hand to him, which he kissed tenderly.

'Come now,' he said as he went out, barely responding to Kitty's reproaches, 'come now, let's not be a fool. This woman is undoubtedly a terrible villain. Let's be on our guard!'

XXXVII
MILADY'S SECRET

DESPITE THE YOUNG GIRL'S APPEALS, d'Artagnan left the townhouse directly rather than go straight up to Kitty's room. He did so for two reasons: first because that way he avoided reproaches, recriminations and entreaties; and secondly, because he was not sorry for the chance to examine his thoughts a little and, if possible, that woman's as well.

The clearest aspect of the whole affair was that d'Artagnan loved Milady madly and she didn't love him in the least. D'Artagnan understood at once that the best thing to do would be to go back home and write Milady a long letter confessing that until then he and de Wardes had been one and the same person, and that consequently he could not undertake, on pain of suicide, to kill de Wardes. But at the same time he was also spurred on by a ferocious desire for revenge. He wanted to possess this woman again under his own name, and as this revenge seemed to him to have a certain sweetness, he did not want to forgo it.

He walked round Place Royale five or six times, turning every ten steps to look at the light in Milady's rooms, which showed through her blinds. The young woman was obviously in less of a hurry to go to her bedroom this time than she had been the first.

But finally the light went out.

And with that glimmer the last hint of indecision was also extinguished in d'Artagnan's heart. He remembered the details of their first night and, his heart leaping, his head on fire, he returned to the townhouse and hurried up to Kitty's room.

Deathly pale, trembling all over, the young girl tried to stop her lover. But Milady, her ears pricked, had heard the noise d'Artagnan made. She opened the door.

'Come,' she said.

All this was so unbelievably impudent, so monstrously bare-faced, that d'Artagnan could scarcely credit what he was seeing and hearing. He thought he was being drawn into one of those fantastical intrigues that unfold in dreams.

Even so he rushed towards Milady, yielding to the attraction she exercised on him, like a magnet on iron.

The door shut behind them.

Kitty rushed in turn to the door.

Jealousy, fury, wounded pride – all the passions, in a word, that vie for the heart of a woman in love urged her to reveal all. But she would be lost if she confessed to assisting such a machination; and, above all, d'Artagnan would be lost to her. This last loving thought counselled her to make this ultimate sacrifice.

D'Artagnan, for his part, had reached the pinnacle of his desires; he was no longer loved as a rival, he was apparently loved as himself. A secret voice deep in his heart, it's true, told him he was merely an instrument of vengeance that one caresses while waiting for it to deal death, but his pride, his vanity, his madness silenced that voice, stifled that murmur. Moreover our Gascon, with his by now familiar confidence, compared himself to de

Wardes and asked why, when all was said and done, he shouldn't be loved simply for himself.

He thus abandoned himself wholeheartedly to the sensations of the moment. Milady was no longer the woman with deadly intentions who had momentarily terrified him; she was an ardent and passionate mistress abandoning herself wholeheartedly to a love that she seemed herself to feel. Two hours or so passed in this fashion.

Nevertheless, the transports of the two lovers eventually abated. Milady, who did not have the same reasons for forgetting as d'Artagnan, came back to reality first and asked the young man if he was clear in his mind as to the measures that would lead to a meeting between him and de Wardes the following day.

But d'Artagnan, whose thoughts had gone off on an entirely different tack, forgot himself like a fool and gallantly replied that it was very late to be concerning oneself with duels at sword-point.

This coolness towards the only interests that concerned her alarmed Milady; her questions became more urgent.

D'Artagnan, who had never seriously considered this impossible duel, tried to change the subject, but it was no longer in his power to do so.

With her irresistible mind and her iron will Milady kept him within the limits she had marked out beforehand.

Thinking himself very witty, d'Artagnan advised Milady to pardon de Wardes and renounce her furious plans.

The moment he spoke, the young woman shuddered and moved away.

'Is it possible you're afraid, dear d'Artagnan?' she said in a shrill, mocking voice that rang out strangely in the darkness.

'You can't think that, dear soul!' replied d'Artagnan. 'But still, what if this poor Count de Wardes were less guilty than you think?'

'At any event,' Milady said gravely, 'he deceived me, and, from that moment, he deserved to die.'

'He will die then, since you condemn him!' d'Artagnan said,

in a tone so firm that Milady thought it an expression of unerring devotion.

She instantly moved close to him.

We could not say how long the night lasted for Milady, but d'Artagnan thought he had been with her barely two hours when daylight appeared through the slats of the blinds, and then, moments later stole into the room with its pallid gleam.

Seeing that d'Artagnan was going to leave her, Milady reminded him of the promise he had made to avenge her on de Wardes.

'I am ready for it,' said d'Artagnan, 'but first I would like to be sure of one thing.'

'What is that?' asked Milady.

'That you love me.'

'I have given you the proof of that, it seems to me.'

'Yes, and I am yours body and soul.'

'Thank you, my brave lover! But just as I have proved my love to you, you will in turn prove yours to me, won't you?'

'Certainly. But if you love me as you say,' d'Artagnan went on, 'aren't you a little afraid for me?'

'What should I fear?'

'Why, that I might be dangerously wounded . . . killed even.'

'Impossible,' said Milady, 'you are so valiant a man and so fine a blade.'

'So you wouldn't prefer,' d'Artagnan went on, 'a means that would avenge you equally well, without there being any need to fight?'

Milady looked at her lover in silence. The pallid gleam of the first rays of dawn lent her limpid eyes a strangely baleful expression.

'Really,' she said, 'I think now you are hesitating.'

'No, I'm not hesitating. But I'm genuinely concerned for this poor Count de Wardes since you no longer love him. It seems to me that the loss of your love must be such a cruel punishment for a man in itself that there is no need to punish him further.'

'Who told you I love him?' asked Milady.

'At least I may now believe without excessive self-conceit that you love another,' said the young man in a caressing tone, 'and, I repeat, I take an interest in the count.'

'You?' asked Milady.

'Yes, I.'

'And why you?'

'Because only I know . . .'

'What?'

'That he is far from being, or rather having been, as guilty towards you as he seems.'

'Indeed?' said Milady uneasily. 'Explain yourself, for I truly don't know what you mean.'

And then she gazed at d'Artagnan, who held her in his arms, his eyes seeming gradually to catch fire.

'Yes, I am a man of honour!' said d'Artagnan, determined to have done with it. 'And since your love is mine, since I am quite sure of possessing it – for I do possess it, don't I?'

'Entirely. Go on.'

'Well, I feel as if transported, then, but a confession lies heavy on me.'

'A confession?'

'If I doubted your love, I wouldn't make it. But you love me, my beautiful mistress, you do love me, don't you?'

'Of course.'

'Then if by an excess of love, I have been guilty of an offence towards you, you will forgive me?'

'Perhaps!'

D'Artagnan tried, with the sweetest smile he could muster, to touch Milady's lips with his own, but she pushed him away.

'This confession,' she said, growing pale, 'what is this confession?'

'You gave de Wardes a rendezvous last Thursday in this very room, isn't that so?'

'I? No, it's not so,' said Milady, so firmly and with such an impassive expression that if d'Artagnan had not been so utterly certain, he would have fallen into doubt.

'Don't lie, my beautiful angel,' said d'Artagnan, smiling, 'it's no use.'

'What's that? Speak! You're killing me!'

'Oh, don't worry, you're not guilty as far as I am concerned, and I have already forgiven you!'

'Well? Well?'

'De Wardes has nothing to boast of.'

'Why? You told me yourself that that ring . . .'

'That ring, my love – I have it myself. The Count de Wardes of Thursday and the d'Artagnan of today are the same person.'

The foolhardy young man was expecting a mixture of surprise and shame, a little storm that would dissolve into tears, but he was strangely mistaken, and his error quickly became apparent.

Pale and terrible, Milady drew herself up, and pushing d'Artagnan away with a violent blow to his chest, leapt out of bed.

It was almost completely light.

D'Artagnan held her back by her peignoir of fine Indies calico to beg her forgiveness, but she jerked herself free with a powerful, resolute movement. The cambric tore, leaving her shoulders bare, and on one of those beautifully rounded white shoulders d'Artagnan, with an inexpressible feeling of shock, recognised a fleur-de-lys, that indelible mark impressed by the executioner's defaming hand.

'Good God!' cried d'Artagnan, letting go of the peignoir.

And then he remained mute, motionless, frozen on the bed.

But d'Artagnan's horror alone was denunciation enough for Milady. He had doubtless seen everything. The young man now knew her secret, a terrible secret that no one else in the world knew except him.

She swung round, less like a furious woman now than a wounded panther.

'Ah, scoundrel!' she said. 'You have cravenly betrayed me, and what's more, you know my secret! You shall die!'

And then she ran to an inlaid box on her dressing table, opened it with a trembling, feverish hand, took out a small dagger with a gold handle and a sharp, thin blade and, in one bound, hurled herself half-naked at d'Artagnan.

The young man was brave, as we know, but he was terrified by that distorted face, those horribly dilated pupils, those pale cheeks and those bloody lips. He shrank back to the wall, as if a snake were slithering towards him. His sweating hand chanced upon his sword, and he drew it from its scabbard.

Milady paid no attention and tried to climb up on to the bed to stab him, only stopping when she felt its sharp point at her throat.

She tried to seize the sword with both her hands, but d'Artagnan kept it out of her reach, and, pointing it now at her eyes, now at her breast, he slid down from the bed, searching for the door to Kitty's room so he could make his retreat.

Meanwhile, Milady kept flinging herself at him in horrible transports of rage, roaring in a fearsome way.

As all this was starting to resemble a duel, however, d'Artagnan gradually recovered his poise.

'Very good, beautiful lady, very good,' he said. 'But, in God's name, calm yourself, otherwise I'll etch you a second fleur-de-lys on the other shoulder!'

'Villain! Villain!' screamed Milady.

But d'Artagnan, still searching for the door, kept on the defensive.

At the noise they were making – she knocking over furniture to get to him, he hiding behind furniture to shield himself from her – Kitty opened the door. D'Artagnan, who had been constantly manoeuvring himself closer to it, was only three paces away. With a single bound he leapt from Milady's room into the maid's, and then, quick as lightning, shut the door behind him and leant against it with all his weight while Kitty shot the bolts.

Then, with a strength far greater than that of an ordinary woman, Milady tried to stave in that barrier confining her to her room. When she found it impossible, she started stabbing the door over and over with her dagger, sometimes driving the blade through the entire thickness of the wood.

Each stab was accompanied by a terrible curse.

'Quick, quick, Kitty,' said d'Artagnan in a whisper when the bolts had been shot, 'get me out of here. If we give her time to collect herself, she'll have me killed by the valets.'

'But you can't go out like that,' said Kitty, 'you're completely naked.'

'That's true,' said d'Artagnan, only now realising his attire, 'that's true. Dress me as best you can, but let's hurry. It's a matter of life and death, you understand?'

Kitty understood only too well. In the twinkling of an eye, she tricked him out in a flowery dress, a big headscarf and a short cape. She gave him a pair of slippers into which he slipped his bare feet, and then led him down the stairs. Not a moment too soon. Milady had already rung the bell and woken the entire building. The doorman pulled the cord at Kitty's request just as Milady, half-naked herself, shouted from the window, 'Don't open up!'

XXXVIII

HOW, WITHOUT STIRRING HIMSELF, ATHOS FOUND HIS OUTFIT

THE YOUNG MAN RAN OFF while she was still threatening him with an impotent gesture. The moment she lost sight of him, Milady fell senseless to her bedroom floor.

D'Artagnan was so traumatised that, without concerning himself about what would become of Kitty, he ran across half Paris and only stopped when he reached Athos's door. The bewilderment of his mind, the terror spurring him on, the cries of several patrols that set off in pursuit after him, and the jeers of some passers-by who, despite the late hour, were going about their business, only made him go all the faster.

He crossed the yard, climbed the two flights of stairs to Athos's rooms and banged on the door as if he wanted to break it down.

Grimaud came to open up, his eyes puffy with sleep. D'Artagnan stormed into the antechamber so forcefully that he almost knocked him over in the process.

Despite the poor lad's habitual muteness, this time he found his tongue.

'Hey there! Hey there!' he cried. 'What do you want, you trollop? What are you after, you strumpet?'

D'Artagnan pushed back his head scarf and took his hands out from under the cape. At the sight of his moustaches and his bare sword, the poor devil saw he was dealing with a man.

He thought it was some assassin.

'Help! To me! Help!' he cried.

'Quiet, wretch!' said the young man. 'I'm d'Artagnan – don't you recognise me? Where is your master?'

'You're Monsieur d'Artagnan?' cried the terrified Grimaud. 'That can't be.'

'Grimaud,' said Athos, coming out of his bedroom in his dressing gown, 'I believe you have given yourself licence to speak.'

'Ah, sir, it's because . . .'

'Silence.'

Grimaud contented himself with pointing out d'Artagnan to his master.

Athos recognised his comrade, and, phlegmatic though he was, burst into laughter at the masquerade that met his eyes: scarf askew, skirts falling over his shoes, sleeves rolled up, moustaches bristling with emotion.

'Don't laugh, my friend,' cried d'Artagnan, 'in heaven's name, don't laugh, for, on my soul, I tell you there's nothing to laugh about.'

And he pronounced these words with so solemn an air and so genuine a sense of dread that Athos immediately grasped his hands and cried, 'Are you wounded, my friend? You're very pale!'

'No, but something terrible has just happened to me. Are you alone, Athos?'

'By God, whom do you expect to be in my home at this hour?'

'Good, good.'

And then d'Artagnan shot into Athos's room.

'Go on, then, speak!' said the latter, closing the door and bolting it so they wouldn't be disturbed. 'Is the king dead? Have you killed the cardinal? You're distraught. Come, come, tell me, for I'm truly dying of worry.'

'Athos,' said d'Artagnan, taking off his women's clothes and appearing in his shirt, 'prepare to hear an unbelievable, an unheard-of story.'

'Take this dressing gown first,' the musketeer told his friend.

D'Artagnan put on the dressing gown, after mixing up the sleeves at first in his agitation.

'Well then?' said Athos.

'Well then,' replied d'Artagnan, bending towards Athos's ear and lowering his voice, 'Milady has a fleur-de-lys branded on her shoulder.'

'Ah!' cried the musketeer, as if he had been shot in the heart.

'Look,' said d'Artagnan, 'are you sure the *other one* is really dead?'

'The *other one*?' said Athos in such a muffled voice d'Artagnan could barely hear him.

'Yes, the one you told me about one day in Amiens.'

Athos groaned and let his head sink into his hands.

'This one,' d'Artagnan went on, 'is a woman of around twenty-six or twenty-eight.'

'Blonde,' said Athos, 'no?'

'Yes.'

'Light blue eyes of a strange brightness, with black lashes and eyebrows?'

'Yes.'

'Tall, shapely? She's missing a tooth next to her left eye-tooth.'

'Yes.'

'The fleur-de-lys is small, a reddish-brown colour, and

looks as if it's been washed out thanks to the layers of paste
applied to it.'

'Yes.'

'Yet you say she's English!'

'She is called Milady, but she may be French. In any case, Lord
de Winter is only her brother-in-law.'

'I wish to see her, d'Artagnan.'

'Careful, Athos, careful! You tried to kill her. She's a woman
who will pay you back in the same coin and she will not fall short.'

'She won't dare say a word, for she'd be denouncing herself.'

'She is capable of anything! Have you ever seen her furious?'

'No,' said Athos.

'A tigress, a panther! Ah, my dear Athos, I am very afraid I
have called down a terrible vengeance on us both!'

D'Artagnan then told Athos everything: Milady's insane rage,
her death threats.

'You're right, and, upon my soul, my life would be hanging
by a hair's breadth,' said Athos. 'But fortunately we're leaving
Paris the day after tomorrow. We'll most likely be going to La
Rochelle, and once we've left . . .'

'She'll follow you to the ends of the earth, Athos, if she recog-
nises you. So let her hatred vent itself on me alone.'

'Ah, my dear friend, what does it matter if she kills me?' said
Athos. 'Do you think I prize life by any chance?'

'There is some horrible mystery behind all this. Athos, that
woman is the cardinal's spy, I'm sure of it!'

'In that case, take great care of yourself. The cardinal does
not hold you in high esteem for the London affair, indeed he
feels great hatred for you. But since, all things considered, he
can't reproach you for anything publicly, and since hatred must
be appeased, especially when it is a cardinal's hatred, you must
be careful! If you go out, don't go out alone. If you eat, take
your precautions. Distrust everything, in a word – even your
shadow.'

'Luckily,' said d'Artagnan, 'it's only a question of making it through to tomorrow evening unscathed, for once we're in the army, we'll only, I hope, have men to fear.'

'Until then,' said Athos, 'I'm renouncing my plans of seclusion and going everywhere with you. You need to go back to Rue des Fossoyeurs; I'll keep you company.'

'Close as it is,' said d'Artagnan, 'I can't go back there like this.'

'Indeed,' said Athos, and rang the bell.

Grimaud came in.

Athos signalled to him to go to d'Artagnan's lodgings and bring back some clothes.

Grimaud replied with another sign that he understood perfectly, and left.

'Now then, none of this gets us any further with fitting ourselves out, my dear friend,' said Athos. 'For, if I am not mistaken, you left all your effects at Milady's, who doubtless has no intention of returning them. Luckily, you have the sapphire.'

'The sapphire is yours, my dear Athos! Didn't you tell me it was a family ring?'

'Yes, my father bought it for two thousand écus, he once told me. It was one of the wedding gifts he gave to my mother, and it is magnificent. My mother gave it to me, and I, madman that I was, rather than guarding the ring like a holy relic, gave it away in turn to that wretch.'

'Then take back the ring, my dear friend. I can understand that you must be attached to it.'

'I, take back that ring after it has passed through that abominable woman's hands? Never. The ring is polluted, d'Artagnan.'

'Sell it, then.'

'Sell a diamond that comes from my mother? I confess, I would regard that as a profanation.'

'Then pawn it. They'll lend you well over a thousand écus. With that sum, you'll put all your affairs in order, and then, with the first money that comes in, you can redeem it, and you'll get it back cleansed of its old stains since it will have passed through usurers' hands.'

Athos smiled.

'You are a charming companion,' he said, 'my dear d'Artagnan. Your eternal merriment lifts the spirits of the afflicted. Well then, yes, let's pawn this ring, but on one condition!'

'What?'

'That it'll be five hundred écus for you and five hundred for me.'

'What are you thinking, Athos? I don't need a quarter of that sum, being in the guards, and I can raise it by selling my saddle. What do I need? A horse for Planchet, that's all. And you're forgetting I have a ring too.'

'To which you're more attached, it seems to me, than I am to mine. At least I think I noticed as much.'

'Yes, for in dire straits, it could rescue us not only from great financial difficulty but also from great danger. It is not merely a precious diamond, it's a magic talisman.'

'I don't understand what you mean, but I'll take your word for it. So, getting back to my ring, or rather yours, you will take half the sum we get for it, or I'll throw it into the Seine, and I doubt whether, as with Polycrates¹, some fish will be amenable enough to return it to us.'

'Well then, I accept!' said d'Artagnan.

At that moment Grimaud came in, accompanied by Planchet. The latter, worried about his master and curious to know what had happened to him, had taken advantage of the situation to bring the clothes himself.

D'Artagnan got dressed, as did Athos. Then, when they were both ready to leave, Athos turned to Grimaud and mimicked a man aiming a gun. The latter took down his carbine and prepared to accompany his master.

Athos and d'Artagnan, followed by their valets, reached Rue des Fossoyeurs without mishap. Bonacieux was at his door. He looked mockingly at d'Artagnan.

'Hey there, my dear tenant,' he said, 'hurry up. You've got a beautiful young girl waiting for you and, as you know, women don't like to be kept waiting!'

'It's Kitty!' cried d'Artagnan.

And then he rushed down the alley.

Sure enough, he found the poor child on the landing outside his rooms, huddled against his door and trembling all over. As soon as she saw him, she said, 'You promised me your protection; you promised to save me from her anger. Remember it's you who's ruined me!'

'Yes, of course,' said d'Artagnan, 'don't worry, Kitty. But what happened after I left?'

'How should I know?' said Kitty. 'At her cries, the valets came running. She was crazed with anger, vomiting up every curse that exists against you. I thought she'd remember it was my room that you'd gone through to get to hers, and would imagine I was your accomplice. I took the little money I had, and my most treasured old rags, and fled.'

'Poor child! But what am I going to do with you? I'm leaving in two days.'

'Anything you like, sir – get me out of Paris, get me out of France!'

'But I can't take you with me to the siege of La Rochelle,' said d'Artagnan.

'No, but you can find me a position in the provinces with a lady of your acquaintance – in your part of the country, for instance.'

'Ah, my dear friend, in my part of the country ladies don't have waiting maids. But, wait, I know just the thing. Planchet, go and find Aramis for me. Tell him to come immediately. We have something very important to tell him.'

'I understand,' said Athos. 'But why not Porthos? I think his marchioness . . .'

'Porthos's marchioness has herself dressed by her husband's clerks,' said d'Artagnan, laughing. 'Besides Kitty wouldn't want to live in Rue aux Ours, would you, Kitty?'

'I'll live wherever you wish,' said Kitty, 'so long as I'm well hidden and no one knows I'm there.'

'Now that we're going to part, Kitty, and as you're therefore
no longer jealous about me . . .'

'Sir, near or far,' said Kitty, 'I will always love you.'

'Where the devil will constancy find its nesting place²?'
murmured Athos.

'I will too,' said d'Artagnan, 'I will always love you, don't
worry. But look, answer this – the question I'm going to ask you
is very important to me. Did you ever hear talk of a young lady
who was abducted one night?'

'Wait a moment . . . Oh, my God, sir, do you still love that
woman?'

'No, it's one of my friends who loves her. Here he is, it's
Athos.'

'I?' cried Athos, like a man who sees he is about to step on a
snake.

'Of course, you!' said d'Artagnan, clasping Athos's hand. 'You
know very well the interest we all take in that poor little Madame
Bonacieux. Besides Kitty won't say anything, will you, Kitty? You
understand, my child,' continued d'Artagnan, 'she's the wife of
that ugly ape you saw on the doorstep when you came in here.'

'Oh, my God!' cried Kitty. 'You're reminding me of how afraid
I was. As long as he hasn't recognised me!'

'What do you mean, recognised? Have you seen that man
before, then?'

'He came to Milady's house twice.'

'I knew it! When was that?'

'Why, some fifteen or eighteen days ago.'

'Exactly.'

'And yesterday evening he came back.'

'Yesterday evening?'

'Yes, a moment before you came yourself.'

'My dear Athos, we are entangled in a web of spies! And do
you think he recognised you, Kitty?'

'I pulled down my hood as soon as I saw him, but it may have
been too late.'

'Go down, Athos – he mistrusts you less than me – and see if he's still by his door.'

Athos went down, but soon came back up.

'He's gone,' he said, 'and the house is locked.'

'He's gone to make his report and say all the pigeons are in the dovecot as he speaks.'

'Well then, let's fly away,' said Athos, 'and only leave Planchet here to bring us news.'

'Wait a moment! What about Aramis? We've sent for him.'

'You're right,' said Athos, 'let's wait for Aramis.'

Aramis came in at that moment.

They explained the affair to him and told him how urgent it was he find a position for Kitty among his array of aristocratic acquaintances.

Aramis thought for a moment, then said, blushing, 'Will this truly be doing you a service, d'Artagnan?'

'I'll be grateful for all my life.'

'Well then, Madame de Bois-Tracy has asked me if I know a reliable lady's maid, for one of her friends, who lives in the country, I believe. And if, my dear d'Artagnan, you can answer for Mademoiselle . . .'

'Oh, sir,' cried Kitty, 'I will be entirely devoted to the person who makes it possible for me to leave Paris, you may count on that.'

'Then,' said Aramis, 'it's all for the best.'

He sat down at a table, wrote a little note which he sealed with a ring, and gave it to Kitty.

'Now, my child,' said d'Artagnan, 'you know it's no easier for us here than it is for you, so let us part. We shall meet again in better days.'

'And whenever we do and wherever it may be,' said Kitty, 'you will find I still love you as I love you today.'

'A gambler's oath,' said Athos, as d'Artagnan went out to see Kitty downstairs.

A moment later, the three young men parted company,

arranging to meet at four o'clock at Athos's, and leaving Planchet to keep an eye on the house.

Aramis went home, while Athos and d'Artagnan set about pawning the sapphire.

As our Gascon had anticipated, they had no trouble getting three hundred pistoles for the ring. Moreover, the Jew announced that if they wanted to sell it to him, as it would make him a magnificent pendant for some earrings, he would give them as much as five hundred pistoles for it.

Athos and d'Artagnan, with the briskness of two soldiers and the expertise of two connoisseurs, needed barely three hours to buy the musketeer's whole outfit. Besides, Athos was accommodating and a great nobleman to his fingertips. Whenever something suited him, he paid the asking price without even trying to negotiate a discount. D'Artagnan wanted to object to this approach but Athos put his hand on his shoulder, smiling, and d'Artagnan realised that, while it may have been fine for a petty Gascon gentleman like him to haggle, it wasn't for a man with the airs of a prince.

The musketeer found a superb Andalusian horse, black as jade, with nostrils of fire and fine, elegant legs, which was getting on for six years old. He examined it and found it faultless. The price was a thousand livres.

He might perhaps have got it for less. But while d'Artagnan was arguing about the price with the horse dealer, Athos counted out the hundred pistoles on the table.

Grimaud was given a squat, powerful Picard horse, which cost three hundred livres.

Once its saddle and Grimaud's arms had been bought, there wasn't a sou of Athos's one hundred and fifty pistoles left. D'Artagnan offered his friend a bite of his share, which he could pay back later.

But Athos's only response was a shrug of his shoulders.

'How much was the Jew going to pay to buy the sapphire outright?' asked Athos.

'Five hundred pistoles.'

'In other words, two hundred pistoles more – a hundred pistoles for you, and a hundred for me. Why, that's an absolute fortune, my friend. Go back to the Jew.'

'What, you want to . . .'

'That ring would undoubtedly bring back too many painful memories. And then we'll never have the three hundred pistoles to give him, so we're losing two thousand livres in the deal. Go and tell him the ring is his, d'Artagnan, and come back with the two hundred pistoles.'

'Think, Athos.'

'Ready money is at a premium these days, and we have to be able to make sacrifices. Go, d'Artagnan, go. Grimaud will accompany you with his carbine.'

Half an hour later, d'Artagnan came back with the two thousand livres without having suffered any accident.

And so this was how Athos found unexpected funds under his own roof.

XXXIX
A VISION

AT FOUR O'CLOCK, THE FOUR FRIENDS met up at Athos's lodgings. Their anxieties about outfitting themselves had entirely disappeared, so each face only bore the marks of its owner's secret concerns – for, behind all present happiness, some fear for the future always lies concealed.

Suddenly Planchet came in, bringing two letters addressed to d'Artagnan.

One was a little note daintily folded lengthwise, with a pretty seal of green wax representing a dove bearing a green branch.

The other was a large, square missive, glittering with the terrible arms of His Eminence the cardinal-duke.

At the sight of the little letter, d'Artagnan's heart leapt, for he thought he recognised the handwriting; and although he had seen that handwriting only once, the memory of it was engraved deep in his heart.

He therefore took the little epistle and quickly unsealed it. It contained the following instructions:

Ride out next Wednesday, between six and seven in the evening, on the Chaillot road, and carefully observe the carriages that pass. But if you value your life and that of the people who love you, do not say a word, do not make a movement that may lead anyone to suspect you have recognised she who is exposing herself to every danger to glimpse you for a moment.

No signature.

'It's a trap,' said Athos. 'Don't go, d'Artagnan.'

'And yet,' said d'Artagnan, 'I really think I recognise the writing.'

'It might be a forgery,' said Athos. 'Between six and seven o'clock, at this time of year, the Chaillot road is completely deserted. You might as well go for a walk in Bondy Forest.'

'But what if we all went?' said d'Artagnan. 'Hang it, they're not going to devour all four of us, plus four valets, plus horses, plus arms.'

'Besides, it will be a chance to show off our outfits,' said Porthos.

'But if it's a woman's writing,' said Aramis, 'and this woman does not wish to be seen, think, d'Artagnan, you'll compromise her – a shameful thing for a gentleman to do.'

'We'll hang back,' said Porthos, 'and he can go ahead on his own.'

'Yes, but it takes just a moment to fire a pistol from a carriage going past at high speed.'

'Bah!' said d'Artagnan, 'they'll miss me. Then we'll catch up the carriage and wipe out whomever's inside. At least we'd reduce the numbers of our enemies.'

'He's right,' said Porthos. 'To battle! Besides, we've got to try out our arms.'

'Why yes, let's treat ourselves to that pleasure,' said Aramis, in his gentle, nonchalant way.

'As you wish,' said Athos.

'Gentlemen,' said d'Artagnan, 'it's half-past four. We barely have time to make the Chaillot road by six.'

'Besides, if we leave too late,' said Porthos, 'no one will see us, which would be a pity. Let's go and get ourselves ready, gentlemen.'

'But you're forgetting the second letter,' said Athos. 'It strikes me, though, that judging by the seal it's well worth opening. Speaking for myself, my dear d'Artagnan, I declare I am much more concerned about it than that little bauble you have just tucked so gently close to your heart.'

D'Artagnan blushed.

'Well then,' said the young man, 'let's see, gentlemen, what His Eminence wants with me.'

And then d'Artagnan unsealed the letter and read:

Monsieur d'Artagnan, of the King's Guards, des Essarts's company, is expected at the Palais-Cardinal this evening at eight o'clock.

La Houdinière,
Captain of the Guards

'Confound it,' said Athos, 'that's a far more troubling appointment than the other.'

'I'll go to the second on my way back from the first,' said d'Artagnan. 'One's for seven o'clock, the other for eight; there'll be time for both.'

'Hmm, I wouldn't go,' said Aramis. 'A gallant cavalier cannot miss a rendezvous granted by a lady, but a prudent gentleman can excuse himself from attending on His Eminence, especially when he has reason to think he has not been summoned for an exchange of compliments.'

'I am of Aramis's opinion,' said Porthos.

'Gentlemen,' replied d'Artagnan, 'I've already had a similar invitation from His Eminence by the hand of Monsieur de Cavois. I ignored it, and the next day I suffered a great misfortune! Constance disappeared. Whatever might happen, I'm going.'

'If you're resolved,' said Athos, 'do so.'

'But the Bastille?' said Aramis.

'Bah, you'll get me out,' replied d'Artagnan.

'Of course,' Aramis and Porthos replied with admirable aplomb, as if it were the simplest thing in the world, 'of course we'll get you out. But, in the meantime, as we're to leave the day after tomorrow, you'd be advised not to risk the Bastille.'

'Let's do better than that,' said Athos. 'Let's not leave him all evening, and each wait at a gate of the palace with three musketeers at our back. If we see any carriage coming out with its curtains closed, looking remotely suspect, we'll fall on it. It's a long time since we've had a score to settle with the cardinal's guards – Monsieur de Tréville must think we're dead.'

'No mistake, Athos,' said Aramis, 'you were born to be a general. What do you say to the plan, gentlemen?'

'Admirable!' chorused the young men.

'Well then,' said Porthos, 'I'll run to Monsieur de Tréville's; I'll tell our comrades to be ready by eight o'clock; the meeting point will be Place du Palais-Cardinal. In the meantime, have the valets saddle the horses.'

'I don't have a horse,' said d'Artagnan. 'But I'll go and get one from Monsieur de Tréville's.'

'No need,' said Aramis, 'you can take one of mine.'

'How many have you got, then?' asked d'Artagnan.

'Three,' answered Aramis with a smile.

'My dear friend!' said Athos. 'You are undoubtedly the best mounted poet in France and Navarre.'

'But listen, my dear Aramis, you won't know what to do with three horses, will you? I don't even understand why you bought three.'

'Actually, I only bought two,' said Aramis.

'So the third fell from heaven?'

'No, the third was brought to me only this morning by an unliveried servant who refused to tell me whose household he belonged to, but simply informed me that he had been ordered by his master . . .'

'Or mistress,' said d'Artagnan.

'That's neither here nor there,' said Aramis, blushing '. . . but simply informed me, as I was saying, that he had been ordered by his mistress to put the horse in my stable without telling me who it came from.'

'Such things only happen to poets,' Athos said gravely.

'Well then, in that case, we can do better,' said d'Artagnan. 'Which of the two horses are you going to ride – the one you bought, or the one that was given to you?'

'Unquestionably the one that was given to me. You understand, d'Artagnan, I cannot insult . . .'

'The unknown donor,' replied d'Artagnan.

'Or mysterious donoress,' said Athos.

'So the one you bought is of no use to you now?'

'More or less.'

'And you chose it yourself?'

'And with the greatest care. The safety of the rider, as you know, almost always depends on his horse!'

'Well then, let me have him for the price you paid!'

'I was going to offer him to you, my dear d'Artagnan, and give you all the time you needed to pay me back such a trifle.'

'And how much did he cost you?'

'Eight hundred livres.'

'Here are forty double pistoles, my dear friend,' said d'Artagnan, taking the sum from his pocket. 'I know that's the coin in which you're paid for your poems.'

'You're in funds, then?' said Aramis.

'I'm rich, fabulously rich, my dear friend!'

D'Artagnan jingled the rest of his pistoles in his pocket.

'Send your saddle to the musketeers' stables, and your horse will be brought back here with ours.'

'Excellent. But it will soon be five o'clock, let's hurry.'

A quarter of an hour later, Porthos appeared at one end of Rue Férou on a magnificent jennet, with Mousqueton following on a small but solid Auvergne horse. Porthos was radiant with joy and pride.

At the same time Aramis appeared at the other end of the street, mounted on a superb English charger. Bazin followed him on a roan, leading a vigorous Mecklenburger – d'Artagnan's mount.

The two musketeers met at the door, watched by Athos and d'Artagnan from the window.

'Hang it,' said Aramis, 'you have a superb horse there, my dear Porthos!'

'Yes,' replied Porthos. 'It's the one they should have sent me first. As a bad joke, the husband swapped it for another, but the husband has since been punished and I have obtained full satisfaction.'

Planchet and Grimaud then appeared in turn, leading their masters' mounts. D'Artagnan and Athos went downstairs, swung themselves into the saddle beside their companions, and all four set off: Athos on the horse he owed to his wife, Aramis on the horse he owed to his mistress, Porthos on the horse he owed to his prosecutor's wife, and d'Artagnan on the horse he owed to his good fortune, the best mistress of all.

The valets followed behind.

As Porthos had thought, their cavalcade made a fine spectacle, and if Madame Coquenard had been in Porthos's path and could have seen what an air of distinction he had on his handsome Spanish jennet, she wouldn't have regretted the bloodletting to which she had subjected her husband's strongbox.

Near the Louvre the four friends came upon Monsieur de Tréville, who was returning from Saint-Germain. He stopped them to compliment them on their outfits, thereby instantly drawing a crowd of several hundred curious onlookers.

D'Artagnan took the opportunity to speak to Monsieur de Tréville about the letter with the great red seal and ducal arms. Understandably enough, he did not breathe a word about the other letter.

Monsieur de Tréville approved of the decision he had taken, and assured him that if he hadn't reappeared by the following day, he would be sure to find him, wherever he might be.

At that moment, the Samaritaine clock struck six. The four friends excused themselves on the grounds of their appointment and took their leave of Monsieur de Tréville.

A short gallop brought them to the Chaillot road. The sun was sinking. Carriages came and went. D'Artagnan, guarded by his friends standing a few paces behind him, peered into every one, but didn't see any face he recognised.

Finally, after waiting for a quarter of an hour, as twilight was falling in earnest, a carriage appeared, racing at full gallop along the Sèvres road. A presentiment told d'Artagnan that it contained the person who had given him the rendezvous. The young man was astonished to feel his heart beating with such violence. Almost instantly, a woman's head leant out of the carriage door with two fingers to her lips, as if calling for silence or blowing a kiss. D'Artagnan let out a faint cry of joy: the woman – or rather the apparition, for the carriage flew past with the speed of a vision – was Madame Bonacieux.

With an involuntary movement, despite the instructions he had been given, d'Artagnan launched his horse into a gallop and in a few bounds caught up with the carriage, but the window of the coach door was shut tight; the vision had disappeared.

Then d'Artagnan remembered the warning: 'If you value your life and the lives of those who love you, stay absolutely still, as if you haven't seen anything.'

He stopped, trembling not for himself but for the poor woman who had evidently exposed herself to great danger in granting him this rendezvous.

Without slacking its tremendous speed the carriage continued on its way, plunged into Paris and disappeared.

D'Artagnan stood rooted to the spot, dumbfounded, not knowing what to think. If it was Madame Bonacieux, and if she was going back to Paris, why this fleeting rendezvous, why this mere exchange of glances, why this lost kiss? If, on the other hand, it wasn't her, which was perfectly possible, for the little daylight remaining made mistakes easy, wasn't this the first move in an attack on him using as bait the woman whom he was known to love?

His three companions came over. All three had clearly seen a woman's head appear at the carriage door, but none of them, apart from Athos, knew Madame Bonacieux. Athos was of the opinion that it was definitely her, but, being less preoccupied by that pretty face than d'Artagnan, he also thought he had seen a second face, a man's, at the back of the carriage.

'If that's so,' said d'Artagnan, 'then they're doubtless transferring her from one prison to another. But what do they want to do to this poor creature, and how will I ever catch up with her again?'

'My friend,' Athos said gravely, 'remember that the dead are the only people we're in no danger of meeting again on this earth. You and I both know something about that, don't we? Now, if your mistress isn't dead, if that was her we just saw, then one day or another you'll find her again. And, my God,' he added with a characteristic note of misanthropy, 'perhaps sooner than you'd like.'

It struck half-past seven. The carriage had been twenty minutes or so late for the rendezvous. D'Artagnan's friends reminded him he had a visit to pay; they also pointed out that he still had time to cry off.

But d'Artagnan was both stubborn and curious. He had got it into his head that he would go to the Palais-Cardinal and find out what His Eminence wanted to say to him, and nothing could shake him in his resolve.

They rode to Rue Saint-Honoré and from there to Place du Palais-Cardinal, where they found the twelve musketeers they had summoned pacing about as they waited for their comrades. Only now was it explained to the musketeers what was afoot.

D'Artagnan was a familiar figure to the honourable corps of the king's musketeers, who knew he would one day take his place in their ranks. They regarded him in anticipation, therefore, as a comrade and consequently each of them wholeheartedly accepted the mission for which he had been summoned. Besides, it would very likely give them the chance to play the cardinal and his men a nasty trick, and for such expeditions these worthy gentlemen were always ready for such expeditions.

Athos divided them into three groups, took command of one, gave the second to Aramis and the third to Porthos. Then each group went to lie in ambush opposite an exit of the palace.

D'Artagnan, for his part, boldly entered by the main gate.

Although he felt vigorously supported, the young man did not climb the sweeping staircase one step at a time without a certain uneasiness. His conduct towards Milady bore some slight resemblance to treachery, and he suspected political dealings between that woman and the cardinal. Moreover, de Wardes, whom he had worked over so badly, was one of His Eminence's loyal followers, and d'Artagnan knew that, inasmuch as His Eminence was implacable towards his enemies, he was also deeply attached to his friends.

If de Wardes has told the cardinal about our whole affair, which he undoubtedly will have, and if he has recognised me, which he probably will have, I should consider myself virtually a condemned man, d'Artagnan said to himself, shaking his head. But why has he waited until today? It's simple enough. With that hypocritical sorrow, which makes her so interesting, Milady must have lodged a complaint against me, and this last crime must have broken the camel's back.

Fortunately, he added, my good friends are downstairs, and they won't let me be taken away without defending me. Still, Monsieur de Tréville's company of musketeers can't single-handedly wage war on the cardinal, who has the forces of France at his command, and robs the queen of her power and the king of his will. D'Artagnan, my friend, you're brave, you have excellent qualities, but women will be the ruin of you!

He came to this sad conclusion as he entered the antechamber. He handed his letter to the usher on duty, who showed him into the waiting room and then disappeared into the heart of the palace.

In the waiting room there were five or six of the cardinal's guards, who, recognising d'Artagnan and, knowing that it was he who had wounded Jussac, looked at him with singular smiles.

These smiles seemed ominous to d'Artagnan. But, as our Gascon was not easily intimidated – or rather, thanks to the great, innate pride of people from his province, as he did not readily betray what was going on in his soul, when what was going on there resembled fear – he planted himself proudly in front of the gentlemen of the guards and waited, hand on hip, in an attitude not without majesty.

The usher came back in and signalled for d'Artagnan to follow him. The young man sensed the guards whispering among themselves as they watched him walk away.

He went down a corridor, crossed a large drawing room, entered a library and found himself facing a man sitting at a desk and writing.

The usher showed him in and withdrew without saying a word. D'Artagnan at first thought he was dealing with a judge who was examining his record, but he soon saw that the man at the desk was writing, or rather editing, lines of unequal length, scanning the words on his fingers. He realised he was in the presence of a poet. After a moment, the poet closed his manuscript, on the cover of which was written: *Mirame, a Tragedy in Five Acts*[1], and raised his head.

D'Artagnan recognised the cardinal.

XL

THE CARDINAL

T HE CARDINAL LEANT HIS ELBOW on his manuscript, cheek in hand, and looked at the young man for a moment. No one had a more profoundly searching eye than Cardinal de Richelieu, and d'Artagnan felt his gaze running through his veins like a fever.

Nevertheless he showed a bold front, holding his felt hat in his hand and awaiting His Eminence's pleasure with neither too much pride, nor too much humility.

'Sir,' the cardinal said to him. 'Are you a d'Artagnan of Béarn?'

'Yes, my lord,' replied the young man.

'There are several branches of the d'Artagnans in Tarbes and the surrounding country,' said the cardinal. 'To which do you belong?'

'I am the son of the man who fought in the wars of religion with the great King Henri, father of His Gracious Majesty.'

'Yes, that's right. Is it you who set out from your province some seven or eight months ago to seek your fortune in the capital?'

'Yes, my lord.'

'You came through Meung, where something happened to you – I can't now remember exactly what, but something at any rate.'

'My lord,' said d'Artagnan, 'this is what happened to me . . .'

'No need, no need,' interrupted the cardinal, with a smile that indicated he knew the story as well as the man who wished to tell it to him. 'You were recommended to Monsieur de Tréville, were you not?'

'Yes, my lord. But actually, in that unfortunate affair at Meung . . .'

'The letter was lost,' His Eminence went on. 'Yes, I know. But Monsieur de Tréville is a gifted physiognomist who can take a man's measure at first sight, and he placed you in the company of his brother-in-law, Monsieur des Essarts, while giving you leave to hope that one day you would enter the musketeers.'

'My lord is impeccably informed,' said d'Artagnan.

'Since then, a great deal has happened to you. You took a stroll behind the Chartreux one day when you would have done better being elsewhere. Then you took a trip with your friends to the waters at Forges. They stopped on the way, but you continued your journey. It was all quite simple: you had business in England.'

'My lord,' said d'Artagnan, completely nonplussed, 'I was going . . .'

'Hunting in Windsor, or elsewhere, it's no one's concern. I know of it, because it is my business to know everything. On your return, you were received by an august personage, and I see with pleasure that you have kept the memento she gave you.'

D'Artagnan reached for the diamond ring he had been given by the queen and quickly turned the stone inwards, but it was too late.

'The following day, you received Cavois's visit,' the cardinal went on. 'He was going to invite you to come to the palace. You did not return the visit, and that was wrong of you.'

'My lord, I fear I have incurred Your Eminence's displeasure.'

'Ah, why is that, sir? For following your superiors' orders with greater intelligence and courage than another would have done? Incur my displeasure when you have merited praise? It's the people who don't obey whom I punish, not those like you, who obey . . . too well. And to prove it, remember the date of the day I sent for you to come and see me, and search your memory for what happened that evening.'

Madame Bonacieux's abduction had taken place that same evening. D'Artagnan shuddered. Then he remembered that half an hour earlier the poor woman had driven past, no doubt carried off once more by the power that was responsible for her disappearance in the first place.

'Eventually,' the cardinal went on, 'as I hadn't heard word of you for some time, I wished to know what you were doing. In any case, you undoubtedly owe me a measure of gratitude. You must have remarked how considerately you have been treated in all these affairs.'

D'Artagnan bowed respectfully.

'This consideration,' the cardinal went on, 'was due not only to a natural sense of fair-mindedness on my part, but also to a plan I had conceived in your regard.'

D'Artagnan was evermore astonished.

'I wanted to inform you of this plan the day you received my first invitation, but you did not show yourself. Happily, nothing has been lost in the delay, and you shall hear it today. Sit down here, in front of me, Monsieur d'Artagnan. You're enough of a gentleman not to have to remain standing.'

And then the cardinal pointed out a chair to the young man, who was so astonished by what was happening that he waited for a second sign from his interlocutor before obeying.

'You're brave, Monsieur d'Artagnan,' continued His Eminence. 'You're also prudent, which is even better. I love men with a head and a heart. Don't be afraid,' he said, smiling, 'by men with a heart, I mean men of courage. But, despite being very young, and only just taking your first steps in the world, you have powerful enemies. If you don't take care, they will destroy you!'

'Alas, my lord,' replied the young man, 'they will doubtless do so with the greatest of ease, for they are strong and well-supported, whilst I am all alone!'

'Yes, that's true. But, alone as you are, you have already done a great deal, and you will do more, I have no doubt. Nonetheless, I believe you need to be guided in the adventurous career you have undertaken, for, if I am not mistaken, you came to Paris with the ambitious idea of making your fortune.'

'I am at the age of wild hopes, my lord,' said d'Artagnan.

'Wild hopes are only for fools, sir, and you have your wits about you. Come now, what would you say to becoming an ensign in my guards, and having your own company after the campaign?'

'Ah, my lord!'

'You accept, do you not?'

'My lord,' d'Artagnan repeated with an embarrassed air.

'What, you refuse?' cried the cardinal, astonished.

'I am in His Majesty's guards, my lord, and I have no cause for dissatisfaction.'

'But it seems to me,' said His Eminence, 'that my guards are also His Majesty's guards, and that, so long as one serves in a French corps, one is serving the king.'

'My lord, Your Eminence has misunderstood me.'

'You want a pretext, do you? I understand. Well then, here it is. Promotion, the new campaign, the opportunity I am giving you – these will suffice as pretexts for the world. For yourself, the need to be under sure protection is reason enough. For you should know, Monsieur d'Artagnan, that I have received serious complaints on your account. You do not devote your days and nights exclusively to the king's service.'

D'Artagnan blushed.

'What's more,' continued the cardinal, putting his hand on a bundle of papers, 'I have here a whole dossier about you. But before reading it, I wanted to talk with you. I know you are a man of resolve, and under proper direction, instead of leading you to harm, your services could profit you greatly. Come, think it over and make up your mind.'

'Your goodness confounds me, my lord,' replied d'Artagnan, 'and I recognise in Your Eminence a greatness of soul that renders me as lowly as a worm. But, after all, since my lord permits me to speak frankly to him . . .'

D'Artagnan paused.

'Yes, speak.'

'Well then, I will say to Your Eminence that all my friends are in the musketeers and the king's guards, and that my enemies, by an inconceivable mischance, are Your Eminence's men. I should therefore be out of place here and ill-regarded there, if I accepted my lord's offer.'

'Can you already have had the vainglorious idea that I am not offering you what you are worth, sir?' the cardinal said with a disdainful smile.

'My lord, Your Eminence is a hundred times too good to me, and I think, on the contrary, that I haven't yet done enough to merit his kindness. The siege of La Rochelle is about to begin, my lord. I shall serve under Your Eminence's eyes, and if I have the good fortune to conduct myself at this siege in such a way as to deserve to attract his gaze, well then, afterwards I shall at least have some brilliant action under my belt to justify the protection with which he would so kindly honour me. Everything at its due time, my lord. Perhaps later I shall be entitled to give myself; now it would look as if I were selling myself.'

'In other words, you refuse to serve me, sir,' said the cardinal spitefully, although still with a certain respect. 'Stay free, then, and persist in your hatreds and your sympathies.'

'My lord . . .'

'Fine, fine,' said the cardinal. 'I don't hold it against you, but you understand, it is occupation enough defending one's friends and rewarding them; one owes nothing to one's enemies. Nevertheless I will give you a piece of advice. Be on your best behaviour, Monsieur d'Artagnan, for the moment I withdraw my hand from above you, I wouldn't give an obole for your life.'

'I will endeavour to, my lord,' the Gascon replied with noble self-assurance.

'Remember later, if at a certain moment misfortune befalls you,' Richelieu said emphatically, 'that it was I who came looking for you, and that I have done all I can to avert that misfortune from you.'

'Come what may,' said d'Artagnan, putting his hand on his breast and bowing, 'I will be eternally grateful to Your Eminence for what he is doing for me at this moment.'

'Well then, as you say, Monsieur d'Artagnan, we shall see each other again after the campaign. I shall keep an eye on you, for I shall be there,' continued the cardinal, indicating to d'Artagnan a magnificent suit of armour which he was to wear, 'and, on our return, we shall have our reckoning!'

'Ah, my lord,' cried d'Artagnan, 'spare me the weight of your displeasure. Remain neutral, my lord, if you find that I act as a man of honour.'

'Young man,' said Richelieu, 'if I have the chance to tell you once again what I have told you today, I promise you I will do so.'

Richelieu's final remark filled d'Artagnan with terrible misgivings. It dismayed d'Artagnan more than a threat. The cardinal was so far seeking to protect him from some misfortune that threatened him. He opened his mouth to reply, but the cardinal dismissed him with a haughty gesture.

D'Artagnan left. At the door, his heart was on the verge of failing him and he almost turned back, but Athos's grave, severe face appeared to him. If he entered into the agreement the cardinal was proposing, Athos would never offer him his hand again; Athos would disown him.

It was this fear that restrained him, so powerful is the influence of a truly noble character on all those who come into contact with him.

D'Artagnan went down the same staircase he had come up, and found Athos and the four musketeers at the door, waiting for him to come back and starting to worry. A word from d'Artagnan reassured them, and Planchet ran to tell the other posts that there was no need to mount guard any longer; his master had emerged safe and sound from the Palais-Cardinal.

When they got back to Athos's, Aramis and Porthos asked the reasons for this strange rendezvous. But d'Artagnan simply told them that Richelieu had sent for him to offer him an ensign's commission in his guards, and that he had refused.

'And you were right!' Porthos and Aramis cried with one voice.

Athos fell into a deep reverie and did not reply. But when he was alone with d'Artagnan, he said, 'You did what you should have done, d'Artagnan. But perhaps you were wrong.'

D'Artagnan heaved a sigh, for this voice echoed a secret voice in his soul, which told him that great misfortunes awaited him.

The following day was spent preparing for their departure. D'Artagnan went to take his leave of Monsieur de Tréville. At that time everyone still thought that the guards and musketeers would only be separated temporarily as the king was holding his parliament that same day and was to start out the next so Monsieur de Tréville simply asked d'Artagnan if he required anything from him. D'Artagnan replied proudly that he had everything he needed.

Night gathered together all the comrades from Monsieur des Essarts's company of guards and Monsieur de Tréville's company of musketeers, who had become friends. They were parting to meet again when, and if, it pleased God. As might be imagined, the night was therefore very rumbustious, for, in such circumstances, extreme unease can be only be countered by extreme insouciance.

The next day, at the first sound of the trumpets, the friends parted: the musketeers rushed to Monsieur de Tréville's, the guards to Monsieur des Essarts's. Each captain then led his company to the Louvre, where the king conducted his review.

The king was downcast and seemingly in ill health, which robbed him of some of his noble bearing. Indeed, the evening before, he had come down with a fever in the middle of parliament, while he was holding a formal session. He was nonetheless determined to leave that same evening and, despite the wealth of remarks passed by others, he wanted to hold his review, hoping to overcome the malady taking hold of him by getting in a first vigorous blow.

When the review was over, the guards marched off. The musketeers were to set out with the king, which enabled Porthos, in his superb outfit, to take a turn in Rue aux Ours.

The prosecutor's wife saw him pass in his new uniform and on his handsome horse. She loved Porthos too much to let him go like that. She made a sign for him to dismount and come in to the house. Porthos was magnificent: his spurs jingled, his breastplate gleamed, his sword slapped proudly against his legs. This time the clerks felt no urge to laugh, so much did Porthos resemble a man who would lop off their ears.

The musketeer was shown in to Monsieur Coquenard, whose

little grey eyes gleamed with anger on seeing his cousin resplendent in his new outfit. Yet he had one private source of consolation; everyone was saying the campaign would be tough. Very quietly, at the bottom of his heart, he hoped that Porthos would be killed.

Porthos presented his compliments to Monsieur Coquenard and bade him farewell. Monsieur Coquenard wished him all manner of prosperity. As for Madame Coquenard, she couldn't control her tears, but no shameful inferences were drawn from her grief. She was known to be very attached to her relatives, on whose count she had always had the cruellest arguments with her husband.

The real farewells, however, took place in Madame Coquenard's bedroom; they were heartbreaking.

As long as the prosecutor's wife could follow her lover with her eyes, she waved her handkerchief, leaning so far out of her window that it seemed as if she wanted to throw herself headlong into the street. Porthos received all these marks of tenderness like a man accustomed to such demonstrations. But, as he turned the corner, he raised his hat and waved it in farewell.

For his part, Aramis wrote a long letter. To whom? No one had an inkling. In the next room, Kitty, who was to leave that evening for Tours, was waiting for this mysterious communication.

Athos drank his last bottle of Spanish wine in little sips.

D'Artagnan, meanwhile, was marching out of Paris with his company.

When they reached the Faubourg Saint-Antoine, he turned to glance merrily at the Bastille. But because it was only the Bastille he was looking at, he did not see Milady, mounted on a light bay horse, who pointed him out to two shady-looking men who immediately drew nearer to the ranks to identify him. To their questioning look, Milady replied with a sign that it was indeed he. Then, certain nothing could go awry in the execution of her orders, she spurred her horse and disappeared.

The two men then followed the company, and, on leaving the Faubourg Saint-Antoine, mounted fully prepared horses, which an unliveried servant was holding in readiness for them.

XLI

THE SIEGE OF LA ROCHELLE

The siege of La Rochelle was not only one of the great political events of Louis XIII's reign but also one of the cardinal's great military undertakings. It will thus be of interest, and even necessary, for us to say a few words about it. Besides, certain details of the siege are connected in too important a way to the story we have undertaken to tell for us to pass them over in silence.

The cardinal's political objectives in embarking on this siege were wide-ranging. Let us set those out first, then address some of his personal objectives, which may have had no less of an influence on His Eminence than his political designs.

Of the major cities given to the Huguenots by Henri IV as safe havens, only La Rochelle remained. The siege aimed, therefore, to destroy this last bulwark of Calvinism, a dangerous leavening into which ferments of civil revolt and foreign war were constantly being mixed.

Spanish, English and Italian malcontents, adventurers of every nation, soldiers of fortune of every sect, rallied at the first call to the banners of the Protestants, organising themselves into a vast association which spread in a shot all over Europe.

Gaining fresh importance from the ruin of the other Calvinist cities, La Rochelle was thus a hotbed of dissension and ambition. Moreover, its port was the last port in the kingdom of France open to the English. By closing it to England, our eternal enemy, the cardinal completed the work of Joan of Arc and the Duke de Guise.

And so Bassompierre, who was simultaneously Protestant and Catholic–Protestant by conviction and Catholic as commander of the Order of the Holy Spirit; who was German by birth and French at heart; and, finally, who commanded his own forces at the siege of La Rochelle – Bassompierre said, as he charged at the head of a number of other Protestant noblemen like him, 'You'll see, gentlemen, we shall be fools enough to take La Rochelle!'

And Bassompierre was right: the cannonade of the Île de Ré heralded the dragonnades of the Cévennes; the capture of La Rochelle was the preface to the revocation of the Edict of Nantes[1].

But, as we have said, alongside these objectives of the levelling and simplifying minister, which are a part of history, the chronicler is also obliged to recognise the pettier aims of the lover and jealous rival.

Richelieu, as is well known, had been in love with the queen. Whether this love was purely political or one of those profound passions Anne of Austria naturally inspired in her entourage, we could not say. But either way, we have seen from previous developments in this story that Buckingham had triumphed, and that he had even in two or three affairs, particularly in that of the diamond tags, outwitted him thanks to the three musketeers' devotion and d'Artagnan's courage.

For Richelieu, therefore, the siege was a question not merely of ridding France of an enemy but also of avenging himself on a rival. Furthermore, this vengeance had to be resounding and momentous, worthy in every way of a man who brandished the forces of an entire kingdom like a sword in his hand.

Richelieu knew that, in fighting England, he was fighting Buckingham; that in triumphing over England, he was triumphing over Buckingham; and, lastly, that in humiliating England in the eyes of Europe, he would be humiliating Buckingham in the eyes of the queen.

For his part, Buckingham, while advancing the honour of England, was motivated by exactly the same interests as the cardinal. Buckingham was also seeking personal revenge. Buckingham couldn't have returned to France as an ambassador under any pretext; he would do so therefore as a conqueror.

Consequently the real stakes in this game, which the two most powerful kingdoms were playing for the pleasure of two men in love, was merely a glance from Anne of Austria.

The Duke of Buckingham had gained the first advantage. Arriving unexpectedly within sight of the Île de Ré with ninety ships and roughly twenty thousand men, he had surprised Count de Toiras, who commanded the island for the king, and, after a bloody battle, had managed to land his troops.

Let us report in passing that Baron de Chantal died in that battle, leaving a little girl of eighteen months an orphan.

This little girl would grow up to be Madame de Sévigné.

Count de Toiras withdrew to the citadel of Saint-Martin with the garrison and threw a hundred men into a small fort which was called the fort of La Prée.

This turn of events had hastened the cardinal's resolve. In the interim before he and the king could take command of the siege of La Rochelle, their fixed objective, he had sent the king's brother, Monsieur, to direct the first operations, and had hurried all the troops at his disposal to the theatre of war.

Our friend d'Artagnan was part of this detachment sent on as a vanguard.

The king, as we've said, was to follow as soon as he had held his formal session. But, on rising from this on the twenty-eighth of June, he felt the onset of a fever. Even so he insisted on setting out, but, his condition worsening, he was forced to stop at Villeroi.

Now, wherever the king stopped, the musketeers stopped too. Consequently, d'Artagnan, who was simply and solely a guard, found himself separated at least temporarily from his good friends Athos, Porthos and Aramis. This separation struck him merely as a nuisance, but it would certainly have become a cause for serious concern if he could have guessed the unknown dangers surrounding him on all sides.

Nevertheless, he reached the camp outside La Rochelle without mishap, towards the tenth of September in the year 1627.

Nothing had changed: the Duke of Buckingham and his Englishmen, masters of the Île de Ré, were still besieging the citadel of Saint-Martin and the fort of La Prée, but without success, and the hostilities with La Rochelle had begun two or three days earlier over a fort the Duke d'Angoulême had just constructed near the city.

The guards, under the command of Monsieur des Essarts, were quartered with the Minims[2].

Preoccupied with his ambition to switch to the musketeers, d'Artagnan, as we know, had made few friends among his comrades, and so found himself isolated and absorbed in his thoughts.

These weren't especially cheerful. He had spent the year since arriving in Paris caught up in public affairs, and consequently his private affairs – love and fortune – had not made a great deal of headway.

As far as love was concerned, the only woman he loved was Madame Bonacieux, and Madame Bonacieux had disappeared, and he hadn't been able to discover what had become of her.

As to fortune, his puny self had managed to become an enemy of the cardinal – that is, of a man before whom the greatest noblemen of the kingdom, starting with the king, quaked.

This man could crush him, and yet he hadn't done so. For a mind as astute as d'Artagnan's, such indulgence was a ray of light revealing a brighter future.

He had also made another enemy, whom he thought was less to be feared, but, he instinctively felt, by no means to be despised. That enemy was Milady.

In return for all this, he had gained the protection and goodwill of the queen, but, as things stood, the queen's goodwill was further grounds for persecution, and her protection, as we know, protected her followers very imperfectly – witness Chalais and Madame Bonacieux.

The clearest benefit he had derived, therefore, was the diamond worth five or six thousand livres that he wore on his finger. But even that diamond, supposing d'Artagnan, in his ambitious designs, wanted to keep it to use it one day as a token to show the queen, had no more value in the meantime – since he couldn't dispose of it – than the pebbles he was treading underfoot.

We say the pebbles he was treading underfoot, for d'Artagnan was thinking these thoughts as he took a solitary stroll along a pretty little path that led from the camp to the village of Angoutin. These thoughts had taken him further than he'd supposed, however, and the light was going when, in the last rays of sunshine, he thought he saw a musket barrel glinting behind a hedge.

D'Artagnan had a sharp eye and a quick mind. He realised the musket hadn't appeared there of its own accord, and that the man holding it hadn't taken cover behind a hedge with friendly intentions. He had already decided, therefore, to make his getaway, when he caught sight of the tip of a second musket on the other side of the road.

Clearly, it was an ambush.

The young man glanced at the first musket and saw with some concern that it was aiming in his direction. As soon as the mouth of the barrel stopped moving, he threw himself flat on the ground. At the same instant, a shot was fired, and he heard the whistle of a bullet passing over his head.

There was no time to lose. D'Artagnan leapt to his feet, and, as he did so, a bullet from the other musket kicked up the pebbles on the path just where he had thrown himself face down on the ground.

D'Artagnan wasn't one of those pointlessly brave men who go to a ridiculous death so people can say they never yielded an inch. Besides, it was no longer a question of courage; d'Artagnan had been caught in a trap.

If there's a third shot, he thought to himself, I'm done for!

And taking to his heels at once, he ran off in the direction of the camp with the swiftness of natives of his province who are so renowned for their agility. But no matter how fast he ran, the man who'd fired first, having had time to reload, could still fire a second shot, which was so well aimed this time that the bullet went through his hat and sent it flying ten paces ahead of him.

As d'Artagnan didn't have another one, he picked up his hat at a run, made it back to his quarters very pale and out of breath, sat down without saying a word to anyone, and set to thinking.

This event could have three causes:

The first and the most natural would be an ambush by the Rochelois, who would not have been sorry to kill one of His Majesty's guards, first because that would mean one enemy fewer, and secondly because that enemy might have a well-lined purse in his pocket.

D'Artagnan reached for his hat, examined the bullet hole, and shook his head. The bullet wasn't from a musket but an harquebus. The accuracy of the shot had already made him think it had been fired by a civilian weapon. It couldn't have been a military ambush, then, because the bullet wasn't the right calibre.

Another possibility was that it was a pleasant souvenir from the cardinal. It will be remembered that, at the very moment when, thanks to that blessed ray of sunshine, he had spotted the gun barrel, he was marvelling at the forbearance of His Eminence in his regard.

But d'Artagnan shook his head. When he only had to reach out his hand to seize a man, His Eminence rarely resorted to such methods.

And finally, it could be Milady's revenge.

That was more probable.

He tried in vain to remember either the features or the dress of the assassins. He had made such a fast getaway that he hadn't had time to notice anything about them.

'Ah, my poor friends,' murmured d'Artagnan, 'where are you? How I miss you!'

D'Artagnan passed a very bad night. Three or four times he woke up with a start, imagining a man was coming towards his bed to stab him. Yet day broke without the darkness having brought any incident.

D'Artagnan, however, had a strong suspicion that what was postponed was not written off.

He kept to his quarters all day. To soothe his conscience, he told himself the weather was bad.

The following day, at nine o'clock, the drums beat the general salute. The Duke d'Orléans[3] was visiting the posts. The guards hurriedly turned out, and d'Artagnan fell in amidst his comrades.

Monsieur passed along the front line. Then all the superior officers approached him to pay their respects, Monsieur des Essarts, the captain of the guards, among them.

After a moment d'Artagnan had the impression Monsieur des Essarts was beckoning him over. Afraid he was mistaken, he waited for another gesture from his superior, but when the gesture was repeated, he left the ranks and stepped forward to receive his orders.

'Monsieur is going to ask for volunteers for a mission, which will be dangerous but will do honour to those who carry it out. I made you a sign so you'd hold yourself in readiness.'

'Thank you, sir!' replied d'Artagnan, who wanted nothing better than to distinguish himself in the sight of the lieutenant-general.

The Rochelois had made a sortie during the night and had recaptured a bastion the royal army had taken two days previously. The plan was to send out a scouting party – 'a forlorn hope' in military parlance – to see how the army was guarding the bastion.

And indeed, after a few moments, Monsieur raised his voice and said:

'I'll need three or four volunteers led by a dependable man for this mission.'

'As to the dependable man, I have him here, my lord,' Monsieur des Essarts said, indicating d'Artagnan. 'And, as to the four or five volunteers, my lord has only to make his intentions known, and he'll have no shortage of men.'

'Four men willing to come and get themselves killed with me!' cried d'Artagnan, flourishing his sword.

Two of his comrades from the guards sprang forward, and were immediately followed by two soldiers, who thus made up the requisite numbers. D'Artagnan rejected everyone after that, not wishing to do an injustice to those who had priority.

It was not known whether, after capturing the bastion, the Rochelois had evacuated it or left a garrison there. The fortification therefore had to be studied at close quarters.

Setting out with his four companions, d'Artagnan followed

the trench. The two guards marched abreast of him, while the soldiers brought up the rear.

Under cover of the revetments, they managed in this manner to get to within no less than a hundred or so paces of the bastion. Then d'Artagnan turned and saw the two soldiers had disappeared.

Thinking they'd stayed behind out of fear, he pushed on.

At the bend of the counterscarp, they found themselves some sixty paces from the bastion.

No one was to be seen, and the bastion seemed abandoned.

The three forlorn hopes were deliberating whether to go on when suddenly a belt of smoke enclosed the giant stone fortification, and a dozen bullets whistled past d'Artagnan and his two companions.

They knew what they needed to know: the bastion was guarded. Staying any longer in that dangerous place would therefore have been pointlessly reckless. D'Artagnan and the two guards thus turned on their heel and began a retreat which bore some resemblance to headlong flight.

As they reached the corner of the trench that would serve as a rampart, one of the guards fell, shot through the chest. The other, unharmed, ran towards the camp.

Not wanting to abandon his fellow guardsman, d'Artagnan bent over to pick him up and help him back to their lines. But, as he did so, two shots rang out. One bullet blew out the brains of the already wounded guard, and the other passed within two inches of him before smashing into a rock.

The young man swung round, for this attack couldn't be coming from the bastion, which was hidden by the angle of the trench. He thought of the two soldiers who had absconded, and was reminded of the assassins from two days previously. This time, he decided, he would get to the bottom of it and collapsed, as if dead, onto his comrade's body.

He instantly saw two heads poking up above an abandoned outwork thirty paces off; it was the heads of our two soldiers. D'Artagnan hadn't been mistaken. Those two men had followed him solely with his murder in mind, hoping the young man's death would be attributed to the enemy.

But now, as he might be wounded and might denounce their crime, they were coming over to finish him off. Fortunately, taken in by d'Artagnan's ruse, they had neglected to reload their guns.

When they were ten paces away, d'Artagnan, who had been very careful not to lose his grip of his sword as he fell, suddenly jumped up and was on them in one bound.

The assassins realised that if they fled towards the camp without having killed their man, he would accuse them, so their first thought was to go over to the enemy. One of them grabbed his gun by the barrel and used it as a club. He aimed a terrible blow at d'Artagnan, who, throwing himself out of the way, avoided it. But, in so doing, he allowed the bandit to pass, and the man immediately raced off towards the bastion. The Rochelois guarding it, however, had no idea what this figure running at them was intending, so they opened fire and he fell, his shoulder shattered by a bullet.

In the meantime, d'Artagnan had flung himself on the second soldier, attacking him with his sword. Their struggle didn't last long; the wretch had nothing to defend himself with except his empty harquebus. Skidding along the barrel of the now-useless weapon, the guard's sword ran the assassin through the thigh, and he fell to the ground. D'Artagnan immediately pressed his sword-point to his throat.

'Oh, don't kill me!' cried the bandit. 'Mercy, mercy, sir, and I will tell you everything.'

'Is your secret worth my sparing your life?' asked the young man, restraining his sword-arm.

'Yes, if you think life has any value when one is twenty-two, like you, and a handsome, brave man who can achieve anything.'

'Scoundrel!' said d'Artagnan. 'Come, talk quickly: who ordered you to murder me?'

'A woman I don't know, but whom people call Milady.'

'But if you don't know this woman, how do you know her name?'

'My comrade knew her and called her that. She dealt with him, not me. He even has a letter from this person in his pocket, which must be of great importance to you, from what I've heard him say.'

'But how did you come to be half of this ambush?'

'He proposed we do the job together and I accepted.'

'And how much did she give you for this fine undertaking?'

'A hundred louis.'

'Well, that's good,' said the young man, laughing, 'at least she thinks I'm worth something. A hundred louis! That's a goodly sum for two scoundrels like you, so I can understand you accepted, and I will let you off, but on one condition.'

'What?' the soldier asked anxiously, seeing it was not all over.

'That you go and fetch the letter your comrade has in his pocket.'

'But,' cried the bandit, 'that's just another means of killing me. How do you expect me to go and fetch that letter under fire from the bastion?'

'You'll have to make your mind up to go and fetch it, though, otherwise I swear you'll die by my hand.'

'Mercy, sir, have pity! In the name of the young lady you love, and perhaps believe is dead, but who isn't!' cried the bandit, falling to his knees and leaning on his hand, his strength ebbing away like his blood.

'And how do you know there is a young woman I love, whom I believed dead?' asked d'Artagnan.

'From the letter my comrade has in his pocket.'

'So, you see I must have that letter,' said d'Artagnan. 'Now, no more delay, no more hesitation, or else, repugnant as I find it to bathe my sword a second time in the blood of a wretch like you, I swear on my faith as an honourable man . . .'

And at these words, d'Artagnan made such a menacing gesture that the wounded man got to his feet.

'Stop! Stop!' he cried, terror giving him fresh courage. 'I'll go . . . I'll go!'

D'Artagnan took the soldier's harquebus, made him walk in front of him, and, prodding him in the back with his sword-point, steered him towards his companion.

He was a frightful sight to behold, that wretch, as, paling at his imminent death and leaving a long trail of blood behind him, he tried to drag himself unobserved to his accomplice's corpse, which lay some twenty paces off.

Terror was painted so starkly on his cold, sweat-drenched face that d'Artagnan took pity on him, and, with a look of scorn, said, 'Fine, I'll show you the difference between a great-hearted man and a coward like you. Stay here, I'll go.'

And then, with an agile step and keeping a sharp lookout, observing the enemy's movements and using all the irregularities of the ground, d'Artagnan made his way to the second soldier.

There were two ways to achieve his goal: search the man on the spot, or carry him back, using his body as a shield, and search him in the trench.

D'Artagnan preferred the second, and hoisted the assassin on to his shoulders just as the enemy opened fire.

A slight jolt, the thud of three bullets piercing flesh, a last cry and a shudder of agony confirmed to d'Artagnan that the man who had wanted to murder him had just saved his life.

D'Artagnan regained the trench and dumped the body next to his wounded accomplice who was deathly pale.

He immediately drew up an inventory: a leather wallet, a purse, which evidently contained part of the sum the bandit had been paid, a dice cup and some dice made up the dead man's inheritance.

He left the dice cup and dice where they fell, tossed the purse to the wounded man, and eagerly opened the wallet.

Among various unimportant papers, he found the following letter. It was the one he had risked his life to go and find:

Since you have lost track of that woman, and she is now
safely in the convent which you should never have let her
reach, try at least not to miss the man. Otherwise, you know

I have a long arm and that you will pay dearly for the
hundred louis you have from me.

No signature. Even so, it was obvious the letter was from Milady.
He kept it as evidence, therefore, and, taking shelter behind the
corner of the trench, began questioning the wounded man. The
latter confessed that he had been engaged with his comrade – the
one who had just been killed – to abduct a young woman, who was
to leave Paris by the Porte de La Villette, but that, having stopped
for a drink in a tavern, they had missed the carriage by ten minutes.

'But what would you have done with this woman?' d'Artagnan
asked in an anguished voice.

'We were to take her to a house on Place Royale,' said the
wounded man.

'Yes, yes!' murmured d'Artagnan, 'that's it – to Milady's own
house.'

The young man understood with a shudder the terrible thirst
for vengeance that was driving this woman to destroy him, and
those who loved him, and how much she knew about the affairs
of court, since she had found out everything. No doubt she owed
her information to the cardinal.

But, in the midst of these revelations, he also realised, with
genuine elation, that the queen had managed to discover the prison
in which Madame Bonacieux was doing penance for her devotion,
and to get her out of there. This explained the letter he had
received from the young woman, and his glimpse of her passing
like a vision on the Chaillot road.

And so, from now on, as Athos had predicted, Madame
Bonacieux could be found – and a convent wasn't impregnable.

This thought restored clemency to his heart. He turned to the
wounded man, who was anxiously following the shifting expressions on his face, held out his arm to him, and said, 'Come, I won't
abandon you like this. Lean on me and let's go back to camp.'

'Yes,' said the wounded man, who found such magnanimity
hard to believe, 'but won't you then just have me hanged?'

'You have my word,' he said. 'I'm granting you your life for the second time.'

The wounded man slid to his knees and kissed his saviour's feet again. But d'Artagnan, who had no further reason to stay in such close proximity to the enemy, cut short these displays of gratitude.

The guard who had returned to camp at the first volley from the Rochelois had announced the death of his four companions. There was thus great astonishment and great joy in the regiment when they saw the young man reappear safe and sound.

D'Artagnan invented a sortie to explain his companion's sword wound, and described the other soldier's death and the perils they had braved. His account was a veritable triumph. The entire army talked of their expedition all day, and Monsieur sent him his compliments.

Moreover, as every fine deed carries its own reward, d'Artagnan's fine deed had the result of restoring his former peace of mind. Indeed d'Artagnan thought he could relax now, since, of his two enemies, one was dead and the other devoted to his interests.

This peace of mind proved only one thing, however: that d'Artagnan didn't know Milady yet.

XLII

THE ANJOU WINE[1]

AFTER A SUCCESSION OF WELL-NIGH desperate reports concerning the king's health, word of his convalescence spread through the camp, and, as he was in great haste to attend the siege in person, it was said that the moment he could mount a horse, he would resume his journey.

Meanwhile, Monsieur, who knew that he was going to be replaced as commander any day soon – either by the Duke d'Angoulême, or Bassompierre, or Schomberg, who were competing for the command – did next to nothing, wasting his days in tentative undertakings and not venturing a major attempt to drive the English off the Île de Ré, where they were still besieging the Citadel of Saint-Martin and the Fort of La Prée, while the French continued to lay siege to La Rochelle.

D'Artagnan, as we have said, had recovered his peace of mind, as so often happens when one has come through some danger and thinks it has now passed. His only worry was that he hadn't heard from his friends.

But, one morning at the start of November, everything was explained to him by the following letter, dated from Villeroi:

> Monsieur d'Artagnan,
>
> Messrs Athos, Porthos and Aramis, having thrown a fine party in my establishment and making very merry, kicked up such a racket that the provost of the castle, a very severe man, confined them to barracks for several days. But I am carrying out their orders to send you twelve bottles of my Anjou wine, of which they have a high opinion. They wish you to drink their health with their favourite wine.
>
> I have done this, and remain, sir, with great respect,
> Your most humble and obedient servant,
> Godeau,
> Hosteller to the gentlemen musketeers

'Excellent!' cried d'Artagnan. 'They think of me in their revels as I think of them in my boredom. Certainly I'll drink their health, but not alone.'

And then d'Artagnan ran to find two of the guards, with whom he had struck up more of a friendship than with the others, to invite them to drink a delicious little Anjou wine that had just arrived from Villeroi. One of the two guards already had an invitation for that evening, and the other one for the following evening, so the gathering was fixed for the day after that.

When he got back, d'Artagnan sent the twelve bottles of wine to the guards' wine shop, with instructions that they should be carefully looked after. Then, on the day of the festivities, as the dinner was arranged for midday, d'Artagnan sent Planchet over at nine o'clock to get everything ready.

Bursting with pride at being raised to the rank of butler, Planchet resolved to plan everything like an intelligent man. To that end, he took on as his assistants the valet of one of his master's guests, named Fourreau, and the sham soldier who had tried to kill d'Artagnan, and who, belonging to no corps, had entered his, or rather Planchet's service, as d'Artagnan had spared his life.

When the hour of the feast arrived, the two guests appeared, took their places, and the dishes lined themselves up on the table. Planchet served the food with a napkin on his arm, Fourreau uncorked the bottles, and Brisemont – that was the convalescent's name – decanted the wine into carafes, as it appeared to have deposited a sediment after being shaken up on its travels. The first bottle was a little cloudy at the bottom. Brisemont poured the lees into a glass, and d'Artagnan gave him permission to drink it, since the poor devil still didn't have much strength.

After finishing the soup, the guests were about to raise the first glass to their lips when suddenly the cannon boomed forth from Fort Louis and Fort Neuf. Thinking it was an unexpected attack by the besieged or the English, the guards immediately leapt for their swords. No less nimble, d'Artagnan did likewise, and all three ran out to go to their posts.

But they had barely left the wine shop before they found themselves face to face with the cause of this great commotion. Shouts of 'Long live the king!' and 'Long live the cardinal!' echoed around on all sides, and drums beat in every direction.

Having covered, in his impatience, which we have mentioned, twice the usual distance in two days' marches, the King had just arrived with all his household and reinforcements of ten thousand men. He was preceded and followed by his musketeers. D'Artagnan, lined up with his company, and waved excitedly to his friends.

They responded with their eyes, as did Monsieur de Tréville, who recognised him instantly.

Once the reception ceremony was complete, the four friends were soon in one another's arms.

'By God!' cried d'Artagnan. 'You couldn't have arrived at a better time. The food won't even have had time to get cold! Isn't that so, gentlemen?' the young man added, turning to the two guards, whom he introduced to his friends.

'Aha, we seem to be banqueting,' said Porthos.

'I trust,' said Aramis, 'there are no women at your dinner!'

'Is there any drinkable wine in your shack?' asked Athos.

'Why, by God, there's yours, my dear friend!' replied d'Artagnan.

'Ours?' said Athos, surprised.

'Yes, the wine you sent me.'

'We sent you wine?'

'Why, you know it very well, that little wine from the slopes of Anjou.'

'Yes, I am well aware of the wine you mean.'

'Your favourite wine.'

'Of course, when I have no champagne or Chambertin[2].'

'Well, for lack of champagne or Chambertin, you can make do with this one.'

'So, gourmets that we are, we sent you some Anjou wine, did we?' said Porthos.

'No, no, the wine was sent on your behalf.'

'On our behalf?' said the three musketeers.

'Was it you, Aramis,' said Athos, 'who sent the wine?'

'No. And you, Porthos?'

'No. And you, Athos?'

'No.'

'If it wasn't you,' said d'Artagnan, 'then it was your hosteller.'

'Our hosteller?'

'Why yes! Your hosteller: Godeau, hosteller to the musketeers.'

'My faith, let it come from wherever it pleases, it makes no difference,' said Porthos. 'Let's try it, and, if it's good, let's drink it.'

'No,' said Athos, 'let's not drink wine when we don't know its origin.'

'You're right, Athos,' said d'Artagnan. 'So none of you instructed the hosteller Godeau to send me wine?'

'No! And yet he sent it to you on our behalf?'

'Here's the letter!' said d'Artagnan.

And then he showed the note to his comrades.

'It's not his writing!' cried Athos. 'I know it. Before we left, I settled the community's accounts.'

'A forgery,' said Porthos. 'We were never confined to barracks.'

'D'Artagnan,' Aramis asked reproachfully, 'how could you think we kicked up a racket . . . ?'

D'Artagnan grew pale, and all his limbs started trembling convulsively.

'You're scaring me,' said Athos, using the familiar 'tu', something he only did on momentous occasions. 'What's happened?'

'Run, run, my friends!' cried d'Artagnan. 'A horrible suspicion has dawned on me! Can this be another of that woman's acts of vengeance?'

Now it was Athos's turn to grow pale.

D'Artagnan rushed to the wine shop, followed by the three musketeers and the two guards.

The first sight that met d'Artagnan's eyes as he went into the dining room was Brisemont stretched out on the ground, racked by atrocious convulsions.

Planchet and Fourreau, both deathly pale, were trying to help him, but it was obvious that all help was useless; the dying man's features were screwed up in agony.

'Ah!' he cried, catching sight of d'Artagnan 'Ah! It's shameful! It seemed as if you had pardoned me, and then you poisoned me!'

'I?' cried d'Artagnan. 'I, you wretch? What are you saying?'

'I say it was you who gave me that wine, I say it was you who told me to drink it, I say that you wanted to avenge yourself on me – I say it's shameful!'

'Don't believe that, Brisemont,' said d'Artagnan, 'don't believe any of it. I swear, I protest . . .'

'Oh, but God is there! God will punish you! My God, let him suffer one day what I am suffering!'

'On the Gospel,' cried d'Artagnan, rushing to the dying man, 'I swear I didn't know the wine was poisoned – I was going to drink it just like you.'

'I don't believe you,' said the soldier.

And then he expired in still greater torment.

'Vile! Vile!' murmured Athos, while Porthos smashed the bottles and Aramis gave somewhat belated orders to fetch a confessor.

'Oh, my friends,' said d'Artagnan, 'you've saved my life again, and not only mine but these gentlemen's too. Gentlemen,' he continued, addressing the guards, 'I will ask you to remain silent about this whole adventure. Persons of rank could have been a party to what you have seen, and the evil of it all would fall on us.'

'Ah, sir!' stammered Planchet, more dead than alive. 'Ah, sir, I had such a narrow escape!'

'What, you rogue?' cried d'Artagnan. 'So you were going to drink my wine?'

'To the king's health, sir. I was going to drink one measly glass, if Fourreau hadn't said someone was calling me.'

'Alas!' said Fourreau, his teeth chattering with terror. 'I wanted to get him out of the way so I could drink on my own!'

'Gentlemen,' said d'Artagnan, addressing the guards, 'you'll understand that after what has just happened our feast couldn't help but be a melancholy affair. So please accept all my apologies and postpone the party to another day.'

The two guards courteously accepted d'Artagnan's apologies, and then, realising the four friends wanted to be alone, withdrew.

Once the young guard and the three musketeers were without witnesses, they looked at one another with an air that indicated they each understood the gravity of the situation.

'First,' said Athos, 'let's leave this room. A dead man is poor company, especially when he has died a violent death.'

'Planchet,' said d'Artagnan, 'I entrust this poor devil's body to your keeping. Let him be buried in consecrated ground. He committed a crime, it's true, but he repented of it.'

And then the four friends went out, leaving Planchet and Fourreau to give Brisemont mortuary honours.

The innkeeper gave them another room, in which he served them boiled eggs and water, which Athos had drawn from the well himself. Porthos and Aramis were apprised of the situation in a few words.

'Well then,' d'Artagnan said to Athos, 'you see, dear friend. It's a fight to the death.'

Athos shook his head.

'Yes, yes,' he said. 'But do you think it's really her?'

'I'm sure of it.'

'Nevertheless, I confess I still have doubts.'

'But that fleur-de-lys on on her shoulder?'

'She's an Englishwoman who has committed some crime in France, and she must have been branded as a result.'

'Athos, she's your wife, I tell you,' repeated d'Artagnan. 'Don't you recall how similar the two descriptions are?'

'Yet I would have sworn the other one was dead, I hanged her so well.'

This time it was d'Artagnan who shook his head.

'Well, what are we to do?' said the young man.

'We certainly can't go on like this, with a sword eternally hanging over our heads,' said Athos. 'We must find our way out of this situation.'

'But how?'

'Listen, try to have a meeting with her and explain everything. Tell her: peace or war! My word as a gentleman that I will never say or do anything against you. For your part, give me your solemn word to remain neutral in my regard. Otherwise I'll go to the chancellor, I'll go to the king, I'll go to the executioner, I'll incite the court against you, I'll denounce you as a branded woman, I'll have you put on trial, and should you be acquitted, then upon my word as a gentleman, I'll kill you by some corner post as I'd kill a rabid dog.'

'I like that plan,' said d'Artagnan, 'but how will I find her?'

'Time, my dear friend. Time brings opportunities, and opportunity is man's martingale³. The more one has ventured, if one can wait, the more one gains.'

'Yes, but to wait surrounded by assassins and poisoners . . .'

'Bah!' said Athos. 'God has preserved us up till now, and God will preserve us henceforward.'

'Us, yes. Besides, we're men, and it's our profession, after all, to risk our lives, but she . . . !' he added in a whisper.

'Who is she?' asked Athos.

'Constance.'

'Madame Bonacieux! Ah, that's right,' said Athos. 'My poor friend! I'd forgotten you were in love.'

'But,' said Aramis, 'didn't you also learn from the letter you found on that dead wretch that she was in a convent? One is very well looked after in a convent, and as soon as the siege of La Rochelle is over, I can tell you, for my part . . .'

'All right!' said Athos. 'All right! Yes, my dear Aramis, we know you have religious inclinations!'

'I am only a musketeer temporarily,' Aramis said humbly.

'He appears not to have had any news of his mistress for a long time,' Athos said in a whisper. 'But pay no attention, we know all about that subject.'

'Well then,' said Porthos, 'it seems to me there is one very simple method.'

'Which is?' asked d'Artagnan.

'She's in a convent, you say?' continued Porthos.

'Yes.'

'Well then, as soon as the siege is over, we will abduct her from this convent.'

'But we still have to know which convent it is.'

'True,' said Porthos.

'But, now I think of it,' said Athos, 'didn't you claim, my dear d'Artagnan, that the queen chose the convent for her?'

'Yes, or at least I think so.'

'Why, then, Porthos will help us with that.'

'And how, if you please?'

'Why, through your marchioness, your duchess, your princess! She must have a long arm.'

'Shh!' said Porthos, putting a finger to his lips. 'I think she's a cardinalist. She mustn't know anything of this.'

'In that case,' said Aramis, 'I'll take it upon myself to get word.'

'You, Aramis?' cried the three friends. 'You? And how will you do that?'

'Through the queen's chaplain, with whom I am great friends . . .' said Aramis, blushing.

And then, on this assurance, the four friends, who had finished their modest meal, parted company, promising to meet up again that evening. D'Artagnan returned to the Minims, and the three musketeers went back to the king's headquarters, where they had to have their lodgings made ready.

XLIII

THE RED DOVECOT INN

ALMOST THE MOMENT HE ARRIVED in camp, the king, who was in great haste to face the enemy – and who shared the cardinal's hatred of Buckingham, although with more justification – wanted to make all the arrangements, first for driving the English off the Île de Ré, then for expediting the siege of La Rochelle.

But, despite his efforts, he was delayed by the dissension that broke out between Messrs de Bassompierre and Schomberg on the one hand, and the Duke d'Angoulême on the other.

Messrs de Bassompierre and Schomberg were marshals of France, and claimed their right to command the army under the king's orders. But, fearing that Bassompierre, a Huguenot at heart, would hold back against his brothers in religion, the English and the Rochelois, the cardinal had put forward the Duke d'Angoulême, whom the king, at his instigation, had appointed lieutenant-general. As a result, to prevent Messrs de Bassompierre and Schomberg deserting the army, they each had to be given a separate command. Bassompierre established his quarters to the north of the town, from La Leu to Dompierre; the Duke d'Angoulême to the east, from Dompierre to Périgny; and Monsieur de Schomberg to the south, from Périgny to Angoutin.

Monsieur had his quarters at Dompierre.

The king had his quarters at times at Étré, and at other times at La Jarrie.

Finally, the cardinal had his quarters on the dunes, at Pont de La Pierre, in a simple house without any entrenchment.

In this way, Monsieur kept an eye on Bassompierre, the king on the Duke d'Angoulême, and the cardinal on Monsieur de Schomberg.

Once organised in that manner, they set about driving the English off the island.

The circumstances were favourable. The English, who, more than anything, need good food to be good soldiers, had nothing but salted meat and bad biscuits, and consequently their camp was full of sick men. Moreover, the sea, which was very rough at that time of the year off the whole Atlantic coast, destroyed some small vessel or other every day, and the beach, from the point of l'Aiguillon to the trenches, was literally covered at low tide by the wrecks of pinnaces, warships and feluccas. As a result, even if the king's men remained in camp, it was obvious that sooner or later Buckingham, who only remained on the

Île de Ré out of stubbornness, would be obliged to raise the siege.

But, as Monsieur de Toiras announced that everything was being prepared in the enemy camp for a new assault, the king thought they must end it and gave the orders for a decisive affair.

As it is not our intention to write a diary of the siege, but, on the contrary, only to report those events that have a bearing on the story we're telling, we will briefly report that the assault succeeded, to the great astonishment of the king and to the great glory of the cardinal. The English, driven back a foot at a time, beaten in every encounter, crushed in the passage of the Île de Loix, were forced to re-embark, leaving on the battlefield two thousand men, among them five colonels, three lieutenant colonels, two hundred and fifty captains, and twenty gentlemen of quality, four cannon, and sixty flags, which were taken to Paris by Claude de Saint-Simon and hung with great pomp from the vault of Notre-Dame.

*Te Deum*s were sung in camp, and from there spread through all of France.

The cardinal was thus left free to pursue the siege without having, at least for the moment, anything to fear from the English.

But, as we have just said, this respite was only temporary.

An envoy from the Duke of Buckingham called Montaigu was captured[1], and proof thereby acquired of a league between the Hapsburg Empire, Spain, England and Lorraine.

This league was directed against France.

What's more, in Buckingham's quarters, which he had been forced to abandon more hurriedly than he had expected, papers had been found that confirmed this league and, as the cardinal states in his memoirs, heavily compromised Madame de Chevreuse, and, in consequence, the queen.

The full weight of responsibility rested on the cardinal, for one is not an absolute minister without being responsible, and so all the resources of his vast genius were exerted day and night, as he listened intently to the least rumour that emanated from any of the great kingdoms of Europe.

The cardinal was aware of the activity and, above all, hatred of Buckingham. Should the league threatening France triumph, all his influence would be lost. Spain's and Austria's interests would have their representatives in the cabinet at the Louvre, where as yet they only had partisans, and he, Richelieu, the French minister, the national minister par excellence, would be destroyed. The king who, while obeying him like a child, hated him as a child hates its schoolmaster, would abandon him to the combined vengeance of Monsieur and the queen. He would be ruined himself, and perhaps France with him. That had to be guarded against.

And so couriers, their numbers increasing by the minute, were to be seen day and night streaming in and out of the small house at the Pont de La Pierre, where the cardinal had established his residence.

There were monks who wore the habit so badly that it was obvious they belonged primarily to the church militant; women slightly ill-at-ease in their pages' costumes, whose loose-fitting hose could not entirely conceal their rounded forms; and peasants with blackened hands but slim legs, whose breeding was obvious a league away.

Then there were other, less agreeable, visits, for rumours circulated on two or three occasions that the cardinal had nearly been assassinated.

His Eminence's enemies did say, it's true, that he had sent those blundering assassins himself, so that, if need be, he would have the right to exact reprisals. But neither ministers nor their enemies should ever be believed.

Besides, those circumstances did not prevent the cardinal, whose personal bravery has never been disputed by his bitterest detractors, from making numerous nocturnal expeditions, at times to give the Duke d'Angoulême important orders, at others to take counsel with the king, and at others to confer with a messenger, whom he did not wish to be admitted into his quarters.

For their part, the musketeers, who did not have a great deal to do in the siege, were not strictly controlled and had a merry time of it. Things were all the easier for them – and for our three companions above all – because, as friends of Monsieur de Tréville, they could always obtain special permission from him to come back late and stay out after the camp was closed.

One evening when d'Artagnan, who was in the trenches, couldn't join them, Athos, Porthos and Aramis, mounted on their warhorses, swathed in their service cloaks, a hand on their pistol butts, were coming back from a tavern called the Red Dovecot, which Athos had discovered two days earlier on the road to La Jarrie. They were riding along the road leading to the camp – on the alert, as we have said, in case of an ambush – when about a quarter of a league from the village of Boisnar, they thought they heard hoofbeats approaching. They all three stopped instantly, closed ranks, and waited in the middle of the road. A moment later, just as the moon came out from behind a cloud, they saw two horsemen appear around a corner of the road. On catching sight of them, the riders stopped in their turn and seemed to deliberate whether they should carry on their way or turn back. This hesitation struck our three friends as suspicious, and Athos, advancing a few paces, called out in a firm voice, 'Who goes there?'

'Who goes there yourself?' replied one of the two riders.

'That's no answer,' said Athos. 'Who goes there? Answer, or we'll charge.'

'Mind what you're about, gentlemen!' declared a ringing voice, which seemed to have the habit of command.

'It's some senior officer making his night rounds,' said Athos. 'What do you want to do, gentlemen?'

'Who are you?' the voice asked in the same commanding tones. 'Answer in your turn, or you may find yourself in trouble for your disobedience.'

'King's musketeers,' said Athos, increasingly certain the man questioning them had the right to do so.

'Which company?'

'Tréville's company.'

'Advance at my order and account to me for what you're doing here at this hour.'

The three companions advanced in a somewhat hangdog fashion, for they were now all convinced they were dealing with someone more powerful than themselves. It was left to Athos to act as their spokesman.

One of the two horsemen – the one who had spoken second – was ten paces in front of his companion. Athos signalled to Porthos and Aramis to stay back and rode forward alone.

'Excuse us, sir!' said Athos. 'But we didn't know whom we were dealing with, and you could see we were keeping a careful lookout.'

'Your name?' asked the officer, who was covering part of his face with his cloak.

'Why, sir,' said Athos, rebelling against this inquisition, 'give me, I beg you, some proof that you have the right to question me.'

'Your name?' the horseman asked for a second time, letting his cloak fall so his face was uncovered.

'Cardinal!' cried the stupefied musketeer.

'Your name?' His Eminence repeated for the third time.

'Athos,' said the musketeer.

The cardinal signalled to his equerry, who came closer.

'These three musketeers will follow us,' he said in a low voice. 'I don't want it known that I have left the camp and, by having them follow us, we will be sure they won't tell anyone.'

'We are gentlemen, my lord,' said Athos. 'Ask us for our word and trouble yourself no further. Thank God, we know how to keep a secret.'

The cardinal fixed his piercing eyes on his bold inter-locutor.

'You have sharp ears, Monsieur Athos,' said the cardinal. 'Now listen to this: it is not out of distrust that I ask you to follow me, it is for my safety. No doubt your two companions are Messrs Porthos and Aramis?'

'Yes, Your Eminence,' said Athos, as the two musketeers who had stayed behind came forward, hat in hand.

'I know you, gentlemen,' said the cardinal. 'I know you. I am aware you are not entirely my friends, and I am sorry for it, but I know that you are brave and loyal gentlemen and that you can be trusted. Do me therefore the honour of accompanying me, Monsieur Athos, you and your two friends, and then I shall have an escort that His Majesty would envy should we meet him.'

The three musketeers bowed low enough to touch their horses' necks.

'Well, on my honour,' said Athos, 'Your Eminence is right to take us with him. We have seen some grim faces on the road. In fact, we had a quarrel with four of them at the Red Dovecot.'

'A quarrel? About what, gentlemen?' said the cardinal. 'I don't like quarrellers, you know!'

'That is precisely why I have the honour of informing Your Eminence of what has just happened, for he might learn of it from others and be persuaded by a false report that we are at fault.'

'And what was the upshot of this quarrel?' the cardinal asked with a frown.

'Why, my friend Aramis here received a slight sword wound in the arm, which will not prevent him, as Your Eminence may see, from mounting the assault tomorrow, if Your Eminence orders us to scale the walls.'

'But you are not the sort of men just to let yourselves be wounded,' said the cardinal. 'Come now, be frank, gentlemen, you must have meted out some punishment in return. Confess yourselves; you know I have the right to give absolution.'

'For my part, my lord,' said Athos, 'I didn't even draw my sword, but I seized the man I was dealing with round the waist and threw him out of the window . . . It seems that, as he fell,' Athos went on slightly hesitantly, 'he broke his thigh.'

'Aha!' said the cardinal. 'And you, Monsieur Porthos?'

'For my part, my lord, knowing that duelling is forbidden, I grabbed a bench and gave one of those brigands a blow with it, which, I think, broke his shoulder.'

'Very well,' said the cardinal. 'And you, Monsieur Aramis?

'For my part, my lord, as I am very gentle by nature and am besides, as my lord may not know, on the point of taking holy orders, I was trying to get my comrades to safety, when one of those scoundrels treacherously ran me through the left arm. My patience ran out at that point. I drew my sword in turn, and, when he returned to the charge, I believe I felt that, as he threw himself on me, he ran himself through. All I'm certain of is that he fell, and I had the impression he was carried out with his two companions.'

'Hang it, gentlemen,' said the cardinal, 'three men put out of action in a tavern row? You go at it hard! And what caused this quarrel?'

'The scoundrels were drunk,' said Athos, 'and knowing that a woman had arrived at the tavern that evening, they wanted to force their way into her room.'

'Force their way into her room?' said the cardinal. 'To do what?'

'To assault her, no doubt,' said Athos. 'I have had the honour of informing Your Eminence that the scoundrels were drunk.'

'And was this woman young and pretty?' the cardinal asked, slightly uneasily.

'We did not see her, my lord,' said Athos.

'You did not see her – ah, very good!' the cardinal smartly replied. 'You were right to defend a woman's honour, and as I'm going to the Red Dovecot inn myself, I shall find out whether you've told me the truth.'

'My lord,' Athos said proudly, 'we are gentlemen, and we would not tell a lie if our lives depended on it.'

'Nor do I doubt what you've told me, Monsieur Athos. Not for a single moment. But,' he added, changing the subject, 'was this woman alone, then?'

'The lady had a gentlemen closeted with her,' said Athos. 'But as the gentleman did not show himself, despite the noise, one must presume he is a coward.'

'"Be not quick to judge," says the Gospel,' the cardinal replied.

Athos bowed.

'Very well, gentlemen,' continued His Eminence, 'now I know all I wanted to know. Follow me.'

The three musketeers fell in behind the cardinal, who covered his face with his cloak again and put his horse into a walk, riding eight or ten paces in front of his companions.

They soon reached the inn which stood lonely. No doubt the innkeeper was expecting an illustrious guest, and had sent away anyone who might cause a nuisance.

Ten paces before he reached the door, the cardinal signalled to his equerry and the three musketeers to stop. A saddled horse was tethered to the outside shutter. The cardinal knocked three times in a distinctive manner.

A man enveloped in a cloak immediately came out and exchanged a few quick words with the cardinal, before getting back on his horse and riding off in the direction of Surgères, which was also the way to Paris.

'Come forward, gentlemen,' said the cardinal. 'You told the truth, sirs, and it will not be my fault if our meeting this evening should not prove advantageous to you. In the meantime, follow me.'

The cardinal dismounted, and the three musketeers did likewise. The cardinal tossed his horse's bridle to his equerry, and the three musketeers tied the bridles of theirs to the shutters.

The innkeeper was standing in the doorway. As far as he was concerned, the cardinal was simply an officer coming to visit a lady.

'Do you have a room on the ground floor where these gentlemen can wait for me in front of a good fire?' said the cardinal.

The innkeeper opened the door to a large room, in which a

pitiful stove had recently been replaced by a large and excellent fireplace.

'I have this one,' he answered.

'Very well,' said the cardinal. 'Go in there, gentlemen, and kindly wait for me. I shan't be more than half-an-hour.'

And then, as the three musketeers went into the room on the ground floor, the cardinal, without further inquiry, set off up the stairs like a man who has no need to be shown the way.

XLIV
ON THE USEFULNESS OF STOVEPIPES

IT WAS EVIDENT THAT, PROMPTED solely by their chivalrous and adventurous natures, our three friends had unwittingly rendered a service to someone whom the cardinal honoured with his special protection.

Now, who was this someone? That was the first question the three musketeers asked themselves. But when they saw that none of the answers their own intelligence could volunteer were satisfactory, Porthos called the innkeeper and asked for some dice.

Porthos and Aramis sat down at a table and started to play, while Athos paced up and down, thinking.

As he paced and thought, Athos kept passing the disconnected stovepipe, which went to the room above, and every time he did so, he heard a murmur of conversation, which finally caught his attention. Athos moved closer and made out several words, which doubtless struck him as deserving of so great an interest that he gestured to his companions to be quiet and remained bent over by the mouth of the pipe, his ear cocked.

'Listen, Milady,' the cardinal was saying, 'this is an important affair. Sit down here and let us talk.'

'Milady!' murmured Athos.

'I am listening to Your Eminence with the greatest attention,' replied a woman's voice which made the musketeer start.

'A little ship with an English crew, whose captain is my man, is waiting for you in the mouth of the Charente, at the Fort de La Pointe. It will sail tomorrow morning.'

'So I must go there tonight?'

'This instant – that is, as soon as you've received my instructions. Two men whom you'll find at the door when you set out will be your escort. Let me leave first, and then, half an hour later, leave in your turn.'

'Yes, my lord. Now let's return to the mission with which you are pleased to entrust me. And, as I am anxious to continue to merit Your Eminence's confidence, deign to explain it in clear and precise terms so that I may make no mistake.'

There was a moment of deep silence between the two inter-locutors. The cardinal was evidently weighing up in advance the terms in which he was going to express himself, while Milady gathered all her intellectual faculties to understand what he was going to say and engrave it on her memory when he was done.

Athos took advantage of this moment to tell his two compan-ions to lock the door from inside and then beckon them over to listen with him.

The two musketeers, who liked their comforts, brought a chair each and one for Athos. Then the three of them sat down with their heads close together and their ears pricked up.

'You're going to leave for London,' the cardinal resumed. 'When you get there, you'll go to find Buckingham.'

'I should point out to His Eminence,' said Milady, 'that since the affair of the diamond tags, of which the duke has always suspected me, His Grace distrusts me.'

'But this time,' said the cardinal, 'it won't be a question of inveigling yourself into his confidence, but of presenting yourself openly and honestly to him as a negotiator.'

'Openly and honestly,' repeated Milady, with an indefinable air of duplicity.

'Yes, openly and honestly,' the cardinal replied in the same tone. 'This whole negotiation must be conducted with complete candour.'

'I will follow His Eminence's instructions to the letter, and wait only for him to give them to me.'

'You will go to find Buckingham on my behalf, and you will tell him that all his preparations, with which I familiar, are of little concern to me, since the moment he ventures anything, I will destroy the queen.'

'Will he believe Your Eminence is in a position to carry out his threat?'

'Yes, for I have proofs.'

'I must be able to submit those proofs to his appraisal.'

'Of course. You will tell him that I am going to publish the report by Bois-Robert and the Marquis de Beautru of the interview the duke had with the queen at the home of the High Constable's wife, on the evening when the High Constable's wife gave a masked ball. You will tell him, so he is left in no doubt, that he went in the Great Mogul costume the Duke de Guise was to have worn, which he bought from the latter for the sum of three thousand pistoles.'

'Very well, my lord.'

'All the details of how he got into the Louvre, where he presented himself in the costume of an Italian fortune-teller, and how he left at night, are known to me. You will tell him, so he does not have any lingering doubts about the authenticity of my information, that he had on under his cloak a great white robe dotted with black tears, skulls and crossbones. The plan was that, if he was surprised, he would pass himself off as the ghost of the White Lady[1] who, as is well known, returns to the Louvre every time a great event is imminent.'

'Is that all, my lord?'

'Tell him that I also know all the details of the Amiens adventure, and that I shall make a wittily contrived little romance out of it, with a map of the garden and portraits of the principal actors in that nocturnal scene.'

'I will tell him that.'

'Tell him also that I've got Montaigu, that Montaigu is in the Bastille, that we haven't found any letters on him, it's true, but that torture may make him say what he knows and even . . . what he does not know.'

'Excellent.'

'Add finally that His Grace, in his haste to leave the Île de Ré, forgot in his quarters a certain letter from Madame de Chevreuse, which singularly compromises the queen, in that it proves not only that Her Majesty can love the king's enemies, but also that she is conspiring with France's. You have remembered everything I've told you, haven't you?'

'Your Eminence may be the judge of that. The High Constable's wife's ball; the night at the Louvre; the evening in Amiens; Montaigu's arrest; Madame de Chevreuse's letter.'

'That's right,' said the cardinal, 'that's right. You're blessed with an excellent memory, Milady.'

'But,' said she to whom the cardinal had just addressed this flattering compliment, 'what if, despite all these reasons, the duke does not yield and continues to threaten France?'

'The duke is madly, or rather idiotically, in love,' Richelieu replied with intense bitterness. 'Like the paladins of old, he undertook this war merely to obtain a glance from his fair lady. If he knows that this war may cost the lady of his thoughts, as they say, her honour and perhaps her liberty, I guarantee you he'll reconsider.'

'And yet,' said Milady, with a tenacity that proved she wanted to understand every aspect of the mission with which she had been instructed, 'and yet what if he persists?'

'If he persists . . .' said the cardinal. 'It's unlikely.'

'But it's possible,' said Milady.

'If he persists . . .' His Eminence paused, and then went on, 'If he persists, well, then I'll hope for one of those events that change the entire face of a state.'

'If His Eminence would cite some examples from history of

these events,' said Milady, 'I shall perhaps share his confidence in the future.'

'Well, think, for example,' said Richelieu, 'of when, in 1610, for a cause almost identical to that which prompts the duke, King Henri IV, of glorious memory, set out to invade Flanders and Italy concurrently, in order to strike Austria from both sides. Wasn't there an event then that saved Austria? Why shouldn't the king of France have the same good fortune as the emperor?'

'Your Eminence is referring to the stabbing in Rue de la Ferronnerie?'

'Precisely,' said the cardinal.

'Isn't Your Eminence afraid that Ravaillac's[2] torture and execution might not scare off anyone who entertained even for a moment the notion of imitating him?'

'In every age and every country, especially those countries that are divided by religion, there will always be fanatics who ask for nothing better than to become martyrs. Why, I've just remembered that the Puritans are furious with the Duke of Buckingham, and that their preachers call him the Antichrist.'

'So?' said Milady.

'So,' continued the cardinal with an air of indifference, 'it would only involve, for example, finding a beautiful, young, able woman who had reason to avenge herself on the duke. Such a woman can certainly be found. The duke has many conquests to his name, and if he has sown a great deal of love with his promises of eternal constancy, he must also have sown a great deal of hatred with his eternal infidelities.'

'There's no doubt such a woman could be found,' Milady said coldly.

'Well, such a woman, who would put the knife of Jacques Clément[3] or Ravaillac in a fanatic's hands, would save France.'

'Yes, but she'd be complicit in an assassination.'

'Have the accomplices of Ravaillac or Jacques Clément ever been discovered?'

'No, for perhaps they were too highly placed for anyone to

dare go looking for them where they were. The Palais de Justice[4] wouldn't be burned down for anybody, my lord.'

'So you believe the fire in the Palais de Justice wasn't an accident?' inquired Richelieu, in a tone he would have used to ask a question of no importance.

'I, my lord?' replied Milady, 'I don't believe anything. I am merely stating a fact. However, I do say that, if I were called Mademoiselle de Monpensier or Queen Marie de Medici, I would take fewer precautions than I do when simply called Lady Clarick.'

'That's perfectly reasonable,' said Richelieu. 'What would you like, then?'

'I would like an order ratifying in advance any step I may believe necessary for the greater good of France.'

'But we'd first have to find the woman I described who has reason to avenge herself on the duke.'

'She has been found,' said Milady.

'Then we'd have to find the wretched fanatic who'd serve as the instrument of God's justice.'

'He will be found.'

'And when he is,' said the duke, 'that will be the time to claim the order you have just requested.'

'Your Eminence is right,' said Milady, 'and it is I who was wrong to see the mission, with which he honours me, as anything other than what it really is – namely, to announce to His Grace, on His Eminence's behalf, that you know the various disguises by means of which he contrived to get close to the queen at the ball given by the High Constable's wife; that you have proofs of the interview in the Louvre granted by the queen to a certain Italian astrologer who was none other than the Duke of Buckingham; that you have commissioned a very witty little romance on the adventure at Amiens, with a map of the garden where this adventure took place, and portraits of the actors who played in it; that Montaigu is in the Bastille, and that torture may make him say what he remembers, and even what he may have forgotten; and, finally, that you possess a certain letter from Madame de Chevreuse, found in His Grace's quarters, which singularly compromises not only she who wrote it, but also she in whose name it was written. Then, if he persists despite all this, as my mission is confined to what I have just told you, there will be nothing left for me to do but pray to God to work a miracle to save France. That is right, isn't it, my lord, and there's nothing else for me to do?'

'That's right,' the cardinal curtly replied.

'And now,' said Milady, without seeming to notice the duke's change of tone, 'now I have received Your Eminence's instructions regarding his enemies, will my lord permit me to say a couple of words to him about mine?'

'You have enemies, then?' asked Richelieu.

'Yes, my lord, enemies against whom you owe me all your support, for I made them serving Your Eminence.'

'And who are they?' replied the duke.

'First, a little intriguer by the name of Bonacieux.'

'She is in Mantes prison.'

'That's to say, she was,' said Milady, 'but the queen intercepted an order from the king and was able to have her moved to a convent.'

'A convent?' said the duke.

'Yes, a convent.'

'And to which one?'

'I don't know, the secret has been carefully guarded . . .'

'I'll find out!'

'And Your Eminence will tell me which convent that woman is in?'

'I see no objection to that,' said the cardinal.

'Very well. Now, I have another enemy, who is far more to be feared than this little Madame Bonacieux.'

'And who is that?'

'Her lover.'

'What is he called?'

'Oh, Your Eminence knows him well!' cried Milady, carried

away by her anger. 'He is our evil genius. It was he who, in a duel with Your Eminence's guards, decided victory in favour of the king's musketeers; it was he who ran de Wardes, your emissary, through three times and thwarted the affair of the diamond tags; and, lastly, it is he who, knowing it was I who had snatched Madame Bonacieux from him, has sworn my death.'

'Aha!' said the cardinal. 'I know who you mean.'

'I mean that scoundrel d'Artagnan.'

'He's a bold character,' said the cardinal.

'And it's precisely because he is a bold character that he's all the more to be feared.'

'We must have some proof of his dealings with Buckingham.'

'Some proof?' cried Milady. 'I'll give you ten instances.'

'Well then, it's the simplest thing in the world. Let me have the proof, and I will send him to the Bastille.'

'Very well, your lordship. And afterwards?'

'When a man is in the Bastille, there is no afterwards,' said the cardinal in a hollow voice. 'Ah, by God,' he continued, 'if it were as easy for me to get rid of my enemies as it is for me to get rid of yours, and if it were against such men that you were asking me for impunity . . .'

'My lord,' Milady interrupted, 'fair exchange: a life for a life, a man for a man. You give me this one, and I'll give you the other.'

'I don't know what you mean,' replied the cardinal, 'nor do I even wish to. But I shall be glad to please you, and I see no objection to giving you what you want concerning such a lowly creature. All the more so since, as you say, this little d'Artagnan is a libertine, a duellist and a traitor.'

'A villain, your lordship, a rank villain!'

'Then give me a pen and ink, and some paper,' said the cardinal.

'Here, your lordship.'

There was a moment's silence, which confirmed the cardinal was either deliberating the terms in which the order should be written, or actually writing it. Athos, who hadn't missed a word of the conversation, took his two companions by the hand and led them to the other end of the room.

'What do you want?' said Porthos, 'Why aren't you letting us hear the end of the conversation?'

'Shh,' said Athos in a whisper. 'We've heard everything we need. Anyway, you can hear the rest, I'm not stopping you, but I have to go.'

'You have to go?' exclaimed Porthos. 'But if the cardinal asks for you, what shall we tell him?'

'You won't wait for him to ask for me, you'll say straightaway that I've gone ahead to scout the road, as some remarks from our landlord made me think it wasn't safe. I'll have a word or two with the cardinal's equerry first. Everything else is my concern, don't trouble yourselves.'

'Be careful, Athos,' said Aramis.

'Don't worry,' replied Athos, 'you know I have a cool head.'

At this, Porthos and Aramis resumed their places by the stovepipe.

As for Athos, he went out without any attempt at concealment, fetched his horse, which was tethered with those of his two friends to the catches of the shutters, convinced the equerry in a matter of words that an advance guard was needed for the return journey, made a show of checking the priming of his pistols, put his sword between his teeth, and then set off as a forlorn hope, on the road to the camp.

XLV

CONJUGAL SCENE

As Athos had anticipated, the cardinal wasn't long in coming downstairs. He opened the door of the room the musketeers had gone into and found Porthos playing a hotly contested game of dice with Aramis. With a rapid glance, he scanned every corner of the room and saw that one of his men was missing.

'What has become of Monsieur Athos?' he asked.

'My lord,' replied Porthos, 'he went ahead to scout the road, as some remarks from our host had made him think it wasn't safe.'

'And what have you been up to, Monsieur Porthos?'

'I've won five pistoles from Aramis.'

'And now you can come back with me?'

'We are Your Eminence's to command.'

'To horse, then, gentlemen, for it's getting late.'

The equerry was at the door, holding the cardinal's horse by the bridle. A little way off, a group of two men and three horses appeared in the shadows. These were the two who were to escort Milady to the Fort de La Pointe and see her on board.

The equerry confirmed to the cardinal what the two musketeers had already told him about Athos. The cardinal made a gesture of approval, then set out again, surrounding himself on his return with the same precautions he had taken at his departure.

Let us leave him heading back to camp, protected by the equerry and the two musketeers, and return to Athos.

He had continued on his way at the same speed for a hundred paces or so, until he was out of sight. Then he had steered his horse to the right and looped back on himself, working his way round to a coppice twenty paces from the inn, so that he could watch the little troop pass by. When he recognised the trimmed hats of his companions and the gold fringe of the cardinal's cloak, he waited until the horsemen turned the corner of the road, and then, when he couldn't see them any more, galloped back to the inn where he was admitted without difficulty.

The innkeeper recognised him.

'My officer,' said Athos, 'forgot to give the lady on the first floor some important instructions. He has sent me to remedy his forgetfulness.'

'Go straight up,' the landlord said, 'she's still in her room.'

Acting on this permission, Athos climbed the stairs, treading as lightly as he could, came to the landing, and, through the half-open door, saw Milady lacing up her hat.

He went into the room and shut the door behind him.

At the sound of the bolt sliding across, Milady turned.

Athos was standing in front of the door, shrouded in his cloak, his hat pulled down over his eyes.

The sight of this figure, as silent and motionless as a statue, frightened Milady.

'Who are you, and what do you want of me?' she cried.

'So, it's really she!' murmured Athos.

And then, letting his cloak fall and taking off his hat, he walked towards Milady.

'Do you recognise me, madam?' he said.

Milady took a step forward, then recoiled as if she'd seen a snake.

'That's good,' said Athos. 'I see you do recognise me.'

'The Count de La Fère!' murmured Milady, turning pale and backing away until the wall stopped her going any further.

'Yes, Milady,' replied Athos, 'the Count de La Fère in person, returned from the other world expressly for the pleasure of seeing you. Sit down here and let us talk, as the cardinal said.'

Overcome by an inexpressible terror, Milady sat down without uttering a word.

'So, are you a demon sent to earth?' said Athos. 'You have great powers, I know, but you must also know that, with God's help, men have often defeated the most terrible demons. You have already crossed my path. I thought I'd crushed you, madam, but either I was wrong, or hell has raised you from the dead.'

At these words, which brought back appalling memories, Milady bowed her head with a low moan.

'Yes, hell has raised you from the dead,' said Athos. 'Hell has made you rich, hell has given you another name, hell has all but fashioned another face for you – but it has not erased the stains on your soul, nor the brand on your body.'

Milady stood up as if propelled by a spring, her eyes flashing lightning. Athos remained seated.

'You believed I was dead, didn't you, as I believed you were?

And this name of "Athos" hid the Count de La Fère, as the name of "Milady Clarick" hid Anne de Breuil! Wasn't that what you were called when your esteemed brother married us? Our situation is strange indeed,' Athos went on, laughing. 'Both of us have only continued living because we thought the other dead – a memory is far less troubling than a living creature, even though memory can sometimes be a devouring thing!'

'Come, though,' Milady said in a hollow voice, 'who has brought you here? And what do you want of me?'

'I want to tell you that, although I've been invisible to your eyes, I haven't lost sight of you!'

'You know what I have been doing?'

'I can detail your every action, one day at a time, from your entry into the cardinal's service to this evening.'

An incredulous smile played on Milady's pale lips.

'Listen. It was you who cut the two diamond tags from the Duke of Buckingham's shoulder; it was you who had Madame Bonacieux abducted; it was you who, in love with de Wardes, and thinking you were spending the night with him, opened your door to Monsieur d'Artagnan; it was you who, believing de Wardes had deceived you, wished to have him killed by his rival; it was you who, when that rival had discovered your infamous secret, tried to have him killed in turn by two assassins whom you sent after him; it was you who, seeing the bullets had missed their target, sent poisoned wine with a forged letter to make your victim believe the wine was from his friends; and, lastly, it was you who, here in this room, sitting in this chair I am sitting in, just undertook with Cardinal de Richelieu to have the Duke of Buckingham assassinated, in exchange for his promise to let you murder d'Artagnan.'

All the colour had drained from Milady's face.

'Are you Satan himself?' she said.

'I may be,' said Athos. 'But, at any rate, listen carefully to this: go ahead, assassinate the Duke of Buckingham or have him assassinated, it matters very little to me. I don't know him, and besides, he's an Englishman. But don't touch with the tip of your finger a single hair on the head of d'Artagnan, who is a loyal friend whom I love and protect, otherwise, I swear on my father's head, your intended crime will be your last.'

'Monsieur d'Artagnan has offended me,' Milady said in a hollow voice, 'Monsieur d'Artagnan will die.'

'Indeed? Is it possible to offend you, madam?' Athos said, laughing. 'He offended you and he will die?'

'He will die,' said Milady. 'She first, then he.'

Athos felt dizzy. The sight of this creature, who hadn't a single feminine quality, brought back terrible memories. He thought of how, one day, in less dangerous circumstances than now, he had tried to sacrifice her to his honour. Murderous lust blazed up again, sweeping through him like a burning fever. He stood up in his turn, brought his hand to his belt, drew a pistol, and cocked it.

Pale as a corpse, Milady tried to cry out, but her frozen tongue could only produce a hoarse sound bearing no resemblance to human speech, like the rattle of a wild beast. With her back pressed against the dark tapestry, her hair wild, she looked like the ghastly image of terror itself.

Athos slowly raised his pistol, stretching out his arm so the weapon was almost touching Milady's forehead, and then, in a voice all the more terrible because it had the supreme calm of an inflexible resolve, said, 'Madam, you're going to give me the paper the cardinal signed for you this instant, or, upon my soul, I will blow your brains out.'

With any other man, Milady might have had her doubts, but she knew Athos. Even so, she didn't move.

'You have one second to make up your mind,' he said.

Milady saw from the way his features tightened that he was about to fire. She quickly brought her hand to her bosom, took out a piece of paper and handed it to Athos.

'Take it,' she said, 'and a curse be on you!'

Athos took the paper, tucked his pistol back in his belt, went over to a lamp to make sure it was the right one, unfolded it and read:

It is by my order, and for the good of the state, that the
bearer has done what has been done.

    5 December 1627

    Richelieu

'And now,' said Athos, picking up his cloak and putting his hat
back on, 'now I have drawn your fangs, viper, bite if you can.'

And then he left the room without looking back.

At the door, he found the two men and the horse they were
holding by the bridle.

'Gentlemen,' he said, 'my lord's orders, as you know, are to
conduct this woman without delay to the Fort de La Pointe and
not leave her until she is on board.'

As these words tallied exactly with the order they'd been given,
they bowed their heads in token of assent.

As for Athos, he vaulted lightly into the saddle and set off at a
gallop. But, instead of taking the road, he cut across country, vigorously spurring his horse and stopping from time to time to listen.

At one of these halts, he heard the hoofbeats of several horses
on the road. He had no doubt it was the cardinal and his escort.
Pushing on for another stretch and then rubbing down his horse
with heather and leaves, he stationed himself in the middle of the
road two hundred paces from the camp.

'Who goes there?' he shouted from a distance, when he saw
the horsemen.

'It's our brave musketeer, I believe,' said the cardinal.

'Yes, my lord,' replied Athos. 'In person.'

'Monsieur Athos,' said Richelieu, 'accept all my thanks for the
excellent job you have done guarding us. Gentlemen, we've
arrived. Take the left-hand gate; the password is *Roi et Ré.*'

Saying which, the cardinal nodded to the three friends and
headed off to the right, followed by his equerry, for he was sleeping
in camp that night himself.

'Well!' Porthos and Aramis said in unison, once the cardinal
was out of earshot. 'He signed the paper she asked for.'

'I know,' Athos said calmly. 'Here it is.'

The three friends did not exchange another word, except to give the password to the sentries, until they reached their quarters.

But they sent Mousqueton to tell Planchet that his master was requested, the moment he was relieved from the trenches, to go immediately to the musketeers' quarters.

Meanwhile, when Milady found the two men waiting for her at the door, as Athos had anticipated, she did not balk at following them. For a moment, it's true, she had thought of asking them to take her to the cardinal so she could tell him everything, but a revelation on her part would bring a revelation on Athos's. She might very well say that Athos had hanged her, but then Athos would say she was branded. So she judged it better to say nothing, leave discreetly, carry out the mission with which she had been entrusted with her usual skill, and then, when everything had been accomplished to the cardinal's satisfaction, return to claim her vengeance.

And so, after travelling all night, she was at the Fort de La Pointe by seven o'clock in the morning, she was on board by eight o'clock, and at nine o'clock the ship, which was ostensibly bound for Bayonne with letters of marque from the cardinal, weighed anchor and set sail for England.

XLVI
THE SAINT-GERVAIS BASTION

W HEN HE GOT TO HIS THREE FRIENDS' quarters, d'Artagnan found them gathered in the same room: Athos was thinking, Porthos was twisting up his moustache, and Aramis was reciting his prayers from a charming little book of hours bound in blue velvet.

'By God, gentlemen!' he said, 'I hope what you've got to tell me is worth it, otherwise, I warn you, I won't forgive you for making me come here rather than letting me rest after a night taking and dismantling a bastion. Ah, why weren't you with us, gentlemen? It was hot out there, I tell you!'

'We were somewhere else, which wasn't too chilly either!' replied Porthos, giving his moustache one of his distinctive twists.

'Shh!' said Athos.

'Oho!' said d'Artagnan, understanding the musketeer's slight frown, 'it seems there's something new here.'

'Aramis,' said Athos, 'you had breakfast at the Parpaillot inn the day before yesterday, I believe?'

'Yes.'

'How's one treated there?'

'Why, I ate very badly myself. The day before yesterday was a fish-day and all they had was meat.'

'What?' said Athos. 'No fish in a sea port?'

'They say,' said Aramis, returning to his pious reading, 'the dyke the cardinal has built drives them out to sea.'

'But I wasn't asking you that, Aramis,' said Athos. 'I was asking you if you were left to your own devices, if no one disturbed you?'

'I don't think we were pestered that much. Yes, in fact, for what you're after, we'd do perfectly well at the Parpaillot.'

'Let's go to the Parpaillot then,' said Athos. 'The walls here are like sheets of paper.'

D'Artagnan, who was used to his friend's manner of doing things, and instantly understood by a word, a gesture, or a sign from him if a situation was serious, took Athos's arm and went out with him without saying a word. Porthos followed, chatting with Aramis.

On the way they met Grimaud, and Athos signalled for him to follow them. Grimaud, as was his way, obeyed in silence; the poor lad had ended up almost forgetting how to speak.

They arrived at the Parpaillot tavern. It was seven o'clock in the morning and day was just breaking. The three friends ordered breakfast and went into a room where, according to the landlord, they would not be disturbed.

Unfortunately the hour was poorly chosen for a conference. Reveille had just sounded; everyone was shaking off the night's sleep and, to drive off the damp morning air, coming to the tavern to take a drop. A succession of dragoons, Swiss guards, guards, musketeers and light horsemen streamed in and out at a speed that must have been very good for the landlord's business, but was very bad for the purposes of the four friends. Consequently they gave only very sullen responses to the greetings, toasts and jests of their companions.

'Right,' said Athos, 'we're going to have a fine quarrel on our hands and that's not what we need just now. D'Artagnan, tell us about your night, and then we'll tell you about ours afterwards.'

'Indeed,' said a light horseman, who swaggered up to them holding a glass of brandy, which he slowly sipped, 'indeed, you were in the trenches last night, you gentlemen of the guards, weren't you? I've a feeling you had a bone to pick with the Rochelois.'

D'Artagnan looked at Athos to know if he should reply to this intruder butting into their conversation.

'Well,' said Athos, 'didn't you hear Monsieur de Busigny, who has done you the honour of addressing you? Relate what happened last night, since these gentlemen wish to know.'

'Haben you nicht tekken a pastion?' asked a Swiss guard, who was drinking rum from a beer glass.

'Yes, sir,' replied d'Artagnan bowing, 'we had that honour. We even, as you may have heard, introduced a powder barrel under one corner which made a very pretty breach when it exploded – not to mention that, since the bastion was no new thing, the rest of the construction was badly shaken up.'

'And what bastion is this?' asked a dragoon, who was carrying a goose spitted on his sabre, which he had brought to have cooked.

'The Saint-Gervais bastion,' replied d'Artagnan, 'under cover of which the Rochelois were harassing our labour battalion.'

'And was it a hot business?'

'Why, yes. We lost five men and the Rochelois eight or ten.'

'Gott's healink balm!' said the Swiss, who, despite the admirable collection of oaths the German language can boast, had acquired the habit of swearing in French.

'But it's likely,' said the light horseman, 'that they'll send pioneers this morning to repair the bastion.'

'Yes, it's likely,' said d'Artagnan.

'Gentlemen,' said Athos, 'a bet!'

'Ach yess, a pet!' said the Swiss man.

'What is it?' asked the light horseman.

'Wait,' said the dragoon, laying his sabre like a spit on the two huge andirons supporting the fire in the hearth, 'I'm in. Hey, you confounded hosteller, a dripping pan so I won't lose a drop of fat from this estimable bird!'

'He hat rriight,' said the Swiss. 'Goose vat ist ferry gut with zuckermeats.'

'There!' said the dragoon. 'Now, what about this bet? We're listening, Monsieur Athos!'

'Yes, the bet!' said the light horseman.

'Well then, Monsieur de Busigny, I bet you,' said Athos, 'that I and my three companions, Messrs Porthos, Aramis and d'Artagnan, can go and breakfast in the Saint-Gervais bastion, and hold it for an hour by the clock, no matter what the enemy may do to dislodge us.'

Porthos and Aramis looked at one another, as comprehension began to dawn on them.

'But,' said d'Artagnan leaning close to Athos's ear, 'you're going to get us all mercilessly killed.'

'We're killed stone dead if we don't go,' replied Athos.

'Ah, my faith, gentlemen,' said Porthos, leaning back in his chair and twirling his moustache, 'you consider this a fine bet, I trust.'

'And I accept!' said Monsieur de Busigny. 'Now we need to set the stakes.'

'Why, you are four, gentlemen,' said Athos, 'and we are four. A dinner for eight, everyone to eat their fill – does that suit you?'

'Marvellously,' said Monsieur de Busigny.

'Perfectly,' said the dragoon.

'Dass ssuits mee,' said the Swiss.

The fourth listener, who had played a silent role in the whole conversation, nodded his head to signify he agreed to the proposal.

'The gentlemen's breakfast is ready,' said the innkeeper.

'Bring it in, then,' said Athos.

The innkeeper obeyed. Athos called Grimaud, pointed to a large basket lying in a corner and mimed wrapping the meal in napkins. Understanding immediately that they were going to eat alfresco, Grimaud took the basket, packed up the food, added the bottles and hooked the basket over this arm.

'But where are you going to eat my breakfast?' said the innkeeper.

'What does it matter to you,' said Athos, 'as long as we pay?'

And with that, he majestically tossed two pistoles on the table.

'Do you need change, sir?' said the innkeeper.

'No, just add two bottles of champagne, and the balance will cover the napkins.'

The innkeeper hadn't done as good a stroke of business as he had at first thought he would, but he made up for it by slipping the four guests two bottles of Anjou wine instead of two bottles of champagne.

'Monsieur de Busigny,' said Athos, 'would you be so kind as to set your watch by mine, or permit me to set mine by yours?'

'Excellent, sir!' said the light horseman, producing an extremely handsome watch from his fob pocket. 'Half-past seven,' he said.

'Twenty-five to eight,' said Athos. 'We now know I am five minutes ahead of you, sir.'

And then, bowing to the astounded onlookers, the four young men set off for the Saint-Gervais bastion, followed by Grimaud, who was carrying the basket. He didn't know where he was going but, with the unquestioning obedience Athos had inculcated in him, it did not even occur to him to ask.

While they were still within the confines of camp, the four friends did not exchange a word. In any case, they were being followed by gawkers who, having heard of the bet, wanted to know how they were going to extricate themselves from their predicament. But once they had crossed the line of circumvallation and were under the open sky, d'Artagnan, who had no idea what was afoot, thought it was time to ask for an explanation.

'And now, my dear Athos,' he said, 'do me the kindness of telling me where we're going?'

'You can see very well,' said Athos, 'we're going to the bastion.'

'But what are we going to do there?'

'You know very well. We're going to breakfast.'

'But why didn't we breakfast at the Parpaillot?'

'Because we have some very important matters to tell you, and it was impossible to have five minutes' conversation in that inn with all those pests coming and going and bowing and accosting us. Here, at least,' continued Athos, pointing to the bastion, 'we won't be disturbed.'

'It seems to me,' said d'Artagnan, with that prudence which combined so happily and naturally with his inordinate bravery, 'it seems to me that we could have found some remote spot in the dunes on the seashore.'

'Where the four of us would have been seen conferring together, and in a quarter of an hour the cardinal would have been informed by his spies that we were holding council.'

'Yes,' said Aramis, 'Athos is right: *Animadvertuntur in desertis*[1].'

'A desert wouldn't have been bad,' said Porthos, 'but there was the matter of finding one.'

'There's no desert where a bird can't fly over your head, or a fish jump out of the water, or a rabbit run out of its burrow, and every bird, fish and rabbit, I believe – everything, in a word, is a spy for the cardinal. So it's better to pursue our enterprise, and, besides, we can't back out of it now without shame. We have made a bet, a bet no one could have predicted, and the true reason for which I defy anyone to guess. To win it, we're going to hold our ground in the bastion for an hour – where we will or will not be attacked. If we're not, we'll have plenty of time to talk and no one will hear us, for I guarantee that that this bastion's walls don't have ears. And if we are, we'll discuss our business all the same, and, what's more, in defending ourselves, we'll cover ourselves with glory. We benefit either way, you see.'

'Yes,' said d'Artagnan, 'but we'll undoubtedly catch a bullet while we're at it.'

'Come, my dear friend,' said Athos, 'you know full well the most dangerous bullets are not the enemy's.'

'But it seems to me that, for such an expedition, we should at least have brought our muskets.'

'You're a fool, friend Porthos. Why load ourselves down with an unnecessary burden?'

'Facing the enemy, I don't consider a good, heavy-calibre musket, twelve cartridges and a powder flask unnecessary.'

'Aha! Well,' said Athos, 'didn't you hear what d'Artagnan said?'

'What did d'Artagnan say?' asked Porthos.

'D'Artagnan said that eight or ten Frenchmen and as many Rochelois were killed in last night's attack.'

'And?'

'They did not have time to strip them, did they? Seeing as they had other more pressing matters to attend to at that moment.'

'Well?'

'Well, we'll find their muskets, their powder flasks and their cartridges, and instead of four carbines and twelve bullets, we'll have about fifteen guns and a hundred rounds of ammunition.'

'Ah, Athos,' said Aramis, 'you truly are a great man!'

Porthos bowed his head in agreement.

Only d'Artagnan seemed unconvinced.

Grimaud evidently shared the young man's doubts, for, seeing they were still walking towards the bastion, something he hadn't believed up until that moment, he pulled his master by the coattail.

'Where are we going?' he inquired with a gesture.

Athos pointed to the bastion.

'But,' said the silent Grimaud, still in the same dialect, 'we'll leave our hides there.'

Athos raised his eyes and finger to heaven.

Grimaud put his basket on the ground and sat down, shaking his head.

Athos took a pistol from his belt, checked to see it was well primed, cocked it and pressed the barrel against Grimaud's ear.

Grimaud found himself back on his feet as if worked by a spring.

Athos gestured for him to take the basket and walk ahead of them.

Grimaud obeyed.

The only thing the poor lad had gained from this brief pantomime was to be transferred from the rearguard to the vanguard.

When they reached the bastion, the four friends turned round.

More than three hundred soldiers of all branches were assembled at the gate of the camp, and in a separate group could be made out Monsieur de Busigny, the dragoon, the Swiss guard and the fourth wagerer.

Athos took off his hat, put it on the tip of his sword and waved it in the air.

All the spectators returned his salute, accompanying this courtesy with a great cheer that carried all the way to them.

After which, the four of them disappeared into the bastion, into which Grimaud had preceeded them.

XLVII

THE COUNCIL OF THE MUSKETEERS

A s Athos had anticipated, the sole occupants of the bastion were a dozen or so dead bodies, French and Rochelois.

'Gentlemen,' said Athos, who had taken command of the

expedition, 'while Grimaud lays the table, let's start by collecting the guns and cartridges. Besides, we can talk while we work. These gentlemen,' he added, indicating the dead, 'aren't listening.'

'All the same, we could just as well throw them in the ditch,' said Porthos, 'after, that is, we've checked there's nothing in their pockets.'

'Yes,' said Aramis, 'but that's Grimaud's affair.'

'Then let Grimaud search them and throw them over the walls, said d'Artagnan.'

'That's the last thing we'll do,' said Athos. 'They may be of use to us.'

'These dead men may be of use to us?' said Porthos. 'Goodness, you're losing your mind, my dear friend.'

'"Be not quick to judge", say the Gospel and the cardinal,' replied Athos. 'How many guns, gentlemen?'

'Twelve,' replied Aramis.

'How many rounds?'

'A hundred.'

'That's all we need; let's load the weapons.'

The four musketeers set to work. As they finished loading the last gun, Grimaud signalled that breakfast was ready.

Athos replied, also by gesture, that he approved, and indicated to Grimaud a sort of pepper-box turret where the latter understood he was to mount guard. To alleviate the boredom of sentry duty, Athos allowed him to take a loaf of bread, two cutlets and a bottle of wine.

'And now, to breakfast,' said Athos.

The four friends sat cross-legged on the ground, like Turks or tailors.

'Ah,' said d'Artagnan, 'now you're no longer afraid of being heard, I hope you're going to let us into your secret, Athos.'

'I trust I shall provide you with both amusement and glory, gentlemen,' said Athos. 'I've led you on a charming outing; here's a most succulent breakfast, and over there are five hundred souls who, as you can see through the loopholes, take us for madmen or heroes, two classes of imbeciles that have a considerable amount in common.'

'But the secret?' asked d'Artagnan.

'The secret,' said Athos, 'is that I saw Milady yesterday evening.'

D'Artagnan was bringing his glass to his lips, but, at the name of Milady, his hand shook so violently he had to set it down so as not to spill its contents.

'You saw your wi—'

'Shh!' interrupted Athos. 'You are forgetting, my dear friend, that these gentlemen are not privy, like you, to my family secrets. I saw Milady.'

'And where was that?' asked d'Artagnan.

'Some two leagues from here, at the Red Dovecot inn.'

'In that case I am done for,' said d'Artagnan.

'No, not quite yet,' replied Athos, 'for she must have left France's shores by now.'

D'Artagnan exhaled.

'But, when all's said and done,' asked Porthos, 'who on earth is this Milady?'

'A charming woman,' said Athos, sipping a glass of sparkling wine. 'That blackguard of a hosteller,' he cried, 'giving us Anjou wine instead of champagne and thinking we'd be fooled! Yes,' he went on, 'a charming woman who radiated kindness towards our friend d'Artagnan, after he had done her some base turn or other. She tried to avenge herself a month ago by having him shot, a week ago by having him poisoned, and yesterday by asking the cardinal for his head.'

'What? By asking the cardinal for my head?' cried d'Artagnan, pale with terror.

'That,' said Porthos, 'is the Gospel truth. I heard it with my own two ears.'

'I did too,' said Aramis.

'Then,' said d'Artagnan, his arms despondently dropping to his side, 'there's no point putting up a fight any more. I might as well blow my brains out and have done with it!'

'That's one act of folly you should not commit,' said Athos, 'seeing as it's the only one for which there is no remedy.'

'But, with enemies like this, I'll never escape,' said d'Artagnan. 'First, the stranger from Meung; then de Wardes, whom I dealt three sword thrusts; then Milady, whose secret I've discovered; and finally the cardinal, whose vengeance I thwarted.'

'Well,' said Athos, 'that only makes four, and we're four, so it's one against one. By God! If we believe Grimaud's signals, we're going to be dealing with much greater numbers. What's the matter, Grimaud? Given the gravity of the situation, you have my permission to speak, my friend, but be laconic, I beg you. What do you see?'

'A troop.'

'Of how many?'

'Twenty men.'

'What sort?'

'Sixteen pioneers, four soldiers.'

'How far away?'

'Five hundred paces.'

'Good, we still have time to finish this chicken and drink a glass of wine to your health, d'Artagnan!'

'To your health!' repeated Porthos and Aramis.

'Very well, to my health! Though I don't think your good wishes will be much help.'

'Bah!' said Athos, 'God is great, as the votaries of Mahomet say, and the future is in His hands.'

Draining the contents of his glass, which he set down next to him, Athos then nonchalantly stood up, took the first musket to hand, and went over to a loophole.

Porthos, Aramis and d'Artagnan did likewise. As for Grimaud, he was positioned behind the four friends to reload their weapons.

After a moment, they saw the troop appear. It was following a sort of approach trench which communicated between the bastion and the town.

'By God,' said Athos, 'it's hardly worth stirring ourselves over twenty characters armed with picks, hoes and spades! Grimaud only had to make a sign to them to be on their way, and I'm certain they would have left us in peace.'

'I doubt it,' observed d'Artagnan, 'for they're advancing very resolutely on this side. Besides, there are four soldiers with the labourers and a corporal, all armed with muskets.'

'That's because they haven't seen us,' said Athos.

'My faith!' said Aramis, 'I confess I'm loath to fire on those poor devils of townsmen.'

'It's a sorry priest,' replied Porthos, 'who takes pity on heretics!'

'Actually,' said Athos, 'Aramis is right, I'm going to warn them.'

'What the devil are you doing?' cried d'Artagnan. 'You're going to get yourself shot, my dear friend.'

But Athos paid no heed to this advice, and climbed on to the breach, his gun in one hand and his hat in the other.

'Gentlemen,' he said, bowing courteously to the soldiers and labourers who, stunned by his appearance, stopped fifty paces or so from the bastion, 'gentlemen, some friends and I are breakfasting in this bastion. Now, you know there's nothing more disagreeable than being disturbed at breakfast. So, if you really have some business to attend to here, we beg you to wait until we have finished our meal, or to come back later, unless that is you feel a salutary desire to leave the side of rebellion and come to drink the health of the king of France with us.'

'Look out, Athos!' cried d'Artagnan. 'Don't you see they're aiming at you?'

'Indeed I do,' said Athos, 'but these townsmen are terrible shots and they have no chance of hitting me.'

And indeed, four shots were fired that very instant, the bullets smashing into the wall around Athos, but none hit him.

Four shots replied almost simultaneously, but, being better aimed than those of the attackers, three soldiers fell dead on the spot, and one of the labourers was wounded.

'Grimaud, another musket!' said Athos, still in the breach.

Grimaud obeyed instantly. For their part, the three friends had already reloaded. A second volley followed the first. The corporal and two of the pioneers fell dead, while the rest of the troop took flight.

'Come, gentlemen, a sortie,' said Athos.

And then the four friends, rushing out of the fort, reached the battlefield, gathered up the soldiers' four muskets and the corporal's half-pike, and then, convinced the runaways wouldn't stop until they got to the town, headed back to the bastion, bringing with them the trophies of their victory.

'Reload the muskets, Grimaud,' said Athos, 'while we, gentlemen, resume our breakfast and our conversation. Where were we?'

'I remember,' said d'Artagnan, extremely concerned about the itinerary of Milady's journey.

'She's going to England,' replied Athos.

'To do what?'

'To assassinate Buckingham, or to have him assassinated.'

D'Artagnan exclaimed with surprise and indignation.

'But that's abominable!' he cried.

'Oh, believe me,' said Athos, 'I'm not too concerned about it. Now you've finished, Grimaud,' continued Athos, 'take our corporal's half-pike, tie a napkin to it, and plant it on top of our bastion, so that those Rochelois rebels can see they're dealing with brave and loyal king's men.'

'What?' said d'Artagnan. 'You're not too concerned if she kills Buckingham or has him killed? But the duke is our friend.'

'The duke is English, the duke is fighting against us – let her do what she likes with the duke, he might as well be an empty bottle for all I care.'

Saying this, Athos tossed the bottle he was holding some fifteen paces away, having poured the last drop of its contents into his glass.

'Wait a moment,' said d'Artagnan, 'I'm not going to forsake Buckingham like this. He gave us some very handsome horses.'

'And, above all, some very handsome saddles,' added Porthos, who at that very moment was wearing the gold braid of his on his cloak.

'Besides,' observed Aramis, 'God wishes for the sinner's conversion, not his death.'

'Amen,' said Athos, 'and we will come back to that later, if you wish. But at the time, as I'm sure you'll understand, d'Artagnan, my main concern was how to relieve that woman of some sort of document giving her full powers she had extorted from the cardinal, which would allow her to do away with you, and perhaps also us, with impunity.'

'This creature is a demon, then, is she?' asked Porthos, holding out his plate to Aramis, who was carving a chicken.

'And these full powers,' said d'Artagnan . . .'is this document still in her hands?'

'No, it came into mine – I won't say entirely straightforwardly, for that would be a lie.'

'My dear Athos,' said d'Artagnan, 'I've given up counting the times I've owed you my life.'

'So you left us to go and see her?' asked Aramis.

'Precisely.'

'And you have this letter from the cardinal?' said d'Artagnan.

'Here it is,' said Athos.

And then he took the precious paper from his tabard pocket.

D'Artagnan unfolded it with a trembling hand, which he made no attempt to conceal, and read:

> It is by my order, and for the good of the state, that the bearer has done what has been done.
>   5 December 1627[1]
>   Richelieu

'Indeed,' said Aramis, 'that is an exemplary absolution.'

'That piece of paper must be torn to pieces!' cried d'Artagnan, who seemed to read his death sentence in it.

'On the contrary,' said Athos, 'it must be kept with the utmost care. I wouldn't give this paper away to a soul, not even if he covered it in gold coins.'

'So what's she going to do now?' asked the young man.

'Why,' Athos said nonchalantly, 'she's probably going to write to the cardinal saying that a damned musketeer by the name of Athos wrested her safe-conduct from her. She will advise him in the same letter to get rid of him – and his two friends Porthos and Aramis while he's about it. The cardinal will remember those are the same men he's always running into. Then, one fine morning, he will have d'Artagnan arrested, and so he won't be bored on his own, he'll send us to keep him company in the Bastille.'

'Now, now,' said Porthos, 'those don't seem to me your best jokes, my dear friend.'

'I'm not joking,' replied Athos.

'You know,' said Porthos, 'I think it would be less of a sin to wring that damned Milady's neck than it would be to wring the necks of those poor Huguenot devils, whose only crime is to sing some psalms in French when we sing them in Latin.'

'What does Monsieur l'abbé say to that?' Athos asked calmly.

'I say that I agree with Porthos,' replied Aramis.

'Then I do too!' said d'Artagnan.

'Luckily she's far away,' observed Porthos. 'For I confess she would trouble me greatly if she were here.'

'She troubles me when she's in England just as much as she does when she's in France,' said Athos.

'She troubles me wherever she is,' continued d'Artagnan.

'But when you had her in your power,' said Porthos, 'why didn't you drown her or strangle her or hang her? It's only the dead who don't reappear.'

'You believe that, Porthos?' replied the musketeer with a melancholy smile that only d'Artagnan understood.

'I've got an idea,' said d'Artagnan.

'Let's hear it,' said the musketeers.

'To arms!' yelled Grimaud.

The young men leapt to their feet and ran for their guns.

This time, a little troop of around twenty or twenty-five men was advancing, but, rather than workers, these were garrison soldiers.

'What if we went back to camp?' said Porthos. 'The sides no longer seem even.'

'Impossible for three reasons,' replied Athos. 'First, we haven't finished our breakfast; second, we still have important matters to discuss; third, there's still another ten minutes until the hour is up.'

'Come,' said Aramis, 'we still have to draw up a plan of battle.'

'It's very simple,' replied Athos. 'As soon as the enemy is within musket range, we open fire. If they keep on advancing, we fire again, and keep firing as long as we still have loaded muskets. If what's left of the troop wants to mount an assault, we let the besiegers get as far as the ditch, then we topple that piece of wall, which is only standing by a miracle of equilibrium, so that it falls on their heads.'

'Bravo!' cried Porthos. 'Truly, Athos, you were born to be a general, and the cardinal, who thinks himself a great military man, is a mere nonentity by comparison.'

'Gentlemen,' said Athos, 'no doubling up, please. Each of you take good aim at your man.'

'I've got mine,' said d'Artagnan.

'And I mine,' said Porthos.

'Ditto,' said Aramis.

'Then fire!' said Athos.

The four gunshots only made a single report, and four men fell to the ground.

The drum immediately began to beat, and the little troop advanced at the double.

Then the gunshots succeeded one another at irregular intervals, yet always with the same accuracy. But, as if they knew the friends' numerical disadvantage, the Rochelois broke into a run.

Three more shots caused two more men to fall, but those that remained standing didn't slacken their pace.

Reaching the foot of bastion, the enemy were still twelve or fifteen strong. A last volley greeted them, but without managing halt them. They leapt into the ditch and prepared to scale the breach.

'Come, my friends,' said Athos, 'let's finish them off with one blow. To the wall! To the wall!'

And then the four friends, aided by Grimaud, set to pushing with their musket barrels an enormous section of wall, which leant forward as if bowing in the wind. It gradually broke loose from its base, before falling with a terrible crash into the ditch. Then a great cry was heard, a cloud of dust rose up into the sky, and it was over.

'Have we crushed every last one of them?' asked Athos.

'My faith, it looks like it,' said d'Artagnan.

'No,' said Porthos, 'there's one or two fellows hobbling off.'

And indeed, three or four of the wretches, covered in dirt and blood, were fleeing along the sunken road back to town. They were all that remained of the little troop.

Athos looked at his watch.

'Gentlemen,' he said, 'we've been here for an hour, and the bet is now won, but we must play the game in the right spirit. Besides, d'Artagnan hasn't told us his idea.'

And then the musketeer, with his customary aplomb, went to sit down at what was left of the breakfast.

'My idea?' said d'Artagnan.

'Yes, you were saying you had an idea,' replied Athos.

'Ah, that's right,' said d'Artagnan. 'I'll cross to England a second time, I'll find the Duke of Buckingham, and I'll warn him of the plot that's being hatched against his life.'

'You won't do that, d'Artagnan,' Athos said coldly.

'And why not? Haven't I already done so once?'

'Yes, but then we weren't at war; then the Duke of Buckingham was an ally, not an enemy. Your plan would be denounced as treason.'

D'Artagnan realised the force of his argument and fell silent.

'Why,' said Porthos, 'I think I've got an idea too.'

'Silence for Monsieur Porthos's idea!' said Aramis.

'I ask Monsieur de Tréville for a leave of absence on a pretext that you'll think of – pretexts are not my forte. Milady doesn't know me, so I'll be able to get close to her without scaring her. And when I have my beauty, I strangle her.'

'You know,' said Athos, 'I'm rather inclined to adopt Porthos's idea.'

'Shame on you!' said Aramis. 'Killing a woman! No, listen, I've got a good idea.'

'Let's hear your idea, Aramis!' demanded Athos, deferring to the young musketeer.

'We must warn the queen.'

'Ah, yes, my faith!' Porthos and d'Artagnan cried out together. 'I think we've found the way.'

'Warn the queen?' said Athos. 'And how are we going to do that? Have we connections at court? Can we send someone to Paris without word of it spreading through camp? It's a hundred and forty leagues from here to Paris; our letter won't have got to Angers before we're under lock and key.'

'As far as conveying a letter safely to Her Majesty is concerned,' proposed Aramis, blushing, 'I can see to that. I know an able person in Tours . . .'

Aramis stopped when he saw Athos smile.

'So, you wouldn't choose this method, Athos?' said d'Artagnan.

'I don't reject it out of hand,' said Athos, 'but I'd just like to point out to Aramis that he can't leave camp; that we are the only ones who can be relied on; that, two hours after the messenger leaves, every capuchin friar, every alguazil, every black cap of the cardinal's will know your letter off by heart, and that you and your able person will have been arrested.'

'Not to mention,' objected Porthos, 'that the queen will save the Duke of Buckingham, but she won't save the rest of us.'

'Gentlemen,' said d'Artagnan, 'Porthos's objection is eminently sensible.'

'Aha, what's happening in the town now?' said Athos.

'They're calling to arms.'

The four friends listened – sure enough, the sound of a drum was audible.

'You'll see, they're going to send a whole regiment now,' said Athos.

'You're not planning to hold out against a whole regiment?' said Porthos.

'Why not?' said the musketeer. 'I feel fine, and I'd hold out against a whole army, if we'd only taken the precaution of bringing a dozen more bottles.'

'On my word, the drum's coming nearer,' said d'Artagnan.

'Let it,' said Athos. 'It's a quarter of an hour from here to the town, and consequently from the town to here. That's more than enough time for us to decide on a plan. If we leave here, we'll never find anywhere as convenient. Wait, gentlemen, that's it – the right idea's just occurred to me.'

'Tell us, then.'

'Let me give Grimaud a few indispensable orders.'

Athos signalled for his valet to come over.

'Grimaud,' said Athos, pointing to the dead bodies lying in the bastion, 'you're going to take these gentlemen, stand them up against the wall, and put their hats on their heads and their muskets in their hands.'

'Oh, you great man!' cried d'Artagnan. 'I understand.'

'You understand?' said Porthos.

'And you, Grimaud, do you understand?' asked Aramis.

Grimaud made a sign that he did.

'That's all that's needed,' said Athos. 'Now, back to my idea.'

'I'd like to understand, though,' observed Porthos.

'Don't trouble yourself.'

'Yes, yes, Athos's idea,' d'Artagnan and Aramis said as one.

'This Milady, this woman, this creature, this demon, from what you tell me, d'Artagnan, has a brother-in-law, I think.'

'Yes, and I know him quite well in fact. I don't think he is very well-inclined towards his sister-in-law.'

'No harm in that,' replied Athos. 'If he detests her, better still.'

'In that case, our needs are met to perfection.'

'Nonetheless,' said Porthos, 'I would really like to know what Grimaud is up to.'

'Quiet, Porthos!' said Aramis.

'What's this brother-in-law called?'

'Lord de Winter.'

'Where is he now?'

'He went back to London at the first rumour of war.'

'Well, there's just the man we need,' said Athos. 'We should warn him. We'll let him know his sister-in-law is about to assassinate someone and entreat him not to let her out of his sight. London should have, I hope, some establishment like the Madelonnettes or the Reformed Girls[2]. He'll put his sister-in-law in there, and then we'll have peace of mind.'

'Yes,' said d'Artagnan, 'until she gets out.'

'Ah, my faith,' said Athos, 'you ask too much, d'Artagnan! I've given you all I have; I warn you, that's the bottom of my sack.'

'I think this is the best plan,' said Aramis. 'We'll alert both the queen and Lord de Winter.'

'Yes, but whom will we get to take the letter to Tours and the one to London?

'I can answer for Bazin,' said Aramis.

'And I for Planchet,' continued d'Artagnan.

'Indeed,' said Porthos, 'we may not be able to leave camp but our valets can.'

'Very true,' said Aramis. 'So we'll write the letters today, give them some money, and they'll set out.'

'Give them money?' said Athos. 'Do you have some, then?'

The four friends looked at one another, as a cloud passed over their brows that had brightened up for a moment.

'To arms!' cried d'Artagnan. 'I see red and black dots swarming over there. What were you saying about a regiment, Athos? It's a veritable army!'

'My faith, yes,' said Athos, 'there they are. Look at those sly dogs coming out without drums and trumpets. Aha! Have you finished, Grimaud?'

Grimaud made a sign of assent, and pointed to a dozen corpses whom he had arranged in the most picturesque of attitudes: some shouldering arms, others seemingly taking aim, others with their sword in hand.

'Bravo!' said Athos. 'That does honour to your imagination!'

'Even so,' said Porthos, 'I'd still like to understand.'

'Let's decamp first,' interrupted d'Artagnan, 'you can understand later.'

'One moment, gentlemen, one moment! Let's give Grimaud time to clear breakfast.'

'Ah!' said Aramis, 'look, the black and red dots are growing bigger before our eyes. I am of d'Artagnan's opinion – I don't think we have any time to waste before getting back to camp.'

'My faith,' said Athos, 'I have nothing against retreating. The bet was for an hour, and we've stayed an hour and a half. There's nothing more to discuss – let's go, gentlemen, let's go!'

Grimaud had already made a head start with the basket and the leftovers.

The four friends followed him for about a dozen paces before Athos cried:

'Hey! what the devil are we about, gentlemen?'

'Have you forgotten something?' asked Aramis.

'The flag, God's teeth! We mustn't let a flag fall into the enemy's hands, even if it's only a napkin.'

And then Athos raced back into the bastion, climbed up to the platform, and took down the flag. But, as the Rochelois were within range, they trained a terrible barrage on this man, exposing himself to their fire as if for sport.

Athos might have been wearing a magic charm, however,

since the bullets whistled past on all sides without hitting him.

Turning his back on the men of the town and saluting those of the camp Athos waved his standard. Great shouts rang out from both directions, shouts of anger on one side, of enthusiasm on the other.

A second barrage followed the first, and three bullets riddled the napkin, turning it into a proper flag. The whole camp could be heard shouting, 'Get down! Get down!'

Athos got down from the platform. His comrades, who were waiting anxiously for him, were thrilled to see him reappear.

'Come on, Athos, come on,' said d'Artagnan, 'let's put our best foot forward. Now we've found everything except the money, it would be stupid to get killed.'

But Athos kept walking at a majestic pace, no matter what remarks his companions made, and, realising all remarks were useless, they adjusted their speed to his.

Grimaud and his basket had gone on ahead and were both out of range.

A moment later, they heard the sound of a mad fusillade.

'What's that?' asked Porthos. 'What are they firing at? I don't hear the whistle of bullets nor do I see anyone.'

'They're firing at our dead,' said Athos.

'But our dead won't fire back.'

'Exactly, so they'll think it's an ambush, they'll mull it over, they'll send a flag of truce, and by the time they realise the joke, we'll be out of range. That's why there's no point getting pleurisy by hurrying.'

'Ah, I understand,' marvelled Porthos.

'That's good,' said Athos, shrugging his shoulders.

On their side, the French, seeing the four friends strolling back, let out shouts of enthusiasm.

In due course, another volley of musket fire was heard, and this time the bullets splattered into the pebbles around the four friends and whistled mournfully in their ears. The Rochelois had finally taken the bastion.

'Those are some very clumsy fellows,' said Athos. 'How many did we kill? Twelve?'

'Or fifteen.'

'How many did we crush?'

'Eight or ten.'

'And in exchange for all that, not a scratch? Ah, no! What's that on your hand there, d'Artagnan? Blood, I think?'

'It's nothing,' said d'Artagnan.

'A stray bullet?'

'Not even.'

'What is it then?'

As we have said, Athos loved d'Artagnan like his own son, and this sombre and inflexible character sometimes felt a paternal concern for the young man.

'A graze,' said d'Artagnan. 'My fingers were caught between the stone of the wall and the stone on my finger, and the skin split.'

'That's what comes from sporting diamonds, my master,' Athos said scornfully.

'Hang on!' cried Porthos, 'that's right, there's a diamond. So why the devil, then, if there's a diamond, are we complaining about not having any money?'

'Yes, why indeed?' said Aramis.

'Good work, Porthos! That's what I call an idea.'

'Naturally,' said Porthos, puffing himself up at Athos's compliment, 'given that there's a diamond, let's sell it.'

'But,' said d'Artagnan, 'it's the queen's diamond.'

'All the more reason,' said Athos. 'The queen saving the Duke of Buckingham, her lover – nothing could be more just; the queen saving us, her friends – nothing could be more moral. Let's sell the diamond. What does Monsieur l'abbé think? I won't ask for Porthos's advice, it has already been volunteered.'

'Why, I think,' said Aramis, blushing, 'that as his ring does not come from a mistress, and so is not a token of love, d'Artagnan can sell it.'

'My dear friend, you are theology personified. So, your advice is . . . ?'

'To sell the diamond,' replied Aramis.

'Well then,' d'Artagnan said merrily, 'let's sell the diamond and say no more about it.'

The fusillade continued, but the friends were out of range and the Rochelois were only shooting to salve their consciences.

'My faith,' said Athos, 'that idea came to Porthos in the nick of time. Here we are in camp. So, gentlemen, not another word about this affair. We're observed, they're coming to meet us, we are going to be borne aloft in triumph.'

And indeed, as we've said, the whole camp was in a ferment. More than two thousand people had watched, as if at a show, the charmed braggadocio of the four friends, a piece of braggadocio for which they were far from suspecting the real reason. All that was to be heard were cries of, 'Long live the guards! Long live the musketeers!' Monsieur de Busigny was the first to come and shake Athos's hand and acknowledge the bet was lost. The dragoon and the Swiss guard followed him, and then all their comrades followed the dragoon and the Swiss guard. There was no end to the congratulations, handshakes, embraces and uncontrollable laughter at the expense of the Rochelois. Eventually, the tumult was so great that the cardinal thought it was a mutiny and sent La Houdinière, the captain of his guards, to find out what was happening.

The exploit was related to his messenger in the full bloom of enthusiasm.

'Well?' asked the cardinal, when he saw La Houdinière.

'Well, my lord,' said the latter, 'three musketeers and a guard bet Monsieur de Busigny they could go and breakfast in the Saint-Gervais bastion, and, while doing so, they held their ground for two hours against the enemy and killed I don't know how many Rochelois.'

'Did you find out the names of these three musketeers?'

'Yes, my lord.'

'What are they?'

'Messrs Athos, Porthos and Aramis.'

'Every time my three brave fellows!' murmured the cardinal. 'And the guard?'

'Monsieur d'Artagnan.'

'My young rascal, every time! I must make those four men mine.'

That same evening, the cardinal spoke to Monsieur de Tréville about the morning's exploit, which was the talk of all the camp. Monsieur de Tréville, who had the story of the adventure from the very mouths of those who were its heroes, related it in every detail to His Eminence, not forgetting the episode of the napkin.

'Very well, Monsieur de Tréville,' said the cardinal, 'please see that I get this napkin. I will have three gold fleur-de-lys embroidered on it, and will give it to your company as a standard.'

'My lord,' said Monsieur de Tréville, 'that would be unjust to the guards. Monsieur d'Artagnan isn't my man, but Monsieur des Essarts's.'

'Well then, take him,' said the cardinal. 'Seeing as these four brave soldiers love each other so much, it's not fair they don't serve in the same company.'

That same evening, Monsieur de Tréville announced the good news to the three musketeers and d'Artagnan, and invited the four of them to lunch the following day.

D'Artagnan was beside himself with joy. As we know, it was his lifelong dream to be a musketeer.

The three friends were equally elated.

'My faith,' d'Artagnan said to Athos, 'you had a triumphant idea, and, as you said, we've won glory by it and have been able to hold a conversation of the highest importance.'

'Which we can now resume without anyone suspecting us. For, with God's help, from now on we'll be thought of as cardinalists.'

That same evening, d'Artagnan went to pay his respects to Monsieur des Essarts and inform him of the promotion he had obtained.

Monsieur des Essarts, who was very fond of d'Artagnan, offered to help him, since his change of corps would entail outfitting expenses.

D'Artagnan declined, but, thinking the moment opportune, he gave him the diamond and asked him to have it appraised, since he wished to turn it into money.

At eight o'clock the following day, Monsieur des Essarts's valet came to d'Artagnan's quarters and handed him a bag containing seven thousands livres in gold.

That was the price of the queen's diamond.

XLVIII

A FAMILY MATTER

A THOS HAD COME UP with the phrase 'a family matter'. A family matter wasn't subject to investigation by the cardinal; a family matter was no one else's concern, and a family matter was something one could attend to in full view of the world.

So, Athos had come up with the phrase: a family matter.

Aramis had come up with the idea: the valets.

Porthos had come up with the means: the diamond.

D'Artagnan was the only one not to have come up with anything, although ordinarily he was the most inventive of the four. But it must also be said that the mere name of Milady paralysed him.

Ah, no, we're mistaken: he had found a buyer for the diamond.

The breakfast at Monsieur de Tréville's was a charmingly merry affair. D'Artagnan already had his uniform. He and Aramis were more or less the same size, and Aramis, having been liberally paid, as will be recalled, by the bookseller for his poem, had ordered two of everything, so he had let his friend have a complete outfit.

All d'Artagnan's wishes would have been fulfilled if it weren't for the fact that he saw Milady looming like a dark cloud on the horizon.

After breakfast, they agreed to meet that evening in Athos's quarters and settle the matter there.

D'Artagnan spent the day showing off his musketeer's uniform in every street of the camp.

That evening, at the appointed hour, the four friends met up. There were only three things left to decide:

What to write to Milady's brother;

What to write to the able person in Tours;

And which of the valets would carry the letters.

Each of them volunteered his own. Athos praised the discretion of Grimaud, who only spoke when his master unstitched his lips. Porthos boasted of the strength of Mousqueton, who was big enough to wipe the floor with four men of ordinary constitution; Aramis, confident of Bazin's tact, delivered a pompous eulogy in honour of his candidate. Finally, d'Artagnan had complete faith in the bravery of Planchet, and recalled how he had borne himself in the thorny matter at Boulogne.

These four virtues contested the prize for a long time, and gave rise to some magnificent perorations, which we will not report here lest they tax the reader's patience.

'Unfortunately,' said Athos, 'the one we send must have all four qualities combined.'

'But where can one find such a valet?'

'One can't,' said Athos. 'I know. So take Grimaud.'

'Take Mousqueton.'

'Take Bazin.'

'Take Planchet; Planchet is brave and clever. That's already two out of the four qualities.'

'Gentlemen,' said Aramis, 'the main thing is not to know which of our four valets is the discreetest, strongest, cleverest, or bravest – the main thing is to know which of them loves money the most.'

'What Aramis says is very sensible,' said Athos. 'One must

speculate on people's failings, not their virtues. Monsieur l'abbé, you are a great moralist!'

'Of course,' replied Aramis. 'For we need to be well served not only if we are to succeed, but also if we are not to fail, since failure will mean the head, not of the valets . . .'

'Not so loud, Aramis!' said Athos.

'You're right. Not of the valets,' Aramis went on, 'but of the master, and even the masters! Are our men devoted enough to risk their lives for us? No.'

'My faith,' said d'Artagnan, 'I'd almost vouch for Planchet.'

'Well then, my dear friend, add to his natural devotion a goodly sum of money, which will give him some independence, and then, instead of vouching for him once, vouch for him twice over.'

'Ah, good God, you'll be tricked all the same!' said Athos, who was an optimist about things and a pessimist about men. 'They'll promise everything to get the money, and on the way fear will stop them acting. Once they're caught, the screws will be turned. Once the screws are turned, they'll confess. What the devil, we're not children! To get to England,' Athos lowered his voice, 'one must cross the whole of France, which is riddled with the cardinal's spies and creatures. One must have a pass to board a ship. One must know English to ask the way to London. Indeed, I think it's a very difficult proposition.'

'Not at all,' said d'Artagnan, who was very anxious for the undertaking to go ahead. 'I think the opposite; that it's simple. Good grief, it goes without saying that if we write to Lord de Winter making extravagant claims about the horrors of the cardinal . . .'

'Not so loud!' said Athos.

'About intrigues and state secrets,' d'Artagnan went on, complying with the instruction, 'it goes without saying we'll all be broken on the wheel. But, for God's sake, don't forget, as you have said yourself, Athos, that we're writing to him on a family matter. That we're writing solely so that, as soon as she arrives in

London, he can make it impossible for Milady to harm us. I'll write him a letter more or less along the following lines . . .'

'Tell us,' said Aramis, assuming a critical expression in anticipation.

'My dear sir and good friend . . .'

'Ah, yes. "Good friend" to an Englishman,' interrupted Athos. 'What a beginning! Bravo, d'Artagnan! For that word alone, you'll be quartered rather than broken on the wheel.'

'Well, so be it. I'll just say, "My dear sir" then.'

'You could even say, "My lord",' remarked Athos, who observed proprieties punctiliously.

'"My lord, do you remember the little paddock for goats behind the Luxembourg?"'

'Good! Now it's the Luxembourg! They'll think it's an allusion to the queen mother. Very ingenious,' said Athos.

'Then we'll just put, "My lord, do you remember a certain little paddock where your life was spared?"'

'My dear d'Artagnan,' said Athos, 'you'll never be anything but a dismal writer. "Where your life was spared"? For shame, that's unworthy. One does not remind a man of honour of such services. A good deed recalled is an insult rendered.'

'Ah, my dear friend,' said d'Artagnan, 'you're unbearable! If I have to write with you censoring me, my faith, I give up.'

'And you're right to do so. Wield the musket and the sword, my dear friend, you perform gallantly in both those disciplines, but leave the pen to Monsieur l'abbé, that is his province.'

'Ah yes, very true,' said Porthos, 'give the pen to Aramis – he writes theses in Latin, no less.'

'Very well,' said d'Artagnan, 'word the note for us, Aramis. But, by our Holy Father the Pope, be concise, for I'll sift it afterwards, I warn you.'

'I'd like nothing better,' said Aramis, with that naive confidence every poet possesses. 'But first acquaint me with the facts. I've certainly heard, here and there, that his sister-in-law is a hussy. I even had proof of it listening to her conversation with the cardinal.'

'Holy heaven, not so loud!' said Athos.

'But,' Aramis went on, 'the particulars escape me.'

'Me too,' said Porthos.

D'Artagnan and Athos looked at one another for a time in silence. Finally Athos, having collected his thoughts, and grown even paler than usual, gave a sign of assent. D'Artagnan understood he had permission to speak.

'Well, here's what there is to say,' said d'Artagnan. '"My lord, your sister-in-law is a villainess, who wished to have you killed to obtain your inheritance. But she was unable to marry your brother, having already married in France, and having been . . ."'

D'Artagnan paused, as if trying to think of the word, and looked at Athos.

'"Driven away by her husband,"' said Athos.

'"Because she had been branded,"' d'Artagnan went on.

'Bah!' cried Porthos. 'It can't be! She wished to kill her brother-in-law?'

'Yes.'

'She was married?' asked Aramis.

'Yes.'

'And her husband saw she had a fleur-de-lys on her shoulder?' cried Porthos.

'Yes.'

These three 'yeses' had been pronounced by Athos, each in an increasingly desolate tone of voice.

'And who saw this fleur-de-lys?' asked Aramis.

'D'Artagnan and I – or rather, to observe chronology, I and d'Artagnan,' replied Athos.

'And this appalling creature's husband is still alive?' said Aramis.

'He's still alive.'

'You're sure?'

'I'm sure.'

There was a moment of frozen silence, as each of them was affected according to his own nature.

'This time,' said Athos, breaking the silence first, 'd'Artagnan has given us an excellent programme, and that's what we must write up first.'

'Hang it, you're right, Athos,' said Aramis, 'but the writing's a knotty business. The chancellor himself would struggle to compose an epistle of this consequence, and yet the chancellor draws up a very agreeable police report. No matter! Keep quiet, while I write.'

Aramis took the pen and thought for a few moments before starting to write eight or ten lines in a small, charming feminine hand. Then, in a soft, slow voice, as if every word had been scrupulously weighed, he read out the following:

> My lord,
>   The person who writes you these few lines had the
> honour to cross swords with you in a little paddock in Rue
> d'Enfer. As you have been kind enough on several
> subsequent occasions, to call yourself this person's friend,
> he owes it to you to acknowledge this friendship with a
> piece of good counsel. You have twice almost fallen victim
> to a close relative, whom you believe to be your heir, since
> you are unaware that, before contracting marriage in
> England, she had already married in France. But the third
> time – presently, that is – you may go to your death. Your
> relative left La Rochelle for England last night. Watch out
> for her arrival, for she has great and terrible plans. If you
> are determined to know what she is capable of, you may
> read her past on her left shoulder.

'Excellently done,' said Athos. 'You have the pen of a secretary of state, my dear Aramis. Lord de Winter will be on his guard now, if the warning reaches him, that is; and if it should fall into the hands of His Eminence himself, we shall not be compromised. But as the valet who is to go could make us believe he went to London when in fact he gets no further than

Châtelleraut, let's only give him half the money with the letter, promising him the other half in exchange for the reply. Have you got the diamond?' Athos went on.

'Better than that; I've got the money.'

And then d'Artagnan tossed the bag on the table. At the sound of the gold, Aramis looked up and Porthos started. Athos, for his part, remained impassive.

'How much is in that little bag?' he said.

'Seven thousand livres in twelve-franc louis.'

'Seven thousand livres!' cried Porthos. 'That puny little diamond was worth seven thousand livres?'

'It appears so,' said Athos, 'since here they are. I presume our friend d'Artagnan hasn't put in any of his own.'

'But, gentlemen,' said d'Artagnan, 'we haven't spared a thought for the queen in all this. Let's take a little care of the health of her dear Buckingham. It's the least we owe her.'

'That's right,' said Athos, 'but this concerns Aramis.'

'Well,' replied the latter, blushing, 'what must I do?'

'Why,' said Athos, 'it's quite simple: write a second letter for the able person who lives in Tours.'

Aramis took up the pen once more, set to thinking again, and then wrote the following lines, which he immediately submitted to his friends' approval:

My dear cousin . . .

'Ah!' said Athos, 'this clever person is a relative!'

'First cousin,' said Aramis.

'Cousin it is!'

Aramis went on:

My dear cousin, His Eminence the cardinal, whom God
preserve for the good fortune of France and the confusion
of the enemies of the realm, is on the verge of putting paid
to the rebellious heretics of La Rochelle. It is probable that

the support of the English fleet will not even arrive in sight of the place. I would even venture to say that I am certain the Duke of Buckingham will be prevented from leaving by some great event. His Eminence is the most illustrious politician of times past, times present, and in all likelihood of times to come. He would put out the sun, if the sun inconvenienced him. Pass on this happy news to your sister, my dear cousin. I dreamt that that cursed Englishman was dead. I cannot remember whether it was by sword or poison. The only thing of which I am certain is that I dreamt he was dead, and, as you know, my dreams never deceive me. Rest assured then that you will see me again soon.

'Excellent!' cried Athos, 'you are the king of poets. My dear Aramis, you speak like the Apocalypse and are as true as the Gospels. All you need now is the address to put on the letter.'

'Easily done,' said Aramis.

He folded the letter coquettishly, turned it over and wrote:

To Mademoiselle Marie Michon, seamstress, Tours.

The three friends looked at each other, laughing. He'd got them.

'Now,' said Aramis, 'you understand, gentlemen, no one but Bazin can take this letter to Tours; my cousin knows only Bazin and trusts only him. Anyone else would skew the affair. Besides, Bazin is ambitious and erudite. Bazin has read history, gentlemen; he knows that Sixtus the Fifth[1] became pope after tending pigs as a young man. Well then, as he plans to enter the Church at the same time as me, he does not despair of becoming pope in his turn, or at least cardinal. You understand that a man with such ambitions won't let himself be caught. Or, if he is caught, will undergo martyrdom sooner than talk.'

'Good, good,' said d'Artagnan. 'I give you Bazin with all my heart, but give me Planchet. Milady had him thrown out one day after seeing he got a good caning. Now, Planchet has a good memory and, you have my word, if he thought he could get his revenge, he would let himself be beaten to within an inch of his life sooner than give up. If your affairs in Tours are your affairs, Aramis, those in London are mine. I beg you therefore to choose Planchet, who in any case has already been to London with me, and knows how to say, "London, sir, if you please," and, "My master, Lord d'Artagnan". So you need not worry, he will make his way there and back.'

'In that case,' said Athos, 'Planchet must be given seven hundred livres for the journey there and seven hundred for the journey back, and Bazin three hundred livres for the journey there and three hundred for the journey back. That will bring the balance down to five thousand livres. We will each take a thousand to use as we see fit, and we'll leave a fund of a thousand which Monsieur l'abbé will keep for exceptional circumstances or our common needs. Does that suit you all?'

'My dear Athos,' said Aramis, 'you speak like Nestor, who, as is well known, was the wisest of the Greeks.'

'Then it's settled,' said Athos. 'Planchet and Bazin will set off. All in all, I'm not sorry to hang on to Grimaud: he's used to my ways and I value that. Yesterday must have disturbed him enough as it is; this journey would be the death of him.'

Planchet was sent for and given his instructions. He had been forewarned by d'Artagnan, who had spoken first of the glory, then of the money, then of the danger the undertaking entailed.

'I'll carry the letter in the lining of my coat,' said Planchet, 'and swallow it if they catch me.'

'But then you won't be able to carry out your mission,' said d'Artagnan.

'You can give me a copy tonight and I'll know it by heart tomorrow.'

D'Artagnan looked at his friends, as if to say, 'Well, what did I promise you?'

'Now,' he went on, addressing Planchet, 'you have eight days to reach Lord de Winter, and eight days to come back here, so sixteen days in all. If there's no sign of you by eight o'clock in the evening on the sixteenth day after your departure, then you'll get no money, even if you arrive at five past eight.'

'Well then, sir,' said Planchet, 'buy me a watch.'

'Take this one,' said Athos, giving him his own with careless generosity, 'and be a brave lad. Remember that if you talk, if you jabber, if you dawdle, you will get your master's throat cut, and he has such confidence in your loyalty that he has vouched for you to us. But also remember that if, through your fault, any misfortune befalls d'Artagnan, I will find you wherever you are and slit open your belly.'

'Oh, sir!' said Planchet, humiliated by the suspicion, and above all, terrified by the musketeer's calm air.

'And I,' said Porthos, rolling his big eyes, 'remember that I will flay you alive.'

'Ah, sir!'

'And I,' said Aramis, in his soft, melodious voice, 'remember that I will roast you over a slow fire like a savage.'

'Ah, sir!'

Planchet started crying – we won't presume to say whether out of terror because of the threats made against him, or emotion at seeing four friends so devoted to one another.

D'Artagnan took his hand and embraced him.

'You see, Planchet,' he said to him, 'these gentlemen have said all this to you out of affection for me, but at heart they love you.'

'Ah, sir!' said Planchet. 'Either I'll succeed, or they'll cut me in quarters. If they cut me in quarters, you may be certain that not one part of me will talk.'

It was decided that Planchet would leave the next morning, at eight o'clock, so that, as he'd said, he could learn the letter by heart overnight. He gained exactly twelve hours by this, as he was to return on the sixteenth day, by eight o'clock in the evening.

The next morning, just as he was about to mount his horse,

d'Artagnan, who at heart had a fondness for the duke, drew Planchet to one side.

'Listen,' he said to him, 'when you've given the letter to Lord de Winter and he's read it, tell him, "Watch over His Grace Lord Buckingham; they want to assassinate him." But this is secret, you realise, Planchet. It is so serious and so important, that I wouldn't even confess to my friends that I had confided it in you, and I wouldn't write it down for you for a captain's commission.'

'Don't worry, sir,' said Planchet, 'you'll see you can depend on me.'

And then, mounted on an excellent horse, which he would have to give up twenty leagues thence to take the post-coach, Planchet sped off at a gallop, somewhat heavy-hearted at the triple promise the musketeers had made him, but otherwise in the best spirits in the world.

Bazin set off for Tours the following morning, with eight days to perform his mission.

While they were both away, the four friends, understandably enough, kept their eyes peeled, their noses to the wind, and their ears pricked. Their days were spent trying to catch the rumours in camp, studying the cardinal's demeanour and nosing out any couriers that arrived. More than once they were seized by uncontrollable trembling on being summoned for some unexpected duty. Besides, they had to be on the lookout for their own safety. Milady was a ghost, who, once she'd appeared to someone, never let him sleep peacefully again.

On the morning of the eighth day, Bazin, fresh as ever, smiling his usual smile, came into the Parpaillot wine shop as the four friends were having breakfast, and said, in the agreed code, 'Monsieur Aramis, here is your cousin's reply.'

The four friends exchanged a joyful glance. Half the job was done – although only the easier and shorter half, it's true.

Blushing in spite of himself, Aramis took the letter, which was poorly spelled and written in a crude hand.

'Good God!' he cried, laughing, 'I truly despair of her. This poor Michon will never write like Monsieur de Voiture.'

'Was doss id mean, dis boor Migeon?' asked the Swiss guard, who was chatting with friends when the letter arrived.

'Oh, my God, less than nothing,' said Aramis. 'A charming little seamstress I was very much in love with, and whom I asked for a few lines in her own hand by way of a souvenir.'

'Gott's firtue!' said the Swiss guard. 'If die iss as grate a leddy as her wrrriting, du are a lucky mensch, kamerade!'

Aramis read the letter and passed it to Athos.

'See what she writes to me, Athos,' he said.

Athos glanced at the epistle, and then, to remove any suspicions that might have arisen, read it aloud:

My dear cousin,
    My sister and I are very good at parsing dreams, and we're even terribly afraid of them. But of yours it may be said, I hope, that every dream is a delusion. Farewell! Be well, and see that we hear from you now and then.
    Aglaé Michon[2].

'And what dream is she talking about?' asked the dragoon, who had come over during the reading.

'Yess, vat tream?' said the Swiss guard.

'Oh, by God,' said Aramis, 'it's quite simple: a dream I had that I told her.'

'Ach yess, by Gott, it's ganz simple to tell fun's treams, aber I nefer tream.'

'You're very fortunate,' said Athos, standing up. 'I would very much like to be able to say as much myself.'

'Nefer!' said the Swiss guard, delighted that a man such as Athos should envy him anything. 'Nefer! Nefer!'

D'Artagnan, seeing Athos stand up, did the same, took his arm, and went out.

Porthos and Aramis stayed to face the gibes of the dragoon and the Swiss guard.

As for Bazin, he went to sleep on a bundle of hay. And as he had more imagination than the Swiss guard, he dreamt that Monsieur Aramis had been made pope and was placing a cardinal's hat on his head.

But, as we've said, Bazin's safe return had only alleviated part of the anxiety goading the four friends. Days spent waiting are always long, and d'Artagnan in particular would have bet there were now forty-eight hours in a day. He forgot the inevitable delays of sailing. He exaggerated Milady's power, endowing that woman, who seemed like a demon to him, with supernatural helpers in her image. At the least noise, he imagined men were coming to arrest him, or bringing Planchet to confront him and his friends. Moreover, his confidence in the worthy Picard, once so great, declined every day. His anxiety was so extreme that it affected Porthos and Aramis. Only Athos remained impassive, as if there were no danger stirring around him and he was breathing his daily air.

On the sixteenth day above all, these signs of agitation were so acute in d'Artagnan and his two friends that they could not stay still, but wandered like ghosts along the road by which Planchet was to return.

'Really,' Athos told them, 'you must be children, not men, if a woman can put such fear into you. What can happen, after all? They can put us in prison? Well, then they can get us out of prison too, as they got Madame Bonacieux out. They can behead us? Every day in the trenches we merrily expose ourselves to far worse, for a cannonball can break your leg, and I'm certain a surgeon would cause you more pain cutting off your thigh than the hangman would cutting off your head. So keep calm. In two hours, or four, or six at the latest, Planchet will be here. He promised he would, and I personally have great faith in any promise Planchet may make – he strikes me as a very brave lad.'

'But what if he doesn't come?' said d'Artagnan.

'Well, if he doesn't come, it means he's been delayed, that's all. He may have fallen from his horse, he may have gone head first off a bridge, he may have ridden so fast he's caught pneumonia.

Come, gentlemen, let's make some allowance for accidents. Life is a rosary of small tribulations, and the philosopher tells its beads with a laugh. Be philosophers like me, gentlemen. Sit down and let's drink. Nothing makes the future so rose-tinted as looking at it through a glass of Chambertin.'

'That's all very well,' replied d'Artagnan. 'But I'm tired, every time I drink a cool glass, of having to worry whether it's come from Milady's cellar.'

'You're very hard to please,' said Athos. 'Such a beautiful woman!'

'Such a branded woman!' said Porthos with his booming laugh.

Athos started, ran a hand over his forehead to wipe away the sweat, and leapt up in his turn with a nervous reflex that he couldn't control.

Nevertheless the day wore on, and evening slowly, but finally, arrived. The taverns filled with customers. Athos, who had pocketed his share of the diamond, didn't stir from the Parpaillot. He had found a drinking partner worthy of himself in Monsieur de Busigny, who, moreover, had laid on a magnificent dinner for them. He and Monsieur de Busigny were as usual playing cards together, when it struck seven. They heard the patrols passing on their way to reinforce the guard. At half-past seven, the tattoo[3] was sounded.

'We're lost,' d'Artagnan whispered in Athos's ear.

'You mean we've lost,' Athos said calmly, taking four pistoles out of his pocket and tossing them on the table. 'Come, gentlemen, they're sounding the tattoo, let's go to bed.'

And then Athos left the Parpaillot, followed by d'Artagnan. Aramis came behind, giving his arm to Porthos. Aramis mumbled verses, and from time to time, Porthos pulled some hairs from his moustache in despair.

But then suddenly a shadow emerged out of the darkness. D'Artagnan recognised its outline, and then a very familiar voice said to him, 'Sir, I've brought you your cloak, it's cool this evening.'

'Planchet!' cried d'Artagnan, drunk with joy.

'Planchet!' repeated Porthos and Aramis.

'Why, yes, it's Planchet,' said Athos. 'What's surprising about that? He had promised to be back by eight o'clock and it's now just striking the hour. Bravo, Planchet, you are a lad of your word, and if you ever leave your master, I'll keep a place for you in my service.'

'Oh, no, never!' said Planchet. 'I'll never leave Monsieur d'Artagnan.'

As he said this, d'Artagnan felt Planchet slip a note into his hand.

D'Artagnan longed to embrace Planchet on his return as he had done on his departure, but he was afraid such an effusive gesture to his valet in the middle of the street might strike a passer-by as extraordinary, and so he restrained himself.

'I've got the note,' he said to Athos and his friends.

'Good,' said Athos. 'Let's go to our quarters and read it.'

The note burned d'Artagnan's hand. He wanted to walk faster, but Athos took his arm and linked it with his, so the young man was compelled to fall into step with his friend.

Finally they entered the tent, lit a lamp, and while Planchet stood at the door so the four friends would not be taken by surprise, d'Artagnan broke the seal with a trembling hand and opened the intensely awaited letter.

It contained half a line in an eminently British hand and of an eminently Spartan brevity.

Thank you, be easy.

Athos took the letter from d'Artagnan's hands, touched it to the lamp so it caught fire, and didn't let go of it until it was reduced to ashes.

Then, calling Planchet, he said, 'Now, my lad, you can claim your seven hundred livres. You weren't running much of a risk with a note like that, though.'

'I still thought of a lot of ways to keep it safe,' said Planchet.

'Well, then,' said d'Artagnan, 'tell us about them.'

'Oh, it's a long story, sir.'

'You're right, Planchet,' said Athos. 'Besides, they've sounded the tattoo and we'll attract attention if we burn our light longer than the others.'

'Very well,' said d'Artagnan, 'let's go to bed. Have a good night's sleep, Planchet!'

'My faith, sir, it will be my first in sixteen days!'

'Mine too!' said d'Artagnan.

'Mine too!' repeated Porthos.

'Mine too!' repeated Aramis.

'Well, do you want me to admit the truth? And mine too!' said Athos.

XLIX

FATALITY

MEANWHILE MILADY, DRUNK WITH FURY, roaring on the deck of the ship as though they had taken a lioness aboard, had been tempted to throw herself in the sea to swim back to shore. She couldn't countenance the thought that, having been insulted by d'Artagnan and threatened by Athos, she was leaving France without avenging herself on them. The thought of this had soon become so intolerable that, at terrible risk to herself, she had begged the captain to put her ashore. But the captain, anxious to escape the false position he was in, caught between the French and English cruisers like a bat between the rats and the birds, was in great haste to get back to England. He stubbornly refused to accede to what he considered was a woman's caprice, instead promising his passenger, whom the cardinal had especially commended to him, to put her ashore, if the sea and the French permitted, at one of the ports of Brittany, either Lorient or Brest. But the wind was adverse, the sea was rough and the ship constantly had to tack about and beat to windward. It was only on the ninth day after leaving the Charente that Milady, ashen from her tribulations and rage, saw the bluish coast of Finisterre.

She estimated she would need at least three days to cross that corner of France and reach the cardinal. Add a day for landing, that made four. Add those four days to the nine others – that was thirteen days lost – thirteen days in which so much of importance could have happened in London. Besides, she thought, the cardinal would doubtless be furious at her return, and thus disposed to listen to the complaints brought against her sooner than the accusations she would bring against others. So she let Lorient and Brest pass without protesting to the captain, and he, for his part, took every care not to alert her to their presence. Milady thus continued on her way, and the very day Planchet embarked at Portsmouth for France, His Eminence's messenger made her triumphant entrance into the port.

The whole town was in an extraordinary fever of activity. Four large ships, newly built, had just been launched. Covered in gold, glittering with diamonds and precious stones, as was his habit, his hat adorned with a white feather that fell to his shoulder, Buckingham was to be seen standing on the jetty, surrounded by a staff almost as resplendent as himself.

It was one of those beautiful, rare winter days when England remembers that there is such a thing as the sun. Pale, but still magnificent, that star was sinking on the horizon, purpling the sky and the sea alike with bands of fire, casting a last ray of sunshine on the towers and old houses of the town, and making the windows glow like a reflected conflagration. Inhaling the sea air, which was fresher and headier with the approach of land, as she contemplated the full might of the preparations she had been ordered to destroy, the full might of the army that she – she, a woman – was to fight single handedly with just a few bags of gold, Milady compared herself in her mind to Judith, the terrible Jewess, when she stole into the camp of the Assyrians and saw the enormous mass of chariots, horses, men and arms that a sweep of her hand was to scatter like a cloud of smoke.

They entered the roads, but as they were preparing to drop anchor, a small, heavily armed cutter approached the merchant vessel, professing to be the coastguard, and lowered its longboat, which made for their boarding ladder. The longboat contained an officer, a bosun's mate and eight oarsmen. Only the officer came on board, where he was received with all the deference a uniform inspires.

The officer conversed with the skipper for a few moments, showed him a letter of which he was the bearer, and then the merchant captain ordered everyone aboard the vessel, sailors and passengers alike, to assemble on deck.

When this sort of summons had been issued, the officer inquired loudly about the brig's port of departure, its course, the stops it had made, and the captain replied without hesitation or difficulty to all his questions. Then the officer began to inspect, one by one, all those on deck. Stopping at Milady, he examined her with great care, but did not address a word to her.

He went back to captain, spoke with him further, and then, as if the boat had to obey him from now on, gave orders for a manoeuvre that the crew carried out immediately. After which the vessel set off again, still escorted by the little cutter sailing alongside, threatening its flank with the mouths of its six cannons, while the longboat followed in its wake, a faint speck next to the ship's enormous mass.

During the officer's examination of her, Milady, as might be imagined, had for her part devoured him with her gaze. But, however accustomed this woman with her eyes of flame was to reading the hearts of those whose secrets she needed to divine, this time she beheld a face of such impassivity that her investigation afforded her no insights. The officer who had stopped in front of her and silently studied her with such care could have been around twenty-five or twenty-six. He had a white face with light blue, slightly deep-set eyes. His thin, finely etched mouth remained motionless in its classic lines. His prominent, vigorous chin denoted that strength of will, which, in the common British type, ordinarily amounts to no more than obstinacy. A slightly receding forehead, of a sort common to poets, enthusiasts and soldiers, was imperfectly shaded by short, thinning hair, which, like the beard covering the lower part of his face, was a handsome deep chestnut colour.

Night had already fallen by the time they came into port. Fog deepened the darkness still further, forming a ring round the jetties' beacons and lanterns like the ring that encircles the moon when rain is imminent. The air was sad, damp and cold.

For all her strength of will, Milady felt herself shiver involuntarily.

The officer had Milady's bags identified and then transferred to the longboat, and, once this operation was completed, invited her to climb down to the vessel by offering her his hand.

Milady looked at the man and hesitated.

'Who are you, sir,' she asked, 'who are so kind as to pay me such particular attention?'

'That should be apparent from my uniform, madam. I am an officer in the English navy,' replied the young man.

'Is it customary, though, for the officers of the English navy to put themselves at the disposal of their countrywomen when they come into a British port, and carry their gallantry so far as to bring them ashore?'

'Yes, my lady, it is customary, not as a matter of gallantry but prudence, that in times of war foreigners are conducted to a designated hotel where they may remain under government observation until full inquiries have been made about them.'

These words were pronounced with the most meticulous politeness and the most perfect composure, and yet they did not have the wherewithal to convince Milady.

'But I am not a foreigner, sir,' she said, in as pure an accent as ever rang out from Portsmouth to Manchester, 'My name is Lady Clarick, and this precaution . . .'

'This precaution applies to everyone, my lady, and it will serve no purpose for you to try to avoid it.'

'Then I will follow you, sir.'

And then, accepting the officer's hand, she began to climb down the ladder, at the bottom of which the longboat was waiting. The officer followed her. A large cloak was spread out in the stern. The officer bade her sit on it and sat next to her.

'Pull away,' he said to the sailors.

The eight oars fell back into the water with a single splash, took a single stroke, and the longboat seemed to fly over the surface of the water.

Five minutes later they touched land.

The officer jumped on to the quay and offered Milady his hand.

A carriage was waiting.

'Is this carriage for us?' asked Milady.

'Yes, madam,' replied the officer.

'The hotel is far, then?'

'At the other end of town.'

'Let us be on our way,' said Milady, and then climbed resolutely into the carriage.

The officer saw to it that the bags were carefully stowed behind the carriage, and, once this was done, took his place next to Milady and shut the door.

In a flash, without any order being given and without needing to be told his destination, the coachman set off at a gallop, plunging into the streets of the town.

Such a strange reception inevitably supplied Milady with ample matter for reflection. Seeing the young officer did not appear at all inclined to get into conversation, she leaned back in a corner of the carriage and reviewed in turn all the suppositions that suggested themselves to her mind.

After a quarter of an hour had passed, however, surprised at the length of their journey, she leant over to the carriage door to see where she was being taken. There were no more houses to be seen; trees loomed in the darkness like great black phantoms chasing one another.

Milady shuddered.

'But we've left the town, sir,' she said.

The young officer remained silent.

'I warn you, sir – I will go no further unless you tell me where you are taking me!'

Her threat obtained no response.

'Oh, this is too much!' cried Milady. 'Help! Help!'

No voice answered hers; the carriage sped along, the officer seemingly like a statue.

Milady turned on him with one of those terrible expressions peculiar to her face that so rarely failed to achieve their effect. Anger made her eyes flash in the gloom.

The young man remained impassive.

Milady tried to open the door to throw herself out.

'Careful, madam,' the young man said coldly, 'you'll kill yourself if you jump.'

Milady sat back down, foaming with rage. Leaning over, the officer looked at her in his turn and seemed surprised to see that face, formerly so beautiful, was now so contorted with rage as to be almost hideous. The guileful creature understood she was damaging her interests by thus exposing her soul. She composed her features and said in a keening voice, 'In heaven's name, sir, tell me whether it's to you, or to your government, or to an enemy that I should impute this violence that is being inflicted on me?'

'No violence is being inflicted on you, madam. The events you are experiencing are the result of a very simple precaution we are obliged to take with everyone landing in England.'

'So you don't know me, sir?'

'It is the first time I have had the honour of seeing you.'

'And, on your honour, you have no cause to hate me?'

'None, I swear.'

There was so much serenity and coolness, even gentleness, in the young man's voice that Milady was reassured.

At last, after travelling for almost an hour, the carriage stopped at an iron gate that sealed off a sunken road leading to a dour, massive, isolated castle. As the carriage wheels rolled through fine sand, Milady heard a great roaring, which she recognised as the sound of the sea breaking on a sheer coast.

The carriage passed under two archways, and stopped finally in a dark, square courtyard. Almost immediately the door opened, the young man jumped lightly down and offered his hand to Milady, who leant on it and, with a fair deal of composure, stepped out in her turn.

'Yet the fact remains,' said Milady, looking round her and then, with the most gracious smile, bringing her gaze back to the young officer, 'that I am a prisoner. But it won't be for long, I'm sure,' she added. 'My conscience and your politeness, sir, stand guarantee for that.'

Flattering though the compliment was, the officer didn't reply, but, drawing from his belt a little silver whistle like those used by bosun's mates on men-of-war, he blew three times, with three different modulations. Several men appeared, unharnessed the steaming horses and took the carriage into a coach house.

Then, with the same calm politeness, the officer invited his prisoner to enter the house. And she, with the same smiling face, took his arm and went in with him under a low, arched doorway, which, through a vaulted chamber which was only lit at the back, led to a stone staircase winding around the rib of the stone vault. They stopped at a massive door, which, after the insertion into the lock of a key the young man carried with him, swung heavily on its hinges and revealed the room intended for Milady.

At a glance, the prisoner took in the chamber in its every last detail.

It was a room whose furnishings were at once very clean for a prison and very severe for the residence of a free man. The bars on the windows and the bolts on the outside of the door, however, decided the case in favour of a prison.

For a moment, all this creature's inner fortitude, tempered

though it was in the most vigorous of springs, failed her. She fell into an armchair, crossed her arms and hung her head, and expected to see a judge enter in at any moment to interrogate her.

But no one came in except two or three marines who brought the trunks and boxes, put them in a corner, and left without a word.

The officer presided over all these details with the calmness Milady had observed in him from the start, saying not a word himself but enforcing his orders with a movement of the hand or a particular note of his whistle.

It was as though spoken language either did not exist or had become obsolete between this man and his inferiors.

Finally Milady could endure it no longer and broke the silence.

'In heaven's name, sir!' she cried, 'what does all this mean? Resolve my doubts! I have sufficient courage to face any danger I can foresee, any misfortune I can comprehend. Where am I? why am I here? If I am free, why these bars and these doors? If I am a prisoner, what crime have I committed?'

'You are in the apartment intended for you, madam. I was given orders to take charge of you at sea and conduct you to this castle. I believe I have carried out those orders not only with all the rigour of a soldier, but also with all the courtesy of a gentleman. There ends, at least for the present, the office I had to perform regarding you. The rest is another person's concern.'

'And this other person – who is he?' asked Milady. 'Can you not tell me his name . . . ?'

At that moment, a great clinking of spurs was heard on the stairs. Some voices passed and died away, and then solitary footsteps could be heard approaching the door.

'Here is that person now, madam,' said the officer, stepping to one side and assuming an attitude of submission and respect.

As he did so, the door opened and a man appeared on the threshold.

He was without a hat, had a sword at his side, and, fingers working, was crumpling a handkerchief in his hand.

Milady thought she recognised this shadow in the shadows. She leant on the arm of the chair with one hand and thrust her head forward, as if going to meet a certainty.

Then the stranger slowly stepped forward. And as he drew nearer, advancing into the circle of light thrown by the lamp, Milady involuntarily shrank back.

At last, when her doubts had been resolved, she cried out in utter amazement, 'What? My brother? Is it you?'

'Yes, fair lady!' replied Lord de Winter, with a half-courteous, half-ironic bow. 'In person.'

'Why, then, this castle . . . ?'

'Is mine.'

'This room?'

'Is yours.'

'So I'm your prisoner?'

'All but.'

'But this is an atrocious abuse of power!'

'No high-flown words, now; let's just sit down and have a quiet chat, as befits a brother and sister.'

Then, turning to the door and seeing that the young officer was waiting for his final orders, he said, 'Very good, thank you. Now, leave us, Mr Felton.'

L

A CHAT BETWEEN A BROTHER AND SISTER

WHILE LORD DE WINTER was closing the door, opening a blind, and moving a chair close to his sister-in-law's armchair, Milady musingly gazed into the depths of possibility and contemplated the whole plot, which she had not even been able to glimpse as long as she was ignorant of the hands into which she had fallen. She knew her brother-in-law to be a nobleman of old family, a keen huntsman, an intrepid gambler, and forward with women, but with lesser powers than hers as far as intrigues were concerned. How then had he been able to find out she was coming and have her seized? And why was he keeping her?

Athos had certainly made some remarks that proved her conversation with the cardinal had reached other ears, but she could not entertain the possibility that he could have so promptly and boldly laid a countermine.

She was more afraid that her previous undertakings in England had been discovered. Buckingham might have guessed that it was she who had cut off the diamond tags, and avenged himself for that petty betrayal. But Buckingham was incapable of committing any excesses against a woman, especially if that woman were considered to have acted from a feeling of jealousy.

This supposition struck her as the most probable. She had the impression they wanted to be revenged for what lay in the past, not forestall something that lay in the future. But, in any case, she congratulated herself on having fallen into the hands of her brother-in-law, of whom she counted on making short work, rather than those of a direct and intelligent enemy.

'Yes, let's have a chat, brother,' she said, in a light-hearted sort of way, determined as she was to enlighten herself from their conversation – no matter how much Lord de Winter might dissimulate – sufficiently to guide her conduct henceforth.

'So, you decided to come back to England,' said Lord de Winter, 'despite the resolve you so often expressed to me in Paris never to set foot on British soil again?'

Milady replied to his question with another question.

'First,' she said, 'tell me how you managed to have me watched so closely that you were informed beforehand not only of my arrival, but also of the day, the hour, and the port I was arriving in.'

Lord de Winter adopted the same tactic as Milady, thinking that, if his sister-in-law was using it, it was bound to be the right one.

'But, tell me yourself, my dear sister,' he said, 'why you have come to England.'

'Why, I have come to see you,' said Milady, not knowing how much this answer exacerbated the suspicions aroused in her brother-in-law's mind by d'Artagnan's letter, and only wishing through a lie to secure the goodwill of her listener.

'Ah, to see me?' Lord de Winter said slyly.

'Of course, to see you. What is there that is surprising about that?'

'And you had no other object in coming to England than to see me?'

'No.'

'So it was just for me that you went to the trouble of crossing the Channel?'

'Just for you.'

'Damn, such affection, sister!'

'But aren't I your closest relative?' asked Milady, in a tone of the most touching naivety.

'And even my sole heir, isn't that so?' Lord de Winter said in his turn, fixing his eyes on Milady's.

Great as her powers of self-control were, Milady couldn't help starting, and since, in pronouncing these last words, Lord de Winter had put his hand on his sister's arm, this start did not escape him.

The hit was direct and deep. The first thought that came to Milady's mind was that she had been betrayed by Kitty, that she had told the baron of her self-interested aversion to him, some signs of which she had rashly let slip in her maid's presence. She remembered also her furious and reckless tirade against d'Artagnan, after he had spared her brother-in-law's life.

'I don't understand, my lord,' she said, to gain time and to get her adversary to speak. 'What do you mean? Is there some unknown significance concealed in your words?'

'Oh, my God, no,' said Lord de Winter, with apparent amiability. 'You have a wish to see me, and you come to England. I learn of that wish, or rather I suspect it, and to spare you all the inconvenience of a nocturnal arrival in port, all the fatigues of landing, I send one of my officers to meet you, I put a carriage at your disposal and he brings you here to this castle, of which I am the governor, where I come every day, and where, to satisfy our mutual desire to see one another, I have had a room prepared for you. What is there in all I've just said that is more surprising than what you have said to me?'

'No, what surprises me is that you were informed of my arrival.'

'But nothing could be simpler, my dear sister. Didn't you see that the captain of your little vessel, when he entered the roads, sent on ahead a little boat carrying his ship's log and the register of his crew so that he might obtain permission to enter port? I am commandant of the port, the book was brought to me, and I recognised your name. My heart told me what your mouth has just confided in me, namely, your purpose in exposing yourself to the dangers of a sea that is so perilous, or at least, so fatiguing, at present, and I sent my cutter to meet you. The rest you know.'

Realising Lord de Winter was lying, Milady was all the more alarmed.

'Brother,' she went on, 'wasn't that my Lord Buckingham I saw on the jetty as I arrived this evening?'

'In person. Ah, I understand why the sight of him struck you,' said Lord de Winter. 'You come from a country where they must pay him a great deal of mind, and I know his arming against France greatly preoccupies your friend the cardinal.'

'My friend the cardinal?' cried Milady, seeing that, on this point, as on the other, Lord de Winter appeared very well informed.

'Isn't he your friend, then?' the baron said carelessly. 'Ah, forgive me, I thought he was. But we will come back to my lord the duke later. Let us not discard the sentimental turn the conversation had taken. You came, you were saying, to see me?'

'Yes.'

'Well, and I replied that your wishes would be answered and that we would see each other every day.'

'Must I stay here forever, then?' asked Milady, a note of fear in her voice.

'Do you find your accommodation unsatisfactory, sister? Ask for whatever you need, and I will hasten to provide it for you.'

'But I don't have my women, my servants . . .'

'And you shall have all that, madam. Tell me how your first husband set up your household, and, although I am only your brother-in-law, I will set this one up in the same style.'

'My first husband!' cried Milady, staring at Lord de Winter with scared eyes.

'Yes, your French husband; I'm not speaking of my brother. But if you've forgotten the details, as he's still alive, I could write to him and he will send me all the particulars.'

Beads of cold sweat stood out on Milady's forehead.

'You're joking,' she said in a hollow voice.

'Do I look as if I am?' asked the baron, standing up and taking a step back.

'Or, rather, you're insulting me,' she went on, pressing hard on the arms of her chair with her clenched hands and raising herself on her wrists.

'I, insult you?' Lord de Winter said contemptuously. 'Really, madam, do you think that's possible?'

'Indeed, sir,' said Milady, 'you are either drunk or mad. Go away and send me a woman.'

'Women are very indiscreet, sister! Couldn't I serve as your lady's maid? That way all our secrets could stay in the family.'

'Insolent wretch!' cried Milady, and, as if worked by a spring, she leapt at the baron, who awaited her impassively, but with one hand on the hilt of his sword.

'Hey, hey!' he said, 'I know you have a habit of killing people, but I will defend myself, I warn you, even against you.'

'Oh, you're right,' said Milady, 'and you do look enough of a coward to raise your hand against a woman.'

'Perhaps. Besides, I'll have my excuse. I don't imagine mine would be the first man's hand to be laid on you.'

And then, with a slow, accusatory gesture, the baron pointed to Milady's left shoulder, almost touching it with his finger.

Milady let out a dull roar and backed away to the corner of the room, like a panther winding itself up to spring.

'Oh, roar as much as you please,' cried Lord de Winter, 'but don't try to bite, for, I warn you, things will turn bad for you. There are no lawyers here to settle successions in advance; there's no knight errant who will seek to pick a quarrel with me for the sake of the fair lady I hold prisoner. But I have judges on hand who will deal with a woman shameless enough to slip bigamously into my older brother Lord de Winter's bed – and those judges, I warn you, will send you to an executioner who will give you two matching shoulders.'

Milady's eyes flashed forth such lightning that, despite being a man armed against an unarmed woman, Lord de Winter felt the chill of fear penetrate to the depths of his heart. Nonetheless, he went on, with mounting fury, 'Yes, I understand, after my brother's inheritance, you would find it agreeable to have mine. But, know this in advance, you can kill me or have me killed, but I have taken my precautions: not a penny of what I own will come into your hands. Aren't you rich enough already, with almost a million to your name? Can't you stop yourself on your fatal course, if, that is, you don't perpetrate evil just for the infinite and ultimate pleasure of so doing? Ah, I tell you, if my brother's memory weren't sacred to me, you would go and rot in some dungeon of the State, or satiate the curiosity of the sailors at Tyburn. I will keep silent, though. But you must endure your captivity peaceably. In two or three weeks, I am leaving for La Rochelle with the army. On the eve of my departure, a ship will come for you, and I will watch it leave to convey you to our southern colonies. And, have no fear, I will furnish you with a companion who will blow your brains out at your first attempt to return to England or the continent.'

Milady listened with intense attention, her burning eyes huge.

'Yes, but for the moment,' went on Lord de Winter, 'you will remain in this castle. The walls are thick, the doors strong, the bars solid. Besides, there is a sheer drop below your window to the sea. My ship's crew, who are devoted to me for life and death, are standing guard around this room and watching every passage to the courtyard. If you reached the courtyard, you'd still have three iron gates to surmount. My orders are precise: any step, any gesture, any word that smacks of an attempt to escape and they will open fire on you. If they kill you, English justice will, I trust, be somewhat obliged to me for sparing her the trouble. Ah, your features are relaxing, your face is regaining its self-assurance. A fortnight, three weeks, you say – bah, I have an inventive mind; some idea is bound to have come to me by then. I have an infernal mind, and I will find some victim. A fortnight from now, you tell yourself, I'll be out of here. Ah, go on, try it!'

Seeing her thoughts read, Milady dug her nails into her flesh to master any impulse that might make her expression suggest anything but anguish.

Lord de Winter went on:

'The officer who has sole command here when I am away – you have seen him, so you will already have got to know him – is good at following orders. You'll have seen that, for, knowing you, you didn't come from Portsmouth without trying to make him talk. What's your verdict? Could a marble statue be more impassive and mute? You have already tried your powers of seduction on many men, and unfortunately you have always succeeded, but try them on this one, by God! If you prevail, I'll declare you the devil himself!'

He went to the door and flung it open.

'Call Mr Felton,' he said. 'Wait another moment, and I'll introduce you to him.'

A strange silence settled over these two individuals, during which the sound of slow, regular footsteps was heard approaching. Soon, in the shadows of the corridor, a human form took shape, and the young lieutenant, with whom we have already become acquainted, stopped on the threshold, awaiting the baron's orders.

'Come in, my dear John,' said Lord de Winter, 'come in and close the door.'

The young officer came in.

'Now,' said the baron, 'look at this woman. She is young, she is beautiful, she has every earthly power of seduction – yes, but she is a monster who, by the age of twenty-five, has been guilty of as many crimes as you could spend a year reading about in our courts's archives. Her voice prepossesses you in her favour, her beauty is a lure for her victims, her body even makes good on her promises – we must give her credit for that. She will try to seduce you; she may even try to kill you. I raised you from poverty, Felton, I had you made lieutenant, I saved your life once, you know on what occasion. I am not only your protector but your friend, not only a benefactor but a father. This woman has come back to England to conspire against my life, and now I have this serpent in my hands. And so I've sent for you to say: friend Felton, John, my child, protect me, and, above all, protect yourself against this woman. Swear on your salvation to keep her for the punishment she deserves. John Felton, I trust in your word; John Felton, I believe in your loyalty.'

'My lord,' said the young officer, imbuing his pure gaze with all the hatred he could find in his heart, 'my lord, I swear that your wishes will be carried out.'

Milady suffered this gaze like a resigned victim. It was impossible to envisage a more submissive and gentle expression than that which then reigned over her beautiful face. Lord de Winter himself could hardly recognise the tigress he was preparing to fight moments before.

'She is never to leave this room, you understand, John,' the baron went on. 'She is to correspond with no one, she is only to speak with you, if, that is, you wish to do her the honour of addressing her.'

'Enough, my lord, I have sworn.'

'And now, madam, try to make your peace with God, for you have been judged by men.'

Milady bowed her head as if crushed by this judgement. Lord de Winter left, gesturing to Felton, who went out after him and shut the door.

A moment later there sounded in the corridor the heavy tread of a marine, who was keeping guard, with his axe in his belt and his musket in his hand.

Milady remained in the same position for a few minutes, thinking she might be being observed through the lock. Then she slowly raised her head, which had regained a fearsome expression of threat and defiance, ran to listen at the door, looked out of the window, and then, coming back to bury herself in a huge armchair, fell to thinking.

LI
THE OFFICER

THE CARDINAL, MEANWHILE, WAS WAITING for news from England, but the only news that came was either exasperating or ominous.

However well invested La Rochelle might be and, however certain success might seem, thanks to the precautions that had been taken and, above all, to the dyke that prevented any ship from reaching the besieged city, the blockade could still go on for a long time. And that was a great affront to the king's arms and a great annoyance to the cardinal, who, it was true, no longer had to set Louis XIII at loggerheads with Anne of Austria – that had been done – but to reconcile Monsieur de Bassompierre, who was at loggerheads with the Duke d'Angoulême.

As for Monsieur, who had begun the siege, he left the job of finishing it to the cardinal.

For its part, despite the incredible perseverance of its mayor, the town had attempted a sort of mutiny to surrender. And the mayor had had the mutineers hanged. These executions calmed down the unruliest, who then decided to let themselves die of hunger. Such a death at least seemed slower and less inexorable than dying by strangulation.

On their side, the besiegers from time to time captured messengers the Rochelois were sending to Buckingham, or spies Buckingham was sending to the Rochelois. In both cases the trial was a summary affair. The cardinal merely said, 'Hang them!' The king was invited to watch the execution. He would languidly come and take up a good position to observe every aspect of the operation. That was always something of a distraction, and gave him a little more patience for the siege, but he was still excruciatingly bored, and constantly talked about going back to Paris. If the flow of spies and messengers had dried up, for all his imagination His Eminence would have found himself at his wits' end.

Nevertheless, time passed, and the Rochelois still did not surrender. The last spy to be captured had been carrying a letter. It was forthright in telling Buckingham that the town was at the last extremity, but instead of adding, 'If your help doesn't get here within a fortnight, we will surrender,' it simply said, 'If your help doesn't get here within a fortnight, we will all have died of hunger by the time it does.'

Thus the Rochelois' only hope was in Buckingham. Buckingham was their Messiah. It was clear that if one day they received reliable information that they could not count on Buckingham any more, their courage would be dashed along with their hopes.

The cardinal was therefore waiting with great impatience for news from England announcing that Buckingham would not be coming.

The question of taking the town by storm, although often debated in the king's council, had always been ruled out. First of all, La Rochelle seemed impregnable. And then the cardinal, whatever he might say, knew that the horror of bloodshed in this encounter, where Frenchman would have to fight against Frenchman, would set back his policy by sixty years and, for those times, the cardinal was what today is called a man of progress. Indeed, the sack of La Rochelle, and the slaughter of the two or three thousand Huguenots, bore far too close a similarity, in 1628, to the Saint Bartholomew massacre[1] in 1572. Lastly, more importantly than all that, this extreme measure, for which the king, as a good Catholic, felt no repugnance, always foundered on the argument of the besieging generals: 'La Rochelle is impregnable, except by starvation.'

The cardinal couldn't banish from his mind the fear his terrible emissary inspired in him, for he too had understood the strange compass of this woman, who was at one moment a serpent, at another a lion. Had she betrayed him? Was she dead? Either way, he knew her well enough to be certain that, whether acting for or against him, whether friend or foe, she wouldn't remain inactive unless faced with great obstacles. What these might be, however, he could not know.

But, all the same, he was counting on Milady, and with good reason. He had divined that there were terrible things in this woman's past that only her red cloak could hide, and he sensed that, for one or other reason, this woman was in accord with him, since his was the only support she could find that was greater than the danger threatening her.

He resolved therefore to wage the war on his own, only waiting for others' success as one waits for a stroke of good fortune. He went on building the famous dyke that was to starve La Rochelle. Meanwhile, he cast his eyes over that unfortunate city, which sheltered so much profound misery and so many heroic virtues, and, remembering the saying of Louis XI, who was his political predecessor, as he was Robespierre's[2] in turn, he murmured this maxim of Tristan's comrade, 'Divide and rule.'

When Henri IV had besieged Paris, he had ordered bread and provisions to be thrown over the walls. The cardinal had little handbills thrown over, in which he told the Rochelois how unjust, selfish and barbaric the conduct of their leaders was. They had wheat in abundance, but did not share it. They adopted as their maxim – for they too had maxims – that it was of little significance if women, children and old men died, so long as the men who had to defend their walls remained strong and healthy. Until then, whether from loyalty or powerlessness to react against it, this maxim, while not generally adopted, had nonetheless passed from theory to practice. But the leaflets undermined it. They reminded the men that those children, those women and those old men who were left to die were their sons, their wives and their fathers; that it would be more just if everyone was reduced to a common misery, and that then their shared circumstances would lead to unanimous decisions.

These handbills had all the effect their author could possibly have hoped for, in that they persuaded a great number of inhabitants to open individual negotiations with the royal army.

But just as the cardinal was seeing his method bear fruit, and was congratulating himself on using it, an inhabitant of La Rochelle, who had managed to get through the royal lines – God knows how, so tight was the surveillance of Bassompierre, Schomberg and the Duke d'Angoulême, who were themselves under the cardinal's surveillance – an inhabitant of La Rochelle, as we were saying, returned from Portsmouth and told the town that he had seen a magnificent fleet ready to set sail within the week. Moreover, Buckingham informed the mayor that the great league against France was finally going to declare itself, and that the kingdom would be invaded simultaneously by English, Imperial and Spanish armies. This letter was read out publicly on all the squares; copies were posted at street corners, and the very people who had started to open negotiations broke them off, resolved to wait for the help thus majestically promised.

This unexpected circumstance revived all of Richelieu's original anxieties and compelled him, in spite of himself, to turn his gaze once more out to sea.

Meanwhile, spared the anxieties of its only real leader, the royal army was having a joyous time of it. There was no shortage of provisions in the camp, or money for that matter, and all the regiments vied with each other in feats of daring and merriment. Catching spies and hanging them, venturing on hazardous expeditions along the dyke or out to sea, dreaming up madcap exploits and coolly executing them, such were the pastimes that made time pass quickly for the army on those days that seemed so long, not only for the Rochelois, racked by famine and anxiety, but also for the cardinal who was blockading them so keenly.

The cardinal rode around constantly like the lowliest soldier in the army, training his pensive gaze on the works being built on his orders, so much more slowly than he wished, by engineers he had brought from the furthest corners of the kingdom of France, Sometimes, if he came across a musketeer of Tréville's company, he would go up to him, observe him in a singular way, and then, seeing he wasn't one of our four companions, he would focus his profound gaze and vast thoughts elsewhere.

One day, consumed by deadly tedium, with no hope of negotiations with the town, with no news from England, the cardinal left camp with no other end in mind than just to go out. Accompanied only by Cahusac and La Houdinière, he rode along the shore, fusing the immensity of his dreams with the immensity of the ocean, until he came at his horse's gentle pace to a hill. From the top of it, he saw seven men lying on the sand behind a hedge, surrounded by empty bottles and catching one of those gleams of sunshine that are so rare at that time of the year. Four of these men were our musketeers, who were preparing to listen to a reading of a letter that one of them had just received. This letter was so important it had caused cards and dice to be abandoned on a drum.

The three others were engaged in uncorking an enormous demijohn of Collioure wine. These were the gentlemen's valets.

The cardinal, as we have said, was in a grim mood, and, in that frame of mind, nothing made him surlier than the high spirits of others. Besides, he had a strange anxiety whereby he would always think that the very causes of his sadness were making others merry. Signalling to La Houdinière and Cahusac to stop, he dismounted and approached the source of the suspicious laughter, hoping the sand muffling his steps, and the hedge hiding his approach, would allow him to hear a few words of the conversation that was of such interest to him. When he was just ten paces from the hedge, he recognised d'Artagnan's Gascon prattle, and, as he already knew these men were musketeers, he was in no doubt that the other three were the ones known as the inseparables, in other words Athos, Porthos and Aramis.

One may imagine how this discovery increased his desire to hear the conversation. His eyes took on a strange expression and, like a tiger-cat, he padded closer to the hedge. But he hadn't been able to catch more than a few vague syllables, with no definite meaning, when a brief, echoing cry made him start and caught the musketeers' attention.

'Officer!' cried Grimaud.

'You spoke, I believe, you rogue,' said Athos, raising himself on an elbow and transfixing Grimaud with his searing gaze.

Grimaud did not add another word, but merely pointed to the hedge with his forefinger, thereby revealing the presence of the cardinal and his escort.

In one bound the four musketeers were on their feet and bowing respectfully. The cardinal seemed furious.

'Apparently the gentlemen of the musketeers have guards!' he said. 'Are the English coming by land, or do the musketeers regard themselves as superior officers?'

'My lord,' replied Athos, for in the midst of the general alarm he alone had retained that lordly coolness and composure which never failed him. 'My lord, when musketeers are not on duty, or have come off duty, they drink and play dice, and their valets certainly regard them as superior officers.'

'Valets!' growled the cardinal. 'Valets who have been detailed to warn their master when someone is passing are not valets, they're sentries.'

'His Eminence can see, nevertheless, that if we had not taken this precaution, we would have risked letting him pass without presenting our respects and offering him our thanks for the favour he has done us by reuniting us. D'Artagnan,' Athos went on, 'you were just asking for an opportunity to express your gratitude to my lord. Well, here it is, make the most of it.'

These words were uttered with that imperturbable coolness, which distinguished Athos in times of danger, and with that extreme

politeness, which at moments made him a king more majestic than
any king by birth.

D'Artagnan approached and stammered some words of thanks,
which soon died away under the cardinal's dour gaze.

'No matter, gentlemen,' the cardinal went on without seeming
deflected in the least from his original intention by the case Athos
had made. 'No matter, gentlemen, I do not it like it when simple
soldiers, because they have the advantage of serving in a privileged
corps, act like great lords. Discipline is the same for them as it is
for everybody.'

Athos allowed the cardinal to conclude and then, bowing in a
sign of assent, said in his turn, 'I trust, my lord, that we have not
failed in any way to keep discipline. We are not on duty, and we
thought that, since we weren't on duty, we might dispose of our
time as we saw fit. If our good fortune is such that His Eminence
has some special order to give us, we are ready to obey him. My
lord can see,' Athos continued, frowning, for this sort of interrogation was beginning to tax his patience, 'that, to be ready for
the least alarm, we have brought our weapons with us.'

And then he pointed out to the cardinal the four muskets stacked
near the drum on which the cards and the dice were spread out.

'Your Eminence must believe,' added d'Artagnan, 'that we
would have gone to meet him if we could have imagined it was
he who was coming towards us in so small a company.'

The cardinal bit his moustaches, and even his lips a little.

'Do you know what you look like, always together as you are
now, armed as you are now, guarded by your lackeys?' said the
cardinal. 'You look like four conspirators.'

'Ah well, my lord, it's true,' said Athos, 'we do conspire, as
Your Eminence could see the other morning, but we do so against
the Rochelois.'

'Ah, gentlemen politicians,' said the cardinal, frowning in his
turn. 'One might perhaps find the secret to many mysteries in your
brains, if one could read them as you were reading that letter you
hid when you saw me coming.'

Athos flushed and took a step towards His Eminence.

'One would think you genuinely suspected us, my lord, and that we are being subjected to a genuine interrogation. If that is the case, let His Eminence deign to explain himself, and we would at least know what we are about.'

'If this does lead to an interrogation,' said the cardinal, 'you won't be the first to undergo it, Monsieur Athos, and everyone else has provided answers.'

'Hence, my lord, why I have told Your Eminence that he has only to ask, and we are ready to answer.'

'What was that letter you were about to read, Monsieur Aramis, that you have hidden?'

'A letter from a woman, my lord.'

'Oh, I understand,' said the cardinal. 'Discretion is essential with those sorts of letters. But still, one can show them to a confessor, and, as you know, I have received holy orders.'

'My lord,' said Athos, with a calmness which was all the more terrible as he was risking his head with his reply, 'the letter is from a woman, but neither Marion de Lorme[3], nor Madame d'Aiguillon have signed it.'

The cardinal grew deathly pale and a savage gleam flashed in his eyes. He turned as if to give an order to Cahusac and La Houdinière. Athos saw the movement. He took a step towards the muskets. The three friends had their eyes riveted on the guns like men who are loath to let themselves be arrested. The cardinal was one of three; the musketeers, valets included, were seven. The game would be even more unequal, the cardinal judged, if Athos and his companions really were conspirators. And so, by one of those complete reversals he could always produce, all his anger melted away to a smile.

'Come, come!' he said, 'you are brave young men, proud in the sunshine, faithful in the dark. There's no harm watching over oneself when one does such a good job of watching over others. Gentlemen, I have not forgotten the night you escorted me to the Red Dovecote. If there were any danger to fear on my road, I would ask you to accompany me. But, as there isn't, stay where you are, and finish your bottles, your game and your letter. Goodbye, gentlemen.'

And then, getting back on to his horse, which Cahusac had brought up, he waved to them and rode off.

Standing stock still, the four young men followed him with their eyes, not saying a word until he had disappeared.

Then they looked at one another.

Blank dismay was written on all their faces, for, despite His Eminence's friendly parting, they realised the cardinal had gone away with rage in his heart.

Only Athos smiled a firm, scornful smile. When the cardinal was out of sight and earshot, Porthos, who had a burning desire to vent his ill humour on someone, said, 'That Grimaud raised the alarm very late!'

Grimaud was about to make an excuse, but Athos raised his finger and he held his tongue.

'Would you have handed over the letter, Aramis?' said d'Artagnan.

'I?' said Aramis in his most melodious voice. 'I'd made up my mind: if he'd demanded the letter, I would have handed it to him with one hand, and run my sword through his body with the other.'

'That's what I was expecting,' said Athos. 'That's why I threw myself between the two of you. Really, that man is very reckless to talk in such a fashion to other men. You'd think he'd only had dealings with women and children.'

'My dear Athos,' said d'Artagnan, 'I admire you, but, after all, we were in the wrong.'

'How so, in the wrong?' said Athos. 'Whose air is this we breathe? Whose ocean is this we look out over? Whose sand is this we were lying on? Whose letter is this from your mistress? Are they all the cardinal's? On my honour, that man thinks the world belongs to him. There you were, stammering, dumbfounded, overwhelmed – you'd have thought the Bastille had reared up in front of you and that gigantic Medusa had turned you to stone. Honestly, is it a conspiracy to be in love? You're in love with a woman the cardinal has locked up. You want to get her out of the cardinal's clutches. It's a game you're playing with His Eminence. This letter is your hand. Why would you show your hand to your opponent? No one does that. If he guesses it, very good! We'll certainly guess his!'

'It's true,' said d'Artagnan. 'What you say makes great sense, Athos.'

'In that case, let's have no further talk of what's just happened, and let Aramis resume reading his cousin's letter at the point where he was interrupted by the cardinal.'

Aramis took the letter from his pocket, the three friends drew near to him, and the three valets once more congregated round the demijohn.

'You had only read a line or two,' said d'Artagnan, 'so start again from the beginning.'

'Gladly,' said Aramis.

My dear cousin,
    I do believe I shall decide to leave for Stenay[4], where my sister has put our little servant into the Carmelite convent. The poor child is resigned. She knows she cannot live elsewhere without the salvation of her soul being in danger. However, if our family affairs are settled as we wish, I believe she will run the risk of damnation, and rejoin those she misses, all the more so because she knows they constantly think of her. In the meantime, she is not too wretched. All she desires is a letter from her intended. I know those sorts of articles are difficult to fit through the grilles, but, after all, as I have proved to you, my dear cousin, I am not too unhandy, and I shall undertake this commission. My sister thanks you for your kind and undying remembrance. She had a moment of great anxiety, but finally she is now somewhat reassured, having sent her agent there so nothing unexpected would happen.

Goodbye, my dear cousin, give us your news as often as you can, that is, whenever you think you can do so safely.

With much love.

Marie Michon

'Oh, is there anything I do not owe you, Aramis?' cried d'Artagnan. 'Dear Constance! So at last I have news of her – she's alive, she's safe in a convent, she's in Stenay! Where do you place Stenay, Athos?'

'Why, a few leagues from the frontiers. Once the siege is raised, we can go and take a tour round there.'

'And that won't be long, one must hope,' said Porthos, 'for they hanged a spy this morning, who declared that the Rochelois were down to their shoe uppers. Supposing they graduate to the soles after eating the uppers, I don't really see what they'll have left after that, unless they eat each other.'

'Poor fools!' said Athos, draining a glass of excellent Bordeaux, which, despite not having the reputation at the time that it has now, deserved it no less. 'Poor fools! As if the Catholic religion wasn't the most advantageous and agreeable of the religions! Still,' he said, after clicking his tongue against the roof of his mouth, 'they're brave souls. But what the devil are you doing, Aramis?' Athos went on. 'Are you putting that letter in your pocket?'

'Yes,' said d'Artagnan, 'Athos is right, it must be burned. And even then, who knows if the cardinal doesn't have a secret way of interrogating ashes?'

'He is bound to have one,' said Athos.

'So what do you want to do with the letter?' asked Porthos.

'Come here, Grimaud,' said Athos.

Grimaud stood up and obeyed.

'To punish you for having spoken without permission, my friend, you are going to eat this piece of paper. Then, to reward you for the service you will have rendered us, you are going to drink this glass of wine. Here's the letter first. Chew it vigorously.'

Grimaud smiled and, his eyes fixed on the glass that Athos had just filled to the brim, ground the piece of paper under his teeth and swallowed it.

'Bravo, Master Grimaud!' said Athos. 'And now take this. Good. I excuse you from saying thank you.'

Grimaud downed the glass of Bordeaux in silence, but, for the duration of this sweet process, his eyes raised to heaven spoke a language, which, although wordless, was no less expressive for all that.

'And now,' said Athos, 'unless the cardinal has the ingenious idea of opening Grimaud's stomach, I believe we can rest more or less easy.'

Meanwhile, His Eminence continued his melancholy progress, murmuring into his moustache:

'There's no question: I must make those four men mine.'

LII
FIRST DAY OF CAPTIVITY

L ET US RETURN TO MILADY, whom we lost sight of for an instant when we turned our gaze to the shores of France.

We shall find her in the desperate position in which we left her, hollowing out an abyss of dark thoughts, a dark hell at the gates of which she had almost abandoned hope, because for the first time she doubted, for the first time she was afraid.

On two occasions her luck had failed her, on two occasions she had seen herself discovered and betrayed, and on both those occasions, she had foundered on that fatal genius who had doubtless been sent by the Lord to oppose her. D'Artagnan had vanquished her – her, the invincible force of evil.

He had exploited her in her love, humiliated her in her pride, outwitted her in her ambition, and now here he was ruining her fortunes, wounding her in her freedom, and even threatening her life. Far worse, he had lifted a corner of her mask, the shield she sheltered behind and made her so strong.

D'Artagnan had deflected from Buckingham, whom she hated, as she hated everything she once loved, the storm with which Richelieu threatened him. D'Artagnan had impersonated de Wardes, for whom she had one of those indomitable tigress's fancies that women of her character conceive. D'Artagnan knew that terrible secret she had sworn no one would know and remain alive. Finally, just as she had obtained the full powers with which she was going to avenge herself on her enemy, the document had been torn from her hands, and now d'Artagnan was holding her prisoner and was going to send her to some filthy Botany Bay, to some vile Tyburn of the Indian Ocean[1].

For there's no doubt all of it came from d'Artagnan. Who else could have heaped such disgrace on her head except him? Only he could have communicated all those terrible secrets to Lord de Winter, who had exposed them one by one as if an agent of inexorable fate. He knew her brother-in-law; he must have written to him.

What hatred she exuded! There, motionless in her empty room, her eyes blazing and fixed, how closely the dull roars that sometimes escaped with a breath from the depths of her breast echoed the sound of the swell as it rose, boomed, roared and broke like eternal, impotent despair against the rocks on which that dark and overweening castle stood! In the lightning flashes her tempestuous anger sent jagging across her mind, how she conjured up magnificent plans of vengeance against Madame Bonacieux, against Buckingham, and, above all, d'Artagnan, plans that stretched into the far distant future!

Yes, but to take revenge, one must be free, and to be free, when one is a prisoner, one must break through a wall, loosen bars, cut a hole through the floor – all enterprises that a strong, patient man might bring off but before which the febrile irritations of woman are doomed to fail. Besides, to do that, one needs time, months, years, and she . . . she had ten or twelve days, according to Lord de Winter, her terrible, brotherly gaoler.

And yet, if she were a man, she would have attempted all that and would perhaps have succeeded. So why had heaven been so mistaken as to put such a virile soul in such a frail and delicate body?

The first moments of her captivity had thus been terrible. Convulsions of fury, which she hadn't been able to control, had paid the debt feminine weakness owes to nature. But gradually she had overcome the eruptions of frenzied anger; the nervous trembling that racked her body had disappeared, and now she was coiled in on herself like a weary serpent taking its rest.

'Come, come, I was insane to get so carried away like that,' she said, her eyes boring into their reflection in the mirror, their burning gaze seeming to take her to task. 'No violence: violence is a proof of weakness. I have never succeeded by that means, for one thing. Perhaps if I used my strength against women, I might find them still weaker than myself, and so might defeat them. But I am fighting men, and to them I am only a woman. Let's fight as a woman. My strength is in my weakness.'

Then, as if to reassure herself of the changes she could conjure from her exceedingly expressive, mobile features, she made them assume every possible expression in turn, from anger, which contorted her features, to the sweetest, most affectionate, most seductive smile. Next her expert hands arranged her hair in a succession of waves that she thought would enhance the charms of her face. Finally, satisfied with herself, she murmured, 'Come now, nothing is lost. I'm still beautiful.'

It was almost eight o'clock in the evening. Noticing a bed, it occurred to Milady that a few hours' rest would refresh not only her mind and her thoughts, but also her complexion. However, before lying down, a better thought presented itself. She had heard talk of supper. She had already been in that room an hour; it couldn't be long before they brought her meal. The prisoner didn't want to waste time, and she resolved to make an attempt to see how the land lay that same evening, by studying the character of the men who had been charged with guarding her.

A light appeared under the door, heralding the return of her gaolers. Milady, who had got up, quickly flung herself back down in her chair, her head thrown back, her beautiful hair loose and tangled, her bosom half showing through her rumpled lace, one hand on her heart, the other dangling at her side.

The bolts were slid back, the door creaked on its hinges, approaching footsteps echoed in the room.

'Put the table there,' said a voice the prisoner recognised as Felton's.

The order was carried out.

'Bring lamps and relieve the sentries,' Felton went on.

This double order of the young lieutenant's proved to Milady that her servants were the same men as her guards, that's to say, soldiers.

Felton's orders, furthermore, were executed with a silence and speed that gave a good idea of the flourishing state of discipline under his command.

At length, Felton, who had not yet looked at Milady, turned towards her.

'Aha!' he said, 'she's asleep. That's good. When she wakes up, she will have supper.'

And he took a few steps to leave.

'But, lieutenant,' said a soldier, who was less stoic than his officer, and who had gone over to Milady, 'this woman's not asleep.'

'What, she's not asleep?' said Felton. 'What is she doing, then?'

'She has fainted. Her face is very pale, and, listen as I may, I can't hear her breathing.'

'You're right,' said Felton, after looking at Milady from where he was, without taking a step towards her. 'Go and tell Lord de Winter that his prisoner has fainted. I don't know what to do. This is an unforeseen circumstance.'

The soldier went out to obey his officer's orders. Felton sat down in an armchair that happened to be near the door and waited without saying a word, without moving a muscle. Milady was an adept of that great art, so assiduously studied by women, of being able to see through her long lashes without appearing to open her eyes. She made out Felton, who had his back to her, and looked at him for ten minutes or so, during which the impassive warder did not turn round once.

She thought that Lord de Winter would soon come and, by his presence, make her gaoler stronger. Her first experiment had failed, but she bore it as a woman who has confidence in her resources. Raising her head, therefore, she opened her eyes and sighed feebly.

At this sigh, Felton finally turned around.

'Ah, you're awake, madam!' he said. 'Then I have nothing more to do here. If you need anything, call.'

'Oh, my God, my God, how I've suffered!' murmured Milady, in that harmonious voice, which, like the voices of ancient enchantresses, charmed all whom she wished to destroy.

And then, sitting up in her armchair, she assumed a more alluring and unrestrained pose than when she was lying back.

Felton stood up.

'You will be served this way three times a day, madam,' he said. 'In the morning, at nine o'clock, in the afternoon, at one o'clock, and in the evening, at eight o'clock. If that does not suit you, you may indicate the hours you prefer to those I propose, and your wishes on this point will be respected.'

'But am I then always to be alone in this huge, cheerless room?' asked Milady.

'A local woman has been instructed. She will be at the castle tomorrow, and will come whenever you desire her presence.'

'I thank you, sir,' the prisoner replied humbly.

Felton gave a faint bow and made for the door. Just as he was about to pass through it, Lord de Winter appeared in the corridor, followed by the soldier who had gone to tell him Milady had fainted. He had a flask of smelling salts in his hand.

'Well then, what's this? What are we up to here?' he said in a mocking voice, as he saw the prisoner on her feet and Felton about to leave. 'The dead woman has been raised from the grave, has she? By God, Felton, my boy, don't you see that she's taking you for a novice, and staging for your benefit the first act of a comedy, of which we will doubtless enjoy all the subsequent twists and turns?'

'I thought as much, my lord,' said Felton. 'But, as the prisoner is a woman, after all, I wanted to show all the consideration a well-born man owes a woman, if not for her sake, then at least for his own.'

Milady shivered all over. These words of Felton's went like ice through all her veins.

'So,' said de Winter, laughing, 'those beautiful locks, so artfully displayed, that white skin and that languorous gaze have not seduced you yet, you heart of stone?'

'No, my lord,' replied the impassive young man, 'and, believe me, it will take more than a woman's wiles and flirtations to corrupt me.'

'In that case, my brave lieutenant, let's leave Milady to think of something else and go to supper. Oh, don't worry, she has a fertile imagination. The second act of the comedy won't be slow in following the first.'

And at these words, Lord de Winter slipped his arm under Felton's and led him away, laughing.

'Ah, I'll find what it takes to get you,' Milady muttered between her teeth. 'Don't worry, you poor failed monk, you poor converted soldier with your uniform cut from a cassock.'

'Incidentally,' said de Winter, stopping in the door, 'you mustn't let this failure rob you of your appetite, Milady. Try the chicken and the fish, neither of which, on my honour, I've had poisoned. I am pleased with my cook, and, as he isn't to inherit anything from me, I have full and complete confidence in him. So treat them as I would. Goodbye, dear sister, until your next fainting fit!'

This was the limit of what Milady could bear: her hands clutched the chair, her teeth ground dully, her eyes followed the door as it closed behind Lord de Winter and Felton, and then, when she found herself alone again, a new wave of despair broke over her. She glanced at the table, saw the gleam of a knife, sprang forward and seized it. But she was cruelly disappointed: the tip was rounded and the blade of flexible silver.

A peal of laughter rang out from behind the half-closed door, which then reopened.

'Ha ha ha!' cried Lord de Winter. 'You see, my good Felton, you see what I told you? That knife was for you, my boy. She would have killed you. You see, it's one of her eccentricities to get rid, in one way or other, of anyone in her way. If I'd listened to you, the knife would have been pointed and of steel – and then, no more Felton! She would have slit your throat and everyone else's after you. Look, John, look how skilfully she holds her knife.'

Indeed, Milady was still holding the weapon in her clenched fist, but these last words, this ultimate insult, dissolved her grip, her strength, and even her will.

The knife fell to the floor.

'You're right, my lord,' said Felton, with a note of profound disgust that resonated to the depths of Milady's heart, 'you're right and it is I who was wrong.'

And then the two of them left again.

But this time, Milady lent a more attentive ear than before, and she heard their footsteps receding and dying away at the end of the corridor.

'I'm lost,' she murmured. 'Here I am in the power of people over whom I have no more hold than over statues of bronze or granite. They know me by heart and are armoured against all my weapons. Yet this cannot end the way they have decided.'

Indeed, as this last thought showed, this instinctive return of hope indicated fear and other such weak sentiments did not survive for long in that deep soul. Milady sat at the table, ate several dishes, drink a little Spanish wine and felt all her resolve flood back.

Before going to bed, she had already commented on, analysed, turned on all sides and examined from all angles the words, steps, gestures, signs and even silence of her gaolers, and the upshot of this profound, skilful, erudite study was that

Felton, all things considered, was the more vulnerable of her two persecutors.

One phrase in particular came back to the prisoner.

'If I'd listened to you,' Lord de Winter had said to Felton.

So, as Lord de Winter had refused to listen to him, Felton must have spoken in her favour.

'Weak or strong,' repeated Milady, 'that man has a spark of pity in his soul. Out of that spark I will create a fire that will devour him. As for the other one, he knows me, fears me, and is sure of what to expect if I escape his clutches. So there's no point trying anything with him. But Felton is another matter. He is a pure, naive, apparently virtuous young man. There are ways to destroy him.'

And then Milady went to bed and fell asleep with a smile on her lips. Anyone seeing her sleep would have thought she was a young girl dreaming of the crown of flowers she was to bind round her forehead at the next dance.

LIII

SECOND DAY OF CAPTIVITY

M ILADY WAS DREAMING that she finally had d'Artagnan in her power and was watching his beheading, and it was the sight of his odious blood flowing under the executioner's axe that was etching that charming smile on her lips.

She slept like a prisoner lulled by the first glimmer of hope.

When they came into her room the next morning, she was still in bed. Felton stayed in the corridor. He had brought the woman he had mentioned the evening before, who had just arrived. She came in and went up to Milady, offering her services.

Milady was naturally paleskinned. Her complexion could therefore deceive someone seeing her for the first time.

'I have a fever,' she said. 'I didn't sleep for an instant that whole long night. I am suffering terribly. Will you be more humane than they were to me yesterday? All I ask, anyhow, is permission to stay in bed.'

'Do you wish a doctor to be sent for?' said the woman.

Felton listened to this conversation without saying a word.

Milady thought that the more people she was surrounded with, the more people she would have to move to pity – but also the tighter Lord de Winter's surveillance would become. Besides, the doctor might declare the illness was feigned, and, after having lost the first game, Milady did not want to lose the second.

'What's the use of sending for a doctor?' she said. 'Those gentlemen declared yesterday that my illness was a comedy. No doubt it will be the same today, for they have had time to inform the doctor since yesterday evening.'

'In that case,' said Felton, out of all patience, 'say yourself, madam, what course of treatment you would like to take.'

'Ah, how should I know? My God! I feel I'm suffering, that's all. Let them give me what they like, it doesn't matter.'

'Go and fetch Lord de Winter,' said Felton, wearied by these eternal complaints.

'Oh, no! No!' cried Milady. 'No, sir, don't call him, I entreat you. I'm fine, I don't need anything, don't call him.'

She imparted such prodigious vehemence, such heart-stirring eloquence into these words that Felton, duly stirred, took a few steps into the room.

He's moved, thought Milady.

'However, madam,' said Felton, 'if you are *really* suffering, we will send for a doctor. If you are deceiving us, well, it will be all the worse for you, but, at least, on our side, we will have nothing to reproach ourselves with.'

Milady did not reply, but, throwing her head back on her pillow, she burst into tears and erupted in sobs.

Felton looked at her for a moment with his usual impassivity, but then, seeing that the paroxysm threatened to go on, he went out, and the woman followed him. Lord de Winter did not appear.

'I think I'm beginning to work it out,' Milady murmured with savage joy, burying herself under the sheets to hide this surge of inner satisfaction from anyone who might be spying on her.

Two hours passed.

'Now it's time the illness cleared up,' she said. 'Let's get out of bed and have some success, starting today. I only have ten days, and by tonight, two will have gone by.'

On coming into Milady's room that morning, they had brought her breakfast. So she thought it wouldn't be long before they came to clear the table, and that then she would see Felton again.

Milady was not mistaken. Felton reappeared and, without paying attention to whether Milady had touched the food or not, gestured for the table, which was ordinarily brought in fully laid, to be taken out of the room.

Felton was the last to leave. He was holding a book in his hand.

Lying in an armchair near the fireplace, beautiful, pale and resigned, Milady looked like a holy virgin awaiting martyrdom.

Felton went over to her and said, 'Lord de Winter, who is a Catholic like you, madam, thought it might be painful for you to be deprived of the rites and ceremonies of your religion. He therefore permits you to read the order of *your mass* every day, and here is a book containing the ritual.'

The air with which Felton put the book on the little table by Milady, the tone in which he pronounced those two words 'your mass', and the disdainful smile with which he accompanied them made Milady raise her head and observe the officer more attentively.

Then, by the severe style in which he wore his hair, the exaggerated plainness of his dress, his forehead that was not only as polished, but also as hard and impenetrable as marble, she recognised one of those sombre Puritans she had so often met not only at the court of King James but also at that of the king of France, where, despite the memory of Saint Bartholomew, they sometimes came to seek refuge.

She then had one of those sudden flashes of inspiration that only geniuses have in great crises, those ultimate moments which will decide their fortunes or their lives.

Those two words, 'your mass', and a quick glance at Felton had revealed to her the crucial importance of the reply she was going to give.

But with that quickness of thought that was characteristic of her, it came to her lips fully formed.

'I?' she said, with a note of scorn pitched at the same level as the one she noticed in the young officer's voice, 'I, sir? *My mass?* Lord de Winter, the corrupted Catholic, knows perfectly well that I am not of his religion, and it is a trap he wishes to set me!'

'And what religion are you then, madam?' asked Felton, with an astonishment which, despite his self-mastery, he could not conceal entirely.

'I will profess it,' cried Milady with feigned exaltation, 'the day I have suffered enough for my faith.'

Felton's look revealed to Milady the extent of the realm she had opened up with this one statement.

The young officer remained mute and unmoving, however. Only his look had spoken.

'I am in the hands of my enemies,' she went on with that note of fervour she knew was normal among Puritans. 'Well then, either let God save me or let me perish for my God! That is the answer I beg you to take to Lord de Winter. And as for this book,' she added, pointing to the ritual with the tip of her finger but making sure not to touch it, as if contact would have defiled her, 'you can take it and use it yourself, for no doubt you are Lord de Winter's accomplice twice over: an accomplice in his persecution and an accomplice in his heresy.'

Felton didn't reply, but took the book with the same sentiment of repugnance he had already manifested and pensively retired. Lord de Winter came at about five o'clock in the evening. Milady had had all day to draw up her plan of action. She received him as a woman who has already regained all her advantages.

'Apparently,' said the baron, sitting in an armchair opposite

Milady's and nonchalantly stretching his feet out to the fire, 'apparently we've committed an act of mild apostasy.'

'What do you mean, sir?'

'I mean that, since we saw each other last, you have changed religion. Have you got married for a third time, to a Protestant, by any chance?'

'Explain yourself, my lord,' said the prisoner majestically, 'for I declare I hear your words, but I do not understand them.'

'In that case, you have no religion at all. I prefer that, I have to say,' sneered Lord de Winter.

'It's certainly more in keeping with your principles,' Milady said coldly.

'Oh, I must confess I don't care either way.'

'Oh, if you didn't confess to this religious indifference, my lord, your debauches and crimes would attest to it.'

'What? You speak of debauches, Madame Messalina¹, you speak of crimes, Lady Macbeth! Either I misheard or, by God, you're very impudent.'

'You speak in this manner because you know people are listening, sir,' Milady replied coldly . . . 'and you wish to turn your gaolers and executioners against me.'

'My gaolers! My executioners! Oh yes, madam, you're striking a poetic tone, and yesterday's comedy is turning to tragedy this evening. At all events, in eight days you will be in your rightful place and my duty will be done.'

'Infamous duty! Impious duty!' Milady said with the exaltation of the victim provoking the judge.

'I think, on my word of honour,' said de Winter, getting to his feet, 'that the hussy is going mad. Come, come, calm yourself, Madame Puritan, or I will have you put in the dungeon. By God, my Spanish wine is going to your head, is that it? But don't worry, that drunkenness isn't dangerous and there won't be any consequences.'

And then Lord de Winter left the room swearing, which at that time was an eminently gentlemanly habit.

Sure enough Felton was behind the door and hadn't missed a word of the whole scene.

Milady had guessed right.

'Yes, go! Go!' she said to her brother. 'The consequences are indeed on their way, but you won't see them, imbecile, until they're too late to avoid.'

Silence fell again and two hours passed. They brought supper and found Milady saying her prayers aloud, prayers she had learnt from an old servant of her second husband's, a very austere Puritan. She seemed in ecstasy and appeared oblivious to what was happening around her. Felton made a sign that she was not to be disturbed, and when everything was in order he went out noiselessly with the soldiers.

Milady knew she might be spied on, so she recited her prayers to the end, and she had the impression that the soldier who was on sentry duty at her door was walking with a different step and seemed to be listening.

For the moment, that was all she wanted. She stood up, went to the table, ate a little and only drank some water.

An hour later they came to take away the table, but Milady noticed that Felton did not accompany the soldiers this time.

So he was afraid of seeing her too often.

She turned her face to the wall to smile, for there was in that smile such an expression of triumph that it alone would have betrayed her.

She let another half an hour pass, and as at that moment everything was quiet in the old castle, as all that could be heard was the eternal murmur of the swell, that immense breathing of the ocean, she began singing in her pure, harmonious and ringing voice, the first verse of that psalm which was then in high favour among the Puritans:

When thou dost abandon us, O Lord,
Tis to see if we are strong,
For then thy heav'nly hand dost us reward
For striving true and long . . .

These verses were not excellent – far from it, in fact – but, as everyone knows, the Protestants did not pride themselves on poetry.

As she sang, Milady listened. The soldier on guard at her door stopped as if turned to stone. So Milady could judge the effect she was having.

Then she continued her singing with an inexpressible fervour and feeling. It seemed to her as if the sound spread into the distance under the vaults, flowing out like a magic charm to soften the hearts of her gaolers. And yet it appeared that the soldier on sentry duty, a zealous Catholic no doubt, shook off the charm, for he said through the door, 'Be quiet now, madam. Your song is as mournful as a *De Profundis*, and if, on top of the delights of being garrisoned here, we have to listen to those sort of things, we won't be able to stand it.'

'Silence!' said a grave voice, which Milady recognised as Felton's. 'What business is it of yours, you rogue? Were you ordered to stop this woman singing? No. You were told to guard her and to shoot her if she tries to escape. So guard her, kill her if she escapes, but don't deviate from your orders.'

An expression of indescribable joy lit up Milady's face, but it was as fleeting as a flash of lightning. Without appearing to have heard the exchange, of which she hadn't missed a word, she resumed singing, lending her voice all the charm, all the range and all the seduction the devil had endowed it with:

For so many tears, such bitter griefs
For my exile and my chains
I have my youth and my beliefs
And God, who records my pains . . .

That voice of unparalleled range and sublime passion gave the crude, uncultured poetry of those psalms a magical expressiveness that the most exalted Puritans rarely found in their brethren's songs, which they were left to adorn with all the resources of their imagination. Felton thought he was listening to the singing of the angel who comforted the three Hebrews in the furnace[2].

Milady went on:

> But freedom's day shall dawn
> O God the just and strong
> And if our hope is forlorn
> To martyrdom and death we shall march on . . .

This verse, into which the terrible enchantress had tried to pour all her soul, completed the job of throwing the young officer's heart into confusion. He tore open the door and Milady saw him appear, as pale as ever, but with fiery, almost wild eyes.

'Why do you sing like that,' he said, 'and in such a voice?'

'Forgive me, sir,' Milady said softly, 'I forgot my songs are out of place in this house. I have doubtless offended you in your beliefs, but it was not my intention, I swear. Forgive me therefore for a fault which may be great but was certainly involuntary.'

Milady was so beautiful at that moment, and the religious ecstasy in which she seemed to be plunged made her countenance so expressive that Felton, completely dazzled, fancied he beheld the angel whom before he had only fancied he heard.

'Yes, yes,' he replied, 'you are disturbing, agitating the inhabitants of the castle.'

The poor madman did not realise the incoherence of his words, as Milady plunged her lynx-eyed gaze into the depths of his heart.

'I shall keep my peace,' said Milady, casting down her eyes, with all the softness she could instil in her voice and all the resignation she could lend her bearing.

'No, no, madam,' said Felton, 'only don't sing so loud, especially at night.'

And at these words, Felton, feeling that he wouldn't be able to keep up his severity towards the prisoner for long, rushed out of the room.

'You did right, lieutenant,' said the soldier. 'Those songs unsettle the soul. Still, you get used to them in the end. Her voice is so beautiful!'

LIV
THIRD DAY OF CAPTIVITY

FELTON HAD COME, but there was another step still to be taken – he had to be made to stay, or rather he had to stay of his own accord. And Milady only had a dim sense of how to bring that about.

But that was not all. He had to be induced to speak, so that she could speak in her turn, for Milady knew only too well that her most seductive quality was her voice, which ran so skilfully through the whole gamut of tones, from human speech to the language of the heavens.

And yet, despite all those powers of seduction, Milady still might fail, since Felton had been forewarned about her, about every possible risk she might pose. Henceforth, she studied her every action, her every word, down to the simplest look in her eyes, the simplest gesture, even her breathing which could be interpreted as a sigh. In a word, she studied everything like a skilful actor, who has just been given a role of a kind he is not used to portraying.

Her behaviour towards Lord de Winter was an easier proposition, and thus she had come to a decision about it the previous evening. To remain silent and dignified in his presence, from time to time to irritate him with an affected disdain, by a scornful word, to provoke him to threats and violence that would contrast with her own resignation – that was her plan. Felton would see. He might not say anything, but he would see.

In the morning, Felton appeared as usual, but Milady let him preside over all the preparations without addressing a word to him. Then, just as he was about to retire, she had a glimmer of hope, for she thought he was about to speak. But his lips moved without any sound coming out of his mouth, and, struggling to control himself, he locked away in his heart the words that were about to escape his lips, and then left.

Towards midday, Lord de Winter came in.

It was rather a beautiful winter's day, and a ray of that pale English sun, which gives light but not warmth, fell through the prison bars.

Milady was looking out of the window and pretended not to hear the door opening.

'Aha!' said Lord de Winter. 'After playing comedy, then tragedy, now it's the turn of melancholy.'

The prisoner did not respond.

'Yes, yes,' Lord de Winter went on, 'I understand. You'd like to be free out there on that shore; you'd like to be cutting through the waves of that sea as green as emerald on a good ship; you'd like to set me one of those lovely ambushes on land or sea that you are so good at contriving. Patience! Patience! In four days, the shore will be yours, the sea will be open to you – more open than you'd like, indeed, for in four days England will be rid of you.'

Milady clasped her hands, and raising her beautiful eyes to heaven, said with an angelic sweetness of gesture and intonation,

'Lord! Lord! Forgive this man as I forgive him myself.'

'Yes, pray, you cursed woman,' cried the baron. 'Your prayer is all the more generous since you are, I swear, in the power of a man who will not forgive.'

And then he left.

As he did so, with a piercing gaze through the half-open door, she spotted Felton who quickly stepped back so as not to be seen by her.

Then she threw herself on her knees and started to pray.

'My God! My God!' she said. 'You know the holy cause for which I suffer – give me then the strength to suffer.'

The door opened softly. The beautiful supplicant pretended not to hear, and, in a tearful voice, went on:

'God of vengeance! God of goodness! Will you permit the atrocious intentions of this man to be fulfilled?'

Only then did she pretend to hear the noise of Felton's foot-steps, and, rising as swiftly as thought, she blushed as if she were ashamed to have been caught on her knees.

'I do not like to disturb those at prayer, madam,' Felton said gravely. 'Do not trouble yourself on my account, I beseech you.'

'How do you know I was praying, sir?' said Milady, her voice choked with sobs. 'You are mistaken, sir, I was not praying.'

'Do you think, then, madam,' replied Felton in the same grave voice, although with a gentler note, 'that I believe I am entitled to prevent a creature from prostrating herself before her Creator? God forbid! Besides, repentance befits the guilty. Whatever crime has been committed, a guilty soul at the feet of God is sacred to me.'

'Guilty? I?' said Milady with a smile that would have disarmed the angel of the Last Judgement. 'Guilty? My God, thou knowest if I am. Say I am condemned, sir, very good. But you know that God, who loves martyrs, sometimes allows the innocent to be condemned.'

'Were you condemned, were you a martyr,' replied Felton, 'then that would be even more reason to pray, and I would help you myself with my prayers.'

'Oh, you are a just man,' cried Milady, throwing herself at his feet. 'Listen, I cannot endure it any longer, for I am afraid my strength shall fail me when I must keep up the struggle and confess my faith. Listen, then, to the supplication of a woman in despair. You are deceived, sir, but that is not the point. I only ask you one favour, and if you grant it me, I will bless you in this world and the next.'

'Speak to the master, madam,' said Felton. 'Fortunately it is not my duty to pardon or punish, and God has given that respon-sibility to one higher than me.'

'To you, no, to you alone. Listen to me, rather than contribute to my destruction, rather than contribute to my ignominy.'

'If you have deserved this shame, madam; if you have incurred this ignominy, you must bear it and offer it up to God.'

'What are you saying? Oh, you don't understand me! When I speak of ignominy, you think I'm speaking of some punishment, of prison or death! Would to heaven I were! What do death and prison matter to me?'

'It is I who do not understand you now, madam.'

'Or who pretend not to understand me, sir,' the prisoner replied with a doubtful smile.

'No, madam, on the honour of a soldier, on the faith of a Christian!'

'What? You don't know about Lord de Winter's designs on me?'

'I don't.'

'Impossible! You are his confidant.'

'I never lie, madam.'

'Oh, but he is so open you must have guessed.'

'I don't try to guess anything, madam. I wait to be confided in, and, apart from what he has said to me in your presence, Lord de Winter hasn't confided anything in me.'

'Why,' cried Milady, with an incredible ring of truth, 'then you are not his accomplice? Then you do not know he intends to cover me with a shame that all the punishments on earth could not equal in horror?'

'You are mistaken, madam,' said Felton, blushing. 'Lord de Winter is incapable of such a crime.'

Good, Milady said to herself, without knowing what it is, he's already calling it a crime!

Then aloud:

'The friend of the beast is capable of anything.'

'Whom do you call the beast?' asked Felton.

'Are there then two men in England to whom such a name applies?'

'You mean Georges Villiers?' said Felton, and his eyes blazed.

'Whom the pagans, the gentiles and the infidels call the Duke of Buckingham,' said Milady. 'I wouldn't have thought there'd be an Englishman in all England who needed such a long explanation to realise whom I meant!'

'The hand of the Lord is stretched over him,' said Felton, 'he will not escape the punishment he deserves.'

Felton was merely expressing the feeling of execration towards the duke that every Englishman vowed to this man whom the Catholics themselves called the extortionist, the peculator, the debauchee, and whom the Puritans simply called Satan.

'Oh, my God! My God!' cried Milady. 'When I beg you to send that man the punishment which is his due, you know I am not pursuing my own vengeance but imploring the deliverance of a whole people.'

'Do you know him, then?' asked Felton.

At last, he's asking me a question, Milady said to herself, overjoyed at having so quickly achieved so great a result.

'Oh yes, I know him! Oh yes – to my misfortune, my eternal misfortune!'

Milady wrung her arms as if in a paroxysm of grief. Doubtless feeling his strength was failing him, Felton took several steps towards the door. But the prisoner, who hadn't let him out of her sight, leapt after him and stopped him.

'Sir!' she cried, 'be good, be merciful, hear my prayer: that knife the fatal prudence of the baron removed from me, because he knew what I wanted to use it for – oh, hear me out! – that knife . . . give it to me for just a minute, for mercy's sake, for pity's sake! I embrace your knees! Look, you can shut the door, I bear you no ill will. God, how could I bear you ill will, the only just, good, compassionate being I have met? You, who may be my saviour! For a minute, that knife, one minute, just one, and I'll give it back to you through the peephole in the door. No more than a minute, Mr Felton, and you will have saved my honour!'

'Kill yourself!' cried Felton in terror, forgetting to withdraw his hands from the prisoner's. 'Kill yourself!'

'I have spoken, sir,' murmured Milady, lowering her voice and letting herself sink to the floor. 'I have revealed my secret! He knows everything! My God, I'm lost!'

Felton remained standing, motionless and undecided.

He still has doubts, thought Milady. I wasn't realistic enough.

They heard someone walking in the corridor. Milady recognised Lord de Winter's tread. Felton recognised it too and went towards the door.

Milady sprang forward.

'Oh, not a word,' she said in a thick voice, 'not a word to that man of everything I've told you, or I am lost, and it's you, you . . .'

Then, as the steps drew nearer, she fell silent lest her voice should be heard, and pressed her beautiful hand to Felton's lips in a gesture of infinite terror. Felton gently pushed Milady away, and she collapsed on to a couch.

Lord de Winter walked past the door without stopping, and the sound of his footsteps could be heard receding down the corridor.

Felton, deathly pale, stood for a few moments with his ears strained, listening, and then, when the sound had entirely died away, he exhaled like a man waking from a dream and rushed out of the room.

'Ah!' said Milady, listening in her turn to the sound of Felton's footsteps, which went off in the opposite direction to those of Lord de Winter, 'so at last you're mine!'

Then her brow darkened.

'If he talks to the baron,' she said, 'I'm lost, because the baron, who knows full well I won't kill myself, will put me in front of him with a knife in my hands, and he'll see that all this great despair was just an act.'

She went and stood before her mirror, and looked at herself. Never had she been so beautiful.

'Oh, yes!' she said, smiling. 'But he won't talk to him.'

That evening, Lord de Winter came in with the supper.

'Sir,' Milady said to him, 'is your presence an obligatory accessory to my captivity? May you not spare me the additional torment
your visits cause me?'

'Why, dear sister!' said de Winter. 'Didn't you sentimentally
announce to me, with that pretty mouth that is so cruel to me
today, that you came to England for the sole purpose of seeing
me at your leisure – a pleasure of which, you told me, you felt the
loss so keenly that you risked everything for its sake: seasickness,
storm, captivity? Well, here I am! Be satisfied. Besides, this time
there's reason for my visit.'

Milady shuddered; she thought Felton had talked. Never in her
life, perhaps, had this woman, who had experienced so many
powerful and contradictory emotions, felt her heart beat so
violently.

She was seated. Lord de Winter took an armchair, pulled it
over to her side and sat down next to her. Then, taking a document
from his pocket and slowly unfolding it, he said, 'Here, I wanted
to show you this sort of passport I have drawn up myself and
which, from now on, will serve you as an official number in the
life I am consenting to let you lead.'

Then, turning his eyes from Milady to the document, he read:

Order to convey to ――――

'The destination is left blank,' de Winter interrupted himself.
'If you have some preference, let me know, and as long as it's a
thousand leagues from London, your request will be granted. So,
I'll start again:

Order to convey to ―――― the woman Charlotte Backson[1],
branded by the justice of the kingdom of France, but
released after punishment. She will reside in this place
without ever travelling more than three leagues hence. In

case of any attempt at escape, the death penalty will be
enacted. She will receive five shillings a day for board and
lodging.

'This order doesn't concern me,' Milady replied coldly, 'since
it's made out in another name than mine.'

'A name! Do you have one?'

'I have your brother's.'

'You're mistaken, my brother is only your second husband,
and the first is still alive. Tell me his name and I'll put it instead
of Charlotte Backson. No? . . . You don't want to? . . . You're
silent? Very well, you'll be imprisoned under the name of Charlotte
Backson.'

Milady remained silent, only this time not out of artifice but
terror. She believed the order could be executed immediately; she
thought Lord de Winter had brought her departure forward; she
believed she was condemned to leave that same night. She imagined
everything was lost for a moment when all of a sudden she noticed
that the order bore no signature.

She felt such joy at this discovery she couldn't conceal it.

'Yes, yes,' said Lord de Winter, who saw what was going
through her mind, 'yes, you're looking for the signature, and you're
thinking: all is not lost since the warrant is unsigned; he's showing
it to me to frighten me, that's all. You're mistaken: tomorrow this
order will be sent to the Duke of Buckingham; the day after
tomorrow it will come back signed by his hand and bearing his
seal, and twenty-four hours later, you have my word, its execution
will begin. Farewell, madam, that is all I have to say to you.'

'And my reply to you, sir, is that this abuse of power, this exile
under a false name, is infamous.'

'Would you rather be hanged under your real name, Milady?
You know that English laws are inexorable towards abuses of
marriage. Explain yourself with all due candour. Though my name,
or rather my brother's, is mixed up in all this, I will risk the scandal
of a public trial to be sure of getting rid of you this time.'

Milady made no reply, but grew as pale as a corpse.

'Oh, I see you prefer to move from place to place. Excellent, madam, and there is an old proverb that says youth is formed by travel. My faith, you're not wrong, now I come to think of it – life is good! That's why I am not keen to have you deprive me of it. It remains, then, to settle the affair of the five shillings. I'm a bit parsimonious, aren't I? That's because I'm not keen to have you corrupting your warders. Besides, you'll always have your charms to seduce them. Employ them then, if your failure with Felton hasn't filled you with disgust for attempts of that sort.'

Felton hasn't talked, Milady said to herself, nothing's lost, then.

'And now, madam, goodbye to you. Tomorrow I will come to announce the departure of my messenger.'

Lord de Winter rose, bowed ironically to Milady, and went out.

Milady exhaled. She still had four days ahead of her. Four days would be enough to finish seducing Felton.

Then she had a terrible thought, that Lord de Winter might send Felton himself to have the order signed by Buckingham. Felton would thus escape her, and, for the prisoner to succeed, the magic spell of her seduction had to be unbroken.

Yet, as we have said, one thing reassured her: Felton had not talked.

Not wanting to appear shaken by Lord de Winter's threats, she sat down at the table and ate.

Then, as she had the previous evening, she got down on her knees and recited her prayers aloud. As on the previous evening, the soldier ceased pacing and stopped to listen.

Soon she heard lighter steps than the sentry's coming from the end of the corridor and stopping outside her door.

'It's he,' she said.

And then she began the same devotional singing that had inflamed Felton so violently the evening before.

But, although her sweet, full, sonorous voice vibrated more harmoniously and heartbreakingly than ever, the door stayed shut. It seemed to Milady, in one of those furtive glances she cast at the little peephole, that she made out the young man's burning eyes, but whether this was real or a vision, he had enough self-control this time not to come in.

But, moments after she had finished her devotional singing, Milady thought she heard a deep sigh. Then the same footsteps she had heard approach went away slowly and as if regretfully.

LV

FOURTH DAY OF CAPTIVITY

THE NEXT DAY, WHEN FELTON came into Milady's room, he found her standing on an armchair, holding a rope fashioned from several cambric handkerchiefs that she had torn into strips and tied together. At the noise Felton made opening the door, Milady jumped lightly down from her chair and tried to hide the improvised rope behind her back.

The young man was even paler than usual, and his eyes, red from sleeplessness, indicated he had passed a feverish night.

And yet his brow was armoured with a serenity more austere than ever.

He advanced slowly towards Milady, who had sat down, and taking hold of one end of the murderous braid that she had inadvertently, or perhaps intentionally, left unconcealed, asked coldly, 'What is this, madam?'

'That? Nothing,' said Milady, smiling with that note of sorrow she was so good at imparting to her smile. 'Boredom is the mortal enemy of prisoners. I was bored, so I amused myself by braiding this rope.'

Felton turned his eyes to that part of the wall where he had found Milady standing on the armchair in which she was now sitting, and saw above her head a gilt hook-nail plugged into the wall, which served for hanging either clothes or arms.

He started, and the prisoner saw this start – for, although her eyes were cast down, nothing escaped her.

'And what were you doing, standing on that armchair?' he asked.

'What does it matter to you?' replied Milady.

'Why,' said Felton, 'I wish to know.'

'Don't question me,' said the prisoner. 'You know very well that we true Christians are forbidden to lie.'

'Well then,' said Felton, 'I will tell you what you were doing, or rather what you were going to do. You were going to finish that fatal piece of work you are nurturing in your mind. Reflect, madam: if our God forbids lying, then how much more strictly does he forbid suicide.'

'When God sees one of his creatures unjustly persecuted, trapped between suicide and dishonour, believe me, sir,' replied Milady, in a tone of profound conviction, 'God pardons his suicide – for suicide is then martyrdom.'

'You either say too much, or too little. Speak, madam, in heaven's name, explain yourself.'

'What, should I tell you my misfortunes so you can call them fables? Should I tell you my plans so you can report them to my persecutor? No, sir. Besides, what does the life or death of a wretched condemned woman matter to you? You're only responsible for my body, aren't you? And so long as you produce a corpse, and it is recognised as mine, nothing more would be required of you, and perhaps your reward will even double.'

'I, madam? I?' cried Felton. 'You suppose I would ever accept a prize for your life? Oh, you're not thinking what you're saying.'

'Let me do it, Felton, let me do it!' said Milady, her excitement mounting. 'Every soldier must be ambitious, isn't that right? You're a lieutenant. Well then, you'll follow my coffin with the rank of captain.'

'But what have I done to you,' said Felton, shaken, 'that you burden me with such responsibility before God and men? In a few days you will be far from here, madam, your life will no longer be in my charge, and,' he added with a sigh, 'then you can do with it what you will.'

'So,' cried Milady, as if she couldn't restrain a surge of holy indignation, 'you, a pious man, you who are called just, you only ask one thing: not to be incriminated in, or inconvenienced by, my death!'

'My duty is to watch over your life, madam, and I shall watch over it.'

'But do you understand the mission you are performing? Cruel enough, if I were guilty, what name will you give it, what name will the Lord give it, if I am innocent?'

'I am a soldier, madam, and I carry out the orders I have been given.'

'Do you believe that, on the day of the Last Judgement, God will separate the blind executioners from the iniquitous judges? You do not want me to kill my body, and yet you make yourself the agent of him who wishes to kill my soul!'

'But, I repeat to you,' said Felton, reeling, 'no danger threatens you, and I will answer for Lord de Winter as for myself.'

'Madman!' cried Milady. 'Poor madman, who dares answer for another man when the wisest, when the greatest in the sight of God, hesitate to answer for themselves, and who sides with the party of the strongest and most fortunate so as to crush the weakest and most unfortunate!'

'Impossible, madam, impossible,' murmured Felton, who in his heart of hearts felt the truth of this argument. 'As a prisoner you will not regain your freedom by any of my doing, and as a living woman, you will not lose your life by any of my doing either.'

'Yes,' cried Milady, 'but I shall lose what is far more precious to me than life; I will lose my honour, Felton. And it is you, you, whom I shall hold responsible before God and men for my shame and my infamy.'

This time Felton, impassive as he was, or as he pretended to be, could not resist the secret influence that had already taken hold of him. To see this woman, so beautiful, as white as the most luminous vision; to see her tearful and threatening by turns, to fall under the spell simultaneously of grief and of beauty – it was too much for a visionary, it was too much for a brain sapped by the fervent dreams of ecstatic faith, it was too much for a heart corroded by a scalding love of heaven, and a consuming hatred of men.

Milady saw the agitation; she sensed intuitively the flame of the antagonistic passions that burned with the blood in the young fanatic's veins; and, like a skilful general who, seeing his enemy about to retreat, bears down on him with a cry of victory, she stood up, beautiful as an ancient priestess, inspired as a Christian virgin, and, her arms outstretched, her neck bared, her hair wild, one hand modestly clasping her dress to her bosom, her gaze lit up by that fire which had already sown confusion in the young Puritan's senses, she walked towards him, singing to a fervent air, a terrifying note in her sweet voice:

Deliver up to Baal his victim
To the lions the martyr feed
God hath thy penitence decreed . . .
From the abyss I cry to Him!

Felton stopped, as if petrified, at this strange reproach.

'Who are you, who are you?' he cried, clasping his hands. 'Are you an envoy from God, are you a minister of hell, are you an angel or a demon, are you called Eloas or Astarte¹?'

'Don't you recognise me, Felton? I am neither an angel nor a demon. I am a daughter of this earth and a sister of your faith; that is all.'

'Yes! Yes!' said Felton. 'I was still in doubt, but now I believe.'

'You believe, and yet you are the accomplice of that son of Belial, who is called Lord de Winter! You believe, and yet you leave me in the hands of my enemies, of the enemy of England, of the enemy of God. You believe, and yet you deliver me up to him who floods and pollutes the world with his heresies and debauches, to that loathsome Sardanapalus[2] whom the blind call the Duke of Buckingham and the believers the Antichrist.'

'I, deliver you up to Buckingham? I? What do you mean?'

'They have eyes,' cried Milady, 'but they see not. They have ears, but they hear not.'

'Yes, yes,' said Felton, running his hands over his sweat-drenched brow, as if to pluck out his last misgiving. 'Yes, I recognise the voice that speaks to me in my dreams; yes, I recognise the features of the angel who comes to me every night, crying out to my unsleeping soul, "Strike, save England, save yourself, for you will die without appeasing the Lord!" Speak, speak!' cried Felton, 'I understand you now.'

A flash of terrible joy, swift as thought, shot through Milady's eyes.

But, fleeting as that murderous gleam was, Felton saw it and shuddered, as if it had lit up the abysses of this woman's heart.

Felton suddenly remembered Lord de Winter's warnings, Milady's seductions, her first attempts on her arrival. He stepped back a pace and bowed his head, but without ceasing to look at her, as if, fascinated by this strange creature, his eyes couldn't tear themselves away from hers.

Milady was not a woman to misunderstand the meaning of this hesitation. Under her apparent emotion, her icy composure did not waver for an instant. Before she was compelled by Felton's reply to resume this conversation that was so difficult to maintain at such a pitch of exaltation, she let her hands fall, and, as if a woman's weakness had prevailed over a mystic's fervour, said, 'No, it is not for me to be the Judith who will deliver Bethulia from that Holofernes. The sword of God is too heavy for my arm. Let me then flee dishonour through death, let me take refuge in martyrdom. I ask you neither for liberty, as would a guilty woman,

nor vengeance, as would a pagan. Let me die, that is all. I beseech
you, I implore you on my knees; let me die, and my last breath
will be a blessing on my saviour.'

At this sweet, supplicating voice, at this timid, downcast look,
Felton drew closer to her again. Gradually the enchantress had
slipped back into that magical finery which she could take up and
set aside at will, that is, beauty, gentleness, tears, and, above all,
the irresistible attraction of voluptuous, mystical delights, the most
devouring of all pleasures.

'Alas!' said Felton, 'all I can do is pity you if you prove to me
that you are a victim! But Lord de Winter has bitter grievances
against you. You are a Christian, you are my sister in religion. I
feel drawn to you, I who have only ever loved my benefactor, I
who have only ever found traitors and the ungodly in this life. But
you, madam, you who are so beautiful in reality, you who are so
pure in appearance, you must have performed iniquitous deeds for
Lord de Winter to pursue you like this.'

'They have eyes,' Milady repeated, with a note of unspeakable
grief, 'but they see not. They have ears, but they hear not.'

'Well then,' cried the young officer, 'speak, speak!'

'Confide my shame in you?' cried Milady, with the blush of
modesty on her face. 'For the crime of one is often the shame of
another. Confide my shame in you, a man, and I, a woman? Oh!'
she went on, modestly shielding her beautiful eyes with her hand.
'Oh, never, never could I do such a thing!'

'To me, to a brother!' cried Felton.

Milady looked at him for a long while with an expression that
the young officer took for hesitation, but in fact was only watchfulness and, above all, a desire to fascinate.

A suppliant in his turn, Felton clasped his hands.

'Well then,' said Milady, 'I will have faith in my brother, I will
venture it!'

At that moment, they heard Lord de Winter's footsteps. But
this time Milady's terrible brother-in-law wasn't content to pass
the door and go on his way, as he had the evening before. He

stopped, exchanged a few words with the sentry, then the door opened and he appeared.

During that brief exchange, Felton had quickly started back and when Lord de Winter entered, he was a few paces away from the prisoner.

The baron came in slowly, and fixing his searching gaze first on the prisoner and then on the young officer, he said:

'You've been here a very long time, John. Has this woman been telling you all her crimes? If so, I can understand the length of the conversation.'

Felton shuddered, and Milady sensed she was lost if she did not come to the assistance of the Puritan in his confusion.

'Ah, you're afraid your prisoner may escape you!' she said. 'Well then, ask your worthy gaoler what favour I was requesting of him just now.'

'You were asking a favour?' said the baron suspiciously.

'Yes, my lord,' said the disconcerted young man.

'And, tell me, what favour was that?' asked Lord de Winter.

'A knife, which she would give back to me through the peep-hole a minute after receiving it,' replied Felton.

'Is there someone hiding in here, then, whose throat this gracious person wishes to slit?' said Lord de Winter in his mocking and disdainful voice.

'Just me,' replied Milady.

'I gave you a choice between America and Tyburn,' said Lord de Winter. 'Choose Tyburn, Milady: the rope, believe me, is more reliable than the knife.'

Felton paled and took a step forward, remembering that when he'd come in, Milady was holding a rope.

'You are right,' said the latter. 'I'd already thought of that.' Then she added in a hollow voice, 'I will do so again.'

Felton shivered to the very marrow of his bones. Lord de Winter most likely noticed this trembling, for he said.

'Beware, John! John, my friend, I am relying on you. Take care, I warned you! Anyway, cheer up, my boy. In three days we will be rid of this creature, and where I'm sending her, she will never harm anyone again.'

'You hear him!' Milady burst out, in such a way that the baron thought she was addressing heaven and Felton understood she was addressing him.

Felton bowed his head musingly.

The baron took the officer by the arm, looking over his shoulder to keep Milady in his sight until he left.

'So,' said the prisoner, when the door was shut again, 'I haven't got as far as I thought. De Winter has swapped his normal stupidity for a hitherto unknown gift for caution. That will be his desire for vengeance, and how that desire schools a man! As for Felton, he's hesitating. Ah, he's not a man like that cursed d'Artagnan. A Puritan only worships virgins, and he clasps his hands together to worship them. A musketeer loves women, and he clasps them in his arms to do so.'

Nevertheless Milady waited impatiently, for she suspected the day wouldn't pass without her seeing Felton again. Finally, an hour after the scene we have just related, she heard low voices talking at the door, and soon afterwards the door opened and she recognised Felton.

The young man strode quickly into the room, leaving the door open behind him and signalling to Milady to keep quiet. His face was distraught.

'What do you want of me?' she said.

'Listen,' replied Felton in a low voice, 'I've just sent the sentry away so I can stay here without anyone knowing I've come, and talk to you without anyone being able to hear what you say. The baron has just told a terrible story.'

Milady assumed her smile of a resigned victim and shook her head.

'Either you are a demon,' Felton went on, 'or the baron, my benefactor, my father, is a monster. I have known you for four days, I have loved him for ten years, so I have every reason to waver between the two of you. Don't be frightened by what I'm saying, I need to be convinced. Tonight, after midnight, I will come and see you, and you will convince me.'

'No, Felton, no, my brother,' she said, 'the sacrifice is too great, and I can feel what it is costing you. No, I am lost, do not be lost with me. My death will be far more eloquent than my life, and the corpse's silence will convince you far better than the prisoner's words.'

'Quiet, madam,' cried Felton, 'do not speak to me in that manner. I have come so that you may promise me on your honour, so that you may swear on what you hold most sacred, that you will make no attempt on your life.'

'I will not promise,' said Milady, 'for no one has more respect for oaths than I, and if I make a promise, I will have to keep it.'

'Well then,' said Felton, 'pledge your word only until the moment you see me again. If, once you've seen me again, you still persist, well, then you will be free, and I will myself give you the weapon you asked me for.'

'Well,' said Milady, 'then I'll wait for you.'

'Swear it.'

'I swear it by our God. Are you satisfied?'

'Very well,' said Felton. 'Till tonight!'

And then he rushed out of the room, closed the door and waited outside, the soldier's half-pike in his hand, as if he were mounting guard in his place.

When the soldier returned, Felton gave him back his weapon.

Then, going over to the peephole, Milady saw the young man cross himself with delirious fervour and walk away down the corridor in transports of joy.

As for her, she went back to her place, a smile of savage contempt on her lips, and blasphemously repeated the terrible name of God, by whom she had sworn, without ever having learnt to know Him.

'My God!' she said. 'That crazed fanatic! My God is myself — myself and whoever helps me take my revenge!'

LVI
FIFTH DAY OF CAPTIVITY

M ILADY HAD ACHIEVED HALF A TRIUMPH, and the success
made her twice as strong.

It was no great challenge to conquer, as she had done hitherto,
men who were ready to let themselves be seduced, and whom the
court's schooling in gallantry swiftly lured into her trap. Milady
was beautiful enough not to meet with any resistance of the flesh,
and skilful enough to overcome any obstacles of the mind.

But this time she was pitted against an untamed spirit, abstracted
and unfeelingly austere. Religion and penitence had made of Felton
a man impervious to ordinary seductions. Such vast plans, such
tumultuous enterprises revolved in that fevered brain that there was
no room left for love, whether capricious or constant, that sentiment
which sustains itself by leisure and grows in corruption. With her
feigned virtue, therefore, Milady had made a breach in the estimation
of a man horribly forewarned against her, and, with her beauty, in
the heart and senses of a man who was chaste and pure. This experiment on the most rebellious subject nature and religion could submit
to her investigation had finally allowed her to gauge the full extent
of her powers, which had remained hidden from her until then.

Even so, there were many times that evening when she had
despaired of fate and of herself. She did not call on God, as we
know but she put her faith in the genius of evil, that infinite sover-
eignty, which rules over all the details of human life, and contrives
it that, as in the Arabian fable[1], a pomegranate seed can suffice to
rebuild a lost world.

Fully prepared to receive Felton, Milady could now lay her
plans for the following day. She knew she had only two days left
and that once the order was signed by Buckingham (and Buckingham
would sign it all the more readily because it bore a false name, so

he wouldn't recognise the woman it concerned), the moment the order was signed, as we were saying, the baron would put her aboard ship. She also knew that women condemned to be transported wield much less powerful weapons in their seductions than those allegedly virtuous women, whose beauty is illuminated by the sun of society, whose minds are vaunted by the voice of fashion, and whose persons are gilded by the enchanted glow of reflected nobility. Being a woman condemned to a wretched and debasing punishment is no hindrance to being beautiful, but it is an obstacle to ever being powerful again. Like all people of genuine merit, Milady knew the milieu that suited her nature and her means. Poverty was repugnant to her; abjection deprived her of two-thirds of her greatness. Milady was only a queen among queens; to dominate, her pride had to be satisfied. Commanding inferiors was a source of humiliation rather than pleasure to her.

Of course she would return from her exile, she didn't doubt that for a moment, but how long would that exile last? For an active and ambitious nature like Milady's, any day not spent rising is an ill-starred day, so what word exactly should one use for days spent falling? Losing a year, two years, three years – in other words an eternity; coming back when a happy, triumphant d'Artagnan and his friends had received their well-earned reward from the queen – those were devouring thoughts a woman like Milady could not endure. And the storm howling within her made her twice as strong. If her body could have assumed for an instant the dimensions of her mind, she would have shattered the walls of her prison.

Amidst all this, the memory of the cardinal still goaded her. What must the distrustful, worried, suspicious cardinal be thinking, what must he be saying about her silence – the cardinal, not only her sole prop, her sole support, her sole protector at present, but also the principal instrument of her fortune and future vengeance? She knew him. It was obvious that, on her return from a futile expedition, she could plead prison all she wished, she could expatiate on her sufferings as much as she pleased, the cardinal would still reply, with the mocking calm of the sceptic, who has both might and genius on his side, 'You shouldn't have let them catch you.'

Milady therefore summoned all her energies, murmuring in the recesses of her mind the name of Felton, the only glimmer of light that reached to the depths of the hell into which she had fallen. And like a snake coiling and uncoiling its body to know its own strength, she enveloped Felton in the myriad folds of her endlessly fertile imagination.

Yet time wore on all the same, the hours seeming to jolt the clock awake as they passed in single file, and each stroke of the bronze clapper reverberated in the prisoner's heart. At nine o'clock, Lord de Winter made his customary visit, tested the windows and the bars, checked the floors and walls, and examined the fireplace and the doors, without either he or Milady uttering a single word during his long and meticulous inspection.

No doubt they both realised the situation had become too serious to waste time on useless words and ineffectual anger.

'There we are,' said the baron, as he left her, 'you won't be escaping tonight!'

At ten o'clock, Felton came to post a sentry. Milady recognised his step. She could tell it the way a mistress can tell the step of her one true lover, and yet Milady both loathed and despised this feeble fanatic.

It wasn't the appointed hour. Felton did not come in.

Two hours later, as midnight struck, the sentry was relieved.

Now the hour had come. Milady began to wait impatiently.

The new sentry began pacing in the corridor.

Ten minutes later, Felton joined him.

Milady listened attentively.

'Listen,' the young man said to the sentry, 'on no pretext whatsoever are you to move away from this door. You know that last night a soldier was punished by my lord for having left his post for a moment, even though it was I who kept watch during his brief absence.'

'Yes, I know,' said the soldier.

'I charge you, then, to observe the strictest vigilance. For my part,' he added, 'I am going to give this woman's room a second inspection. I fear she has sinister designs on herself and I have been ordered to keep watch on her.'

'Good,' murmured Milady, 'listen to the austere Puritan lying!'

The soldier, for his part, merely smiled.

'Damn, lieutenant,' he said, 'your luck can't be all bad if you get jobs like that, especially if my lord has given you permission to watch until she's in bed.'

Felton blushed. In any other circumstances, he would have reprimanded the soldier who took the liberty to make such a joke. But his conscience murmured too loudly for his tongue to dare speak.

'If I call,' he said, 'come. And if someone comes, call me.'

'Yes, lieutenant,' said the soldier.

Felton went into Milady's room. Milady rose to her feet.

'You're here?' she said.

'I promised you I'd come,' said Felton, 'and I have come.'

'You promised me something else as well.'

'But what? My God!' said the young man, who, despite his powers of self-control, felt his knees trembling and the sweat beading on his forehead.

'You promised to bring me a knife, and to leave it with me after our talk.'

'Don't speak of that, madam,' said Felton. 'There is no situation, however terrible, that permits a creature of God to take his own life.'

'Ah, you have been thinking!' said the prisoner, sitting down in her armchair with a contemptuous smile. 'I have been thinking too.'

'About what?'

'That I had nothing to say to a man who does not keep his word.'

'Oh, my God!' murmured Felton.

'You may retire,' said Milady. 'I shall not speak.'

'Here's the knife!' said Felton, taking from his pocket the weapon he had brought as he promised, but hesitating to pass it to his prisoner.

'Let's see it,' said Milady.

'What for?'

'On my honour, I'll give it back immediately. You can put it on the table and stand between me and it.'

Felton handed the weapon to Milady, who carefully examined its temper, and tested the point on the tip of her finger.

'Good,' she said, giving the knife back to the young officer. 'It's a fine one, of good steel. You are a loyal friend, Felton.'

Felton took the weapon and put it on the table, as had just been agreed with his prisoner.

Milady followed him with her eyes and made a gesture of satisfaction.

'Now,' she said, 'listen to me.'

The instruction was redundant; the young officer stood face to face with her, poised to devour her words.

'Felton,' said Milady, with a melancholy solemnity, 'Felton, if your sister, your father's daughter, said to you, "While I was still young, and unfortunately possessed of a certain beauty, I was lured into a trap, but I resisted. Ambushes and attacks were multiplied around me, but I resisted. The religion I serve and the God I adore were blasphemed because I called to my aid that God and that religion, but I resisted. Then outrages were heaped upon me, and as they couldn't destroy my soul, they wanted to stain my body forever. Finally . . ."'

Milady paused, and a bitter smile played over her lips.

'Finally,' said Felton, 'finally what did they do?'

'Finally, one evening, they resolved to paralyse that resistance they could not vanquish. One evening, they added a powerful narcotic to my water. I had barely finished my meal when I felt myself gradually sinking into a strange torpor. Although I was unsuspecting, a vague fear seized me, and I tried to fight against sleep. I got up, wanting to run to the window and call for help, but my legs wouldn't support me. It seemed as if the ceiling was falling on my head and crushing me with its weight. I stretched out my arms and tried to talk, but I could only make garbled sounds. An irresistible numbness came over me, I held on to a chair, feeling I was going to fall, but soon that wasn't enough support for my limp arms and I fell on one knee, then two. I wanted to cry out but my tongue was frozen. Doubtless God did not see or hear me as I slid to the floor, in the grips of a deathlike sleep.

'Of everything that happened during that sleep, and of all the time that passed while it lasted, I have no memory. The only thing I recall is that I woke up in a round room, which was sumptuously furnished, and inaccessible to daylight other than through an opening in the ceiling. Moreover, there seemed to be no door to it; a prison.

'It was a long time before I could take in where I was, or any of the details I am relaying. My mind seemed to struggle futilely to shake off the heavy shadows of that sleep from which I could not wrench myself free. I had a vague awareness of having travelled some distance, of the rolling of a carriage, of a horrible dream in which all my strength was used up – but it was all so dark and indistinct in my thoughts that these events seemed to belong to a life that was not mine, and yet entangled with it in a fantastic duality.

'For some time, the state I found myself in seemed so strange to me that I thought I was having a dream. I staggered to my feet. My clothes were near me on a chair. I didn't remember either getting undressed or going to bed. Then reality gradually dawned on me, full of shameful terrors: I was no longer in the house I lived in. As far as I could judge by the light of the sun, two thirds of the day were already over! It was on the previous evening I had fallen asleep; my sleep had thus lasted almost twenty-four hours. What had happened during that long sleep?

'I got dressed as fast as I could. All my slow, torpid movements indicated the influence of the narcotic had still not entirely ceased. Moreover, that room had been furnished to receive a woman, and the most consummate coquette could not have conceived of a desire, which, on looking round the room, she did not find already gratified.

'I was definitely not the first captive to find herself locked away in that splendid prison. But, you understand, Felton, the more beautiful the prison was, the more it terrified me.

'Yes, it was a prison, for I tried in vain to get out. I tested all the walls looking for a door, but everywhere the walls gave back a solid, dead sound.

'I went round that room perhaps twenty times, searching for some way out. There wasn't one. Overwhelmed by exhaustion and terror, I collapsed into an armchair.

'In the meantime, night was rapidly falling, and with night my terrors increased. I didn't know whether I should stay sitting where I was. It seemed to me I was surrounded by unknown dangers into which I might fall at every step. I hadn't eaten anything since the day before but my fears kept me from feeling any hunger.

'No sound reached me from outside, allowing me to gauge the time. I merely presumed that it was perhaps seven or eight o'clock in the evening, for it was October and it was pitch dark.

'Suddenly the sound of a door swinging on its hinges made me start. A flaming globe appeared above the glass opening in the ceiling, casting a bright light into the room, and I saw with terror that a man was standing a few paces away from me.

'A table with two settings, bearing a supper all prepared, had appeared as if by magic in the middle of the room.

'This man was he who had been pursuing me for a year, who had sworn my dishonour, and who, with the first words that came out of his mouth, made me understand he had accomplished this the previous night.'

'The beast!' murmured Felton.

'Oh, yes, the beast!' cried Milady, seeing the interest the young officer, whose soul seemed to hang on her lips, took in this strange story. 'Yes, the beast! He had thought triumphing over me in my sleep would mean there was nothing more to be said. He came hoping I would accept my shame because my shame had already been consummated. He came to offer me his fortune in exchange for my love.

'All that a woman's heart could contain of proud contempt and disdainful speech I poured on this man. No doubt he was used to such reproaches, for he listened to me calmly, smiling, his arms crossed over his chest. Then, when he thought I had said all I had to say, he started towards me. I leapt for the table, seized the knife and pressed it to my breast.

'"Take one step further," I said to him, "and besides my dishonour, you will have my death to lay at your door."

'Doubtless there was in my look, in my voice, in my whole person, that sincerity of gesture, of pose and accent that has the power to convince the most perverse souls, for he stopped.

'"Your death?" he said to me. "Oh, no, you are too charming a mistress for me to consent to losing you like that, after only having the happiness of possessing you once. Goodbye, my enchanting beauty! I shall wait until you are in a better frame of mind before I pay you my next visit."

'At these words, he blew a whistle. The flaming globe that lit my room rose up and disappeared, and I found myself in darkness again. The same noise of a door opening and shutting repeated itself a moment later, the flaming globe came down again, and I was alone.

'It was a terrible moment. If I had still entertained some doubts about my misfortune, those doubts had vanished before a desperate reality. I was in the power of a man whom I not only detested but despised. A man capable of anything, who had already given me a fatal proof of what he might dare to do.'

'But who was this man?' asked Felton.

'I spent the night on a chair, starting at the least noise, for around midnight, the lamp went out and I found myself in darkness again. But the night passed without any new attempt by my persecutor. Dawn broke. The table had disappeared, but I still had the knife in my hand.

'That knife was my only hope.

'I was overwhelmed with exhaustion. My eyes burned from lack of sleep. I hadn't dared drift off for a single moment. The dawn reassured me, and I went to throw myself on my bed, not taking my hand off the liberating knife which I hid under my pillow.

'When I woke up, a new table had been laid.

'But this time, despite my terrors, despite my anguish, a gnawing hunger gripped me. I hadn't had any sustenance for forty-eight hours. I ate some bread and some fruit. Then, remembering the narcotic mixed into the water I'd drunk, I didn't touch what was on the table, but went to fill my glass from a marble fountain fixed in the wall above my washstand.

'However, despite this safeguard, I remained in terrible anguish for some while. But my fears this time were unfounded, I spent the day without feeling anything resembling that which I dreaded.

'I took the precaution of emptying half the carafe, so that my distrust wouldn't be noticed.

'Evening came, and, with it, darkness. But, deep as it was, my eyes began to accustom themselves to it. In the midst of the gloom, I saw the table sink into the floor. A quarter of an hour later, it reappeared bearing my supper. The next moment, thanks to the same lamp, my room grew light again.

'I was resolved only to eat things to which it was impossible to add a sleeping draught; two eggs and some fruit made up my meal. Then I went to draw a glass of water from my protecting fountain, and I drank it.

'At the first mouthful, it seemed to me as if didn't have the same taste as in the morning. Gripped by a sudden suspicion, I stopped. But I had already drunk half a glass.

'I threw away the rest, horrified, and waited, the sweat of terror on my brow.

'Some invisible witness had clearly seen me take the water from that fountain, and had taken advantage of my very self-confidence to guarantee all the more surely my ruin, so coldly decided, so cruelly pursued.

'Half an hour had not passed before the same symptoms took hold. But, as this time I had only drunk half a glass, I struggled longer, and instead of falling into a deep sleep, I lapsed into a soporific state that left me aware of what was happening around me, while robbing me of the strength either to defend myself or to flee.

'I dragged myself towards the bed, to seek the only defence left me, my protector knife, but I couldn't reach the pillow. I fell on my knees, my hands clamped to one of the bedposts at the foot of the bed. Then I realised I was lost.'

Felton turned terribly pale, and a convulsive shudder ran through his whole body.

'And the most terrible thing,' went on Milady, her voice broken as though she was again experiencing the anguish of that dreadful moment, 'was that this time I was aware of the danger threatening me. My soul, if I can put it like this, was awake in my sleeping body. I could see, I could hear. It's true that it was all like a dream, but that only made it more terrifying.

'I saw the lamp going back up, gradually leaving me in darkness, then I heard the creak of that door that I knew so well, though the door had only opened twice.

'I sensed instinctively that someone was coming towards me. They say a wretch lost in the deserts of America can sense the approach of a serpent in the same way.

'I wanted to struggle, I tried to cry out; by an incredible act of will, I even managed to raise myself up, but only to fall back down again . . . down into the arms of my persecutor.'

'Tell me, then – who was this man?' cried the young officer.

Milady saw at a glance all the suffering she was causing Felton by dwelling on every detail of her story, but she did not want to spare him any torment. The more thoroughly she broke his heart, the more remorselessly he would avenge her. She thus went on as if she hadn't heard his exclamation, or as if she thought the moment to answer it had not arrived.

'Only this time, it was no longer some sort of inert, insensible corpse the beast was dealing with. I've told you that, although unable to regain the full use of my faculty, I could still feel I was in danger. So I fought with all my might and no doubt, weakened though I was, I put up a long resistance, for I heard him cry out, "These wretched Puritan women! I knew they wearied their executioners but I thought them less strong against their seducers."

'Alas, this desperate resistance couldn't last! I felt my strength give out, and this time it was not my sleep but a dead faint the coward took advantage of.'

Felton listened without emitting any sound other than a muffled growl, but his marble brow ran with sweat, and his hand, hidden under his jacket, tore at his breast.

'My first impulse, when I came to, was to search under my pillow for that knife I hadn't been able to reach. Not having served my defence, it might at least serve my expiation.

'But as I grasped that knife, Felton, a terrible thought came into my mind. I've sworn to tell all and I will tell all. I've promised you the truth, and I will tell it, even if it should damn me.'

'The thought came to you of avenging yourself on this man, isn't that so?' cried Felton.

'Ah, yes!' said Milady. 'That thought was not worthy of a Christian, I know. Our soul's eternal enemy, that lion constantly roaring around us, had no doubt breathed it into my mind. Truly, what can I say, Felton?' Milady went on, in the tone of a woman accusing herself of a crime. 'The thought came to me and doubtless has never left me since. It is for that murderous thought that I stand punished today.'

'Go on, go on,' said Felton. 'I'm impatient to see you attain your vengeance.'

'Oh, I was determined it would happen as soon as possible! I had no doubt he would come back the next night. During the day I had nothing to fear.

'So, when it was time for breakfast, I did not hesitate to eat and drink. I had decided to pretend to have supper, but to take nothing. So I had to use the morning's food to combat the evening's fast.

'I also hid a glass of water from my breakfast, thirst having caused me most suffering when I passed forty-eight hours without eating or drinking.

'The day passed without having any other influence on me than to strengthen me in my resolve. But I took care my face didn't betray any of the thoughts in my heart, for I had no doubt that I was being observed. Several times, even, I felt a smile on my lips. Felton, I dare not tell you what idea I was smiling at, you would abhor me . . .'

'Go on, go on,' said Felton. 'You can see I'm listening and impatient to reach the end.'

'Evening came, the usual things happened. My supper was served in the dark, as ever, then the lamp was lit, and I sat down at the table.

'I only ate some fruit. I pretended to pour out some water from the carafe, but only drank what I'd kept in my glass. I managed the changeover deftly enough not to cause my spies, if I had any, to entertain any suspicion.

'After supper, I gave the same signs of torpor as the evening before, but this time, as if I was overcome with fatigue, or inured to danger, I dragged myself to the bed and pretended to fall asleep.

'This time I found my knife under my pillow and, as I feigned sleep, my hand convulsively gripped its hilt.

'Two hours passed without anything new happening. This time – oh, my God, who would have imagined it the day before – I began to be afraid he might not come.

'At last I saw the lamp gently rise and disappear into the furthest reaches of the ceiling. My room filled with darkness, but I made an effort to peer through the gloom.

'Some ten minutes passed. I heard nothing but the beating of my heart.

'I implored heaven that he would come.

'At last I heard the familiar sound of the door opening and shutting. Despite the thick carpet, I heard footsteps that made the floor creak. Despite the darkness, I saw a shadow coming towards my bed.'

'Hurry, hurry!' said Felton. 'Don't you see your every word burns me like molten lead?'

'Then,' went on Milady, 'then I summoned up all my strength. I remembered that the hour of vengeance, or rather justice, had sounded. I saw myself as another Judith. I crouched, my knife in my hand, and when I saw him near me, stretching out his arms to search for his victim, then, with a last cry of grief and despair, I stabbed him in the middle of the chest.

'The scoundrel! He had anticipated everything. His chest was clad in mail. The knife skidded off, blunted.

'"Aha!" he cried, seizing my arm and tearing away the weapon that had so ill served me. "You have designs on my life, my beautiful Puritan! But that's worse than hatred, that's ingratitude! Come, come, calm yourself, my beautiful child! I thought you'd softened. I'm not one of those tyrants that keep women against their will. You don't love me. With my usual self-conceit, I had my doubts, but now I'm convinced of it. Tomorrow you'll be free."

'I had only one desire – that he should kill me.

'"Beware!" I told him. "For my freedom will be your dishonour. Yes, for, the moment I am out of here, I will tell everything, I will tell of the violence you have used against me, I will tell of my captivity. I will denounce this palace of infamy. You are very high in the world, my lord, but tremble! Above you there is the king, and above the king there is God."

'For all his seeming self-mastery, my persecutor allowed a flash of anger to slip. I couldn't see the expression on his face, but I felt the arm on which my arm rested tremble.

'"Then you won't leave here," he said.

'"Good, good!" I cried. "Then the site of my torment will also be the site of my grave. Good, I will die here and you will see if a ghost with her accusations is not more terrible than a living person with her threats!"

'"You won't have a weapon."

'"There's one despair has placed within the reach of every creature who has the courage to use it. I will let myself starve to death."

'"Come," said the scoundrel, "isn't peace preferable to a war like this? I will give you back your freedom this instant, I will proclaim you a virtuous woman, I will call you the Lucretia of England[2]."

'"And I will say you are the Sextus, I will denounce you before men as I have denounced you before God, and if, like Lucretia, I have to sign my accusation in my blood, I will sign it."

'"Aha!" said my enemy mockingly. "Then that's a different matter. My faith, all things considered, you're perfectly well off here, you lack nothing, and if you let yourself starve to death, it will be your fault."

'At these words, he went out. I heard the door open and shut again, and I was left overwhelmed – less, I confess, by my grief, than by shame at not having avenged myself.

'He kept his word. All the next day and all the next night passed without my seeing him again. But I kept my word too, and I neither ate nor drank; I was resolved, as I had told him, to let myself starve to death.

'I passed that day and night in prayer, for I hoped that God would forgive my suicide.

'The second night, the door opened. I was lying on the floor, my strength starting to ebb away.

'At the noise I raised myself on one hand.

'"Well," said a voice that vibrated in my ear too terribly for me not to recognise it, "well, have we softened a little now? Will we buy our freedom for just a promise of silence? You know, I am a good prince," he added, "and although I have no fondness for the Puritans, I do them justice, as I do their women – when they're pretty. Come, swear me a little oath on the cross. That's all I ask of you."

'"On the cross!" I cried, getting to my feet, for that abhorred voice had restored all my strength. "On the cross I swear that no promise, no threat, no torture will ever seal my lips! On the cross, I swear to denounce you everywhere as a murderer, as a despoiler of honour, as a coward! On the cross, I swear, if I ever get out of here, I will demand vengeance against you from the entire human race!"

'"Be careful!" said the voice, in a tone of menace I hadn't heard before. "I have an ultimate method, which I will only use in the direst extremity, for sealing your lips, or at least for preventing people from believing a single word you say."

'I summoned up all my strength to reply with a burst of laughter.

'He saw that from then on it was eternal war between us, a war to the death.

'"Listen," he said, "I give you the rest of tonight and the daylight hours of tomorrow. Think on it. Promise to be silent, and riches, respect, even honours shall surround you. Threaten to speak, and I condemn you to infamy."

'"You?" I cried. "You?"

'"To eternal, ineradicable infamy!"

'"You?" I repeated. 'Oh, I tell you, Felton, I thought he was mad!

'"Yes, I!" he said.

'"Ah, leave me," I said, "go, if you don't want me to batter my head against the wall before your eyes!"

'"Very well," he said, "if that's what you want, till tomorrow evening!"

'"Till tomorrow evening," I replied, sinking to the floor and biting the carpet in rage . . .'

Felton was leaning on a chair, and Milady saw with a devilish joy that his strength might give out before the end of the story.

LVII
A DEVICE FROM CLASSICAL TRAGEDY

AFTER A MOMENT'S SILENCE, which Milady used to observe the young man listening to her, she continued her story:

'It was almost three days since I had drunk or eaten anything, and I was suffering horrendous torments: sometimes it felt as if clouds were tightening around my forehead, veiling my eyes: delirium had set in.

'Evening came. I was so weak that I fainted constantly, and every time I fainted, I thanked God because I thought I was going to die.

'In the midst of one of those fainting fits, I heard the door open; terror called me back to myself.

'My persecutor entered, followed by a masked man. He was masked himself, but I recognised his step, I recognised that commanding air hell has bestowed on his person for the misfortune of mankind.

'"Well," he said to me, "have you made up your mind to swear the oath I asked of you?"

'"You said yourself that Puritans only have one word. You have heard mine: it is to pursue you on earth before the tribunal of men, and in heaven before the tribunal of God!"

'"So, you persist?"

'"I swear before that God who hears me: I will take the whole world as witness to your crime, and I will only cease when I have found an avenger."

'"You are a prostitute," he said in a voice of thunder, "and you will suffer the punishment of prostitutes! Branded in the eyes of the world you would invoke, try to prove to that world that you are neither guilty nor mad!"

'Then, addressing the man who was with him, he said, "Executioner, do your duty."'

'Oh, his name, his name!' cried Felton. 'Tell me his name!'

'Then, despite my cries, despite my resistance, for I began to understand something far worse than death was intended for me, the executioner seized me, threw me down on the floor, bruised me with his grip, and, choking with sobs, almost unconscious, calling to God Who did not listen, I suddenly let out a terrible scream of pain and shame. A burning iron, a red-hot iron, the executioner's iron, had left its stamp on my shoulder.'

Felton let out a roar.

'Here,' said Milady, getting to her feet with queenly majesty, 'here, Felton, see how they invented a new martyrdom for the young girl who was pure and yet the victim of a villain's brutality. Learn to know the hearts of men, and from now on be less ready to serve as the instrument of their unjust vengeance.'

With a quick movement, Milady opened her dress, tore the cambric covering her breast, and, blushing with feigned rage and affected shame, showed the young man the ineradicable mark that dishonoured so beautiful a shoulder.

'But,' cried Felton, 'that is a fleur-de-lys I see there!'

'And that is the true horror,' replied Milady. 'With the brand of England, he would have had to have proved which court had decreed it, and I could have made a public appeal to all the courts of the realm. But the brand of France . . . oh, by that I was truly branded!'

This was too much for Felton.

Pale, motionless, crushed by this terrible revelation, dazzled by the superhuman beauty of this woman who unveiled herself before him with a shamelessness he found sublime, he finally fell on his knees before her, as the first Christians did before those pure and holy martyrs whom the persecution of the emperors delivered up to the bloodlust of the rabble in the circus. The brand disappeared, only the beauty remained.

'Forgive me! Forgive me!' cried Felton. 'Oh, forgive me!'

Milady read in his eyes: Love! Love!

'Forgive you for what?' she asked.

'Forgive me for having thrown in my lot with your persecutors.'

Milady held out her hand to him.

'So beautiful, so young!' cried Felton, covering that hand with kisses.

Milady bestowed one of those looks on him that make a slave into a king.

Felton was a Puritan. He released the woman's hand to kiss her feet.

He no longer loved her, he adored her.

When this crisis was over, when Milady appeared to have recovered the composure she had never lost, when Felton had seen the veil of chastity drawn back over those treasures of love that were only hidden from him so that he would desire them more ardently, he said, 'Ah, now, I have only one other thing to ask you, and that is the name of your real executioner, since for me, there is only one. The other was an instrument, that's all.'

'What, brother!' cried Milady. 'Must I still name him? Haven't you guessed it?'

'What!' said Felton. 'Him! . . . him again! . . . Always him! . . . What, the one who is truly guilty . . .'

'The one who is truly guilty,' said Milady, 'is the ravager of England, the persecutor of true believers, the cowardly ravisher of the honour of so many women, he who on a whim of his corrupt heart is going to shed so much blood in the two kingdoms, who protects the Protestants today and will betray them tomorrow . . .'

'Buckingham! Then it is Buckingham!' cried the deranged Felton.

Milady hid her face in her hands, as if she couldn't bear the shame that name brought back to her mind.

'Buckingham, the executioner of this angelic creature!' cried Felton. 'Oh God, You did not crush him! You left him noble, honoured, powerful, for the ruin of us all!'

'God forsakes those who forsake themselves,' said Milady.

'He wants to draw down on his head the punishment reserved

for the cursed!' went on Felton, with mounting exaltation. 'He wants human justice to anticipate divine justice!'

'Men fear him and spare him.'

'Oh!' said Felton. 'I don't fear him, and I won't spare him! . . .'

Milady felt infernal joy bathe her soul.

'But how does Lord de Winter, my protector, my father,' asked Felton, 'find himself mixed up in all this?'

'Listen, Felton,' said Milady, 'alongside the cowardly and contemptible, there are also great and generous natures. I had a fiancé, a man whom I loved and who loved me. A heart like yours, Felton, a man like you. I came to him and I told him everything. That man knew me and didn't doubt me for an instant. He was a great nobleman, Buckingham's equal in every respect. Without saying a word, he girded on his sword, wrapped himself in his cloak, and went to Buckingham Palace.

'Yes, yes,' said Felton, 'I understand, although with men like that, one shouldn't use a sword but a dagger.'

'Buckingham had set out the previous evening as an ambassador to Spain¹, where he was going to ask the hand of the Infanta for King Charles I, who was then only the Prince of Wales. My fiancé came back.

'"Listen," he said to me, "the man has left, thereby escaping my vengeance for the present. But, let us be married meanwhile, as we should be, and then Lord de Winter shall maintain his honour and that of his wife."'

'Lord de Winter!' cried Felton.

'Yes,' said Milady, 'Lord de Winter. And now you must understand everything, don't you? Buckingham was gone for more than a year. Eight days before his return, Lord de Winter died suddenly, leaving me his sole heir. Who dealt him this blow? God, who knows everything, no doubt knows that. I accuse no one myself . . .'

'Oh, what an abyss, what an abyss!' cried Felton.

'Lord de Winter died without saying anything to his brother. The terrible secret was to have been hidden from everyone, until it broke like thunder on the head of the guilty man. Your brother had looked askance at this marriage of his elder brother to a young girl of no means. I felt I couldn't expect any support from a man disappointed in his hopes of an inheritance. I crossed to France, resolved to stay there for the rest of my life. But all my fortune is in England. With communications cut off by the war, my funds ran short, so I was compelled to return. Six days ago I landed at Portsmouth.'

'Well?' said Felton.

'Well, Buckingham doubtless learnt of my return, informed Lord de Winter, who was already prejudiced against me, and told him his sister-in-law was a prostitute, a branded woman. My husband's pure and noble voice was no longer there to defend me. Lord de Winter believed everything he was told, all the more readily because it was in his interest to do so. He had me arrested, brought me here, put me under your guard. You know the rest. The day after tomorrow, he exiles me, deports me; the day after tomorrow he sends me to be surrounded by the vilest of the vile. Oh, the intrigue is well woven! Yes, it's a skilful plot and my honour will not survive it. You can see that I must die, Felton. Felton, give me that knife.'

And at these words, as if all her strength were exhausted, Milady collapsed, weak and languishing, into the arms of the young officer, who, drunk with love, with rage, with unknown pleasures, caught her ecstatically and pressed her to his heart, quivering at the breath of that beautiful mouth, frenzied at the touch of that heaving breast.

'No, no,' he said, 'no, you shall live, honoured and pure. You shall live to triumph over your enemies.'

Milady slowly pushed him away with her hand, while drawing him closer with her gaze, but Felton, in his turn, seized hold of her, imploring her like a deity.

'Oh, death, death!' she said, lowering her voice and her eyelids. 'Oh, death sooner than shame! Felton, my brother, my friend, I beseech you!'

'No,' cried Felton, 'no, you shall live, and you shall be avenged!'

'Felton, I bring misfortune to all around me! Felton, forsake me! Felton, let me die!'

'Well, then we shall die together!' he cried, pressing his lips to his prisoner's.

A knocking rang out on the door. This time Milady pushed him away in earnest.

'Listen,' she said, 'they've heard us, they're coming! It's over, we're done for!'

'No,' said Felton, 'it's only the sentry telling me a patrol is coming.'

'Run to the door, then, and open it yourself.'

Felton obeyed. This woman was his every thought now, his entire soul.

He found himself facing a sergeant commanding a watch patrol.

'Well, what is it?' asked the young lieutenant.

'You told me to open the door if I heard a cry for help,' said the soldier, 'but you forgot to leave me the key. I heard you cry out without understanding what you were saying. I tried to open the door, it was locked from inside, so I called the sergeant.'

'And here I am,' said the sergeant.

Distraught, almost out of his mind, Felton couldn't speak.

Milady realised it was up to her to take control of the situation. She ran to the table and picked up the knife Felton had put there.

'And by what right do you wish to prevent me from dying?' she said.

'Holy God!' cried Felton, seeing the knife glinting in her hand.

At that moment, a burst of ironic laughter rang out in the corridor.

Attracted by the noise, the baron was standing in the doorway, in his dressing gown, with his sword under his arm.

'Aha!' he said. 'Here we are at the final act of the tragedy. You see, Felton, the drama has followed all the stages I suggested. But don't worry, no blood will be shed.'

Milady realised she was lost if she didn't give Felton immediate and terrible proof of her courage.

'You're mistaken, my lord. Blood will be shed, and may that blood be visited on those who caused it to flow!'

Felton cried out and rushed towards her. It was too late: Milady had stabbed herself. But luckily, or deftly, as we should say, the knife had hit the metal corset that in those days shielded women's bosoms like a cuirass. It had glanced off, tearing her dress, and gone in at angle between the flesh and ribs.

Milady's dress was nonetheless stained with blood in a second.

Milady fell backwards, seemingly unconscious.

Felton snatched the knife away.

'You see, my lord,' he said sombrely, 'here is a woman who was under my guard and who has killed herself!'

'Set your mind at rest, Felton,' said Lord de Winter, 'she's not dead. Demons don't die that easily. Set your mind at rest, and go and wait for me in my rooms.'

'But, my lord . . .'

'Go: that's an order.'

At this command from his superior, Felton obeyed, but, as he left, he slipped the knife into his shirt.

As for Lord de Winter, he simply sent for the woman who served Milady and, when she came, he commended the still-unconscious prisoner to her care and left the two of them alone.

Nevertheless, since the wound might, after all, be serious, despite his suspicions, he at once sent a man on horseback to fetch a doctor.

LVIII
ESCAPE

As Lord de Winter had thought, Milady's wound wasn't dangerous. And so, as soon as she found herself alone with the woman the baron had sent for, who was hurriedly undressing her, she opened her eyes.

She still had to feign weakness and pain. But that wasn't a difficult task for an actress like Milady, and the poor woman was so completely fooled by her prisoner that, despite her entreaties, she insisted on watching over her all night.

This woman's presence, however, did not stop Milady thinking.

There was no longer any doubt about it: Felton was convinced, Felton was hers. If an angel had appeared to the young man to accuse Milady, he would certainly, in his current state of mind, have taken it for an envoy of the devil.

Milady smiled at this thought, for henceforth Felton was her only hope, her only means of safety.

But Lord de Winter might have suspected that, and Felton might now be under surveillance himself.

Around four o'clock in the morning, the doctor arrived. But, in the time since Milady had stabbed herself, the wound had already closed up. The doctor was thus unable to determine its direction or its depth. He could only tell from the patient's pulse that the case was not serious.

Next morning, on the pretext that she hadn't slept that night and needed rest, Milady dismissed the woman who was watching over her.

She had one hope, which was that Felton would come at breakfast time, but Felton didn't come.

Had her fears come true? Suspected by the baron, was Felton going to fail her at the critical moment? She only had one day left: Lord de Winter had told her she was embarking on the twenty-third, and it was now the morning of the twenty-second.

Nevertheless, she waited patiently enough until dinnertime.

Although she hadn't eaten in the morning, dinner was brought at the usual time. Milady noticed with alarm that the uniforms of the soldiers guarding her were different.

She ventured to ask what had become of Felton. The reply came that Felton had taken a horse an hour ago and ridden off.

She asked if the baron was still in the castle. The soldier replied that he was, and that he had orders to inform him if the prisoner wished to speak with him.

Milady replied that she was too weak at present, and that her wish was to be left alone.

The soldier went out, leaving dinner served on the table.

Felton had been sent away, the marines changed – so, Felton was distrusted.

This was the final blow for the prisoner.

Left alone, she got up. She had stayed in bed out of prudence, and to make them believe she was seriously wounded, but now it burned her like live coals. She glanced at the door. The baron had had the peephole boarded up. No doubt he feared that through this opening, she could still find some diabolical means to seduce the guards.

Milady smiled with joy. She could now give way to her passions without being observed. She paced the room, as frenzied as a raving madwoman or a tigress locked in an iron cage. If the knife was still there, she would definitely have considered killing not herself this time but the baron.

At six o'clock, Lord de Winter came in. He was armed to the teeth. This man, whom Milady had regarded until then as no more than a slightly foolish gentleman, had become an admirable gaoler: he seemed to foresee, guess and anticipate everything.

A single glance at Milady told him what was going on in her soul.

'So be it,' he said, 'but you won't kill me today either. You have no weapons left, and besides, I'm on my guard. You had begun to pervert my poor Felton: he was already succumbing to your infernal influence, but I will save him. He won't be seeing you again. It's over. Gather your rags, you're leaving tomorrow. I had arranged for you to go aboard on the twenty-fourth, but I think the sooner it happens, the safer it will be. By noon tomorrow I will have the order for your exile, signed by Buckingham. If you say a single word to anyone at all before you're on the ship, my sergeant will blow your brains out – he's been ordered to do so.

If, once aboard, you say a word to anyone at all before the captain gives you his permission, the captain will have you thrown in the sea – that is agreed. Goodbye, that's all I have to say to you today. I will see you again tomorrow to bid you farewell!'

And, with these words, the baron left.

Milady had listened to this whole threatening tirade with a smile of contempt on her lips, but fury in her heart.

Supper was served. Milady felt she needed strength. She didn't know what might happen during that night, which was menacingly drawing near. Great clouds rolled across the sky, and distant lightning heralded a storm.

The storm broke around ten o'clock in the evening. Milady found it comforting to see nature share the chaos in her heart. Thunder rumbled in the air like the rage in her mind. She thought the gusts of wind dishevelled her hair like the trees whose branches they bent, scattering their leaves. She howled like the thunderstorm, and her voice was drowned out by the great voice of nature which also seemed to moan and despair.

Suddenly she heard a rapping on the windowpane, and, in a flash of lightning, she saw a man's face appear at the bars.

She ran to the window and opened it.

'Felton!' she cried. 'I'm saved!'

'Yes,' said Felton, 'but quiet, quiet! I need time to saw through your bars. Just be careful they don't see you through the peephole.'

'Oh, that's proof the Lord is with us, Felton,' said Milady; 'they've boarded up the peephole.'

'Good. God has robbed them of their senses!' said Felton.

'But what should I do?' asked Milady.

'Nothing, nothing, just shut the window. Go to bed, or at least get into bed fully clothed. When I've finished, I'll rap on the windowpane. But are you able to go with me?'

'Oh, yes!'

'Your wound?'

'It's painful, but I can still walk.'

'Be ready, then, for the first signal.'

Milady shut the window, put out her lamp, and, as Felton had counselled, went and huddled in the bed. Amidst the wailing of the storm, she heard the grating of the file on the bars, and, at every flash of lightning, she saw Felton's shadow on the other side of the window.

She spent an hour breathless, panting, her forehead drenched in sweat, her heart gripped by terrible anguish at every movement she heard in the corridor.

There are some hours that last a year.

After one had passed, Felton tapped again.

Milady sprang out of bed and opened the window. Two bars had been removed, leaving an opening the size of a man.

'Are you ready?' asked Felton.

'Yes. Need I bring anything?'

'Gold, if you have any.'

'I do. Luckily they left me what I had when I came.'

'So much the better: I used all mine to charter a boat.'

'Take it,' said Milady, putting a bag of gold into Felton's hands.

Felton took the bag and threw it down by the foot of the wall.

'Now,' he said, 'will you?'

'Here I come.'

Milady climbed on a chair and leant halfway out of the window. She saw the young officer hanging over the abyss on a rope ladder.

For the first time, a rush of terror reminded her she was a woman.

The sheer void appalled her.

'I'd thought that might happen,' said Felton.

'It's nothing, it's nothing,' said Milady. 'I'll go down with my eyes shut.'

'Do you trust me?' Felton said.

'Do you have to ask?'

'Join your hands together. Cross them – that's right.'

Felton tied her wrists with his handkerchief, then, over the handkerchief, with a rope.

'What are you doing?' Milady asked in surprise.

'Put your arms around my neck, and don't be afraid of anything.'

'But I'll knock you off balance. We'll both be dashed on the rocks.'

'I'm a sailor, don't worry.'

There wasn't a moment to lose. Milady put both arms around Felton's neck and let herself slide out of the window.

Felton began to climb down the ladder slowly, rung by rung. Despite the weight of the two bodies, the blast of the storm buffeted them from side to side.

Felton suddenly stopped.

'What's wrong?' asked Milady.

'Quiet,' said Felton, 'I hear footsteps.'

'We've been found out!'

There was silence for a few moments.

'No,' said Felton, 'it's nothing.'

'But what's that noise then?'

'The patrol coming past on the walkway.'

'Where's the walkway?'

'Just below us.'

'They'll see us.'

'Not if there isn't any lightning.'

'They'll bump into the foot of the ladder.'

'Luckily it's six feet short.'

'There they are, my God!'

'Silence!'

The two of them remained suspended, motionless, not breathing, twenty feet above the ground, while the soldiers passed under them, laughing and talking.

It was agony for the fugitives.

The patrol passed. They heard the sound of footsteps receding and the murmur of voices growing fainter.

'Now,' said Felton, 'we're safe.'

Milady breathed a sigh and fainted.

Felton continued down. Reaching the bottom of the ladder and feeling nothing to support his feet, he lowered himself hand over hand, until finally, on the last rung, he hung, arms outstretched, and touched the ground. He bent down, gathered up the bag of gold, and put it between his teeth.

Then he picked up Milady in his arms, and quickly set off in the opposite direction to the one the patrol had taken. Soon he turned off the walkway, climbed down over the rocks, and, reaching the seashore, blew a whistle.

An identical whistle replied, and five minutes later a boat crewed by four men appeared.

The boat came in as close to shore as it could but the water wasn't deep enough for it to ground. Felton waded into the water up to his belt, refusing to entrust his precious load to anyone else.

Fortunately the storm was abating, although the sea was still rough. The little boat jumped on the waves like a nutshell.

'To the sloop,' said Felton, 'and pull hard.'

The four men set to, but the swell was too heavy for their oars to find much purchase on it.

Nonetheless, they drew away from the castle – that was the main thing. The night was pitch black, and it was already impossible to make out the shore from the boat, let alone the boat from the shore.

A black speck rocked on the waves.

It was the sloop.

While the boat made for it with all the strength of its four rowers, Felton untied the rope and then the handkerchief binding Milady's hands.

Then, when her hands were loose, he scooped up some seawater and threw it in her face.

Milady breathed a sigh and opened her eyes.

'Where am I?' she said.

'Safe,' replied the young officer.

'Oh, safe, safe!' she cried. 'Yes, here's the sky, here's the sea!

This air I'm breathing is the air of freedom. Ah! . . . Thank you, Felton, thank you!'

The young man clasped her to his heart.

'But what's the matter with my hands?' asked Milady. 'It feels as though my wrists have been crushed in a vice.'

Milady raised her arms, and, indeed, there were bruises all over her wrists.

'Alas!' said Felton, looking at those beautiful hands and gently shaking his head.

'Oh, it's nothing, it's nothing!' cried Milady. 'I remember now!'

Milady looked around, searching for something.

'Here it is,' said Felton, nudging the bag of gold with his foot.

They drew up to the sloop. The sailor on watch hailed the boat, and the boat answered.

'What is that vessel?' asked Milady.

'The one I've chartered for you.'

'Where will it take me?'

'Wherever you wish, provided you put me ashore at Portsmouth.'

'What are you going to do in Portsmouth?'

'Carry out Lord de Winter's orders,' said Felton with a sombre smile.

'What orders?' asked Milady.

'You don't understand, then?' said Felton.

'No. Oh, explain yourself, please.'

'As he distrusted me, he wanted to guard you himself, and sent me in his place to have Buckingham sign the order for your deportation.'

'But if he distrusted you, how did he come to entrust you with this order?'

'Was I supposed to know what I was carrying?'

'True. And you're going to Portsmouth?'

'I've no time to lose: tomorrow is the twenty-third and Buckingham leaves tomorrow with the fleet.'

'He's leaving tomorrow? Where's he going?'

'To La Rochelle.'

'He mustn't leave!' cried Milady, her usual presence of mind forgotten.

'Don't worry,' replied Felton, 'he won't leave.'

Milady thrilled with joy. She had just read to the bottom of the young man's heart: Buckingham's death was spelled out in capital letters there.

'Felton . . .' she said, 'you are as great as Judas Maccabeus[1]! If you die, I will die with you, that's all there is to it.'

'Quiet!' said Felton. 'We're here.'

The side of the boat was indeed touching the sloop.

Felton climbed the ladder first and gave his hand to Milady, while the sailors steadied her, for the sea was still choppy.

A moment later they were on deck.

'Captain,' said Felton, 'here's the person of whom I spoke to you. She must be conveyed, safe and sound, to France.'

'For a thousand pistoles,' said the captain.

'I've given you five hundred already.'

'True,' said the captain.

'And here's the other five hundred,' said Milady, reaching for the bag of gold.

'No,' said the captain, 'I can only give my word once, and I did that to this young man. The other five hundred pistoles aren't due to me until we land in Boulogne.'

'Will we do that?'

'Safe and sound,' said the captain, 'as sure as my name is Jack Butler.'

'Well then,' said Milady, 'if you keep your word, instead of five hundred, I'll give you a thousand pistoles.'

'Hurrah for you, then, my fair lady,' cried the captain, 'and may God send me a constant stream of passengers like Your Ladyship!'

'In the meantime,' said Felton, 'take us to the little bay off Chichester, just before Portsmouth. You know we agreed you'd take us there.'

The captain replied by giving orders for the necessary

manoeuvre, and towards seven o'clock in the morning, the vessel dropped anchor in the aforementioned bay.

On the way, Felton told Milady everything: how, instead of going to London, he had chartered the little vessel, how he had made his way back, how he had scaled the wall by fixing crampons in the gaps between the stones to rest his feet on, and how finally, when he reached the bars, he had fastened the ladder to them. The rest Milady knew.

For her part, Milady wanted to encourage Felton in his mission. But, as soon as she spoke, she saw the young fanatic needed moderating rather than inciting.

It was agreed that Milady would wait for Felton until ten o'clock. If he hadn't come back by ten, she would leave.

In that case, supposing he was at liberty, he would join her in France, at the Carmelite convent at Béthune.

LIX

WHAT HAPPENED IN PORTSMOUTH
ON 23 AUGUST 1628

FELTON TOOK HIS LEAVE of Milady like a brother going for a walk takes his leave of his sister with a kiss of her hand.

He seemed his usual calm self, only a strange light shone in his eyes, like the sparkle of a fever, his brow was paler than normal, his teeth were clenched, and he spoke in a curt staccato, which indicated that something dark was moving within him.

As long as he was in the boat taking him to land, he kept his face turned towards Milady, who, standing on the deck, followed him with her eyes. Both were fairly sure they need have no fear of being pursued. No one ever came into Milady's room before nine o'clock, and it was a journey of three hours to get from the castle to London.

Felton stepped ashore, climbed the little rise that led to the top of the cliff, saluted Milady a last time, and set off towards the town.

After a hundred paces, the ground sloped down and all he could see was the sloop's mast.

He hastened off at once in the direction of Portsmouth, the towers and houses of which he saw before him, about half a mile away, emerging from the morning mist.

The sea off Portsmouth was covered with ships, whose masts, like a forest of poplars stripped of their leaves by winter, could be seen swaying in the puffs of wind.

As he raced along, Felton reviewed what ten years of ascetic meditation and a long sojourn among the Puritans had furnished him by way of true and false accusations against the favourite of James VI[1] and Charles I.

When he compared the public crimes of this minister – blatant crimes, European crimes, if one can put it like that – with the private and unknown crimes with which Milady had charged him, Felton found the guiltier of the two men Buckingham comprised was the one whose life was unknown to the public. His love, so strange, so new, and so ardent, made him view the loathsome and fictitious accusations of Milady the way, through a magnifying glass, one sees horrific monsters that, in reality, are but atoms barely visible next to an ant.

The speed at which he ran inflamed his blood still further. The thought that he was leaving behind him, prey to a terrible vengeance, a woman whom he loved, or rather worshipped as a saint; his past emotions and present fatigue all exalted his soul beyond human feeling.

He entered Portsmouth around eight o'clock in the morning. All the town's inhabitants were abroad, drums were beating in the streets and at the port, the troops were marching down to the sea to embark.

Felton reached the Admiralty covered in dust and dripping with perspiration. Ordinarily so pale, his face was purple with heat and rage. The sentry wanted to turn him away but Felton called for the senior officer in the guard post, and, taking from his pocket the letter of which he was the bearer, he said, 'An urgent message from Lord de Winter.'

At the name of Lord de Winter, who was known to be one of His Grace's most intimate friends, the officer gave the order to admit Felton, who was, in any case, wearing the uniform of a naval officer himself.

Felton rushed into the palace.

Just as he entered the vestibule, another man came in too, dusty and out of breath, who left a post horse at the gate, which, on arriving, fell to its knees.

He and Felton went simultaneously to speak to Patrick, the duke's confidential valet. Felton named Baron de Winter; the stranger would not give a name, claiming he might only make himself known to the duke. Each insisted on going in first.

Patrick, who knew that Lord de Winter had both official and amicable relations with the duke, gave preference to the one who came in his name. The other was forced to wait, and it was plain to see how bitterly he cursed this delay.

The valet led Felton through a large hall where the deputies from La Rochelle led by the Prince de Soubise[2] were waiting, and steered him into a dressing room where Buckingham, just out of the bath, was finishing his toilet, to which, now as ever, he was paying extraordinary attention.

'Lieutenant Felton,' said Patrick, 'on the part of Lord de Winter.'

'On the part of Lord de Winter?' repeated Buckingham. 'Show him in.'

Felton went in. As he did so, Buckingham threw a sumptuous, gold-brocaded dressing gown on to a sofa, in order to put on a doublet of blue velvet, all embroidered with pearls.

'Why didn't the baron come himself?' asked Buckingham. 'I was expecting him this morning.'

'He asked me to tell Your Grace,' replied Felton, 'that he deeply regrets not having that honour, but that he was prevented by his guard duties at the castle.'

'Yes, yes,' said Buckingham, 'I know, he has a prisoner.'

'That prisoner is just what I wanted to speak with Your Grace about,' said Felton.

'Well, speak then.'

'What I have to say is only for your attention, my lord.'

'Leave us, Patrick,' said Buckingham, 'but keep within earshot of the bell. I'll call you presently.'

Patrick went out.

'We are alone, sir,' said Buckingham. 'Speak.'

'My lord,' said Felton, 'Baron de Winter wrote to you the other day requesting you sign an order of transportation concerning a young woman by the name of Charlotte Backson.'

'Yes, sir, and I replied that he should bring me or send me the order, and I would sign it.'

'Here it is, my lord.'

'Give it to me,' said the duke.

And, taking it from Felton, he cast a rapid glance over the paper. Then, seeing that it was indeed the one that had been mentioned to him, he placed it on the table, took a pen, and prepared to sign it.

'Excuse me, my lord,' said Felton, stopping the duke; 'but does Your Grace know that Charlotte Backson is not the real name of this young woman?'

'Yes, sir, I know that,' replied the duke, dipping his pen in the ink.

'Then Your Grace knows her real name?' Felton asked curtly. 'I do.'

The duke's pen hovered over the paper. Felton grew pale.

'And knowing her real name,' said Felton, 'my lord will sign it all the same?'

'Of course,' said Buckingham, 'twice, ideally.'

'I cannot believe,' continued Felton, in increasingly curt, staccato tones, 'that Your Grace knows that it concerns Lady de Winter.'

'I am fully aware of it, although I am surprised you are too!'

'And Your Grace will sign this order without remorse?'

Buckingham looked at the young man haughtily.

'Do you have any notion, sir,' he said to him, 'that you are asking me questions, and that it is rather foolish of me to answer them?'

'Answer, my lord,' said Felton; 'the circumstances are more serious than you may think.'

Buckingham thought that the young man, coming on the part of Lord de Winter, was probably speaking in his name, and he recovered his temper.

'Without a shred of remorse,' he said. 'The baron knows, as do I, that Milady de Winter is a hardened criminal, and it is almost a mark of favour only to punish her with transportation.'

The duke put his pen to the paper.

'You will not sign that order, my lord!' said Felton, taking a step towards the duke.

'I will not sign this order?' said Buckingham. 'And why not?'

'Because you will look into your soul, and you will do justice to Milady.'

'It would be doing her justice to send her to Tyburn,' said Buckingham. 'Milady is a vile creature.'

'My lord, Milady is an angel, as you well know, and I demand you set her free.'

'What?' said Buckingham. 'Have you gone mad, speaking to me in that way?'

'My lord, forgive me, I speak as I can. I shall restrain myself. But, my lord, think of what you're about to do, and beware of committing an excess!'

'What did you say? Lord have mercy,' cried Buckingham, 'but I think he's threatening me!'

'No, my lord, I am still begging. And I say to you: a drop of water is enough to make the cup run over; one slight fault can draw down punishment upon a head that has been spared despite so many crimes.'

'Mr Felton,' said Buckingham, 'you will leave here and place yourself under arrest immediately.'

'You are going to hear me out, my lord. You have seduced this young girl; you have outraged her, defiled her. Atone for your crimes against her; let her go free, and I will demand nothing more of you.'

'Demand nothing more?' said Buckingham, looking at Felton in astonishment, and stressing every syllable of the three words as he uttered them.

'My lord,' continued Felton, growing more agitated as he spoke, 'my lord, take care, all England is tired of your iniquities. My lord, you have abused the royal power that you have almost usurped. My lord, you are abhorred by God and men. God will punish you hereafter, but I − I will punish you today!'

'Ah, this is too much!' cried Buckingham, taking a step towards the door.

Felton barred his way.

'I ask you humbly,' he said, 'to sign the order setting Lady de Winter free. Consider that she is a woman you have dishonoured.'

'Withdraw, sir,' said Buckingham, 'or I shall call and have you put in irons.'

'You will not call,' said Felton, flinging himself between the duke and the bell placed on a silver-inlaid stand. 'Careful, my lord, for now you are in God's hands!'

'In the devil's hands, you mean,' cried Buckingham, raising his voice to attract people, although not calling out directly.

'Sign, my lord, sign the release of Lady de Winter,' said Felton, pushing a piece of paper towards the duke.

'Under duress? Are you joking? Ho there, Patrick!'

'Sign, my lord!'

'Never!'

'Never?'

'To me!' yelled the duke, leaping for his sword as he did so.

But Felton gave him no time to draw it. The knife Milady had stabbed herself with was hidden, unsheathed, in his doublet. In one bound he was on the duke.

As he did so, Patrick came into the room, crying, 'My lord, a letter from France!'

'From France?' cried Buckingham, forgetting everything as he thought whom this letter might be from.

Felton seized the moment and drove the knife into his side up to the hilt.

'Ah, traitor!' cried Buckingham. 'You've killed me . . .'

'Murder!' yelled Patrick.

Felton cast his eyes around him for a way to escape and, seeing the door free, raced into the next room, which, as we have said, was where the deputies from La Rochelle were waiting. He crossed it at a run and rushed for the stairs. But on the top step he ran into Lord de Winter, who, seeing him pale, wild, livid, his hand and face stained with blood, grabbed him by the neck, crying, 'I knew it, I guessed it – but I've come a minute too late! Oh, luckless, luckless wretch that I am!'

Felton put up no resistance. Lord de Winter handed him over to the guards – who took him, while awaiting further orders, to a small terrace overlooking the sea – and then hurried to the duke's dressing room.

At the duke's cry and Patrick's call, the man whom Felton had met in the antechamber rushed into the room.

He found the duke lying on a sofa, his clenched hand pressed to the wound.

'La Porte,' said the duke, in a dying voice, 'La Porte, do you come from her?'

'Yes, my lord,' replied Anne of Austria's faithful servant, 'but too late, perhaps.'

'Silence, La Porte, you might be overheard. Patrick, let no one in. Oh, I'll never know what she wants to tell me! My God, I'm dying!'

And then the duke fell unconscious.

Meanwhile, Lord de Winter, the deputies, the leaders of the

expedition, the officers of Buckingham's household had all burst into the room. On all sides cries of despair rang out. Filling the palace with tears and groans, the news quickly overflowed in all directions and spread through the town.

A cannon fired, announcing that something new and unexpected had happened.

Lord de Winter tore his hair.

'A minute too late!' he cried. 'A minute too late! Oh, my God, my God, what cursed ill fortune!'

It was seven o'clock that morning, in fact, that he had been informed that a rope ladder was dangling from one of the castle windows. He had immediately run to Milady's room, found the room empty and the window opened, the bars cut through. Remembering the verbal warning from d'Artagnan by his messenger, he had trembled for the duke, and, running to the stable, without waiting to have a horse saddled, he had leapt on the first one to hand and ridden hell for leather. Jumping off the horse in the courtyard, he had raced up the stairs and, on the top step, as we have said, run into Felton.

The duke wasn't dead, however. He came to, reopened his eyes, and hope flooded back into all their hearts.

'Gentlemen,' he said, 'leave me alone with Patrick and La Porte. Ah, it's you, de Winter! You sent me a strange madman this morning – look at the state he's left me in!'

'Oh, my lord!' cried the baron. 'I'll never get over it!'

'And that would be wrong of you, my dear de Winter,' said Buckingham, giving him his hand. 'I know of no man who deserves to be mourned the length of another man's life. But leave us, I beg you.'

The baron went out, sobbing.

Only the wounded duke, La Porte and Patrick remained in the dressing room.

A doctor had been sent for, but was nowhere to be found.

'You will live, my lord, you will live,' Anne of Austria's messenger repeated, kneeling by the duke's sofa.

'What has she written to me?' Buckingham said weakly, blood streaming from him, fighting against excruciating pain to talk of her he loved. 'What has she written to me? Read me the letter.'

'Oh, my lord!' said La Porte.

'Obey, La Porte. Don't you see I have no time to lose?'

La Porte broke the seal and held the parchment in front of the duke's eyes, but Buckingham's attempts to make out the writing were in vain.

'Read it, then,' he said, 'go on, read it. I can't see any more. Read it! For soon I may no longer be able to hear and I'll die without knowing what she wrote to me.'

La Porte raised no more objections, and read:

My lord,

By all that I have suffered through you and for you, since I have known you, I beseech you, if you have any concern for my peace of mind, to cut short the great armament you are engaged in against France, and to call off a war of which it is said openly that religion is the visible cause, and secretly that your love for me is the hidden cause. This war may not only bring great calamities on France and England but also on you, my lord, misfortunes for which I could never be consoled.

Pay great care to your life, which is threatened, and which will be dear to me the moment I am no longer obliged to think of you as an enemy.

Your affectionate

Anne

Buckingham summoned all the life left in him to listen to this reading. Then, when it was finished, as if he found the letter a bitter disappointment, he asked, 'Have you nothing else to tell me by word of mouth, La Porte?'

'I have, my lord. The queen bade me tell you to take care of yourself, for she had been warned that there was a plot to assassinate you.'

'And is that all? Is that all?' said Buckingham impatiently.

'She also bade me tell that she always loved you.'

'Ah!' said Buckingham, 'God be praised! So my death will not be the death of a stranger for her! . . .'

La Porte burst into tears.

'Patrick,' said the duke, 'bring me the box the diamond tags were in.'

Patrick brought the object he asked for, which La Porte recognised as having belonged to the queen.

'Now the white satin bag with her monogram embroidered on it in pearls.'

Patrick obeyed again.

'Here, La Porte,' said Buckingham, 'here are the only tokens I had from her, this silver box and these two letters. Give them back to Her Majesty. And as a last souvenir . . .' he added, looking around him for some precious object '. . . add . . .'

He carried on looking, but his gaze, darkened by death, only lighted on the knife that had fallen from Felton's hands, the crimson blood still steaming on its blade.

'And add this knife,' said the duke, pressing La Porte's hand.

He was still able to put the bag in the bottom of the box and drop the knife in, as he made a sign to La Porte that he couldn't speak any more. Then, with a last convulsion, which this time he no longer had the strength to resist, he slid from the sofa on to the floor.

Patrick let out a great cry.

Buckingham tried to smile one last time, but death arrested the thought, which remained engraved on his brow like a last loving kiss.

At that moment the duke's doctor arrived in a terrible flurry. He had been on the admiral's ship already, and they had had to go and find him there.

He went over to the duke, took his hand, held it in his own for a moment, and then let it fall again.

'There's no point,' he said, 'he's dead.'

'Dead! dead!' cried Patrick.

At the cry, the whole throng came back into the room, and on all sides there was only consternation and uproar.

As soon as Lord de Winter saw Buckingham lying dead, he ran to Felton, whom the soldiers were still guarding on the palace terrace.

'Wretch!' he said to the young man, who, since Buckingham's death, had recovered that calm and coolness which were never to leave him again. 'Wretch! What have you done?'

'I have taken my revenge,' he said.

'You?' said the baron. 'You mean you've served as the instrument of that cursed woman. But, I swear to you, this crime will be her last.'

'I don't know what you mean,' Felton said calmly, 'and I have no idea to whom you refer, my lord. I killed the Duke of Buckingham because he twice refused your own request to make me captain. I have punished him for his injustice, that's all.'

De Winter looked on in stupefaction as Felton's hands were tied, not knowing what to think of such indifference.

One thing, however, clouded Felton's pure brow. At every sound he heard, the naive Puritan thought he recognised the footsteps and voice of Milady, coming to throw herself in his arms, to accuse herself and go to her doom with him.

Suddenly he started. His gaze was fixed on a part of the sea, which one could see in its full sweep from the terrace where he was standing. With his sailor's eagle eye, he had recognised, where anyone else would have seen only a seagull bobbing on the waves, the sail of a sloop that was making for the shores of France.

He paled, brought his hand to his heart, which was breaking and understood the betrayal in its entirety.

'A last favour, my lord!' he said to the baron.

'What?' asked the latter.

'What time is it?'

The baron took out his watch.

'Ten minutes to nine,' he said.

Milady had left an hour and a half earlier than planned. As soon as she had heard the cannon shot announcing the fatal event, she had given the order to weigh anchor.

The boat could be seen far from shore, sailing away under a blue sky.

'It was God's will,' said Felton, with the resignation of the fanatic, and yet without being able to tear his eyes away from that ship, on board which he doubtless thought he could make out the white ghost of her to whom his life was about to be sacrificed.

De Winter followed his gaze, considered his suffering, and guessed everything.

'Suffer your punishment alone for now, wretch,' Lord de Winter said to Felton, who let himself be dragged off with his eyes still turned towards the sea, 'but I swear to you, on the memory of my brother, whom I loved so dearly, your accomplice will not get away.'

Felton bowed his head without uttering a syllable.

As for de Winter, he went quickly down the stairs and made for the port.

LX

IN FRANCE

THE IMMEDIATE FEAR OF CHARLES I, the King of England, on learning of this death, was that such terrible news would discourage the Rochelois. According to Richelieu's memoirs, he tried to hide it from them for as long as possible, closing all the ports in the kingdom, and being scrupulously careful that no vessel left until after the army Buckingham had been preparing had sailed, taking it upon himself, now Buckingham was no more, to oversee its departure.

He enforced this order so strictly as to detain in England even the ambassador of Denmark, who had taken leave, and the ambassador ordinary of Holland, who was to bring back to the port of Flushing the Indian merchantmen that Charles I had restored to the United Provinces.

But as he had not thought of giving this order until five hours after the event, that is to say, at two o'clock in the afternoon, two ships had already left port, the one carrying, as we know, Milady, who, already suspecting what had happened, was further confirmed in her belief by seeing the black flag unfurl from the mast of the admiral's ship.

As to the second vessel, we will say later whom it carried, and how it made its departure.

In the meantime, nothing of note had happened in the La Rochelle camp. The only piece of news was that the king, who was excruciatingly bored, as always, but perhaps a little more so in camp than elsewhere, had resolved to go incognito to spend the feast of St Louis at Saint-Germain, and asked the cardinal to arrange a small escort of just twenty musketeers. The cardinal, who was infected by the king's boredom himself on occasion, took great pleasure in granting this leave of absence to his royal lieutenant, who promised to come back around the fifteenth of September.

Informed by His Eminence, Monsieur de Tréville packed his bags, and as he knew the keen desire and even imperious need which his friends had to return to Paris, although not the cause of those sentiments, we hardly need to say that he selected them to be part of the escort.

The four young men learnt of this development a quarter of an hour after Monsieur de Tréville, for they were the first he told. And then d'Artagnan appreciated the favour the cardinal had granted him by finally transferring him to the musketeers. If it weren't for that, he would have been forced to stay in camp while his companions left.

It will become apparent later that the cause for this impatience to go back to Paris was the danger Madame Bonacieux would be in if she encountered Milady, her mortal enemy, in the convent of Béthune. So, as we have said, Aramis had written immediately to

Marie Michon, the seamstress of Tours with such an array of fine acquaintances, so that she might obtain from the queen an order authorising Madame Bonacieux to leave the convent and retire either to Lorraine or Belgium. The reply had not been slow in coming, and, eight or ten days later, Aramis had received this letter:

> My dear cousin,
> Here is the authorisation from my sister to withdraw our little servant from the convent of Béthune, where you think the air is bad for her. My sister sends you this authorisation with great pleasure, for she loves the little girl very much and intends to be of more service to her later.
> With much love.
> Marie Michon

Appended to this letter was an authorisation in the following terms:

> The mother superior of the convent of Béthune will place in the hands of the person who shall present this note to her the novice who entered the convent upon my recommendation and under my patronage.
> At the Louvre, 10 August 1628
> Anne

One can imagine how these family relations between Aramis and a seamstress who called the queen her sister had lifted the young men's spirits. But Aramis, after blushing two or three times to the roots of his hair at Porthos's coarse jokes, had begged his friends not to bring the subject up again, declaring that if another word was said to him about it, he would stop using his cousin as an intermediary in these sorts of affairs.

Marie Michon's name, therefore, was never mentioned again among the four musketeers, who in any case had what they wanted:

the authorisation to remove Madame Bonacieux from the Carmelite convent of Béthune. It is true this authorisation wouldn't be of great use to them while they were in camp at La Rochelle, that is, at the other end of France[1]. And so d'Artagnan was going to ask for a leave of absence from Monsieur de Tréville, confessing to him in all candour the importance of his going, when the news reached him and his three friends that the king was about to set out for Paris with an escort of twenty musketeers, and that they were part of its number.

They were overjoyed. The valets were sent ahead with the baggage, and they set out on the morning of the sixteenth.

The cardinal escorted His Majesty from Surgères to Mauzé, and there the king and his minister took leave of each other with great displays of friendship.

However, the king, who sought entertainment even while trying to travel as fast as possible, for he wished to be in Paris by the twenty-third, stopped from time to time to hunt magpie, a pastime for which he had acquired a taste from de Luynes[2], and had remained very fond of. Whenever this happened, sixteen of the twenty musketeers were delighted at the prospect of good sport, four cursed it with a will. D'Artagnan, in particular, had a constant buzzing in his ears, which Porthos explained by saying:

'A very grand lady told me that means someone is talking about you somewhere.'

Finally the escort rode through Paris on the night of the twenty-third. The king thanked Monsieur de Tréville, and permitted him to hand out four-day leaves, on condition that none of the favoured parties should appear in any public place, on pain of the Bastille.

The first four leaves granted, as may be imagined, were to our four friends. Furthermore, Athos obtained six days leave rather than four from Monsieur de Tréville, with two more nights thrown in, for they were to set out on the twenty-fourth at five o'clock in the afternoon, and as a further kindness Monsieur de Tréville post-dated the leave to the morning of the twenty-fifth.

'My God,' said d'Artagnan, who, as we know, never balked at anything, 'it seems to me that we are making a great to-do over a very simple matter. In two days, if I ride two or three horses into the ground – I don't mind, I've got money – I'll be in Béthune. I give the queen's letter to the superior and escort the dear treasure I'm seeking, not to Lorraine, not to Belgium, but to Paris, where she will be better hidden, particularly while the cardinal is at La Rochelle. Then, once I'm back from the country, partly through the good offices of her cousin, partly in consideration for what we've done for her personally, we shall obtain from the queen what we desire. So stay here, don't wear yourselves out to no purpose. Planchet and I are all that's required for such a simple expedition.'

Athos replied quietly:

'We have money too, because I haven't drunk all of what's left of the diamond, and Porthos and Aramis haven't eaten their way through it either. So we can just as well run four horses into the ground as one. But consider, d'Artagnan,' he added, in a such a sombre tone of voice that it made the young man shudder, 'consider that Béthune is a town where the cardinal gave a rendezvous to a woman who brings misery in her train wherever she goes. If you were only dealing with four men, d'Artagnan, I'd let you go alone, but you're dealing with that woman, so let's all four of us go, and God grant that, with our four valets, we will be enough.'

'You're terrifying me, Athos,' cried d'Artagnan. 'My God, what are you afraid of?'

'Everything!' replied Athos.

D'Artagnan examined the faces of his companions, which, like Athos's, bore the mark of deep anxiety; and then they set off again as fast as their horses could carry them, without adding another word.

On the evening of the twenty-fifth, they rode into Arras, and just as d'Artagnan dismounted at the Golden Harrow inn to drink a glass of wine, a horseman came out of the post yard, where he had just changed his horse, and galloped off on the road to Paris.

As he came out of the main gate on to the street, the wind blew open the cloak in which he was wrapped, despite it being the month of August, and tugged at his hat, which he grabbed as it lifted off his head, and jammed back down over his eyes.

D'Artagnan, whose eyes were fixed on this man, became very pale and dropped his glass.

'What is the matter, sir?' said Planchet. 'Ho there, quickly, gentlemen, my master is unwell!'

The three friends came running and found d'Artagnan not unwell, but racing for his horse. They stopped him at the gate.

'Hey, where the devil are you going like this?' cried Athos.

'It is he!' cried d'Artagnan, pale with anger, his brow beaded with sweat. 'It is he! Let me catch him!'

'But he who?' asked Athos.

'He, that man!'

'What man?'

'That cursed man, my evil genius, whom I've seen every time I've been threatened by some misfortune, the one who was with that horrible woman when I met her for the first time, the one I was looking for when I provoked Athos, the one I saw the morning of the day Madame Bonacieux was abducted! You know, the man from Meung! I saw him, it's he! I recognised him when the wind blew open his cloak.'

'Confound it!' Athos said pensively.

'To horse, gentlemen, to horse! Let's go after him, we'll catch him up!'

'My dear friend,' said Aramis, 'remember that he's going in the opposite direction to us, that he has a fresh horse, while ours are fatigued, and consequently we will disable our own horses without even a chance of catching him. Let's let the man go, d'Artagnan, and save the woman.'

'Hey, sir!' cried a stable lad, running after the stranger. 'Hey, sir, this note fell out of your hat! Hey, sir!'

'My friend,' said d'Artagnan, 'a half-pistole for that note!'

'My faith, sir, with great pleasure! Here it is!'

Delighted with the good day's work he had done, the stable boy returned to the hotel yard. D'Artagnan unfolded the note.

'Well?' asked his three friends, gathering round him.

'Only one word!' said d'Artagnan.

'Yes,' said Aramis, 'but it's the name of some town or village.'

'Armentières[3],' read Porthos. 'Armentières . . . no, not a clue!'

'And this name of a town or village is written in her hand!' cried Athos.

'Come on, let's look after this note very carefully,' said d'Artagnan. 'Perhaps I haven't wasted my last pistole after all. To horse, my friends, to horse!'

And then the four companions set off at a gallop on the road to Béthune.

LXI

THE CARMELITE CONVENT OF BÉTHUNE

GREAT CRIMINALS HAVE SOMETHING PREDESTINED about them, which enables them to surmount all obstacles, to escape all dangers, until that moment arrives which a wearied Providence has marked out as the rock on which their impious fortunes shall come to grief.

Such was the case with Milady. She slipped between the cruisers of both nations, and arrived at Boulogne without incident.

Landing at Portsmouth, Milady had been an Englishwoman driven out of La Rochelle by the persecutions of the French; landing at Boulogne, after a two-day crossing, she presented herself as a Frenchwoman harassed by the English at Portsmouth in their hatred for France.

Besides, Milady had the most effective of passports: her beauty, her noble appearance, and the generosity with which she scattered her pistoles. Spared the usual formalities by the affable smile and gallant manners of an old governor of the port, who kissed her hand, she only remained in Boulogne long enough to post a letter that read:

To His Eminence the Lord Cardinal de Richelieu, in his
camp before La Rochelle.
     My lord,
     Your Eminence may rest assured, His Grace the Duke
of Buckingham will not leave for France.
     Boulogne, the evening of the 25th.
     Milady de ——

P.S. As Your Eminence wished, I am going to the Carmelite convent in Béthune, where I shall await your orders.

And indeed, Milady set out that same evening. Night overtook her on the road; she stopped, and slept at an inn. Then, at five o'clock the next morning she left, and three hours later drove into Béthune.

She was directed to the Carmelite convent, and went in at once.

The mother superior came to meet her. Milady showed her the cardinal's order, and the abbess had her assigned a room and served breakfast.

The past had already been entirely erased, as far as Milady was concerned; and, her gaze fixed on the future, she saw only the high fortune reserved for her by the cardinal, whom she had served so successfully without his name being mixed up in any way with that bloody affair. The ever-new passions which consumed her gave her life the appearance of those clouds which float across the sky, sometimes reflecting azure, sometimes fire, sometimes the opaque black of the storm, and which leave no trace on the earth but devastation and death.

After breakfast, the abbess came to pay her a visit. There was very little in the way of distraction in the cloister, and the good mother superior was eager to make the acquaintance of her new boarder.

Milady wished to please the abbess, an easy matter for such a genuinely superior woman. She tried to be amiable and was charming, captivating the good mother superior with the variety of her conversation and the grace that animated every aspect of her person.

The abbess, who was a daughter of the nobility, took particular delight in stories of the court, which so seldom reach the furthest corners of the kingdom, and, above all, have terrible difficulty getting over the walls of convents, at the thresholds of which the noises of the world come to expire.

Milady, by contrast, was extremely conversant with all the aristocratic intrigues, which she had been living in the thick of constantly for the last five or six years. She therefore began discoursing with the good abbess on the worldly practices of the court of France, throwing a few remarks on the extravagant devotions of the king. She regaled her with a scandalous chronicle of the lords and ladies of the court, whom the abbess knew perfectly by name, touched lightly on the amours of the queen and the Duke of Buckingham, and generally spoke a great deal so that she would hardly be spoken to.

The abbess simply smiled and listened, and did not say a word in reply. However, Milady saw that these sorts of stories amused her very much, and kept going; only now she steered her conversation towards the cardinal.

She was rather perplexed, though. She did not know whether the abbess was a royalist or a cardinalist, so she kept to a prudent middle course. But the abbess, for her part, out of a still more prudent reserve, contented herself with merely bowing her head down very low each time the traveller pronounced His Eminence's name.

Milady began to think she was going to be bored to tears in that convent.

She thus resolved to venture something in order to find out which side to choose. Wanting to see how far the discretion of the good abbess would go, she began to denigrate the cardinal – veiled terms at first, then in great detail – relating the amours of the minister with Madame d'Aiguillon, Marion de Lorme, and several other gallant ladies.

The abbess listened more attentively, gradually smiling and becoming animated.

Good, thought Milady; she's developing a taste for my conversation. If she is a cardinalist, at least she's not a fanatical one.

Then she moved on to the cardinal's persecutions of his enemies. The abbess simply crossed herself, neither approving nor disapproving.

This confirmed Milady in her opinion that the nun was more of a royalist than cardinalist. She went on, each story capping the last.

'I am very ignorant of all these matters,' the abbess said finally, 'but remote as we are from the court, outside the interests of the world as we find ourselves here, we still have some very sad examples of what you have just been relating, and one of our boarders has suffered greatly from the vengeance and persecutions of the cardinal.'

'One of your boarders?' said Milady. 'Oh, my God, poor woman, I pity her then!'

'And you are right to do so, for she is much to be pitied: prison, threats, ill treatment – she has suffered everything. But then,' said the abbess, 'perhaps the cardinal had plausible reasons for acting in such a way. And, although she seems like an angel, we must not always judge people by their appearance.'

Good! said Milady to herself. Who knows, perhaps I'll find something out here. I am on a lucky streak.

And she concentrated on giving her face an expression of perfect candour.

'Alas,' said Milady, 'I know it. They say one must not believe in physiognomies; but what should we believe in then, if not in the Lord's most beautiful handiwork? As for me, perhaps I shall be deceived all my life, but I shall always trust a person whose face inspires sympathy in me.'

'You would be tempted to believe, then,' said the abbess, 'that this young woman is innocent?'

'The cardinal does not only punish crimes,' she said. 'There are certain virtues that he prosecutes more severely than any heinous crime.'

'Allow me, madam, to express my surprise,' said the abbess.

'At what?' asked Milady artlessly.

'Why, at the language you use.'

'What do you find surprising about my language?' Milady asked with a smile.

'You are the cardinal's friend, since he sends you here, and yet . . .'

'And yet I speak ill of him,' said Milady, finishing the mother superior's thought.

'At least, you don't speak well of him.'

'That's because I'm not his friend,' she said, sighing, 'but his victim.'

'And yet this letter in which he recommends you to me . . . ?'

'Is an order to me to stay in a kind of prison from which he will have me removed by one of his henchmen.'

'But why haven't you run away?'

'Where should I go? Do you think there's a place on earth the cardinal cannot reach, if he troubles himself to stretch out his hand? If I was a man, it might conceivably be possible, but a woman – what would you have a woman do? This young boarder you have here – has she tried to run away?'

'No, it's true. But it's different with her. I believe some love keeps her in France.'

'In that case,' said Milady with a sigh, 'if she's in love, she cannot be entirely unfortunate.'

'So,' said the abbess, looking at Milady with mounting interest, 'Is this another poor persecuted woman I see?'

'Alas, yes,' said Milady.

The abbess looked at Milady anxiously for a moment, as if a new thought was forming in her mind.

'You're not an enemy of our holy faith?' she stammered.

'I?' cried Milady, 'I, a Protestant? Oh, no! I call on God who hears as my witness that, quite the opposite, I am a fervent Catholic.'

'Well then, madam,' said the abbess, smiling, 'rest assured: the house you are in will not be a very harsh prison for you, and we will do everything necessary to make you cherish your captivity. What's more, you will find that young woman here, who is no doubt persecuted as the result of some court intrigue. She is kind, gracious.'

'What is her name?'

'She was recommended to me by someone of very high rank, under the name of Kitty. I have not thought to ask her other name.'

'Kitty?' cried Milady. 'What? Are you sure?'

'That she calls herself that? Yes, madam. Is it possible that you know her?'

Milady smiled to herself at the notion she had just had that this young woman might be her former chambermaid. Mingled with her memory of the young girl was a memory of anger, and a desire for vengeance twisted Milady's features. Almost immediately, however, they recovered the calm, benevolent expression that this woman of a hundred faces had momentarily mislaid.

'And when will I be able to see this young lady, for whom I feel so great a sympathy?' asked Milady.

'Why, this evening,' said the abbess, 'or even before. But you have been travelling for four hours, you told me. This morning you got up at five o'clock. You must need to rest. Lie down and sleep; we will wake you at dinnertime.'

Although Milady could very well have forgone sleep, sustained as she was by all the excitement that a new adventure awakened in her heart, with its hunger for intrigues, she nonetheless accepted the mother superior's offer. In the past twelve or fifteen days she had experienced so many different emotions that, while her iron constitution could still endure fatigue, her soul needed repose.

She therefore took leave of the abbess, and lay down, lulled by the thoughts of vengeance which the name of Kitty had naturally prompted. She remembered the almost unconditional promise the cardinal had made her, if she succeeded in her enterprise. She had succeeded, and so could be revenged on d'Artagnan.

Only one thing frightened Milady: the memory of her husband, the Count de La Fère, whom she had believed dead or at least banished, and whom she had rediscovered in the person of Athos, d'Artagnan's best friend.

But, if he was d'Artagnan's friend, he must have helped him in all the schemings by means of which the queen had thwarted His Eminence's plans. If he was d'Artagnan's friend, he was the cardinal's enemy; and she would no doubt manage to envelop him in the folds of the vengeance in which she expected to smother the young musketeer.

All these hopes were sweet thoughts for Milady, and so, lulled by them, she soon fell asleep.

She was woken by a soft voice, which was speaking at the foot of her bed. She opened her eyes and saw the abbess accompanied by a young woman with blonde hair and a delicate complexion, who fixed upon her a look full of benevolent curiosity.

The face of this young woman was completely unknown to her. Each examined the other with meticulous attention, while exchanging the customary compliments; both were very beautiful, but of very different kinds of beauty. Milady, however, smiled on seeing herself far superior to the young woman in the nobility of her bearing and her aristocratic manner. It was true that the novice's habit, which the young woman wore, was not very advantageous in such a contest.

The abbess introduced them to one another. Then, when this formality had been performed, as her duties called her to church, she left the two young women alone.

The novice, seeing Milady in bed, was about to follow the mother superior, but Milady stopped her.

'What, madam,' she said to her, 'I have barely caught sight of you and already you want to deprive me of your presence? I was counting on it rather, I must confess, for my stay here.'

'No, madam,' replied the novice, 'I was simply afraid of having chosen the wrong time. You were sleeping, you must be tired.'

'Well,' said Milady, 'what do all sleepers wish for? A good awakening. You have granted me that awakening, so let me enjoy it at my ease.'

And taking her hand, she drew her to a chair by the bed.

The novice sat down.

'My God!' she said. 'How luckless I am! For six months I've been here without the shadow of a distraction, then you arrive, your presence would provide me with charming company, and now, in all likelihood, I'll be leaving the convent at any moment.'

'What?' said Milady. 'You're leaving soon?'

'At least I hope so,' said the novice, with an expression of joy which she made not the least effort to disguise.

'I believe I heard you had suffered at the hands of the cardinal,' continued Milady. 'That would have been another bond between us.'

'So what our good mother told me is true, that you were also a victim of that wicked cardinal?'

'Hush!' said Milady. 'Don't let's even talk about him like that. All my misfortunes have come from saying something similar to what you said in the presence of a woman whom I thought was my friend and who betrayed me. But what about you? Have you been the victim of a betrayal too?'

'No,' said the novice, 'but of my devotion to a woman whom I loved, for whom I would have given my life, and for whom I still would give it.'

'And who abandoned you, did she?'

'I was unjust enough to think so, but two or three days ago I received proof to the contrary, and I thank God for it: it would have cost me dearly to think she had forgotten me. But you, madam,' the novice went on, 'it seems to me that you are free, and that if you wanted to flee, it would only depend on you.'

'Where would you have me go, without friends, without money, in a part of France I don't know, where I have never been?'

'Oh!' cried the novice. 'As for friends, you will have them wherever you show your face, you seem so good and are so beautiful!'

'All the same,' said Milady, softening her smile in a way that lent her face an angelic expression, 'I am alone and persecuted.'

'Listen,' said the novice, 'one must gladly put one's trust in heaven, you see. There always comes a moment when the good one has done pleads one's case before God, and, besides, perhaps it is a stroke of good fortune for you that you have met me, humble and powerless as I am. For if I leave here, well, I shall have some powerful friends, who, after they have campaigned on my behalf, will also campaign on yours.'

'Oh, when I said I was alone,' said Milady, hoping to make the novice speak by speaking herself, 'it's not that I don't also have some eminent acquaintances, but these acquaintances tremble themselves before the cardinal. The queen herself does not dare take a stand against the terrible minister. I have proof that Her Majesty, despite her excellent heart, has been obliged more than once to abandon people who have served her to His Eminence's wrath.'

'Believe me, madam, the queen may seem to have abandoned those people, but one mustn't believe appearances. The more they are persecuted, the more she thinks of them, and often, when they least expect it, they receive proof of her kind remembrance.'

'Alas!' said Milady. 'I believe it. The queen is so good.'

'Oh, you must know her then, the beautiful and noble queen, if you speak of her in that fashion!' the novice cried fervently.

'Actually,' said Milady, forced to retreat, 'I don't have the honour of knowing her personally, but I know a good number of her most intimate friends. I know Monsieur de Putange; I knew Monsieur Dujart in England[1]; I know Monsieur de Tréville.'

'Monsieur de Tréville!' cried the novice. 'Do you know Monsieur de Tréville?'

'Yes, indeed. Quite well even.'

'The captain of the king's musketeers?'

'The captain of the king's musketeers.'

'Oh, but you shall see,' cried the novice, 'in a moment we shall be established acquaintances, almost friends. If you know Monsieur de Tréville, you must have been to his residence?'

'Often!' said Milady, who, having entered on this path, and seeing the lie was working, wanted to pursue it to its conclusion.

'In his residence you must have seen some of his musketeers?'

'All his regular guests!' replied Milady, for whom this conversation was beginning to acquire a real interest.

'Name some of those you know, and you'll see they are my friends.'

'Why,' said Milady, embarrassed, 'I know Monsieur de Louvigny, Monsieur de Courtivron, Monsieur de Férussac . . .'

The novice let her speak, and then seeing her pause, said, 'You don't know a gentleman called Athos?'

Milady became as pale as the sheets on which she lay, and, for all her self-mastery, couldn't help letting out a cry, as she seized the novice's hand, and devouring her with her gaze.

'What? What's wrong? Oh, my God!' asked the poor woman, 'Have I said something that has caused you offence?'

'No, but that name struck me because I have also been acquainted with this gentleman, and it seemed strange to find someone who knows him well.'

'Oh, yes, very well, very well! Not just him, but also his friends Messrs Porthos and Aramis!'

'Indeed? I know them too!' cried Milady, who felt a chill seep into her heart.

'Well then, if you are acquainted with them, you must know they are good and true companions. Why don't you go to them, if you need support?'

'Well,' stammered Milady, 'I'm not really close to any of them. I know them from hearing them spoken of a great deal by one of their friends, Monsieur d'Artagnan.'

'You know Monsieur d'Artagnan?' cried the novice in her turn, seizing Milady's hand and devouring her with her eyes.

Then, noticing the strange expression on Milady's face, she said, 'Excuse me, madam, but how do you know him?'

'Why,' said Milady, embarrassed, 'why, as a friend.'

'You are deceiving me, madam,' said the novice. 'You were his mistress.'

'That was you, madam,' cried Milady in her turn.

'Me?' said the novice.

'Yes, you. I know who you are now. You're Madame Bonacieux.'

The young woman drew back, stricken with amazement and terror.

'Oh, don't deny it! Answer!' said Milady.

'Well then – yes, madam, I love him!' said the novice. 'Are we rivals?'

Milady's face lit up with such a savage fire that, in any other circumstances, Madame Bonacieux would have fled in terror. But jealousy had her completely in its grip.

'Come, tell me, madam,' said Madame Bonacieux with a forcefulness of which one would have believed her incapable, 'were you or are you his mistress?'

'Oh, no!' cried Milady in a voice that left no doubt as to its truthfulness. 'Never! Never!'

'I believe you,' said Madame Bonacieux. 'But then why did you cry out like that?'

'What, you don't understand?' said Milady, who had already mastered her confusion and recovered all her presence of mind.

'How do you expect me to understand? I don't know anything.'

'You don't understand that, being my friend, Monsieur d'Artagnan took me as a confidante?'

'Really?'

'You don't understand that I know everything: your abduction from the little house at Saint-Germain, his despair, the despair of his friends, their futile searching ever since? And how do you expect me not to be astonished, when, without suspecting it, I find myself

face to face with you, about whom we have so often spoken together
– with you whom he loves with all the strength of his soul, with
you whom he has made me love before I ever saw you? Ah, dear
Constance, so I've found you! At last I have set eyes on you!'

And then Milady held out her arms to Madame Bonacieux,
who, convinced by what she had just said, no longer saw this
woman, who a moment before she had thought her rival, as
anything other than a sincere and devoted friend.

'Oh, forgive me, forgive me!' she cried, falling on Milady's
shoulder. 'I love him so much!'

The two women held their embrace for a moment. If Milady's
strength had been equal to her hatred, Madame Bonacieux would
certainly never have emerged from her arms alive. But, since she
couldn't suffocate her, Milady merely smiled.

'Oh, my dear, beautiful little one!' said Milady. 'How happy I
am to see you! Let me look at you.' And, saying these words, she
did indeed devour her with her eyes. 'Yes, it's really you. Ah, I
recognise you now from what he's told me, I recognise you
perfectly.'

The poor young woman couldn't suspect the dreadful cruelty
of the thoughts that were working behind the ramparts of that
immaculate brow, behind those sparkling eyes in which she read
nothing but concern and compassion.

'Then you know what I've suffered,' said Madame Bonacieux,
'since he told you all he suffered. But to suffer for him is
happiness.'

Milady said mechanically:

'Yes, it is happiness.'

She was thinking of something else.

'Besides,' Madame Bonacieux went on, 'my torment is drawing
to its close. Tomorrow, tonight perhaps, I will see him again, and
then the past will be no more.'

'Tonight? Tomorrow?' cried Milady, jolted out of her reverie
by these words. 'What do you mean? Are you expecting some
news from him?'

'I'm expecting him himself.'

'Himself? D'Artagnan, here?'

'In person.'

'But that's impossible! He's at the siege of La Rochelle with the cardinal. He won't return to Paris until the town is taken.'

'So you think, but is there anything that's impossible for my d'Artagnan, that noble and loyal gentleman?'

'Oh, I can't believe you!'

'Well, then read this!' said the unfortunate young woman, carried away with pride and joy, handing a letter to Milady.

'Madame de Chevreuse's handwriting!' Milady said to herself. 'Ah, I was sure they had communications in that quarter!'

And then she avidly read these few lines:

My dear child,

Keep yourself ready. Our friend will see you soon, and he will see you only to snatch you from that prison where your safety required that you be hidden. So prepare yourself for your departure, and never despair of us.

Our charming Gascon has again shown himself as brave and faithful as ever. Tell him there is much gratitude to him in a certain place for the warning which he gave.

'Yes, yes,' said Milady, 'yes, the letter is definite. Do you know what this warning was?'

'No. I only suspect that he must have alerted the queen to some new machination of the cardinal's.'

'Yes, I daresay that's right,' said Milady, giving the letter back to Madame Bonacieux and letting her head sink pensively on to her breast.

At that moment they heard the gallop of a horse.

'Oh!' cried Madame Bonacieux, rushing to the window. 'Can it be him already?'

Milady stayed in bed, petrified by surprise. So many unexpected things had happened to her all at once that, for the first time, she couldn't think.

'He? He?' she murmured. 'Might it be he?'

And she remained in bed, her eyes vacant.

'Alas, no!' said Madame Bonacieux. 'It's some man I don't know, and yet he seems to be coming here. Yes, he's slowing down, he's stopping at the gate, he's ringing.'

Milady leapt out of bed.

'You're quite sure it's not him?' she said.

'Oh, yes, quite sure!'

'Perhaps you didn't have a clear sight of him?'

'Oh, I'd only have to see the plume of his hat or the hem of his cloak to recognise him!'

Milady was still dressing.

'No matter! The man is coming here, you say?'

'Yes, he's come in.'

'The visitor is either for you or for me.'

'Oh, my God, how agitated you seem!'

'Yes, I admit it, I don't have your confidence, I fear everything to do with the cardinal.'

'Shh!' said Madame Bonacieux. 'Someone's coming!'

Indeed, the door opened and the mother superior came in.

'Is it you who came from Boulogne?' she asked Milady.

'Yes, it is I,' replied the latter, trying to regain her composure. 'Who is asking for me?'

'A man who does not want to say his name, but has come on the cardinal's behalf.'

'And he wishes to speak with me?' asked Milady.

'He wishes to speak with a lady who has come from Boulogne.'

'Then send him in, madam, I beg you.'

'Oh, my God! My God!' said Madame Bonacieux. 'Can this be some bad news?'

'I fear it might.'

'I'll leave you with this stranger, but as soon as he leaves, if you'll permit me, I will come back.'

'Why of course, you must.'

The mother superior and Madame Bonacieux went out.

Milady remained alone, her eyes fixed on the door. A moment later, there was a jingling of spurs on the stairs, then footsteps coming closer, then the door opened, and a man appeared.

Milady let out a cry of joy. The man was the Count de Rochefort, His Eminence's hound.

LXII

TWO VARIETIES OF DEMON

'AH!' ROCHEFORT AND MILADY CRIED out together. 'It's you!'

'Yes, it's I.'

'And you've come . . . ?' asked Milady.

'From La Rochelle. And you?'

'From England.'

'Buckingham?'

'Dead or dangerously wounded. As I was leaving, not having been able to get anything from him, a fanatic had just assassinated him.'

'Ah,' said Rochefort, with a smile, 'that's a very fortunate coincidence, and one that will delight His Eminence! Have you informed him of it?'

'I wrote to him from Boulogne. But how is it that you're here?'

'His Eminence was worried and sent me to look for you.'

'I only arrived yesterday.'

'And what have you been doing since yesterday?'

'Not wasting my time.'

'Ah, I daresay you haven't!'

'Do you know whom I've found here?'

'No.'

'Guess.'

'How can I?'

'That young woman the queen got out of prison.'

'Little d'Artagnan's mistress?'

'Yes, Madame Bonacieux, whose whereabouts the cardinal didn't know.'

'Well,' said Rochefort, 'there's a coincidence on a par with the first. The cardinal is truly privileged!'

'Fancy my astonishment,' continued Milady, 'when I found myself face to face with that woman!'

'Does she know you?'

'No.'

'So she considers you a stranger?'

Milady smiled.

'I am her best friend!'

'On my honour,' said Rochefort, 'No one but you, my dear countess, could perform such miracles!'

'It's a good thing too, sir,' said Milady, 'for do you know what's afoot?'

'No.'

'They're coming to fetch her tomorrow or the day after with an order from the queen.'

'Indeed? Who's coming?'

'D'Artagnan and his friends.'

'Really, they'll go so far that one day we'll be obliged to send them to the Bastille.'

'Why hasn't that happened already?'

'What can you do? The cardinal has a weakness for these men that I cannot comprehend.'

'Indeed?'

'Yes.'

'Well, then, tell him this, Rochefort. Tell him that our conversation at the Red Dovecot inn was overheard by those four men; tell him that after he left, one of them came upstairs and forcibly took from me the safe conduct he had given me; tell him they

warned Lord de Winter of my crossing to England; that they
almost thwarted my mission as they thwarted the affair of the
tags; tell him that, of those four men, only two are to be feared
– d'Artagnan and Athos; tell him that the third, Aramis, is the
lover of Madame de Chevreuse: he must be allowed to live, we
know his secret, he may be useful; as for the fourth, Porthos,
he's a fool, a fop and a clod, he needn't trouble himself about
him.'

'But those four men should be at the siege of La Rochelle as
we speak.'

'I thought so too, but a letter Madame Bonacieux received from
Madame de Chevreuse, which she was rash enough to show me,
leads me to believe that, on the contrary, these four men are on
their way here to take her away.'

'Confound it! What should we do?'

'What did the cardinal say about me?'

'I am to take your written or verbal dispatches and return by
post, and when he knows what you've been doing, he will see to
what you should do.'

'I must stay here, then?'

'Here, or nearby.'

'You can't take me with you?'

'No, the order is categorical. You might be recognised in
the vicinity of the camp, and as you will understand, your presence would compromise His Eminence, especially after what
has just happened over there. But be sure to tell me where you
go to await news from the cardinal, so I'll know where to find
you.'

'Listen, it's likely I won't be able to stay here.'

'Why?'

'You forget that my enemies may come at any minute.'

'That's right. But is this little woman going to escape His
Eminence, then?'

'Bah!' said Milady, with a smile that only she could smile. 'You
forget I am her best friend.'

'Ah, that's true! So, with regard to this woman, I may tell the cardinal . . .'

'That he may be at his ease.'

'Is that all?'

'He'll know what that means.'

'He'll guess it, anyway. Now, what should I do?'

'Leave straightaway. It seems to me the news you're bringing is worth the trouble of making haste.'

'My post-chaise broke down coming into Lillers.'

'Perfect!'

'Why's it perfect?'

'Because I need your post-chaise,' said the countess.

'And how shall I travel, then?'

'At full gallop.'

'That's easy for you to say — it's a hundred and eighty leagues.'

'What does that matter?'

'It will be done. What next?'

'When you go through Lillers, you will send me your post-chaise, with orders for your servant to place himself at my disposal.'

'Very well.'

'You no doubt have some order from the cardinal?'

'I have full authority.'

'Show it to the abbess and say that someone will come for me, either today or tomorrow, and that I am to go with the person who presents himself in your name.'

'Very well.'

'Don't forget to speak harshly of me when you talk to the abbess.'

'Why?'

'I am a victim of the cardinal. I must inspire confidence in this poor little Madame Bonacieux.'

'Indeed. Now, will you make me a report of all that's happened?'

'But I've related all the events to you, and you've got a good memory – repeat everything as I told it to you. Papers get lost.'

'You're right. Only let me know where to find you so I don't go scouring the countryside in vain.'

'True . . . wait!'

'Do you want a map?'

'Oh, I know this country perfectly!'

'You do? When were you here?'

'I was brought up here.'

'Indeed?'

'You see, it is of some use being raised somewhere.'

'So you'll wait for me . . . ?'

'Let me think for a moment . . . Ah, that's the place: at Armentières.'

'What is Armentières?'

'A little town on the Lys'. I'll only have to cross the river to be in another country.'

'Perfect! But, of course, you'll only cross the river in case of danger.'

'Of course.'

'And, in that case, how will I know where you are?'

'You don't need your valet?'

'No.'

'Is he reliable?'

'Absolutely.'

'Give him to me, then. Nobody knows him. He'll stay behind when I leave and then bring you to me.'

'And you say you'll wait for me in Armentières?'

'In Armentières,' replied Milady.

'Write the name on a slip of paper, in case I forget it. There's nothing compromising in the name of a town, is there?'

'Ah, who knows? Never mind,' said Milady, writing the name on half a sheet of paper, 'I'll compromise myself.'

'Good!' said Rochefort, taking the paper from Milady, folding it and placing it in the lining of his hat, 'Anyway, don't worry. I will do as children do and repeat the name as I go in case I lose the paper. Now, is that all?'

'I think so.'

'Let's check: Buckingham dead or grievously wounded; your conversation with the cardinal overheard by the four musketeers; Lord de Winter warned of your arrival at Portsmouth; d'Artagnan and Athos to the Bastille; Aramis the lover of Madame de Chevreuse; Porthos a fop; Madame Bonacieux found again; send you the post-chaise as soon as possible; put my valet at your disposal; make you a victim of the cardinal so the abbess has no suspicions; Armentières, on the banks of the Lys. Is that it?'

'Truly, my dear sir, your memory is miraculous. By the way, add one thing . . .'

'What?'

'I saw some very pretty woods which back on to the convent garden. Say that I have permission to walk in those woods. Who knows, perhaps I'll need to leave by a back door.'

'You think of everything.'

'And you're forgetting something . . .'

'What's that?'

'To ask if I need money.'

'That's right, how much do you want?'

'All the gold you have.'

'I have some five hundred pistoles.'

'I have the same. With a thousand pistoles, one can face anything. Empty your pockets.'

'There you are, countess.'

'Good, my dear count! And you're leaving . . . ?'

'In an hour. Time to have a bite to eat while I send for a post-horse.'

'Perfect! Goodbye, chevalier!'

'Goodbye, countess!'

'Commend me to the cardinal,' said Milady.

'Commend me to Satan,' replied Rochefort.

Milady and Rochefort smiled at one another and parted.

An hour later, Rochefort set off at full gallop. Five hours later, he passed through Arras.

Our readers already know how he was recognised by d'Artagnan, and how this recognition, arousing fears in the musketeers, lent a new urgency to their journey.

LXIII

A DROP OF WATER

ROCHEFORT HAD SCARCELY LEFT before Madame Bonacieux came in. She found Milady with a smile on her face.

'So,' said the young woman, 'what you were afraid of has happened. The cardinal is sending someone for you tonight or tomorrow, is that right?'

'Who told you that, my child?' asked Milady.

'I heard it from the mouth of the messenger himself.'

'Come and sit down next to me,' said Milady.

'Here I am.'

'Wait while I check nobody's listening.'

'Why all these precautions?'

'You'll find out.'

Milady got up and went to the door, opened it, looked in the corridor, and then came back and sat down next to Madame Bonacieux.

'So,' she said, 'he played his part well.'

'Who did?'

'The man who presented himself to the abbess as the cardinal's envoy.'

'So he was playing a part?'

'Yes, my child.'

'Then that man is not . . .'

'That man,' said Milady, lowering her voice, 'is my brother.'

'Your brother?' cried Madame Bonacieux

'You're the only person who knows this secret, my child. If you reveal it to anyone in the world, I shall be lost, and you too perhaps.'

'Oh, my God!'

'Listen, this is what's happening: my brother, who was coming to my aid to take me away from here by force, if necessary, chanced upon the cardinal's emissary, who was on his way to fetch me. He followed him. Reaching a solitary and remote place on the road, he drew his sword, and called on the messenger to surrender the papers he was carrying. The messenger tried to defend himself. My brother killed him.'

'Oh!' exclaimed Madame Bonacieux, shuddering.

'It was the only way, you understand. So then my brother resolved to substitute cunning for force. He took the papers, presented himself here as the cardinal's emissary, and in an hour or two a carriage is to come to take me away on the part of His Eminence.'

'I see. Your brother is sending the carriage.'

'Exactly. But that's not all. That letter you received, which you believe to be from Madame Chevreuse . . .'

'Well?'

'It's a forgery.'

'What?'

'Yes, a forgery: it's a trap so you won't put up any resistance when they come to get you.'

'But d'Artagnan's coming.'

'Don't you believe it! D'Artagnan and his friends are detained at the siege of La Rochelle.'

'How do you know?'

'My brother met emissaries from the cardinal dressed as musketeers. They would have met you at the door, you would have thought you were dealing with friends, and then they would have abducted you and taken you back to Paris.'

'Oh, my God, my mind's becoming unhinged in all this chaos

of iniquity. If this goes on,' said Madame Bonacieux, holding her forehead, 'I feel I'll go mad!'

'Wait . . .'

'What?'

'I hear hoofbeats. It's my brother setting off again. I want to say a last goodbye. Come!'

Milady opened the window and made a sign to Madame Bonacieux to join her. The young woman went over.

Rochefort galloped past.

'Goodbye, brother!' cried Milady.

The horseman raised his head, saw the two young women, and, as he raced past, gave Milady a friendly wave.

'That lovely Georges!' she said, closing the window with an affectionate, melancholic expression on her face.

And then she went to sit down in her place again, as though immersed in the most personal of thoughts.

'Dear lady!' said Madame Bonacieux, 'forgive me for interrupting you, but what do you advise me to do? My God, you have more experience than me. Speak, I'm listening.'

'In the first place,' said Milady, 'it may be that I'm mistaken, and that d'Artagnan and his friends really are coming to your assistance.'

'Oh, that would be too perfect!' cried Madame Bonacieux. 'Such happiness isn't meant for me!'

'So, you understand, it's simply a question of time, a sort of race to see who'll get here first. If it's your friends who are the faster, you're saved, and if it's the cardinal's henchmen, you're lost.'

'Oh, yes, yes, lost irredeemably! So what am I to do? What am I to do?'

'There's one very simple, very obvious thing to do . . .'

'What? Tell me.'

'Wait nearby in hiding, so you can be sure which of the two bands of men is coming to ask for you.'

'But wait where?'

'Oh, that's not difficult. I am going to hide a few leagues from here while I wait for my brother to come and find me. So I can take you with me, and we can hide and wait together.'

'But they won't let me leave. I'm almost a prisoner here.'

'They think I'm leaving on the cardinal's orders, so they won't imagine you're in a great hurry to come with me.'

'Well?'

'Well, when the carriage is at the gate and you're saying goodbye, you step up on the footboard to give me one last hug. My brother's servant, who is coming to fetch me, will have been informed what to do. He will give the postilion a sign, and then we'll race off at a gallop.'

'But d'Artagnan? What if d'Artagnan comes?'

'Won't we know?'

'How?'

'Nothing could be easier. We send my brother's servant back to Béthune. As I told you, we can trust him. He disguises himself and takes lodgings across from the convent. If it's the cardinal's emissaries who come, he doesn't stir. If it is Monsieur d'Artagnan and his friends, he brings them to us.'

'He knows them, then?'

'Of course. Hasn't he seen Monsieur d'Artagnan at my house?'

'Oh, yes, yes, you're right. So, all is well, all is for the best. But let's not go far from here.'

'Seven or eight leagues at most. We can stay close to the border, for instance, and at the first alarm, leave France.'

'And what do we do until then?'

'Wait.'

'But what if they come?'

'My brother's carriage will come before them.'

'What if I'm far away when they come to take you – at dinner or supper, for instance?'

'Do one thing.'

'What is that?'

'Tell your good mother superior that, in order that we may be apart as little as possible, you ask her permission to share my meals.'

'Will she permit it?'

'What objection could there be?'

'Oh, very good! This way we won't be apart for an instant.'

'Well, go down to her, then, to make your request. My head feels heavy, I'm going to take a turn in the garden.'

'You must. But where shall I find you?'

'Here, in an hour.'

'Here, in an hour, then. Oh, you're so kind, and I'm so grateful!'

'How can I not take an interest in you? Set aside the fact you're beautiful and charming, aren't you the friend of one of my best friends?'

'Dear d'Artagnan! Oh, how he'll thank you!'

'I hope so. Now, all is agreed. Let's go down.'

'You're going to the garden?'

'Yes.'

'Follow this corridor, a little staircase takes you there.'

'Excellent! Thank you.'

And then, with an exchange of charming smiles, the two women went their separate ways.

Milady had told the truth: her head was heavy, for her jumbled plans were colliding in her brain as if in total chaos. She needed to be alone to order her thoughts a little. She had a vague picture of the future, but she needed some peace and quiet to give her still-confused ideas a distinct shape, a definite plan.

The most urgent priority was to make off with Madame Bonacieux, get her somewhere safe, and, if need be, use her as a hostage. Milady was beginning to dread the outcome of this terrible duel, in which her enemies were proving to be every bit as persistent as she was relentless.

Besides, she sensed, as one senses a coming storm, that the outcome was close at hand and could not fail to be fearsome.

The main thing for her, as we've said, was thus to have Madame

Bonacieux in her grasp. Madame Bonacieux was d'Artagnan's life. She was more than that: she was the life of the woman he loved. If Milady's fortunes soured, she would be a bargaining tool and a way to obtain favourable terms.

So, that point was settled: Madame Bonacieux would trustingly follow wherever she led. Once they were both in hiding in Armentières, it would be easy to convince her that d'Artagnan hadn't come to Béthune. In a fortnight at most, Rochefort would be back. In that time, she could also work out what needed to be done to avenge herself on the four friends. She wouldn't be bored, thank God, for she would have the sweetest pastime events can afford a woman of her character: honing a goodly act of vengeance to perfection.

As she mused in that fashion, she glanced around her and mapped out the topography of the garden in her mind. Milady was like a general, who anticipates both victory and defeat, and who is always prepared, depending on the accidents of battle, to advance or retreat.

After an hour, she heard a sweet voice calling her. It was Madame Bonacieux. The good abbess had naturally agreed to everything, and, to begin with, they were going to have supper together.

As they came into the courtyard, they heard the sound of a carriage stopping at the gate.

'Do you hear?' she said.

'Yes, the wheels of a carriage.'

'It's the one my brother is sending us.'

'Oh, my God!'

'Come now, take courage!'

There was a ring at the convent gate. Milady had not been mistaken.

'Go up to your room,' she said to Madame Bonacieux. 'You must have some jewellery you want to bring with you.'

'I have his letters,' she said.

'Well, go and fetch them, and then meet me in my room. We'll have supper quickly. We may be travelling part of the night, we have to build up our strength.'

'Good God!' said Madame Bonacieux, pressing her hand to her breast. 'My heart's going to burst, I can't walk.'

'Courage, come now, courage! Think that in a quarter of an hour you'll be safe, and remember that what you are about to do, you're doing for him.'

'Oh, yes, all for him! You've restored my courage with a single word. Go ahead, I'll join you.'

Milady quickly went up to her room. She found Rochefort's valet there and gave him instructions.

He was to wait at the gate. If by chance the musketeers should appear, the carriage would set off at a gallop, drive around the convent, and wait for Milady in a little village on the other side of the wood. In that case, Milady would cross the garden and reach the village on foot. As we've already said, Milady knew that part of France perfectly.

If the musketeers did not appear, they would follow the agreed plan. Madame Bonacieux would get into the carriage on the pretext of saying goodbye and Milady would make off with her.

Madame Bonacieux came in, and to remove any last hint of suspicion she might have, Milady repeated in her presence the last part of her instructions to the valet.

Milady asked several questions about the carriage. It was a post-chaise drawn by three horses and driven by the postilion. Rochefort was to ride ahead as a courier.

Milady was wrong to fear that Madame Bonacieux might have any suspicions. The poor young woman was too pure to suspect such perfidy in another woman. Beside, the name of the Countess de Winter, which she had heard mentioned by the abbess, was entirely unknown to her, and she didn't even know that a woman had played such a large and fatal part in the misfortunes of her life.

'You see,' said Milady, when the valet had left, 'everything is ready. The abbess doesn't suspect in the least, and believes they're fetching me on the part of the cardinal. That man is going off to give the final orders. Eat a little bite, drink a thimbleful of wine, and then let's be off.'

'Yes,' Madame Bonacieux said mechanically, 'yes, let's be off.'

Milady gestured for her to sit down opposite her, poured her a little glass of Spanish wine and helped her to some chicken breast.

'See,' she said, 'everything is in our favour: night is falling; by daybreak we will have reached our haven, and no one will know where we are. Come, take courage, eat something.'

Madame Bonacieux mechanically ate a few mouthfuls and touched her lips to her glass.

'No, come now,' said Milady, raising her glass, 'do as I do.'

But, as she brought the glass to her mouth, her hand froze. She had just heard what sounded like the distant rumbling of hoofbeats galloping along the road. Then, almost at the same moment, she seemed to hear the neighing of horses.

The noise dashed her high spirits, like the crash of a storm waking a sleeper in the midst of a pleasant dream. She turned pale and ran to the window, while Madame Bonacieux, rising tremblingly to her feet, leant on a chair to stop herself falling over.

There was nothing to be seen, but the galloping hoofbeats could be heard coming ever closer.

'Oh, my God!' said Madame Bonacieux. 'What is that noise?'

'Either our friends or our enemies,' said Milady, with terrible self-possession. 'Stay where you are, I'll tell you.'

Madame Bonacieux remained standing, as silent, motionless and pale as a statue.

The noise grew louder; the horses couldn't have been more than a hundred and fifty paces away. A bend in the road hid them from sight, but the noise was so distinct, one could have counted the number of horses from the staccato clatter of their iron shoes.

Milady watched with all her powers of concentration. There would be just enough light for her to recognise whoever was approaching.

Suddenly, around the bend in the road, she saw the gleam of gold-laced hats and the flutter of feathers. She counted two, then five, then eight horsemen. One of them rode two lengths ahead of the rest.

Milady let out a dull roar. The rider at the front, she realised, was d'Artagnan.

'Oh, my God! My God!' cried Madame Bonacieux. 'What is it?'

'It's the uniform of the cardinal's guards. There's not a moment to lose!' cried Milady. 'We must flee, we must flee!'

'Yes, yes, we must flee,' repeated Madame Bonacieux, but she couldn't take a step, rooted to the ground as she was by terror.

They heard the horsemen passing under the window.

'Come on! Quick, come on!' cried Milady, trying to drag the young woman by the arm. 'There's the garden, we can still flee. I've got the key. But we must hurry, in five minutes it will be too late.'

Madame Bonacieux tried to walk, took two steps, then fell to her knees.

Milady tried to pick her up and carry her, but without success.

At that moment they heard the wheels of the carriage, which had set off at a gallop at the sight of the musketeers. Then three or four shots rang out.

'For the last time, are you coming?' cried Milady.

'Oh, my God! My God! You can see I have no strength, you can see I can't walk. Flee by yourself!'

'Flee by myself, and leave you here? No, no, never!' cried Milady.

Suddenly a livid gleam flared in her eyes. In one frantic bound, she was at the table and pouring into Madame Bonacieux's glass the contents of a gemstone on her ring, which she had opened with singular speed.

The reddish grain dissolved immediately.

Then, grasping the glass, she said, 'Drink – this wine will give you strength. Drink.'

And she brought the glass to the lips of the young woman, who drank mechanically.

'Ah, this isn't how I wanted to avenge myself,' said Milady, setting the glass back down on the table with an infernal smile, 'but, my faith, one does what one can!'

And then she rushed out of the room.

Madame Bonacieux watched her flee without being able to follow her. She was like those people who dream they are being chased and try in vain to take a step.

A few minutes went by. A terrible noise was heard at the gate. Madame Bonacieux expected to see Milady reappear at any moment, but she did not.

Several times, from terror, no doubt, cold sweat stood out on her burning brow.

Finally she heard the creak of the gates being opened. The sound of boots and spurs reverberated on the stairs. There was a loud murmur of voices coming nearer, in the midst of which she seemed to hear her name pronounced.

All at once she uttered a great cry of joy, and rushed for the door; she had recognised d'Artagnan's voice.

'D'Artagnan! d'Artagnan!' she cried. 'Is that you?'

'Constance! Constance!' replied the young man. 'My God, where are you?'

At the same moment the door of the cell didn't so much open as give way under a massive impact and several men stormed into the room. Madame Bonacieux had collapsed into an armchair, unable to move.

D'Artagnan threw aside the still-smoking pistol he was holding, and fell on his knees before his mistress. Athos tucked his pistol back into his belt; Porthos and Aramis, who were holding their drawn swords, sheathed them.

'Oh, d'Artagnan! My beloved d'Artagnan! So you've come at last, you didn't deceive me, it's really you!'

'Yes, yes, Constance, we're together again!'

'Oh, no matter how much she said you wouldn't come, I

secretly hoped. I didn't want to flee. Oh, how right I was, how happy I am!'

At the word 'she', Athos, who had calmly sat down, leapt up.

'She? She who?' asked d'Artagnan.

'Why, my companion: she who, out of friendship for me, wanted to hide me from my persecutors; she who, taking you for the cardinal's guards, has just fled.'

'Your companion?' cried d'Artagnan, paler than his mistress's white veil. 'What companion do you mean?'

'The one whose carriage was at the gate; a woman who said she was your friend; a woman to whom you had told everything.'

'Her name, her name!' cried d'Artagnan. 'My God, don't you know her name?'

'Yes, I do. Someone said it when I was in the room. Wait . . . but that's strange . . . oh, my God, my head's confused! I can't see any more!'

'Help me, my friends, help! Her hands are ice cold,' cried d'Artagnan. 'She is ill! Good God, she's passed out!'

While Porthos was calling for help at the top of his lungs, Aramis ran to the table to get a glass of water. But he stopped on seeing the terrible change in Athos's expression. Standing by the table, his hair on end, his eyes glazed, Athos was looking at one of the glasses, seemingly possessed by the most terrible misgivings.

'Oh, no!' said Athos. 'No, it can't be! God wouldn't permit such a crime.'

'Water, water,' cried d'Artagnan, 'water!'

'Oh, poor woman, poor woman!' murmured Athos, his voice breaking.

Madame Bonacieux opened her eyes again as d'Artagnan kissed her.

'She's coming to!' cried the young man. 'Oh, my God, my God, thank you!'

'Madam,' said Athos, 'madam, in heaven's name, whose empty glass is this?'

'Mine, sir . . .' replied the young woman, her voice failing.

'But who poured you the wine that was in this glass?'

'*She.*'

'But who is this *she?*'

'Ah, I remember,' said Madame Bonacieux, 'the Countess de Winter . . .'

The four friends cried out as one, but Athos's voice overpowered the others.

At that moment, Madame Bonacieux's face became livid, a dull, crushing pain engulfed her, and she fell gasping into the arms of Porthos and Aramis.

D'Artagnan seized Athos's hands in indescribable anguish.

'And what?' he said. 'You think . . .'

His voice died away in a sob.

'I think everything,' said Athos, biting his lips till he drew blood.

'D'Artagnan, d'Artagnan!' cried Madame Bonacieux. 'Where are you? Don't leave me, you can see that I'm going to die.'

D'Artagnan let go of Athos's hands, which he held clenched in his own, and ran to her.

Her beautiful face was completely distorted, her glassy eyes couldn't focus, her body shook convulsively, sweat streamed down her forehead.

'In heaven's name, run and fetch someone! Porthos, Aramis, call for help!'

'No use,' said Athos, 'no use. The poison she dispenses has no antidote.'

'Yes, yes,' murmured Madame Bonacieux, 'help, help!'

Then, gathering all her strength, she held the young man's head in her hands, looked at him for a moment as if all her soul were concentrated in her gaze, and, with a sobbing cry, pressed her lips to his.

'Constance! Constance!' cried d'Artagnan.

A sigh escaped from Madame Bonacieux's mouth as it brushed against d'Artagnan's; that sigh was her chaste and loving soul returning to heaven.

Now d'Artagnan held only a lifeless body in his arms.

The young man cried out and fell down at his mistress's side, as pale and cold as she was.

Porthos wept, Aramis raised his fist to heaven, Athos made the sign of the cross.

At that moment a man appeared at the door, almost as pale as those who were in the room, looked all round him, and saw Madame Bonacieux dead and d'Artagnan unconscious.

He entered at that moment of stupor that always succeeds great catastrophes.

'I wasn't mistaken,' he said, 'here is Monsieur d'Artagnan, and you are his three friends, Messrs Athos, Porthos and Aramis.'

Those whose names had just been pronounced looked at the stranger in astonishment. All three felt as if they recognised him.

'Gentlemen,' the newcomer went on, 'you, like me, are searching for a woman, who,' he added with a terrible smile, 'must have passed this way, for I see a dead body!'

The three friends remained mute. Only the man's voice, like his face, reminded them of someone they had already met, although they couldn't remember in what circumstances.

'Gentlemen,' continued the stranger, 'since you are not willing to recognise a man who probably owes you his life twice over, then clearly I must tell you my name. I am Lord de Winter, that woman's brother-in-law.'

The three friends let out a cry of surprise.

Athos stood up and gave him his hand.

'Welcome, my lord,' he said, 'you are one of us.'

'I left Portsmouth five hours after her,' said Lord de Winter, 'I got to Boulogne three hours after her, I missed her by twenty minutes at Saint-Omer; finally, at Lillers, I lost track of her. I was going around haphazardly, questioning everybody, when I saw you pass at a gallop. I recognised Monsieur d'Artagnan and called out, but you didn't reply. I wanted to follow you, but my horse was too tired to keep up with yours. And yet it seems that, despite all your haste, you still got here too late!'

'As you see,' said Athos, indicating to Lord de Winter Madame Bonacieux's dead body, and d'Artagnan whom Porthos and Aramis were trying to bring round.

'Are they both dead, then?' Lord de Winter asked coldly.

'No, fortunately,' replied Athos, 'Monsieur d'Artagnan has merely fainted.'

'Ah, so much the better!' said Lord de Winter.

Indeed, at that moment d'Artagnan opened his eyes again.

He tore himself away from the arms of Porthos and Aramis and threw himself like a madman on his mistress's body.

Athos got up, walked towards his friend with a slow and solemn step, embraced him tenderly, and, as he burst into sobs, said to him in his noble and persuasive voice, 'Be a man, my friend: women weep for the dead, men avenge them!'

'Oh, yes!' said d'Artagnan. 'Yes, if it's to avenge her, I'm ready to follow you!'

Athos took advantage of his unfortunate friend's momentary revival, prompted by the hope of vengeance, to make a sign to Porthos and Aramis to go and fetch the mother superior.

The two friends came upon her in the corridor, still very dismayed and bewildered by so many events. She called several nuns, who, contrary to all monastic custom, found themselves in the presence of five men.

'Madam,' said Athos, tucking d'Artagnan's arm under his own, 'we entrust to your pious care the body of this unfortunate woman. She was an angel on earth before becoming an angel in heaven. Treat her as one of your sisters; we shall come back one day to pray on her grave.'

D'Artagnan buried his face in Athos's chest and burst into sobs.

'Weep,' said Athos, 'weep, heart full of love, youth and life! Alas, would that I could weep like you!'

And then, affectionate as a father, comforting as a priest, noble as a man who has suffered much, he led his friend away.

Then all five, followed by their valets, who led the horses by the bridle, headed for the town of Béthune, the outskirts of which were in sight, and stopped at the first inn they came across.

'But,' said d'Artagnan, 'aren't we going after that woman?'

'Later,' said Athos, 'I must take some measures first.'

'She'll escape,' said the young man, 'she'll escape, Athos, and it'll be your fault.'

'I'll answer for her,' said Athos.

D'Artagnan had so much confidence in his friend's word that he bowed his head and went into the inn without making any reply.

Porthos and Aramis looked at one another, not comprehending Athos's assurance in the least.

Lord de Winter thought he spoke in that fashion to dull d'Artagnan's grief.

'Now, gentlemen,' said Athos, when he had ascertained there were five unoccupied rooms in the hotel, 'let each of us retire to his room. D'Artagnan needs to be alone to shed his tears and you to sleep. Rest assured, I'll see to everything.'

'It seems to me, however,' said Lord de Winter, 'that if any measures are to be taken against the countess, they are my concern: she is my sister-in-law.'

'But they are mine too,' said Athos. 'She is my wife.'

D'Artagnan shuddered, for he realised that Athos must be certain of his revenge to reveal such a secret. Porthos and Aramis looked at one another and grew pale. Lord de Winter thought Athos was mad.

'Retire, then,' said Athos, 'and leave it in my hands. It must be obvious to you that, in my capacity as husband, it is my concern. One thing: d'Artagnan, if you haven't lost it, give me the note, which fell from that man's hat and on which the name of the town was written . . .'

'Ah!' said d'Artagnan. 'I understand – that name written in her hand . . .'

'You see,' said Athos, 'there is a God in heaven!'

LXIV
THE MAN IN THE RED CLOAK

A THOS'S DESPAIR HAD GIVEN WAY to a concentrated grief, which rendered his remarkable intellectual faculties even more lucid.

Wholly absorbed by a single thought, that of the promise he had made and the responsibility he had assumed, he was the last to go up to his room. He asked the innkeeper to bring him a map of the province, bent over it, studied its tracery of lines, established that four separate roads went from Béthune to Armentières, and then had the valets summoned.

Planchet, Grimaud, Mousqueton and Bazin entered and were given his clear, precise, solemn orders.

They were to set out at daybreak the following morning and each go to Armentières by a different route. Planchet, the most intelligent of the four, was to take the road along which the carriage at which the four friends had fired had disappeared – accompanied, it will be remembered, by Rochefort's servant.

Athos had decided to put the valets into the field, first, because, since they had been in his and his friends' service, he had discovered different and essential qualities in each of them.

Secondly, because valets who question passers-by arouse less mistrust than their masters, and encounter more sympathy in those they engage in conversation.

And finally, because Milady knew the masters but did not know the valets, whereas the valets were well acquainted with Milady.

All four were to meet again the next day at eleven o'clock in the appointed place. If they had discovered Milady's hiding place, three would stay to keep watch and the fourth would return to Béthune to inform Athos and serve as guide for the four friends.

Once these arrangements were made, the valets went up in turn to their rooms.

Then Athos got up from his chair, buckled on his sword, wrapped himself up in his cloak and left the hotel. It was around ten o'clock. Ten at night in provincial towns is a time when, it's well known, the streets are very far from busy. Nevertheless it was apparent Athos was looking for someone whom he could ask a question. Eventually he saw a passerby out late, went up to him, and said a few words. The man he addressed backed away, terrified, but answered the musketeer's questions by pointing his finger. Athos offered the man a half-pistole to come with him to his destination, but the man refused.

Athos went down the street the man had pointed out, but, when he reached a crossroads, he stopped again, evidently perplexed. As a crossroads was a more likely place at which to meet someone than any other, however, he stopped. And indeed, a moment later, a night watchman passed by. Athos repeated the same question he had already asked of the first person he had met. The night watchman reacted with the same terror, similarly refusing to accompany Athos, and merely pointed out the road he was to take.

Athos set off in the direction indicated and came to the outskirts at the other end of the town to that by which he and his friends had entered. There again he seemed worried and perplexed, and he stopped for the third time.

Fortunately, a beggar appeared and went up to Athos to ask for alms. Athos offered him an écu to accompany him on his way. The beggar hesitated for an instant, but seeing the silver coin glinting in the darkness, he made up his mind and set off in front of Athos.

Coming to a street corner, he pointed out from a distance an isolated, solitary, sad little house. Athos set off towards it, while the beggar, who had received his wage, ran off as fast as his legs could carry him.

Athos had to walk round the entire house before he made out

a door amidst the reddish coloured walls. No light appeared through the slats of the shutters, no sound gave reason to suppose the place was inhabited. It was dark and silent as a tomb.

Three times Athos knocked without response. At the third knock, however, footsteps approached from inside. The door finally opened a little, and a tall, pale man with a black beard and black hair appeared.

He and Athos exchanged a few words in low voices, then the tall man signalled to the musketeer that he might enter. Athos immediately availed himself of his permission, and the door closed again behind him.

The man whom Athos had gone so far to look for, and had found with such difficulty, led him into his laboratory, where he was engaged in wiring together the rattling bones of a skeleton. The body was already in one piece, only the head lay apart on the table.

All the other furnishings indicated that the owner of the house was a student of the natural sciences: there were jars filled with snakes, labelled according to species; dried lizards glinting like emeralds in large black wooden frames; and, finally, bunches of fragrant wild herbs, no doubt endowed with virtues unknown to the common man, were tied to the ceiling and hung down in the corners of the room.

Otherwise, no family, no servants. The tall man lived alone in the house.

Athos cast a cold and indifferent glance at all the objects we have just described and, at an invitation of the man he had come looking for, sat down by him.

Then he explained the reason for his visit and the service he required of him. His request was barely out of his mouth, however, before the stranger, who had remained standing in front of the musketeer, started back in terror and refused. Then Athos produced from his pocket a small piece of paper on which were written two lines, accompanied by a signature and a seal, and handed it to the man who had been so premature in his display of repugnance. The tall man had scarcely read the two lines, seen the signature and recognised the seal, before he nodded as a sign that he had no further objections and was ready to obey.

Athos asked for nothing more. He got up, bowed and left. Following the same route he had come by, he returned to the hotel and shut himself in his room.

At daybreak, d'Artagnan came in and asked him what they were to do.

'Wait,' replied Athos.

Moments later, the mother superior of the convent sent word to the musketeers that the burial of Milady's victim would take place at noon. As for the poisoner, there had been no news of her; except that she must have fled through the garden. Her footprints had been identified on the sandy path and the door had been found locked; its key had disappeared.

At the appointed hour, Lord de Winter and the four friends went to the convent. The bells were pealing, the chapel was open, the choir screen was closed. In the middle of the choir, dressed in her novice's habit, the victim's body was laid out. On either side of the choir and behind the screens leading to the convent, the whole community of the Carmelites was assembled, listening to the service and mingling their singing with the strains of the priests, without seeing the laity or being seen by them.

At the door to the chapel, d'Artagnan felt his courage fail him once more. He turned to look for Athos, but Athos had disappeared.

Faithful to his mission of vengeance, Athos had asked to be shown the garden, and there, following the light steps on the sandy path of that woman, who had left a trail of blood wherever she went, had gone as far as the gate that gave on to the wood. He had it unlocked, and plunged into the forest.

There all his suspicions were confirmed. The road down which the carriage had disappeared skirted the forest. Athos followed it for a time, his eyes fixed on the ground. Little flecks of blood dotted the road, which must have come either from a wound to the courier accompanying the carriage, or to one of the horses. About three quarters of a league away – fifty paces from Festubert, that is – a larger patch of blood was visible, a stretch of ground that had been trampled by horses. Between the forest and this incriminating spot, a little way past the flattened ground, he found traces of the same small footprints as in the garden. The carriage had stopped there.

So that was where Milady had left the wood and been picked up by the driver.

Satisfied with this discovery, which confirmed what he had suspected, Athos went back to the hotel, where he found Planchet waiting impatiently for him.

Everything was as Athos had anticipated.

Planchet had followed the same road. Like Athos, he had noticed the bloodstains; like Athos he had remarked the place where the horses had stopped; but he had gone on further than Athos, and in the village of Festubert, while having a drink in a tavern, had learnt, without needing to ask any questions, that the night before, at half-past eight, a wounded man, who was accompanying a lady travelling in a post-chaise, had been forced to stop, too ill to go any further. The accident had been blamed on robbers, who had ostensibly stopped the post-chaise in the woods. The man had stayed in the village, while the woman had changed horses and continued on her way.

Planchet set off in search of the postilion who had driven the post-chaise, and found him. He had taken the lady as far as Fromelles, and from Fromelles she had made for Armentières. Planchet cut across country, and by seven in the morning he was in Armentières.

There was only one hotel there, the Post. Planchet went in, saying he was a valet without employment who was looking for a position. He hadn't chatted for ten minutes to the staff of the inn before he knew that a woman had arrived on her own at eleven o'clock in the evening, had taken a room, had sent for the landlord and told him she wished to stay a while in the neighbourhood.

That was all Planchet needed to know. He ran to the rendezvous, found the three valets punctually at their posts, placed them as sentries at all the exits of the hotel, and went to find Athos. Planchet had just finished his report, when Athos's friends came in.

Their faces were grim and drawn, even Aramis's mild countenance.

'What are we to do?' asked d'Artagnan.

'Wait,' replied Athos.

Each of them retired to his room.

At eight o'clock in the evening, Athos gave orders to saddle the horses, and told Lord de Winter and his friends to make their preparations for the expedition.

All five were ready in a moment. Each of them inspected his weapons and made them ready. Athos went down first and found d'Artagnan already on horseback, waiting restlessly.

'Patience,' said Athos, 'we're still missing someone.'

The four riders looked round them in astonishment, vainly racking their brains to think who this someone they were missing could be.

At that moment Planchet brought up Athos's horse and the musketeer vaulted lightly into the saddle.

'Wait for me,' he said. 'I'll be back presently.'

And then he set off at a gallop.

A quarter of an hour later, he indeed came back, accompanied by a man wearing a mask and wrapped in a large red cloak.

Lord de Winter and the three musketeers looked questioningly at each other. None of them could enlighten the others, for none of them knew who this man was. However, they thought there must be good reason for it, since it had come about on Athos's orders.

At nine o'clock, guided by Planchet, the little cavalcade set off, taking the road the carriage had followed.

They made a sad sight, those four men riding in silence, each plunged in his thoughts, bleak as despair, grim as retribution.

LXV

THE JUDGEMENT

I T WAS A DARK AND STORMY NIGHt. Great clouds scudded
across the sky, veiling the brightness of the stars. The moon
would not rise before midnight.

Sometimes, by a flash of lightning that glittered on the horizon,
the road could be seen stretching ahead, white and solitary, but
then, when the lightning died away, everything would sink back
into darkness.

Athos constantly had to ask d'Artagnan, who insisted on
riding at the head of the little troop, to return to his place in the
ranks. Moments after he had done so, however, he would leave
it again. D'Artagnan had only one thought: forward! And forward
he went.

They passed silently through the village of Festubert, where
the wounded servant had stopped, then skirted the Richebourg
Wood. When they reached Herlies, Planchet, who was still guiding
the column, turned left.

Several times one of Lord de Winter, Porthos and Aramis tried
to address a word to the man in the red cloak, but at each question
put to him, he nodded without replying. After a while the travellers
understood the stranger must have some reason to keep silent, and
so stopped speaking to him.

In any case, the storm was building, flashes of lightning came
in swift succession, the thunder began to roll, and the wind,
forerunner of the tempest, whistled over the plain, shaking the
horsemen's plumes.

The cavalcade spurred their horses into a fast trot.

A little way beyond Fromelles, the storm broke. They spread
their cloaks. There were still three leagues to go; they covered
them in torrential rain.

D'Artagnan had taken off his hat, and wasn't wearing his cloak. He took pleasure in letting the water stream down his burning brow and over his feverish, trembling body.

Just as the little troop passed Goskal and was approaching the post-house, a man sheltering under a tree stepped away from the trunk, which he had merged into in the darkness, and came out into the middle of the road with his finger to his lips.

Athos recognised Grimaud.

'What is it?' cried d'Artagnan. 'Has she left Armentières?'

Grimaud nodded in the affirmative. D'Artagnan ground his teeth.

'Silence, d'Artagnan!' said Athos. 'I've taken charge of everything, so it's for me to question Grimaud. Where is she?'

Grimaud stretched out his hand in the direction of the Lys.

'Far from here?' asked Athos.

Grimaud raised a bent forefinger.

'Alone?' asked Athos.

Grimaud made a sign in the affirmative.

'Gentlemen,' said Athos, 'she is alone, a half-league from here, in the direction of the river.'

'Very good,' said d'Artagnan. 'Lead on, Grimaud.'

Grimaud set off across the fields, guiding the cavalcade.

After some five hundred paces, they came to a stream, which they forded.

In a flash of lightning, they spied the village of Erquinghem.

'Is it here?' asked d'Artagnan.

Grimaud shook his head.

'Silence!' said Athos.

And then the troop continued on its way.

Another bolt of lightning blazed across the sky. Grimaud stretched out his arm, and in the bluish light of the fiery serpent, they made out an isolated little house on the bank of the river, a hundred paces from the ferry. There was a light at one window.

'We're here,' said Athos.

At that moment, a man lying in a ditch got to his feet. It was Mousqueton. He pointed to the lighted window.

'She's there,' he said.

'And Bazin?' asked Athos.

'While I've been watching the window, he's been guarding the door.'

'Good,' said Athos, 'you are all faithful servants.'

Athos leapt off his horse, handed the bridle to Grimaud, and, after signalling to the rest of the troop to go round to the side of the house where the door was, made for the window.

The little house was surrounded by a quickset hedge two or three feet high. Athos slipped through it and went up to the window. Instead of shutters, it had half-length curtains which were tightly drawn.

He climbed on the stone windowsill to look over the curtains.

By the light of a lamp, he saw a woman wrapped in a dark-coloured cloak sitting on a stool by a dying fire. Her elbows were propped on a rickety table, and she was resting her head in her two ivory-white hands.

Her face was hidden, but a sinister smile played on Athos's lips. There was no mistaking it; that was the woman he was searching for.

At that moment, a horse neighed. Milady raised her head, saw Athos's pale face pressed to the window, and let out a cry.

Realising he'd been recognised, Athos pushed the window with his knee and hand; the window gave, the panes broke.

And then Athos, like the spectre of vengeance, leapt into the room.

Milady ran to the door and opened it. Paler and still more threatening than Athos, d'Artagnan stood on the threshold.

Milady started back with a scream. Thinking she had some means of escape, fearing she would slip from their grasp, d'Artagnan drew his pistol from his belt. But Athos raised his hand.

'Put back that weapon, d'Artagnan,' he said. 'This woman must be tried not murdered. Wait a while longer, d'Artagnan, and you shall be satisfied. Come in, gentlemen.'

D'Artagnan obeyed, for Athos had the solemn voice and commanding gestures of a judge sent by the Lord Himself. And so, after d'Artagnan, Porthos came into the room followed by Aramis, Lord de Winter and the man in the red cloak.

The four valets stood guard at the door and the window.

Milady had fallen into her chair with her arms outstretched, as if to ward off this terrible apparition. When she saw her brother-in-law, she let out a terrible scream.

'What do you want?' cried Milady.

'We want,' said Athos, 'Charlotte Backson, who was called first the Countess de La Fère, then Lady de Winter, Baroness Sheffield.

'I am that person,' she murmured in extreme terror. 'What do you want of me?'

'We want to judge you according to your crimes,' said Athos. 'You will be free to defend yourself. Justify yourself, if you can. Monsieur d'Artagnan, you will lay your accusations first.'

D'Artagnan stepped forward.

'Before God and men,' he said, 'I accuse this woman of having poisoned Constance Bonacieux, who died last night.'

He turned to Porthos and Aramis.

'We bear witness to this,' the two musketeers burst out as one.

D'Artagnan went on.

'Before God and men, I accuse this woman of having tried to poison me with adulterated wine, which she sent me from Villeroi with a forged letter to make it seem as if the wine came from my friends. God spared me, but a man by the name of Brisemont died in my place.'

'We bear witness to this,' Porthos and Aramis said with one voice.

'Before God and men, I accuse this woman of having incited me to murder Baron de Wardes, and as no one is here to bear witness to the truth of this accusation, I bear witness to it myself. There, I have spoken.'

And then d'Artagnan crossed to the other side of the room to join Porthos and Aramis.

'Now you, my lord!' said Athos.

The baron came forward in his turn.

'Before God and men,' he said, 'I accuse this woman of having the Duke of Buckingham assassinated.'

'The Duke of Buckingham assassinated?' all those present cried out in one voice.

'Yes,' said the baron, 'assassinated! Prompted by your letter of warning, I had this woman arrested, and I placed her in the charge of a loyal servant. She corrupted that man, put the dagger in his hand and had the duke assassinated, and at this very moment Felton may be paying for this Fury's crime with his life.'

A shudder ran through the judges at the revelation of these hitherto unknown crimes.

'That is not all,' said Lord de Winter. 'My brother, who made you his heir, died in three hours of a strange sickness which left livid bruises all over his body. My sister, how did your husband die?'

'Horrific!' cried Porthos and Aramis.

'Murderer of Buckingham, murderer of Felton, murderer of my brother, I demand justice against you, and I declare that if it is not done, I shall do it myself.'

And then Lord de Winter went to stand by d'Artagnan, leaving the floor open to another accuser.

Milady buried her brow in her hands and tried to gather her thoughts, her head swimming in deadly turmoil.

'It is my turn,' said Athos, trembling as the lion trembles at the sight of a snake, 'it is my turn. I married this woman when she was a young girl. I married her against the wishes of all my family. I gave her my property, I gave her my name, and one day I discovered that this woman was branded; this woman was marked with a fleur-de-lys on her left shoulder.'

'Oh!' said Milady, getting to her feet. 'I defy you to find the court that pronounced that loathsome sentence against me. I defy you to find the man who carried it out.'

'Silence,' said a voice. 'That is for me to answer!'

And then the man in the red cloak stepped forward in his turn.

'Who is this man, who is this man?' cried Milady, choking with terror, her hair falling loose and standing up on her livid brow as though alive.

All eyes turned to this man, for he was unknown to all of them except Athos.

But even Athos looked at him with as much amazement as the others, for he didn't know how he could be involved in the awful drama that was drawing to a close.

After approaching Milady with a slow, solemn step, until only the table stood between them, the stranger took off his mask.

Milady gazed for a long time with mounting terror at that pale face framed by black hair and side-whiskers, whose sole expression was one of icy impassivity. Then suddenly, standing up and backing away towards the wall, she said, 'Oh, no, no, it's a ghost from hell! No, no, it's not he! . . . Help! Help!' she cried in a hoarse voice, turning to the wall as if she could tear a hole in it with her bare hands.

'But who are you?' cried all the witnesses to the scene.

'Ask this woman,' said the man in the red cloak, 'for you can see she's recognised me.'

'The executioner of Lille, the executioner of Lille!' cried Milady, stricken with mad terror and clinging desperately to the wall so as not to fall down.

Everyone drew back, and the man in the red cloak was left standing alone in the middle of the room.

'Oh, mercy! Mercy! Forgive me!' cried the wretched woman, falling to her knees.

The stranger allowed the room to fall silent.

'I told you she had recognised me!' he said. 'Yes, I am the executioner of the town of Lille, and here is my story.'

All eyes were fixed on this man, as they avidly and anxiously awaited what he would say.

'This young woman was once a young girl, as beautiful as she is today. She was a nun in the Benedictine convent of Templemar. A young priest, with a heart full of simplicity and belief, served in the convent's church. She undertook to seduce him, and she succeeded – she could have seduced a saint.

'The vows they had both taken were sacred, irrevocable, and their liaison could not last without ruining them both. She persuaded him that they should leave that part of the country. But to leave, to run off together, to get to some other part of France, where they could live in peace as unknowns, required money, and neither of them had any. So the priest stole the sacred vessels and sold them, but just as they were preparing to leave together, they were both arrested.

'Within eight days she had seduced the gaoler's son and escaped. The young priest was sentenced to branding and ten years in irons. I was the executioner of the town of Lille, as this woman said. I was obliged to brand the guilty man, and the guilty man, gentlemen, was my own brother!

'I swore then that this woman who had ruined him, who was more than his accomplice, since she had incited him to commit the crime, would at least share his punishment. I suspected where she was hiding, pursued her, caught her, bound her and branded her with the same mark as I had branded my brother.

'The day after my return to Lille, my brother managed to escape in his turn. I was accused of being complicit and sentenced to remain in prison in his place until he gave himself up to justice. My poor brother had no knowledge of this sentence. He had rejoined this woman and they had fled together to Berry. There he had obtained a small parish. This woman passed herself off as his sister.

'The lord of the manor, on whose lands the curate's church stood, saw this alleged sister and fell in love with her, so in love that he proposed to marry her. Then she left the man she had ruined for the one she was to ruin, and became Countess de La Fère . . .'

All eyes turned towards Athos, whose real name that was.

He nodded as a sign that everything the executioner said was true.

'Then,' the latter continued, 'crazed, desperate, resolved to rid himself of an existence which she had robbed of all honour and happiness, my poor brother returned to Lille, and, learning of the sentence that had condemned me in his place, gave himself up and hanged himself that same night from the grating in his cell.

'To do them justice, those who had condemned me kept their word. The identity of the body had scarcely been confirmed before they restored my liberty.

'That is the crime of which I accuse her, that is the reason why I branded her.'

'Monsieur d'Artagnan,' said Athos, 'what is the penalty you call for against this woman?'

'The death penalty,' replied d'Artagnan.

'My Lord de Winter,' Athos went on, 'what is the penalty you call for against this woman?'

'The death penalty,' said Lord de Winter.

'Messrs Porthos and Aramis,' said Athos, 'as her judges, what is the penalty you inflict on this woman?'

'The death penalty,' replied the two musketeers in hollow voices.

Milady let out a dreadful scream and dragged herself on her knees a few paces closer to her judges.

Athos stretched out his hand towards her.

'Anne de Breuil, Countess de La Fère, Milady de Winter,' he said, 'your crimes have wearied men on earth and God in heaven. If you know a prayer, say it, for you are condemned and you will die.'

At these words, which left her no hope, Milady drew herself up to her full height and tried to speak, but her strength failed her. She felt a strong and implacable hand seize her by the hair and drag her away as irrevocably as fate drags man. Not even attempting to resist, therefore, she left the cottage.

Lord de Winter, d'Artagnan, Athos, Porthos and Aramis went

out after her. The valets followed their masters, and the room was left empty with its broken window, its open door and its lamp smoking sadly on the table.

LXVI
THE EXECUTION

I T WAS ALMOST MIDNIGHT. The moon, eaten into by its waning and bloodied by the last traces of the storm, rose behind the little village of Armentières, which stood out against its pallid light with the dark silhouette of its houses and the skeleton of its tall latticed bell tower. Opposite, the Lys rolled its waters like a river of molten tin, while, on the far bank, a black mass of trees was outlined against a stormy sky overrun by dense, coppery clouds, which created a sort of twilight in the middle of the night. To the left rose an old abandoned mill, its sails unmoving, in the ruins of which a screech owl was raising its shrill, recurrent, monotonous cry. Here and there on the plain, to right and left of the path taken by the lugubrious procession, a few low, squat trees appeared, which looked like misshapen dwarfs, crouching to spy on mankind at that sinister hour.

From time to time, a great flash of lightning revealed the full breadth of the horizon, snaking over the black mass of trees, cleaving the sky and water in two like a terrible scimitar. Not a breath of wind stirred in the heavy atmosphere. A deathlike silence weighed on the whole of nature. The ground was wet and slippery from the recent rain, and, refreshed, the grasses discharged their scent with redoubled vigour.

Two valets dragged Milady, each holding her by an arm. The executioner walked behind them, and Lord de Winter, d'Artagnan, Athos, Porthos and Aramis walked behind the executioner.

Planchet and Bazin brought up the rear.

The two valets led Milady to the riverbank. Her mouth was

mute, but her eyes spoke with inexpressible eloquence, beseeching everyone she looked at by turn.

Finding herself a few paces in front of the others, she said to the valets:

'A thousand pistoles for each of you if you cover my escape. But if you give me up to your masters, I have avengers close at hand, who will make you pay dearly for my death.'

Grimaud hesitated. Mousqueton trembled in every limb.

Athos, who had heard Milady's voice, strode up, as did Lord de Winter.

'Send these valets away,' he said, 'she's spoken to them. They're not to be trusted any more.'

They called Planchet and Bazin, who took the places of Grimaud and Mousqueton.

Reaching the water's edge, the executioner went over to Milady and bound her hands and feet.

Then she broke her silence to cry out, 'You are cowards, you are vile murderers – ten of you banding together to cut a woman's throat. Watch out – there may be no one to help me, but there will be to avenge me.'

'You are not a woman,' Athos said coldly, 'you do not belong to the human race. You are a demon escaped from hell, and we are going to send you back there.'

'Ah, such virtuous gentlemen!' said Milady. 'Remember that he who touches a hair on my head is a murderer in his turn.'

'An executioner may kill without being a murderer for all that, madam,' said the man in the red cloak, tapping his broadsword. 'He is the last judge, that's all: *Nachrichter*[1], as our German neighbours say.'

And, as he was binding her while saying these words, Milady gave two or three wild screams, which made a grim and strange impression as they flew off into the night and lost themselves in the depths of the wood.

'But if I am guilty, if I have committed the crimes you accuse me of,' cried Milady, 'bring me before a court. You are no judges to condemn me!'

'I offered you Tyburn,' said Lord de Winter. 'Why didn't you choose that?'

'Because I don't want to die!' Milady cried, struggling. 'Because I'm too young to die!'

'The woman you poisoned in Béthune was even younger than you, madam, and yet she is dead,' said d'Artagnan.

'I'll enter a convent, I'll become a nun,' said Milady.

'You were in a convent,' said the executioner, 'and you left it to ruin my brother.'

Milady screamed with terror and fell to her knees.

The executioner picked her up in his arms and made to take her to the boat.

'Oh, my God!' she cried. 'My God! Are you going to drown me?'

There was something so heartrending in those cries that d'Artagnan, who at first had been the most unrelenting in his pursuit of Milady, sank down on a tree stump and hung his head, blocking his ears with the palms of his hands. But even so, he could still heard her threatening and screaming.

D'Artagnan was the youngest of all those men, and his courage failed him.

'Oh, I can't bear to see this frightful spectacle! I can't consent to that woman dying like this!'

Milady heard these few words and they gave her a glimmer of hope.

'D'Artagnan! D'Artagnan!' she cried. 'Remember I loved you!'

The young man stood up and took a step towards her.

But Athos suddenly drew his sword and stood in his way.

'If you take one more step, d'Artagnan,' he said, 'we will cross swords.'

D'Artagnan fell on his knees and prayed.

'Come, executioner,' Athos went on, 'do your duty.'

'Willingly, my lord,' said the executioner, 'for, though it's true that I am a good Catholic, I solemnly believe that it is with justice that I carry out my office on this woman.'

'Very well.'

Athos took a step towards Milady.

'I forgive you,' he said, 'the evil you have done me. I forgive you my destroyed future, my lost honour, my defiled love and my salvation forever compromised by the despair into which you have thrown me. Die in peace.'

Lord de Winter stepped forward in his turn.

'I forgive you,' he said, 'the poisoning of my brother, the assassination of His Grace the Duke of Buckingham; I forgive you the death of poor Felton, and I forgive you your attempts on my life. Die in peace.'

'And I,' said d'Artagnan, 'forgive me, madam, for having provoked your anger by an imposture unworthy of a gentleman – and, in exchange, I forgive you the murder of my poor love and your cruel vengeance on me. I forgive you and I weep for you. Die in peace!'

'I am lost!' Milady murmured in English. 'I must die.'

Then she stood up and cast around her one of those bright glances that seemed to flash forth from an eye of flame.

She saw nothing.

She listened and heard nothing.

She had only enemies on all sides.

'Where am I going to die?' she said.

'On the other bank,' replied the executioner.

Then he put her in the boat, and, as he was stepping in after her, Athos handed him a sum of money.

'Here,' he said, 'this is the price of the execution. Let it be plain to all that we are acting as judges.'

'Very well,' said the executioner. 'But let this woman now know, in her turn, that I am carrying out not my trade, but my duty.'

And then he threw the money in the river.[2]

The boat struck out towards the left bank of the Lys, bearing the guilty woman and the executioner. The others stayed on the right bank, where they had fallen to their knees.

The boat glided slowly along the rope of the ferry, under the reflection of a pale cloud that hung over the water at that moment.

They saw it land on the other bank. The figures were black outlines against the reddish horizon.

During the crossing, Milady had managed to untie the rope binding her feet. When they reached the shore, she lightly jumped out and ran off.

But the ground was wet. Reaching the top of the bank, she slipped and fell on her knees.

A superstitious thought had no doubt struck her. She understood that heaven was refusing her its help, and she remained in the position in which she had fallen, her head bowed and her hands clasped.

Then, from the other bank, they saw the executioner slowly raise both arms; a ray of moonlight was reflected on the blade of his broadsword; both arms fell again; they heard the whistle of the scimitar and the cry of the victim, and a truncated mass slumped to the ground under the blow.

Then the executioner took off his red cloak, spread it on the ground, laid the body on it, threw in the head, tied it up by its four corners, swung it on to his shoulder, and got back into the boat.

Reaching the middle of the Lys, he stopped the boat, and, holding his burden over the water, cried in a loud voice, 'Let God's justice take its course!'

And then he dropped the body into the deepest part of the waters, which closed over it.

Three days later, the four musketeers returned to Paris. They had not exceeded their leaves of absence, and that same evening, they went to pay their customary visit to Monsieur de Tréville.

'Well, gentlemen,' the brave captain asked them, 'did you enjoy yourselves on your excursion?'

'Prodigiously,' replied Athos through gritted teeth.

LXVII
CONCLUSION

O N THE SIXTH OF THE FOLLOWING MONTH, the king, keeping the promise he'd made to the cardinal to leave Paris to return to La Rochelle, rode out of his capital still stunned by the news just circulating there that Buckingham had been assassinated.

Although the queen had been warned that the man she loved so much was in danger, she refused to believe it when his death was announced to her. She even recklessly cried out, 'It's a lie! He's just written to me!'

But the following day she had no choice but to believe the fatal news. La Porte, having been detained in England like everyone else by the orders of King Charles I, arrived bearing the last grim present Buckingham had sent to the queen.

The king's joy was intense, and he was not at any pains to hide it. On occasion, in fact, he even made a great show of it in front of the queen. Like all weak-hearted men, Louis XIII lacked generosity.

But he soon lapsed back into melancholy and ill health. His brow was not the sort that remains clear for long. Going back to camp, he felt, was like returning to bondage, and yet he went back all the same.

The cardinal was to him the snake that casts its mesmerising spell, and he was the bird that flutters from branch to branch but can never escape.

And so the return to La Rochelle was a deeply unhappy one. Our four friends, especially, amazed their comrades. They travelled together, side by side, their eyes bleak, their heads bowed. Only Athos would raise his broad brow from time to time; his eyes would flash, a bitter smile would play over his lips, and then, like his comrades, he would let himself sink back into his reveries.

As soon as the escort arrived in a town, once they had conducted the king to his quarters, the four friends would withdraw either to their own lodgings or to some out-of-the-way tavern, where they neither gambled nor drank, but only spoke among themselves in low voices, looking around carefully to make sure no one was listening to them.

One day when the king had made a stop to hunt magpies, and the four friends, as ever, instead of following the hunt, had stopped in a tavern on the main road, a man who came post-haste from La Rochelle pulled up at the door to drink a glass of wine, and looked into the room where the four musketeers were sitting at a table.

'Ho there, Monsieur d'Artagnan!' he said. 'That's not you I see there, is it?'

D'Artagnan raised his head and let out a shout of joy. It was he, his phantom, as he called him – the stranger from Meung, Rue des Fossoyeurs and Arras.

D'Artagnan drew his sword and rushed for the door.

But this time, instead of fleeing, the stranger leapt from his horse and came forward to meet d'Artagnan.

'Ah, sir!' said the young man. 'I've caught up with you at last! This time you won't escape me.'

'Nor is it my intention to, sir, for this time I'm looking for you. In the name of the king, I arrest you and inform you that you must surrender your sword to me, sir. Without resistance, at that. Your life depends on it, I warn you.'

'Who are you, then?' asked d'Artagnan, lowering his sword, but not surrendering it yet.

'I am the Chevalier de Rochefort,' replied the stranger, 'equerry to Cardinal Richelieu, and I have orders to take you to His Eminence.'

'We are on our way back to His Eminence, sir,' said Athos, stepping forward, 'and you will surely accept Monsieur d'Artagnan's word that he will go directly to La Rochelle.'

'I must hand him over to the guards who will take him back to camp.'

'We will serve him as guards, sir, on our word as gentlemen . . . But, also on our word as gentlemen,' added Athos, frowning, 'Monsieur d'Artagnan will not be parted from us.'

The Chevalier de Rochefort glanced over his shoulder and saw that Porthos and Aramis had placed themselves between him and the door. He realised that he was entirely at the mercy of these four men.

'Gentlemen,' he said, 'if Monsieur d'Artagnan will surrender his sword to me, and join his word to yours, I will be satisfied with your promise to escort Monsieur d'Artagnan to the cardinal's quarters.'

'You have my word, sir,' said d'Artagnan, 'and here is my sword.'

'That suits me much better,' added Rochefort, 'for I must continue my journey.'

'If it is to rejoin Milady,' Athos said coldly, 'there's no use, you won't find her.'

'What's become of her?' Rochefort demanded hotly.

'Go back to camp and you'll find out.'

Rochefort stood thinking for a moment, then, as they were no more than a day's journey from Surgères, where the cardinal was to meet the king, he decided to follow Athos's advice and go back with them.

Besides, this return had the advantage of enabling him to keep watch on his prisoner himself.

They set out again.

The next day, at three o'clock in the afternoon, they reached Surgères. The cardinal was waiting there for Louis XIII. The minister and the king exchanged many endearments, and congratu-lated one another on the happy chance that had rid France of the rabid enemy who was stirring up Europe against her. After which, the cardinal, who had been informed by Rochefort that d'Artagnan had been arrested, and who was anxious to see him, took his leave of the king, inviting him to come the next day to see the work on the dyke, which was finished.

On returning in the evening to his quarters at Pont de La Pierre, the cardinal found, standing at the door of his house, d'Artagnan without a sword and the three musketeers under arms.

This time, as he had his full retinue with him, he looked sternly at them and made a sign with his eye and hand for d'Artagnan to follow him.

D'Artagnan obeyed.

'We will wait for you, d'Artagnan,' said Athos, loudly enough for the cardinal to hear.

His Eminence frowned, stopped for a moment, then continued on his way without a word.

D'Artagnan went in after the cardinal, and Rochefort after d'Artagnan. The door was guarded.

His Eminence went to the room that served as his study, and signalled to Rochefort to bring in the young musketeer.

Rochefort obeyed and then withdrew.

D'Artagnan remained alone facing the cardinal. It was his second interview with Richelieu, and he subsequently confessed that he was utterly convinced it would be his last.

Richelieu remained standing, leaning against the fireplace. A table stood between him and d'Artagnan.

'Sir,' said the cardinal, 'you have been arrested on my orders.'

'I was informed of that, my lord.'

'Do you know why?'

'No, my lord, for the only thing I could be arrested for is still unknown to His Eminence.'

Richelieu looked hard at the young man.

'Oho!' he said. 'What does that mean?'

'If my lord will first tell me the crimes I am accused of, I will then tell him the actions I have performed.'

'You are accused of crimes that have caused heads higher than yours to roll, sir!' said the cardinal.

'What are they, my lord?' asked d'Artagnan, with a calm that amazed the cardinal.

'You are accused of corresponding with the enemies of the

realm, you are accused of seeking knowledge of state secrets, you're accused of trying to bring your general's plans to naught.'

'And who accuses me of that, my lord?' said d'Artagnan, suspecting the accusation came from Milady. 'A woman branded by the justice of her country, a woman who married one man in France and another in England, a woman who poisoned her second husband and tried to poison me?'

'What are you saying, sir?' cried the astonished cardinal. 'What woman are you talking about in this fashion?'

'Milady de Winter,' replied d'Artagnan. 'Yes, Milady de Winter, of all of whose crimes Your Eminence was doubtless unaware when he honoured her with his trust.'

'Sir,' said the cardinal, 'if Milady de Winter has committed the crimes you speak of, she will be punished.'

'She has been, my lord.'

'And who punished her?'

'We did.'

'She's in prison?'

'She's dead.'

'Dead?' repeated the cardinal, who couldn't believe what he was hearing. 'Dead? Did you say she was dead?'

'Three times she tried to kill me and I forgave her. But she killed the woman I loved. Then my friends and I caught her, tried her and condemned her.'

And then d'Artagnan related Madame Bonacieux's poisoning in the Carmelite convent at Béthune, the trial in the isolated house, the execution on the banks of the Lys.

A shudder passed through the cardinal's body, although he did not shudder easily.

But suddenly, as if under the influence of some mute thought, the cardinal's expression, which had been sombre until then, brightened gradually until it displayed the most perfect serenity.

'So,' he said, in a voice whose gentleness contrasted with the severity of his words, 'you set yourselves up as judges, not thinking that those who have no right to punish and yet punish anyway are murderers!'

'My lord, I swear that I do not for a moment intend to defend myself before you. I will submit to whatever punishment Your Eminence pleases to inflict on me. I don't value life enough to fear death.'

'Yes, I know, you are a man of courage, sir,' said the cardinal, in an almost affectionate voice. 'So I can tell you that you will be tried, and even condemned.'

'Another man might tell Your Eminence that he has his pardon in his pocket. But I will simply say to you, "Give your orders, my lord, I am ready."'

'Your pardon?' Richelieu asked in surprise.

'Yes, my lord,' said d'Artagnan.

'And signed by whom? The king?'

The cardinal pronounced these words with a singular expression of contempt.

'No, by Your Eminence.'

'By me? Are you mad, sir?'

'My lord will doubtless recognise his own handwriting.'

And then d'Artagnan presented to the cardinal the precious document Athos had taken from Milady, and given to d'Artagnan as a safeguard.

His Eminence took the paper and read in a slow voice, stressing every syllable:

It is by my order and for the good of the state that the bearer has done what has been done.

In the camp before La Rochelle, this 5 August 1628.
Richelieu.

After reading these two lines, the cardinal fell into a deep reverie, without giving the paper back to d'Artagnan.

He's debating the mode of execution by which he will put me to death, d'Artagnan said to himself. Well then, my faith, he'll see how a gentleman dies!

The young musketeer was ready to depart this life in a heroic manner.

Richelieu went on thinking, rolling and unrolling the document in his hands. Finally he raised his head, fixed his eagle eye on that loyal, open, intelligent countenance, read in that tear-tracked face all the sufferings d'Artagnan had endured in the last month, and thought for the third or fourth time how much of a future awaited this boy of twenty-one, and what resources his energy, courage and intelligence could offer a good master.

Another thing: the crimes, the power, the infernal genius of Milady had scared him on more than one occasion. He felt a sort of secret joy at being rid of that dangerous accomplice forever.

He slowly tore up the document d'Artagnan had so generously given him.

I'm lost, d'Artagnan said to himself.

And he made the cardinal a low bow, as one who says, 'Lord, Thy will be done!'

The cardinal went to the table, and, without sitting down, wrote a few lines on a parchment, which was already two-thirds full, and appended his seal to it.

That's my sentence, said d'Artagnan to himself. He's sparing me the tedium of the Bastille and the torpor of a trial. It's very good of him.

'Here, sir,' the cardinal said to the young man, 'I took one full power from you and I'm giving you another back. The name on this commission is blank: you may fill it in.'

D'Artagnan hesitantly took the document and glanced at it.

It was a lieutenancy in the musketeers.

D'Artagnan fell at the cardinal's feet.

'My lord,' he said, 'my life is yours, use it as you will henceforth. But this favour you're granting me I do not deserve. I have three friends who are more deserving and more worthy . . .'

'You are a brave lad, d'Artagnan,' interrupted the cardinal, clapping him familiarly on the shoulder, delighted to have conquered his rebellious nature. 'Do as you please with this commission. But remember that, although the name's blank, you are the one to whom I'm giving it.'

'I will never forget,' replied d'Artagnan. 'Your Eminence may be certain of it.'

The cardinal turned and said in a loud voice,

'Rochefort!'

The chevalier, who no doubt was waiting behind the door, entered immediately.

'Rochefort,' said the cardinal, 'you see Monsieur d'Artagnan. I am receiving him into my circle of friends. Kiss each other, then. And be sensible if you're keen to preserve your heads.'

Rochefort and d'Artagnan grudgingly made a show of kissing one another, while the cardinal stood there, observing them with his vigilant eye.

They left the study together.

'We shall see each other again, shall we not, sir?'

'Whenever you please,' said d'Artagnan.

'An opportunity will present itself,' replied Rochefort.

'Eh?' said the cardinal, opening the door.

The two men smiled at one another, shook hands, and bowed to His Eminence.

'We were starting to get impatient,' said Athos.

'Here I am, my friends,' replied d'Artagnan, 'not only free, but in favour.'

'You'll tell us about it?'

'This evening.'

Accordingly, that same evening d'Artagnan went to Athos's lodgings, where he found him emptying a bottle of his Spanish wine, a mission he religiously carried out every night.

D'Artagnan told him what had transpired between the cardinal and himself, and, taking the commission out of his pocket, said, 'Here, my dear Athos, this naturally belongs to you.'

Athos smiled one of his sweet, charming smiles.

'My friend,' said he, 'this is too much for Athos, and too little for the Count de La Fère. Keep this commission, it's yours. Alas, my God, you've paid a high price for it.'

D'Artagnan left Athos's rooms and went to see Porthos.

He found him wearing a magnificent coat covered with splendid embroidery, and looking at himself in a mirror.

'Aha, it's you, dear friend!' exclaimed Porthos. 'How do you think this suits me?'

'Marvellously,' said d'Artagnan, 'but I've come to offer you an outfit that will suit you even better.'

'What?' asked Porthos.

'That of a lieutenant in the musketeers.'

D'Artagnan told Porthos about his interview with the cardinal, and, taking the commission from his pocket, said, 'Here, my dear friend, write your name on it, and be a good leader for me.'

Porthos glanced at the commission and, to the young man's great astonishment, handed it back to him.

'Yes,' he said, 'that would be very flattering, but I wouldn't have long enough to enjoy the favour. During our Béthune expedition, my duchess's husband died, and so, my dear friend, with the deceased's strongbox holding out its arms to me, I'm marrying the widow. You see, I'm trying on my wedding attire. Keep the lieutenancy, my dear friend, keep it.'

And then he returned the commission to d'Artagnan.

The young man then went to Aramis's lodgings.

He found him kneeling in front of a prayer stool, his forehead resting on his open Book of Hours.

He told him about his interview with the cardinal, and taking the commission from his pocket for the third time, he said, 'You, our friend, our light, our invisible protector, accept this commission. You have deserved it more than anyone by your wisdom and your counsels, which have always been attended by such fortunate outcomes.'

'Alas, my dear friend!' said Aramis. 'Our latest adventures have made me thoroughly sick of a soldier's life. This time my decision is irrevocable. After the siege I shall enter the Lazarists. Keep the commission, d'Artagnan. The profession of arms suits you; you will be a brave and adventurous captain.'

D'Artagnan, his eyes moist with gratitude and shining with joy, went back to Athos, whom he found still sitting at his table, studying his last glass of Malaga against the light of the lamp.

'Well,' he said, 'they've refused me too.'

'That's because no one, my dear friend, is more worthy of it than you.'

He took a pen, wrote d'Artagnan's name on the commission, and gave it back to him.

'I won't have any more friends,' said the young man. 'Alas, nothing but bitter memories . . .'

And then he let his head drop into his hands, while two tears rolled down his cheeks.

'You're young,' replied Athos, 'and there's still time for your bitter memories to turn to sweet ones.'

EPILOGUE

L A ROCHELLE, DEPRIVED OF THE SUPPORT of the English fleet and the division promised by Buckingham, surrendered after a year's siege. On the twenty-eighth of October 1628, the capitulation was signed.

The king made his entrance into Paris on the twenty-third of December of the same year. He was cheered wildly, as if he was returning from conquering an enemy rather than his fellow Frenchmen. He entered under verdant arches by the Faubourg Saint-Jacques.

D'Artagnan took his promotion. Porthos left the service and, in the course of the following year, married Madame Coquenard. The strongbox which he had coveted with such feeling, proved to contain eight hundred thousand livres'.

Mousqueton was given a magnificent livery, and, what's more, the chance to fulfil his lifelong dream of riding behind a gilded carriage.

Aramis suddenly disappeared after a trip to Lorraine, and stopped writing to his friends. It emerged later, from Madame de Chevreuse, who had told two or three of her lovers, that he had taken the habit in a monastery at Nancy[2].

Bazin became a lay brother.

Athos remained a musketeer under d'Artagnan's command until 1633, at which time, after a trip to Touraine, he also left the service, on the pretext that he had just inherited a small property in Roussillon[3].

Grimaud accompanied Athos.

D'Artagnan fought Rochefort three times and wounded him three times.

'I'll probably kill you the fourth time,' he said to him, offering him a hand to help him to his feet.

'Then it would be better for both of us if we left it there,' replied the wounded man. 'God's teeth, I'm more of a friend to you than you think, for, ever since our first meeting, with just a word to the cardinal, I could have had you beheaded.'

They kissed, but this time gladly and without dissembling[4].

Through the offices of Rochefort, Planchet was awarded the rank of sergeant in the guards[5].

Monsieur Bonacieux lived a very peaceful life, entirely unaware of what had become of his wife and not too concerned about it either. One day, he was rash enough to send the cardinal a reminder of his existence. By reply, the cardinal assured him he would see to it that in future he never lacked for anything.

And indeed, after leaving his home at seven o'clock the following evening to go to the Louvre, Monsieur Bonacieux was never seen again in Rue des Fossoyeurs. Those who seemed to be best informed were of the opinion that he was being lodged and fed in some royal castle at the expense of His Generous Eminence.

THE END

NOTES

PREFACE

1   MY HISTORY OF LOUIS XIV: Dumas's work of narrative history, *Louis XIV and His Century,* was published just after *The Three Musketeers* in 1844–5. *The Memoirs of M. d'Artagnan* by Gatien Courtilz de Sandras was published in Cologne in 1700, then reprinted there and in Amsterdam. For Dumas's use of the apocryphal memoirs as a source, see Introduction.

2   MONSIEUR ANQUETIL'S HISTORY: the works of historian Louis-Pierre Anquetil (1723–1806), in particular his *History of France,* provided Dumas with numerous ideas for plots. His first resounding theatrical success, *Henri III and His Court,* came from a story in Anquetil. Suspecting his wife of infidelity, the Duke de Guise offers her the choice of death by dagger or poison. She chooses the latter, drinks the potion, falls to her knees in prayer, and the Duke leaves her room. After an hour, he returns to reveal that, rather than poison, she has in fact swallowed 'an excellent consommé'.

3   AN ENTIRE INSTALMENT: the instalments (*feuilletons*), in which *The Three Musketeers* was initially published in *Le Siècle* newspaper between 14 March and 14 July 1844, roughly correspond to the chapters in this book.

4   ACADÉMIE FRANÇAISE: Dumas's preface is essentially playful, a gently self-deprecating attempt to convince the reader that what follows is the non-existent *Memoirs of the Count de la Fère,* and that he is merely an editor, rather than author. The fiction is not subsequently maintained with great vigour (in this respect, Dumas is like Athos when he tells the story of his marriage on pp. 323–4). Yet its plea for intellectual respectability, that Dumas be taken as seriously as Louis-Pierre Anquetil or

the historian and editor of medieval texts Paulin Paris (1800–1881), is not entirely unserious. The Académie des Inscriptions et Belles Lettres, founded in 1694 and still an important institute of historical, archaeological and oriental scholarship, may have been out of reach, but Dumas's lifelong dream was to enter the Académie Française, founded by Cardinal Richelieu in 1635 and still France's pre-eminent literary and intellectual institution. Appropriately enough, given their complicated relationship, his son, Alexandre Dumas fils, was elected to the Académie Française four years after his death in 1874.

5   WE UNDERTAKE TO PUBLISH THE SECOND PART FORTHWITH: sure enough, the sequel, *Twenty Years After,* came out in 1845, and the third part of the trilogy, *The Vicomte de Bragelonne* in 1847.

I. THE THREE GIFTS OF MONSIEUR D'ARTAGNAN PÈRE

1   MEUNG: Courtilz de Sandras sets d'Artagnan's first (mis)adventure at Saint-Dié on the left bank of the Loire (now Saint-Dyé-sur-Loire). Dumas changes it to Meung-sur Loire, 30 km north, presumably to establish the literary credentials of his hero. Begun in the thirteenth century by Guillaume de Lorris and completed by Jean de Meung in the fourteenth, *The Romance of the Rose* was the most popular of all medieval romances, an allegory of courtly love tracing the trials of The Lover in his quest for the rose of his affections. Dumas's subsequent allusions to Don Quixote emphasise the point: d'Artagnan is to be seen as the latest in a line of knights errant who seek to apply the chivalric code in different times.

2   THE HONEST MILLER INN: 'honest' here implies both 'straightforward/forthright' – the French is 'l'hôtel du Franc Meunier' – and 'trustworthy', unscrupulous millers being notorious for keeping a share of the grain they were given to mill. All the other translations the translator has seen, however, translate this as the Happy Miller inn, so this reading may be mistaken.

3   THE SPANISH, WHO WERE MAKING WAR ON THE KING: Louis
    XIII in fact only declared war on Spain on 21 May 1635.

4   YELLOW AND RED FLAG: the colours of Spain.

5   ROCINANTE: Don Quixote's ageing horse in Miguel de
    Cervantes's novel, *Don Quixote. Rocin* is the Spanish word for
    workhorse or low-quality horse, like *roussin* in French. When
    Aramis sees d'Artagnan's trusty steed on p. 390, he will exclaim,
    'Oh! l'affreux roussin,' 'Oh what a frightful workhorse!'

6   THICK BÉARNAIS TWANG: Dumas uses the term 'patois', and
    indeed Béarnais is recognised as a dialect of the province of
    Béarn in south-west France in the Pyrénées-Atlantiques. It is
    considered by some to be a local variant of the Gascon dialect
    just as Béarn may be considered a part of the ancient duchy
    of Gascony, a large and ill-defined area stretching from the
    Garonne river in the east to the Atlantic coast in the west. To
    the south Gascony borders with Basque and Spain (interest-
    ingly, 'Gascony' derives from *Vasconia*, its Latin name, so
    called because it had been invaded by the *Vascones* – or
    Basques). The dialect of Béarn, to the south-west and near
    neighbour to Basque and Spain, has a distinctive twang.

    Dumas's references to Béarn and Gascony make it clear that
    he saw the two regions as virtually interchangeable: his young
    hero is sometimes 'the Béarnais' (like his king's father) but he
    is usually referred to as a Gascon. His father, with his Béarnais
    twang, might well have come (like Monsieur de Tréville and
    Henri IV, who was born in Pau, the capital of Béarn) from
    the Béarn region: in *Twenty Years After*, d'Artagnan mentions
    having gone to Béarn on account of his father's death. On the
    other hand, d'Artagnan sets off on his adventures (on his
    'Béarnais nag') from Tarbes, which is a part of Gascony well
    to the east of Béarn.

    As for Henri IV, father of Louis XIII, it is possible that
    sauce Béarnaise was named – indirectly – after him: it is thought
    that the sauce was first served at the opening in 1836 of a
    restaurant not far from Paris called Le Pavillon Henri IV.

7   THE WARS OF RELIGION: conflicts between Catholics and Protestants racked France throughout the sixteenth century, until largely brought to an end by Henri IV with his signature of the Edict of Nantes in 1598.

8   THE UNFORTUNATE TOWN OF MEUNG: Meung is around 600 km, or 125 leagues, from Tarbes. At the Béarnais nag's average speed of eight leagues a day, d'Artagnan will therefore have travelled without incident for about a fortnight.

9   TWELVE ÉCUS: d'Artagnan appears to have spent three écus – eighteen livres, almost the price of his nag – during his journey.

10   MILADY: Dumas, in one of his occasional attempts to assert that he is merely the editor of the *Memoirs of the Count de la Fère*, inserted a footnote in the original edition saying, 'We are fully aware that the expression *Milady* is properly used only in conjunction with a family name. But it is written thus in the manuscript and we shall not change it.'

11   THE DUKE: George Villiers, first Duke of Buckingham (1592–1628). He came to Paris in May 1625 to negotiate the marriage of the English king, Charles I, to Henrietta, Louis XIII's sister and Henri IV's daughter.

12   THE HERON AND THE SNAIL: the moral of La Fontaine's fable 'The Heron' (*Fables*, VII. 4) is not to be too fussy: 'would you be strong and great, learn to accommodate'. After scorning all manner of fish by day, the heron is ravenous by evening and ends up tucking into a snail.

13   ORTOLANS; songbirds in the bunting family, they were long considered one of France's great gastronomic delicacies. They were fattened on millet, doused in Armagnac, roasted and then eaten whole, with a napkin over the diner's head. The former French president, François Mitterand, ate one at his 'last supper' before dying of cancer in 1996.

14   FATHER JOSEPH: the original *Éminence Grise*, François Leclerc de Tremblay, known as 'le père Joseph', was a monk and diplomat and confidant of Cardinal Richelieu, who was

known as *Éminence Rouge*, 'red eminence'. Their soubriquets reflect the respective colours of their habits.

15 RUE DES FOSSOYEURS: 'Gravediggers Street', a narrow street near Place Saint-Sulpice in Paris's 6th arrondissement. It was renamed Rue Servandoni in 1806, which leads to an amusingly confusing moment later in the story. The Luxembourg Palace was built between 1615 and 1620 for Louis XIII's mother, Marie de' Medici. It now houses the French Senate, and its gardens are one of Paris's largest and most popular public parks.

16 QUAI DE LA FERRAILLE: now the Quai de la Mégisserie, between the Châtelet and the Pont-Neuf.

17 RUE DU VIEUX-COLOMBIER: this street runs across the north of Place Saint-Sulpice.

II. MONSIEUR DE TRÉVILLE'S ANTECHAMBER

1 THE LEAGUE: *la Sainte Ligue*, an association of Catholics set up by the Duke de Guise (1550–1588) during the Wars of Religion, partly to defend the Catholic faith against the Protestants, partly so he could replace Henri III. The Duke de Guise was assassinated on Henri III's orders in 1588, and Henri III was himself assassinated the following year. Aided by Philip II of Spain, the League was finally defeated when Henri IV converted to Catholicism in 1593.

2 HIS COAT OF ARMS: the language of heraldry is a contemporary anglicisation of Norman French. The *field* is the background of the shield. The coat of arms would have shown a gold (*or*) lion *passant* (walking towards the *dexter*, or right, side, with the *dexter* fore-paw raised, the other three paws on the ground) on a red (*gules*) field. The motto *Fidelis et fortis* – faithful and brave – is just one variant of the many carrying the same meaning. All Monsieur de Tréville's heraldic details are Dumas's invention.

3 A BESME, A MAUREVERS, A POLTROT DE MÉRÉ, OR A VITRY: all assassins. The latter, for instance, Nicholas de l'Hôpital,

Duke de Vitry (1581–1644), killed the minister (and favourite of Marie de' Medici) Concini, Maréchal d'Ancre, on Louis XIII's orders in 1617. The affair is referred to on p. 177.

4   AND SO LOUIS XIII MADE DE TRÉVILLE CAPTAIN OF HIS MUSKET-EERS: Arnaud-Jean du Peyrer (1598–1672), first Count de Troisvilles, or Tréville, was a sublieutenant of the musketeers in 1625 and captain-lieutenant in 1634. Only the king could be captain of the musketeers.

5   LOUIS XI'S SCOTS GUARD: this Garde Écossaise had no connection with the British Army's famous regiment, which did not exist at the time. It was a result of the longstanding 'Auld Alliance' against England between the two countries, ratified by a treaty signed in 1295. The Garde Écossaise, made up of Scots soldiers, was founded in 1418 by Charles VII of France. They were considered an elite force and Charles VII's son Louis XI appointed them personal bodyguards to the French monarchy. As time went on, the unit came to include more French than Scots soldiers; its final dissolution came in 1830. The British Scots Guards was a regiment of Scottish soldiers raised in 1642 to protect the Scottish settlers in Ireland.

6   PLURIBUS IMPAR: meaning 'equalled by many', this is a slightly awkward play on the motto of Louis XIV, the Sun King, '*nec pluribus impar*', 'unequalled by many'.

7   WHERE GULLIVER WAS TO GO LATER AND BE SO TERRIFIED: an engaging attempt to avoid anachronism. *Gulliver's Travels* by Jonathan Swift, who invented Brobdingnag, the land of giants, was published in 1726.

8   MADAME D'AIGUILLON, HIS MISTRESS, AND MADAME DE COMBALET, HIS NIECE: these were in fact the same woman, Marie-Madeleine de Vignerot, Dame de Combalet, Duchess d'Aiguillon, Richelieu's niece by marriage and probably also his mistress.

9   THE CROWN OF FRANCE WITH AN HEIR: Louis XIV wasn't born until 5 September 1638 (see p. 351), a birth that, after twenty-three childless years of marriage between Louis XIII and

Anne of Austria, was described by contemporaries as 'a marvel when it was least expected'. The long wait had caused all manner of rumours about sterility and homosexuality, and allowed Dumas to create Louis XIV's putative twin brother, the Man in the Iron Mask.

10 MADAME DE BOIS-TRACY: she seems to be an invention of Dumas's, unlike Madame de Chevreuse. Marie-Aimée de Rohan-Montbazon (1600–1679), the Duchess de Luynes by her first marriage and Duchess de Chevreuse by her second, was an extremely influential figure at court, close confidante of Anne of Austria and implacable opponent of Richelieu. Mentioned above (inaccurately as far as chronology is concerned), her lovers included Henri de Chalais (1599–1626), Count de Chalais, who failed in his attempt to kill Richelieu in 1626, and Geoffrey, Marquis de Laigues (1614–1674), who assisted her during the uprisings of the nobility against the crown, from 1648 onwards, known as the Fronde. Madame de Chevreuse is a shadowy but insistent presence throughout the book, and emerges as a central figure in *Twenty Years After* and the third part of the trilogy of d'Artagnan romances, *The Vicomte de Bragelonne*.

III. THE AUDIENCE

1 RUE FÉROU: the street, where, it will emerge, Athos lives, still runs from Place Saint-Sulpice to Rue de Vaugirard in the 6th arrondissement of Paris.

2 ACADÉMIE ROYALE: a private military academy, one of many at the time in Paris and the provinces.

IV. ATHOS'S SHOULDER, PORTHOS'S BALDRIC AND ARAMIS'S HANDKERCHIEF

1 CARMES-DÉSCHAUX: written without the 's,' the Carmes-Déchaux were an order of Carmelite monks who went barefoot (*déchaussés*). The church still stands on Rue de Vaugirard.

2   WENT DOWN TO THE FERRY: using a rope to pull boats across the
     Seine, a ferry was established in 1550 between the Rue du Bac
     (the French for 'ferry') and the Tuileries to help the construction
     of the Château des Tuileries. Rue de Seine runs from the
     Luxembourg Palace to the Seine and Rue de Croix-Rouge is the
     other side of Rue de Rennes from Place Saint-Sulpice.

3   D'AIGUILLON MANSION: the *hôtel d'Aiguillon* (*hôtel* in the French
     sense of townhouse) was known at the time as the Petit-
     Luxembourg. In 1627, Marie de' Medici gave it to Richelieu,
     who lived there while the Palais Cardinal (subsequently Palais
     Royal) was being built. He gave it to his niece, the Duchess
     d'Aiguillon, in 1639.

V. THE KING'S MUSKETEERS AND THE CARDINAL'S GUARDS

1   POMPEY'S SOLDIERS: another allusion to the battle of Pharsalus
     (48 BC) between Pompey and Julius Caesar, like Porthos's on
     p. 37. According to Lucan's *Pharsalia*, Caesar told his men to
     strike their patrician opponents in the face, since their vanity
     mattered more to them than their lives.

2   PRÉ-AUX-CLERCS: part of the charm of *The Three Musketeers*
     for its nineteenth-century audience would have been its
     evocation of pre-industrial Paris with its patches of rural
     tranquillity. The Pré-aux-Clercs was one of the meadows,
     prés, commemorated in the name of the Left Bank *quartier*,
     Saint-Germain-des-Prés.

3   THE SAMARITAINE CLOCK: a hydraulic pump near the Pont-Neuf,
     which provided water for the Louvre Palace from 1609 to 1813.
     It was topped by a bell tower with a gilded bas relief depicting
     the Woman of Samaria, who, in the fourth chapter of John's
     Gospel in the Bible, draws water from Jacob's well and gives
     it to Christ to drink. The owner of the famous department
     store, La Samaritaine, which ran from 1900 to 2005, started
     selling ties on this spot.

4   BISCARAT: Biscarat's son, who is a credit to his father, appears in *The Vicomte de Bragelonne*.

VI. HIS MAJESTY KING LOUIS XIII

1   KING LOUIS XIII: played for comic effect, Dumas's portrait of Louis XIII (1601–1643) is nonetheless broadly accurate. His marriage with Anne of Austria was unhappy, he relied heavily on Cardinal Richelieu to rule France, and his reign was over-shadowed by the intriguing of his mother, Marie de' Medici, and his struggles with the Huguenots and the Hapsburgs. Not the most distinguished of French monarchs, Geoffrey Parker describes him in *Europe in Crisis, 1598–1648*, as 'Morose, unhappy, irritable, a stammerer – he was also intensely proud and possessed a great awareness of his own importance. "Remember that the greatest honour you have in this world is to be my brother," he once arrogantly informed the older (illegitimate) duke of Vendôme.'

2   THE KING'S GAMING TABLE: Louis XIII only played chess. Forty-seven gaming houses were shut down during his reign, although the nobility continued to gamble as furiously as ever – the Maréchal d'Ancre, for instance, commonly staked 20,000 pistoles. Louis's passion for chess was so fervent, however, (like the love of hunting Dumas accurately ascribes to him), that he had his carriage fitted with a chessboard designed to prevent the pieces falling over.

3   MAKE CHARLEMAGNE: *faire Charlemagne* means to stop playing while you're winning, thereby leaving your opponent no chance to win back his or her losses. It may derive from Charlemagne's refusal to give up any of his conquests in his lifetime.

4   EIGHTY LOUIS D'OR IN MY PILE: an anachronism on Dumas's part – the louis d'or was not in fact issued until 1641 as part of Louis XIII's bid to sort out a number of anomalies in France's currency.

5 PONT-DE-CÉ: in 1620, Louis XIII's army defeated a revolt by Marie de' Medici and the nobility at Pont-de-Cé near Angers.

6 A GAME OF TENNIS: real, or royal, tennis, played without rackets until the late seventeenth century, hence its original French name, *jeu de paume*, 'palm game'. 'Tennis', as a name, is thought to derive from the server's warning when about to serve – *Tenez!* 'Take heed' – a detail d'Artagnan might appreciate in what follows.

7 ONLY THE POPE IS INFALLIBLE: papal infallibility, as David Coward points out, was a nineteenth rather than a seventeenth century preoccupation. It was declared dogma by the Vatican Council of 1870.

8 BY THE HOLY GREY BELLY: One explanation for Henri IV's oath, *Ventre-saint-gris*, is that it is an euphemistic variant, referring to Christ, of the more common *Ventredieu*, 'God's wounds', the wounds suffered during Christ's Passion. Possible translations would therefore be 'Holy cris's wounds', 'Holy Crist's wounds', or 'Holy crying wounds'. This version refers to another tradition, noted in the 1898 edition of *Brewer's Dictionary of Phrase and Fable*, that Henri IV was prone to swearing as a child, and, as the lesser of two evils, his preceptors therefore allowed him to use *Ventre-saint-gris*, a term of disparagement for the grey-robed Franciscans. Appropriately enough there is a popular restaurant called Le Ventre Saint-Gris in Brussels.

VII. THE MUSKETEERS AT HOME

1 A FIRST-RATE MEAL AT THE PINE CONE: The *Pomme de Pin* was a famous tavern on the Île de la Cité, on what is now the Rue de la Cité, near Notre-Dame. Richard Pevear points out that it should not be confused with the still more famous *Pomme de Pin* on Place de Contrescarpe, which is mentioned by Villon and Rabelais, and was popular with such seventeenth-century writers as Molière, Racine and La Fontaine.

2 THE PONT DE LA TOURNELLE: a bridge running from the Île de la Cité to the Quai de la Tournelle on the left bank of the Seine.

3 THE ORDER OF THE HOLY SPIRIT: *L'Ordre du Saint-Esprit*, also known as The Order of the Knights of the Holy Spirit, was France's most prestigious Order of Chivalry, created by Henri III in 1578 to fight the League.

4 ANOTHER ACHILLES . . . ANOTHER AJAX . . . ANOTHER JOSEPH: Achilles is the brooding hero of Homer's *Iliad*, bravest of the Greeks, lovelorn, invincible save for one fatal weakness. Also from the *Iliad*, Ajax is the second bravest of the Greeks, the enormously tall and powerful 'bulwark of the Achaeans', who survives the Trojan War unscathed. The Biblical figure of Joseph, meanwhile, he of the coat of many colours, is the son of Rachel and Jacob in the Book of Genesis, the paradigmatic true believer.

VIII. A COURT INTRIGUE

1 ARCHIMEDES: (*c.*287–212 BC), celebrated Greek scientist and mathematician (hence the reference on p. 338). Archimedes's explanation of the principle of the lever prompted him to say, 'Give me a place to stand on, and I will move the Earth.'

2 MONSIEUR DE LA PORTE: a vital go-between for Anne of Austria, allowing her to correspond with the Spanish court and Madame de Chevreuse. Pierre de la Porte (1603–1680) entered the queen's service in 1621 as her *porte-manteau*, 'cloak bearer'. He was sent to the Bastille in 1637, then exiled, then rehabilitated after Richelieu's death in 1642.

3 THE SARABAND INCIDENT: a scurrilous rumour had it that, such was his infatuation for the queen, Richelieu had once danced a Saraband – a stately court dance in slow triple time – for her, dressed as a clown.

4 ON THE HONOUR OF THE BONACIEUX: as will become apparent, Monsieur Bonacieux's name is a gleeful play on *bonasse*: 'nice, easily pushed around, possibly stupid'.

5 JEAN MOCQUET: an explorer and keeper of the king's cabinet of curiosities, Jean Mocquet (1575–1617), wrote an account of his travels, *Travels in Africa, Asia, the East and the West Indies*, which was published the year he died and reprinted in 1831.

IX. D'ARTAGNAN SHOWS HIMSELF

1 SAMUEL'S SPIRIT APPEARED TO SAUL: at war with the Philistines, Saul in his despair commands the witch of Endor to summon the ghost of the prophet Samuel so he can ask for advice. 1 Samuel 28: 7-25

2 WHEN HE SCATTERED HIS PEARLS: Dumas was very fond of the story, which also appears in *The Vicomte de Bragelonne*, of how, in an attempt to court Anne of Austria in 1625, the Duke of Buckingham deliberately snapped his necklace and let her courtiers pick up its pearls. As David Coward says, such 'aristocratic' liberality is later displayed, to general admiration, by Athos, and was a feature of Dumas's life.

3 IN THE GARDEN AT AMIENS: the Duke of Buckingham caused a diplomatic incident in 1625, rather than earlier, as Aramis implies, when he got carried away in the garden of a house at Amiens and tried to snatch a kiss from the queen. Guillaume Morel, sieur de Putange, was one of the queen's equerries.

X. A SEVENTEENTH-CENTURY MOUSETRAP

1 RUE DE JÉRUSALEM: site of the main Paris police station. Dumas's dates the start of his writing career to 1829, when the success of his play, *Henri III and His Court*, made him an acclaimed, and notorious, flagbearer of Romanticism.

2 THE QUEEN OFTEN LAY AWAKE AND CRIED A GREAT DEAL: Anne of Austria (1601–1666), eldest daughter of Philip III of Spain, was betrothed to Louis XIII when she was eleven. She was slow to adapt to French court life, under suspicion given France's relations with Spain, rarely close to the king, suffered

repeated miscarriages, and, thanks to her closest confidante, the Duchess de Luynes, subsequently Duchess de Chevreuse, drawn into numerous intrigues against Richelieu. Dumas's portrait is unnuanced, however, in its depiction of her as entirely helpless. Many see her as a brilliant political operator, and certainly her position improved over time. She overruled Louis XIII's objections to her becoming regent after his death, and was very close to her son, Louis XIV.

XI. THE INTRIGUE GROWS TANGLED

1 RUE DU CHERCHE-MIDI: running from the Boulevard du Montparnasse to the Carrefour de la Croix-Rouge, this street was originally called 'Cherche-Midy,' then renamed 'Chasse-Midy' after 1628, then re-renamed 'Cherche-Midi'.

2 RUE SERVANDONI: in a dizzying turn of events, d'Artagnan travels through time to some time after 1806, the year in which Rue des Fossoyeurs, the street he lives on, was renamed Rue de Servandoni after the Italian architect who designed the façade of the church of Saint-Sulpice. Umberto Eco makes this the starting point for an engaging essay in *Six Walks in the Fictional Woods* (Harvard University Press, 1994).

3 CB, CONSTANCE BONACIEUX: Madame Bonacieux's first name promises 'constancy,' a quality much in demand in a world where no one is what they seem and everything changes at incredible speed. See Athos's rhetorical question on p. 439.

4 FOR-L'ÉVÊQUE: originally an ecclesiastical prison, For-l'Évêque was a royal prison from 1652-1780, mainly for actors and actresses.

XII. GEORGE VILLIERS, THE DUKE OF BUCKINGHAM

1 ONE OF THOSE FABULOUS EXISTENCES: Dumas accurately describes George Villiers, 1st Duke of Buckingham (1592–1648), as the favourite of successive kings of England, James I and Charles I – James I went so far as to call him his 'sweet

child and wife' – and hence extremely rich and powerful. Buckingham's dashing role in *The Three Musketeers*, however, gives no idea of his military incompetence – he was responsible for failed expeditions to Germany, Cadiz and, on two occasions, to La Rochelle, the first attacking the Huguenots and the second defending them. He was roundly loathed in England, again something that does not come across very clearly in the book. Later Milady will cast such a long and dark shadow that, as one of her adversaries, much about Buckingham is obscured.

2   HOLLAND: Henry Rich (1589–1649), Earl of Holland, became Madame de Chevreuse's lover while negotiating the marriage of Henrietta, Louis XIII's sister, to Charles I. He may have set up the meeting of Anne of Austria and Buckingham at Amiens, and later negotiated the peace of La Rochelle in 1628.

XIII. MONSIEUR BONACIEUX

1   CRUSHED BY THE SUCCESSIVE WAVES OF EMOTION: Monsieur Bonacieux takes a tour of some of Paris's places of execution. The Bastille was in the parish of the church of Saint-Paul-des-Champs, hence prisoners were buried – although not executed – in the church's cemetery. State criminals were executed on Place de Grève. La Croix-du-Trahoir was on Rue Saint-Honoré at the junction with Rue de l'Arbre-Sec – *l'arbre sec*, 'the dry tree', being a nickname for a gibbet.

XIV. THE MAN FROM MEUNG

1   A MAN OF MEDIUM HEIGHT: as David Coward points out, the average height for men at the time was 5 foot, 6 inches. We learn from *The Three Musketeers* that Athos was also this height, and from *Twenty Years After*, that d'Artagnan was too.

2   IMPERIAL: a narrow pointed beard extending from the chin, also known as a 'royal', familiar from portraits of Richelieu.

3   CARDINAL RICHELIEU: Armand-Jean du Plessis (1585–1642),

Cardinal-Duke de Richelieu, is considered the world's first Prime Minister. On becoming Head of the Royal Council in 1624, he set about uniting the kingdom, destroying the power of the Protestants and the nobility, combating the influence of the Austro-Spanish Hapsburg dynasty, and ensuring France's success in the Thirty Years War. Dumas's depiction of him is more ambivalent than it initially appears – he tries to protect d'Artagnan, after all – but nonetheless the notion of him as a cold, calculating villain, while reflecting his avowed Machiavellianism, ignores Richelieu's role in making France a centralised nation and thus paving the way for Louis XIV's glorious reign.

4   HAVING SUPPORTED THE DUKE DE NEVERS: Dumas reverses the order of events. The British landed on the Île de Ré off La Rochelle in July 1627 and were driven out in November of the same year. Richelieu besieged La Rochelle from 1627–28.

5   THE DIAMOND TAGS HIS MAJESTY GAVE THE QUEEN: alternative translations of 'les ferrets en diamants' would be diamond studs, pendants or aiglets. As defined by Webster's they are:

> 1.1 The metal tag of a lace (formerly called point), intended primarily to make it easier to thread through the eyelet-holes, but afterwards also as an ornament to the pendant ends.
>
> 2.2 An ornament consisting of a gold or silver tag or pendant attached to a fringe; whence extended to any metallic stud, plate, or spangle worn on the dress.

6   THE DUCHESS IS IN TOURS AND THE DUKE IN BOULOGNE: Madame de Chevreuse was exiled to Poitou after the execution of Chalais in 1626, and to Tours only in 1636. Boulogne signifies the Duke of Buckingham was on his way back to England.

XV. MEN OF THE LAW AND MEN OF THE SWORD

1   CRIMINAL LIEUTENANT: a magistrate in charge of civil and criminal justice.

2 SAMSON: Judges 15: 14–15. 'And when he came unto Lehi, the Philistines shouted against him: and the Spirit of the Lord came mightily upon him, and the cords that were upon his arms became as flax that was burnt with fire, and his bands loosed from off his hands. And he found a new jawbone of an ass, and put forth his hand, and took it, and slew a thousand men therewith.'

XVI. IN WHICH SÉGUIER, THE KEEPER OF THE SEALS, SEARCHES MORE THAN ONCE FOR THE BELL IN ORDER TO RING IT AS HE USED TO

1 MARÉCHALE D'ANCRE: Leonora 'Galigaï' Dori, wife of Concino Concini, Maréchal d'Ancre, the minister and favourite of Marie de' Medici, who was killed on Louis XIII's orders in 1617.

2 MARIE DE' MEDICI: the Italian Queen Mother (1573–1642), Marie de' Medici was Queen of France as Henri IV's second wife, ruling as regent after her husband's assassination in 1610 until her son, Louis XIII, took power in 1617. Her pro-Hapsburg, pro-Spanish policies and intriguing led to constant conflict with her son and Richelieu. Balzac spoke for many of the Romantic generation when he damningly wrote, 'Marie de' Medici, all of whose actions were prejudicial to France, has escaped the shame which ought to cover her name. Marie de' Medici wasted the wealth amassed by Henry IV; she never purged herself of the charge of having known of the king's assassination; her intimate was d'Épernon, who did not ward off Ravaillac's blow, and who was proved to have known the murderer personally for a long time. Marie's conduct was such that she forced her son to banish her from France, where she was encouraging her other son, Gaston, to rebel; and the victory Richelieu at last won over her (on the Day of the Dupes) was due solely to the discovery the cardinal made, and imparted to Louis XIII, of secret documents relating to the death of Henri IV.'

3 LAFFEMAS, RICHELIEU'S CHIEF GAMEKEEPER IN FRANCE: Isaac de Laffemas (1584–1657) was a magistrate who worked closely

with Richelieu. 'Chief gamekeeper' refers to the severity of his judgements in his mission to purge the king's lands of enemies. For the Chalais Affair, see p. 31.

4 THE CHANCELLOR DELIVERED THE LETTER TO THE KING: Pierre Séguier (1588–1672) did not become keeper of seals until 1633, or chancellor until 1635. He did search the queen, but not until 1637, when he was after a letter to the Spanish court. No doubt it is far-fetched to think Dumas's character assassination of him has anything to do with the fact that Séguier was one of the founding members of the Académie Française, which, as mentioned in the note to p. 4, never accepted Dumas into its ranks.

5 THE KING OF SPAIN: Philip IV (1605–1665).

XVII. THE BONACIEUX HOUSEHOLD

1 LEAVING NO TRACE OF THEIR PASSAGE: Proverbs 30: 18–20. 'There be three things which are too wonderful for me, yea, four which I know not: the way of an eagle in the air; the way of a serpent upon a rock; the way of a ship in the midst of the sea; and the way of a man with a maid.'

XVIII. THE LOVER AND THE HUSBAND

1 ANOTHER EAR OF DIONYSIUS: the Ear of Dionysius is a vast limestone cave in Sicily, thought to have been carved in the eighth century BC by Greek builders quarrying rock to build the city of Syracuse. It is said to have been named by the painter Caravaggio who in 1608 sought refuge from the law there. With its high sides and S-shape, it picked up and amplified sound like an ear. The story goes that in the fourth century BC the tyrant Dionysius I used the cave as a prison for political dissidents, taking advantage of the extraordinary acoustics to eavesdrop on them. Another legend has it that Dionysius actually had the cave carved in order that the screams of prisoners being tortured

might be magnified. (Caravaggio with his dark imagination might well have been responsible for one or both of these stories). D'Artagnan's cunning surveillance technique foreshadows the 'stakeout' scenes of myriad crime and espionage films, Gene Hackman's *The Conversation* in 1974 being a notable example.

XIX. THE PLAN OF CAMPAIGN

1   BONDY: the forest of Bondy north-east of Paris, a notorious haunt of bandits and robbers, see p. 427.
2   FORGES: with its thermal springs, Forges-les-Eaux in Normandy, 120 km from Paris, was a popular spa town then, as now.
3   ST JOHN GOLDEN MOUTH: St John Chrysostom, Archbishop of Constantinople 398–404 AD, was born between 344 and 349 AD in Antioch. He studied rhetoric under the most famous orator of the age, Libanius, but was soon drawn into the Church and was ordained in 486 AD. He became known as the most eloquent of the early Church Fathers. The name Chrysostom, from the Greek 'chrysostomos', meaning 'golden-mouthed', was given to him after his death in 407 AD.

XX. THE JOURNEY

1   COUNT DE WARDES: in Courtilz de Sandras's *The Memoirs of M. d'Artagnan*, an Englishwoman, 'Milédi,' is in love with the wealthy Marquis de Wardes, who was perhaps inspired by François-René Crespin du Bec (1620–1688). A favourite of Louis XIV's, he would only have been seven at the time of *The Three Musketeers*.

XXI. THE COUNTESS DE WINTER

1   HIS TOWNHOUSE: not in fact Buckingham House, as the first building of the present Buckingham Palace was called in 1703, but York House in the Strand in London. It was sold by the family in 1672 on condition the neighbouring streets would

commemorate the Duke of Buckingham's ownership, hence the current Duke Street and Villiers Street, for instance.

XXII. THE BALLET OF THE MERLAISON

1 THE BALLET OF THE MERLAISON; a ballet possibly composed by Louis XIII on the theme of blackbird (*merle*) hunting, one of his favourite winter pastimes.

XXIII. THE RENDEZVOUS

1 MONSIEUR DE BENSERADE: Isaac de Benserade (1613–91), poet and dramatist, who would have been in his mid-teens at the time. *Timeo Danaos et dona ferentes* – more accurately, 'I fear the Danaans even when they bring gifts' – is the prophet Laocoön's warning to his fellow Trojans when the Greeks produce the Trojan Horse. Virgil, *Aeneid*, II. 49.

XXV. PORTHOS

1 MONSIEUR DE CAVOIS: captain of Richelieu's guards, François d'Oger, sieur de Cavois.
2 PALAIS-ROYAL: Richelieu began planning a residence on Place Royale, near the Louvre, in 1624. The Palais-Cardinal, as it was known, (and as Dumas correctly calls it on pp. 428, 429, and 433) was completed in 1636. In 1639, Richelieu bequeathed it to the king and in 1642 Anne of Austria moved in, at which point it was renamed the Palais-Royal. Dumas worked there as a copyist on the secretarial staff of Louis-Philippe, Duke d'Orléans, the future king, when he first arrived in Paris.
3 LANSQUENET: from the German *Landskecht*, 'mercenary,' a card game.
4 RUE AUX OURS: the Grand Châtelet, a former fortress, housed Paris's criminal courts. As if this wasn't grim enough, the surrounding streets smelled of drying blood from nearby

slaughterhouses, and worse from nearby sewers opening into the Seine. Rue aux Ours, which still exists in Paris's third arrondissement, was originally called Rue aux Oies (geese) because of the number of rôtisseries it contained.

5   HARQUEBUS: relatively light and accurate, the harquebus was reserved for private use when the heavier musket, which needed a fork-rest to fire it, was introduced into the French army towards the end of the sixteenth century. Hence d'Artagnan's deduction on p. 449.

XXVI. ARAMIS'S THESIS

1   ARMIDA: in Torquato Tasso's *Jerusalem Delivered* (1581), a mythical version of the First Crusade, Armida is a witch who holds the Christian knight Rinaldo captive on a magical island. Her garden is full of defences, such as poisoned spring 'one sup thereof the drinker's heart doth bring to sudden joy, whence laughter vain doth rise, nor that strange merriment once stops or stays, till, with his laughter's end, he end his days.'

2   PRORSUS ADMIRABILE!: 'utterly admirable!', and in the exchange that follows: *facilius natans*: 'swimming more easily'; *exordium*: in rhetoric, the introductory part of a speech; *Quemadmodum inter cœlorum immensitatem*: 'as amidst the vastness of the heavens'.

3   ARGUMENTUM OMNI DENUDATUM ORNAMENTO: 'the argument stripped of all ornament'.

4   THE AUGUSTINUS OF THE HERESIARCH JANSEN: Cornelius Jansen (1583–1638) thought salvation could never be attained through human will; only predestination can determine one's fate after death through the concept of God's 'efficient grace'. His *Augustinus* was not published until 1640. The career of great criminals in general, and Milady in particular, is said to be predestined on p. 634.

5   THE PELAGIANS AND SEMI-PELAGIANS: by contrast to Jansen, the fifth-century heretic Pelagius preached salvation through good works.

6 MONSIEUR VOITURE: Vincent Voiture (1597–1648) was a fashionable poet who specialised in *vers de société*, witty, elegant poems for the amusement of friends that were seen as a sign of good breeding.

7 SEVERUS SIT CLERICORUM SERMO: 'let a cleric's conversation be austere.' Confusion reigns: the curate of Montdidier thinks *severus* means 'clear', but the Jesuit superior also seems to think *sermo* means 'sermon'.

8 ONE OF MASTER PATRU'S PLEADINGS: Olivier Patru (1604–1681), a renowned lawyer and prose stylist.

9 AVES CÆLI COMEDERUNT ILLAM: the parable of the sower, Matthew 13: 3–9, specifically verse 4, 'And when he sowed, some seeds fell by the way side, and the fowls came and devoured them up . . .'

10 EFFICIENT GRACE: d'Artagnan mocks the central tenet of Jansenism.

11 CONFESS ONE TO ANOTHER: James 5:16: 'Confess your faults one to another, and pray one for another, that ye may be healed.'

12 JUDITH: The Book of Judith, part of the Apocrypha of the Old Testament, describes how Judith, a beautiful Hebrew widow, seduces and beheads Holofernes, a general in the Babylonian King Nebuchadnezzar's army, who has besieged the town of Bethulia. Milady identifies with Judith on pp. 528, 582 and 599.

13 LA FORCE: La Force prison near Rue des Francs-Bourgeois in the Marais district of Paris had two buildings: La Petite-Force, for women, in Rue Pavée, and La Grande-Force, for men, in Rue du Roi-de-Sicile.

XXVII. ATHOS'S WIFE

1 MONSIEUR DE NOGARET DE LA VALETTE: Archbishop of Toulouse in 1613 and cardinal in 1621, Louis de Nogaret de La Valette (1593–1639) commanded an army in the Thirty

Years War. He served under Richelieu and was nicknamed *cardinal valet*, 'the valet cardinal'.

2   THE GIANT: as David Coward points out, Porthos is described in *Twenty Years After* as six feet tall (in French feet) – in other words 6 foot 4 inches.

3   THE LORD'S SEVENTH COMMANDMENT: 'Thou shalt not steal.'

4   RUBENS: Dumas was a great admirer of the Baroque artist, Peter Paul Rubens (1577–1640), Marie de' Medici's court painter.

5   A DANDOLO OR A MONTMORENCY: patrician families, Venetian and French respectively.

6   SHE WAS BRANDED: the practice of branding to identify (and punish) prostitutes and criminals of all sorts was widespread and had been so for many centuries. It seems strange that the fleur-de-lys, a decorative emblem, and associated with royalty, in particular with the French royal family, should be used in France to mark criminals (known as *fleurdeliser*); possibly it was to indicate that the criminal was owned by the monarchy.

XXVIII. RETURN

1   YOU KNOW THE PROVERB: *faute d'un point, Martin perdit son âne*, 'For want of a nail the shoe was lost.' So near and yet so far, in other words.

2   AS MINERVA SEIZED ACHILLES IN THE ILIAD : 'The son of Peleus [Achilles] was furious, and his heart within his shaggy breast was divided whether to draw his sword, push the others aside, and kill the son of Atreus [Agamemnon], or to restrain himself and check his anger. While he was thus in two minds, and was drawing his mighty sword from its scabbard, Minerva came down from heaven (for Juno had sent her in the love she bore to them both), and seized the son of Peleus by his yellow hair . . .'. *Iliad*, 1, tr. Samuel Butler.

3   SONS OF AYMON: one of the most popular tales of chivalry revolved around the Duke of Aymon's four sons who had to

flee Charlemagne on their magical horse, Bayard. The horse's powers included being able to carry all four of them on its back and leap across valleys.

4 SISTER ANNE: the sister of Bluebeard's wife. She desperately watches from the tower of Bluebeard's castle as she waits for their brothers to come to her and her sister's rescue.

5 'ERAT, EST, FUIT': should read, '*Erit, est, fuit,*' 'It will be, it is, it has been.' '*Erat, est, fuit,*' 'It was, it is, it has been,' may be one of the rudimentary errors Dumas mentions on p. 309

6 LARDED FRICANDEAU: veal braised and glazed in its own juices.

7 THE FAVOUR OF JOINING THE MUSKETEERS: in fact, d'Artagnan only joins the musketeers after the Saint-Gervais bastion affair, see p. 511.

XXIX. THE HUNT FOR OUTFITS

1 THE COURSERS OF HIPPOLYTUS: in Jean Racine's tragedy *Phèdre*, Hippolytus's horses are said to have mourned his death.

2 THE CHURCH OF SAINT-LEU: still in the Rue Saint-Denis, near the Rue aux Ours.

3 CLOISTER OF SAINT-MAGLOIRE: the abbey of Saint-Magloire on Rue Saint-Denis.

XXX. MILADY

1 SAINT-GERMAIN: Saint-Germain-en-Laye.

XXXI. ENGLISHMEN AND FRENCHMEN

1 PLACE ROYALE: renamed Place des Vosges after the French Revolution, Place Royale is the oldest planned square in Paris. Inaugurated in 1612 to celebrate the marriage of Louis XIII and Anne of Austria, its great innovation was to have all the house fronts built to the same design. Richelieu would have been Milady's neighbour at no. 21.

2 THIS INTRODUCTION TO MILADY: As mentioned above in connection with Count de Wardes, Dumas's idea for Milady came from the Englishwoman, 'Milédi', in Courtilz Gatien de Sandras's Memoirs. Milédi has a brother, and a maid who is enamoured of d'Artagnan, and, once crossed, is a ruthless adversary. Milady, however, is in an entirely different league of villainy.

3 A WIDOW WITH A CHILD: see *Twenty Years After*. '(See also chapter LXVI. 'The Execution', note 2 below.)

XXXII. A PROSECUTOR'S DINNER

1 BASSET, PASSE-DIX: basset is a card game, passe-dix, also known as 'hazard,' a dice game.

2 EPULAE EPULARUM!: 'banquet of banquets!' A successful and extremely wealthy general, who perfected a way of eating thrushes all year, Lucius Lucullus (118–57 BC) was a byword for Epicureanism. Served a less than impressive dinner one night when he was eating alone, he reprimanded his servant, saying 'What, did not you know, then, that today Lucullus dines with Lucullus?'

3 A HEAD START ON HARPAGON: Molière's *The Miser*, with Harpagon as its main character, wasn't performed until 1688.

XXXVI. THE DREAM OF VENGEANCE

1 CIRCE: goddess and sorceress in Homer's *Odyssey* who turns Odysseus' companions into swine.

2 DON JAPHET OF ARMENIA: bombastic nobleman in Paul Scarron's comedy, *Don Japhet of Armenia*, 1652.

XXXVIII. HOW, WITHOUT STIRRING HIMSELF, ATHOS FOUND HIS OUTFIT

1 POLYCRATES: tyrant of Samos in the sixth century BC, Polycrates was warned by the Pharaoh of Egypt, who wanted to make an

alliance with him, that he was too successful: so much good fortune had to turn bad sometime. In an attempt to prevent this, Polycrates threw his most precious possession, a ring, into the sea. A few days later, however, a fisherman brought a large fish as a gift, and, while it was being prepared, Polycrates's cooks found out that it had swallowed the ring. The Pharaoh broke off the alliance and Polycrates was finally assassinated and possibly impaled.

2   FIND ITS NESTING PLACE: a play on Molière's question, *Où la vertu va-t-elle se nicher?* 'Where will virtue find its nesting place?'

XXXIX. A VISION

I   MIRAME: a play in fact written by the poet Desmarets de Saint-Sorlin (1596–1676). Richelieu, who founded the Académie Française, was fascinated by the theatre and commissioned authors such as Pierre Corneille to write plays under his supervision.

XLI. THE SIEGE OF LA ROCHELLE

I   REVOCATION OF THE EDICT OF NANTES: seventy years after Henri IV gave them religious freedom, the position of Protestants in France became increasingly insecure under his grandson, Louis XIV. In the 1680s they were deliberately terrorised by the billeting of unruly troops in their homes, 'the Dragonnades', and Louis XIV finally revoked the Edict of Nantes in 1685. Despite the risk of execution or being sent as galley slaves to the French fleet in the Mediterranean, many Protestants subsequently emigrated.

2   MINIMS: the order of the Minims, founded by St Francis of Assisi, built a monastery by the entrance to La Rochelle harbour in 1634.

3   THE DUKE D'ORLÉANS: Gaston d'Orléans, Louis XIII's brother, also known as 'Monsieur'. With Marie de' Medici he mounted the 'Day of the Dupes' in 1630, an unsuccessful attempt to overthrow Richelieu.

XLII. THE ANJOU WINE

1 THE ANJOU WINE: produced in the Loire Valley (Anjou and its neighbour Saumur constitute what's known as the 'Middle Loire') Anjou wine comes in every variety: red, white, rosé and dessert wines such as the Coteaux du Layon.

2 CHAMBERTIN: sometimes known as the 'King of Wines', Chambertin, a red Burgundy, was Napoleon's favourite wine, supplies of which he took on every campaign.

3 MARTINGALE: as suggested by the reference to d'Artagnan's Béarnais nag on p. 8, the martingale is the piece of harness that keeps a horse's head down. Roughly, therefore, this dictum suggests that one must not only be able to wait for opportunities to present themselves, but that opportunity itself is the true measure of life, a very Dumas sentiment.

XLIII. THE RED DOVECOT INN

1 MONTAIGU HAD BEEN CAPTURED: Walter 'Wat' Montagu (without the 'i') was sent to Italy and Lorraine to raise alliances against Richelieu, partly to prepare for the invasion of the Île de Ré and partly for a full-blown invasion of France. He was arrested in 1627 and held in the Bastille for a year.

XLIV. ON THE USEFULNESS OF STOVEPIPES

1 THE GHOST OF THE WHITE LADY: the Louvre, the palace of the French kings until Louis XIV moved the court to Versailles in 1682, was popularly believed to be haunted until the eighteenth century. Then there was a lull, now there's the Internet. See, for instance, the Top Ten Most Haunted Places in France on the Haunted America Tours website: 'Many believe that thousands of lost and crazed, starving and tortured souls still walk the many galleries, looking for a way out. Many locals will tell

you they also believe quite frankly that many of the great
works of art on display have ghosts attached to them.'

2 RAVAILLAC: A fanatical Catholic, François Ravaillac (1578–
1610) stabbed Henri IV to death in Paris's Rue de la Ferronnerie
in 1610. He was tortured – scalded with burning sulphur, molten
lead, boiling oil and resin, his flesh torn by pincers – and then
drawn and quartered on Place de Grève, which so terrifies
Monsieur Bonacieux earlier in the novel.

3 JACQUES CLÉMENT: Henri III's assassin in 1589.

4 PALAIS DE JUSTICE: a fire severely damaged the Palais de Justice
in 1618.

XLVI. THE SAINT-GERVAIS BASTION

1 ANIMADVERTUNTUR IN DESERTIS: 'They are noticed in desert
wastes.'

XLVII. THE COUNCIL OF THE MUSKETEERS

1 5 DECEMBER 1627: the date has changed from the 3 December.
Later it will become 5 August 1628.

2 MADELONNETTES OR THE REFORMED GIRLS: two convents in
Paris, the *Filles de la Madeleine* or *Madelonnettes*, and the *Filles
Repenties*, which took in penitent women of various sorts.

XLVIII. A FAMILY MATTER

1 SIXTUS THE FIFTH: the son of a farmer, Felix Peretti (1520–1590)
became Pope Sixtus V in 1585.

2 AGLAÉ MICHON; this is subsequently changed to Marie Michon.
Dumas's first love, when he was seventeen, was a seamstress
called Aglaé Tellier. In his memoirs, he describes the moment
he saw her getting married to another man: 'My first dream
had just vanished, my first illusion had just died.' The actress
Gabrielle-Anne di Cisterne, with whom Dumas was

enamoured, wrote a gossip column in his newspaper *Le Mousquetaire* under the name Marie Michon.

3 TATTOO: the signal to return to barracks.

LI. THE OFFICER

1 THE SAINT BARTHOLOMEW MASSACRE: a notorious massacre of Protestants on 24 August 1572 in Paris.

2 ROBESPIERRE: the fiction that Dumas is editing the Count de la Fère's memoirs has been left far behind. Maximilien Robespierre (1754–1794) was a powerful leader of the French Revolution, associated in particular with the Reign of Terror. Tristan l'Hermite was grand provost of the marshals in the fifteenth century. *Divide ut regnes* was the motto of the Roman Senate and Machiavelli.

3 MARION DE LORME: Like the Duchess d'Aiguillon mentioned on p. 28, Marion de Lorme (1611–1650) was one of Richelieu's mistresses.

4 STENAY: as we find out on p. 630, Stenay, which is in the Lorraine near the German border, proves to be a red herring. Constance is in fact in the Carmelite convent at Béthune, 40 or so km west of Lille near the Belgium border.

LII. FIRST DAY OF CAPTIVITY

1 BOTANY BAY...TYBURN: Captain Cook only entered Botany Bay in 1770; it became a penal colony in 1787. Tyburn was the main place of public execution in London until 1783, at the junction of what are now Oxford Street, Edgware Road and Bayswater Road.

LIII. SECOND DAY OF CAPTIVITY

1 MADAME MESSALINA: the third wife of the Roman Emperor Claudius, Valeria Messalina (15–48 AD) was a byword for sexual depravity, thanks in part to the historians Suetonius and Tacitus.

2 THE THREE HEBREWS IN THE FURNACE: for refusing to worship

a golden image, Shadrach, Meschach and Abednego (or 'Hurry-Up-To-Bed-You-Go, in the English childrens' rhyme) escaped unscathed after being thrown into a fiery furnace by the Babylonian King Nebuchadnezzar.

LIV. THIRD DAY OF CAPTIVITY

1 CHARLOTTE BACKSON: Milady's other names, that we know of, are Lady Clarick, Lady de Winter and Anne de Breuil. We never find out her real name, just as we never find out Athos's, Porthos's or Aramis's.

LV. FOURTH DAY OF CAPTIVITY

1 ELOAS OR ASTARTE: in Alfred de Vigny's poem, *Eloa or The Sister of the Angels,* Eloa is an angel seduced by Satan. Astarte was a Mesopotamian goddess whose cult included temple prostitution and human sacrifice.
2 SARDANAPALUS: the spectacular decadence of this Assyrian king, as described by the Greek historian Diodorus Siculus, made him a favourite subject of the Romantics.

LVI. FIFTH DAY OF CAPTIVITY

1 ARABIAN FABLE: no doubt identifying with Scheherazade, Dumas was an avid reader of *The Thousand and One Nights.*
2 THE LUCRETIA OF ENGLAND: the Roman heroine Lucretia, whose rape by Sextus, son of the Etruscan king Tarquin, and subsequent suicide led to the establishment of the Roman Republic in 510 BC.

LVII. A DEVICE FROM CLASSICAL TRAGEDY

1 AMBASSADOR TO SPAIN: Buckingham went with Charles to Spain in 1623 on an unsuccessful mission by the Prince of Wales to marry Maria, Anne of Austria's younger sister.

LVIII. ESCAPE

1   JUDAS MACCABEUS: acclaimed Jewish warrior, who led a
    successful uprising against the Syrian Seleucid dynasty. The
    feast of Hannukah commemorates the restoration of Jewish
    worship at the temple in Jerusalem in 165 BC after Maccabeus
    cleared it of Hellenistic statuary.

LIX. WHAT HAPPENED IN PORTSMOUTH ON 23 AUGUST 1628

1   JAMES VI: James VI of Scotland (1567–1625), who became
    James I of England in 1603.
2   PRINCE DE SOUBISE: Benjamin de Rohan (1583–1642), Baron
    de Soubise, commanded the Protestant forces in La Rochelle.
3   JOHN FELTON: the historical John Felton (1595–1628) was a
    professional soldier wounded in Buckingham's expedition
    against the Île de Ré in 1627. He stabbed Buckingham to
    death in Portsmouth as he was preparing to set sail for La
    Rochelle, partly because he had been passed over for promo-
    tion, as Dumas mentions, but largely out of Protestant and
    patriotic feeling. The murder was acclaimed, such was
    Buckingham's unpopularity, but Felton was brought to trial
    on the instigation of Charles I and hanged at Tyburn on 29
    November 1628.

LX. IN FRANCE

1   AT THE OTHER END OF FRANCE, THAT IS: Béthune is roughly
    700 km from La Rochelle.
2   DE LUYNES: Madame de Chevreuse's first husband, Honoré
    d'Albert, Duke de Luynes, was a favourite of Louis XIII and
    worked hard to bring about a rapprochement between the king
    and Anne of Austria.
3   ARMENTIÈRES: 19 km north of Lille near the Belgian border.

LXI. THE CARMELITE CONVENT OF BÉTHUNE

1   I KNOW MONSIEUR DE PUTANGE; I KNEW MONSIEUR DUJART IN ENGLAND: for Guillaume Morel, sieur de Putange, see above, chapter IX, note 3, 'IN THE GARDEN OF AMIENS'. 'Dujart' is François de Rochechouart, who was also close to the queen and an enemy of Richelieu. He was initially sentenced to death, then pardoned, for his part in the Chalais Affair.

LXII. TWO VARIETIES OF DEMON

1   LYS: a tributary of the Scheldt, the Lys is part of France's border with Belgium. Is there an echo of Milady's fleur-de-lys?

LXVI. THE EXECUTION

1   NACHRICHTER: German for 'he who comes after the judge'.
2   THREW THE MONEY IN THE RIVER: Frank Wild Reed, in *A Bibliography of Alexandre Dumas Père*, points out that early editions of the novel contained the following sentence at this point, *Voyez, dit Athos, cette femme a un enfant, et cependant elle n'a pas dit un mot de son enfant!* 'Mark,' said Athos, 'this woman has a child, and yet she has not spoken one word about him.'

EPILOGUE

1   PORTHOS: life has worked out very well for Porthos at the start of *Twenty Years After*. With Madame de Coquenard's money, he has become a landowner with the grandiose name of Monsieur du Vallon de Bracieux de Pierrefonds.
2   ARAMIS: Aramis initially becomes the Abbé d'Herblay, but in *The Vicomte de Bragelonne*, rises to Bishop of Vannes and Vicar-General of the Jesuits. As Bazin had predicted, there is every chance he will be made a cardinal, or even pope.

3   ATHOS: d'Artagnan finds Athos living on a small estate in Blois
    in *Twenty Years After*. He has a son, and therein, as they say,
    lies a tale.

4   ROCHEFORT: Dumas has plans in mind for Rochefort in *Twenty
    Years After*, as one would expect from his build-up in *The Three
    Musketeers*.

5   PLANCHET: all the valets report for duty in the sequels.